ALSO BY STEPHEN KING

FICTION

Carrie
'Salem's Lot
The Shining
Night Shift
The Stand
The Dead Zone
Firestarter
Cujo
Creepshow
Different Seasons
The Body
Apt Pupil
Cycle of the Werewolf
Christine
Pet Sematary
IT
Skeleton Crew
The Mist
The Eyes of the Dragon
Misery
The Tommyknockers
The Dark Half
Four Past Midnight
Needful Things
Gerald's Game
Dolores Claiborne
Nightmares & Dreamscapes
Insomnia
Rose Madder
The Green Mile
Desperation
The Girl Who Loved Tom Gordon
Hearts in Atlantis
Dreamcatcher
Everything's Eventual
From a Buick 8
The Colorado Kid
Cell
Lisey's Story
Duma Key
Just After Sunset
Stephen King Goes to the Movies
Under the Dome
Full Dark, No Stars
11/22/63
Doctor Sleep
Mr. Mercedes
Revival
Finders Keepers
The Bazaar of Bad Dreams
End of Watch
The Outsider
Elevation

NOVELS IN THE DARK TOWER SERIES

The Dark Tower I: The Gunslinger
The Dark Tower II: The Drawing of the Three
The Dark Tower III: The Waste Lands
The Dark Tower IV: Wizard and Glass
The Dark Tower V: Wolves of the Calla
The Dark Tower VI: Song of Susannah
The Dark Tower VII: The Dark Tower
The Wind Through the Keyhole: A Dark Tower Novel

BY STEPHEN KING AS RICHARD BACHMAN

Thinner
The Running Man
The Long Walk
Roadwork
The Regulators
Blaze

WITH OWEN KING

Sleeping Beauties

WITH PETER STRAUB

The Talisman
Black House

NONFICTION

Danse Macabre
On Writing (A Memoir of the Craft)

STEPHEN KING

THE SUN DOG

SCRIBNER
New York London Toronto Sydney New Delhi

Scribner
An Imprint of Simon & Schuster, Inc.
1230 Avenue of the Americas
New York, NY 10020

Originally published in 1990 in *Four Past Midnight* by Scribner, an imprint of Simon & Schuster, Inc.

This Scribner trade paperback edition December 2018

Manufactured in the United States of America

9 10 8

Library of Congress Cataloging-in-Publication Data is available.

ISBN 978-1-9821-1542-5
ISBN 978-1-9821-1543-2 (ebook)

THIS IS IN MEMORY OF JOHN D. MACDONALD.
I MISS YOU, OLD FRIEND—AND YOU WERE RIGHT
ABOUT THE TIGERS.

A NOTE ON THE SUN DOG

Every now and then someone will ask me, "When are you going to get tired of this horror stuff, Steve, and write something serious?"

I used to believe the implied insult in this question was accidental, but as the years go by I have become more and more convinced that it is not. I watch the faces of the people who drop that particular dime, you see, and most of them look like bombardiers waiting to see if their last stick of bombs is going to fall wide or hit the targeted factory or munitions dump dead on.

The fact is, almost all of the stuff I have written—and that includes a lot of the funny stuff—was written in a serious frame of mind. I can remember very few occasions when I sat at the typewriter laughing uncontrollably over some wild and crazy bit of fluff I had just finished churning out. I'm never going to be Reynolds Price or Larry Woiwode—it isn't in me—but that doesn't mean I don't care as deeply about what I do. I have to do what I *can* do, however—as Nils Lofgren once put it, "I gotta be my dirty self . . . I won't play no jive."

If *real*—meaning!! SOMETHING THAT COULD ACTUALLY HAPPEN!!—is your definition of serious, you are in the wrong place and you should by all means leave the building. But please remember as you go that I'm not the only one doing business at this particular site; Franz Kafka had an office here, and George Orwell, and Shirley Jackson, and Jorge Luis Borges, and Jonathan Swift, and Lewis Carroll. A glance at the directory in the lobby shows the present tenants include Thomas Berger, Ray Bradbury, Jonathan Carroll, Thomas

Pynchon, Thomas Disch, Kurt Vonnegut, Jr., Peter Straub, Joyce Carol Oates, Isaac Bashevis Singer, Katherine Dunn, and Mark Halpern.

I am doing what I do for the most serious reasons: love, money, and obsession. The tale of the irrational is the sanest way I know of expressing the world in which I live. These tales have served me as instruments of both metaphor and morality; they continue to offer the best window I know on the question of how we perceive things and the corollary question of how we do or do not behave on the basis of our perceptions. I have explored these questions as well as I can within the limits of my talent and intelligence. I am no one's National Book Award or Pulitzer Prize winner, but I'm serious, all right. If you don't believe anything else, believe this: when I take you by your hand and begin to talk, my friend, I believe every word I say.

A lot of the things I have to say—those Really Serious Things—have to do with the small-town world in which I was raised and where I still live. Stories and novels are scale models of what we laughingly call "real life," and I believe that lives as they are lived in small towns are scale models of what we laughingly call "society." This idea is certainly open to argument, and argument is perfectly fine (without it, a lot of literature teachers and critics would be looking for work); I'm just saying that a writer needs some sort of launching pad, and aside from the firm belief that a story may exist with honor for its own self, the idea of the small town as social and psychological microcosm is mine. I began experimenting with this sort of thing in *Carrie*, and continued on a more ambitious level with *'Salem's Lot.* I never really hit my stride, however, until *The Dead Zone.*

That was, I think, the first of my Castle Rock stories (and Castle Rock is really just the town of Jerusalem's Lot without the vampires). In the years since it was written, Castle Rock has increasingly become "my town," in the sense that the mythical city of Isola is Ed McBain's town and the West Virginia village of Glory was Davis Grubb's town. I have been called back there time and time again to examine the lives of its residents and the geographies which seem to rule their lives—Castle Hill and Castle View, Castle Lake and the Town Roads which lie around it in a tangle at the western end of the town.

As the years passed, I became more and more interested in—almost entranced by—the secret life of this town, by the hidden relationships which seemed to come clearer and clearer to me. Much of this history remains either unwritten or unpublished: how the late Sheriff George Bannerman lost his virginity in the back seat of his dead father's car, how Ophelia Todd's husband was killed by a walking windmill, how Deputy Andy Clutterbuck lost the index finger on his left hand (it was cut off in a fan and the family dog ate it).

Following *The Dead Zone,* which is partly the story of the psychotic Frank Dodd, I wrote a novella called "The Body"; *Cujo,* the novel in which good old Sheriff Bannerman bit the dust; and a number of short stories and novelettes about the town (the best of them, at least in my mind, are "Mrs. Todd's Shortcut" and "Uncle Otto's Truck"). All of which is very well, but a state of entrancement with a fictional setting may not be the best thing in the world for a writer. It was for Faulkner and J. R. R. Tolkien, but sometimes a couple of exceptions just prove the rule, and besides, I don't play in that league.

So at some point I decided—first in my subconscious mind, I think, where all that Really Serious Work takes place—that the time had come to close the book on Castle Rock, Maine, where so many of my own favorite characters have lived and died. Enough, after all, is enough. Time to move on (maybe all the way next door to Harlow, ha-ha). But I didn't just want to walk away; I wanted to *finish* things, and do it with a bang.

Little by little I began to grasp how that could be done, and over the last four years or so I have been engaged in writing a

Castle Rock Trilogy, if you please—the *last* Castle Rock stories. They were not written in order (I sometimes think "out of order" is the story of my life), but now they *are* written, and they are serious enough . . . but I hope that doesn't mean that they are sober-sided or boring.

The first of these stories, *The Dark Half,* was published in 1989. While it is primarily the story of Thad Beaumont and is in large part set in a town called Ludlow (the town where the Creeds lived in *Pet Sematary)*, the town of Castle Rock figures in the tale, and the book serves to introduce Sheriff Bannerman's replacement, a fellow named Alan Pangborn. Sheriff Pangborn is at the center of the last story in this sequence, a long novel called *Needful Things,* which is scheduled to be published next year and will conclude my doings with what local people call The Rock.

The connective tissue between these longer works is the story which follows. You will meet few if any of Castle Rock's larger figures in "The Sun Dog," but it will serve to introduce you to Pop Merrill, whose nephew is town bad boy (and Gordie LaChance's *bête noire* in "The Body") Ace Merrill. "The Sun Dog" also sets the stage for the final fireworks display . . . and, I hope, exists as a satisfying story on its own, one that can be read with pleasure even if you don't give a hang about *The Dark Half* or *Needful Things.*

One other thing needs to be said: every story has its own secret life, quite separate from its setting, and "The Sun Dog" is a story about cameras and photographs. About five years ago, my wife, Tabitha, became interested in photography, discovered she was good at it, and began to pursue it in a serious way, through study, experiment, and practice-practice-practice. I myself take bad photos (I'm one of those guys who always manage to cut off my subjects' heads, get pictures of them with their mouths hanging open, or both), but I have a great deal of respect for those who take good ones . . . and the whole process fascinates me.

In the course of her experiments, my wife got a Polaroid camera, a simple one accessible even to a doofus like me. I became fascinated with this camera. I had seen and used Polaroids before, of course, but I had never really *thought* about them much, nor had I ever looked closely at the images these cameras produce. The more I thought about them, the stranger they seemed. They are, after all, not just images but moments of time . . . and there is something so *peculiar* about them.

This story came almost all at once one night in the summer of 1987, but the thinking which made it possible went on for almost a year. And that's enough out of me, I think. It's been great to be with all of you again, but that doesn't mean I'm letting you go home just yet.

I think we have a birthday party to attend in the little town of Castle Rock.

CHAPTER ONE

September 15th was Kevin's birthday, and he got exactly what he wanted: a Sun.

The Kevin in question was Kevin Delevan, the birthday was his fifteenth, and the Sun was a Sun 660, a Polaroid camera which does everything for the novice photographer except make bologna sandwiches.

There *were* other gifts, of course; his sister, Meg, gave him a pair of mittens she had knitted herself, there was ten dollars from his grandmother in Des Moines, and his Aunt Hilda sent—as she always did—a string tie with a horrible clasp. She had sent the first of these when Kevin was three, which meant he already had twelve unused string ties with horrible clasps in a drawer of his bureau, to which this would be added—lucky thirteen. He had never worn any of them but was not allowed to throw them away. Aunt Hilda lived in Portland. She had never come to one of Kevin's or Meg's birthday parties, but she might decide to do just that one of these years. God knew she *could*; Portland was only fifty miles south of Castle Rock. And suppose she *did* come . . . and asked to see Kevin in one of his *other* ties (or Meg in one of her other scarves, for that matter)? With some relatives, an excuse might do. Aunt Hilda, however, was different. Aunt Hilda presented a certain golden possibility at a point where two essential facts about her crossed: she was Rich, and she was Old.

Someday, Kevin's Mom was convinced, she might DO SOMETHING for Kevin and Meg. It was understood that the SOMETHING would probably come after Aunt Hilda finally kicked it, in the form of a clause in her will. In the meantime, it was thought wise to keep the horrible string ties and the equally horrible scarves. So this thirteenth string tie (on the clasp of which was a bird Kevin thought was a woodpecker) would join the others, and Kevin would write Aunt Hilda a thank-you note, not because his mother would insist on it and not because he thought or even cared that Aunt Hilda might DO SOMETHING for him and his kid sister someday, but because he was a generally thoughtful boy with good habits and no real vices.

He thanked his family for all his gifts (his mother and father had, of course, supplied a number of lesser ones, although the Polaroid was clearly the centerpiece, and they were delighted with *his* delight), not forgetting to give Meg a kiss (she giggled and pretended to rub it off but her own delight was equally clear) and to tell her he was sure the mittens would come in handy on the ski team this winter—but most of his attention was reserved for the Polaroid box, and the extra film packs which had come with it.

He was a good sport about the birthday cake and the ice cream, although it was clear he was itching to get at the camera and try it out. And as soon as he decently could, he did.

That was when the trouble started.

He read the instruction booklet as thoroughly as his eagerness to begin would allow, then loaded the camera while the family watched with anticipation and unacknowledged dread (for some reason, the gifts which seem the most wanted are the ones which so often don't work). There was a little collective sigh—more puff than gust—when the camera obediently spat out the cardboard square on top of the film packet, just as the instruction booklet had promised it would.

There were two small dots, one red and one green, separated by a zig-zag lightning-bolt on the housing of the camera. When Kevin loaded the camera, the red light came on. It stayed on for a couple of seconds. The family watched in silent fascination as the Sun 660 sniffed for light. Then the red light went out and the green light began to blink rapidly.

"It's ready," Kevin said, in the same straining-to-be-off-hand-but-not-quite-making-it tone with which Neil Armstrong had reported his first step upon the surface of Luna. "Why don't all you guys stand together?"

"I hate having my picture taken!" Meg cried, covering her face with the theatrical anxiety and pleasure which only sub-teenage girls and really bad actresses can manage.

"Come on, Meg," Mr. Delevan said.

"Don't be a goose, Meg," Mrs. Delevan said.

Meg dropped her hands (and her objections), and the three of them stood at the end of the table with the diminished birthday cake in the foreground.

Kevin looked through the viewfinder. "Squeeze a little closer to Meg, Mom," he said, motioning with his left hand. "You too, Dad." This time he motioned with his right.

"You're *squishing* me!" Meg said to her parents.

Kevin put his finger on the button which would fire the camera, then remembered a briefly glimpsed note in the instructions about how easy it was to cut off your subjects' heads in a photograph. *Off with their heads,* he thought, and it should have been funny, but for some reason he felt a little tingle at the base of his spine, gone and forgotten almost before it was noticed. He raised the camera a little. There. They were all in the frame. Good.

"Okay!" he sang. "Smile and say Intercourse!"

"Kevin!" his mother cried out.

His father burst out laughing, and Meg screeched the sort of mad laughter not even bad actresses often essay; girls between the ages of ten and twelve own sole title to that particular laugh.

Kevin pushed the button.

The flashbulb, powered by the battery in the film pack, washed the room in a moment of righteous white light.

It's mine, Kevin thought, and it should have been the surpassing moment of his fifteenth birthday. Instead, the thought brought back that odd little tingle. It was more noticeable this time.

The camera made a noise, something between a squeal and a whirr, a sound just a little beyond description but familiar enough to most people, just the same: the sound of a Polaroid camera squirting out what may not be art but what is often serviceable and almost always provides instant gratification.

"Lemme see it!" Meg cried.

"Hold your horses, muffin," Mr. Delevan said. "They take a little time to develop."

Meg was staring at the stiff gray surface of what was not yet a photograph with the rapt attention of a woman gazing into a crystal ball.

The rest of the family gathered around, and there was that same feeling of anxiety which had attended the ceremony of Loading the Camera: still life of the American Family waiting to let out its breath.

Kevin felt a terrible tenseness stealing into his muscles, and this time there was no question of ignoring it. He could not explain it . . . but it was there. He could not seem to take his eyes from that solid gray square within the white frame which would form the borders of the photograph.

"I think I see me!" Meg cried brightly. Then, a moment later: "No. I guess I don't. I think I see—"

They watched in utter silence as the gray cleared, as the mists are reputed to do in a seer's crystal when the vibrations or feelings or whatever they are are right, and the picture became visible to them.

Mr. Delevan was the first to break the silence.

"What is this?" he asked no one in particular. "Some kind of joke?"

Kevin had absently put the camera down rather too close to the edge of the table in order to watch the picture develop. Meg saw what the picture was and took a single step away. The expression on her face was neither fright nor awe but just ordinary surprise. One of her hands came up as she turned toward her father. The rising hand struck the camera and knocked it off the table and onto the floor. Mrs. Delevan had been looking at the emerging picture in a kind of trance, the expression on her face either that of a woman who is deeply puzzled or who is feeling the onset of a migraine headache. The sound of the camera hitting the floor startled her. She uttered a little scream and recoiled. In doing this, she tripped over Meg's foot and lost her balance. Mr. Delevan reached for her, propelling Meg, who was still between them, forward again, quite forcefully. Mr. Delevan not only caught his wife, but did so with some grace; for a moment they would have made a pretty picture indeed: Mom and Dad, showing they still know how to Cut A Rug, caught at the end of a spirited tango, she with one hand thrown up and her back deeply bowed, he bent over her in that ambiguous male posture which may be seen, when divorced from circumstance, as either solicitude or lust.

Meg was eleven, and less graceful. She went flying back toward the table and smacked into it with her stomach. The hit was hard enough to have injured her, but for the last year and a half she had been taking ballet lessons at the YWCA three afternoons a week. She did not dance with much grace, but she enjoyed ballet, and the dancing had fortunately toughened the muscles of her stomach enough for them to absorb the blow as efficiently as good shock absorbers absorb the pounding a road full of potholes can administer to a car. Still, there was a band of black and blue just above her hips the next day. These bruises took almost two weeks to first purple, then yellow, then fade . . . like a Polaroid picture in reverse.

At the moment this Rube Goldberg accident happened, she didn't even feel it; she simply banged into the table and cried out. The table tipped. The birthday cake, which should have been in the foreground of Kevin's first picture with his new camera, slid off the table. Mrs. Delevan didn't even have time to start her *Meg, are you all right?* before the remaining half of the cake fell on top of the Sun 660 with a juicy *splat!* that sent frosting all over their shoes and the baseboard of the wall.

The viewfinder, heavily smeared with Dutch chocolate, peered out like a periscope. That was all.

Happy birthday, Kevin.

Kevin and Mr. Delevan were sitting on the couch in the living room that evening when Mrs. Delevan came in, waving two dog-eared sheets of paper which had been stapled together. Kevin and Mr. Delevan both had open books in their laps (*The Best and the Brightest* for the father; *Shoot-Out at Laredo* for the son), but what they were mostly doing was staring at the Sun camera, which sat in disgrace on the coffee table amid a litter of Polaroid pictures. All the pictures appeared to show exactly the same thing.

Meg was sitting on the floor in front of them, using the VCR to watch a rented movie. Kevin wasn't sure which one it was, but there were a lot of people running around and screaming, so he guessed it was a horror picture. Megan had a passion for them. Both parents considered this a low taste (Mr. Delevan in particular was often outraged by what he called "that useless junk"), but tonight neither of them had said a word. Kevin guessed they were just grateful she had quit complaining about her bruised stomach and wondering aloud what the exact symptoms of a ruptured spleen might be.

"Here they are," Mrs. Delevan said. "I found them at the bottom of my purse the second time through." She handed the papers—a sales slip from J. C. Penney's and a MasterCard receipt—to her husband. "I can never find anything like this the first time. I don't think anyone can. It's like a law of nature."

She surveyed her husband and son, hands on her hips.

"You two look like someone just killed the family cat."

"We don't *have* a cat," Kevin said.

"Well, you know what I mean. It's a shame, of course, but

we'll get it sorted out in no time. Penney's will be happy to exchange it—"

"I'm not so sure of that," John Delevan said. He picked up the camera, looked at it with distaste (almost sneered at it, in fact), and then set it down again. "It got chipped when it hit the floor. See?"

Mrs. Delevan took only a cursory glance. "Well, if Penney's won't, I'm positive that the Polaroid company *will.* I mean, the fall obviously didn't cause whatever is wrong with it. The first picture looked just like all these, and Kevin took *that* one before Meg knocked it off the table."

"I didn't mean to," Meg said without turning around. On the screen, a pint-sized figure—a malevolent doll named Chucky, if Kevin had it right—was chasing a small boy. Chucky was dressed in blue overalls and waving a knife.

"I know, dear. How's your stomach?"

"Hurts," Meg said. "A little ice cream might help. Is there any left over?"

"Yes, I think so."

Meg gifted her mother with her most winning smile. "Would you get some for me?"

"Not at all," Mrs. Delevan said pleasantly. "Get it yourself. And what's that horrible thing you're watching?"

"Child's Play," Megan said. "There's this doll named Chucky that comes to life. It's neat."

Mrs. Delevan wrinkled her nose.

"Dolls don't come to life, Meg," her father said. He spoke heavily, as if knowing this was a lost cause.

"Chucky did," Meg said. "In movies, anything can happen." She used the remote control to freeze the movie and went to get her ice cream.

"Why does she want to watch that crap?" Mr. Delevan asked his wife, almost plaintively.

"I don't know, dear."

Kevin had picked up the camera in one hand and several of

the exposed Polaroids in the other—they had taken almost a dozen in all. "I'm not so sure I *want* a refund," he said.

His father stared at him. "*What?* Jesus wept!"

"Well," Kevin said, a little defensively, "I'm just saying that maybe we ought to think about it. I mean, it's not exactly an ordinary defect, is it? I mean, if the pictures came out overexposed . . . or underexposed . . . or just plain blank . . . that would be one thing. But how do you get a thing like this? The same picture, over and over? I mean, look! And they're outdoors, even though we took every one of these pictures inside!"

"It's a practical joke," his father said. "It must be. The thing to do is just exchange the damned thing and forget about it."

"I don't think it's a practical joke," Kevin said. "First, it's too *complicated* to be a practical joke. How do you rig a camera to take the same picture over and over? Plus, the psychology is all wrong."

"Psychology, yet," Mr. Delevan said, rolling his eyes at his wife.

"Yes, psychology!" Kevin replied firmly. "When a guy loads your cigarette or hands you a stick of pepper gum, he hangs around to watch the fun, doesn't he? But unless you or Mom have been pulling my leg—"

"Your father isn't much of a leg-puller, dear," Mrs. Delevan said, stating the obvious gently.

Mr. Delevan was looking at Kevin with his lips pressed together. It was the look he always got when he perceived his son drifting toward that area of the ballpark where Kevin seemed most at home: left field. *Far* left field. There was a hunchy, intuitive streak in Kevin that had always puzzled and confounded him. He didn't know where it had come from, but he was sure it hadn't been *his* side of the family.

He sighed and looked at the camera again. A piece of black plastic had been chipped from the left side of the housing, and there was a crack, surely no thicker than a human hair, down the center of the viewfinder lens. The crack was so thin it disappeared completely when you raised the camera to your eye to set the shot you would not get—what you *would* get was on the coffee table, and there were nearly a dozen other examples in the dining room.

What you got was something that looked like a refugee from the local animal shelter.

"All right, what in the devil are you going to do with it?" he asked. "I mean, let's think this over reasonably, Kevin. What practical good is a camera that takes the same picture over and over?"

But it was not practical good Kevin was thinking about. In fact, he was not thinking at all. He was feeling . . . and remembering. In the instant when he had pushed the shutter release, one clear idea

(it's mine)

had filled his mind as completely as the momentary white flash had filled his eyes. That idea, complete yet somehow inexplicable, had been accompanied by a powerful mixture of emotions which he could still not identify completely . . . but he thought fear and excitement had predominated.

And besides—his father *always* wanted to look at things reasonably. He would never be able to understand Kevin's intuitions or Meg's interest in killer dolls named Chucky.

Meg came back in with a huge dish of ice cream and started the movie again. Someone was now attempting to toast Chucky with a blowtorch, but he went right on waving his knife. "Are you two still arguing?"

"We're having a discussion," Mr. Delevan said. His lips were pressed more tightly together than ever.

"Yeah, right," Meg said, sitting down on the floor again and crossing her legs. "You always say that."

"Meg?" Kevin said kindly.

"What?"

"If you dump that much ice cream on top of a ruptured

spleen, you'll die horribly in the night. Of course, your spleen might not actually be ruptured, but—"

Meg stuck her tongue out at him and turned back to the movie.

Mr. Delevan was looking at his son with an expression of mingled affection and exasperation. "Look, Kev—it's your camera. No argument about that. You can do whatever you want with it. But—"

"Dad, aren't you even the least bit interested in *why* it's doing what it's doing?"

"Nope," John Delevan said.

It was Kevin's turn to roll his eyes. Meanwhile, Mrs. Delevan was looking from one to the other like someone who is enjoying a pretty good tennis match. Nor was this far from the truth. She had spent years watching her son and her husband sharpen themselves on each other, and she was not bored with it yet. She sometimes wondered if they would ever discover how much alike they really were.

"Well, I want to think it over."

"Fine. I just want *you* to know that I can swing by Penney's tomorrow and exchange the thing—if you want me to and they agree to swap a piece of chipped merchandise, that is. If you want to keep it, that's fine, too. I wash my hands of it." He dusted his palms briskly together to illustrate.

"I suppose you don't want *my* opinion," Meg said.

"Right," Kevin said.

"Of course we do, Meg," Mrs. Delevan said.

"I think it's a supernatural camera," Meg said. She licked ice cream from her spoon. "I think it's a Manifestation."

"That's utterly ridiculous," Mr. Delevan said at once.

"No, it's not," Meg said. "It happens to be the only explanation that fits. You just don't think so because you don't believe in stuff like that. If a ghost ever floated up to you, Dad, you wouldn't even see it. What do you think, Kev?"

For a moment Kevin didn't—couldn't—answer. He felt

as if another flashbulb had gone off, this one behind his eyes instead of in front of them.

"Kev? Earth to Kevin!"

"I think you might just have something there, squirt," he said slowly.

"Oh my dear God," John Delevan said, getting up. "It's the revenge of Freddy and Jason—my kid thinks his birthday camera's haunted. I'm going to bed, but before I do, I want to say just one more thing. A camera that takes photographs of the same thing over and over again—especially something as ordinary as what's in *these* pictures—is a *boring* manifestation of the supernatural."

"Still . . ." Kevin said. He held up the photos like a dubious poker hand.

"I think it's time we all went to bed," Mrs. Delevan said briskly. "Meg, if you absolutely need to finish that cinematic masterpiece, you can do it in the morning."

"But it's almost over!" Meg cried.

"I'll come up with her, Mom," Kevin said, and, fifteen minutes later, with the malevolent Chucky disposed of (at least until the sequel), he did. But sleep did not come easily for Kevin that night. He lay long awake in his bedroom, listening to a strong late-summer wind rustle the leaves outside into whispery conversation, thinking about what might make a camera take the same picture over and over and over again, and what such a thing might mean. He only began to slip toward sleep when he realized his decision had been made: he would keep the Polaroid Sun at least a little while longer.

It's mine, he thought again. He rolled over on his side, closed his eyes, and was sleeping deeply forty seconds later.

CHAPTER TWO

Amid the tickings and tockings of what sounded like at least fifty thousand clocks and totally undisturbed by them, Reginald "Pop" Merrill shone a pencil-beam of light from a gadget even more slender than a doctor's ophthalmoscope into Kevin's Polaroid 660 while Kevin stood by. Pop's eyeglasses, which he didn't need for close work, were propped on the bald dome of his head.

"Uh-huh," he said, and clicked the light off.

"Does that mean you know what's wrong with it?" Kevin asked.

"Nope," Pop Merrill said, and snapped the Sun's film compartment, now empty, closed. "Don't have a clue." And before Kevin could say anything else, the clocks began to strike four o'clock, and for a few moments conversation, although possible, seemed absurd.

I want to think it over, he had told his father on the evening he had turned fifteen—three days ago now—and it was a statement which had surprised both of them. As a child he had made a career of *not* thinking about things, and Mr. Delevan had in his heart of hearts come to believe Kevin never *would* think about things, whether he ought to or not. They had been seduced, as fathers and sons often are, by the idea that their behavior and very different modes of thinking would never change, thus fixing their relationship eternally . . . and childhood would thus go on forever. *I want to think it over:* there was a world of potential change implicit in that statement.

Further, as a human being who had gone through his life to that point making most decisions on instinct rather than reason (and he was one of those lucky ones whose instincts were almost always good—the sort of person, in other words, who drives reasonable people mad), Kevin was surprised and intrigued to find that he was actually On the Horns of a Dilemma.

Horn #1: he had wanted a Polaroid camera and he had gotten one for his birthday, but, dammit, he had wanted a Polaroid camera that *worked.*

Horn #2: he was deeply intrigued by Meg's use of the word *supernatural.*

His younger sister had a daffy streak a mile wide, but she wasn't stupid, and Kevin didn't think she had used the word lightly or thoughtlessly. His father, who was of the Reasonable rather than Instinctive tribe, had scoffed, but Kevin found he wasn't ready to go and do likewise . . . at least, not yet. That word. That fascinating, exotic word. It became a plinth which his mind couldn't help circling.

I think it's a Manifestation.

Kevin was amused (and a little chagrined) that only Meg had been smart enough—or brave enough—to actually say what should have occurred to all of them, given the oddity of the pictures the Sun produced, but in truth, it wasn't really that amazing. They were not a religious family; they went to church on the Christmas Day every third year when Aunt Hilda came to spend the holiday with them instead of her other remaining relatives, but except for the occasional wedding or funeral, that was about all. If any of them truly believed in the invisible world it was Megan, who couldn't get enough of walking corpses, living dolls, and cars that came to life and ran down people they didn't like.

Neither of Kevin's parents had much taste for the bizarre. They didn't read their horoscopes in the daily paper; they would never mistake comets or falling stars for signs from the Almighty; where one couple might see the face of Jesus on the bottom of an enchilada, John and Mary Delevan would see only an overcooked enchilada. It was not surprising that Kevin, who had never seen the man in the moon because neither mother nor father had bothered to point it out to him, had been likewise unable to see the possibility of *a supernatural Manifestation* in a camera which took the same picture over and over again, inside or outside, even in the dark of his bedroom closet, until it was suggested to him by his sister, who had once written a fan-letter to Jason and gotten an autographed glossy photo of a guy in a bloodstained hockey mask by return mail.

Once the possibility *had* been pointed out, it became difficult to unthink; as Dostoyevsky, that smart old Russian, once said to his little brother when the two of them were both smart *young* Russians, try to spend the next thirty seconds *not* thinking of a blue-eyed polar bear.

It was hard to do.

So he had spent two days circling that plinth in his mind, trying to read hieroglyphics that weren't even *there,* for pity's sake, and trying to decide which he wanted more: the camera or the possibility of a Manifestation. Or, put another way, whether he wanted the Sun . . . or the man in the moon.

By the end of the second day (even in fifteen-year-olds who are clearly destined for the Reasonable tribe, dilemmas rarely last longer than a week), he had decided to take the man in the moon . . . on a trial basis, at least.

He came to this decision in study hall period seven, and when the bell rang, signalling the end of both the study hall and the school-day, he had gone to the teacher he respected most, Mr. Baker, and had asked him if he knew of anyone who repaired cameras.

"Not like a regular camera-shop guy," he explained. "More like a . . . you know . . . a thoughtful guy."

"An F-stop philosopher?" Mr. Baker asked. His saying things like that was one of the reasons why Kevin respected him. It was just a cool thing to say. "A sage of the shutter? An alchemist of the aperture? A—"

"A guy who's seen a lot," Kevin said cagily.

"Pop Merrill," Mr. Baker said.

"Who?"

"He runs the Emporium Galorium."

"Oh. *That* place."

"Yeah," Mr. Baker said, grinning. "*That* place. If, that is, what you're looking for is a sort of homespun Mr. Fixit."

"I guess that's what I am looking for."

"He's got damn near everything in there," Mr. Baker said, and Kevin could agree with that. Even though he had never actually been inside, he passed the Emporium Galorium five, ten, maybe fifteen times a week (in a town the size of Castle Rock, you had to pass *everything* a lot, and it got amazingly boring in Kevin Delevan's humble opinion), and he had looked in the windows. It seemed crammed literally to the rafters with objects, most of them mechanical. But his mother called it "a junk-store" in a sniffing voice, and his father said Mr. Merrill made his money "rooking the summer people," and so Kevin had never gone in. If it had *only* been a "junk-store," he might have; almost certainly would have, in fact. But doing what the summer people did, or buying something where summer people "got rooked" was unthinkable. He would be as apt to wear a blouse and skirt to high school. Summer people could do what they wanted (and did). They were all mad, and conducted their affairs in a mad fashion. *Exist* with them, fine. But be *confused* with them? No. No. And no *sir.*

"Damn near everything," Mr. Baker repeated, "and most of what he's got, he fixed himself. He thinks that crackerbarrel philosopher act he does—glasses up on top of the head, wise pronouncements, all of that—fools people. No one who knows him disabuses him. I'm not sure anyone would *dare* disabuse him."

"Why? What do you mean?"

Mr. Baker shrugged. An odd, tight little smile touched his mouth. "Pop—Mr. Merrill, I mean—has got his fingers in a lot of pies around here. You'd be surprised, Kevin."

Kevin didn't care about how many pies Pop Merrill was currently fingering, or what their fillings might be. He was left with only one more important question, since the summer people were gone and he could probably slink into the Emporium Galorium unseen tomorrow afternoon if he took advantage of the rule which allowed all students but freshmen to cut their last-period study hall twice a month.

"Do I call him Pop or Mr. Merrill?"

Solemnly, Mr. Baker replied, "I think the man kills anyone under the age of sixty who calls him Pop."

And the thing was, Kevin had an idea Mr. Baker wasn't exactly joking.

"You really don't know, huh?" Kevin said when the clocks began to wind down.

It had not been like in a movie, where they all start and finish striking at once; these were real clocks, and he guessed that most of them—along with the rest of the appliances in the Emporium Galorium—were not really running at all but sort of lurching along. They had begun at what his own Seiko quartz watch said was 3:58. They began to pick up speed and volume gradually (like an old truck fetching second gear with a tired groan and jerk). There were maybe four seconds when all of them really *did* seem to be striking, bonging, chiming, clanging, and cuckoo-ing at the same time, but four seconds was all the synchronicity they could manage. And "winding down" was not exactly what they did. What they did was sort of give up, like water finally consenting to gurgle its way down a drain which is almost but not quite completely plugged.

He didn't have any idea why he was so disappointed. Had he really expected anything else? For Pop Merrill, whom Mr. Baker had described as a crackerbarrel philosopher and homespun Mr. Fixit, to pull out a spring and say, "Here it is—this is the bastard causing that dog to show up every time you push the shutter release. It's a dog-spring, belongs in one of those toy dogs a kid winds up so it'll walk and bark a little, some joker on the Polaroid Sun 660 assembly line's *always* putting them in the damn cameras."

Had he expected that?

No. But he had expected . . . *something.*

"Don't have a friggin clue," Pop repeated cheerfully. He reached behind him and took a Douglas MacArthur corncob pipe from a holder shaped like a bucket seat. He began to tamp tobacco into it from an imitation-leather pouch with the words EVIL WEED stamped into it. "Can't even take these babies apart, you know."

"You can't?"

"Nope," Pop said. He was just as chipper as a bird. He paused long enough to hook a thumb over the wire ridge between the lenses of his rimless specs and give them a yank. They dropped off his bald dome and fell neatly into place, hiding the red spots on the sides of his nose, with a fleshy little thump. "You could take apart the old ones," he went on, now producing a Diamond Blue Tip match from a pocket of his vest (of course he was wearing a vest) and pressing the thick yellow thumbnail of his right hand on its head. Yes, this was a man who could rook the summer people with one hand tied behind his back (always assuming it wasn't the one he used to first fish out his matches and then light them)—even at fifteen years of age, Kevin could see that. Pop Merrill had *style.* "The Polaroid Land cameras, I mean. Ever seen one of those beauties?"

"No," Kevin said.

Pop snapped the match alight on the first try, which of course he would always do, and applied it to the corncob, his words sending out little smoke-signals which looked pretty and smelled absolutely foul.

"Oh yeah," he said. "They looked like those old-time cameras people like Mathew Brady used before the turn of the century—or before the Kodak people introduced the Brownie box camera, anyway. What I mean to say is" (Kevin was rapidly learning that this was Pop Merrill's favorite phrase; he used it the way some of the kids in school used "you know," as intensifier, modifier, qualifier, and most of all as a convenient thought-gathering pause) "they tricked it up some, put on chrome and real leather side-panels, but it still looked old-fashioned, like the sort of camera folks used to make daguerreotypes with. When you opened one of those old Polaroid Land cameras, it snapped out an accordion neck, because the lens needed half a foot, maybe even nine inches, to focus the image. It looked old-fashioned as hell when you put it next to one of the Kodaks in the late forties and early fifties, and it was like those old daguerreotype cameras in another way—it only took black-and-white photos."

"Is that so?" Kevin asked, interested in spite of himself.

"Oh, ayuh!" Pop said, chipper as a chickadee, blue eyes twinkling at Kevin through the smoke from his fuming stew-pot of a pipe and from behind his round rimless glasses. It was the sort of twinkle which may indicate either good humor or avarice. "What I mean to say is that people laughed at those cameras the way they laughed at the Volkswagen Beetles when *they* first come out . . . but they bought the Polaroids just like they bought the VWs. Because the Beetles got good gas mileage and didn't go bust so often as American cars, and the Polaroids did one thing the Kodaks and even the Nikons and Minoltas and Leicas didn't."

"Took instant pictures."

Pop smiled. "Well . . . not exactly. What I mean to say is you took your pitcher, and then you yanked on this flap to pull it out. It didn't have no motor, didn't make that squidgy little whining noise like modern Polaroids."

So there *was* a perfect way to describe that sound after all, it was just that you had to find a Pop Merrill to tell it to you: the sound that Polaroid cameras made when they spat out their product was *a squidgy little whine.*

"Then you had to time her," Pop said.

"Time—?"

"Oh, ayuh!" Pop said with great relish, bright as the early bird who has found that fabled worm. "What I mean to say is they didn't have none of this happy automatic crappy back in those days. You yanked and out come this long strip which you put on the table or whatever and timed off sixty seconds on your watch. Had to be sixty, or right around there, anyway. Less and you'd have an underexposed pitcher. More and it'd be overexposed."

"Wow," Kevin said respectfully. And this was not bogus respect, jollying the old man along in hopes he would get back to the point, which was not a bunch of long-dead cameras that had been wonders in their day but his *own* camera, the damned balky Sun 660 sitting on Pop's worktable with the guts of an old seven-day clock on its right and something which looked suspiciously like a dildo on its left. It wasn't bogus respect and Pop knew it, and it occurred to Pop (it wouldn't have to Kevin) how fleeting that great white god "state-of-the-art" really was; ten years, he thought, and the phrase itself would be gone. From the boy's fascinated expression, you would have thought he was hearing about something as antique as George Washington's wooden dentures instead of a camera everyone had thought was the ultimate only thirty-five years ago. But of course this boy had still been circling around in the unhatched void thirty-five years ago, part of a female who hadn't yet even met the male who would provide his other half.

"What I mean to say is it was a regular little darkroom goin on in there between the pitcher and the backing," Pop resumed, slow at first but speeding up as his own mostly genuine interest in the subject resurfaced (but the thoughts of who this kid's father was and what the kid might be worth to him and the strange thing the kid's camera was up to never completely left his mind). "And at the end of the minute, you peeled the pitcher off the back—had to be careful when you did it, too, because there was all this goo like jelly on the back, and if your skin was in the least bit sensitive, you could get a pretty good burn."

"Awesome," Kevin said. His eyes were wide, and now he looked like a kid hearing about the old two-holer outhouses which Pop and all his childhood colleagues (they were almost all colleagues; he had had few childhood friends in Castle Rock, perhaps preparing even then for his life's work of rooking the summer people and the other children somehow sensing it, like a faint smell of skunk) had taken for granted, doing your business as fast as you could in high summer because one of the wasps always circling around down there between the manna and the two holes which were the heaven from which the manna fell might at any time take a notion to plant its stinger in one of your tender little boycheeks, and also doing it as fast as you could in deep winter because your tender little boycheeks were apt to freeze solid if you didn't. *Well,* Pop thought, *so much for the Camera of the Future. Thirty-five years and to this kid it's interestin in the same way a backyard shithouse is interestin.*

"The negative was on the back," Pop said. "And your positive—well, it was black and white, but it was *fine* black and white. It was just as crisp and clear as you'd ever want even today. And you had this little pink thing, about as long as a school eraser, as I remember; it squeegeed out some kind of chemical, smelled like ether, and you had to rub it over the pitcher as fast as you could, or that pitcher'd roll right up, like the tube in the middle of a roll of bung-fodder."

Kevin burst out laughing, tickled by these pleasant antiquities.

Pop quit long enough to get his pipe going again. When he had, he resumed: "A camera like that, nobody but the Polaroid people really knew what it was doing—I mean to say those people were *close*—but it was *mechanical.* You could take it *apart.*"

He looked at Kevin's Sun with some distaste.

"And, lots of times when one went bust, that was as much as you needed. Fella'd come in with one of those and say it wouldn't work, moanin about how he'd have to send it back to the Polaroid people to get it fixed and that'd prob'ly take months and would I take a look. 'Well,' I'd say, 'prob'ly nothin I can do, what I mean to say is nobody really knows about these cameras but the Polaroid people and they're goddam close, but I'll take a look.' All the time knowin it was prob'ly just a loose screw inside that shutter-housin or maybe a fouled spring, or hell, maybe Junior slathered some peanut butter in the film compartment."

One of his bright bird-eyes dropped in a wink so quick and so marvellously sly that, Kevin thought, if you hadn't known he was talking about summer people, you would have thought it was your paranoid imagination, or, more likely, missed it entirely.

"What I mean to say is you had your perfect situation," Pop said. "If you could fix it, you were a goddam wonder-worker. Why, I have put eight dollars and fifty cents in my pocket for takin a couple of little pieces of potato-chip out from between the trigger and the shutter-spring, my son, and the woman who brought that camera in kissed me on the lips. Right . . . on . . . the lips."

Kevin observed Pop's eye drop momentarily closed again behind the semi-transparent mat of blue smoke.

"And of course, if it was somethin you couldn't fix, they didn't hold it against you because, what I mean to say, they never really expected you to be able to do nothin in the first place. You was only a last resort before they put her in a box and stuffed newspaper around her to keep her from bein broke even worse in the mail, and shipped her off to Schenectady.

"But—*this* camera." He spoke in the ritualistic tone of distaste all philosophers of the crackerbarrel, whether in Athens of the golden age or in a small-town junk-shop during this current one of brass, adopt to express their view of entropy without having to come right out and state it. "Wasn't put together, son. What I mean to say is it was *poured.* I could maybe pop the lens, and will if you want me to, and I *did* look in the film compartment, although I knew I wouldn't see a goddam thing wrong—that I recognized, at least—and I didn't. But beyond that I can't go. I could take a hammer and wind it right to her, could *break* it, what I mean to say, but fix it?" He spread his hands in pipe-smoke. "Nossir."

"Then I guess I'll just have to—" *return it after all,* he meant to finish, but Pop broke in.

"Anyway, son, I think you knew that. What I mean to say is you're a bright boy, you can see when a thing's all of a piece. I don't think you brought that camera in to be *fixed.* I think you know that even if it *wasn't* all of a piece, a man couldn't fix what *that* thing's doing, at least not with a screwdriver. I think you brought it in to ask me if I knew what it's *up* to."

"Do you?" Kevin asked. He was suddenly tense all over.

"I might," Pop Merrill said calmly. He bent over the pile of photographs—twenty-eight of them now, counting the one Kevin had snapped to demonstrate, and the one Pop had snapped to demonstrate to himself. "These in order?"

"Not really. Pretty close, though. Does it matter?"

"I think so," Pop said. "They're a little bit different, ain't they? Not much, but a little."

"Yeah," Kevin said. "I can see the difference in *some* of them, but . . ."

"Do you know which one is the first? I could prob'ly figure it out for myself, but time is money, son."

"That's easy," Kevin said, and picked one out of the untidy little pile. "See the frosting?" He pointed at a small brown spot on the picture's white edging.

"Ayup." Pop didn't spare the dab of frosting more than a glance. He looked closely at the photograph, and after a moment he opened the drawer of his worktable. Tools were littered untidily about inside. To one side, in its own space, was an object wrapped in jeweler's velvet. Pop took this out, folded the cloth back, and removed a large magnifying glass with a switch in its base. He bent over the Polaroid and pushed the switch. A bright circle of light fell on the picture's surface.

"That's neat!" Kevin said.

"Ayup," Pop said again. Kevin could tell that for Pop he was no longer there. Pop was studying the picture closely.

If one had not known the odd circumstances of its taking, the picture would hardly have seemed to warrant such close scrutiny. Like most photographs which are taken with a decent camera, good film, and by a photographer at least intelligent enough to keep his finger from blocking the lens, it was clear, understandable . . . and, like so many Polaroids, oddly undramatic. It was a picture in which you could identify and name each object, but its content was as flat as its surface. It was not well composed, but composition wasn't what was wrong with it—that undramatic flatness could hardly be called *wrong* at all, any more than a real day in a real life could be called wrong because nothing worthy of even a made-for-television movie happened during its course. As in so many Polaroids, the things in the picture were only *there,* like an empty chair on a porch or an unoccupied child's swing in a backyard or a passengerless car sitting at an unremarkable curb without even a flat tire to make it interesting or unique.

What was wrong with the picture was the *feeling* that it was wrong. Kevin had remembered the sense of unease he had felt while composing his subjects for the picture he *meant* to take, and the ripple of gooseflesh up his back when, with the glare of the flashbulb still lighting the room, he had thought, *It's mine.* That was what was wrong, and as with the man in the moon you can't unsee once you've seen it, so, he was discovering, you couldn't *unfeel* certain feelings . . . and when it came to these pictures, those feelings were bad.

Kevin thought: *It's like there was a wind—very soft, very cold—blowing out of that picture.*

For the first time, the idea that it might be something supernatural—that this was part of a Manifestation—did something more than just intrigue him. For the first time he found himself wishing he had simply let this thing go. *It's mine*—that was what he had thought when his finger had pushed the shutter-button for the first time. Now he found himself wondering if maybe he hadn't gotten that backward.

I'm scared of it. Of what it's doing.

That made him mad, and he bent over Pop Merrill's shoulder, hunting as grimly as a man who has lost a diamond in a sandpile, determined that, no matter what he saw (always supposing he *should* see something new, and he didn't think he would; he had studied all these photographs often enough now to believe he had seen all there was to see in them), he would *look* at it, *study* it, and under no circumstances allow himself to unsee it. Even if he could . . . and a dolorous voice inside suggested very strongly that the time for unseeing was now past, possibly forever.

What the picture showed was a large black dog in front of a white picket fence. The picket fence wasn't going to be white much longer, unless someone in that flat Polaroid world painted or at least whitewashed it. That didn't seem likely; the fence looked untended, forgotten. The tops of some pickets were broken off. Others sagged loosely outward.

The dog was on a sidewalk in front of the fence. His hindquarters were to the viewer. His tail, long and bushy, drooped. He appeared to be smelling one of the fence-pickets—probably, Kevin thought, because the fence was what his dad called a "letter-drop," a place where many dogs would lift their legs and leave mystic yellow squirts of message before moving on.

The dog looked like a stray to Kevin. Its coat was long and tangled and sown with burdocks. One of its ears had the crumpled look of an old battle-scar. Its shadow trailed long enough to finish outside the frame on the weedy, patchy lawn inside the picket fence. The shadow made Kevin think the picture had been taken not long after dawn or not long before sunset; with no idea of the direction the photographer (*what* photographer, ha-ha) had been facing, it was impossible to tell which, just that he (or she) must have been standing only a few degrees shy of due east or west.

There was something in the grass at the far left of the picture which looked like a child's red rubber ball. It was inside the fence, and enough behind one of the lackluster clumps of grass so it was hard to tell.

And that was all.

"Do you recognize anything?" Pop asked, cruising his magnifying glass slowly back and forth over the photo's surface. Now the dog's hindquarters swelled to the size of hillocks tangled with wild and ominously exotic black undergrowth; now three or four of the scaly pickets became the size of old telephone poles; now, suddenly, the object behind the clump of grass clearly became a child's ball (although under Pop's glass it was as big as a soccer ball): Kevin could even see the stars which girdled its middle in upraised rubber lines. So something new *was* revealed under Pop's glass, and in a few moments Kevin would see something else himself, without it. But that was later.

"Jeez, no," Kevin said. "How could I, Mr. Merrill?"

"Because there are *things* here," Pop said patiently. His glass went on cruising. Kevin thought of a movie he had seen once where the cops sent out a searchlight-equipped helicopter to look for escaped prisoners. "A dog, a sidewalk, a picket fence that needs paintin or takin down, a lawn that needs tendin. The sidewalk ain't much—you can't even see all of it—and the house, even the foundation, ain't in the frame, but what I mean to say is there's that dog. You recognize *it?*"

"No."

"The fence?"

"No."

"What about that red rubber ball? What about that, son?"

"No . . . but you look like you think I should."

"I look like I thought you *might,*" Pop said. "You never had a ball like that when you were a tyke?"

"Not that I remember, no."

"You got a sister, you said."

"Megan."

"She never had a ball like that?"

"I don't think so. I never took that much interest in Meg's toys. She had a BoLo bouncer once, and the ball on the end of it was red, but a different shade. Darker."

"Ayuh. I know what a ball like that looks like. This ain't one. And that mightn't be your lawn?"

"Jes—I mean jeepers, no." Kevin felt a little offended. He and his dad took good care of the lawn around their house. It was a deep green and would stay that way, even under the fallen leaves, until at least mid-October. "We don't have a picket fence, anyway." *And if we did,* he thought, *it wouldn't look like that mess.*

Pop let go of the switch in the base of the magnifying glass, placed it on the square of jeweler's velvet, and with a care which approached reverence folded the sides over it. He returned it to its former place in the drawer and closed the drawer. He looked at Kevin closely. He had put his pipe aside, and there was now no smoke to obscure his eyes, which were still sharp but not twinkling anymore.

"What I mean to say is, could it have been your house before you owned it, do you think? Ten years ago—"

"We owned it ten years ago," Kevin replied, bewildered.

"Well, twenty? Thirty? What I mean to say, do you recognize how the land lies? Looks like it climbs a little."

"Our front lawn—" He thought deeply, then shook his head. "No, ours is flat. If it does anything, it goes down a little. Maybe that's why the cellar ships a little water in a wet spring."

"Ayuh, ayuh, could be. What about the back lawn?"

"There's no sidewalk back there," Kevin said. "And on the sides—" He broke off. "You're trying to find out if my camera's taking pictures of the past!" he said, and for the first time he was really, actively frightened. He rubbed his tongue on the roof of his mouth and seemed to taste metal.

"I was just askin." Pop rapped his fingers beside the photographs, and when he spoke, it seemed to be more to himself than to Kevin. "You know," he said, "some goddam funny things seem to happen from time to time with two gadgets we've come to take pretty much for granted. I ain't sayin they *do* happen; only if they don't, there are a lot of liars and out-n-out hoaxers in the world."

"What gadgets?"

"Tape recorders and Polaroid cameras," Pop said, still seeming to talk to the pictures, or himself, and there was no Kevin in this dusty clock-drumming space at the back of the Emporium Galorium at all. "Take tape recorders. Do you know how many people claim to have recorded the voices of dead folks on tape recorders?"

"No," Kevin said. He didn't particularly mean for his own voice to come out hushed, but it did; he didn't seem to have a whole lot of air in his lungs to speak with, for some reason or other.

"Me neither," Pop said, stirring the photographs with one finger. It was blunt and gnarled, a finger which looked made for rude and clumsy motions and operations, for poking people and knocking vases off endtables and causing nosebleeds if it tried to do so much as hook a humble chunk of dried snot from one of its owner's nostrils. Yet Kevin had watched the man's hands and thought there was probably more grace in that one finger than in his sister Meg's entire body (and maybe in his own; Clan Delevan was not known for its light-footedness or -handedness, which was probably one reason why he thought that image of his father so nimbly catching his mother on the way down had stuck with him, and might forever). Pop Merrill's finger looked as if it would at any moment sweep all the photographs onto the floor—by mistake; this sort of clumsy finger would always poke and knock and tweak by mistake—but it did not. The Polaroids seemed to barely stir in response to its restless movements.

Supernatural, Kevin thought again, and shivered a little. An *actual* shiver, surprising and dismaying and a little embarrassing even if Pop had not seen it.

"But there's even a way they do it," Pop said, and then, as if Kevin had asked: "Who? Damn if I know. I guess some of them are 'psychic investigators,' or at least call themselves that or some such, but I guess it's more'n likely most of em are just playin around, like folks that use Ouija Boards at parties."

He looked up at Kevin grimly, as if rediscovering him.

"You got a Ouija, son?"

"No."

"Ever played with one?"

"No."

"Don't," Pop said more grimly than ever. "Fucking things are dangerous."

Kevin didn't dare tell the old man he hadn't the slightest idea what a weegee board was.

"Anyway, they set up a tape machine to record in an empty room. It's supposed to be an old house, is what I mean to say, one with a History, if they can find it. Do you know what I mean when I say a house with a History, son?"

"I guess . . . like a haunted house?" Kevin hazarded. He found he was sweating lightly, as he had done last year every time Mrs. Whittaker announced a pop quiz in Algebra I.

"Well, that'll do. These . . . people . . . like it best if it's a house with a *Violent* History, but they'll take what they can get. Anyhow, they set up the machine and record that empty room. Then, the next day—they always do it at night, is what I mean to say, they ain't happy unless they can do it at night, and midnight if they can get it—the next day they play her back."

"An empty room?"

"Sometimes," Pop said in a musing voice that might or might not have disguised some deeper feeling, "there are voices."

Kevin shivered again. There were hieroglyphics on the plinth after all. Nothing you'd want to read, but . . . yeah. They were there.

"*Real* voices?"

"Usually imagination," Pop said dismissively. "But once or twice I've heard people I trust say they've heard real voices."

"But *you* never have?"

"Once," Pop said shortly, and said nothing else for so long Kevin was beginning to think he was done when he added, "It was one word. Clear as a bell. 'Twas recorded in the parlor of an empty house in Bath. Man killed his wife there in 1946."

"What was the word?" Kevin asked, knowing he would not be told just as surely as he knew no power on earth, certainly not his own willpower, could have kept him from asking.

But Pop *did* tell.

"Basin."

Kevin blinked. "Basin?"

"Ayuh."

"That doesn't mean anything."

"It might," Pop said calmly, "if you know he cut her throat and then held her head over a basin to catch the blood."

"Oh my God!"

"Ayuh."

"Oh my God, really?"

Pop didn't bother answering that.

"It couldn't have been a fake?"

Pop gestured with the stem of his pipe at the Polaroids. "Are those?"

"Oh my God."

"Polaroids, now," Pop said, like a narrator moving briskly

to a new chapter in a novel and reading the words *Meanwhile, in another part of the forest,* "I've seen pitchers with people in em that the other people in the pitcher swear weren't there with em when the pitcher was taken. And there's one—this is a famous one—that a lady took over in England. What she did was snap a pitcher of some fox-hunters comin back home at the end of the day. You see em, about twenty in all, comin over a little wooden bridge. It's a tree-lined country road on both sides of that bridge. The ones in front are off the bridge already. And over on the right of the pitcher, standin by the road, there's a lady in a long dress and a hat with a veil on it so you can't see her face and she's got her pocketbook over her arm. Why, you can even see she's wearin a locket on her boosom, or maybe it's a watch.

"Well, when the lady that took the pitcher saw it, she got wicked upset, and wasn't nobody could blame her, son, because what I mean to say is she meant to take a pitcher of those fox-hunters comin home and no one else, because there wasn't nobody else *there.* Except in the pitcher there is. And when you look real close, it seems like you can see the trees right through that lady."

He's making all this up, putting me on, and when I leave he'll have a great big horselaugh, Kevin thought, knowing Pop Merrill was doing nothing of the sort.

"The lady that took that pitcher was stayin at one of those big English homes like they have on the education-TV shows, and when she showed that pitcher, I heard the man of the house fainted dead away. That part could be made up. Prob'ly is. *Sounds* made up, don't it? But I seen that pitcher in an article next to a painted portrait of that fella's great-grandmother, and it could be her, all right. Can't tell for certain because of the veil. But it *could* be."

"Could be a hoax, too," Kevin said faintly.

"Could be," Pop said indifferently. "People get up to all

sorts of didos. Lookit my nephew, there, for instance, Ace." Pop's nose wrinkled. "Doin four years in Shawshank, and for what? Bustin into The Mellow Tiger. He got up to didos and Sheriff Pangborn slammed him in the jug for it. Little ring-meat got just what he deserved."

Kevin, displaying a wisdom far beyond his years, said nothing.

"But when ghosts show up in photographs, son—or, like you say, what people *claim* to be ghosts—it's almost always in *Polaroid* photographs. And it almost always seems to be by accident. Now your pitchers of flyin saucers and that Lock Nest Monster, they almost always show up in the other kind. The kind some smart fella can get up to didos with in a darkroom."

He dropped Kevin a third wink, expressing all the didos (whatever *they* were) an unscrupulous photographer might get up to in a well-equipped darkroom.

Kevin thought of asking Pop if it was possible someone could get up to didos with a weegee and decided to continue keeping his mouth shut. It still seemed by far the wisest course.

"All by way of sayin I thought I'd ask if you saw somethin you knew in *these* Polaroid pitchers."

"I don't, though," Kevin said so earnestly that he believed Pop would believe he was lying, as his mom always did when he made the tactical mistake of even controlled vehemence.

"Ayuh, ayuh," Pop said, believing him so dismissively Kevin was almost irritated.

"Well," Kevin said after a moment which was silent except for the fifty thousand ticking clocks, "I guess that's it, huh?"

"Maybe not," Pop said. "What I mean to say is I got me a little idear. You mind takin some more pitchers with that camera?"

"What good is it? They're all the same."

"That's the point. They ain't."

Kevin opened his mouth, then closed it.

"I'll even chip in for the film," Pop said, and when he saw the amazed look on Kevin's face he quickly qualified: "A little, anyway."

"How many pictures would you want?"

"Well, you got . . . what? Twenty-eight already, is that right?"

"Yes, I think so."

"Thirty more," Pop said after a moment's thought.

"Why?"

"Ain't gonna tell you. Not right now." He produced a heavy purse that was hooked to a belt-loop on a steel chain. He opened it and took out a ten-dollar bill, hesitated, and added two ones with obvious reluctance. "Guess that'd cover half of it."

Yeah, right, Kevin thought.

"If you really *are* int'rested in the trick that camera's doing, I guess you'd pony up the rest, wouldn't you?" Pop's eyes gleamed at him like the eyes of an old, curious cat.

Kevin understood the man did more than expect him to say yes; to Pop it was inconceivable that he could say no. Kevin thought, *If I said no he wouldn't hear it; he'd say "Good, that's agreed, then," and I'd end up back on the sidewalk with his money in my pocket whether I wanted it or not.*

And he *did* have his birthday money.

All the same, there was that chill wind to think about. That wind that seemed to blow not from the surface but right out of those photographs in spite of their deceptively flat, deceptively shiny surfaces. He felt that wind coming from them despite their mute declaration which averred *We are Polaroids, and for no reason we can tell or even understand, we show only the undramatic surfaces of things.* That wind was there. What about that wind?

Kevin hesitated a moment longer and the bright eyes behind the rimless spectacles measured him. *I ain't gonna ask you if you're a man or a mouse,* Pop Merrill's eyes said. *You're fifteen years old, and what I mean to say is at fifteen you may not be a man yet, not quite, but you are too goddam old to be a mouse and both of us know it. And besides you're not from Away; you're from town, just like me.*

"Sure," Kevin said with a hollow lightness in his voice. It fooled neither of them. "I can get the film tonight, I guess, and bring the pictures in tomorrow, after school."

"Nope," Pop said.

"You're closed tomorrow?"

"Nope," Pop said, and because he *was* from town, Kevin waited patiently. "You're thinkin about takin thirty pitchers all at once, aren't you?"

"I guess so."

"That ain't the way I want you to do it," Pop said. "It don't matter *where* you take them, but it *does* matter *when.* Here. Lemme figure."

Pop figured, and then even wrote down a list of times, which Kevin pocketed.

"So!" Pop said, rubbing his hands briskly together so that they made a dry sound that was like two pieces of used-up sandpaper rubbing together. "You'll see me in . . . oh, three days or so?"

"Yes . . . I guess so."

"I'll bet you'd just as lief wait until Monday after school, anyway," Pop said. He dropped Kevin a fourth wink, slow and sly and humiliating in the extreme. "So your friends don't see you coming in here and tax you with it, is what I mean to say."

Kevin flushed and dropped his eyes to the worktable and began to gather up the Polaroids so his hands would have something to do. When he was embarrassed and they didn't, he cracked his knuckles.

"I—" He began some sort of absurd protest that would convince neither of them and then stopped, staring down at one of the photos.

"What?" Pop asked. For the first time since Kevin had approached him, Pop sounded entirely human, but Kevin hardly heard his words, much less his tone of faint alarm. "Now you look like *you* seen a ghost, boy."

"No," Kevin said. "No ghost. I see who took the picture. Who *really* took the picture."

"What in glory are you talking about?"

Kevin pointed to a shadow. He, his father, his mother, Meg, and apparently Mr. Merrill himself had taken it for the shadow of a tree that wasn't itself in the frame. But it wasn't a tree. Kevin saw that now, and what you had seen could never be unseen.

More hieroglyphics on the plinth.

"I don't see what you're gettin at," Pop said. But Kevin knew the old man knew he was getting at *something,* which was why he sounded put out.

"Look at the shadow of the dog first," Kevin said. "Then look at this one here again." He tapped the left side of the photograph. "In the picture, the sun is either going down or coming up. That makes all the shadows long, and it's hard to tell what's throwing them. But looking at it, just now, it clicked home for me."

"*What* clicked home, son?" Pop reached for the drawer, probably meaning to get the magnifying glass with the light in it again . . . and then stopped. All at once he didn't need it. All at once it had clicked into place for him, too.

"It's the shadow of a man, ain't it?" Pop said. "I be go to hell if that one ain't the shadow of a man."

"Or a woman. You can't tell. Those are legs, I'm sure they are, but they could belong to a woman wearing pants. Or even a kid. With the shadow running so long—"

"Ayuh, you can't tell."

Kevin said, "It's the shadow of whoever took it, isn't it?"

"Ayuh."

"But it wasn't *me,*" Kevin said. "It came out of my camera—all of them did—but I didn't take it. So who did, Mr. Merrill? Who did?"

"Call me Pop," the old man said absently, looking at the shadow in the picture, and Kevin felt his chest swell with pleasure as those few clocks still capable of running a little fast began to signal the others that, weary as they might be, it was time to charge the half-hour.

CHAPTER THREE

When Kevin arrived back at the Emporium Galorium with the photographs on Monday after school, the leaves had begun to turn color. He had been fifteen for almost two weeks and the novelty had worn off.

The novelty of that plinth, *the supernatural,* had not, but this wasn't anything he counted among his blessings. He had finished taking the schedule of photographs Pop had given him, and by the time he had, he had seen clearly—clearly enough, anyway—why Pop had wanted him to take them at intervals: the first ten on the hour, then let the camera rest, the second ten every two hours, and the third at three-hour intervals. He'd taken the last few that day at school. He had seen something else as well, something none of them *could* have seen at first; it was not clearly visible until the final three pictures. They had scared him so badly he had decided, even before taking the pictures to the Emporium Galorium, that he wanted to get rid of the Sun 660. Not exchange it; that was the last thing he wanted to do, because it would mean the camera would be out of his hands and hence out of his control. He couldn't have that.

It's mine, he had thought, and the thought kept recurring, but it wasn't a *true* thought. If it was—if the Sun only took pictures of the black breedless dog by the white picket fence when he, Kevin, was the one pushing the trigger—that would have been one thing. But that wasn't the case. Whatever the nasty magic inside the Sun might be, he was not its sole initiator. His father had taken the same (well, *almost* the same) picture, and so had Pop Merrill, and so had Meg when Kevin had let her take a couple of the pictures on Pop's carefully timed schedule.

"Did you number em, like I asked?" Pop asked when Kevin delivered them.

"Yes, one to fifty-eight," Kevin said. He thumbed through the stack of photographs, showing Pop the small circled numbers in the lower lefthand corner of each. "But I don't know if it matters. I've decided to get rid of the camera."

"Get rid of it? That ain't what you mean."

"No. I guess not. I'm going to break it up with a sledgehammer."

Pop looked at him with those shrewd little eyes. "That so?"

"Yes," Kevin said, meeting the shrewd gaze steadfastly. "Last week I would have laughed at the idea, but I'm not laughing now. I think the thing is dangerous."

"Well, I guess you could be right, and I guess you could tape a charge of dynamite to it and blow it to smithereens if you wanted. It's yours, is what I mean to say. But why don't you hold off a little while? There's somethin I want to do with these pitchers. You might be interested."

"What?"

"I druther not say," Pop answered, "case it don't turn out. But I might have somethin by the end of the week that'd help you decide better, one way or the other."

"I *have* decided," Kevin said, and tapped something that had shown up in the last two photographs.

"What *is* it?" Pop asked. "I've looked at it with m'glass, and I feel like I *should* know what it is—it's like a name you can't quite remember but have right on the tip of your tongue, is what I mean to say—but I don't quite."

"I suppose I could hold off until Friday or so," Kevin said, choosing not to answer the old man's question. "I really don't want to hold off much longer."

"Scared?"

"Yes," Kevin said simply. "I'm scared."

"You told your folks?"

"Not all of it, no."

"Well, you might want to. Might want to tell your dad, anyway, is what I mean to say. You got time to think on it while I take care of what it is I want to take care of."

"No matter what you want to do, I'm going to put my dad's sledgehammer on it come Friday," Kevin said. "I don't even *want* a camera anymore. Not a Polaroid or any other kind."

"Where is it now?"

"In my bureau drawer. And that's where it's going to stay."

"Stop by the store here on Friday," Pop said. "Bring the camera with you. We'll take a look at this little idear of mine, and then, if you want to bust the goddam thing up, I'll provide the sledgehammer myself. No charge. Even got a chopping block out back you can set it on."

"That's a deal," Kevin said, and smiled.

"Just what *have* you told your folks about all this?"

"That I'm still deciding. I didn't want to worry them. My mom, especially." Kevin looked at him curiously. "Why did you say I might want to tell my dad?"

"You bust up that camera, your father is going to be mad at you," Pop said. "That ain't so bad, but he's maybe gonna think you're a little bit of a fool, too. Or an old maid, squallin burglar to the police on account of a creaky board, is what I mean to say."

Kevin flushed a little, thinking of how angry his father had gotten when the idea of the supernatural had come up, then sighed. He hadn't thought of it in that light at all, but now that he did, he thought Pop was probably right. He didn't like the idea of his father being mad at him, but he could live with it. The idea that his father might think him a coward, a fool, or both, though . . . that was a different kettle of fish altogether.

Pop was watching him shrewdly, reading these thoughts as they crossed Kevin's face as easily as a man might read the headlines on the front page of a tabloid newspaper.

"You think he could meet you here around four in the afternoon on Friday?"

"No way," Kevin said. "He works in Portland. He hardly ever gets home before six."

"I'll give him a call, if you want," Pop said. "He'll come if I call."

Kevin gave him a wide-eyed stare.

Pop smiled thinly. "Oh, I know him," he said. "Know him of old. He don't like to let on about me any more than you do, and I understand that, but what I mean to say is I know him. I know a lot of people in this town. You'd be surprised, son."

"How?"

"Did him a favor one time," Pop said. He popped a match alight with his thumbnail, and veiled those eyes behind enough smoke so you couldn't tell if it was amusement, sentiment, or contempt in them.

"What kind of favor?"

"That," Pop said, "is between him and me. Just like this business here"—he gestured at the pile of photographs—"is between me and you. *That's* what I mean to say."

"Well . . . okay . . . I guess. Should I say anything to him?"

"Nope!" Pop said in his chipper way. "You let me take care of everything." And for a moment, in spite of the obfuscating pipe-smoke, there was something in Pop Merrill's eyes Kevin Delevan didn't care for. He went out, a sorely confused boy who knew only one thing for sure: he wanted this to be over.

When he was gone, Pop sat silent and moveless for nearly five minutes. He allowed his pipe to go out in his mouth and drummed his fingers, which were nearly as knowing and talented as those of a concert violinist but masqueraded as equipment which should more properly have belonged to a digger of ditches or a pourer of cement, next to the stack of photographs. As the smoke dissipated, his eyes stood out clearly, and they were as cold as ice in a December puddle.

Abruptly he put the pipe in its holder and called a camera-and-video shop in Lewiston. He asked two questions. The answer to both of them was yes. Pop hung up the phone and went back to drumming his fingers on the table beside the Polaroids. What he was planning wasn't really fair to the boy, but the boy had uncovered the corner of something he not only didn't understand but didn't *want* to understand.

Fair or not, Pop didn't believe he intended to let the boy do what the boy wanted to do. He hadn't decided what he himself meant to do, not yet, not entirely, but it was wise to be prepared.

That was *always* wise.

He sat and drummed his fingers and wondered what that thing was the boy had seen. He had obviously felt Pop would know—or might know—but Pop hadn't a clue. The boy might tell him on Friday. Or not. But if the boy didn't, the father, to whom Pop had once loaned four hundred dollars to cover a bet on a basketball game, a bet he had lost and which his wife knew nothing about, certainly would. If, that was, he could. Even the best of fathers didn't know all about their sons anymore once those sons were fifteen or so, but Pop thought Kevin was a very *young* fifteen, and that his dad knew most things . . . or could find them out.

He smiled and drummed his fingers and all the clocks began to charge wearily at the hour of five.

CHAPTER FOUR

Pop Merrill turned the sign which hung in his door from OPEN to CLOSED at two o'clock on Friday afternoon, slipped himself behind the wheel of his 1959 Chevrolet, which had been for years perfectly maintained at Sonny's Texaco at absolutely no cost at all (the fallout of another little loan, and Sonny Jackett another town fellow who would prefer hot coals pressed against the soles of his feet to admitting that he not only knew but was deeply indebted to Pop Merrill, who had gotten him out of a desperate scrape over in New Hampshire in '69), and took himself up to Lewiston, a city he hated because it seemed to him that there were only two streets in the whole town (maybe three) that weren't one-ways. He arrived as he always did when Lewiston and only Lewiston would do: not by driving to it but arriving somewhere near it and then spiraling slowly inward along those beshitted one-way streets until he reckoned he was as close as he could get and then walking the rest of the way, a tall thin man with a bald head, rimless specs, clean khaki pants with creases and cuffs, and a blue workman's shirt buttoned right up to the collar.

There was a sign in the window of Twin City Camera and Video that showed a cartoon man who appeared to be battling a huge tangle of movie-film and losing. The fellow looked just about ready to blow his stack. The words over and under the picture read: TIRED OF FIGHTING? WE TRANSFER YOUR 8 MM MOVIES (SNAPSHOTS TOO!) ONTO VIDEO TAPE!

Just another goddam gadget, Pop thought, opening the door and going in. World's dying of em.

But he was one of those people—world's dying of em—not

at all above using what he disparaged if it proved expedient. He spoke briefly with the clerk. The clerk got the proprietor. They had known each other for many years (probably since Homer sailed the wine-dark sea, some wits might have said). The proprietor invited Pop into the back room, where they shared a nip.

"That's a goddam strange bunch of photos," the proprietor said.

"Ayuh."

"The videotape I made of them is even stranger."

"I bet so."

"That all you got to say?"

"Ayuh."

"Fuck ya, then," the proprietor said, and they both cackled their shrill old-man's cackles. Behind the counter, the clerk winced.

Pop left twenty minutes later with two items: a video cassette, and a brand-new Polaroid Sun 660, still in its box.

When he got back to the shop, he called Kevin's house. He was not surprised when it was John Delevan who answered.

"If you've been fucking my boy over, I'll kill you, you old snake," John Delevan said without preamble, and distantly Pop could hear the boy's wounded cry: *"Da-ad!"*

Pop's lips skinned back from his teeth—crooked, eroded, pipe-yellow, but his own, by the bald-headed Christ—and if Kevin had seen him in that moment he would have done more than *wonder* if maybe Pop Merrill was something other than the Castle Rock version of the Kindly Old Sage of the Crackerbarrel: he would have *known.*

"Now, John," he said. "I've been trying to *help* your boy with that camera. That's all in the world I've been trying to do." He paused. "Just like that one time I gave you a help when you got a little too proud of the Seventy-Sixers, is what I mean to say."

A thundering silence from John Delevan's end of the line which meant he had plenty to say on *that* subject, but the kiddo was in the room and that was as good as a gag.

"Now, your kid don't know nothing about *that,*" Pop said, that nasty grin broadening in the tick-tock shadows of the Emporium Galorium, where the dominant smells were old magazines and mouse-turds. "I told him it wasn't none of his business, just like I told him that this business here *was.* I wouldn't have even brought up that bet if I knew another way to get you here, is what I mean to say. And you ought to see what I've got, John, because if you don't you won't understand why the boy wants to smash that camera you bought him—"

"*Smash* it!"

"—and why I think it's a hell of a good idea. Now are you going to come down here with him, or not?"

"I'm not in Portland, am I, dammit?"

"Never mind the CLOSED sign on the door," Pop said in the serene tone of a man who has been getting his own way for many years and expects to go right on getting it for many more. "Just knock."

"Who in hell gave my boy your name, Merrill?"

"I didn't ask him," Pop said in that same infuriatingly serene tone of voice, and hung up the telephone. And, to the empty shop: "All I know is that he came. Just like they always do."

While he waited, he took the Sun 660 he had bought in Lewiston out of its box and buried the box deep in the trash-can beside his worktable. He looked at the camera thoughtfully, then loaded the four-picture starter-pack that came with the camera. With that done, he unfolded the body of the camera, exposing the lens. The red light to the left of the lightning-bolt shape came on briefly, and then the green one began to stutter. Pop was not very surprised to find he was filled with trepidation. *Well,* he thought, *God hates a coward,* and pushed the shutter-release. The clutter of the Emporium Galorium's barnlike interior was bathed in an instant of merciless and improbable white light. The camera made its squidgy little whine and spat out what would be a Polaroid picture—perfectly adequate but somehow lacking; a picture that was all surfaces depicting a world where ships undoubtedly *would* sail off the fuming and monster-raddled edge of the earth if they went far enough west.

Pop watched it with the same mesmerized expression Clan Delevan had worn as it waited for Kevin's first picture to develop. He told himself this camera would not do the same thing, of course not, but he was stiff and wiry with tension just the same and, tough old bird or not, if a random board had creaked in the place just then, he almost certainly would have cried out.

But no board *did* creak, and when the picture developed it showed only what it was supposed to show: clocks assembled, clocks in pieces, toasters, stacks of magazines tied with twine, lamps with shades so horrible only women of the British upper classes could truly love them, shelves of quarter paperbacks (six for a buck) with titles like *After Dark My Sweet* and *Fire in the Flesh* and *The Brass Cupcake,* and, in the distant background, the dusty front window. You could read the letters EMPOR backward before the bulky silhouette of a bureau blocked off the rest.

No hulking creature from beyond the grave; no knife-wielding doll in blue overalls. Just a camera. He supposed the whim which had caused him to take a picture in the first place, just to see, showed how deeply this thing had worked its way under his skin.

Pop sighed and buried the photograph in the trash-can. He opened the wide drawer of the worktable and took out a small hammer. He held the camera firmly in his left hand and then swung the hammer on a short arc through the dusty tick-tock air. He didn't use a great deal of force. There was no need. Nobody took any pride in workmanship anymore. They talked about the wonders of modern science, synthetics, new alloys, polymers, Christ knew what. It didn't matter. Snot. That was what everything was *really* made out of these days, and you didn't have to work very hard to bust a camera that was made of snot.

The lens shattered. Shards of plastic flew from around it, and that reminded Pop of something else. Had it been the left or right side? He frowned. Left. He thought. They wouldn't notice anyway, or remember which side themselves if they did, you could damn near take that to the bank, but Pop hadn't feathered his nest with damn-nears. It was wise to be prepared.

Always wise.

He replaced the hammer, used a small brush to sweep the broken chunks of glass and plastic off the table and onto the floor, then returned the brush and took out a grease-pencil with a fine tip and an X-Act-O knife. He drew what he thought was the approximate shape of the piece of plastic which had broken off Kevin Delevan's Sun when Meg knocked it on the floor, then used the X-Act-O to carve along the lines. When he thought he had dug deep enough into the plastic, he put the X-Act-O back in the drawer, and then knocked the Polaroid camera off the worktable. What had happened once ought to happen again, especially with the fault-lines he had pre-carved.

It worked pretty slick, too. He examined the camera, which now had a chunk of plastic gone from the side as well as a busted lens, nodded, and placed it in the deep shadow under the worktable. Then he found the piece of plastic that had split off from the camera, and buried it in the trash along with the box and the single exposure he had taken.

Now there was nothing to do but wait for the Delevans to arrive. Pop took the video cassette upstairs to the cramped little apartment where he lived. He put it on top of the VCR he had bought to watch the fuck-movies you could buy nowadays, then sat down to read the paper. He saw there had been a plane-crash in Pakistan. A hundred and thirty people killed. Goddam fools were always getting themselves killed, Pop thought, but that was all right. A few less woggies in the world was a good thing all around. Then he turned to the sports to see how the Red Sox had done. They still had a good chance of winning the Eastern Division.

CHAPTER FIVE

"What was it?" Kevin asked as they prepared to go. They had the house to themselves. Meg was at her ballet class, and it was Mrs. Delevan's day to play bridge with her friends. She would come home at five with a large loaded pizza and news of who was getting divorced or at least thinking of it.

"None of your business," Mr. Delevan said in a rough voice which was both angry and embarrassed.

The day was chilly. Mr. Delevan had been looking for his light jacket. Now he stopped and turned around and looked at his son, who was standing behind him, wearing his own jacket and holding the Sun camera in one hand.

"All right," he said. "I never pulled that crap on you before and I guess I don't want to start now. You know what I mean."

"Yes," Kevin said, and thought: *I know exactly what you're talking about, is what I mean to say.*

"Your mother doesn't know anything about this."

"I won't tell her."

"Don't say that," his father told him sharply. "Don't start down that road or you'll never stop."

"But you said you never—"

"No, I never told her," his father said, finding the jacket at last and shrugging into it. "She never asked and I never told her. If she never asks you, you never have to tell her. That sound like a bullshit qualification to you?"

"Yeah," Kevin said. "To tell the truth, it does."

"Okay," Mr. Delevan said. "Okay . . . but that's the way we do it. If the subject ever comes up, you—*we*—have to tell. If it doesn't, we don't. That's just the way we do things in the grown-up world. It sounds fucked up, I guess, and sometimes it is fucked up, but that's how we do it. Can you live with that?"

"Yes. I guess so."

"Good. Let's go."

They walked down the driveway side by side, zipping their jackets. The wind played with the hair at John Delevan's temples, and Kevin noted for the first time—with uneasy surprise—that his father was starting to go gray there.

"It was no big deal, anyway," Mr. Delevan said. He might almost have been talking to himself. "It never is with Pop Merrill. He isn't a big-deal kind of guy, if you know what I mean."

Kevin nodded.

"He's a fairly wealthy man, you know, but that junk-shop of his isn't the reason why. He's Castle Rock's version of Shylock."

"Of who?"

"Never mind. You'll read the play sooner or later if education hasn't gone entirely to hell. He loans money at interest rates that are higher than the law allows."

"Why would people borrow from him?" Kevin asked as they walked toward downtown under trees from which leaves of red and purple and gold sifted slowly down.

"Because," Mr. Delevan said sourly, "they can't borrow anyplace else."

"You mean their credit's no good?"

"Something like that."

"But we . . . you . . ."

"Yeah. We're doing all right now. But we weren't *always* doing all right. When your mother and I were first married, how we were doing was all the way across town from all right."

He fell silent again for a time, and Kevin didn't interrupt him.

"Well, there was a guy who was awful proud of the Celtics one year," his father said. He was looking down at his feet, as if afraid to step on a crack and break his mother's back. "They were going into the play-offs against the Philadelphia Seventy-Sixers. They—the Celtics—were favored to win, but by a lot less than usual. I had a feeling the Seventy-Sixers were going to take them, that it was their year."

He looked quickly at his son, almost snatching the glance as a shoplifter might take a small but fairly valuable item and tuck it into his coat, and then went back to minding the cracks in the sidewalk again. They were now walking down Castle Hill and toward the town's single signal-light at the crossing of Lower Main Street and Watermill Lane. Beyond the intersection, what locals called the Tin Bridge crossed Castle Stream. Its overstructure cut the deep-blue autumn sky into neat geometrical shapes.

"I guess it's that feeling, that special *sureness,* that infects the poor souls who lose their bank accounts, their houses, their cars, even the clothes they stand up in at casinos and back-room poker games. That feeling that you got a telegram from God. I only got it that once, and I thank God for that.

"In those days I'd make a friendly bet on a football game or the World Series with somebody, five dollars was the most, I think, and usually it was a lot less than that, just a token thing, a quarter or maybe a pack of cigarettes."

This time it was Kevin who shoplifted a glance, only Mr. Delevan caught it, cracks in the sidewalk or no cracks.

"Yes, I smoked in those days, too. Now I don't smoke and I don't bet. Not since that last one. That last one cured me.

"Back then your mother and I had only been married two years. You weren't born yet. I was working as a surveyor's assistant, bringing home just about a hundred and sixteen dollars a week. Or that was what I cleared, anyway, when the government finally let go of it.

"This fellow who was so proud of the Celtics was one of the engineers. He even wore one of those green Celtics warm-up jackets to work, the kind that have the shamrock on the back.

The week before the play-offs, he kept saying he'd like to find someone brave enough and stupid enough to bet on the Seventy-Sixers, because he had four hundred dollars just waiting to catch him a dividend.

"That voice inside me kept getting louder and louder, and the day before the championship series started, I went up to him on lunch-break. My heart felt like it was going to tear right out of my chest, I was so scared."

"Because you didn't have four hundred dollars," Kevin said. "The other guy did, but you didn't." He was looking at his father openly now, the camera completely forgotten for the first time since his first visit to Pop Merrill. The wonder of what the Sun 660 was doing was lost—temporarily, anyway—in this newer, brighter wonder: as a young man his father had done something spectacularly stupid, just as Kevin knew other men did, just as he might do himself someday, when he was on his own and there was no adult member of the Reasonable tribe to protect him from some terrible impulse, some misbegotten instinct. His father, it seemed, had briefly been a member of the Instinctive tribe himself. It was hard to believe, but wasn't this the proof?

"Right."

"But you bet him."

"Not right away," his father said. "I told him I thought the Seventy-Sixers would take the championship, but four hundred bucks was a lot to risk for a guy who was only a surveyor's assistant."

"But you never came right out and told him you didn't have the money."

"I'm afraid it went a little further than that, Kevin. I implied I *did* have it. I said I couldn't afford to *lose* four hundred dollars, and that was disingenuous, to say the least. I told him I couldn't risk that kind of money on an even bet—still not lying, you see, but skating right up to the edge of the lie. *Do* you see?"

"Yes."

"I don't know what would have happened—maybe nothing—if the foreman hadn't rung the back-to-work bell right then. But he did, and this engineer threw up his hands and said, 'I'll give you two-to-one, sonny, if that's what you want. It don't matter to me. It's still gonna be four hundred in my pocket.' And before I knew what was happening we'd shook on it with half a dozen men watching and I was in the soup, for better or worse. And going home that night I thought of your mother, and what she'd say if she knew, and I pulled over to the shoulder of the road in the old Ford I had back then and I puked out the door."

A police car came rolling slowly down Harrington Street. Norris Ridgewick was driving and Andy Clutterbuck was riding shotgun. Clut raised his hand as the cruiser turned left on Main Street. John and Kevin Delevan raised their hands in return, and autumn drowsed peacefully around them as if John Delevan had never sat in the open door of his old Ford and puked into the road-dust between his own feet.

They crossed Main Street.

"Well . . . you could say I got my money's worth, anyway. The Sixers took it right to the last few seconds of the seventh game, and then one of those Irish bastards—I forget which one it was—stole the ball from Hal Greer and went to the hole with it and there went the four hundred dollars I didn't have. When I paid that goddam engineer off the next day he said he 'got a little nervous there near the end.' That was all. I could have popped his eyes out with my thumbs."

"You paid him off the next *day*? How'd you do that?"

"I told you, it was like a fever. Once we shook hands on the bet, the fever passed. I hoped like hell I'd win that bet, but I knew I'd have to *think* like I was going to lose. There was a lot more at stake than just four hundred dollars. There was the question of my job, of course, and what might happen if I wasn't able to pay off the guy I'd bet with. He was an engineer, after all, and technically my boss. That fellow had just enough son of a bitch in him to have fired my ass if I didn't pay the wager. It wouldn't have been the bet, but he would have found something, and it would have been something that would go on my work-record in big red letters, too. But that wasn't the biggest thing. Not at all."

"What was?"

"Your mother. Our marriage. When you're young and don't have either a pot to piss in or a window to throw it out of, a marriage is under strain all the time. It doesn't matter how much you love each other, that marriage is like an overloaded packhorse and you know it can fall to its knees or even roll over dead if all the wrong things happen at all the wrong times. I don't think she would have divorced me over a four-hundred-dollar bet, but I'm glad I never had to find out for sure. So when the fever passed, I saw that I might have bet a little more than four hundred dollars. I might just have bet my whole goddam future."

They were approaching the Emporium Galorium. There was a bench on the verge of the grassy town common, and Mr. Delevan gestured for Kevin to sit down.

"This won't take long," he said, and then laughed. It was a grating, compressed sound, like an inexperienced driver working a transmission lever. "It hurts too much to stretch out, even after all these years."

So they sat on the bench and Mr. Delevan finished the story of how he happened to know Pop Merrill while they looked across the grassy common with the bandstand in the middle.

"I went to him the same night I made the bet," he said. "I told your mother I was going out for cigarettes. I went after dark, so no one would see me. From town, I mean. They would have known I was in some kind of trouble, and I didn't want that. I went in and Pop said, 'What's a professional man like you doing in a place like this, Mr. John Delevan?' and I told him what I'd done and he said, 'You made a bet and already you have got your head set to the idea you've lost it.' 'If I do lose it,' I said, 'I want to make sure I don't lose anything else.'

"That made him laugh. 'I respect a wise man,' he said. 'I reckon I can trust you. If the Celtics win, you come see me. I'll take care of you. You got an honest face.' "

"And that was *all*?" Kevin asked. In eighth-grade math, they had done a unit on loans, and he still remembered most of it. "He didn't ask for any, uh, collateral?"

"People who go to Pop don't have collateral," his father said. "He's not a loan-shark like you see in the movies; he doesn't break any legs if you don't pay up. But he has ways of fixing people."

"What ways?"

"Never mind," John Delevan said. "After that last game ended, I went upstairs to tell your mother I was going to go out for cigarettes—again. She was asleep, though, so I was spared that lie. It was late, late for Castle Rock, anyway, going on eleven, but the lights were on in his place. I knew they would be. He gave me the money in tens. He took them out of an old Crisco can. All tens. I remember that. They were crumpled but he had made them straight. Forty ten-dollar bills, him counting them out like a bank-clerk with that pipe going and his glasses up on his head and for just a second there I felt like knocking his teeth out. Instead I thanked him. You don't know how hard it can be to say thank you sometimes. I hope you never do. He said, 'You understand the terms, now, don't you?' and I said I did, and he said, 'That's good. I ain't worried about you. What I mean to say is you got an honest face. You go on and take care of your business with that fella at work, and then take care of your business with me. And don't make any more bets. Man only has to look in your face to see you weren't cut out to be a gambler.' So I took the money and went home and put it under the floor-mat of the old Chevy and lay next to your mother and didn't sleep a wink all night long because I felt filthy. Next day I gave the tens to the engineer

I bet with, and *he* counted them out, and then he just folded them over and tucked them into one of his shirt pockets and buttoned the flap like that cash didn't mean any more than a gas receipt he'd have to turn in to the chief contractor at the end of the day. Then he clapped me on the shoulder and said, 'Well, you're a good man, Johnny. Better than I thought. I won four hundred but I lost twenty to Bill Untermeyer. He bet you'd come up with the dough first thing this morning and I bet him I wouldn't see it till the end of the week. If I ever did.' 'I pay my debts,' I said. 'Easy, now,' he said, and clapped me on the shoulder again, and I think that time I really *did* come close to popping his eyeballs out with my thumbs."

"How much interest did Pop charge you, Dad?"

His father looked at him sharply. "Does he let you call him that?"

"Yeah, why?"

"Watch out for him, then," Mr. Delevan said. "He's a snake."

Then he sighed, as if admitting to both of them that he was begging the question, and knew it. "Ten per cent. That's what the interest was."

"That's not so m—"

"Compounded weekly," Mr. Delevan added.

Kevin sat struck dumb for a moment. Then: "But that's not *legal!*"

"How true," Mr. Delevan said dryly. He looked at the strained expression of incredulity on his son's face and his own strained look broke. He laughed and clapped his son on the shoulder. "It's only the world, Kev," he said. "It kills us all in the end, anyhow."

"But—"

"But nothing. That was the freight, and he knew I'd pay it. I knew they were hiring on the three-to-eleven shift at the mill over in Oxford. I told you I'd gotten myself ready to lose, and going to Pop wasn't the only thing I did. I'd talked to your mother, said I might take a shift over there for awhile. After all, she'd been wanting a newer car, and maybe to move to a better apartment, and get a little something into the bank in case we had some kind of financial setback."

He laughed.

"Well, the financial setback had happened, and she didn't know it, and I meant to do my damnedest to keep her from finding out. I didn't know if I could or not, but I meant to do my damnedest. She was dead set against it. She said I'd kill myself, working sixteen hours a day. She said those mills were dangerous, you were always reading about someone losing an arm or leg or even getting crushed to death under the rollers. I told her not to worry, I'd get a job in the sorting room, minimum wage but sit-down work, and if it really *was* too much, I'd give it up. She was still against it. She said she'd go to work herself, but I talked her out of *that.* That was the last thing I wanted, you know."

Kevin nodded.

"I told her I'd quit six months, eight at the outside, anyway. So I went up and they hired me on, but not in the sorting room. I got a job in the rolling shed, feeding raw stock into a machine that looked like the wringer on a giant's washing machine. It was dangerous work, all right; if you slipped or if your attention wandered—and it was hard to keep that from happening because it was so damned monotonous—you'd lose part of yourself or all of it. I saw a man lose his hand in a roller once and I never want to see anything like that again. It was like watching a charge of dynamite go off in a rubber glove stuffed with meat."

"God-*damn,*" Kevin said. He had rarely said that in his father's presence, but his father did not seem to notice.

"Anyway, I got two dollars and eighty cents an hour, and after two months they bumped me to three ten," he said. "It was hell. I'd work on the road project all day long—at least it was early spring and not hot—and then race off to the mill, pushing that Chevy for all it was worth to keep from being late. I'd take off my khakis and just about jump into a pair of blue-jeans and a tee-shirt and work the rollers from three until eleven. I'd get home around midnight and the worst part was the nights when your mother waited up—which she did two or three nights a week—and I'd have to act cheery and full of pep when I could hardly walk a straight line, I was so tired. But if she'd seen that—"

"She would have made you stop."

"Yes. She would. So I'd act bright and chipper and tell her funny stories about the sorting room where I wasn't working and sometimes I'd wonder what would happen if she ever decided to drive up some night—to give me a hot dinner, or something like that. I did a pretty good job, but some of it must have showed, because she kept telling me I was silly to be knocking myself out for so little—and it really *did* seem like chicken-feed once the government dipped their beak and Pop dipped his. It seemed like just about what a fellow working in the sorting room for minimum wage would clear. They paid Wednesday afternoons, and I always made sure to cash my check in the office before the girls went home.

"Your mother never saw one of those checks.

"The first week I paid Pop fifty dollars—forty was interest, and ten was on the four hundred, which left three hundred and ninety owing. I was like a walking zombie. On the road I'd sit in my car at lunch, eat my sandwich, and then sleep until the foreman rang his goddamned bell. I *hated* that bell.

"I paid him fifty dollars the second week—thirty-nine was interest, eleven was on the principal—and I had it down to three hundred and seventy-nine dollars. I felt like a bird trying to eat a mountain one peck at a time.

"The third week I almost went into the roller myself, and it scared me so bad I woke up for a few minutes—enough to have an idea, anyway, so I guess it was a blessing in disguise. I had to give up smoking. I couldn't understand why I hadn't seen it before. In those days a pack of smokes cost forty cents.

I smoked two packs a day. That was five dollars and sixty cents a week!

"We had a cigarette break every two hours and I looked at my pack of Tareytons and saw I had ten, maybe twelve. I made those cigarettes last a week and a half, and I never bought another pack.

"I spent a month not knowing if I could make it or not. There were days when the alarm went off at six o'clock and I knew I couldn't, that I'd just have to tell Mary and take whatever she wanted to dish out. But by the time the second month started, I knew I was probably going to be all right. I think to this day it was the extra five sixty a week—that, and all the returnable beer and soda bottles I could pick up along the sides of the road—that made the difference. I had the principal down to three hundred, and that meant I could knock off twenty-five, twenty-six dollars a week from it, more as time went on.

"Then, in late April, we finished the road project and got a week off, with pay. I told Mary I was getting ready to quit my job at the mill and she said thank God, and I spent that week off from my regular job working all the hours I could get at the mill, because it was time and a half. I never had an accident. I saw them, saw men fresher and more awake than I was have them, but I never did. I don't know why. At the end of that week I gave Pop Merrill a hundred dollars and gave my week's notice at the paper mill. After that last week I had whittled the nut down enough so I could chip the rest off my regular pay-check without your mother noticing."

He fetched a deep sigh.

"Now you know how I know Pop Merrill, and why I don't trust him. I spent ten weeks in hell and he reaped the sweat off my forehead and my ass, too, in ten-dollar bills that he undoubtedly took out of that Crisco can or another one and passed on to some other sad sack who had got himself in the same kind of mess I did."

"Boy, you must hate him."

"No," Mr. Delevan said, getting up. "I don't hate him and I don't hate myself. I got a fever, that's all. It could have been worse. My marriage could have died of it, and you and Meg never would have been born, Kevin. Or I might have died of it myself. Pop Merrill was the cure. He was a *hard* cure, but he worked. What's hard to forgive is *how* he worked. He took every damned cent and wrote it down in a book in a drawer under his cash register and looked at the circles under my eyes and the way my pants had gotten a way of hanging off my hip-bones and he said nothing."

They walked toward the Emporium Galorium, which was painted the dusty faded yellow of signs left too long in country store windows, its false front both obvious and unapologetic. Next to it, Polly Chalmers was sweeping her walk and talking to Alan Pangborn, the county sheriff. She looked young and fresh with her hair pulled back in a horsetail; he looked young and heroic in his neatly pressed uniform. But things were not always the way they looked; even Kevin, at fifteen, knew that. Sheriff Pangborn had lost his wife and youngest son in a car accident that spring, and Kevin had heard that Ms. Chalmers, young or not, had a bad case of arthritis and might be crippled up with it before too many more years passed. Things were not always the way they looked. This thought caused him to glance toward the Emporium Galorium again . . . and then to look down at his birthday camera, which he was carrying in his hand.

"He even did me a favor," Mr. Delevan mused. "He got me to quit smoking. But I don't trust him. Walk careful around him, Kevin. And no matter what, let me do the talking. I might know him a little better now."

So they went into the dusty ticking silence, where Pop Merrill waited for them by the door, with his glasses propped on the bald dome of his head and a trick or two still up his sleeve.

CHAPTER SIX

"Well, and here you are, father and son," Pop said, giving them an admiring, grandfatherly smile. His eyes twinkled behind a haze of pipe-smoke and for a moment, although he was clean-shaven, Kevin thought Pop looked like Father Christmas. "You've got a fine boy, Mr. Delevan. *Fine.*"

"I know," Mr. Delevan said. "I was upset when I heard he'd been dealing with you because I want him to stay that way."

"That's hard," Pop said, with the faintest touch of reproach. "That's hard comin from a man who when he had nowhere else to turn—"

"That's over," Mr. Delevan said.

"Ayuh, ayuh, that's just what I mean to say."

"But this isn't."

"It will be," Pop said. He held a hand out to Kevin and Kevin gave him the Sun camera. "It will be today." He held the camera up, turning it over in his hands. "This is a piece of work. What *kind* of piece I don't know, but your boy wants to smash it because he thinks it's dangerous. I think he's right. But I told him, 'You don't want your daddy to think you're a sissy, do you?' That's the only reason I had him ho you down here, John—"

"I liked 'Mr. Delevan' better."

"All right," Pop said, and sighed. "I can see you ain't gonna warm up none and let bygones be bygones."

"No."

Kevin looked from one man to the other, his face distressed.

"Well, it don't matter," Pop said; both his voice and face

went cold with remarkable suddenness, and he didn't look like Father Christmas at all. "When I said the past is the past and what's done is done, I meant it . . . except when it affects what people do in the here and now. But I'm gonna say this, Mr. Delevan: I don't bottom deal, and you know it."

Pop delivered this magnificent lie with such flat coldness that both of them believed it; Mr. Delevan even felt a little ashamed of himself, as incredible as that was.

"Our business was our business. You told me what you wanted, I told you what I'd have to have in return, and you give it to me, and there was an end to it. This is another thing." And then Pop told a lie even more magnificent, a lie which was simply too towering to be disbelieved. "I got no stake in this, Mr. Delevan. There is nothing I want but to help your boy. I like him."

He smiled and Father Christmas was back so fast and strong that Kevin forgot he had ever been gone. Yet more than this: John Delevan, who had for months worked himself to the edge of exhaustion and perhaps even death between the rollers in order to pay the exorbitant price this man demanded to atone for a momentary lapse into insanity—John Delevan forgot that other expression, too.

Pop led them along the twisting aisles, through the smell of dead newsprint and past the tick-tock clocks, and he put the Sun 660 casually down on the worktable a little too near the edge (just as Kevin had done in his own house after taking that first picture) and then just went on toward the stairs at the back which led up to his little apartment. There was a dusty old mirror propped against the wall back there, and Pop looked into it, watching to see if the boy or his father would pick the camera up or move it further away from the edge. He didn't think either would, but it was possible.

They spared it not so much as a passing glance and as Pop led them up the narrow stairway with the ancient eroded rubber treads he grinned in a way it would have been bad business for anyone to see and thought, *Damn, I'm good!*

He opened the door and they went into the apartment.

Neither John nor Kevin Delevan had ever been in Pop's private quarters, and John knew of no one who had. In a way this was not surprising; no one was ever going to nominate Pop as the town's number-one citizen. John thought it was not *impossible* that the old fuck had a friend or two—the world never exhausted its oddities, it seemed—but if so, he didn't know who they were.

And Kevin spared a fleeting thought for Mr. Baker, his favorite teacher. He wondered if, perchance, Mr. Baker had ever gotten into the sort of crack he'd need a fellow like Pop to get him out of. This seemed as unlikely to him as the idea of Pop having friends seemed to his father . . . but then, an hour ago the idea that his own father—

Well. It was best let go, perhaps.

Pop *did* have a friend (or at least an acquaintance) or two, but he didn't bring them here. He didn't want to. It was his place, and it came closer to revealing his true nature than he wanted anyone to see. It struggled to be neat and couldn't get there. The wallpaper was marked with water-stains; they weren't glaring, but stealthy and brown, like the phantom thoughts that trouble anxious minds. There were crusty dishes in the old-fashioned deep sink, and although the table was clean and the lid on the plastic waste-can was shut, there was an odor of sardines and something else—unwashed feet, maybe—which was almost not there. An odor as stealthy as the water-stains on the wallpaper.

The living room was tiny. Here the smell was not of sardines and (maybe) feet but of old pipe-smoke. Two windows looked out on nothing more scenic than the alley that ran behind Mulberry Street, and while their panes showed some signs of having been washed—at least swiped at occasionally—the corners were bleared and greasy with years of condensed smoke. The whole place had an air of nasty things swept under the faded hooked rugs and hidden beneath the old-fashioned, overstuffed easy-chair and sofa. Both of these articles were light green, and your eye wanted to tell you they matched but couldn't, because they didn't. Not quite.

The only new things in the room were a large Mitsubishi television with a twenty-five-inch screen and a VCR on the endtable beside it. To the left of the endtable was a rack which caught Kevin's eye because it was totally empty. Pop had thought it best to put the better than seventy fuck-movies he owned in the closet for the time being.

One video cassette rested on top of the television in an unmarked case.

"Sit down," Pop said, gesturing at the lumpy couch. He went over to the TV and slipped the cassette out of its case.

Mr. Delevan looked at the couch with a momentary expression of doubt, as if he thought it might have bugs, and then sat down gingerly. Kevin sat beside him. The fear was back, stronger than ever.

Pop turned on the VCR, slid the cassette in, and then pushed the carriage down. "I know a fellow up the city," he began (to residents of Castle Rock and its neighboring towns, "up the city" always meant Lewiston), "who's run a camera store for twenty years or so. He got into this VCR business as soon as it started up, said it was going to be the wave of the future. He wanted me to go halves with him, but I thought he was nuts. Well, I was wrong on that one, is what I mean to say, but—"

"Get to the point," Kevin's father said.

"I'm tryin," Pop said, wide-eyed and injured. "If you'll let me."

Kevin pushed his elbow gently against his father's side, and Mr. Delevan said no more.

"Anyway, a couple of years ago he found out rentin tapes for folks to watch wasn't the only way to make money with these gadgets. If you was willin to lay out as little as eight hundred bucks, you could take people's movies and snapshots and put em on a tape for em. Lots easier to watch."

Kevin made a little involuntary noise and Pop smiled and nodded.

"Ayuh. You took fifty-eight pitchers with that camera of yours, and we all saw each one was a little different than the last one, and I guess we knew what it meant, but I wanted to see for myself. You don't have to be from Missouri to say show me, is what I mean to say."

"You tried to make a movie out of those snapshots?" Mr. Delevan asked.

"Didn't *try,*" Pop said. "*Did.* Or rather, the fella I know up the city did. But it was my idea."

"*Is* it a movie?" Kevin asked. He understood what Pop had done, and part of him was even chagrined that he hadn't thought of it himself, but mostly he was awash in wonder (and delight) at the idea.

"Look for yourself," Pop said, and turned on the TV. "Fifty-eight pitchers. When this fella does snapshots for folks, he generally videotapes each one for five seconds—long enough to get a good look, he says, but not long enough to get bored before you go on to the next one. I told him I wanted each of these on for just a single second, and to run them right together with no fades."

Kevin remembered a game he used to play in grade school when he had finished some lesson and had free time before the next one began. He had a little dime pad of paper which was called a Rain-Bo Skool Pad because there would be thirty pages of little yellow sheets, then thirty pages of little pink sheets, then thirty pages of green, and so on. To play the game, you went to the very last page and at the bottom you drew a stick-man wearing baggy shorts and holding his arms out. On the next page you drew the same stick-man in the same place and wearing the same baggy shorts, only this time you drew his arms further up . . . but just a little bit. You did that on every page until the arms came together over the stick-man's head. Then, if you still had time, you went on drawing the stick-man, but now with the arms going down. And if you flipped the pages very fast when you were done, you had a crude sort of cartoon which showed a boxer celebrating a KO: he raised his hands over his head, clasped them, shook them, lowered them.

He shivered. His father looked at him. Kevin shook his head and murmured, "Nothing."

"So what I mean to say is the tape only runs about a minute," Pop said. "You got to look close. Ready?"

No, Kevin thought.

"I guess so," Mr. Delevan said. He was still trying to sound grumpy and put-out, but Kevin could tell he had gotten interested in spite of himself.

"Okay," Pop Merrill said, and pushed the PLAY button.

Kevin told himself over and over again that it was stupid to feel scared. He told himself this and it didn't do a single bit of good.

He knew what he was going to see, because he and Meg had both noticed the Sun was doing something besides simply reproducing the same image over and over, like a photocopier; it did not take long for them to realize that the photographs were expressing movement from one to the next.

"Look," Meg had said. "The dog's moving!"

Instead of responding with one of the friendly-but-irritating wisecracks he usually reserved for his little sister, Kevin had said, "It *does* look like it . . . but you can't tell for sure, Meg."

"Yes, you can," she said. They were in his room, where he had been morosely looking at the camera. It sat on the middle of his desk with his new schoolbooks, which he had been meaning to cover, pushed to one side. Meg had bent the gooseneck of his study-lamp so it shone a bright circle of light on the middle of his desk blotter. She moved the camera aside and put the first picture—the one with the dab of cake-frosting on it—in the center of the light. "Count the fence-posts between the dog's behind and the righthand edge of the picture," she said.

"Those are pickets, not fence-posts," he told her. "Like what you do when your nose goes on strike."

"Ha-ha. Count them."

He did. He could see four, and part of a fifth, although the dog's scraggly hindquarters obscured most of that one.

"Now look at this one."

She put the fourth Polaroid in front of him. Now he could see *all* of the fifth picket, and part of the sixth.

So he knew—or believed—he was going to see a cross between a very old cartoon and one of those "flip-books" he used to make in grammar school when the time weighed heavy on his hands.

The last twenty-five seconds of the tape were indeed like that, although, Kevin thought, the flip-books he had drawn in the second grade were really better . . . the perceived action of the boxer raising and lowering his hands smoother. In the last twenty-five seconds of the videotape the action moved in rams and jerks which made the old Keystone Kops silent films look like marvels of modern filmmaking in comparison.

Still, the key word was *action,* and it held all of them—even Pop—spellbound. They watched the minute of footage three times without saying a word. There was no sound but breathing: Kevin's fast and smooth through his nose, his father's deeper, Pop's a phlegmy rattle in his narrow chest.

And the first thirty seconds or so . . .

He had expected action, he supposed; there was action in the flip-books, and there was action in the Saturday-morning cartoons, which were just a slightly more sophisticated version of the flip-books, but what he had not expected was that for the first thirty seconds of the tape it wasn't like watching notebook pages rapidly thumbed or even a primitive cartoon like *Possible Possum* on TV: for thirty seconds (twenty-eight, anyway), his single Polaroid photographs looked eerily like a real movie. Not a Hollywood movie, of course, not even a low-budget horror movie of the sort Megan sometimes pestered him to rent for their own VCR when their mother and father went out for the evening; it was more like a snippet of home movie made by someone who has just gotten an eight-millimeter camera and doesn't know how to use it very well yet.

In those first twenty-eight seconds, the black no-breed dog walked with barely perceptible jerks along the fence, exposing five, six, seven pickets; it even paused to sniff a second time at one of them, apparently reading another of those canine telegrams. Then it walked on, head down and toward the fence, hindquarters switched out toward the camera. And, halfway through this first part, Kevin noted something else he hadn't seen before: the photographer had apparently swung his camera to keep the dog in the frame. If he (or she) hadn't done so, the dog would have simply walked out of the picture, leaving nothing to look at but the fence. The pickets at the far right of the first two or three photographs disappeared beyond the righthand border of the picture and new pickets appeared at the left. You could tell, because the tip of one of those two rightmost pickets had been broken off. Now it was no longer in the frame.

The dog started to sniff again . . . and then its head came up. Its good ear stiffened; the one which had been slashed and laid limp in some long-ago fight tried to do the same. There was no sound, but Kevin felt with a certainty beyond repudiation that the dog had begun to growl. The dog had sensed something or someone. What or who?

Kevin looked at the shadow they had at first dismissed as the branch of a tree or maybe a phone-pole and knew.

Its head began to turn . . . and that was when the second half of this strange "film" began, thirty seconds of snap-jerk action that made your head ache and your eyeballs hot. Pop had had a hunch, Kevin thought, or maybe he had even read about something like this before. Either way, it had proved out and was too obvious to need stating. With the pictures taken quite closely together, if not exactly one after another, the action in the makeshift "movie" almost flowed. Not quite, but almost. But when the time between photographs was spaced, what they were watching became something that nauseated your eye because it wanted to see either a moving picture or a series of still photographs and instead it saw both and neither.

Time was passing in that flat Polaroid world. Not at the same speed it passed in this

(real?)

one, or the sun would have come up (or gone down) over there three times already and whatever the dog was going to do would be done (if it *had* something to do), and if it did not, it would just be gone and there would be only the moveless and seemingly eternal eroded picket fence guarding the listless patch of lawn, but it *was* passing.

The dog's head was coming around to face the photographer, owner of the shadow, like the head of a dog in the grip of a fit: at one moment the face and even the shape of the head was obscured by that floppy ear; then you saw one black-brown eye enclosed by a round and somehow mucky corona that made Kevin think of a spoiled egg-white; then you saw half the muzzle with the lips appearing slightly wrinkled, as if the dog were getting ready to bark or growl; and last of all you saw three-quarters of a face somehow more awful than the face of any mere dog had a right to be, even a mean one. The white spackles along its muzzle suggested it was no longer young. At the very end of the tape you saw the dog's lips were indeed pulling back. There was one blink of white Kevin thought was a tooth. He didn't see that until the third run-through. It was the eye that held him. It was homicidal. This breedless dog almost screamed rogue. And it was nameless; he knew that, as well. He knew beyond a shadow of a doubt that no Polaroid man or Polaroid woman or Polaroid child had ever named that Polaroid dog; it was a stray, born stray, raised stray, grown old and mean stray, the avatar of all the dogs who had ever wandered the world, unnamed and un-homed, killing chickens, eating garbage out of the cans they had long since learned to knock over, sleeping in culverts and beneath the porches of deserted houses. Its wits would be dim, but its instincts would be sharp and red. It—

When Pop Merrill spoke, Kevin was so deeply and fundamentally startled out of his thoughts that he nearly screamed.

"The man who took those pictures," he said. "If there *was* a person, is what I mean to say. What do you suppose happened to *him?*"

Pop had frozen the last frame with his remote control. A line of static ran through the picture. Kevin wished it ran through the dog's eye, but the line was below it. That eye stared out at them, baleful, stupidly murderous—no, not stupidly, not entirely, that was what made it not merely frightening but terrifying—and no one needed to answer Pop's question. You needed no more pictures to understand what was going to happen next. The dog had perhaps heard something: of course it had, and Kevin knew what. It had heard that squidgy little whine.

Further pictures would show it continuing to turn, and then beginning to fill more and more of each frame until there was nothing to see but dog—no listless patchy lawn, no fence, no sidewalk, no shadow. Just the dog.

Who meant to attack.

Who meant to kill, if it could.

Kevin's dry voice seemed to be coming from someone else. "I don't think it likes getting its picture taken," he said.

Pop's short laugh was like a bunch of dry twigs broken over a knee for kindling.

"Rewind it," Mr. Delevan said.

"You want to see the whole thing again?" Pop asked.

"No—just the last ten seconds or so."

Pop used the remote control to go back, then ran it again. The dog turned its head, as jerky as a robot which is old and running down but still dangerous, and Kevin wanted to tell them, *Stop now. Just stop. That's enough. Just stop and let's break the camera.* Because there was something else, wasn't there? Something he didn't want to think about but soon would, like it or not; he could feel it breaching in his mind like the broad back of a whale.

"Once more," Mr. Delevan said. "Frame by frame this time. Can you do that?"

"Ayuh," Pop said. "Goddam machine does everything but the laundry."

This time one frame, one picture, at a time. It was not like a robot now, or not exactly, but like some weird clock, something that belonged with Pop's other specimens downstairs. Jerk. Jerk. Jerk. The head coming around. Soon they would be faced by that merciless, not-quite-idiotic eye again.

"What's that?" Mr. Delevan asked.

"What's what?" Pop asked, as if he didn't know it was the thing the boy hadn't wanted to talk about the other day, the thing, he was convinced, that had made up the boy's mind about destroying the camera once and for all.

"Underneath its neck," Mr. Delevan said, and pointed. "It's not wearing a collar or a tag, but it's got something around its neck on a string or a thin rope."

"I dunno," Pop said imperturbably. "Maybe your boy does. Young folks have sharper eyes than us old fellas."

Mr. Delevan turned to look at Kevin. "Can you make it out?"

"I—" He fell silent. "It's really small."

His mind returned to what his father had said when they were leaving the house. *If she never asks you, you never have to tell her. . . . That's just the way we do things in the grown-up world.* Just now he had asked Kevin if he could make out what that thing under the dog's neck was. Kevin hadn't really answered that question; he had said something else altogether. *It's really small.* And it was. The fact that he knew what it was in spite of that . . . well . . .

What had his father called it? Skating up to the edge of a lie?

And he *couldn't* actually see it. Not *actually.* Just the same, he knew. The eye only suggested; the heart understood. Just as his heart understood that, if he was right, the camera must be destroyed. *Must* be.

At that moment, Pop Merrill was suddenly struck by an agreeable inspiration. He got up and snapped off the TV. "I've got the pitchers downstairs," he said. "Brought em back with the videotape. I seen that thing m'self, and ran my magnifying glass over it, but still couldn't tell . . . but it *does* look familiar, God cuss it. Just let me go get the pitchers and m'glass."

"We might as well go down with you," Kevin said, which was the last thing in the world Pop wanted, but then Delevan stepped in, God bless him, and said he might like to look at the tape again after they looked at the last couple of pictures under the magnifying glass.

"Won't take a minute," Pop said, and was gone, sprightly as a bird hopping from twig to twig on an apple tree, before either of them could have protested, if either had had a mind to.

Kevin did not. That thought had finally breached its monstrous back in his mind, and, like it or not, he was forced to contemplate it.

It was simple, as a whale's back is simple—at least to the eye of one who does not study whales for a living—and it was colossal in the same way.

It wasn't an idea but a simple certainty. It had to do with that odd flatness Polaroids always seemed to have, with the way they showed you things only in two dimensions, although all photographs did that; it was that other photographs seemed to at least *suggest* a third dimension, even those taken with a simple Kodak 110.

The things in *his* photographs, photographs which showed things he had never seen through the Sun's viewfinder or anywhere else, for that matter, were that same way: flatly, unapologetically two-dimensional.

Except for the dog.

The dog wasn't *flat.* The dog wasn't *meaningless,* a thing you could recognize but which had no emotional impact. The dog not only seemed to *suggest* three dimensions but to really *have* them, the way a hologram seems to really have them, or one of those 3-D movies where you had to wear special glasses to reconcile the double images.

It's not a Polaroid dog, Kevin thought, *and it doesn't belong in the world Polaroids take pictures of. That's crazy, I know it is, but I also know it's true. So what does it mean? Why is my camera taking pictures of it over and over . . . and what Polaroid man or Polaroid woman is snapping pictures of it? Does he or she even see it? If it is a three-dimensional dog in a two-dimensional world, maybe he or she doesn't see it . . . can't see it. They say for us time is the fourth dimension, and we know it's there, but we can't see it. We can't even really feel it pass, although sometimes, especially when we're bored, I guess, it seems like we can.*

But when you got right down to it, all that might not even matter, and the questions were far too tough for him, anyway. There were other questions that seemed more important to him, vital questions, maybe even mortal ones.

Like why was the dog in *his* camera?

Did it want something of *him,* or just of anybody? At first he had thought the answer was anybody, anybody would do because anybody could take pictures of it and the movement always advanced. But the thing around its neck, that thing that wasn't a collar . . . that had to do with him, Kevin Delevan, and nobody else. Did it want to do something *to* him? If the answer to *that* question was yes, you could forget all the other ones, because it was pretty goddamned obvious what the dog wanted to do. It was in its murky eye, in the snarl you could just see beginning. He thought it wanted two things.

First to escape.

Then to kill.

There's a man or woman over there with a camera who maybe doesn't even see that dog, Kevin thought, *and if the photographer can't see the dog, maybe the dog can't see the photographer, and so the photographer is safe. But if the dog really is three-dimensional, maybe he sees out—maybe he sees whoever is using my camera. Maybe it's still not me, or not specifically me; maybe whoever is using the camera is its target.*

Still—the thing it was wearing around its neck. What about that?

He thought of the cur's dark eyes, saved from stupidity by a single malevolent spark. God knew how the dog had gotten into that Polaroid world in the first place, but when its picture was taken, it could see *out,* and it wanted to *get* out, and Kevin believed in his heart that it wanted to kill him first, the thing it was wearing around its neck *said* it wanted to kill him first, *proclaimed* that it wanted to kill him first, but after that?

Why, after Kevin, anyone would do.

Anyone at all.

In a way it was like another game you played when you were a little kid, wasn't it? It was like Giant Step. The dog had been walking along the fence. The dog had heard the Polaroid, that squidgy little whine. It turned, and saw . . . what? Its own world or universe? A world or universe enough *like* its own so it saw or sensed it could or at least might be able to live and hunt here? It didn't matter. Now, every time someone took a picture of it, the dog would get closer. It would get closer and closer until . . . well, until what? Until it burst through, somehow?

"That's stupid," he muttered. "It'd never fit."

"What?" his father asked, roused from his own musings.

"Nothing," Kevin said. "I was just talking to myse—"

Then, from downstairs, muffled but audible, they heard Pop Merrill cry out in mingled dismay, irritation, and surprise: "Well shit fire and save matches! *Goddammit!*"

Kevin and his father looked at each other, startled.

"Let's go see what happened," his father said, and got up. "I hope he didn't fall down and break his arm, or something. I mean, part of me *does* hope it, but . . . you know."

Kevin thought: *What if he's been taking pictures? What if that dog's down there?*

It hadn't sounded like fear in the old man's voice, and of course there really was no way a dog that looked as big as a medium-sized German shepherd could come through either a camera the size of the Sun 660 or one of the prints it made. You might as well try to drag a washing machine through a knothole.

Still, he felt fear enough for both of them—for all three of them—as he followed his father back down the stairs to the gloomy bazaar below.

Going down the stairs, Pop Merrill was as happy as a clam at high tide.

He had been prepared to make the switch right in front of them if he had to. Might have been a problem if it had just been the boy, who was still a year or so away from thinking he knew everything, but the boy's dad—ah, fooling *that* fine fellow would have been like stealing a bottle from a baby. Had he told the boy about the jam he'd gotten into that time? From the way the boy looked at him—a new, cautious way—Pop thought Delevan probably had. And what else had the father told the son? Well, let's see. *Does he let you call him Pop? That means he's planning to pull a fast one on you.* That was for starters. *He's a lowdown snake in the grass, son.* That was for seconds.

And, of course, there was the prize of them all: *Let me do the talking, boy. I know him better than you do. You just let me handle everything.* Men like Delevan were to Pop Merrill what a nice platter of fried chicken was to some folks—tender, tasty, juicy, and all but falling off the bone. Once Delevan had been little more than a kid himself, and he would never fully understand that it wasn't Pop who had stuck his tit in the wringer but he himself. The man could have gone to his wife and she would have tapped that old biddy aunt of hers whose tight little ass was lined with hundred-dollar bills, and Delevan would have spent some time in the doghouse, but she would have let him out in time. He not only hadn't seen it that way; he hadn't seen it at all. And now, for no reason but idiot time, which came and went without any help from anyone, he thought he knew all there was to know about Reginald Marion Merrill.

Which was just the way Pop liked it.

Why, he could have swapped one camera for the other right in front of the man and Delevan never would have seen a goddamned thing—that was how sure he was he had old Pop figured out.

But this was better.

You never ever asked Lady Luck for a date; she had a way of standing men up just when they needed her the most. But if she showed up on her own . . . well, it was wise to drop whatever it was you were doing and take her out and wine her and dine her just as lavishly as you could. That was one bitch who always put out if you treated her right.

So he went quickly to the worktable, bent, and extracted the Polaroid 660 with the broken lens from the shadows underneath. He put it on the table, fished a key-ring from his pocket (with one quick glance over his shoulder to be sure neither of them had decided to come down after all), and selected the small key which opened the locked drawer that formed the entire left side of the table. In this deep drawer were a number of gold Krugerrands; a stamp album in which the least valuable stamp was worth six hundred dollars in the latest *Scott Stamp Catalogue*; a coin collection worth approximately nineteen thousand dollars; two dozen glossy photographs of a bleary-eyed woman having sexual congress with a Shetland pony; and an amount of cash totalling just over two thousand dollars.

The cash, which he stowed in a variety of tin cans, was Pop's loan-out money. John Delevan would have recognized the bills. They were all crumpled tens.

Pop deposited Kevin's Sun 660 in this drawer, locked it, and put his key-ring back in his pocket. Then he pushed the camera with the broken lens off the edge of the worktable (again) and cried out "Well shit fire and save matches! *Goddammit!*" loud enough for them to hear.

Then he arranged his face in the proper expression of dismay and chagrin and waited for them to come running to see what had happened.

"Pop?" Kevin cried. "Mr. Merrill? Are you okay?"

"Ayuh," he said. "Didn't hurt nothin but my goddam pride. That camera's just bad luck, I guess. I bent over to open the tool-drawer, is what I mean to say, and I knocked the fucking thing right off onto the floor. Only I guess it didn't come through s'well this time. I dunno if I should say I'm sorry or not. I mean, you was gonna—"

He held the camera apologetically out to Kevin, who took it, looked at the broken lens and shattered plastic of the housing around it. "No, it's okay," Kevin told him, turning the camera over in his hands—but he did not handle it in the same gingerly, tentative way he had before: as if it might really be constructed not of plastic and glass but some sort of explosive. "I meant to bust it up, anyhow."

"Guess I saved you the trouble."

"I'd feel better—" Kevin began.

"Ayuh, ayuh. I feel the same way about mice. Laugh if you want to, but when I catch one in a trap and it's dead, I beat it with a broom anyway. Just to be sure, is what I mean to say."

Kevin smiled faintly, then looked at his father. "He said he's got a chopping block out back, Dad—"

"Got a pretty good sledge in the shed, too, if ain't nobody took it."

"Do you mind, Dad?"

"It's your camera, Kev," Delevan said. He flicked a distrustful glance at Pop, but it was a glance that said he distrusted Pop on general principles, and not for any specific reason. "But if it will make you feel any better, I think it's the right decision."

"Good," Kevin said. He felt a tremendous weight go off his shoulders—no, it was from his *heart* that the weight was lifted. With the lens broken, the camera was surely useless . . . but he wouldn't feel really at ease until he saw it in fragments around Pop's chopping block. He turned it over in his hands, front to back and back to front, amused and amazed at how much he liked the broken way it looked and felt.

"I think I owe you the cost of that camera, Delevan," Pop said, knowing exactly how the man would respond.

"No," Delevan said. "Let's smash it and forget this whole crazy thing ever hap—" He paused. "I almost forgot—we were going to look at those last few photos under your magnifying glass. I wanted to see if I could make out the thing the dog's wearing. I keep thinking it looks familiar."

"We can do that after we get rid of the camera, can't we?" Kevin asked. "Okay, Dad?"

"Sure."

"And then," Pop said, "it might not be such a bad idear to burn the pitchers themselves. You could do it right in my stove."

"I think that's a *great* idea," Kevin said. "What do you think, Dad?"

"I think Mrs. Merrill never raised any fools," his father said.

"Well," Pop said, smiling enigmatically from behind folds of rising blue smoke, "there was five of us, you know."

• • •

The day had been bright blue when Kevin and his father walked down to the Emporium Galorium; a perfect autumn day. Now it was four-thirty, the sky had mostly clouded over, and it looked like it might rain before dark. The first real chill of the fall touched Kevin's hands. It would chap them red if he stayed out long enough, but he had no plans to. His mom would be home in half an hour, and already he wondered what she would say when she saw Dad was with him, and what his dad would say.

But that was for later.

Kevin set the Sun 660 on the chopping block in the little backyard, and Pop Merrill handed him a sledgehammer. The haft was worn smooth with usage. The head was rusty, as if someone had left it carelessly out in the rain not once or twice but many times. Yet it would do the job, all right. Kevin had no doubt of that. The Polaroid, its lens broken and most of the housing around it shattered as well, looked fragile and defenseless sitting there on the block's chipped, chunked, and splintered surface, where you expected to see a length of ash or maple waiting to be split in two.

Kevin set his hands on the sledgehammer's smooth handle and tightened them.

"You're sure, son?" Mr. Delevan asked.

"Yes."

"Okay." Kevin's father glanced at his own watch. "Do it, then."

Pop stood to one side with his pipe clamped between his wretched teeth, hands in his back pockets. He looked shrewdly from the boy to the man and then back to the boy, but said nothing.

Kevin lifted the sledgehammer and, suddenly surprised by an anger at the camera he hadn't even known he felt, he brought it down with all the force he could muster.

Too hard, he thought. *You're going to miss it, be lucky not to mash your own foot, and there it will sit, not much more than a piece of hollow plastic a little kid could stomp flat without half trying, and even if you're lucky enough to miss your foot, Pop will look at you. He won't say anything: he won't have to. It'll all be in the way he looks at you.*

And thought also: *It doesn't matter if I hit it or not. It's magic, some kind of magic camera, and you* CAN'T *break it. Even if you hit it dead on the money the sledge will just bounce off it, like bullets off Superman's chest.*

But then there was no more time to think anything, because the sledge connected squarely with the camera. Kevin really *had* swung much too hard to maintain anything resembling control, but he got lucky. And the sledgehammer didn't just bounce back up, maybe hitting Kevin square between the eyes and killing him, like the final twist in a horror story.

The Sun didn't so much shatter as detonate. Black plastic flew everywhere. A long rectangle with a shiny black square at one end—a picture which would never be taken, Kevin supposed—fluttered to the bare ground beside the chopping block and lay there, face-down.

There was a moment of silence so complete they could hear not only the cars on Lower Main Street but kids playing tag half a block away in the parking lot behind Wardell's Country Store, which had gone bankrupt two years before and had stood vacant ever since.

"Well, that's *that,*" Pop said. "You swung that sledge just like Paul Bunyan, Kevin! I should smile n kiss a pig if you didn't.

"No need to do that," he said, now addressing Mr. Delevan, who was picking up broken chunks of plastic as prissily as a man picking up the pieces of a glass he has accidentally knocked to the floor and shattered. "I have a boy comes in and cleans up the yard every week or two. I know it don't look like much as it is, but if I didn't have that kid . . . Glory!"

"Then maybe we ought to use your magnifying glass and take

a look at those pictures," Mr. Delevan said, standing up. He dropped the few pieces of plastic he had picked up into a rusty incinerator that stood nearby and then brushed off his hands.

"Fine by me," Pop said.

"Then burn them," Kevin reminded. "Don't forget that."

"I didn't," Pop said. "I'll feel better when they're gone, too."

"Jesus!" John Delevan said. He was bending over Pop Merrill's worktable, looking through the lighted magnifying glass at the second-to-last photograph. It was the one in which the object around the dog's neck showed most clearly; in the last photo, the object had swung back in the other direction again. "Kevin, look at that and tell me if it's what I think it is."

Kevin took the magnifying glass and looked. He had known, of course, but even so it still wasn't a look just for form's sake. Clyde Tombaugh must have looked at an actual photograph of the planet Pluto for the first time with the same fascination. Tombaugh had known it was there; calculations showing similar distortions in the orbital paths of Neptune and Uranus had made Pluto not just a possibility but a necessity. Still, to *know* a thing was there, even to know what it *was* . . . that did not detract from the fascination of actually *seeing* it for the first time.

He let go of the switch and handed the glass back to Pop. "Yeah," he said to his father. "It's what you think it is." His voice was as flat as . . . as flat as the things in that Polaroid world, he supposed, and he felt an urge to laugh. He kept the sound inside, not because it would have been inappropriate to laugh (although he supposed it would have been) but because the sound would have come out sounding . . . well . . . flat.

Pop waited and when it became clear to him they were going to need a nudge, he said: "Well, don't keep me hoppin from one foot to the other! What the hell is it?"

Kevin had felt reluctant to tell him before, and he felt reluctant now. There was no reason for it, but—

Stop being so goddamned dumb! He helped you when you needed helping, no matter how he earns his dough. Tell him and burn the pictures and let's get out of here before all those clocks start striking five.

Yes. If he was around when *that* happened, he thought it would be the final touch; he would just go completely bananas and they could cart him away to Juniper Hill, raving about real dogs in Polaroid worlds and cameras that took the same picture over and over again except not quite.

"The Polaroid camera was a birthday present," he heard himself saying in that same dry voice. "What it's wearing around its neck was another one."

Pop slowly pushed his glasses up onto his bald head and squinted at Kevin. "I don't guess I'm followin you, son."

"I have an aunt," Kevin said. "Actually she's my great-aunt, but we're not supposed to call her that, because she says it makes her feel old. Aunt Hilda. Anyway, Aunt Hilda's husband left her a lot of money—my mom says she's worth over a million dollars—but she's a tightwad."

He stopped, leaving his father space to protest, but his father only smiled sourly and nodded. Pop Merrill, who knew all about *that* situation (there was not, in truth, much in Castle Rock and the surrounding areas Pop didn't know at least something about), simply held his peace and waited for the boy to get around to spilling it.

"She comes and spends Christmas with us once every three years, and that's about the only time we go to church, because *she* goes to church. We have lots of broccoli when Aunt Hilda comes. None of us like it, and it just about makes my sister puke, but Aunt Hilda likes broccoli a *lot,* so we have it. There was a book on our summer reading list, *Great Expectations,* and there was a lady in it who was just like Aunt Hilda. She got her kicks dangling her money in front of her relatives. Her name was Miss Havisham, and when Miss Havisham said frog, people jumped. We jump, and I guess the rest of our family does, too."

"Oh, your Uncle Randy makes your mother look like a piker," Mr. Delevan said unexpectedly. Kevin thought his dad meant it to sound amused in a cynical sort of way, but what came through was a deep, acidic bitterness. "When Aunt Hilda says frog in Randy's house, they all just about turn cartwheels over the roofbeams."

"Anyway," Kevin told Pop, "she sends me the same thing for my birthday every year. I mean, each one is different, but each one's really the same."

"What is it she sends you, boy?"

"A string tie," Kevin said. "Like the kind you see guys wearing in old-time country-music bands. It has something different on the clasp every year, but it's always a string tie."

Pop snatched the magnifying glass and bent over the picture with it. "Stone the crows!" he said, straightening up. "A string tie! That's just what it is! Now how come I didn't see that?"

"Because it isn't the sort of thing a dog would wear around his neck, I guess," Kevin said in that same wooden voice. They had been here for only forty-five minutes or so, but he felt as if he had aged another fifteen years. *The thing to remember,* his mind told him over and over, *is that the camera is gone. It's nothing but splinters. Never mind all the King's horses and all the King's men; not even all the guys who work making cameras at the Polaroid factory in Schenectady could put* that *baby back together again.*

Yes, and thank God. Because this was the end of the line. As far as Kevin was concerned, if he never encountered *the supernatural* again until he was eighty, never so much as brushed up against it, it would still be too soon.

"Also, it's very small," Mr. Delevan pointed out. "I was there when Kevin took it out of the box, and we all knew what it was going to be. The only mystery was what would be on the clasp this year. We joked about it."

"What *is* on the clasp?" Pop asked, peering into the photograph again . . . or peering *at* it, anyway: Kevin would testify in any court in the land that peering *into* a Polaroid was simply impossible.

"A bird," Kevin said. "I'm pretty sure it's a woodpecker. And that's what the dog in the picture is wearing around its neck. A string tie with a woodpecker on the clasp."

"Jesus!" Pop said. He was in his own quiet way one of the world's finer actors, but there was no need to simulate the surprise he felt now.

Mr. Delevan abruptly swept all the Polaroids together. "Let's put these goddam things in the woodstove," he said.

When Kevin and his father got home, it was ten minutes past five and starting to drizzle. Mrs. Delevan's two-year-old Toyota was not in the driveway, but she had been and gone. There was a note from her on the kitchen table, held down by the salt and pepper shakers. When Kevin unfolded the note, a ten-dollar bill fell out.

Dear Kevin,

At the bridge game Jane Doyon asked if Meg and I would like to have dinner with her at Bonanza as her husband is off to Pittsburgh on business and she's knocking around the house alone. I said we'd be delighted. Meg especially. You know how much she likes to be "one of the girls"! Hope you don't mind eating in "solitary splendor." Why not order a pizza & some soda for yourself, and your father can order for himself when he gets home. He doesn't like reheated pizza & you know he'll want a couple of beers.

Luv you,
Mom

They looked at each other, both saying *Well, there's one thing we don't have to worry about* without having to say it out loud.

Apparently neither she nor Meg had noticed that Mr. Delevan's car was still in the garage.

"Do you want me to—" Kevin began, but there was no need to finish because his father cut across him: "Yes. Check. Right now."

Kevin went up the stairs by twos and into his room. He had a bureau and a desk. The bottom desk drawer was full of what Kevin simply thought of as "stuff": things it would have seemed somehow criminal to throw away, although he had no real use for any of them. There was his grandfather's pocket-watch, heavy, scrolled, magnificent . . . and so badly rusted that the jeweler in Lewiston he and his mother had brought it to only took one look, shook his head, and pushed it back across the counter. There were two sets of matching cufflinks and two orphans, a *Penthouse* gatefold, a paperback book called *Gross Jokes,* and a Sony Walkman which had for some reason developed a habit of eating the tapes it was supposed to play. It was just stuff, that was all. There was no other word that fit.

Part of the stuff, of course, was the thirteen string ties Aunt Hilda had sent him for his last thirteen birthdays.

He took them out one by one, counted, came up with twelve instead of thirteen, rooted through the stuff-drawer again, then counted again. Still twelve.

"Not there?"

Kevin, who had been squatting, cried out and leaped to his feet.

"I'm sorry," Mr. Delevan said from the doorway. "That was dumb."

"That's okay," Kevin said. He wondered briefly how fast a person's heart could beat before the person in question simply blew his engine. "I'm just . . . on edge. Stupid."

"It's not." His father looked at him soberly. "When I saw that tape, I got so scared I felt like maybe I'd have to reach into my mouth and push my stomach back down with my fingers."

Kevin looked at his father gratefully.

"It's not there, is it?" Mr. Delevan asked. "The one with the woodpecker or whatever in hell it was supposed to be?"

"No. It's not."

"Did you keep the camera in that drawer?"

Kevin nodded his head slowly. "Pop—Mr. Merrill—said to let it rest every so often. That was part of the schedule he made out."

Something tugged briefly at his mind, was gone.

"So I stuck it in there."

"Boy," Mr. Delevan said softly.

"Yeah."

They looked at each other in the gloom, and then suddenly Kevin smiled. It was like watching the sun burst through a raft of clouds.

"What?"

"I was remembering how it felt," Kevin said. "I swung that sledgehammer so hard—"

Mr. Delevan began to smile, too. "I thought you were going to take off your own damned—"

"—and when it hit it made this CRUNCH! sound—"

"—flew every damn whichway—"

"BOOM!" Kevin finished. "Gone!"

They began to laugh together in Kevin's room, and Kevin found he was almost—*almost*—glad all this had happened. The sense of relief was as inexpressible and yet as perfect as the sensation one feels when, either by happy accident or by some psychic guidance, another person manages to scratch that one itchy place on one's back that one cannot scratch oneself, hitting it exactly, bang on the money, making it wonderfully worse for a single second by the simple touch, pressure, arrival, of those fingers . . . and then, oh blessed relief.

It was like that with the camera and with his father's knowing.

"It's gone," Kevin said. "Isn't it?"

"As gone as Hiroshima after the *Enola Gay* dropped the

A-bomb on it," Mr. Delevan replied, and then added: "Smashed to shit, is what I mean to say."

Kevin gawped at his father and then burst into helpless peals—screams, almost—of laughter. His father joined him. They orderd a loaded pizza shortly after. When Mary and Meg Delevan arrived home at twenty past seven, they both still had the giggles.

"Well, you two look like you've been up to no good," Mrs. Delevan said, a little puzzled. There was something in their hilarity that struck the woman center of her—that deep part which the sex seems to tap into fully only in times of childbirth and disaster—as a little unhealthy. They looked and sounded like men who may have just missed having a car accident. "Want to let the ladies in on it?"

"Just two bachelors having a good time," Mr. Delevan said.

"*Smashing* good time," Kevin amplified, to which his father added, "Is what we mean to say," and they looked at each other and were howling again.

Meg, honestly bewildered, looked at her mother and said: "Why are they doing that, Mom?"

Mrs. Delevan said, "Because they have penises, dear. Go hang up your coat."

Pop Merrill let the Delevans, *père et fils,* out, and then locked the door behind them. He turned off all the lights save for the one over the worktable, produced his keys, and opened his own stuff-drawer. From it he took Kevin Delevan's Polaroid Sun 660, chipped but otherwise undamaged, and looked at it fixedly. It had scared both the father and the son. That was clear enough to Pop; it had scared him as well, and still did. But to put a thing like this on a block and smash it to smithereens? That was crazy.

There was a way to turn a buck on this goddam thing.

There always was.

Pop locked it away in the drawer. He would sleep on it, and

by the morning he would know how to proceed. In truth, he already had a pretty goddam good idea.

He got up, snapped off the work-light, and wove his way through the gloom toward the steps leading up to his apartment. He moved with the unthinking surefooted grace of long practice.

Halfway there, he stopped.

He felt an urge, an amazingly strong urge, to go back and look at the camera again. What in God's name for? He didn't even have any *film* for the Christless thing . . . not that *he* had any intentions of taking any pictures with it. If someone *else* wanted to take some snapshots, watch that dog's progress, the buyer was welcome. Caveet emperor, as he always said. Let the goddam emperor caveet or not as it suited him. As for him, he'd as soon go into a cage filled with lions without even a goddam whip and chair.

Still . . .

"Leave it," he said roughly in the darkness, and the sound of his own voice startled him and got him moving and he went upstairs without another look back.

CHAPTER SEVEN

Very early the next morning, Kevin Delevan had a nightmare so horrible he could only remember parts of it, like isolated phrases of music heard on a radio with a defective speaker.

He was walking into a grungy little mill-town. Apparently he was on the bum, because he had a pack on his back. The name of the town was Oatley, and Kevin had the idea it was either in Vermont or upstate New York. *You know anyone hiring here in Oatley?* he asked an old man pushing a shopping-cart along a cracked sidewalk. There were no groceries in the cart; it was full of indeterminate junk, and Kevin realized the man was a wino. *Get away!* the wino screamed. *Get away! Feef! Fushing feef! Fushing* FEEF!

Kevin ran, darted across the street, more frightened of the man's madness than he was of the idea anyone might believe that he, Kevin, was a thief. The wino called after him: *This ain't Oatley! This is Hildasville! Get out of town, you fushing feef!*

It was then that he realized that this town wasn't Oatley or Hildasville or any other town with a normal name. How could an utterly abnormal town have a normal name?

Everything—streets, buildings, cars, signs, the few pedestrians—was two-dimensional. Things had height, they had width . . . but they had no thickness. He passed a woman who looked the way Meg's ballet teacher might look if the ballet teacher put on a hundred and fifty pounds. She was wearing slacks the color of Bazooka bubble gum. Like the wino, she was pushing a shopping-cart. It had a squeaky wheel. It was full of Polaroid Sun 660 cameras. She looked at Kevin with narrow suspicion as they drew closer together. At the moment when they passed each other on the sidewalk, she disappeared. Her *shadow* was still there and he could still hear that rhythmic squeaking, but she was no longer there. Then she reappeared, looking back at him from her fat flat suspicious face, and Kevin understood the reason why she had disappeared for a moment. It was because the concept of "a side view" didn't exist, *couldn't* exist, in a world where everything was perfectly flat.

This is Polaroidsville, he thought with a relief which was strangely mingled with horror. *And that means this is only a dream.*

Then he saw the white picket fence, and the dog, and the photographer standing in the gutter. There were rimless spectacles propped up on his head. It was Pop Merrill.

Well, son, you found him, the two-dimensional Polaroid Pop said to Kevin without removing his eye from the shutter. *That's the dog, right there. The one tore up that kid out in Schenectady.* YOUR *dog, is what I mean to say.*

Then Kevin woke up in his own bed, afraid he had screamed but more concerned at first not about the dream but to make sure he was *all there,* all three dimensions of him.

He was. But something was wrong.

Stupid dream, he thought. *Let it go, why can't you? It's over. Photos are burned, all fifty-eight of them. And the camera's bus—*

His thought broke off like ice as that something, that something *wrong,* teased at his mind again.

It's not over, he thought. *It's n—*

But before the thought could finish itself, Kevin Delevan fell deeply, dreamlessly asleep. The next morning, he barely remembered the nightmare at all.

CHAPTER EIGHT

The two weeks following his acquisition of Kevin Delevan's Polaroid Sun were the most aggravating, infuriating, *humiliating* two weeks of Pop Merrill's life. There were quite a few people in Castle Rock who would have said it couldn't have happened to a more deserving guy. Not that anyone in Castle Rock did know . . . and that was just about all the consolation Pop could take. He found it cold comfort. Very cold indeed, thank you very much.

But who would have ever believed the Mad Hatters would have, *could* have, let him down so badly?

It was almost enough to make a man wonder if he was starting to slip a little.

God forbid.

CHAPTER NINE

Back in September, he hadn't even bothered to wonder if he would sell the Polaroid; the only questions were how soon and how much. The Delevans had bandied the word *supernatural* about, and Pop hadn't corrected them, although he knew that what the Sun was doing would be more properly classed by psychic investigators as a paranormal rather than supernatural phenomenon. He *could* have told them that, but if he *had,* they might both have wondered how come the owner of a small-town used-goods store (and part-time usurer) knew so much about the subject. The fact was this: he knew a lot because it was *profitable* to know a lot, and it was profitable to know a lot because of the people he thought of as "my Mad Hatters."

Mad Hatters were people who recorded empty rooms on expensive audio equipment not for a lark or a drunken party stunt, but either because they believed passionately in an unseen world and wanted to prove its existence, or because they wanted passionately to get in touch with friends and/or relatives who had "passed on" ("passed on": that's what they always called it; Mad Hatters never had relatives who did something so simple as die).

Mad Hatters not only owned and used Ouija Boards, they had regular conversations with "spirit guides" in the "other world" (never "heaven," "hell," or even "the rest area of the dead" but the "other world") who put them in touch with friends, relatives, queens, dead rock-and-roll singers, even arch-villains. Pop knew of a Mad Hatter in Vermont who had twice-weekly conversations with Hitler. Hitler had told him it was all a bum rap, he had sued for peace in January of 1943 and that son of a bitch Churchill had turned him down. Hitler had also told him Paul Newman was a space alien who had been born in a cave on the moon.

Mad Hatters went to séances as regularly (and as compulsively) as drug addicts visited their pushers. They bought crystal balls and amulets guaranteed to bring good luck; they organized their own little societies and investigated reputedly haunted houses for all the usual phenomena: teleplasm, table-rappings, floating tables and beds, cold spots, and, of course, ghosts. They noted all of these, real or imagined, with the enthusiasm of dedicated bird-watchers.

Most of them had a ripping good time. Some did not. There was that fellow from Wolfeboro, for instance. He hanged himself in the notorious Tecumseh House, where a gentleman farmer had, in the 1880s and '90s, helped his fellow men by day and helped himself to them by night, dining on them at a formal table in his cellar. The table stood upon a floor of sour packed dirt which had yielded the bones and decomposed bodies of at least twelve and perhaps as many as thirty-five young men, all vagabonds. The fellow from Wolfeboro had left this brief note on a pad of paper beside his Ouija Board: *Can't leave the house. Doors all locked. I hear him eating. Tried cotton. Does no good.*

And the poor deluded asshole probably thought he really did, Pop had mused after hearing this story from a source he trusted.

Then there was a fellow in Dunwich, Massachusetts, to whom Pop had once sold a so-called spirit trumpet for ninety dollars; the fellow had taken the trumpet to the Dunwich Cemetery and must have heard something exceedingly unpleasant, because he had been raving in a padded cell in Arkham for almost six years now, totally insane. When he had gone into the boneyard, his hair had been black; when his screams awoke the few neighbors who lived close enough to the cemetery to hear them and the police were summoned, it was as white as his howling face.

And there was the woman in Portland who lost an eye when

a session with the Ouija Board went cataclysmically wrong . . . the man in Kingston, Rhode Island, who lost three fingers on his right hand when the rear door of a car in which two teenagers had committed suicide closed on it . . . the old lady who landed in Massachusetts Memorial Hospital short most of one ear when her equally elderly cat, Claudette, supposedly went on a rampage during a séance . . .

Pop believed some of these things, disbelieved others, and mostly held no opinion—not because he didn't have enough hard evidence one way or the other, but because he didn't give a fart in a high wind about ghosts, séances, crystal balls, spirit trumpets, rampaging cats, or the fabled John the Con-querer Root. As far as Reginald Marion "Pop" Merrill was concerned, the Mad Hatters could all take a flying fuck at the moon.

As long, of course, as one of them handed over some mighty tall tickets for Kevin Delevan's camera before taking passage on the next shuttle.

Pop didn't call these enthusiasts Mad Hatters because of their spectral interests; he called them that because the great majority—he was sometimes tempted to say *all* of them—seemed to be rich, retired, and just begging to be plucked. If you were willing to spend fifteen minutes with them nodding and agreeing while they assured you they could pick a fake medium from a real one just by walking into the *room,* let alone sitting down at the séance table, or if you spent an equal amount of time listening to garbled noises which might or might not be words on a tape player with the proper expression of awe on your face, you could sell them a four-dollar paperweight for a hundred by telling them a man had once glimpsed his dead mother in it. You gave them a smile and they wrote you a check for two hundred dollars. You gave them an encouraging word and they wrote you a check for two *thousand* dollars. If you gave them both things at the same time, they just kind of passed the checkbook over to you and asked you to fill in an amount.

It had always been as easy as taking candy from a baby.

Until now.

Pop didn't keep a file in his cabinet marked MAD HATTERS any more than he kept one marked COIN COLLECTORS or STAMP COLLECTORS. He didn't even *have* a file-cabinet. The closest thing to it was a battered old book of phone numbers he carried around in his back pocket (which, like his purse, had over the years taken on the shallow ungenerous curve of the spindly buttock it lay against every day). Pop kept his files where a man in his line of work should *always* keep them: in his head. There were eight full-blown Mad Hatters that he had done business with over the years, people who didn't just dabble in the occult but who got right down and rolled around in it. The richest was a retired industrialist named McCarty who lived on his own island about twelve miles off the coast. This fellow disdained boats and employed a full-time pilot who flew him back and forth to the mainland when he needed to go.

Pop went to see him on September 28th, the day after he obtained the camera from Kevin (he didn't, couldn't, exactly think of it as robbery; the boy, after all, had been planning to smash it to shit anyway, and what he didn't know surely couldn't hurt him). He drove to a private airstrip just north of Boothbay Harbor in his old but perfectly maintained car, then gritted his teeth and slitted his eyes and held onto the steel lockbox with the Polaroid Sun 660 in it for dear life as the Mad Hatter's Beechcraft plunged down the dirt runway like a rogue horse, rose into the air just as Pop was sure they were going to fall off the edge and be smashed to jelly on the rocks below, and flew away into the autumn empyrean. He had made this trip twice before, and had sworn each time that he would never get into that goddam flying coffin again.

They bumped and jounced along with the hungry Atlantic less than five hundred feet below, the pilot talking cheerfully the whole way. Pop nodded and said ayuh in what seemed like the right places, although he was more concerned with his imminent demise than with anything the pilot was saying.

Then the island was ahead with its horribly, dismally, suicidally short landing strip and its sprawling house of redwood and fieldstone, and the pilot swooped down, leaving Pop's poor old acid-shrivelled stomach somewhere in the air above them, and they hit with a thud and then, somehow, miraculously, they were taxiing to a stop, still alive and whole, and Pop could safely go back to believing God was just another invention of the Mad Hatters . . . at least until he had to get back in that damned plane for the return journey.

"Great day for flying, huh, Mr. Merrill?" the pilot asked, unfolding the steps for him.

"Finest kind," Pop grunted, then strode up the walk to the house where the Thanksgiving turkey stood in the doorway, smiling in eager anticipation. Pop had promised to show him "the goddamnedest thing I ever come across," and Cedric McCarty looked like he couldn't wait. He'd take one quick look for form's sake, Pop thought, and then fork over the lettuce. He went back to the mainland forty-five minutes later, barely noticing the thumps and jounces and gut-goozling drops as the Beech hit the occasional air-pocket. He was a chastened, thoughtful man.

He had aimed the Polaroid at the Mad Hatter and took his picture. While they waited for it to develop, the Mad Hatter took a picture of Pop . . . and when the flashbulb went off, had he heard something? Had he heard the low, ugly snarl of that black dog, or had it been his imagination? Imagination, most likely. Pop had made some magnificent deals in his time, and you couldn't do that without imagination.

Still—

Cedric McCarty, retired industrialist *par excellence* and Mad Hatter *extraordinaire,* watched the photographs develop with that same childlike eagerness, but when they finally came clear, he looked amused and even perhaps a little contemptuous and Pop knew with the infallible intuition which had developed over almost fifty years that arguing, cajolery, even vague hints that he had another customer just *slavering* for a chance to buy this camera—none of those usually reliable techniques would work. A big orange NO SALE card had gone up in Cedric McCarty's mind.

By why?

Goddammit, *why?*

In the picture Pop took, that glint Kevin had spotted amid the wrinkles of the black dog's muzzle had clearly become a tooth—except *tooth* wasn't the right word, not by any stretch of the imagination. That was a *fang.* In the one McCarty took, you could see the beginnings of the neighboring teeth.

Fucking dog's got a mouth like a bear-trap, Pop thought. Unbidden, an image of his arm in that dog's mouth rose in his mind. He saw the dog not *biting* it, not *eating* it, but *shredding* it, the way the many teeth of a wood-chipper shred bark, leaves, and small branches. *How long would it take?* he wondered, and looked at those dirty eyes staring out at him from the overgrown face and knew it wouldn't take long. Or suppose the dog seized him by the crotch, instead? Suppose—

But McCarty had said something and was waiting for a response. Pop turned his attention to the man, and any lingering hope he might have held of making a sale evaporated. The Mad Hatter *extraordinaire,* who would cheerfully spend an afternoon with you trying to call up the ghost of your dear departed Uncle Ned, was gone. In his place was McCarty's other side: the hardheaded realist who had made *Fortune* magazine's listing of the richest men in America for twelve straight years—not because he was an airhead who had had the good fortune to inherit both a lot of money and an honest, capable staff to husband and expand it, but because he had been a genius in the field of aerodynamic design and development. He was not as rich as Howard Hughes but not quite as crazy as Hughes had been at the end, either. When it came to psychic phenomena, the man was a Mad Hatter. Outside that one area, however, he was a shark that made the likes of Pop Merrill look like a tadpole swimming in a mud-puddle.

"Sorry," Pop said. "I was woolgatherin a little, Mr. McCarty."

"I said it's fascinating," McCarty said. "Especially the subtle indications of passing time from one photo to the next. How does it work? Camera in camera?"

"I don't understand what you're gettin at."

"No, not a camera," McCarty said, speaking to himself. He picked the camera up and shook it next to his ear. "More likely some sort of roller device."

Pop stared at the man with no idea what he was talking about . . . except it spelled NO SALE, whatever it was. That goddam Christless ride in the little plane (and soon to do over again), all for nothing. But why? *Why?* He had been so *sure* of this fellow, who would probably believe the Brooklyn Bridge was a spectral illusion from the "other side" if you *told* him it was. So *why?*

"Slots, of course!" McCarty said, as delighted as a child. "*Slots!* There's a circular belt on pulleys inside this housing with a number of slots built into it. Each slot contains an exposed Polaroid picture of this dog. Continuity suggests"—he looked carefully at the pictures again—"yes, that the dog might have been *filmed,* with the Polaroids made from individual frames. When the shutter is released, a picture drops from its slot and emerges. The battery turns the belt enough to position the next photo, and—*voilà!*"

His pleasant expression was suddenly gone, and Pop saw a man who looked like he might have made his way to fame and fortune over the broken, bleeding bodies of his competitors . . . and enjoyed it.

"Joe will fly you back," he said. His voice had gone chill and impersonal. "You're good, Mr. Merrill"—this man, Pop realized glumly, would never call him Pop again—"I'll admit that. You've finally overstepped yourself, but for a long time you had me fooled. How much did you take me for? Was it all claptrap?"

"I didn't take you for one red cent," Pop said, lying stoutly. "I never sold you one single thing I didn't b'lieve was the genuine article, and what I mean to say is that goes for that camera as well."

"You make me sick," McCarty said. "Not because I trusted you; I've trusted others who were fakes and shams. Not because you took my money; it wasn't enough to matter. You make me sick because it's men like you that have kept the scientific investigation of psychic phenomena in the dark ages, something to be laughed at, something to be dismissed as the sole province of crackpots and dimwits. The one consolation is that sooner or later you fellows always overstep yourselves. You get greedy and try to palm off something ridiculous like *this.* I want you out of here, Mr. Merrill."

Pop had his pipe in his mouth and a Diamond Blue Tip in one shaking hand. McCarty pointed at him, and the chilly eyes above that finger made it look like the barrel of a gun.

"And if you light that stinking thing in here," he said, "I'll have Joe yank it out of your mouth and dump the coals down the back of your pants. So unless you want to leave my house with your skinny ass in flames, I suggest—"

"What's the *matter* with you, Mr. McCarty?" Pop bleated. "These pitchers didn't come out all developed! *You watched em develop with your own eyes!*"

"An emulsion any kid with a twelve-dollar chemistry set could whip up," McCarty said coldly. "It's not the catalyst-fixative the Polaroid people use, but it's close. You expose your Polaroids—or create them from movie-film, if that's what you did—and then you take them in a standard darkroom and paint them with goop. When they're dry, you load them. When they pop out, they look like any Polaroid that hasn't started to develop yet. Solid gray in a white border. Then the light hits your home-made emulsion, creating a chemical change, and it evaporates, showing a picture you yourself took hours or days or weeks before. Joe?"

Before Pop could say anything else, his arms were seized and he was not so much walked as propelled from the spacious, glass-walled living room. He wouldn't have said anything, anyway. Another of the many things a good businessman had to know was when he was licked. And yet he wanted to shout over his shoulder: *Some dumb cunt with dyed hair and a crystal ball she ordered from* Fate *magazine floats a book or a lamp or a page of goddam sheet-music through a dark room and you bout shit yourself, but when I show you a camera that takes pitchers of some other world, you have me thrown out by the seat of m'pants! You're mad as a hatter, all right! Well, fuck ya! There's other fish in the sea!*

So there were.

On October 5th, Pop got into his perfectly maintained car and drove to Portland to pay a visit on the Pus Sisters.

The Pus Sisters were identical twins who lived in Portland. They were eighty or so but looked older than Stonehenge. They chain-smoked Camel cigarettes, and had done so since they were seventeen, they were happy to tell you. They never coughed in spite of the six packs they smoked between them each and every day. They were driven about—on those rare occasions when they left their red brick Colonial mansion—in a 1958 Lincoln Continental which had the somber glow of a hearse. This vehicle was piloted by a black woman only a little younger than the Pus Sisters themselves. This female chauffeur was probably a mute, but might just be something a bit more special: one of the few truly taciturn human beings God ever made. Pop did not know and had never asked. He had dealt with the two old ladies for nearly thirty years, the black woman had been with them all that time, mostly driving the car, sometimes washing it, sometimes mowing the lawn or clipping the hedges around the house, sometimes stalking down to the mailbox on the corner with letters from the Pus Sisters to God alone knew who (he didn't know if the black woman ever went or was allowed inside the house, either, only that he had never seen her there), and during all that time he had never heard this marvellous creature speak.

The Colonial mansion was in Portland's Bramhall district, which is to Portland what the Beacon Hill area is to Boston. In that latter city, in the land of the bean and the cod, it's said the Cabots speak only to Lowells and the Lowells speak only to God, but the Pus Sisters and their few remaining contemporaries in Portland would and did calmly assert that the Lowells had turned a private connection into a party line some years after the Deeres and their Portland contemporaries had set up the original wire.

And of course no one in his right mind would have called them the Pus Sisters to their identical faces any more than anyone in his right mind would have stuck his nose in a bandsaw to take care of a troublesome itch. They were the Pus Sisters when they weren't around (and when one was fairly sure one was in company which didn't contain a tale-bearer or two), but their real names were Miss Eleusippus Deere and Mrs. Meleusippus Verrill. Their father, in his determination to combine devout Christianity with an exhibition of his own erudition, had named them for two of three triplets who had all become saints . . . but who, unfortunately, had been *male* saints.

Meleusippus's husband had died a great many years before, during the Battle of Leyte Gulf in 1944, as a matter of fact, but she had resolutely kept his name ever since, which made it impossible to take the easy way out and simply call them the Misses Deere. No; you had to practice those goddamned tongue-twister names until they came out as smooth as shit from a waxed asshole. If you fucked up once, they held it against you, and you might lose their custom for as long as six months or a year. Fuck up twice, and don't even bother to call. Ever again.

Pop drove with the steel box containing the Polaroid camera on the seat beside him, saying their names over and over again in a low voice: "Eleusippus. Meleusippus. Eleusippus and Meleusippus. Ayuh. *That's* all right."

But, as it turned out, that was the only thing that *was* all right. They wanted the Polaroid no more than McCarty had wanted it . . . although Pop had been so shaken by *that* encounter he went in fully prepared to take ten thousand dollars less, or fifty per cent of his original confident estimate of what the camera might fetch.

The elderly black woman was raking leaves, revealing a lawn which, October or not, was still as green as the felt on a billiard table. Pop nodded to her. She looked at him, looked *through* him, and continued raking leaves. Pop rang the bell and, somewhere in the depths of the house, a bell bonged. *Mansion* seemed the perfectly proper word for the Pus Sisters' domicile. Although it was nowhere near as big as some of the old homes in the Bramhall district, the perpetual dimness which reigned inside made it seem much bigger. The sound of the bell really *did* seem to come floating through a depth of rooms and corridors, and the sound of that bell always stirred a specific image in Pop's mind: the dead-cart passing through the streets of London during the plague year, the driver ceaselessly tolling his bell and crying, "Bring outcher dead! Bring outcher dead! For the luvva Jaysus, bring outcher dead!"

The Pus Sister who opened the door some thirty seconds later looked not only dead but embalmed; a mummy between whose lips someone had poked the smouldering butt of a cigarette for a joke.

"Merrill," the lady said. Her dress was a deep blue, her hair colored to match. She tried to speak to him as a great lady would speak to a tradesman who had come to the wrong door by mistake, but Pop could see she was, in her way, every bit as excited as that son of a bitch McCarty had been; it was just that the Pus Sisters had been born in Maine, raised in Maine, and would die in Maine, while McCarty hailed from someplace in the Midwest, where the art and craft of taciturnity were apparently not considered an important part of a child's upbringing.

A shadow flitted somewhere near the parlor end of the hallway, just visible over the bony shoulder of the sister who had opened the door. The other one. Oh, they were eager, all right. Pop began to wonder if he couldn't squeeze twelve grand out of them after all. Maybe even fourteen.

Pop knew he *could* say, "Do I have the honor of addressing Miss Deere or Mrs. Verrill?" and be completely correct and completely polite, but he had dealt with this pair of eccentric old bags before and he knew that, while the Pus Sister who had opened the door wouldn't raise an eyebrow or flare a nostril, would simply tell him which one he was speaking to, he would lose at least a thousand by doing so. They took great pride in their odd masculine names, and were apt to look more kindly on a person who tried and failed than one who took the coward's way out.

So, saying a quick mental prayer that his tongue wouldn't fail him now that the moment had come, he gave it his best and was pleased to hear the names slip as smoothly from his tongue as a pitch from a snake-oil salesman: "Is it Eleusippus or Meleusippus?" he asked, his face suggesting he was no more concerned about getting the names right than if they had been Joan and Kate.

"Meleusippus, Mr. Merrill," she said, ah, good, now he was *Mister* Merrill, and he was sure everything was going to go just as slick as ever a man could want, and he was just as wrong as ever a man could be. "Won't you step in?"

"Thank you kindly," Pop said, and entered the gloomy depths of the Deere Mansion.

"Oh *dear,*" Eleusippus Deere said as the Polaroid began to develop.

"What a *brute* he looks!" Meleusippus Verrill said, speaking in tones of genuine dismay and fear.

The dog *was* getting uglier, Pop had to admit that, and

there was something else that worried him even more: the time-sequence of the pictures seemed to be speeding up.

He had posed the Pus Sisters on their Queen Anne sofa for the demonstration picture. The camera flashed its bright white light, turning the room for one single instant from the purgatorial zone between the land of the living and that of the dead where these two old relics somehow existed into something flat and tawdry, like a police photo of a museum in which a crime had been committed.

Except the picture which emerged did not show the Pus Sisters sitting together on their parlor sofa like identical bookends. The picture showed the black dog, now turned so that it was full-face to the camera and whatever photographer it was who was nuts enough to stand there and keep snapping pictures of it. Now all of its teeth were exposed in a crazy, homicidal snarl, and its head had taken on a slight, predatory tilt to the left. That head, Pop thought, would continue to tilt as it sprang at its victim, accomplishing two purposes: concealing the vulnerable area of its neck from possible attack and putting the head in a position where, once the teeth were clamped solidly in flesh, it could revolve upright again, ripping a large chunk of living tissue from its target.

"It's so *awful!*" Eleusippus said, putting one mummified hand to the scaly flesh of her neck.

"So *terrible!*" Meleusippus nearly moaned, lighting a fresh Camel from the butt of an old one with a hand shaking so badly she came close to branding the cracked and fissured left corner of her mouth.

"It's totally in-ex-PLICK-able!" Pop said triumphantly, thinking: *I wish you was here, McCarty, you happy asshole. I just wish you was. Here's two ladies been round the Horn and back a few times that don't think this goddam camera's just some kind of a carny magic-show trick!*

"Does it show something which *has* happened?" Meleusippus whispered.

"Or something which *will* happen?" Eleusippus added in an equally awed whisper.

"I dunno," Pop said. "All I know for sure is that I have seen some goldarn strange things in my time, but I've never seen the beat of these pitchers."

"I'm not surprised!" Eleusippus.

"Nor I!" Meleusippus.

Pop was all set to start the conversation going in the direction of price—a delicate business when you were dealing with *anyone,* but never more so than when you were dealing with the Pus Sisters: when it got down to hard trading, they were as delicate as a pair of virgins—which, for all Pop knew, at least one of them was. He was just deciding on the *To start with, it never crossed my mind to sell something like this, but . . .* approach (it was older than the Pus Sisters themselves—although probably not by much, you would have said after a good close look at them—but when you were dealing with Mad Hatters, that didn't matter a bit; in fact, they *liked* to hear it, the way small children like to hear the same fairy tales over and over) when Eleusippus absolutely floored him by saying, "I don't know about my sister, Mr. Merrill, but I wouldn't feel comfortable looking at anything you might have to"—here a slight, pained pause—"offer us in a business way until you put that . . . that camera, or whatever God-awful thing it is . . . back in your car."

"I couldn't agree more," Meleusippus said, stubbing out her half-smoked Camel in a fish-shaped ashtray which was doing everything but *shitting* Camel cigarette butts.

"*Ghost* photographs," Eleusippus said, "are one thing. They have a certain—"

"Dignity," Meleusippus suggested.

"Yes! Dignity! But that *dog*—" The old woman actually shivered. "It looks as if it's ready to jump right out of that photograph and *bite* one of us."

"*All* of us!" Meleusippus elaborated.

Up until this last exchange, Pop had been convinced—

perhaps because he *had* to be—that the sisters had merely begun their own part of the dickering, and in admirable style. But the tone of their voices, as identical as their faces and figures (if they could have been said to *have* such things as figures), was beyond his power to disbelieve. They had no doubt that the Sun 660 was exhibiting some sort of paranormal behavior . . . *too* paranormal to suit them. They weren't dickering; they weren't pretending; they weren't playing games with him in an effort to knock the price down. When they said they wanted no part of the camera and the weird thing it was doing, that was exactly what they meant—nor had they done him the discourtesy (and that's just what it would have been, in their minds) of supposing or even *dreaming* that selling it had been his purpose in coming.

Pop looked around the parlor. It was like the old lady's room in a horror movie he'd watched once on his VCR—a piece of claptrap called *Burnt Offerings,* where this big old beefy fella tried to drown his son in the swimming pool but nobody even took their clothes off. That lady's room had been filled, overfilled, actually *stuffed* with old and new photographs. They sat on the tables and the mantel in every sort of frame; they covered so much of the walls you couldn't even tell what the pattern on the frigging paper was supposed to be.

The Pus Sisters' parlor wasn't quite that bad, but there were still plenty of photographs; maybe as many as a hundred and fifty, which seemed like three times that many in a room as small and dim as this one. Pop had been here often enough to notice most of them at least in passing, and he knew others even better than that, for he had been the one to sell them to Eleusippus and Meleusippus.

They had a great many more "ghost photographs," as Eleusippus Deere called them, perhaps as many as a thousand in all, but apparently even they had realized a room the size of their parlor was limited in terms of display-space, if not in those of taste. The rest of the ghost photographs were distributed among the mansion's other fourteen rooms. Pop had seen them all. He was one of the fortunate few who had been granted what the Pus Sisters called, with simple grandiosity, The Tour. But it was here in the parlor that they kept their *prize* "ghost photographs," with the prize of prizes attracting the eye by the simple fact that it stood in solitary splendor atop the closed Steinway baby grand by the bow windows. In it, a corpse was levitating from its coffin before fifty or sixty horrified mourners. It was a fake, of course. A child of ten—hell, a child of *eight*—would have known it was a fake. It made the photographs of the dancing elves which had so bewitched poor Arthur Conan Doyle near the end of his life look accomplished by comparison. In fact, as Pop ranged his eye about the room, he saw only two photographs that weren't obvious fakes. It would take closer study to see how the trickery had been worked in those. Yet these two ancient pussies, who had collected "ghost photographs" all their lives and claimed to be great experts in the field, acted like a couple of teenage girls at a horror movie when he showed them not just a paranormal *photograph* but a goddam Jesus-jumping paranormal *camera* that didn't just do its trick once and then quit, like the one that had taken the picture of the ghost-lady watching the fox-hunters come home, but one that did it *again* and *again* and *again,* and how much had they spent on this stuff that was nothing but *claptrap?* Thousands? Tens of thousands? *Hundreds* of—

"—show us?" Meleusippus was asking him.

Pop Merrill forced his lips to turn up in what must have been at least a reasonable imitation of his Folksy Cracker-barrel Smile, because they registered no surprise or distrust.

"Pardon me, dear lady," Pop said. "M'mind went wool-gatherin all on its own for a minute or two there. I guess it happens to all of us as we get on."

"We're eighty-three, and *our* minds are as clear as window-glass," Eleusippus said with clear disapproval.

"*Freshly washed* window-glass," Meleusippus added. "I asked if you have some new photographs you would care to show us . . . once you've put that wretched thing away, of course."

"It's been *ages* since we saw any really *good* new ones," Eleusippus said, lighting a fresh Camel.

"We went to The New England Psychic and Tarot Convention in Providence last month," Meleusippus said, "and while the lectures were enlightening—"

"—and uplifting—"

"—so many of the photographs were *arrant* fakes! Even a child of ten—"

"—of *seven!*—"

"—could have seen through them. So . . ." Meleusippus paused. Her face assumed an expression of perplexity which looked as if it might hurt (the muscles of her face having long since atrophied into expressions of mild pleasure and serene knowledge). "I am puzzled. Mr. Merrill, I must admit to being a bit puzzled."

"I was about to say the same thing," Eleusippus said.

"Why *did* you bring that awful thing?" Meleusippus and Eleusippus asked in perfect two-part harmony, spoiled only by the nicotine rasp of their voices.

The urge Pop felt to say *Because I didn't know what a pair of chickenshit old cunts you two were* was so strong that for one horrified second he believed he *had* said it, and he quailed, waiting for the twin screams of outrage to rise in the dim and hallowed confines of the parlor, screams which would rise like the squeal of rusty bandsaws biting into tough pine-knots, and go on rising until the glass in the frame of every bogus picture in the room shattered in an agony of vibration.

The idea that he had spoken such a terrible thought aloud lasted only a split-second, but when he relived it on later wakeful nights while the clocks rustled sleepily below (and while Kevin Delevan's Polaroid crouched sleeplessly in the locked drawer of the worktable), it seemed much longer. In those sleepless hours, he sometimes found himself wishing he *had* said it, and wondered if he was maybe losing his mind.

What he *did* do was react with a speed and a canny instinct for self-preservation that were nearly noble. To blow up at the Pus Sisters would give him immense gratification, but it would, unfortunately, be *short-lived* gratification. If he buttered them up—which was exactly what they expected, since they had been basted in butter all their lives (although it hadn't done a goddam thing for their skins)—he could perhaps sell them another three or four thousand dollars' worth of claptrap "ghost photographs," if they continued to elude the lung cancer which should surely have claimed one or both at least a dozen years ago.

And there were, after all, other Mad Hatters in Pop's mental file, although not quite so many as he'd thought on the day he'd set off to see Cedric McCarty. A little checking had revealed that two had died and one was currently learning how to weave baskets in a posh northern California retreat which catered to the incredibly rich who also happened to have gone hopelessly insane.

"Actually," he said, "I brought the camera out so you ladies could look at it. What I mean to say," he hastened on, observing their expressions of consternation, "is I know how much experience you ladies have in this field."

Consternation turned to gratification; the sisters exchanged smug, comfy looks, and Pop found himself wishing he could douse a couple of their goddam packs of Camels with barbecue lighter fluid and jam them up their tight little old-maid asses and then strike a match. They'd smoke then, all right. They'd smoke just like plugged chimneys, was what he meant to say.

"I thought you might have some advice on what I should do with the camera, is what I mean to say," he finished.

"Destroy it," Eleusippus said immediately.

"I'd use dynamite," Meleusippus said.

"Acid first, *then* dynamite," Eleusippus said.

"Right," Meleusippus finished. "It's dangerous. You don't have to look at that devil-dog to know that." She did look though; they both did, and identical expressions of revulsion and fear crossed their faces.

"You can feel *eee*vil coming out of it," Eleusippus said in a voice of such portentousness that it should have been laughable, like a high-school girl playing a witch in *Macbeth,* but which somehow wasn't. "Destroy it, Mr. Merrill. Before something awful happens. Before—perhaps, you'll notice I only say *perhaps*—it destroys *you.*"

"Now, now," Pop said, annoyed to find he felt just a little uneasy in spite of himself, "that's drawing it a little strong. It's just a camera, is what I mean to say."

Eleusippus Deere said quietly: "And the planchette that put out poor Colette Simineaux's eye a few years ago—that was nothing but a piece of fiberboard."

"At least until those foolish, foolish, *foolish* people put their fingers on it and woke it up," Meleusippus said, more quietly still.

There seemed nothing left to say. Pop picked up the camera—careful to do so by the strap, not touching the actual camera itself, although he told himself this was just for the benefit of these two old pussies—and stood.

"Well, you're the experts," he said. The two old women looked at each other and preened.

Yes; retreat. Retreat was the answer . . . for now, at least. But he wasn't done yet. Every dog had its day, and you could take *that* to the bank. "I don't want to take up any more of y'time, and I surely don't want to discommode you."

"Oh, you haven't!" Eleusippus said, also rising.

"We have so very few guests these days!" Meleusippus said, also rising.

"Put it in your car, Mr. Merrill," Eleusippus said, "and then—"

"—come in and have tea."

"*High* tea!"

And although Pop wanted nothing more in his life than to be *out* of there (and to tell them exactly that: *Thanks but no thanks, I want to get the fuck* OUT *of here),* he made a courtly little half-bow and an excuse of the same sort. "It would be my pleasure," he said, "but I'm afraid I have another appointment. I don't get to the city as often as I'd like." If you're going to tell one lie, you might as well tell a pack, Pop's own Pop had often told him, and it was advice he had taken to heart. He made a business of looking at his watch. "I've stayed too long already. You girls have made me late, I'm afraid, but I suppose I'm not the first man you've done *that* to."

They giggled and actually raised identical blushes, like the glow of very old roses. "Why, Mr. *Merrill!*" Eleusippus trilled.

"Ask me next time," he said, smiling until his face felt as if it would break. "Ask me next time, by the Lord Harry! You just ask and see if I don't say yes faster'n a hoss can trot!"

He went out, and as one of them quickly closed the door behind him (maybe they think the sun'll fade their goddam fake ghost photographs, Pop thought sourly), he turned and snapped the Polaroid at the old black woman, who was still raking leaves. He did it on impulse, as a man with a mean streak may on impulse swerve across a country road to kill a skunk or raccoon.

The black woman's upper lip rose in a snarl, and Pop was stunned to see she was actually forking the sign of the evil eye at him.

He got into his car and backed hurriedly down the driveway.

The rear end of his car was halfway into the street and he was turning to check for traffic when his eye happened upon the Polaroid he had just taken. It wasn't fully developed; it had the listless, milky look of all Polaroid photographs which are still developing.

Yet it had come up enough so that Pop only stared at it, the breath he had begun to unthinkingly draw into his lungs suddenly ceasing like a breeze that unaccountably drops away to nothing for a moment. His very heart seemed to cease in mid-beat.

What Kevin had imagined was now happening. The dog had finished its pivot, and had now begun its relentless ordained irrefutable approach toward the camera and whoever held it . . . ah, but *he* had held it this time, hadn't he? *He,* Reginald Marion "Pop" Merrill, had raised it and snapped it at the old black woman in a moment's pique like a spanked child that shoots a pop bottle off the top of a fence-post with his BB gun because he can't very well shoot his father, although in that humiliating, bottom-throbbing time directly after the paddling he would be more than happy to.

The dog was coming. Kevin had known that would happen next, and Pop would have known it, too, if he'd had occasion to think on it, which he hadn't—although from this moment on he would find it hard to think of anything else when he thought of the camera, and he would find those thoughts filling more and more of his time, both waking and dreaming.

It's coming, Pop thought with the sort of frozen horror a man might feel standing in the dark as some Thing, some unspeakable and unbearable Thing, approaches with its razor-sharp claws and teeth. *Oh my God, it's coming, that dog is coming.*

But it wasn't just *coming;* it was *changing.*

It was impossible to say how. His eyes hurt, caught between what they should be seeing and what they *were* seeing, and in the end the only handle he could find was a very small one: it was as if someone had changed the lens on the camera, from the normal one to a fish-eye, so that the dog's forehead with its clots of tangled fur seemed somehow to bulge and recede at the same time, and the dog's murderous eyes seemed to have taken on filthy, barely visible glimmers of red, like the sparks a Polaroid flash sometimes puts in people's eyes.

The dog's *body* seemed to have elongated but not thinned; if anything, it seemed thicker—not fatter, but more heavily muscled.

And its teeth were bigger. Longer. Sharper.

Pop suddenly found himself remembering Joe Camber's

Saint Bernard, Cujo—the one who had killed Joe and that old tosspot Gary Pervier and Big George Bannerman. The dog had gone rabid. It had trapped a woman and a young boy in their car up there at Camber's place and after two or three days the kid had died. And now Pop found himself wondering if *this* was what they had been looking at during those long days and nights trapped in the steaming oven of their car; this or something like this, the muddy red eyes, the long sharp teeth—

A horn blared impatiently.

Pop screamed, his heart not only starting again but *gunning,* like the engine of a Formula One racing-car.

A van swerved around his sedan, still half in the driveway and half in the narrow residential street. The van's driver stuck his fist out his open window and his middle finger popped up.

"Eat my dick, you son of a whore!" Pop screamed. He backed the rest of the way out, but so jerkily that he bumped up over the curb on the far side of the street. He twisted the wheel viciously (inadvertently honking his horn in the process) and then drove off. But three blocks south he had to pull over and just sit there behind the wheel for ten minutes, waiting for the shakes to subside enough so he could drive.

So much for the Pus Sisters.

During the next five days, Pop ran through the remaining names on his mental list. His asking price, which had begun at twenty thousand dollars with McCarty and dropped to ten with the Pus Sisters (not that he had gotten far enough into the business to mention price in either case), dropped steadily as he ran out the string. He was finally left with Emory Chaffee, and the possibility of realizing perhaps twenty-five hundred.

Chaffee presented a fascinating paradox: in all Pop's experience with the Mad Hatters—an experience that was long and amazingly varied—Emory Chaffee was the only believer in the "other world" who had absolutely no imagination whatsoever.

That he had ever spared a single thought for the "other world" with such a mind was surprising; that he *believed* in it was amazing; that he paid good money to collect objects connected with it was something Pop found absolutely astounding. Yet it was so, and Pop would have put Chaffee much higher on his list save for the annoying fact that Chaffee was by far the least well off of what Pop thought of as his "rich" Mad Hatters. He was doing a game but poor job of holding onto the last unravelling threads of what had once been a great family fortune. Hence, another large drop in Pop's asking price for Kevin's Polaroid.

But, he had thought, pulling his car into the overgrown driveway of what had in the '20s been one of Sebago Lake's finest summer homes and which was now only a step or two away from becoming one of Sebago Lake's shabbiest year-round homes (the Chaffee house in Portland's Bramhall district had been sold for taxes fifteen years before), *if anyone'll buy this beshitted thing, I reckon Emory will.*

The only thing that really distressed him—and it had done so more and more as he worked his way fruitlessly down the list—was the demonstration part. He could *describe* what the camera did until he was black in the face, but not even an odd duck like Emory Chaffee would lay out good money on the basis of a description alone.

Sometimes Pop thought it had been stupid to have Kevin take all those pictures so he could make that videotape. But when you got right down to where the bear shit in the buckwheat, he wasn't sure it would have made any difference. Time passed over there in that world (for, like Kevin, he had come to think of it as that: an actual world), and it passed much more slowly than it did in this one . . . but wasn't it speeding up as the dog approached the camera? Pop thought it was. The movement of the dog along the fence had been barely visible at first; now only a blind man could fail to see that the dog was closer each time the shutter was pressed. You could see the difference in distance even if you snapped two photographs one right after the other. It was almost as if time over there were trying to . . . well, trying to *catch up* somehow, and get in sync with time over here.

If that had been all, it would have been bad enough. But it *wasn't* all.

That was no *dog,* goddammit.

Pop didn't know what it *was,* but he knew as well as he knew his mother was buried in Homeland Cemetery that it was no *dog.*

He thought it *had* been a dog, when it had been snuffling its way along that picket fence which it had now left a good ten feet behind; it had *looked* like one, albeit an exceptionally mean one once it got its head turned enough so you could get a good look at its phiz.

But to Pop it now looked like no creature that had ever existed on God's earth, and probably not in Lucifer's hell, either. What troubled him even more was this: the few people for whom he had taken demonstration photographs did not seem to see this. They inevitably recoiled, inevitably said it was the ugliest, meanest-looking junkyard mongrel they had ever seen, but that was all. Not a single one of them suggested that the dog in Kevin's Sun 660 was turning into some kind of monster as it approached the photographer. As it approached the lens which might be some sort of portal between that world and this one.

Pop thought again (as Kevin had), *But it could never get through. Never. If something is going to happen, I'll tell you what that something will be, because that thing is an* ANIMAL, *maybe a goddam ugly one, a scary one, even, like the kind of thing a little kid imagines in his closet after his momma turns off the lights, but it's still an* ANIMAL, *and if anything happens it'll be this: there'll be one last pitcher where you can't see nothing but blur because that devil-dog will have jumped, you can see that's what it means to do, and after that the camera either won't work, or if it does, it won't take pitchers that develop into anything but black squares, because you can't take pitchers with a camera that has a busted lens or with one that's broke right in two for that matter, and if whoever owns that shadow drops the camera when the devil-dog hits it and him, and I imagine he will, it's apt to fall on the sidewalk and it probably* WILL *break. Goddam thing's nothing but plastic, after all, and plastic and cement don't get along hardly at all.*

But Emory Chaffee had come out on his splintery porch now, where the paint on the boards was flaking off and the boards themselves were warping out of true and the screens were turning the rusty color of dried blood and gaping holes in some of them; Emory Chaffee wearing a blazer which had once been a natty blue but had now been cleaned so many times it was the nondescript gray of an elevator operator's uniform; Emory Chaffee with his high forehead sloping back and back until it finally disappeared beneath what little hair he had left and grinning his *Pip-pip, jolly good, old boy, jolly good, wot, wot?* grin that showed his gigantic buck teeth and made him look the way Pop imagined Bugs Bunny would look if Bugs had suffered some cataclysmic mental retardation.

Pop took hold of the camera's strap—God, how he had come to hate the thing!—got out of his car, and forced himself to return the man's wave and grin.

Business, after all, was business.

"That's one ugly pup, wouldn't you say?"

Chaffee was studying the Polaroid which was now almost completely developed. Pop had explained what the camera did, and had been encouraged by Chaffee's frank interest and curiosity. Then he had given the Sun to the man, inviting him to take a picture of anything he liked.

Emory Chaffee, grinning that repulsive buck-toothed grin, swung the Polaroid Pop's way.

"Except me," Pop said hastily. "I'd ruther you pointed a shotgun at my head instead of that camera."

"When you sell a thing, you really sell it," Chaffee said

admiringly, but he had obliged just the same, turning the Sun 660 toward the wide picture window with its view of the lake, a magnificent view that remained as rich now as the Chaffee family itself had been in those years which began after World War I, golden years which had somehow begun to turn to brass around 1970.

He pressed the shutter.

The camera whined.

Pop winced. He found that now he winced every time he heard that sound—that squidgy little whine. He had tried to control the wince and had found to his dismay that he could not.

"Yes, sir, one goddamned ugly brute!" Chaffee repeated after examining the developed picture, and Pop was sourly pleased to see that the repulsive buck-toothed wot-ho, bit-of-a-sticky-wicket grin had disappeared at last. The camera had been able to do that much, at least.

Yet it was equally clear to him that the man wasn't seeing what he, Pop, was seeing. Pop had had some preparation for this eventuality; he was, all the same, badly shaken behind his impassive Yankee mask. He believed that if Chaffee *had* been granted the power (for that was what it seemed to be) to see what Pop was seeing, the stupid fuck would have been headed for the nearest door, and at top speed.

The dog—well, it wasn't a dog, not anymore, but you had to call it *something*—hadn't begun its leap at the photographer yet, but it was getting ready; its hindquarters were simultaneously bunching and lowering toward the cracked anonymous sidewalk in a way that somehow reminded Pop of a kid's souped-up car, trembling, barely leashed by the clutch during the last few seconds of a red light; the needle on the rpm dial already standing straight up at 60 × 10, the engine screaming through chrome pipes, fat deep-tread tires ready to smoke the macadam in a hot soul-kiss.

The dog's face was no longer a recognizable thing at all. It had twisted and distorted into a carny freak-show thing that seemed to have but a single dark and malevolent eye, neither round nor oval but somehow *runny,* like the yolk of an egg that has been stabbed with the tines of a fork. Its nose was a black beak with deep flared holes drilled into either side. And was there *smoke* coming from those holes—like steam from the vents of a volcano? Maybe—or maybe that part was just imagination.

Don't matter, Pop thought. *You just keep workin that shutter, or lettin people like this fool work it, and you are gonna find out, aren't you?*

But he didn't *want* to find out. He looked at the black, murdering thing whose matted coat had caught perhaps two dozen wayward burdocks, the thing which no longer had fur, exactly, but stuff like living spikes, and a tail like a medieval weapon. He observed the shadow it had taken a damned snot-nosed kid to extract meaning from, and saw it had changed. One of the shadow-legs appeared to have moved a stride backward—a very *long* stride, even taking the effect of the lowering or rising sun (but it was going down; Pop had somehow become very sure it was going down, that it was night coming in that world over there, not day) into account.

The photographer over there in that world had finally discovered that his subject did not mean to sit for its portrait; that had never been a part of its plan. It intended to *eat,* not *sit. That* was the plan.

Eat, and, maybe, in some way he didn't understand, escape.

Find out! he thought ironically. *Go ahead! Just keep taking pitchers! You'll find out! You'll find out* PLENTY*!*

"And you, sir," Emory Chaffee was saying, for he had only been stopped for a moment; creatures of little imagination are rarely stopped for long by such trivial things as consideration, "are one hell of a salesman!"

The memory of McCarty was still very close to the surface of Pop's mind, and it still rankled.

"If you think it's a fake—" he began.

"A fake? Not at all! Not . . . at *all!*" Chaffee's buck-toothed smile spread wide in all its repulsive splendor. He spread his hands in a surely-you-jest motion. "But I'm afraid, you see, that we can't do business on this particular item, Mr. Merrill. I'm sorry to say so, but—"

"Why?" Pop bit off. "If you don't think the goddam thing's a fake, why in the hell don't you want it?" And he was astonished to hear his voice rising in a kind of plaintive, balked fury. There had never been anything like this, never in the history of the *world,* Pop was sure of it, nor ever would be again. Yet it seemed he couldn't *give* the goddam thing away.

"But . . ." Chaffee looked puzzled, as if not sure how to state it, because whatever it was he had to say seemed so obvious to him. In that moment he looked like a pleasant but not very capable pre-school teacher trying to teach a backward child how to tie his shoes. "But it doesn't *do* anything, does it?"

"Doesn't *do* anything?" Pop nearly screamed. He couldn't believe he had lost control of himself to such a degree as this, and was losing more all the time. What was happening to him? Or, cutting closer to the bone, what was the son-of-a-bitching *camera* doing to him? "Doesn't *do* anything? What are you, blind? It takes pitchers of *another world!* It takes pitchers that move in time from one to the next, no matter *where* you take em or *when* you take em in *this* world! And that . . . that thing . . . that *monster—*"

Oh. Oh dear. He had finally done it. He had finally gone too far. He could see it in the way Chaffee was looking at him.

"But it's just a dog, isn't it?" Chaffee said in a low, comforting voice. It was the sort of voice you'd use to try and soothe a madman while the nurses ran for the cabinet where they kept the hypos and the knock-out stuff.

"Ayuh," Pop said slowly and tiredly. "Just a dog is all it is. But you said yourself it was a hell of an ugly brute."

"That's right, that's right, I did," Chaffee said, agreeing much too quickly. Pop thought if the man's grin got any wider and broader he might just be treated to the sight of the top three-quarters of the idiot's head toppling off into his lap. "But . . . surely you see, Mr. Merrill . . . what a problem this presents for the collector. The *serious* collector."

"No, I guess I don't," Pop said, but after running through the entire list of Mad Hatters, a list which had seemed so promising at first, he was beginning to. In fact, he was beginning to see a whole *host* of problems the Polaroid Sun presented for the serious collector. As for Emory Chaffee . . . God knew what Emory thought, exactly.

"There are most certainly such things as ghost photographs," Chaffee said in a rich, pedantic voice that made Pop want to strangle him. "But these are not ghost photographs. They—"

"They're sure as hell not *normal* photographs!"

"My point exactly," Chaffee said, frowning slightly. "But what sort of photographs *are* they? One can hardly say, can one? One can only display a perfectly normal camera that photographs a dog which is apparently preparing to leap. And once it leaps, it will be gone from the frame of the picture. At that point, one of three things may happen. The camera may start taking normal pictures, which is to say, pictures of the things it is aimed at; it may take no more pictures at all, its one purpose, to photograph—to *document,* one might even say—that dog, completed; or it may simply go on taking pictures of that white fence and the ill-tended lawn behind it." He paused and added, "I suppose someone might walk by at some point, forty photographs down the line—or four hundred—but unless the photographer raised his angle, which he doesn't seem to have done in any of these, one would only see the passerby from the waist down. More or less." And, echoing Kevin's father without even knowing who Kevin's father was, he added: "Pardon me for saying so, Mr. Merrill, but you've shown me something I thought I'd never see: an inexplicable and almost irrefutable paranormal occurrence that is really quite boring."

This amazing but apparently sincere remark forced Pop to disregard whatever Chaffee might think about his sanity and ask again: "It really *is* only a dog, as far as you can see?"

"Of course," Chaffee said, looking mildly surprised. "A stray mongrel that looks exceedingly bad-tempered."

He sighed.

"And it wouldn't be taken seriously, of course. What I mean is it wouldn't be taken seriously by people who don't know you personally, Mr. Merrill. People who aren't familiar with your honesty and reliability in these matters. It looks like a trick, you see? And not even a very good one. Something on the order of a child's Magic Eight-Ball."

Two weeks ago, Pop would have argued strenuously against such an idea. But that was before he had been not walked but actually *propelled* from that bastard McCarty's house.

"Well, if that's your final word," Pop said, getting up and taking the camera by the strap.

"I'm very sorry you made a trip to such little purpose," Chaffee said . . . and then his horrid grin burst forth again, all rubbery lips and huge teeth shining with spit. "I was about to make myself a Spam sandwich when you drove in. Would you care to join me, Mr. Merrill? I make quite a nice one, if I do say so myself. I add a little horseradish and Bermuda onion—that's my secret—and then I—"

"I'll pass," Pop said heavily. As in the Pus Sisters' parlor, all he really wanted right now was to get out of here and put miles between himself and this grinning idiot. Pop had a definite allergy to places where he had gambled and lost. Just lately there seemed to be a lot of those. Too goddam many. "I already had m'dinner, is what I mean to say. Got to be gettin back."

Chaffee laughed fruitily. "The lot of the toiler in the vineyards is busy but yields great bounty," he said.

Not just lately, Pop thought. *Just lately it ain't yielded no fuckin bounty at all.*

"It's a livin, anyway," Pop replied, and was eventually

allowed out of the house, which was damp and chill (what it must be like to live in such a place come February, Pop couldn't imagine) and had that mousy, mildewed smell that might be rotting curtains and sofa-covers and such . . . or just the smell money leaves behind when it has spent a longish period of time in a place and then departed. He thought the fresh October air, tinged with just a small taste of the lake and a stronger tang of pine-needles, had never smelled so good.

He got into his car and started it up. Emory Chaffee, unlike the Pus Sister who had shown him as far as the door and then closed it quickly behind him, as if afraid the sun might strike her and turn her to dust like a vampire, was standing on the front porch, grinning his idiot grin and actually *waving,* as if he were seeing Pop off on a goddam ocean cruise.

And, without thinking, just as he had taken the picture of (or *at,* anyway) the old black woman without thinking, he had snapped Chaffee and the just-starting-to-moulder house which was all that remained of the Chaffee family holdings. He didn't remember picking the camera up off the seat where he had tossed it in disgust before closing his door, was not even aware that the camera was in his hands or the shutter fired until he heard the whine of the mechanism shoving the photograph out like a tongue coated with some bland gray fluid—Milk of Magnesia, perhaps. That sound seemed to vibrate along his nerve-endings now, making them scream; it was like the feeling you got when something too cold or hot hit a new filling.

He was peripherally aware that Chaffee was laughing as if it was the best goddam joke in the world before snatching the picture from the slot in a kind of furious horror, telling himself he had imagined the momentary, blurred sound of a snarl, a sound like you might hear if a power-boat was approaching while you had your head ducked under water; telling himself he had imagined the momentary feeling that the camera had *bulged* in his hands, as if some huge pressure inside had pushed the sides out momentarily. He punched the glove-compartment button and threw the picture inside and then closed it so hard and fast that he tore his thumbnail all the way down to the tender quick.

He pulled out jerkily, almost stalling, then almost hitting one of the hoary old spruces which flanked the house end of the long Chaffee driveway, and all the way up that driveway he thought he could hear Emory Chaffee laughing in loud mindless cheery bellows of sound: *Haw! Haw! Haw! Haw!*

His heart slammed in his chest, and his head felt as if someone was using a sledgehammer inside there. The small cluster of veins which nestled in the hollows of each temple pulsed steadily.

He got himself under control little by little. Five miles, and the little man inside his head quit using the sledgehammer. Ten miles (by now he was almost halfway back to Castle Rock), and his heartbeat was back to normal. And he told himself: *You ain't gonna look at it. You* AIN'T. *Let the goddam thing rot in there. You don't need to look at it, and you don't need to take no more of em, either. Time to mark the thing off as a dead loss. Time to do what you should have let the boy do in the first place.*

So of course when he got to the Castle View rest area, a turnout from which you could, it seemed, see all of western Maine and half of New Hampshire, he swung in and turned off his motor and opened the glove compartment and brought out the picture which he had taken with no more intent or knowledge than a man might have if he did a thing while walking in his sleep. The photograph had developed in there, of course; the chemicals inside that deceptively flat square had come to life and done their usual efficient job. Dark or light, it didn't make any difference to a Polaroid picture.

The dog-thing was crouched all the way down now. It was as fully coiled as it was going to get, a trigger pulled back to full cock. Its teeth had outgrown its mouth so that the thing's snarl seemed now to be not only an expression of rage but a simple necessity; how could its lips ever fully close over those teeth? How could those jaws ever chew? It looked more like a weird species of wild boar than a dog now, but what it really looked like was nothing Pop had ever seen before. It did more than hurt his eyes to look at it; it hurt his *mind.* It made him feel as if he was going crazy.

Why not get rid of that camera right here? he thought suddenly. *You can. Just get out, walk to the guardrail there, and toss her over. All gone. Goodbye.*

But that would have been an impulsive act, and Pop Merrill belonged to the Reasonable tribe—belonged to it body and soul, is what I mean to say. He didn't want to do anything on the spur of the moment that he might regret later, and—

If you don't *do this, you'll regret it later.*

But no. And no. And no. A man couldn't run against his nature. It was unnatural. He needed time to think. To be sure.

He compromised by throwing the print out instead and then drove on quickly. For a minute or two he felt as if he might throw up, but the urge passed. When it did, he felt a little more himself. Safely back in his shop, he unlocked the steel box, took out the Sun, rummaged through his keys once more, and located the one for the drawer where he kept his "special" items. He started to put the camera inside . . . and paused, brow furrowed. The image of the chopping block out back entered his mind with such clarity, every detail crisply limned, that it was like a photograph itself.

He thought: *Never mind all that about how a man can't run against his nature. That's crap, and you know it. It ain't in a man's nature to eat dirt, but you could eat a whole bowl of it, by the bald-headed Christ, if someone with a gun pointed at your head told you to do it. You know what time it is, chummy—time to do what you should have let the boy do in the first place. After all, it ain't like you got any investment in this.*

But at this, another part of his mind rose in angry, fist-waving protest. *Yes I* do! *I* do *have an investment, goddammit! That kid smashed a perfectly good Polaroid camera! He may not know it, but that don't change the fact that I'm out a hundred and thirty-nine bucks!*

"Oh, shit on toast!" he muttered agitatedly. "It ain't that! It ain't the fuckin *money!*"

No—it wasn't the fucking money. He could at least admit that it wasn't the money. He could afford it; Pop could indeed have afforded a great deal, including his own mansion in Portland's Bramhall district and a brand-new Mercedes-Benz to go in the carport. He never would have bought those things—he pinched his pennies and chose to regard almost pathological miserliness as nothing more than good old Yankee thrift—but that didn't mean he couldn't have had them if he so chose.

It wasn't about money; it was about something more important than money ever could be. It was about *not getting skinned.* Pop had made a life's work out of *not getting skinned,* and on the few occasions when he had been, he had felt like a man with red ants crawling around inside his skull.

Take the business of the goddam Kraut record-player, for instance. When Pop found out that antique dealer from Boston—Donahue, his name had been—had gotten fifty bucks more than he'd ought to have gotten for a 1915 Victor-Graff gramophone (which had actually turned out to be a much more common 1919 model), Pop had lost three hundred dollars' worth of sleep over it, sometimes plotting various forms of revenge (each more wild-eyed and ridiculous than the last), sometimes just damning himself for a fool, telling himself he must really be slipping if a city man like that Donahue could skin Pop Merrill. And sometimes he imagined the fucker telling his poker-buddies about how easy it had been, hell, they were all just a bunch of rubes up there, he believed that if you tried to sell the Brooklyn Bridge to a fellow like that country mouse Merrill in Castle Rock, the damned fool would ask "How much?" Then him and his cronies rocking back in their chairs around that poker-table (why he always saw them around such a table in this morbid daydream Pop didn't know, but he did), smoking dollar cigars and roaring with laughter like a bunch of trolls.

The business of the Polaroid was eating into him like acid, but he still wasn't ready to let go of the thing yet.

Not quite yet.

You're crazy! a voice shouted at him. *You're crazy to go on with it!*

"Damned if I'll eat it," he muttered sulkily to that voice and to his empty shadowed store, which ticked softly to itself like a bomb in a suitcase. "*Damned* if I will."

But that didn't mean he had to go haring off on any more stupid goddam trips trying to sell the sonofawhore, and he *certainly* didn't mean to take any more pictures with it. He judged there were at least three more "safe" ones left in it, and there were *probably* as many as seven, but he wasn't going to be the one to find out. Not at all.

Still, something might come up. You never knew. And it could hardly do him or anyone else any harm locked up in a drawer, could it?

"Nope," Pop agreed briskly to himself. He dropped the camera inside, locked the drawer, repocketed his keys, and then went to the door and turned CLOSED over to OPEN with the air of a man who has finally put some nagging problem behind him for good.

CHAPTER TEN

Pop woke up at three the next morning, bathed with sweat and peering fearfully into the dark. The clocks had just begun another weary run at the hour.

It was not this sound which awakened him, although it could have done, since he was not upstairs in his bed but down below, in the shop itself. The Emporium Galorium was a cave of darkness crowded with hulking shadows created by the streetlamp outside, which managed to send just enough light through the dirty plate-glass windows to create the unpleasant feeling of things hiding beyond the borders of vision.

It wasn't the *clocks* that woke him; it was the *flash.*

He was horrified to find himself standing in his pajamas beside his worktable with the Polaroid Sun 660 in his hands. The "special" drawer was open. He was aware that, although he had taken only a single picture, his finger had been pushing the button which triggered the shutter again and again and again. He would have taken a great many more than the one that protruded from the slot at the bottom of the camera but for simple good luck. There had only been a single picture left in the film pack currently in the camera.

Pop started to lower his arms—he had been holding the camera pointed toward the front of the shop, the viewfinder with its minute hairline crack held up to one open, sleeping eye—and when he got them down as far as his ribcage, they began to tremble and the muscles holding the hinges of his elbows just seemed to give way. His arms fell, his fingers opened, and the camera tumbled back into the "special" drawer with a clatter. The picture he had taken slipped from the slot and fluttered. It struck one edge of the open drawer, teetered first one way as if it would follow the camera in, and then the other. It fell on the floor.

Heart attack, Pop thought incoherently. *I'm gonna have a goddam Christing heart attack.*

He tried to raise his right arm, wanting to massage the left side of his chest with the hand on the end of it, but the arm wouldn't come. The hand on the end of it dangled as limp as a dead man at the end of a hangrope. The world wavered in and out of focus. The sound of the clocks (the tardy ones were just finishing up) faded away to distant echoes. Then the pain in his chest diminished, the light seemed to come back a little, and he realized all he was doing was trying to faint.

He made to sit down in the wheeled chair behind the worktable, and the business of lowering himself into the seat, like the business of lowering the camera, began all right, but before he had gotten even halfway down, *those* hinges, the ones that strapped his thighs and calves together by way of his knees, also gave way and he didn't so much sit in the chair as cave into it. It rolled a foot backward, struck a crate filled with old *Life* and *Look* magazines, and stopped.

Pop put his head down, the way you were supposed to do when you felt lightheaded, and time passed. He had no idea at all, then or later, how much. He might even have gone back to sleep for a little while. But when he raised his head, he was more or less all right again. There was a steady dull throbbing at his temples and behind his forehead, probably because he had stuffed his goddam noodle with blood, hanging it over so long that way, but he found he could stand up and he knew what he had to do. When the thing had gotten hold of him so badly it could make him walk in his sleep, then make him (his mind tried to revolt at that verb, that *make,* but he wouldn't let it) take pictures with it, that was enough. He had no idea what the goddam thing was, but one thing was clear: you couldn't compromise with it.

Time to do what you should have let the boy do in the first place.

Yes. But not tonight. He was exhausted, drenched with sweat, and shivering. He thought he would have his work cut out for him just climbing the stairs to his apartment again, let alone swinging that sledge. He supposed he could do the job in here, simply pick it out of the drawer and dash it against the floor again and again, but there was a deeper truth, and he'd better own up to it: he couldn't have any more truck with that camera tonight. The morning would be time enough . . . and the camera couldn't do any damage between now and then, could it? There was no film in it.

Pop shut the drawer and locked it. Then he got up slowly, looking more like a man pushing eighty than seventy, and tottered slowly to the stairs. He climbed them one at a time, resting on each, clinging to the bannister (which was none too solid itself) with one hand while he held his heavy bunch of keys on their steel ring in the other. At last he made the top. With the door shut behind him, he seemed to feel a little stronger. He went back into his bedroom and got into bed, unaware as always of the strong yellow smell of sweat and old man that puffed up when he lay down—he changed the sheets on the first of every month and called it good.

I won't sleep now, he thought, and then: *Yes you will. You will because you can, and you can because tomorrow morning you're going to take the sledge and pound that fucking thing to pieces and there's an end to it.*

This thought and sleep came simultaneously, and Pop slept without dreaming, almost without moving, all the rest of that night. When he woke he was astonished to hear the clocks downstairs seeming to chime an extra stroke, all of them: eight instead of seven. It wasn't until he looked at the light falling across the floor and wall in a slightly slanted oblong that he realized it really *was* eight; he had overslept for the first time in ten years. Then he remembered the night before. Now, in daylight, the whole episode seemed less weird; had he nearly *fainted?* Or was that maybe just a natural sort of weakness that came to a sleepwalker when he was unexpectedly wakened?

But of course, that was it, wasn't it? A little bright morning sunshine wasn't going to change that central fact: he *had* walked in his sleep, he *had* taken at least one picture and would have taken a whole slew of them if there had been more film in the pack.

He got up, got dressed, and went downstairs, meaning to see the thing in pieces before he even had his morning's coffee.

CHAPTER ELEVEN

Kevin wished his *first* visit to the two-dimensional town of Polaroidsville had also been his *last* visit there, but that was not the case. During the thirteen nights since the first one, he'd had the dream more and more often. If the dumb dream happened to take the night off—*little vacation, Kev, but seeya soon, okay?*—he was apt to have it twice the next night. Now he always *knew* it was a dream, and as soon as it started he would tell himself that all he had to do was wake himself up, *dammit, just wake yourself up!* Sometimes he *did* wake up, and sometimes the dream just faded back into deeper sleep, but he never succeeded in waking *himself* up.

It was always Polaroidsville now—never Oatley or Hildasville, those first two efforts of his fumbling mind to identify the place. And like the photograph, each dream took the action just a little bit further. First the man with the shopping-cart, which was never empty now even to start with but filled with a jumble of objects . . . mostly clocks, but all from the Emporium Galorium, and all with the eerie look not of real things but rather of *photographs* of real things which had been cut out of magazines and then somehow, impossibly, paradoxically, stuffed into a shopping-cart, which, since it was as two-dimensional as the objects themselves, had no breadth in which to store them. Yet there they were, and the old man hunched protectively over them and told Kevin to get out, that he was a fushing feef . . . only now he also told Kevin that if he *didn't* get out, "I'll sic Pop's dawg on you! Fee if I don't!"

The fat woman who couldn't be fat since she was perfectly flat but who was fat anyway came next. She appeared pushing her own shopping-cart filled with Polaroid Sun cameras. She also spoke to him before he passed her. "Be careful, boy," she'd say in the loud but toneless voice of one who is utterly deaf, "Pop's dog broke his leash and he's a mean un. He tore up three or four people at the Trenton Farm in Camberville before he came here. It's hard to take his pitcher, but you can't do it at all, 'less you have a cam'ra."

She would bend to get one, would sometimes get as far as holding it out, and he would reach for the camera, not knowing why the woman would think he should take the dog's picture or why he'd want to . . . or maybe he was just trying to be polite?

Either way, it made no difference. They both moved with the stately slowness of underwater swimmers, as dream-people so often do, and they always just missed making connections; when Kevin thought of this part of the dream, he often thought of the famous picture of God and Adam which Michelangelo had painted on the ceiling of the Sistine Chapel: each of them with an arm outstretched, and each with the hand at the end of the arm also outstretched, and the forefingers almost—not quite, but *almost*—touching.

Then she would disappear for a moment because she had no width, and when she reappeared again she was out of reach. *Well just go back to her, then,* Kevin would think each time the dream reached this point, but he couldn't. His feet carried him heedlessly and serenely onward to the peeling white picket fence and Pop and the dog . . . only the dog was no longer a dog but some horrible mixed thing that gave off heat and smoke like a dragon and had the teeth and twisted, scarred snout of a wild pig. Pop and the Sun dog would turn toward him at the same time, and Pop would have the camera—*his* camera, Kevin knew, because there was a piece chipped out of the side—up to his right eye. His left eye was squinted shut. His rimless spectacles glinted on top of his head in hazy sunlight. Pop and the Sun dog had all three dimensions. They were the only things in this seedy, creepy little dreamtown that did.

"He's the one!" Pop cried in a shrill, fearful voice. "He's the thief! Sic em, boy! *Pull his fuckin guts out, is what I mean to say!*"

And as he screamed out this last, heatless lightning flashed in the day as Pop triggered the shutter and the flash, and Kevin turned to run. The dream had stopped here the second time he had had it. Now, on each subsequent occasion, things went a little further. Again he was moving with the aquatic slowness of a performer in an underwater ballet. He felt that, if he had been outside himself, he would even have *looked* like a dancer, his arms turning like the blades of a propeller just starting up, his shirt twisting with his body, pulling taut across his chest and his belly at the same time he heard the shirt's tail pulling free of his pants at the small of his back with a magnified rasp like sandpaper.

Then he was running back the way he came, each foot rising slowly and then floating dreamily (of *course* dreamily, what else, you fool? he would think at this point every time) back down until it hit the cracked and listless cement of the sidewalk, the soles of his tennis shoes flattening as they took his weight and spanking up small clouds of grit moving so slowly that he could see the individual particles revolving like atoms.

He ran slowly, yes, of course, and the Sun dog, nameless stray Grendel of a thing that came from nowhere and signified nothing and had all the sense of a cyclone but existed nevertheless, chased him slowly . . . but not *quite* as slowly.

On the third night, the dream faded into normal sleep just as Kevin began to turn his head in that dragging, maddening slow motion to see how much of a lead he had on the dog. It then skipped a night. On the following night it returned—twice. In the first dream he got his head halfway around so he could see the street on his left disappearing into limbo behind him as he ran along it; in the second (and from this one his alarm-clock woke him, sweating lightly in a crouched fetal position on the far side of the bed) he got his head turned enough to see the dog just as its forepaws came down in his own tracks, and he saw the paws were digging crumbly little craters in the cement because they had sprouted claws . . . and from the back of each lower leg-joint there protruded a long thorn of bone that looked like a spur. The thing's muddy reddish eye was locked on Kevin. Dim fire blew and dripped from its nostrils. *Jesus, Jesus Christ, its SNOT'S on fire,* Kevin thought, and when he woke he was horrified to hear himself whispering it over and over, very rapidly: ". . . snot's on fire, snot's on fire, snot's on fire."

Night by night the dog gained on him as he fled down the sidewalk. Even when he wasn't turning to look he could *hear* the Sun dog gaining. He was aware of a spread of warmth from his crotch and knew he was in enough fear to have wet himself, although the emotion came through in the same diluted, numbed way he seemed to have to move in this world. He could hear the Sun dog's paws striking the cement, could hear the dry crack and squall of the cement breaking. He could hear the hot blurts of its breath, the suck of air flowing in past those outrageous teeth.

And on the night Pop woke up to find he had not only walked in his sleep but taken at least one picture in it, Kevin *felt* as well as heard the Sun dog's breath for the first time: a warm rush of air on his buttocks like the sultry suck of wind a subway on an express run pulls through a station where it needn't stop. He knew the dog was close enough to spring on his back now, and that would come next; he would feel one more breath, this one not just warm but *hot,* as hot as acute indigestion in your throat, and then that crooked living bear-trap of a mouth would sink deep into the flesh of his back, between the shoulderblades, ripping the skin and meat off his spine, and did he think this was really just a dream? *Did* he?

He awoke from this last one just as Pop was gaining the top of the stairs to his apartment and resting one final time before going inside back to bed. This time Kevin woke sitting bolt upright, the sheet and blanket which had been over him puddled around his waist, his skin covered with sweat and yet *freezing,* a million stiff little white goose-pimples standing out all over his belly, chest, back, and arms like stigmata. Even his cheeks seemed to crawl with them.

And what he thought about was not the dream, or at least not directly; he thought instead: *It's wrong, the number is wrong, it says three but it can't—*

Then he flopped back and, in the way of children (for even at fifteen most of him was still a child and would be until later that day), he fell into a deep sleep again.

The alarm woke him at seven-thirty, as it always did on school mornings, and he found himself sitting up in bed again, wide-eyed, every piece suddenly in place. The Sun he had smashed hadn't been *his* Sun, and that was why he kept having this same crazy dream over and over and over again. Pop Merrill, that kindly old crackerbarrel philosopher and repairer of cameras and clocks and small appliances, had euchred him and his father as neatly and competently as a riverboat gambler does the tenderfeet in an old Western movie.

His father—!

He heard the door downstairs slam shut and leaped out of bed. He took two running strides toward the door in his underwear, thought better of it, turned, yanked the window up, and hollered *"Dad!"* just as his father was folding himself into the car to go to work.

CHAPTER TWELVE

Pop dredged his key-ring up from his pocket, unlocked the "special" drawer, and took out the camera, once again being careful to hold it by the strap only. He looked with some hope at the front of the Polaroid, thinking he might see that the lens had been smashed in its latest tumble, hoping that the goddam thing's eye had been poked out, you might say, but his father had been fond of saying that the devil's luck is always in, and that seemed to be the case with Kevin Delevan's goddamned camera. The chipped place on the thing's side had chipped away a little more, but that was all.

He closed the drawer and, as he turned the key, saw the one picture he'd taken in his sleep lying face-down on the floor. As unable not to look at it as Lot's wife had been unable not to turn back and look at the destruction of Sodom, he picked it up with those blunt fingers that hid their dexterity from the world so well and turned it over.

The dog-creature had begun its spring. Its forepaws had barely left the ground, but along its misshapen backbone and in the bunches of muscle under the hide with its hair like the stiff filaments sticking out of black steel brushes he could see all that kinetic energy beginning to release itself. Its face and head were actually a little blurred in this photograph as its mouth yawned wider, and drifting up from the picture, like a sound heard under glass, he seemed to hear a low and throaty snarl beginning to rise toward a roar. The shadow-photographer looked as if he were trying to stumble back another pace, but what did it matter? That was smoke jetting from the holes in the dog-thing's muzzle, all right, *smoke,* and more smoke drifting back from the hinges of its open jaws in the little space where the croggled and ugly stake-wall of its teeth ended, and any man would stumble back from a horror like *that,* any man would try to turn and run, but all Pop had to do was look to tell you that the man (of *course* it was a man, maybe once it had been a boy, a teenage boy, but who had the camera now?) who had taken that picture in mere startled reflex, with a kind of wince of the finger . . . that man didn't have a nickel's worth of chances. That man could keep his feet or trip over them, and all the difference it would make would be as to how he died: while he was on his feet or while he was on his ass.

Pop crumpled the picture between his fingers and then stuck his key-ring back into his pocket. He turned, holding what had been Kevin Delevan's Polaroid Sun 660 and was now *his* Polaroid Sun 660 by the strap and started toward the back of the store; he would pause on the way just long enough to get the sledge. And as he neared the door to the back shed, a shutterflash, huge and white and soundless, went off not in front of his eyes but behind them, in his brain.

He turned back, and now his eyes were as empty as the eyes of a man who has been temporarily blinded by some bright light. He walked past the worktable with the camera now held in his hands at chest level, as one might carry a votive urn or some other sort of religious offering or relic. Halfway between the worktable and the front of the store was a bureau covered with clocks. To its left was one of the barnlike structure's support beams, and from a hook planted in this there hung another clock, an imitation German cuckoo clock. Pop grasped it by the roof and pulled it off its hook, indifferent to the counterweights, which immediately became entangled in one another's chains, and to the pendulum, which snapped off when one of the disturbed chains tried to twine around it. The little door below the roofpeak of the clock sprang ajar; the wooden bird poked out its beak and one startled eye. It gave a single choked sound—*kook!*—as if in protest of this rough treatment before creeping back inside again.

Pop hung the Sun by its strap on the hook where the clock had been, then turned and moved toward the back of the store for the second time, his eyes still blank and dazzled. He clutched the clock by its roof, swinging it back and forth indifferently, not hearing the cluds and clunks from inside it, or the occasional strangled sound that might have been the bird trying to escape, not noticing when one of the counterweights smacked the end of an old bed, snapped off, and went rolling beneath, leaving a deep trail in the undisturbed dust of years. He moved with the blank mindless purpose of a robot. In the shed, he paused just long enough to pick up the sledgehammer by its smooth shaft. With both hands thus filled, he had to use the elbow of his left arm to knock the hook out of the eyebolt so he could push open the shed door and walk into the backyard.

He crossed to the chopping block and set the imitation German cuckoo clock on it. He stood for a moment with his head inclined down toward it, both of his hands now on the handle of the sledge. His face remained blank, his eyes dim and dazzled, but there was a part of his mind which not only thought clearly but thought *all* of him was thinking—and acting—clearly. This part of him saw not a cuckoo clock which hadn't been worth much to begin with and was now broken in the bargain; it saw Kevin's Polaroid. This part of his mind really believed he had come downstairs, gotten the Polaroid from the drawer, and proceeded directly out back, pausing only to get the sledge.

And it was this part that would do his remembering later . . . unless it became convenient for him to remember some other truth. Or any other truth, for that matter.

Pop Merrill raised the sledgehammer over his right shoulder and brought it down hard—not as hard as Kevin had done, but hard enough to do the job. It struck squarely on the roof of the imitation German cuckoo clock. The clock did not so much break or shatter as *splatter;* pieces of plastic wood and little gears and springs flew everywhere. And what that little piece of Pop which saw would remember (unless, of course, it became convenient to remember otherwise) were pieces of *camera* splattering everywhere.

He pulled the sledge off the block and stood for a moment with his meditating, unseeing eyes on the shambles. The bird, which to Pop looked exactly like a film-case, a Polaroid Sun film-case, was lying on its back with its little wooden feet sticking straight up in the air, looking both deader than any bird outside of a cartoon ever looked and yet somehow miraculously unhurt at the same time. He had his look, then turned and headed back toward the shed door.

"There," he muttered under his breath. "Good 'nuff."

Someone standing even very close to him might have been unable to pick up the words themselves, but it would have been hard to miss the unmistakable tone of relief with which they were spoken.

"*That's* done. Don't have to worry about *that* anymore. Now what's next? Pipe-tobacco, isn't it?"

But when he got to the drugstore on the other side of the block fifteen minutes later, it was not pipe-tobacco he asked for (although that was what he would *remember* asking for). He asked for film.

Polaroid film.

CHAPTER THIRTEEN

"Kevin, I'm going to be late for work if I don't—"

"Will you call in? Can you? Call in and say you'll be late, or that you might not get there at all? If it was something really, really, *really* important?"

Warily, Mr. Delevan asked, "What's the something?"

"*Could* you?"

Mrs. Delevan was standing in the doorway of Kevin's bedroom now. Meg was behind her. Both of them were eyeing the man in his business suit and the tall boy, still wearing only his Jockey shorts, curiously.

"I suppose I—yes, say I could. But I won't until I know what it *is*."

Kevin lowered his voice, and, cutting his eyes toward the door, he said: "It's about Pop Merrill. And the camera."

Mr. Delevan, who had at first only looked puzzled at what Kevin's eyes were doing, now went to the door. He murmured something to his wife, who nodded. Then he closed the door, paying no more attention to Meg's protesting whine than he would have to a bird singing a bundle of notes on a telephone wire outside the bedroom window.

"What did you tell Mom?" Kevin asked.

"That it was man-to-man stuff." Mr. Delevan smiled a little. "I think *she* thinks you want to talk about masturbating."

Kevin flushed.

Mr. Delevan looked concerned. "You don't, do you? I mean, you know about—"

"I know, I know," Kevin said hastily; he was not about to tell his father (and wasn't sure he would have been able to put the right string of words together, even if he had wanted to) that what had thrown him momentarily off-track was finding out that not only did his *father* know about whacking off—which of course shouldn't have surprised him at all but somehow did, leaving him with feelings of surprise at his own surprise—but that his *mother* somehow did, too.

Never mind. All this had nothing to do with the nightmares, or with the new certainty which had locked into place in his head.

"It's about Pop, I told you. And some bad dreams I've been having. But mostly it's about the camera. Because Pop stole it somehow, Dad."

"Kevin—"

"I beat it to pieces on his chopping block, I know. But it wasn't *my* camera. It was *another* camera. And that isn't even the worst thing. The worst thing is that *he's still using mine to take pictures!* And that dog is going to get out! When it does, I think it's going to kill me. In that other world it's already started to j-j-j—"

He couldn't finish. Kevin surprised himself again—this time by bursting into tears.

By the time John Delevan got his son calmed down it was ten minutes of eight, and he had resigned himself to at least being late for work. He held the boy in his arms—whatever it was, it really had the kid shook, and if it really *was* nothing but a bunch of dreams, Mr. Delevan supposed he would find sex at the root of the matter someplace.

When Kevin was shivering and only sucking breath deep into his lungs in an occasional dry-sob, Mr. Delevan went to the door and opened it cautiously, hoping Mary had taken Meg downstairs. She had; the hallway was empty. *That's one for our side, anyway,* he thought, and went back to Kevin.

"Can you talk now?" he asked.

"Pop's got my camera," Kevin said hoarsely. His red eyes,

still watery, peered at his father almost myopically. "He got it somehow, and he's using it."

"And this is something you *dreamed?*"

"Yes . . . and I remembered something."

"Kevin . . . that *was* your camera. I'm sorry, son, but it *was.* I even saw the little chip in the side."

"He must have rigged that somehow—"

"Kevin, that seems pretty farf—"

"Listen," Kevin said urgently, "will you just *listen?*"

"All right. Yes. I'm listening."

"What I remembered was that when he handed me the camera—when we went out back to crunch it, remember?"

"Yes—"

"I looked in the little window where the camera keeps count of how many shots there are left. And it said three, Dad! It said *three!*"

"Well? What about it?"

"It had film in it, too! *Film!* I know, because I remember one of those shiny black things jumping up when I squashed the camera. It jumped up and then it fluttered back down."

"I repeat: so what?"

"*There wasn't any film in my camera when I gave it to Pop!* That's so-what. I had twenty-eight pictures. He wanted me to take thirty more, for a total of fifty-eight. I might have bought more film if I'd known what he was up to, but probably not. By then I was scared of the thing—"

"Yeah. I was, a little, too."

Kevin looked at him respectfully. "Were you?"

"Yeah. Go on. I think I see where you're heading."

"I was just going to say, he chipped in for the film, but not enough—not even half. He's a *wicked* skinflint, Dad."

John Delevan smiled thinly. "He is that, my boy. One of the world's greatest, is what I mean to say. Go on and finish up. *Tempus* is *fugiting* away like mad."

Kevin glanced at the clock. It was almost eight. Although

neither of them knew it, Pop would wake up in just under two minutes and start about his morning's business, very little of which he would remember correctly.

"All right," Kevin said. "All I'm trying to say is I couldn't have bought any more film even if I'd wanted to. I used up all the money I had buying the three film packs. I even borrowed a buck from Megan, so I let her shoot a couple, too."

"Between the two of you, you used up *all* the exposures? Every single one?"

"Yes! *Yes!* He even *said* it was fifty-eight! And between the time when I finished shooting all the pictures he wanted and when we went to look at the tape he made, I never bought any more film. It was *dead empty* when I brought it in, Dad! The number in the little window was a *zero!* I saw it, I remember! So if it was my camera, how come it said *three* in the window when we went back downstairs?"

"He *couldn't* have—" Then his father stopped, and a queer look of uncharacteristic gloom came over his face as he realized that Pop *could* have, and that the truth of it was this: he, John Delevan, didn't want to believe that Pop *had;* that even bitter experience had not been sufficient vaccination against foolishness, and Pop might have pulled the wool over his own eyes as well as those of his son.

"Couldn't have *what?* What are you thinking about, Dad? Something just hit you!"

Something had hit him, all right. How eager Pop had been to go downstairs and get the original Polaroids so they could all get a closer look at the thing around the dog's neck, the thing that turned out to be Kevin's latest string tie from Aunt Hilda, the one with the bird on it that was probably a woodpecker.

We might as well go down with you, Kevin had said when Pop had offered to get the photos, but hadn't Pop jumped up himself, chipper as a chickadee? *Won't take a minute,* the old man had said, or some such thing, and the truth was, Mr. Delevan told himself, I hardly noticed *what* he was saying or doing, because I wanted to watch that goddamned tape again. And the truth *also* was this: Pop hadn't even had to pull the old switcheroo right in front of them—although, with his eyes unwooled, Mr. Delevan was reluctantly willing to believe the old son of a bitch had probably been prepared to do just that, if he had to, and probably *could* have done it, too, pushing seventy or not. With them upstairs and him downstairs, presumably doing no more than getting Kevin's photographs, he could have swapped *twenty* cameras, at his leisure.

"Dad?"

"I suppose he could have," Mr. Delevan said. "But why?"

Kevin could only shake his head. He didn't know why. But that was all right; Mr. Delevan thought *he* did, and it was something of a relief. Maybe honest men *didn't* have to learn the world's simplest truths over and over again; maybe some of those truths eventually stuck fast. He'd only had to articulate the question aloud in order to find the answer. Why did the Pop Merrills of this world do anything? To make a profit. That was the reason, the whole reason, and nothing but the reason. Kevin had wanted to destroy it. After looking at Pop's videotape, Mr. Delevan had found himself in accord with that. Of the three of them, who had been the only one capable of taking a longer view?

Why, Pop, of course. Reginald Marion "Pop" Merrill.

John Delevan had been sitting on the edge of Kevin's bed with an arm about his son's shoulders. Now he stood up. "Get dressed. I'll go downstairs and call in. I'll tell Brandon I'll probably just be late, but to assume I won't be in at all."

He was preoccupied with this, already talking to Brandon Reed in his mind, but not so preoccupied he didn't see the gratitude which lighted his son's worried face. Mr. Delevan smiled a little and felt that uncharacteristic gloom first ease and then let go entirely. There was this much, at least: his son was as yet not too old to take comfort from him, or accept him as a higher power to whom appeals could sometimes be directed in the knowledge that they would be acted upon; nor was he himself too old to take comfort from his son's comfort.

"I think," he said, moving toward the door, "that we ought to pay a call on Pop Merrill." He glanced at the clock on Kevin's night-table. It was ten minutes after eight, and in back of the Emporium Galorium, a sledgehammer was coming down on an imitation German cuckoo clock. "He usually opens around eight-thirty. Just about the time we'll get there, I think. If you get a wiggle on, that is."

He paused on his way out and a brief, cold smile flickered on his mouth. He was not smiling at his son. "I think he's got some explaining to do, is what I mean to say."

Mr. Delevan went out, closing the door behind him. Kevin quickly began to dress.

CHAPTER FOURTEEN

The Castle Rock LaVerdiere's Super Drug Store was a lot more than just a drugstore. Put another way, it was really only a drugstore as an afterthought. It was as if someone had noticed at the last moment—just before the grand opening, say—that one of the words in the sign was still "Drug." That someone might have made a mental note to tell someone else, someone in the company's management, that here they were, opening yet another LaVerdiere's, and they had by simple oversight neglected yet again to correct the sign so it read, more simply and accurately, LaVerdiere's Super Store . . . and, after making the mental note, the someone in charge of noticing such things had delayed the grand opening a day or two so they could shoe-horn in a prescription counter about the size of a telephone booth in the long building's furthest, darkest, and most neglected corner.

The LaVerdiere's Super Drug Store was really more of a jumped-up five-and-dime than anything else. The town's last *real* five-and-dime, a long dim room with feeble, fly-specked overhead globes hung on chains and reflected murkily in the creaking but often-waxed wooden floor, had been The Ben Franklin Store. It had given up the ghost in 1978 to make way for a video-games arcade called Galaxia and E-Z Video Rentals, where Tuesday was Toofers Day and no one under the age of twenty could go in the back room.

LaVerdiere's carried everything the old Ben Franklin had carried, but the goods were bathed in the pitiless light of Maxi-Glo fluorescent bars which gave every bit of stock its own hectic, feverish shimmer. *Buy me!* each item seemed to shriek. *Buy me or you may die! Or your wife may die! Or your kids! Or your best friend! Possibly all of them at once! Why? How should* I *know? I'm just a brainless item sitting on a pre-fab LaVerdiere's shelf! But doesn't it feel true? You know it does! So buy me and buy me* RIGHT . . . NOW!

There was an aisle of notions, two aisles of first-aid supplies and nostrums, an aisle of video and audio tapes (both blank and pre-recorded). There was a long rack of magazines giving way to paperback books, a display of lighters under one digital cash-register and a display of watches under another (a third register was hidden in the dark corner where the pharmacist lurked in his lonely shadows). Halloween candy had taken over most of the toy aisle (the toys would not only come back after Halloween but eventually take over two whole aisles as the days slid remorselessly down toward Christmas). And, like something too neat to exist in reality except as a kind of dumb admission that there *was* such a thing as Fate with a capital F, and that Fate might, in its own way, indicate the existence of that whole "other world" about which Pop had never before cared (except in terms of how it might fatten his pocketbook, that was) and about which Kevin Delevan had never before even thought, at the front of the store, in the main display area, was a carefully arranged work of salesmanship which was billed as the FALL FOTO FESTIVAL.

This display consisted of a basket of colorful autumn leaves spilling out on the floor in a bright flood (a flood too large to actually have come from that one basket alone, a careful observer might have concluded). Amid the leaves were a number of Kodak and Polaroid cameras—several Sun 660s among the latter—and all sorts of other equipment: cases, albums, film, flashbars. In the midst of this odd cornucopia, an old-fashioned tripod rose like one of H. G. Wells's Martian death-machines towering over the crispy wreck of London. It bore a sign which told all patrons interested enough to look that this week one could obtain SUPER REDUCTIONS ON ALL POLAROID CAMERAS & ACCESSORIES!

At eight-thirty that morning, half an hour after LaVerdiere's opened for the day, "all patrons" consisted of Pop Merrill and Pop alone. He took no notice of the display but marched straight to the only open counter, where Molly Durham had just finished laying out the watches on their imitation-velvet display-cloth.

Oh no, here comes old Eyeballs, she thought, and grimaced. Pop's idea of a really keen way to kill a stretch of time about as long as Molly's coffee-break was to kind of *ooze* up to the counter where she was working (he always picked hers, even if he had to stand in line; in fact, she thought he liked it better when there *was* a line) and buy a pouch of Prince Albert tobacco. This was a purchase an ordinary fellow could transact in maybe thirty seconds, but if she got Eyeballs out of her face in under three minutes, she thought she was doing very well indeed. He kept all of his money in a cracked leather purse on a chain, and he'd haul it out of his pocket—giving his doorbells a good feel on the way, it always looked to Molly—and then open it. It always gave out a little *screeeeek!* noise, and honest to God if you didn't expect to see a moth flutter out of it, just like in those cartoons people draw of tightwads. On top of the purse's contents there would be a whole mess of paper money, bills that looked somehow as if you shouldn't handle them, as if they might be coated with disease germs of some kind, and jingling silver underneath. Pop would fish out a dollar bill and then kind of hook the other bills to one side with one of those thick fingers of his to get to the change underneath—he'd never give you a couple of bucks, hunh-uh, that would make everything too quick to suit him—and then he'd work *that* out, too. And all the time his eyes would be busy, flicking down to the purse for a second or two but mostly letting the fingers sort out the proper coins by touch while his eyes crawled over her boobs, her belly, her hips, and then back up to her boobs again. Never once her face; not even so far as her mouth, which *was* a part of a girl in which most men seemed to be interested; no, Pop Merrill was strictly interested in the lower portions of the female anatomy. When he finally finished—and no matter how quick that was, it always seemed like three times as long to Molly—and got the hell out of the store again, she always felt like going somewhere and taking a long shower.

So she braced herself, put on her best it's-only-eight-thirty-and-I've-got-seven-and-a-half-hours-to-go smile, and stood at the counter as Pop approached. She told herself, *He's only looking at you, guys have been doing that since you sprouted,* and that was true, but this wasn't the same. Because Pop Merrill wasn't like most of the guys who had run their eyes over her trim and eminently watchable superstructure since that time ten years ago. Part of it was that Pop was *old,* but that wasn't all of it. The truth was that some guys looked at you and some—a very few—seemed to actually be feeling you up with their eyes, and Merrill was one of *those.* His gaze actually seemed to have weight; when he fumbled in his creaky old-maid's purse on its length of incongruously masculine chain, she seemed to actually *feel* his eyes squirming up and down her front, lashing their way up her hills on their optic nerves like tadpoles and then sliding bonelessly down into her valleys, making her wish she had worn a nun's habit to work that day. Or maybe a suit of armor.

But her mother had been fond of saying *What can't be cured must be endured, sweet Molly,* and until someone discovered a method of weighing gazes so those of dirty men both young and old could be outlawed, or, more likely, until Pop Merrill did everyone in Castle Rock a favor by dying so that eyesore of a tourist trap he kept could be torn down, she would just have to deal with it as best she could.

But today she was in for a pleasant surprise—or so it seemed at first. Pop's usual hungry appraisal was not even an ordinary patron's look; it seemed utterly blank. It wasn't that he looked through her, or that his gaze struck her and bounced off. It seemed to Molly that he was so deep in his thoughts that his usually penetrating look did not even reach her, but made it about halfway and then petered out—like a man trying to locate and observe a star on the far side of the galaxy with just the naked eye.

"May I help you, Mr. Merrill?" she asked, and her feet were already cocking so she could turn quickly and reach up for where the pouches of tobacco were kept. With Pop, this was a task she always did as quickly as possible, because when she turned and reached, she could feel his eyes crawling busily over her ass, dropping for a quick check of her legs, then rising again to her butt for a final ocular squeeze and perhaps a pinch before she turned back.

"Yes," he said calmly and serenely, and he might as well have been talking to one of those automated bank machines for all the interest in her he showed. That was fine by Molly. "I'd like some" and then either a word she didn't hear right or one that was utter gibberish. If it was gobbledegook, she thought with some hope, maybe the first few parts of the complicated network of dikes, levees, and spillways the old crock had constructed against the rising sea of senility were finally giving way.

It *sounded* as if he had said *toefilmacco,* which wasn't a product they stocked . . . unless it was a prescription drug of some sort.

"I beg pardon, Mr. Merrill?"

"Film," he said, so clearly and firmly that Molly was more than disappointed; she was convinced he must have said it just that way the first time and her ears had picked it up wrong. Maybe *she* was the one who was beginning to lose her dikes and levees.

"What kind would you like?"

"Polaroid," he said. "Two packs." She didn't know exactly what was going on here, but it was beyond doubt that Castle Rock's premier dirty old man was not himself today. His eyes would still not focus, and the words . . . they reminded her of something, something she associated with her five-year-old niece, Ellen, but she couldn't catch hold of it.

"For what model, Mr. Merrill?"

She sounded brittle and actressy to herself, but Pop Merrill didn't even come close to noticing. Pop was lost in the ozone.

After a moment's consideration in which he did not look at her at all but seemed instead to study the racks of cigarettes behind her left shoulder, he jerked out: "For a Polaroid Sun camera. Model 660." And then it came to her, even as she told him she'd have to get it from the display. Her niece owned a big soft panda toy, which she had, for reasons which would probably make sense only to another little girl, named Paulette. Somewhere inside of Paulette was an electronic circuit-board and a memory chip on which were stored about four hundred short, simple sentences such as "I like to hug, don't you?" and "I wish you'd *never* go away." Whenever you poked Paulette above her fuzzy little navel, there was a brief pause and then one of those lovesome little remarks would come out, almost *jerk* out, in a somehow remote and emotionless voice that seemed by its tone to deny the content of the words. Ellen thought Paulette was the nuts. Molly thought there was something creepy about it; she kept expecting Ellen to poke the panda-doll in the guts someday and it would surprise them all (except for Aunt Molly from Castle Rock) by saying what was *really* on its mind. "I think tonight after you're asleep I'll strangle you dead," perhaps, or maybe just "I have a knife."

Pop Merrill sounded like Paulette the stuffed panda this morning. His blank gaze was uncannily like Paulette's. Molly had thought any change from the old man's usual leer would be a welcome one. She had been wrong.

Molly bent over the display, for once totally unconscious of the way her rump was poking out, and tried to find what the old man wanted as quickly as she could. She was sure that when she turned around, Pop would be looking at anything but her. This time she was right. When she had the film and started back (brushing a couple of errant fall leaves from one of the boxes), Pop was still staring at the cigarette racks, at first glance appearing to look so closely he might have been inventorying the stock. It took a second or two to see that that expression was no expression at all, really, but a gaze of almost divine blankness.

Please get out of here, Molly prayed. *Please, just take your film and go. And whatever else you do, don't touch me. Please.*

If he touched her while he was looking like that, Molly thought she would scream. Why did the place have to be empty? Why couldn't at least one other customer be in here, preferably Sheriff Pangborn, but since he seemed to be otherwise engaged, anyone at all? She supposed Mr. Constantine, the pharmacist, was in the store someplace, but the drug counter looked easily a quarter of a mile away, and while she knew it *couldn't* be that far, not really, it was still too far for him to reach her in a hurry if old man Merrill decided to touch her. And suppose Mr. Constantine had gone out to Nan's for coffee with Mr. Keeton from the selectmen's office? The more she thought about that possibility, the more likely it seemed. When something genuinely weird like this happened, wasn't it an almost foregone conclusion that it should happen while one was alone?

He's having a mental breakdown of some kind.

She heard herself saying with glassy cheerfulness: "Here you are, Mr. Merrill." She put the film on the counter and scooted to her left and behind the register at once, wanting it between her and him.

The ancient leather purse came out of Pop Merrill's pants, and her stuttering fingers miskeyed the purchase so she had to clear the register and start again.

He was holding two ten-dollar bills out to her.

She told herself they were only *rumpled* from being squashed up with the other bills in that little pocketbook, probably not even old, although they *looked* old. That didn't stop her galloping mind, however. Her mind insisted that they weren't just *rumpled,* they were rumpled and *slimy.* It further insisted that *old* wasn't the right word, that *old* wasn't even in the ballpark. For those particular items of currency, not even the word *ancient* would do. Those were *prehistoric* tens, somehow printed before Christ was born and Stonehenge was built, before the first low-browed, no-neck Neanderthal had crawled out of his cave. They belonged to a time when even God had been a baby.

She didn't want to touch them.

She *had* to touch them.

The man would want his change.

Steeling herself, she took the bills and shoved them into the cash register as fast as she could, banging a finger so hard she ripped most of the nail clear off, an ordinarily exquisite pain she would not notice, in her extreme state of distress, until sometime later . . . when, that was, she had chivvied her willing mind around enough to scold herself for acting like a whoopsy little girl on the edge of her first menstrual period.

At the moment, however, she only concentrated on getting the bills into the register as fast as she could and getting her hand *off* them, but even later she would remember what the surfaces of those tens had felt like. It felt as if they were actually crawling and moving under the pads of her fingers; as if billions of germs, *huge* germs almost big enough to be seen with the naked eye, were sliding along them toward her, eager to infect her with whatever *he* had.

But the man would want his change.

She concentrated on that, lips pressed together so tightly they were dead white; four singles that did not, absolutely did *not* want to come out from beneath the roller that held them down in the cash drawer. Then a dime, but oh Jesus-please-us, there *were* no dimes, and what the hell was *wrong* with her, what had she done to be saddled for so long with this weird old man on the one morning in recorded history when he actually seemed to want to get out of here in a hurry?

She fished out a nickel, feeling the silent, stinky loom of him so close to her (and she felt that when she was finally forced to look up she would see he was even closer, that he was leaning over the counter toward her), then three pennies, four, five . . . but the last one dropped back into the drawer among the quarters and she had to fish for it with one of her cold, numb fingers. It almost squirted away from her again; she could feel sweat popping out on the nape of her neck and on the little strip of skin between her nose and her upper lip. Then, clutching the coins tightly in her fist and praying he wouldn't have his hand outstretched to receive them so she would have to touch his dry, reptilian skin, but knowing, somehow *knowing* that he would, she looked up, feeling her bright and cheery LaVerdiere's smile stretching the muscles of her face in a kind of frozen scream, trying to steel herself for even *that,* telling herself it would be the last, and never mind the image her stupid, insisting mind kept trying to make her see, an image of that dry hand suddenly snapping shut over hers like the talon of some old and horrid bird, a bird not of prey, no, not even that, but one of carrion; she told herself she did not see those images, absolutely did *NOT,* and, seeing them all the same, she looked up with that smile screaming off her face as brightly as a cry of murder on a hot still night, and the store was empty.

Pop was gone.

He had left while she was making change.

Molly began to shudder all over. If she had needed concrete proof that the old geezer was not right, this was it. This was proof positive, proof indubitable, proof of the purest ray serene: for the first time in her memory (and in the living memory of the town, she would have bet, and she would have won her bet), Pop Merrill, who refused to tip even on those rare occasions when he was forced to eat in a restaurant that had no take-out service, had left a place of business without waiting for his change.

Molly tried to open her hand and let go of the four ones,

the nickel, and the five pennies. She was stunned to find she couldn't do it. She had to reach over with her other hand and pry the fingers loose. Pop's change dropped to the glass top of the counter and she swept it off to one side, not wanting to touch it.

And she never wanted to see Pop Merrill again.

CHAPTER FIFTEEN

Pop's vacant gaze held as he left LaVerdiere's. It held as he crossed the sidewalk with the boxes of film in his hand. It broke and became an expression of somehow unsettling alertness as he stepped off into the gutter . . . and stopped there, with one foot on the sidewalk and one planted amid the litter of squashed cigarette butts and empty potato-chip bags. Here was another Pop Molly would not have recognized, although there were those who had been sharp-traded by the old man who would have known it quite well. This was neither Merrill the lecher nor Merrill the robot, but Merrill the animal with its wind up. All at once he was *there,* in a way he seldom allowed himself to be *there* in public. Showing so much of one's true self in public was not, in Pop's estimation, a good idea. This morning, however, he was far from being in command of himself, and there was no one out to observe him, anyway. If there had been, that person would not have seen Pop the folksy crackerbarrel philosopher or even Pop the sharp trader, but something like the *spirit* of the man. In that moment of being totally *there,* Pop looked like a rogue dog himself, a stray who has gone feral and now pauses amid a midnight henhouse slaughter, raggedy ears up, head cocked, bloodstreaked teeth showing a little as he hears some sound from the farmer's house and thinks of the shotgun with its wide black holes like a figure eight rolled onto its side. The dog knows nothing of figure eights, but even a dog may recognize the dim shape of eternity if its instincts are honed sharp enough.

Across the town square he could see the urine-yellow front of the Emporium Galorium, standing slightly apart from its nearest neighbors: the vacant building which had housed The Village Wash tub until earlier that year, Nan's Luncheonette, and You Sew and Sew, the dress-and-notions shop run by Evvie Chalmers's great-granddaughter, Polly—a woman of whom we must speak at another time.

There were slant-parking spaces in front of all the shops on Lower Main Street, and all of them were empty . . . except for one, which was just now being filled with a Ford station-wagon Pop recognized. The light throb of its engine was clearly audible in the morning-still air. Then it cut off, the brakelights went out, and Pop pulled back the foot which had been in the gutter and prudently withdrew himself to the corner of LaVerdiere's. Here he stood as still as that dog who has been alerted in the henhouse by some small sound, the sort of sound which might be disregarded in the killing frenzy of dogs neither so old nor so wise as this one.

John Delevan got out from behind the wheel of the station-wagon. The boy got out on the passenger side. They went to the door of the Emporium Galorium. The man began to knock impatiently, loud enough so the sound of it came as clearly to Pop as the sound of the engine had done. Delevan paused, they both listened, and then Delevan started in again, not knocking now but *hammering* at the door, and you didn't have to be a goddam mind-reader to know the man was steamed up.

They know, Pop thought. *Somehow they know. Damned good thing I smashed the fucking camera.*

He stood a moment longer, nothing moving except his hooded eyes, and then he slipped around the corner of the drugstore and into the alley between it and the neighboring bank. He did it so smoothly that a man fifty years younger might have envied the almost effortless agility of the movement.

This morning, Pop figured, it might be a little wiser to go back home by backyard express.

CHAPTER SIXTEEN

When there was still no answer, John Delevan went at the door a third time, hammering so hard he made the glass rattle loosely in its rotting putty gums and hurt his hand. It was hurting his hand that made him realize how angry he was. Not that he felt the anger was in any way unjustified if Merrill had done what Kevin thought he had done—and yes, the more he thought about it, the more John Delevan was sure that Kevin was right. But he was surprised that he hadn't recognized the anger for what it was until just now.

This seems to be a morning for learning about myself, he thought, and there was something schoolmarmish in that. It allowed him to smile and relax a little.

Kevin was not smiling, nor did he look relaxed.

"It seems like one of three things has happened," Mr. Delevan said to his son. "Merrill's either not up, not answering the door, or he figured we were getting warm and he's absconded with your camera." He paused, then actually laughed. "I guess there's a fourth, too. Maybe he died in his sleep."

"He didn't die." Kevin now stood with his head against the dirty glass of the door he mightily wished he had never gone through in the first place. He had his hands cupped around his eyes to make blinders, because the sun rising over the east side of the town square ran a harsh glare across the glass. "Look."

Mr. Delevan cupped his own hands to the sides of his face and pressed his nose to the glass. They stood there side by side, backs to the square, looking into the dimness of the Emporium Galorium like the world's most dedicated window-shoppers.

"Well," he said after a few seconds, "it looks like if he absconded he left his shit behind."

"Yeah—but that's not what I mean. Do you see it?"

"See what?"

"Hanging on that post. The one by the bureau with all the clocks on it."

And after a moment, Mr. Delevan did see it: a Polaroid camera, hanging by its strap from a hook on the post. He thought he could even see the chipped place, although that might have been his imagination.

It's not your imagination.

The smile faded off his lips as he realized he was starting to feel what Kevin was feeling: the weird and distressing certainty that some simple yet terribly dangerous piece of machinery was running . . . and unlike most of Pop's clocks, it was running right on time.

"Do you think he's just sitting upstairs and waiting for us to go away?" Mr. Delevan spoke aloud, but he was really talking to himself. The lock on the door looked both new and expensive . . . but he was willing to bet that if one of them—probably Kevin was in better shape—hit the door hard enough, it would rip right through the old wood. He mused randomly: *A lock is only as good as the door you put it in. People never think.*

Kevin turned his strained face to look at his father. In that moment, John Delevan was as struck by Kevin's face as Kevin had been by his not long ago. He thought: *I wonder how many fathers get a chance to see what their sons will look like as men? He won't always look this strained, this tightly drawn—God, I hope not—but this is what he will look like. And, Jesus, he's going to be handsome!*

He, like Kevin, had that one moment in the midst of whatever it was that was going on here, and the moment was a short one, but he also never forgot; it was always within his mind's reach.

"What?" Kevin asked hoarsely. "What, Dad?"

"You want to bust it? Because I'd go along."

"Not yet. I don't think we'll have to. I don't think he's here . . . but he's close."

You can't know any such thing. Can't even think it.

But his son *did* think it, and he believed Kevin was right. Some sort of link had been formed between Pop and his son. "Some sort" of link? Get serious. He knew perfectly well what the link was. It was that fucking camera hanging on the wall in there, and the longer this went on, the longer he felt that machinery running, its gears grinding and its vicious unthinking cogs turning, the less he liked it.

Break the camera, break the link, he thought, and said: "Are you sure, Kev?"

"Let's go around to the back. Try the door there."

"There's a gate. He'll keep it locked."

"Maybe we can climb over."

"Okay," Mr. Delevan said, and followed his son down the steps of the Emporium Galorium and around to the alley, wondering as he went if he had lost his mind.

But the gate wasn't locked. Somewhere along the line Pop had forgotten to lock it, and although Mr. Delevan hadn't liked the idea of climbing over the fence, or maybe *falling* over the fence, quite likely tearing the hell out of his balls in the process, he somehow liked the open gate even less. All the same, he and Kevin went through it and into Pop's littered backyard, which not even the drifts of fallen October leaves could improve.

Kevin wove his way through the piles of junk Pop had thrown out but not bothered to take to the dump, and Mr. Delevan followed him. They arrived at the chopping block at about the same time Pop was coming out of Mrs. Althea Linden's backyard and onto Mulberry Street, a block west. He would follow Mulberry Street until he reached the offices of the Wolf Jaw Lumber Company. Although the company's pulp trucks would already be coursing the roads of western Maine and the yowl and yark of the cutters' chainsaws would have been rising from the area's diminishing stands of hardwood since six-thirty or so, no one would come in to man the office until nine, which was still a good fifteen minutes away. At the rear of the lumber company's tiny backyard was a high board fence. It was gated, and this gate *was* locked, but Pop had the key. He would unlock the gate and step through into his own backyard.

Kevin reached the chopping block. Mr. Delevan caught up, followed his son's gaze, and blinked. He opened his mouth to ask what in the hell *this* was all about, then shut it again. He was starting to have an idea of what in the hell it was all about without any aid from Kevin. It wasn't *right* to have such ideas, wasn't *natural,* and he knew from bitter experience (in which Reginald Marion "Pop" Merrill himself had played a part at one point, as he had told his son not so long ago) that doing things on impulse was a good way to reach the wrong decision and go flying off half-cocked, but it didn't matter. Although he did not think it in such terms, it would be fair to say Mr. Delevan just hoped he could apply for readmittance to the Reasonable tribe when this was over.

At first he thought he was looking at the smashed remains of a Polaroid camera. Of course that was just his mind, trying to find a little rationality in repetition; what lay on and around the chopping block didn't look anything at all like a camera, Polaroid or otherwise. All those gears and flywheels could only belong to a clock. Then he saw the dead cartoon-bird and even knew what kind of clock. He opened his mouth to ask Kevin why in God's name Pop would bring a cuckoo clock out back and then sledgehammer it to death. He thought it over again and decided he didn't have to ask, after all. The answer to that was also beginning to come. He didn't *want* it to come, because it pointed to madness on what seemed to Mr. Delevan a grand scale, but that didn't matter; it came anyway.

You had to hang a cuckoo clock on something. You had to hang it because of the pendulum weights. And what did you hang it on? Why, a hook, of course.

Maybe a hook sticking out of a beam.

Like the beam Kevin's Polaroid had been hanging on.

Now he spoke, and his words seemed to come from some long distance away: "What in the hell is wrong with him, Kevin? Has he gone nuts?"

"Not *gone,*" Kevin answered, and his voice also seemed to come from some long distance away as they stood above the chopping block, looking down on the busted timepiece. "*Driven* there. By the camera."

"We've got to smash it," Mr. Delevan said. His voice seemed to float to his ears long after he had felt the words coming out of his mouth.

"Not yet," Kevin said. "We have to go to the drugstore first. They're having a special sale on them."

"Having a special sale on wh—"

Kevin touched his arm. John Delevan looked at him. Kevin's head was up, and he looked like a deer scenting fire. In that moment the boy was more than handsome; he was almost divine, like a young poet at the hour of his death.

"What?" Mr. Delevan asked urgently.

"Did you hear something?" Alertness slowly changing to doubt.

"A car on the street," Mr. Delevan said. How much older was he than his son? he wondered suddenly. Twenty-five years? Jesus, wasn't it time he started acting it?

He pushed the strangeness away from him, trying to get it at arm's length. He groped desperately for his maturity and found a little of it. Putting it on was like putting on a badly tattered overcoat.

"You sure that's all it was, Dad?"

"Yes. Kevin, you're wound up too tight. Get hold of yourself or . . ." Or what? But he knew, and laughed shakily. "Or you'll have us both running like a pair of rabbits."

Kevin looked at him thoughtfully for a moment, like someone coming out of a deep sleep, perhaps even a trance, and then nodded. "Come on."

"Kevin, why? What do you want? He could be upstairs, just not answering—"

"I'll tell you when we get there, Dad. Come *on.*" And almost dragged his father out of the littered backyard and into the narrow alleyway.

"Kevin, do you want to take my arm off, or what?" Mr. Delevan asked when they got back to the sidewalk.

"He was back there," Kevin said. "Hiding. Waiting for us to go. I felt him."

"He was—" Mr. Delevan stopped, then started again. "Well . . . let's say he was. Just for argument, let's say he was. Shouldn't we go back there and collar him?" And, belatedly: "*Where* was he?"

"On the other side of the fence," Kevin said. His eyes seemed to be floating. Mr. Delevan liked this less all the time. "He's already been. He's already got what *he* needs. We'll have to hurry."

Kevin was already starting for the edge of the sidewalk, meaning to cut across the town square to LaVerdiere's. Mr. Delevan reached out and grabbed him like a conductor grabbing a fellow he's caught trying to sneak aboard a train without a ticket. *"Kevin, what are you talking about?"*

And then Kevin actually said it: looked at him and *said* it. "It's coming, Dad. Please. It's my life." He looked at his father, pleading with his pallid face and his fey, floating eyes. "The dog is coming. It won't do any good to just break in and take the camera. It's gone way past that now. Please don't stop me. Please don't wake me up. It's my *life.*"

Mr. Delevan made one last great effort not to give in to this creeping craziness . . . and then succumbed.

"Come on," he said, hooking his hand around his son's elbow and almost dragging him into the square. "Whatever it is, let's get it done." He paused. "Do we have enough time?"

"I'm not sure," Kevin said, and then, reluctantly: "I don't think so."

CHAPTER SEVENTEEN

Pop waited behind the board fence, looking at the Delevans through a knothole. He had put his tobacco in his back pocket so that his hands would be free to clench and unclench, clench and unclench.

You're on my property, his mind whispered at them, and if his mind had had the power to kill, he would have reached out with it and struck them both dead. *You're on my property, goddammit, you're on my property!*

What he ought to do was go get old John Law and bring him down on their fancy Castle View heads. That was what he *ought* to do. And he would have done it, too, right then, if they hadn't been standing over the wreckage of the camera the boy himself had supposedly destroyed with Pop's blessing two weeks ago. He thought maybe he would have tried to bullshit his way through anyway, but he knew how they felt about him in this town. Pangborn, Keeton, all the rest of them. Trash. That's what they thought of him. Trash.

Until they got their asses in a crack and needed a fast loan and the sun was down, that was.

Clench, unclench. Clench, unclench.

They were talking, but Pop didn't bother listening to what they were saying. His mind was a fuming forge. Now the litany had become: *They're on my goddam property and I can't do a thing about it! They're on my goddam property and I can't do a thing about it! Goddam them! Goddam them!*

At last they left. When he heard the rusty screech of the gate in the alley, Pop used his key on the one in the board fence. He slipped through and ran across the yard to his back door—ran with an unsettling fleetness for a man of seventy, with one hand clapped firmly against his upper right leg, as if, fleet or not, he was fighting a bad rheumatism pain there. In fact, Pop was feeling no pain at all. He didn't want either his keys or the change in his purse jingling, that was all. In case the Delevans were still there, lurking just beyond where he could see. Pop wouldn't have been surprised if they were doing just that. When you were dealing with skunks, you expected them to get up to stinking didos.

He slipped his keys out of his pocket. *Now* they rattled, and although the sound was muted, it seemed very loud to him. He cut his eyes to the left for a moment, sure he would see the brat's staring sheep's face. Pop's mouth was set in a hard, strained grin of fear. There was no one there.

Yet, anyway.

He found the right key, slipped it into the lock, and went in. He was careful not to open the door to the shed too wide, because the hinges picked up a squeal when you exercised them too much.

Inside, he turned the thumb-bolt with a savage twist and then went into the Emporium Galorium. He was more than at home in these shadows. He could have negotiated the narrow, junk-lined corridors in his sleep . . . *had,* in fact, although that, like a good many other things, had slipped his mind for the time being.

There was a dirty little side window near the front of the store that looked out upon the narrow alleyway the Delevans had used to trespass their way into his backyard. It also gave a sharply angled view on the sidewalk and part of the town common.

Pop slipped up to this window between piles of useless, valueless magazines that breathed their dusty yellow museum scent into the dark air. He looked out into the alley and saw it was empty. He looked to the right and saw the Delevans, wavery as fish in an aquarium through this dirty, flawed glass, crossing the common just below the bandstand. He didn't watch them out of sight in this window or go to the front windows to get a better angle on them. He guessed they were going over to LaVerdiere's, and since they had already been here, they would be asking about him. What could the little counter-slut tell them? That he had been and gone. Anything else?

Only that he had bought two pouches of tobacco.

Pop smiled.

That wasn't likely to hang him.

He found a brown bag, went out back, started for the chopping block, considered, then went to the gate in the alleyway instead. Careless once didn't mean a body had to be careless again.

After the gate was locked, he took his bag to the chopping block and picked up the pieces of shattered Polaroid camera. He worked as fast as he could, but he took time to be thorough.

He picked up everything but little shards and splinters that could be seen as no more than anonymous litter. A Police Lab investigating unit would probably be able to ID some of the stuff left around; Pop had seen TV crime shows (when he wasn't watching X-rated movies on his VCR, that was) where those scientific fellows went over the scene of a crime with little brushes and vacuums and even pairs of tweezers, putting things in little plastic bags, but the Castle Rock Sheriff's Department didn't have one of those units. And Pop doubted if Sheriff Pangborn could talk the State Police into sending their crime wagon, even if Pangborn himself could be persuaded to make the effort—not for what was no more than a case of camera theft, and that was all the Delevans could accuse him of without sounding crazy. Once he had policed the area, he went back inside, unlocked his "special" drawer, and deposited the brown bag inside. He relocked the drawer and put his keys back in his pocket. *That* was all right, then. He knew all about search warrants, too. It would be a snowy day in hell before the

Delevans could get Pangborn into district court to ask for one of those. Even if he was crazy enough to try, the remains of the goddamned camera would be gone—*permanently*—long before they could turn the trick. To try and dispose of the pieces for good right now would be more dangerous than leaving them in the locked drawer. The Delevans would come back and catch him right in the middle of it. Best to wait.

Because they *would* be back.

Pop Merrill knew that as well as he knew his own name.

Later, perhaps, after all this hooraw and foolishment died down, he would be able to go to the boy and say *Yes. That's right. Everything you think I did, I did. Now why don't we just leave her alone and go back to not knowin each other . . . all right? We can afford to do that. You might not think so, at least not at first, but we can. Because look—you wanted to bust it up because you thought it was dangerous, and I wanted to sell it because I thought it was valuable. Turned out you was right and I was wrong, and that's all the revenge you're ever gonna need. If you knew me better, you'd know why—there ain't many men in this town that have ever heard me say such a thing. It sticks in my gut, is what I mean to say, but that don't matter; when I'm wrong, I like to think I'm big enough to own up to it, no matter how bad it hurts. In the end, boy, I did what you meant to do in the first place. We all came out on the same street, is what I mean to say, and I think we ought to let bygones be bygones. I know what you think of me, and I know what I think of you, and neither of us would ever vote for the other one to be Grand Marshal in the annual Fourth of July parade, but that's all right; we can live with that, can't we? What I mean to say is just this: we're both glad that goddam camera is gone, so let's call it quits and walk away.*

But that was for later, and even then it was only perhaps. It wouldn't do for right now, that was for sure. They would need time to cool down. Right now both of them would be raring to tear a chunk out of his ass, like

(the dog in that pitcher)

like . . . well, never mind what they'd be like. The important thing was to be down here, business as usual and as innocent as a goddam baby when they got back.

Because they *would* be back.

But that was all right. It was all right because—

"B'cause things are under control," Pop whispered. "*That's* what I mean to say."

Now he did go to the front door, and switched the CLOSED sign over to OPEN (he then turned it promptly back to CLOSED again, but this Pop did not observe himself doing, nor would he remember it later). All right; that was a start. What was next? Make it look like just another normal day, no more and no less. He had to be all surprise and what-in-the-tar-nation-are-you-talking-about when they came back with steam coming out of their collars, all ready to do or die for what had already been killed just as dead as sheepdip.

So . . . what was the most normal thing they could find him doing when they came back, with Sheriff Pangborn or without him?

Pop's eye fixed on the cuckoo clock hanging from the beam beside that nice bureau he'd gotten at an estate sale in Sebago a month or six weeks ago. Not a very nice cuckoo clock, probably one originally purchased with trading stamps by some soul trying to be thrifty (people who could only *try* to be thrifty were, in Pop's estimation, poor puzzled souls who drifted through life in a vague and constant state of disappointment). Still, if he could put it right so it would run a little, he could maybe sell it to one of the skiers who would be up in another month or two, somebody who needed a clock at their cottage or ski-lodge because the last bargain had up and died and who didn't understand yet (and probably never would) that another bargain wasn't the solution but the problem.

Pop would feel sorry for that person, and would dicker with him or her as fairly as he thought he could, but he wouldn't disappoint the buyer. *Caveet emperor* was not only what he *meant* to say but often *did* say, and he had a living to make, didn't he?

Yes. So he would just sit back there at his worktable and fuss around with that clock, see if he could get it running, and when the Delevans got back, that was what they would find him doing. Maybe there'd even be a few prospective customers browsing around by then; he could hope, although this was always a slack time of year. Customers would be icing on the cake, anyway. The important thing was how it would look: just a fellow with nothing to hide, going through the ordinary motions and ordinary rhythms of his ordinary day.

Pop went over to the beam and took the cuckoo clock down, being careful not to tangle up the counterweights. He carried it back to his worktable, humming a little. He set it down, then felt his back pocket. Fresh tobacco. That was good, too.

Pop thought he would have himself a little pipe while he worked.

CHAPTER EIGHTEEN

"You can't *know* he was in here, Kevin!" Mr. Delevan was still protesting feebly as they went into LaVerdiere's.

Ignoring him, Kevin went straight to the counter where Molly Durham stood. Her urge to vomit had passed off, and she felt much better. The whole thing seemed a little silly now, like a nightmare you have and then wake up from and after the initial relief you think: *I was afraid of* THAT*? How could I ever have thought* THAT *was really happening to me, even in a dream?*

But when the Delevan boy presented his drawn white face at the counter, she *knew* how you could be afraid, yes, oh yes, even of things as ridiculous as the things which happened in dreams, because she was tumbled back into her own waking dreamscape again.

The thing was, Kevin Delevan had almost the same *look* on his face: as though he were so deep inside somewhere that when his voice and his gaze finally reached her, they seemed almost expended.

"Pop Merrill was in here," he said. "What did he buy?"

"Please excuse my son," Mr. Delevan said. "He's not feeling w—"

Then *he* saw *Molly's* face and stopped. She looked like she had just seen a man lose his arm to a factory machine.

"Oh!" she said. "Oh my God!"

"Was it film?" Kevin asked her.

"What's wrong with him?" Molly asked faintly. "I *knew* something was the minute he walked in. What is it? Has he . . . done something?"

Jesus, John Delevan thought. *He* DOES *know. It's all true, then.*

At that moment, Mr. Delevan made a quietly heroic decision: he gave up entirely. He gave up entirely and put himself and what he believed could and could not be true entirely in his son's hands.

"It was, wasn't it?" Kevin pressed her. His urgent face rebuked her for her flutters and tremors. "Polaroid film. From *that*." He pointed at the display.

"Yes." Her complexion was as pale as china; the bit of rouge she had put on that morning stood out in hectic, flaring patches. "He was so . . . strange. Like a talking doll. What's wrong with him? What—"

But Kevin had whirled away, back to his father.

"I need a camera," he rapped. "I need it right now. A Polaroid Sun 660. They have them. They're even on special. See?"

And in spite of his decision, Mr. Delevan's mouth would not quite let go of the last clinging shreds of rationality. "Why—" he began, and that was as far as Kevin let him get.

"I don't KNOW why!" he shouted, and Molly Durham moaned. She didn't want to throw up now; Kevin Delevan was scary, but not *that* scary. What she wanted to do right now was simply go home and creep up to her bedroom and draw the covers over her head. *"But we have to have it, and time's almost up, Dad!"*

"Give me one of those cameras," Mr. Delevan said, drawing his wallet out with shaking hands, unaware that Kevin had already darted to the display.

"Just take one," she heard a trembling voice entirely unlike her own say. "Just take one and go."

CHAPTER NINETEEN

Across the square, Pop Merrill, who believed he was peacefully repairing a cheap cuckoo clock, innocent as a babe in arms, finished loading Kevin's camera with one of the film packs. He snapped it shut. It made its squidgy little whine.

Damn cuckoo sounds like he's got a bad case of laryngitis. Slipped a gear, I guess. Well, I got the cure for that.

"I'll fix you," Pop said, and raised the camera. He applied one blank eye to the viewfinder with the hairline crack which was so tiny you didn't even see it when you got your eye up to it. The camera was aimed at the front of the store, but *that* didn't matter; wherever you pointed it, it was aimed at a certain black dog that wasn't any dog God had ever made in a little town called for the want of a better word Polaroidsville, which He also hadn't ever made.

FLASH!

That squidgy little whine as Kevin's camera pushed out a new picture.

"There," Pop said with quiet satisfaction. "Maybe I'll do more than get you talking, bird. What I mean to say is I might just get you *singing.* I don't promise, but I'll give her a try."

Pop grinned a dry, leathery grin and pushed the button again.

FLASH!

They were halfway across the square when John Delevan saw a silent white light fill the dirty windows of the Emporium Galorium. The *light* was silent, but following it, like an aftershock, he heard a low, dark rumble that seemed to come to his ears from the old man's junk-store . . . but only because the old man's junk-store was the only place it could find a way to get out. Where it seemed to be *emanating* from was under the earth . . . or was it just that the earth itself seemed the only place large enough to cradle the owner of that voice?

"Run, Dad!" Kevin cried. *"He's started doing it!"*

That flash recurred, lighting the windows like a heatless stroke of electricity. It was followed by that subaural growl again, the sound of a sonic boom in a wind-tunnel, the sound of some animal which was horrible beyond comprehension being kicked out of its sleep.

Mr. Delevan, helpless to stop himself and almost unaware of what he was doing, opened his mouth to tell his son that a light that big and bright could not possibly be coming from the built-in flash of a Polaroid camera, but Kevin had already started to run.

Mr. Delevan began to run himself, knowing perfectly well what he meant to do: catch up to his son and collar him and drag him away before something dreadful beyond his grasp of all dreadful things could happen.

CHAPTER TWENTY

The second Polaroid Pop took forced the first one out of the slot. It fluttered down to the top of the desk, where it landed with a thud heavier than such a square of chemically treated cardboard could possibly make. The Sun dog filled almost the entire frame now; the foreground was its impossible head, the black pits of the eyes, the smoking, teeth-filled jaws. The skull seemed to be elongating into a shape like a bullet or a teardrop as the dog-thing's speed and the shortening distance between it and the lens combined to drive it further out of focus. Only the tops of the pickets in the fence behind it were visible now; the bulk of the thing's flexed shoulders ate up the rest of the frame.

Kevin's birthday string tie, which had rested next to the Sun camera in his drawer, showed at the bottom of the frame, winking back a shaft of hazy sunlight.

"Almost got you, you son of a whore," Pop said in a high, cracked voice. His eyes were blinded by the light. He saw neither dog nor camera. He saw only the voiceless cuckoo which had become his life's mission. "You'll sing, damn you! I'll *make* you sing!"

FLASH!

The third picture pushed the second from the slot. It fell too fast, more like a chunk of stone than a square of cardboard, and when it hit the desk, it dug through the ancient frayed blotter there and sent startled splinters flying up from the wood beneath.

In this picture, the dog's head was torn even further out of focus; it had become a long column of flesh that gave it a strange, almost three-dimensional aspect.

In the third one, still poking out of the slot in the bottom of the camera, the Sun dog's snout seemed, impossibly, to be coming back into focus again. It was impossible because it was as close to the lens as it could get; so close it seemed to be the snout of some sea-monster just below that fragile meniscus we call the surface.

"Damn thing still ain't quite right," Pop said.

His finger pushed the Polaroid's trigger again.

CHAPTER TWENTY-ONE

Kevin ran up the steps of the Emporium Galorium. His father reached for him, caught nothing but the air an inch from the fluttering tail of Kevin's shirt, stumbled, and landed on the heels of his hands. They slid across the second step from the top, sending a quiver of small splinters into his skin.

"Kevin!"

He looked up and for a moment the world was almost lost in another of those dazzling white flashes. This time the roar was much louder. It was the sound of a crazed animal on the verge of making its weakening cage give it up. He saw Kevin with his head down, one hand shielding his eyes from the white glare, frozen in that stroboscopic light as if he himself had turned into a photograph. He saw cracks like quicksilver jig-jag their way down the show windows.

"Kevin, look ou—"

The glass burst outward in a glittery spray and Mr. Delevan ducked his own head. Glass flew around him in a squall. He felt it patter into his hair and both cheeks were scratched, but none of the glass dug deeply into either the boy or the man; most of it had been pulverized to crumbs.

There was a splintering crunch. He looked up again and saw that Kevin had gained entry just as Mr. Delevan had thought they might earlier: by ramming the now-glassless door with his shoulder and tearing the new locking bolt right through the old, rotted wood.

"KEVIN, GODDAMMIT!" he bawled. He got up, almost stumbled to one knee again as his feet tangled together, then lurched upright and plunged after his son.

• • •

Something had happened to the goddam cuckoo clock. Something *bad.*

It was striking again and again—bad enough, but that wasn't all. It had also gained weight in Pop's hands . . . and it seemed to be growing uncomfortably hot, as well.

Pop looked down at it, and suddenly tried to scream in horror through jaws which felt as if they had been wired together somehow.

He realized he had been struck blind, and he *also* suddenly realized that what he held was not a cuckoo clock at all.

He tried to make his hands relax their death-grip on the camera and was horrified to find he could not open his fingers. The field of gravity around the camera seemed to have increased. And the horrid thing was growing steadily hotter. Between Pop's splayed, white-nailed fingers, the gray plastic of the camera's housing had begun to smoke.

His right index finger began to crawl upward toward the red shutter-button like a crippled fly.

"No," he muttered, and then, in a plea: *"Please . . ."*

His finger paid no attention. It reached the red button and settled upon it just as Kevin slammed his shoulder into the door and burst in. Glass from the door's panes crunched and sprayed.

Pop didn't push the button. Even blind, even feeling the flesh of his fingers begin to smoulder and scorch, he knew he didn't push the button. But as his finger settled upon it, that gravitational field first seemed to double, then treble. He tried to hold his finger up and off the button. It was like trying to hold the push-up position on the planet Jupiter.

"Drop it!" the kid screamed from somewhere out on the rim of his darkness. "Drop it, *drop it!*"

"NO!" Pop screamed back. *"What I mean to say is I CAN'T!"*

The red button began to slide in toward its contact point.

• • •

Kevin was standing with his legs spread, bent over the camera they had just taken from LaVerdiere's, the box it had come in lying at his feet. He had managed to hit the button that released the front of the camera on its hinge, revealing the wide loading slot. He was trying to jam one of the film packs into it, and it stubbornly refused to go—it was as if this camera had turned traitor, too, possibly in sympathy to its brother.

Pop screamed again, but this time there were no words, only an inarticulate cry of pain and fear. Kevin smelled hot plastic and roasting flesh. He looked up and saw the Polaroid was melting, actually *melting,* in the old man's frozen hands. Its square, boxy silhouette was rearranging itself into an odd, hunched shape. Somehow the glass of both the viewfinder and the lens had also become plastic. Instead of breaking or popping out of the camera's increasingly shapeless shell, they were elongating and drooping like taffy, becoming a pair of grotesque eyes like those in a mask of tragedy.

Dark plastic, heated to a sludge like warm wax, ran over Pop's fingers and the backs of his hands in thick runnels, carving troughs in his flesh. The plastic cauterized what it burned, but Kevin saw blood squeezing from the sides of these runnels and dripping down Pop's flesh to strike the table in smoking droplets which sizzled like hot fat.

"Your film's still wrapped up!" his father bawled from behind him, breaking Kevin's paralysis. *"Unwrap it! Give it to me!"*

His father reached around him, bumping Kevin so hard he almost knocked him over. He snatched the film pack, with its heavy paper-foil wrapping still on it, and ripped the end. He stripped it off.

"HELP ME!" Pop screeched, the last coherent words either of them heard him say.

"Quick!" his father yelled, putting the fresh film pack back in his hands. "Quick!"

The sizzle of hot flesh. The patter of hot blood on the desk, what had been a shower now becoming a storm as the bigger veins and arteries in Pop's fingers and the backs of his hands began to let go. A brook of hot, running plastic braceleted his left wrist and the bundle of veins so close to the surface there let go, spraying out blood as if through a rotten gasket which has first begun to leak in several places and now begins to simply disintegrate under the insistent, beating pressure.

Pop howled like an animal.

Kevin tried to jam the film pack in again and cried out *"Fuck!"* as it still refused to go.

"It's backwards!" Mr. Delevan hollered. He tried to snatch the camera from Kevin, and Kevin tore away, leaving his father with a scrap of shirt and no more. He pulled the film pack out and for a moment it jittered on the ends of his fingers, almost dropping to the floor—which, he felt, longed to actually hump itself up into a fist and smash it when it came down.

Then he had it, turned it around, socked it home, and slammed the front of the camera, which was hanging limply downward like a creature with a broken neck, shut on its hinge.

Pop howled again, and—

FLASH!

CHAPTER TWENTY-TWO

This time it was like standing in the center of a sun which goes supernova in one sudden, heatless gust of light. Kevin felt as if his shadow had actually been hammered off his heels and driven into the wall. Perhaps this was at least partly true, for all of the wall behind him was instantly flash-baked and threaded with a thousand crazy cracks except for one sunken area where his shadow fell. His outline, as clear and unmistakable as a silhouette cut-out, was tattooed there with one elbow stuck out in a flying wedge, caught and frozen even as the arm which cast the shadow left its frozen image behind, rising to bring the new camera up to his face.

The top of the camera in Pop's hands tore free of the rest with a thick sound like a very fat man clearing his throat. The Sun dog growled, and this time that bass thunder was loud enough, clear enough, *near* enough, to shatter the glass in the fronts of the clocks and to send the glass in the mirrors and in the frames of pictures belching across the floor in momentary crystal arcs of amazing and improbable beauty.

The camera did not moan or whine this time; the sound of its mechanism was a scream, high and drilling, like a woman who is dying in the throes of a breech delivery. The square of paper which shoved and bulled its way out of that slitted opening smoked and fumed. Then the dark delivery-slot itself began to melt, one side drooping downward, the other wrinkling upward, all of it beginning to yawn like a toothless mouth. A bubble was forming upon the shiny surface of the last picture, which still hung in the widening mouth of the channel from which the Polaroid Sun gave birth to its photographs.

As Kevin watched, frozen, looking through a curtain of flashing, zinging dots that last white explosion had put in front of his eyes, the Sun dog roared again. The sound was smaller now, with less of that sense that it was coming from beneath and from everywhere, but it was also more deadly because it was more *real,* more *here.*

Part of the dissolving camera blew backward in a great gray gobbet, striking Pop Merrill's neck and expanding into a necklace. Suddenly both Pop's jugular vein and carotid artery gave way in spraying gouts of blood that jetted upward and outward in bright-red spirals. Pop's head whipped bonelessly backward.

The bubble on the surface of the picture grew. The picture itself began to jitter in the yawning slot at the bottom of the now-decapitated camera. Its sides began to spread, as if the picture was no longer on cardboard at all but some flexible substance like knitted nylon. It wiggled back and forth in the slot, and Kevin thought of the cowboy boots he had gotten for his birthday two years ago, and how he had had to wiggle his feet into them, because they were a little too tight.

The edges of the picture struck the edges of the camera delivery-slot, where they should have stuck firmly. But the camera was no longer a solid; was, in fact, losing all resemblance to what it had been. The edges of the picture sliced through its sides as cleanly as the razor-sharp sides of a good double-edged knife slide through tender meat. They poked through what had been the Polaroid's housing, sending gray drops of smoking plastic flying into the dim air. One landed on a dry, crumbling stack of old *Popular Mechanics* magazines and burrowed a fuming, charred hole into them.

The dog roared again, an angry, ugly sound—the cry of something with nothing but rending and killing on its mind. Those things, and nothing else.

The picture teetered on the edge of the sagging, dissolving slit, which now looked more like the bell of some misshapen wind instrument than anything else, and then fell forward to the desk with the speed of a stone tumbling into a well.

Kevin felt a hand claw at his shoulder.

"What's it doing?" his father asked hoarsely. "Jesus Christ almighty, Kevin, *what's it doing?*"

Kevin heard himself answer in a remote, almost disinterested voice: "Being born."

CHAPTER TWENTY-THREE

Pop Merrill died leaning back in the chair behind his worktable, where he had spent so many hours sitting: sitting and smoking; sitting and fixing things up so they would run for at least awhile and he could sell the worthless to the thoughtless; sitting and loaning money to the impulsive and the improvident after the sun went down. He died staring up at the ceiling, from which his own blood dripped back down to splatter on his cheeks and into his open eyes.

His chair overbalanced and spilled his lolling body onto the floor. His purse and his key-ring clattered.

On his desk, the final Polaroid continued to jiggle about restlessly. Its sides spread apart, and Kevin seemed to sense some unknown thing, both alive and not alive, groaning in horrid, unknowable labor pains.

"We've got to get out of here," his father panted, pulling at him. John Delevan's eyes were large and frenzied, riveted on that spreading, moving photograph which now covered half of Merrill's worktable. It no longer resembled a photograph at all. Its sides bulged out like the cheeks of someone trying frantically to whistle. The shiny bubble, now a foot high, humped and shuddered. Strange, unnameable colors raced aimlessly back and forth across a surface which seemed to have broken some oily sort of sweat. That roar, full of frustration and purpose and frantic hunger, ripped through his brain again and again, threatening to split it and let in madness.

Kevin pulled away from him, ripping his shirt along the shoulder. His voice was full of a deep, strange calm. "No—it would just come after us. I think it wants me, because if it wanted Pop it's already got him and I was the one who owned the camera first, anyway. But it wouldn't stop there. It'd take you, too. And it might not stop there, either."

"You can't do anything!" his father screamed.

"Yes," Kevin said. "I've got one chance."

And raised the camera.

The edges of the picture reached the edges of the worktable. Instead of lolling over, they curled up and continued to twist and spread. Now they resembled odd wings which were somehow equipped with lungs and were trying to breathe in some tortured fashion.

The entire surface of the amorphous, pulsing thing continued to puff up; what should have been flat surface had become a horrid tumor, its lumped and cratered sides trickling with vile liquid. It gave off the bland smell of head cheese.

The dog's roars had become continuous, the trapped and furious belling of a hell-hound bent on escape, and some of the late Pop Merrill's clocks began to strike again and again, as if in protest.

Mr. Delevan's frantic urge to escape had deserted him; he felt overcome by a deep and dangerous lassitude, a kind of lethal sleepiness.

Kevin held the camera's viewfinder to his eye. He had only been deer-hunting a few times, but he remembered how it was when it was your turn to wait, hidden, with your rifle as your hunting partners walked through the woods toward you, deliberately making as much noise as they could, hoping to drive something out of the trees and into the clearing where you were waiting, your field of fire a safe angle that would cross in front of the men. You didn't have to worry about hitting them; you only had to worry about hitting the deer.

There was time to wonder if you *could* hit it, when and if it showed itself. There was also time to wonder if you could bring yourself to fire at all. Time to hope that the deer would remain hypothetical, so the test did not have to be made . . . and so it had always turned out to be. The one time there *had* been a deer, his father's friend Bill Roberson had been lying up in the blind. Mr. Roberson had put the bullet just where you were supposed to put it, at the juncture of neck and shoulder, and they had gotten the game-warden to take their pictures around it, a twelve-point buck any man would be happy to brag on.

Bet you wish it'd been your turn in the puckies, don't you, son? the game-warden had asked, ruffling Kevin's hair (he had been twelve then, the growth spurt which had begun about seventeen months ago and which had so far taken him to just an inch under six feet still a year away . . . which meant he had not been big enough to be resentful of a man who wanted to ruffle his hair). Kevin had nodded, keeping his secret to himself: he was *glad* it hadn't been his turn in the puckies, his the rifle which must be responsible for throwing the slug or not throwing it . . . and, if he had turned out to have the courage to do the shooting, his reward would have been only another troublesome responsibility: to shoot the buck clean. He didn't know if he could have mustered the courage to put another bullet in the thing if the kill *wasn't* clean, or the strength to chase the trail of its blood and steaming, startled droppings and finish what he had started if it ran.

He had smiled up at the game-warden and nodded and his dad had snapped a picture of *that,* and there had never been any need to tell his dad that the thought going on behind that upturned brow and under the game-warden's ruffling hand had been *No. I don't wish it. The world is full of tests, but twelve's too young to go hunting them. I'm glad it was Mr. Roberson. I'm not ready yet to try a man's tests.*

But now he was the one in the blind, wasn't he? And the animal was coming, wasn't it? And it was no harmless eater of grasses this time, was it? This was a killing engine big enough and mean enough to swallow a tiger whole, and it meant to kill *him,* and that was only for starters, and he was the only one that could stop it.

The thought of turning the Polaroid over to his father crossed his mind, but only momentarily. Something deep inside himself knew the truth: to pass the camera would be tantamount to murdering his father and committing suicide himself. His father believed *something,* but that wasn't specific enough. The camera wouldn't work for his father even if his father managed to break out of his current stunned condition and press the shutter.

It would only work for him.

So he waited on the test, peering through the viewfinder of the camera as if it were the gunsight of a rifle, peering at the photograph as it continued to spread and force that shiny, liquescent bubble wider and wider and higher and higher.

Then the actual birthing of the Sun dog into this world began to happen. The camera seemed to gain weight and turn to lead as the thing roared again with a sound like a whiplash loaded with steel shot. The camera trembled in his hands and he could feel his wet, slippery fingers simply wanting to uncurl and let go. He held on, his lips pulling back from his teeth in a sick and desperate grin. Sweat ran into one eye, momentarily doubling his vision. He threw his head back, snapping his hair off his forehead and out of his eyebrows, and then nestled his staring eye back into the viewfinder as a great ripping sound, like heavy cloth being torn in half by strong, slow hands, filled the Emporium Galorium.

The shiny surface of the bubble tore open. Red smoke, like the blast from a tea-kettle set in front of red neon, billowed out.

The thing roared again, an angry, homicidal sound. A gigantic jaw, filled with croggled teeth, burst up through the shrivelling membrane of the now-collapsing bubble like the jaw of a breaching pilot whale. It ripped and chewed and gnawed at the membrane, which gave way with gummy splattering sounds.

The clocks struck wildly, crazily.

His father grabbed him again, so hard that Kevin's teeth rapped against the plastic body of the camera and it came within a hair of spilling out of his hands and shattering on the floor.

"Shoot it!" his father screamed over the thing's bellowing din. *"Shoot it, Kevin, if you can shoot it, SHOOT IT NOW, Christ Jesus, it's going to—"*

Kevin yanked away from his father's hand. "Not yet," he said. "Not just y—"

The thing *screamed* at the sound of Kevin's voice. The Sun dog lunged up from wherever it was, driving the picture still wider. It gave and stretched with a groaning sound. This was replaced by the thick cough of ripping fabric again.

And suddenly the Sun dog was up, its head rising black and rough and tangled through the hole in reality like some weird periscope which was all tangled metal and glittering, glaring lenses . . . except it wasn't metal but that twisted, spiky fur Kevin was looking at, and those were not lenses but the thing's insane, raging eyes.

It caught at the neck, the spines of its pelt shredding the edges of the hole it had made into a strange sunburst pattern. It roared again, and sickly yellow-red fire licked out of its mouth.

John Delevan took a step backward and struck a table overloaded with thick copies of *Weird Tales* and *Fantastic Universe.* The table tilted and Mr. Delevan flailed helplessly against it, his heels first rocking back and then shooting out from under him. Man and table went over with a crash. The Sun dog roared again, then dipped its head with an unsuspected delicacy and tore at the membrane which held it. The membrane ripped. The thing barked out a thin stream of fire which ignited the membrane and turned it to ash. The beast lunged upward again and Kevin saw that the thing on the tie around its neck was no longer a tie-clasp but the spoon-shaped tool which Pop Merrill had used to clean his pipe.

In that moment a clean calmness fell over the boy. His father bellowed in surprise and fear as he tried to untangle himself from the table he had fallen over, but Kevin took no notice. The cry seemed to come from a great distance away.

It's all right, Dad, he thought, fixing the struggling, emerging beast more firmly in the viewfinder. *It's all right, don't you see? It* can *be all right, anyway . . . because the charm it wears has changed.*

He thought that perhaps the Sun dog had its master, too . . . and its master had realized that Kevin was no longer sure prey.

And perhaps there was a dog-catcher in that strange nowhere town of Polaroidsville; there must be, else why had the fat woman been in his dream? It was the fat woman who had told him what he must do, either on her own or because that dog-catcher had put her there for him to see and notice: the two-dimensional fat woman with her two-dimensional shopping-cart full of two-dimensional cameras. *Be careful, boy. Pop's dog broke his leash and he's a mean un. . . . It's hard to take his pitcher, but you can't do it at all, 'less you have a cam'ra.*

And now he had his camera, didn't he? It was not sure, not by any means, but at least he had it.

The dog paused, head turning almost aimlessly . . . until its muddy, burning gaze settled on Kevin Delevan. Its black lips peeled back from its corkscrewed boar's fangs, its muzzle opened to reveal the smoking channel of its throat, and it gave a high, drilling howl of fury. The ancient hanging globes that lit Pop's place at night shattered one after another in rows, sending down spinning shards of frosted fly-beshitted glass. It lunged, its broad, panting chest bursting through the membrane between the worlds.

Kevin's finger settled on the Polaroid's trigger.

It lunged again, and now its front legs popped free, and those cruel spurs of bone, so like gigantic thorns, scraped and scrabbled for purchase on the desk. They dug long vertical scars in the heavy rock-maple. Kevin could hear the dusky thud-and-scratch of its pistoning rear legs digging for a grip down there (wherever *down there* was), and he knew that this was the final short stretch of seconds in which it would be trapped and at his mercy; the next convulsive lunge would send it flying over the desk, and once free of the hole through which it was squirming, it would move as fast as liquid death, charging across the space between them, setting his pants ablaze with its fiery breath split-seconds before it tore into his warm innards.

Very clearly, Kevin instructed: "Say *cheese,* you motherfucker."

And triggered the Polaroid.

CHAPTER TWENTY-FOUR

The flash was so bright that Kevin could not conceive of it later; could, in fact, barely remember it at all. The camera he was holding did not grow hot and melt; instead there were three or four quick, decisive breaking sounds from inside it as its ground-glass lenses burst and its springs either snapped or simply disintegrated.

In the white afterglare he saw the Sun dog *frozen,* a perfect black-and-white Polaroid photograph, its head thrown back, every twisting fold and crevasse in its wildly bushed-out fur caught like the complicated topography of a dry river-valley. Its teeth shone, no longer subtly shaded yellow but as white and nasty as old bones in that sterile emptiness where water had quit running millennia ago. Its single swollen eye, robbed of the dark and bloody porthole of iris by the merciless flash, was as white as an eye in the head of a Greek bust. Smoking snot drizzled from its flared nostrils and ran like hot lava in the narrow gutters between its rolled-back muzzle and its gums.

It was like a negative of all the Polaroids Kevin had ever seen: black-and-white instead of color, and in three dimensions instead of two. And it was like watching a living creature turned instantly to stone by a careless look at the head of Medusa.

"You're *done,* you son of a bitch!" Kevin screamed in a cracked, hysterical voice, and as if in agreement, the thing's frozen forelegs lost their hold on the desk and it began to disappear, first slowly and then rapidly, into the hole from which it had come. It went with a rocky coughing sound, like a landslide.

What would I see if I ran over now and looked into that hole? he wondered incoherently. *Would I see that house, that fence, the old man with his shopping-cart, staring with wide-eyed wonder at the face of a giant, not a boy but a Boy, staring back at him from a torn and charred hole in the hazy sky? Would it suck me in? What?*

Instead, he dropped the Polaroid and raised his hands to his face.

Only John Delevan, lying on the floor, saw the final act: the twisted, dead membrane shrivelling in on itself, pulling into a complicated but unimportant node around the hole, crumpling there, and then falling (or being *inhaled*) into itself.

There was a whooping sound of air, which rose from a broad gasp to a thin tea-kettle whistle.

Then it turned inside-out and was gone. Simply gone, as if it had never been.

Getting slowly and shakily to his feet, Mr. Delevan saw that the final inrush (or outrush, he supposed, depending on which side of that hole you were on) of air had pulled the desk-blotter and the other Polaroids the old man had taken in with it.

His son was standing in the middle of the floor with his hands over his face, weeping.

"Kevin," he said quietly, and put his arms around his boy.

"I had to take its picture," Kevin said through his tears and through his hands. "It was the only way to get rid of it. I had to take the rotten whoredog's picture. *That's* what I mean to say."

"Yes." He hugged him tighter. "Yes, and you did it."

Kevin looked at his father with naked, streaming eyes. "*That's* how I had to shoot it, Dad. Do you see?"

"Yes," his father said. "Yes, I see that." He kissed Kevin's hot cheek again. "Let's go home, son."

He tightened his grip around Kevin's shoulders, wanting to lead him toward the door and away from the smoking, bloody body of the old man (Kevin hadn't really noticed yet, Mr. Delevan thought, but if they spent much longer here, he would), and for a moment Kevin resisted him.

"What are people going to *say?*" Kevin asked, and his tone was so prim and spinsterish that Mr. Delevan laughed in spite of his own sizzling nerves.

"Let them say whatever they want," he told Kevin. "They'll never get within shouting distance of the truth, and I don't think anyone will try very hard, anyway." He paused. "No one really liked him much, you know."

"I never *want* to be in shouting distance of the truth," Kevin whispered. "Let's go home."

"Yes. I love you, Kevin."

"I love you, too," Kevin said hoarsely, and they went out of the smoke and the stink of old things best left forgotten and into the bright light of day. Behind them, a pile of old magazines burst into flame . . . and the fire was quick to stretch out its hungry orange fingers.

EPILOGUE

It was Kevin Delevan's sixteenth birthday, and he got exactly what he wanted: a WordStar 70 PC and word processor. It was a seventeen-hundred-dollar toy, and his parents could never have afforded it in the old days, but in January, about three months after that final confrontation in the Emporium Galorium, Aunt Hilda had died quietly in her sleep. She had indeed Done Something for Kevin and Meg; had, in fact, Done Quite a Lot for the Whole Family. When the will cleared probate in early June, the Delevans found themselves richer by nearly seventy thousand dollars . . . and that was after taxes, not before.

"Jeez, it's neat! Thank you!" Kevin cried, and kissed his mother, his father, and even his sister, Meg (who giggled but, being a year older, made no attempt to rub it off; Kevin couldn't decide if this change was a step in the right direction or not). He spent much of the afternoon in his room, fussing over it and trying out the test program.

Around four o'clock, he came downstairs and into his father's den. "Where's Mom and Meg?" he asked.

"They've gone out to the crafts fair at . . . Kevin? Kevin, what's wrong?"

"You better come upstairs," Kevin said hollowly.

At the door to his room, he turned his pale face toward his father's equally pale face. There was something more to pay, Mr. Delevan had been thinking as he followed his son up the stairs. Of course there was. And hadn't he also learned that from Reginald Marion "Pop" Merrill? The debt you incurred was what hurt you.

It was the *interest* that broke your back.

"Can we get another one of these?" Kevin asked, pointing to the laptop computer which stood open on his desk, glowing a mystic yellow oblong of light onto the blotter.

"I don't know," Mr. Delevan said, approaching the desk. Kevin stood behind him, a pallid watcher. "I guess, if we *had* to—"

He stopped, looking down at the screen.

"I booted up the word-processing program and typed 'The quick brown fox jumped over the lazy sleeping dog,'" Kevin said. "Only *that* was what came out of the printer."

Mr. Delevan stood, silently reading the hard copy. His hands and forehead felt very cold. The words there read:

```
The dog is loose again.
It is not sleeping.
It is not lazy.
It's coming for you, Kevin.
```

The original debt was what hurt you, he thought again; it was the interest that broke your back. The last two lines read:

```
It's very hungry.
And it's VERY angry.
```

Also by Stephen King

FICTION

Carrie
'Salem's Lot
The Shining
Night Shift
The Stand
The Dead Zone
Firestarter
Cujo
Creepshow
Different Seasons
The Body
Cycle of the Werewolf
Christine
Pet Sematary
IT
Skeleton Crew
The Eyes of the Dragon
Misery
The Tommyknockers
The Dark Half
Four Past Midnight
Needful Things
Gerald's Game
Dolores Claiborne
Nightmares & Dreamscapes
Insomnia
Rose Madder
The Green Mile
Desperation
Bag of Bones
The Girl Who Loved Tom Gordon
Hearts in Atlantis
Dreamcatcher
Everything's Eventual
From a Buick 8
The Colorado Kid
Cell
Lisey's Story
Duma Key
Just After Sunset
Stephen King Goes to the Movies
Under the Dome
Full Dark, No Stars
11/22/63
Doctor Sleep
Mr. Mercedes
Revival
Finders Keepers
The Bazaar of Bad Dreams
End of Watch
The Outsider

NOVELS IN THE DARK TOWER SERIES

The Dark Tower I: The Gunslinger
The Dark Tower II: The Drawing of the Three
The Dark Tower III: The Waste Lands
The Dark Tower IV: Wizard and Glass
The Dark Tower V: Wolves of the Calla
The Dark Tower VI: Song of Susannah
The Dark Tower VII: The Dark Tower
The Wind Through the Keyhole: A Dark Tower Novel

BY STEPHEN KING AS RICHARD BACHMAN

Thinner
The Running Man
The Long Walk
Roadwork
The Regulators
Blaze

WITH OWEN KING

Sleeping Beauties

WITH PETER STRAUB

The Talisman
Black House

NONFICTION

Danse Macabre
On Writing (A Memoir of the Craft)

STEPHEN KING

THE MIST

SCRIBNER
New York London Toronto Sydney New Delhi

Scribner
An Imprint of Simon & Schuster, Inc.
1230 Avenue of the Americas
New York, NY 10020

This book is a work of fiction. Any references to historical events, real people, or real places are used fictitiously. Other names, characters, places, and events are products of the author's imagination, and any resemblance to actual events or places or persons, living or dead, is entirely coincidental.

"The Mist" first appeared in *Dark Forces*, edited by Kirby McCauley

First Scribner trade paperback edition June 2018

Interior design by Erich Hobbing

Manufactured in the United States of America

10

Library of Congress Cataloging-in-Publication Data is available.

ISBN 978-1-9821-0352-1
ISBN 978-1-5011-7624-1 (ebook)

THE MIST

I. The Coming of the Storm

This is what happened. On the night that the worst heat wave in northern New England history finally broke—the night of July 19—the entire western Maine region was lashed with the most vicious thunderstorms I have ever seen.

We lived on Long Lake, and we saw the first of the storms beating its way across the water toward us just before dark. For an hour before, the air had been utterly still. The American flag that my father put up on our boathouse in 1936 lay limp against its pole. Not even its hem fluttered. The heat was like a solid thing, and it seemed as deep as sullen quarry-water. That afternoon the three of us had gone swimming, but the water was no relief unless you went out deep. Neither Steffy nor I wanted to go deep because Billy couldn't. Billy is five.

We ate a cold supper at five-thirty, picking listlessly at ham sandwiches and potato salad out on the deck that faces the lake. Nobody seemed to want anything but Pepsi, which was in a steel bucket of ice cubes.

After supper Billy went out back to play on his monkey bars for a while. Steff and I sat without talking much, smoking and looking across the sullen flat mirror of the lake to Harrison on the far side. A few powerboats droned back and forth. The evergreens over there looked dusty and beaten. In the west, great purple thunderheads were slowly building up, massing like an army. Lightning flashed inside them. Next door, Brent Norton's radio, tuned to that classical-music station that broadcasts from the top of Mount Washington, sent out a loud bray of static each time the lightning flashed. Norton was a lawyer from New Jersey and his place on Long Lake was only a summer cottage with no furnace or insulation. Two years before, we had a boundary dispute that finally wound up in county court. I won. Norton claimed I won because he was an out-of-towner. There was no love lost between us.

Steff sighed and fanned the top of her breasts with the edge of her halter. I doubted if it cooled her off much but it improved the view a lot.

"I don't want to scare you," I said, "but there's a bad storm on the way, I think."

She looked at me doubtfully. "There were thunderheads last night and the night before, David. They just broke up."

"They won't do that tonight."

"No?"

"If it gets bad enough, we're going to go downstairs."

"How bad do you think it can get?"

My dad was the first to build a year-round home on this side of the lake. When he was hardly more than a kid he and his brothers put up a summer place where the house now stood, and in 1938 a summer storm knocked it flat, stone walls and all. Only the boathouse escaped. A year later he started the big house. It's the trees that do the damage in a bad blow. They get old, and the wind knocks them over. It's mother nature's way of cleaning house periodically.

"I don't really know," I said, truthfully enough. I had only heard stories about the great storm of thirty-eight. "But the wind can come off the lake like an express train."

Billy came back a while later, complaining that the monkey bars were no fun because he was "all sweated up." I ruffled his hair and gave him another Pepsi. More work for the dentist.

The thunderheads were getting closer, pushing away the blue. There was no doubt now that a storm was coming. Norton had turned off his radio. Billy sat between his mother and me, watching the sky, fascinated. Thunder boomed, rolling slowly across the lake and then echoing back again. The clouds twisted and rolled, now black, now purple, now veined, now black again. They gradually overspread the lake, and I could see a delicate caul of rain extending down from them. It was still a distance away. As we watched, it was probably raining on Bolster's Mills, or maybe even Norway.

The air began to move, jerkily at first, lifting the flag and then dropping it again. It began to freshen and grew steady, first cooling the perspiration on our bodies and then seeming to freeze it.

That was when I saw the silver veil rolling across the lake. It blotted out Harrison in seconds and then came straight at us. The powerboats had vacated the scene.

Billy stood up from his chair, which was a miniature replica of our director's chairs, complete with his name printed on the back. "Daddy! Look!"

"Let's go in," I said. I stood up and put my arm around his shoulders.

"But do you see it? Dad, what is it?"

"A water-cyclone. Let's go in."

Steff threw a quick, startled glance at my face and then said, "Come on, Billy. Do what your father says."

We went in through the sliding glass doors that give on the living room. I slid the door shut on its track and paused for another look out. The silver veil was three-quarters of the way across the lake. It had resolved itself into a crazily spinning teacup between the lowering black sky and the surface of the water, which had gone the color of lead streaked with white chrome. The lake had begun to look eerily like the ocean, with high waves rolling in and sending spume up from the docks and breakwaters. Out in the middle, big whitecaps were tossing their heads back and forth.

Watching the water-cyclone was hypnotic. It was nearly on top of us when lightning flashed so brightly that it printed everything on my eyes in negative for thirty seconds afterward. The telephone gave out a startled *ting!* and I turned to see my wife and son standing directly in front of the big picture window that gives us a panoramic view of the lake to the northwest.

One of those terrible visions came to me—I think they are reserved exclusively for husbands and fathers—of the picture window blowing in with a low hard coughing sound and sending jagged arrows of glass into my wife's bare stomach, into my boy's face and neck. The horrors of the Inquisition are nothing compared to the fates your mind can imagine for your loved ones.

I grabbed them both hard and jerked them away. "What the hell are you doing? Get away from there!"

Steff gave me a startled glance. Billy only looked at me as if he had been partially awakened from a deep dream. I led them into the kitchen and hit the light switch. The phone ting-a-linged again.

Then the wind came. It was as if the house had taken off like a 747. It was a high, breathless whistling, sometimes deepening to a bass roar before glissading up to a whooping scream.

"Go downstairs," I told Steff, and now I had to shout to make myself heard. Directly over the house thunder whacked mammoth planks together and Billy shrank against my leg.

"You come too!" Steff yelled back.

I nodded and made shooing gestures. I had to pry Billy off my leg. "Go with your mother. I want to get some candles in case the lights go off."

He went with her, and I started opening cabinets. Candles are funny things, you know. You lay them by every spring, knowing that a summer storm may knock out the power. And when the time comes, they hide.

I was pawing through the fourth cabinet, past the half-ounce of grass that Steff and I bought four years ago and had still not smoked much of, past Billy's wind-up set of chattering teeth from the Auburn Novelty Shop, past the drifts of photos Steffy kept forgetting to glue in our album. I looked under a Sears catalogue and behind a Kewpie doll from Taiwan that I had won at the Fryeburg Fair knocking over wooden milk bottles with tennis balls.

I found the candles behind the Kewpie doll with its glazed dead man's eyes. They were still wrapped in their cellophane. As my hand closed around them the lights went out and the only electricity was the stuff in the sky. The dining room was lit in a series of shutterflashes that were white and purple. Downstairs I heard Billy start to cry and the low murmur of Steff soothing him.

I had to have one more look at the storm.

The water-cyclone had either passed us or broken up when it reached the shoreline, but I still couldn't see twenty yards out onto the lake. The water was in complete turmoil. I saw someone's dock—the Jassers', maybe—hurry by with its main supports alternately turned up to the sky and buried in the churning water.

I went downstairs. Billy ran to me and clung to my legs. I lifted him up and gave him a hug. Then I lit the candles. We sat in the guest room down the hall from my little studio and looked at each other's faces in the flickering yellow glow and listened to the storm roar and bash at our house. About twenty minutes later we heard a ripping, rending crash as one of the big pines went down nearby. Then there was a lull.

"Is it over?" Steff asked.

"Maybe," I said. "Maybe only for a while."

We went upstairs, each of us carrying a candle, like monks going to vespers. Billy carried his proudly and carefully. Carrying a candle, carrying the *fire*, was a very big deal for him. It helped him forget about being afraid.

It was too dark to see what damage had been done around the house. It was past Billy's bedtime, but neither of us suggested putting him in. We sat in the living room, listened to the wind, and looked at the lightning.

About an hour later it began to crank up again. For three weeks the temperature had been over ninety, and on six of those twenty-one days the National Weather Service station at the Portland Jetport had reported temperatures of over one hundred degrees. Queer weather. Coupled with the grueling winter we had come through and the late spring, some people had dragged out that old chestnut about the long-range results of the fifties A-bomb tests again. That, and of course, the end of the world. The oldest chestnut of them all.

The second squall wasn't so hard, but we heard the crash of several trees weakened by the first onslaught. As the wind began to die down again, one thudded heavily on the roof, like a fist dropped on a coffin lid. Billy jumped and looked apprehensively upward.

"It'll hold, champ," I said.

Billy smiled nervously.

Around ten o'clock the last squall came. It was bad. The

wind howled almost as loudly as it had the first time, and lightning seemed to be flashing all around us. More trees fell, and there was a splintering crash down by the water that made Steff utter a low cry. Billy had gone to sleep on her lap.

"David, what was that?"

"I think it was the boathouse."

"Oh. Oh, Jesus."

"Steffy, I want us to go downstairs again." I took Billy in my arms and stood up with him. Steff's eyes were big and frightened.

"David, are we going to be all right?"

"Yes."

"Really?"

"Yes."

We went downstairs. Ten minutes later, as the final squall peaked, there was a splintering crash from upstairs—the picture window. So maybe my vision earlier hadn't been so crazy after all. Steff, who had been dozing, woke up with a little shriek, and Billy stirred uneasily in the guest bed.

"The rain will come in," she said. "It'll ruin the furniture."

"If it does, it does. It's insured."

"That doesn't make it any better," she said in an upset, scolding voice. "Your mother's dresser . . . our new sofa . . . the color TV . . ."

"Shhh," I said. "Go to sleep."

"I can't," she said, and five minutes later she had.

I stayed awake for another half hour with one lit candle for company, listening to the thunder walk and talk outside. I had a feeling that there were going to be a lot of people from the lakefront communities calling their insurance agents in the morning, a lot of chainsaws burring as cottage owners cut up the trees that had fallen on their roofs and battered through their windows, and a lot of orange CMP trucks on the road.

The storm was fading now, with no sign of a new squall coming in. I went back upstairs, leaving Steff and Billy on the bed, and looked into the living room. The sliding glass door had held. But where the picture window had been there was now a jagged hole stuffed with birch leaves. It was the top of the old tree that had stood by our outside basement access for as long as I could remember. Looking at its top, now visiting in our living room, I could understand what Steff had meant by saying insurance didn't make it any better. I had loved that tree. It had been a hard campaigner of many winters, the one tree on the lakeside of the house that was exempt from my own chainsaw. Big chunks of glass on the rug reflected my candle-flame over and over. I reminded myself to warn Steff and Billy. They would want to wear their slippers in here. Both of them liked to slop around barefoot in the morning.

I went downstairs again. All three of us slept together in the guest bed, Billy between Steff and me. I had a dream that I saw God walking across Harrison on the far side of the lake, a God so gigantic that above the waist He was lost in a clear blue sky. In the dream I could hear the rending crack and splinter of breaking trees as God stamped the woods into the shape of His footsteps. He was circling the lake, coming toward the Bridgton side, toward us, and all the houses and cottages and summer places were bursting into purple-white flame like lightning, and soon the smoke covered everything. The smoke covered everything like a mist.

II. After the Storm. Norton. A Trip to Town.

"Jeee-pers," Billy said.

He was standing by the fence that separates our property

from Norton's and looking down our driveway. The driveway runs a quarter of a mile to a camp road which, in its turn, runs about three-quarters of a mile to a stretch of two-lane blacktop, called Kansas Road. From Kansas Road you can go anywhere you want, as long as it's Bridgton.

I saw what Billy was looking at and my heart went cold.

"Don't go any closer, champ. Right there is close enough."

Billy didn't argue.

The morning was bright and as clear as a bell. The sky, which had been a mushy, hazy color during the heat wave, had regained a deep, crisp blue that was nearly autumnal. There was a light breeze, making cheerful sun-dapples move back and forth in the driveway. Not far from where Billy was standing there was a steady hissing noise, and in the grass there was what you might at first have taken for a writhing bundle of snakes. The power lines leading to our house had fallen in an untidy tangle about twenty feet away and lay in a burned patch of grass. They were twisting lazily and spitting. If the trees and grass hadn't been so completely damped down by the torrential rains, the house might have gone up. As it was, there was only that black patch where the wires had touched directly.

"Could that lectercute a person, Daddy?"

"Yeah. It could."

"What are we going to do about it?"

"Nothing. Wait for the CMP."

"When will they come?"

"I don't know." Five-year-olds have as many questions as Hallmark has cards. "I imagine they're pretty busy this morning. Want to take a walk up to the end of the driveway with me?"

He started to come and then stopped, eyeing the wires nervously. One of them humped up and turned over lazily, as if beckoning.

"Daddy, can lectricity shoot through the ground?"

A fair question. "Yes, but don't worry. Electricity wants the ground, not you, Billy. You'll be all right if you stay away from the wires."

"Wants the ground," he muttered, and then came to me. We walked up the driveway holding hands.

It was worse than I had imagined. Trees had fallen across the drive in four different places, one of them small, two of them middling, and one old baby that must have been five feet through the middle. Moss was crusted onto it like a moldy corset.

Branches, some half-stripped of their leaves, lay everywhere in jackstraw profusion. Billy and I walked up to the camp road, tossing the smaller branches off into the woods on either side. It reminded me of a summer's day that had been maybe twenty-five years before; I couldn't have been much older than Billy was now. All my uncles had been here, and they had spent the day in the woods with axes and hatchets and Darcy poles, cutting brush. Later that afternoon they had all sat down to the trestle picnic table my dad and mom used to have and there had been a monster meal of hot dogs and hamburgers and potato salad. The 'Gansett beer had flowed like water and my uncle Reuben took a dive into the lake with all his clothes on, even his deck-shoes. In those days there were still deer in these woods.

"Daddy, can I go down to the lake?"

He was tired of throwing branches, and the thing to do with a little boy when he's tired is to let him go do something else. "Sure."

We walked back to the house together and then Billy cut right, going around the house and giving the downed wires a large berth. I went left, into the garage, to get my McCullough.

As I had suspected, I could already hear the unpleasant song of the chainsaw up and down the lake.

I topped up the tank, took off my shirt, and was starting back up the driveway when Steff came out. She eyed the downed trees lying across the driveway nervously.

"How bad is it?"

"I can cut it up. How bad is it in there?"

"Well, I got the glass cleaned up, but you're going to have to do something about that tree, David. We can't have a tree in the living room."

"No," I said. "I guess we can't."

We looked at each other in the morning sunlight and got giggling. I set the McCullough down on the cement areaway, and kissed her, holding her buttocks firmly.

"Don't," she murmured. "Billy's—"

He came tearing around the corner of the house just then. "Dad! Daddy! Y'oughta see the—"

Steffy saw the live wires and screamed for him to watch out. Billy, who was a good distance away from them, pulled up short and stared at his mother as if she had gone mad.

"I'm okay, Mom," he said in the careful tone of voice you use to placate the very old and senile. He walked toward us, showing us how all right he was, and Steff began to tremble in my arms.

"It's all right," I said in her ear. "He knows about them."

"Yes, but people get killed," she said. "They have ads all the time on television about live wires, people get—Billy, I want you to come in the house right now!"

"Aw, come on, Mom! I wanna show Dad the boathouse!" He was almost bug-eyed with excitement and disappointment. He had gotten a taste of poststorm apocalypse and wanted to share it.

"You go in right now! Those wires are dangerous and—"

"Dad said they want the ground, not me—"

"Billy, don't you argue with me!"

"I'll come down and look, champ. Go on down yourself." I could feel Steff tensing against me. "Go around the other side, kiddo."

"Yeah! Okay!"

He tore past us, taking the stone steps that led around the west end of the house two by two. He disappeared with his shirttail flying, trailing back one word—"Wow!"—as he spotted some other piece of destruction.

"He knows about the wires, Steffy." I took her gently by the shoulders. "He's scared of them. That's good. It makes him safe."

One tear tracked down her cheek. "David, I'm scared."

"Come on! It's over."

"Is it? Last winter . . . and the late spring . . . they called it a black spring in town . . . they said there hadn't been one in these parts since 1888—"

"They" undoubtedly meant Mrs. Carmody, who kept the Bridgton Antiquary, a junk shop that Steff liked to rummage around in sometimes. Billy loved to go with her. In one of the shadowy, dusty back rooms, stuffed owls with gold-ringed eyes spread their wings forever as their feet endlessly grasped varnished logs; stuffed raccoons stood in a trio around a "stream" that was a long fragment of dusty mirror; and one moth-eaten wolf, which was foaming sawdust instead of saliva around his muzzle, snarled a creepy eternal snarl. Mrs. Carmody claimed the wolf was shot by her father as it came to drink from Stevens Brook one September afternoon in 1901.

The expeditions to Mrs. Carmody's Antiquary shop worked well for my wife and son. She was into carnival glass and he was into death in the name of taxidermy. But I thought that the old woman exercised a rather unpleasant hold over Steff's mind, which was in all other ways practical and hardheaded. She had found Steff's vulnerable spot, a mental Achilles' heel. Nor was Steff the only one in town who was fascinated by Mrs. Carmody's gothic pronouncements and folk remedies (which were always prescribed in God's name).

Stump-water would take off bruises if your husband was the sort who got a bit too free with his fists after three drinks. You could tell what kind of a winter was coming by counting the rings on the caterpillars in June or by measuring the thickness of August honeycomb. And now, good God protect and preserve us, THE BLACK SPRING OF 1888 (add your own exclamation points, as many as you think it deserves). I had also heard the story. It's one they like to pass around up here—if the spring is cold enough, the ice on the lakes will eventually turn as black as a rotted tooth. It's rare, but hardly a once-in-a-century occurrence. They like to pass it around, but I doubt that many could pass it around with as much conviction as Mrs. Carmody.

"We had a hard winter and a late spring," I said. "Now we're having a hot summer. And we had a storm but it's over. You're not acting like yourself, Stephanie."

"That wasn't an ordinary storm," she said in that same husky voice.

"No," I said. "I'll go along with you there."

I had heard the Black Spring story from Bill Giosti, who owned and operated—after a fashion—Giosti's Mobil in Casco Village. Bill ran the place with his three tosspot sons (with occasional help from his four tosspot grandsons . . . when they could take time off from tinkering with their snowmobiles and dirtbikes). Bill was seventy, looked eighty, and could still drink like twenty-three when the mood was on him. Billy and I had taken the Scout in for a fill-up the day after a surprise mid-May storm dropped nearly a foot of wet, heavy snow on the region, covering the new grass and flowers. Giosti had been in his cups for fair, and happy to pass along the Black Spring story, along with his own original twist. But we get snow in May sometimes; it comes and it's gone two days later. It's no big deal.

Steff was glancing doubtfully at the downed wires again. "When will the power company come?"

"Just as soon as they can. It won't be long. I just don't want you to worry about Billy. His head's on pretty straight. He forgets to pick up his clothes, but he isn't going to go and step on a bunch of live lines. He's got a good, healthy dose of self-interest." I touched a corner of her mouth and it obliged by turning up in the beginning of a smile. "Better?"

"You always make it seem better," she said, and that made me feel good.

From the lakeside of the house Billy was yelling for us to come and see.

"Come on," I said. "Let's go look at the damage."

She snorted ruefully. "If I want to look at damage, I can go sit in my living room."

"Make a little kid happy, then."

We walked down the stone steps hand in hand. We had just reached the first turn in them when Billy came from the other direction at speed, almost knocking us over.

"Take it easy," Steff said, frowning a little. Maybe, in her mind, she was seeing him skidding into that deadly nest of live wires instead of the two of us.

"You gotta come see!" Billy panted. "The boathouse is all bashed! There's a dock on the rocks . . . and trees in the boat cove . . . Jesus *Christ!*"

"Billy Drayton!" Steff thundered.

"Sorry, Ma—but you gotta—wow!" He was gone again.

"Having spoken, the doomsayer departs," I said, and that made Steff giggle again. "Listen, after I cut up those trees across the driveway, I'll go by the Central Maine Power office on Portland Road. Tell them what we got. Okay?"

"Okay," she said gratefully. "When do you think you can go?"

Except for the big tree—the one with the moldy corset of moss—it would have been an hour's work. With the big one added in, I didn't think the job would be done until eleven or so.

"I'll give you lunch here, then. But you'll have to get some things at the market for me . . . we're almost out of milk and butter. Also . . . well, I'll have to make you a list."

Give a woman a disaster and she turns squirrel. I gave her a hug and nodded. We went on around the house. It didn't take more than a glance to understand why Billy had been a little overwhelmed.

"Lordy," Steff said in a faint voice.

From where we stood we had enough elevation to be able to see almost a quarter of a mile of shoreline—the Bibber property to our left, our own, and Brent Norton's to our right.

The huge old pine that had guarded our boat cove had been sheared off halfway up. What was left looked like a brutally sharpened pencil, and the inside of the tree seemed a glistening and defenseless white against the age-and-weather-darkened outer bark. A hundred feet of tree, the old pine's top half, lay partly submerged in our shallow cove. It occurred to me that we were very lucky our little Star-Cruiser wasn't sunk underneath it. The week before, it had developed engine trouble and it was still at the Naples marina, patiently waiting its turn.

On the other side of our little piece of shorefront, the boathouse my father had built—the boathouse that had once housed a sixty-foot Chris-Craft when the Drayton family fortunes had been at a higher mark than they were today—lay under another big tree. It was the one that had stood on Norton's side of the property line, I saw. That raised the first flush of anger. The tree had been dead for five years and he should have long since had it taken down. Now it was three-quarters of the way down; our boathouse was propping it up. The roof had taken on a drunken, swaybacked look. The wind had swirled shingles from the hole the tree had made all over the point of land the boathouse stood on. Billy's description, "bashed," was as good as any.

"That's Norton's tree!" Steff said. And she said it with such hurt indignation that I had to smile in spite of the pain I felt. The flagpole was lying in the water and Old Glory floated soggily beside it in a tangle of lanyard. And I could imagine Norton's response: Sue me.

Billy was on the rock breakwater, examining the dock that had washed up on the stones. It was painted in jaunty blue and yellow stripes. He looked back over his shoulder at us and yelled gleefully, "It's the Martinses', isn't it?"

"Yeah, it is," I said. "Wade in and fish the flag out, would you, Big Bill?"

"Sure!"

To the right of the breakwater was a small sandy beach. In 1941, before Pearl Harbor paid off the Great Depression in blood, my dad hired a man to truck in that fine beach sand—six dumptrucks full—and to spread it out to a depth that is about nipple-high on me, say five feet. The workman charged eighty bucks for the job, and the sand has never moved. Just as well, you know, you can't put a sandy beach in on your land now. Now that the sewerage runoff from the booming cottage-building industry has killed most of the fish and made the rest of them unsafe to eat, the EPA has forbidden installing sand beaches. They might upset the ecology of the lake, you see, and it is presently against the law for anyone except land developers to do that.

Billy went for the flag—then stopped. At the same moment I felt Steff go rigid against me, and I saw it myself. The Harrison side of the lake was gone. It had been buried under a line of bright-white mist, like a fair-weather cloud fallen to earth.

My dream of the night before recurred, and when Steff asked me what it was, the word that nearly jumped first from my mouth was *God.*

"David?"

You couldn't see even a hint of the shoreline over there, but years of looking at Long Lake made me believe that the shoreline wasn't hidden by much; only yards, maybe. The edge of the mist was nearly ruler-straight.

"What is it, Dad?" Billy yelled. He was in the water up to his knees, groping for the soggy flag.

"Fogbank," I said.

"On the *lake?"* Steff asked doubtfully, and I could see Mrs. Carmody's influence in her eyes. Damn the woman. My own moment of unease was passing. Dreams, after all, are insubstantial things, like mist itself.

"Sure. You've seen fog on the lake before."

"Never like that. That looks more like a cloud."

"It's the brightness of the sun," I said. "It's the same way clouds look from an airplane when you fly over them."

"What would do it? We only get fog in damp weather."

"No, we've got it right now," I said. "Harrison does, anyway. It's a little leftover from the storm, that's all. Two fronts meeting. Something along that line."

"David, are you sure?"

I laughed and hauled my arm around her neck. "No, actually, I'm bullshitting like crazy. If I was sure, I'd be doing the weather on the six-o'clock news. Go on and make your shopping list."

She gave me one more doubtful glance, looked at the fog-bank for a moment or two with the flat of her hand held up to shade her eyes, and then shook her head. "Weird," she said, and walked away.

For Billy, the mist had lost its novelty. He had fished the flag and a tangle of lanyard out of the water. We spread it on the lawn to dry.

"I heard it was wrong to ever let the flag touch the ground, Daddy," he said in a businesslike, let's-get-this-out-of-the-way tone.

"Yeah?"

"Yeah. Victor McAllister says they lectercute people for it."

"Well, you tell Vic he's full of what makes the grass grow green."

"Horseshit, right?" Billy is a bright boy, but oddly humorless. To the champ, everything is serious business. I'm hoping that he'll live long enough to learn that in this world that is a very dangerous attitude.

"Yeah, right, but don't tell your mother I said so. When the flag's dry, we'll put it away. We'll even fold it into a cocked hat, so we'll be on safe ground there."

"Daddy, will we fix the boathouse roof and get a new flagpole?" For the first time he looked anxious. He'd maybe had enough destruction for a while.

I clapped him on the shoulder. "You're damn tooting."

"Can I go over to the Bibbers' and see what happened there?"

"Just for a couple of minutes. They'll be cleaning up, too,

and sometimes that makes people feel a little ugly." The way I presently felt about Norton.

"Okay. Bye!" He was off.

"Stay out of their way, champ. And Billy?"

He glanced back.

"Remember about the live wires. If you see more, steer clear of them."

"Sure, Dad."

I stood there for a moment, first surveying the damage, then glancing out at the mist again. It seemed closer, but it was very hard to tell for sure. If it was closer, it was defying all the laws of nature, because the wind—a very gentle breeze—was against it. That, of course, was patently impossible. It was very, very white. The only thing I can compare it to would be fresh-fallen snow lying in dazzling contrast to the deep-blue brilliance of the winter sky. But snow reflects hundreds and hundreds of diamond points in the sun, and this peculiar fogbank, although bright and clean-looking, did not sparkle. In spite of what Steff had said, mist isn't uncommon on clear days, but when there's a lot of it, the suspended moisture almost always causes a rainbow. But there was no rainbow here.

The unease was back, tugging at me, but before it could deepen I heard a low mechanical sound—*whut-whut-whut!*—followed by a barely audible "Shit!" The mechanical sound was repeated, but this time there was no oath. The third time the chuffing sound was followed by "Mother-fuck!" in that same low I'm-all-by-myself-but-boy-am-I-pissed tone.

Whut-whut-whut-whut—

—Silence—

—then: "You cunt."

I began to grin. Sound carries well out here, and all the buzzing chainsaws were fairly distant. Distant enough for me to recognize the not-so-dulcet tones of my next-door neighbor, the renowned lawyer and lakefront-property-owner, Brenton Norton.

I moved down a little closer to the water, pretending to stroll toward the dock beached on our breakwater. Now I could see Norton. He was in the clearing beside his screened-in porch, standing on a carpet of old pine needles and dressed in paint-spotted jeans and a white strappy T-shirt. His forty-dollar haircut was in disarray and sweat poured down his face. He was down on one knee, laboring over his own chainsaw. It was much bigger and fancier than my little $79.95 Value House job. It seemed to have everything, in fact, but a starter button. He was yanking a cord, producing the listless *whut-whut-whut* sounds and nothing more. I was gladdened in my heart to see that a yellow birch had fallen across his picnic table and smashed it in two.

Norton gave a tremendous yank on the starter cord.

Whut-whut-whutwhutwhut-WHAT! WHAT! WHAT! . . . WHAT! . . . Whut.

Almost had it there for a minute, fella.

Another Herculean tug.

Whut-whut-whut.

"Cocksucker," Norton whispered fiercely, and bared his teeth at his fancy chainsaw.

I went back around the house, feeling really good for the first time since I got up. My own saw started on the first tug, and I went to work.

Around ten o'clock there was a tap on my shoulder. It was Billy with a can of beer in one hand and Steff's list in the other. I stuffed the list in the back pocket of my jeans and took the beer, which was not exactly frosty-cold but at least cool. I chugged almost half of it at once—rarely does a beer taste that good—and tipped the can in salute at Billy. "Thanks, champ."

"Can I have some?"

I let him have a swallow. He grimaced and handed the can back. I offed the rest and just caught myself as I started to crunch it up in the middle. The deposit law on bottles and cans has been in effect for over three years, but old ways die hard.

"She wrote something across the bottom of the list, but I can't read her writing," Billy said.

I took out the list again. "I can't get WOXO on the radio," Steff's note read. "Do you think the storm knocked them off the air?"

WOXO is the local automated FM rock outlet. It broadcast from Norway, about twenty miles north, and was all that our old and feeble FM receiver would haul in.

"Tell her probably," I said, after reading the question over to him. "Ask her if she can get Portland on the AM band."

"Okay, Daddy, can I come when you go to town?"

"Sure. You and Mommy both, if you want."

"Okay." He ran back to the house with the empty can.

I had worked my way up to the big tree. I made my first cut, sawed through, then turned the saw off for a few moments to let it cool down—the tree was really too big for it, but I thought it would be all right if I didn't rush it. I wondered if the dirt road leading up to Kansas Road was clear of falls, and just as I was wondering, an orange CMP truck lumbered past, probably on its way to the far end of our little road. So that was all right. The road was clear and the power guys would be here by noon to take care of the live lines.

I cut a big chunk off the tree, dragged it to the side of the driveway, and tumbled it over the edge. It rolled down the slope and into the underbrush that had crept back since the long-ago day when my dad and his brothers—all of them artists, we have always been an artistic family, the Draytons—had cleared it away.

I wiped sweat off my face with my arm and wished for another beer; one really only sets your mouth. I picked up the chainsaw and thought about WOXO being off the air. That was the direction that funny fogbank had come from. And it was the direction Shaymore (pronounced *Shammore* by the locals) lay in. Shaymore was where the Arrowhead Project was.

That was old Bill Giosti's theory about the so-called Black Spring: the Arrowhead Project. In the western part of Shaymore, not far from where the town borders on Stoneham, there was a small government preserve surrounded with wire. There were sentries and closed-circuit television cameras and God knew what else. Or so I had heard; I'd never actually seen it, although the Old Shaymore Road runs along the eastern side of the government land for a mile or so.

No one knew for sure where the name Arrowhead Project came from and no one could tell you for one hundred percent sure that that really was the name of the project—if there was a project. Bill Giosti said there was, but when you asked him how and where he came by his information, he got vague. His niece, he said, worked for the Continental Phone Company, and she had heard things. It got like that.

"Atomic things," Bill said that day, leaning in the Scout's window and blowing a healthy draught of Pabst into my face. "That's what they're fooling around with up there. Shooting atoms into the air and all that."

"Mr. Giosti, the air's full of atoms," Billy had said. "That's what Mrs. Neary says. Mrs. Neary says everything's full of atoms."

Bill Giosti gave my son Bill a long, bloodshot glance that finally deflated him. "These are *different* atoms, son."

"Oh, yeah," Billy muttered, giving in.

Dick Muehler, our insurance agent, said the Arrowhead Project was an agricultural station the government was running, no more or less. "Bigger tomatoes with a longer growing season," Dick said sagely, and then went back to showing me how I could help my family most efficiently by dying young. Janine Lawless, our postlady, said it was a geological survey having something to do with shale oil. She knew for a fact, because her husband's brother worked for a man who had—

Mrs. Carmody, now . . . she probably leaned more to Bill Giosti's view of the matter. Not just atoms, but *different* atoms.

I cut two more chunks off the big tree and dropped them over the side before Billy came back with a fresh beer in one hand and a note from Steff in the other. If there's anything Big Bill likes to do more than run messages, I don't know what it could be.

"Thanks," I said, taking them both.

"Can I have a swallow?"

"Just one. You took two last time. Can't have you running around drunk at ten in the morning."

"Quarter past," he said, and smiled shyly over the top of the can. I smiled back—not that it was such a great joke, you know, but Billy makes them so rarely—and then read the note.

"Got JBQ on the radio," Steffy had written. "Don't get drunk before you go to town. You can have one more, but that's it before lunch. Do you think you can get up our road okay?"

I handed him the note back and took my beer. "Tell her the road's okay because a power truck just went by. They'll be working their way up here."

"Okay."

"Champ?"

"What, Dad?"

"Tell her everything's okay."

He smiled again, maybe telling himself first. "Okay."

He ran back and I watched him go, legs pumping, soles of his zori showing. I love him. It's his face and sometimes the way his eyes turn up to mine that make me feel as if things are really okay. It's a lie, of course—things are not okay and never have been—but my kid makes me believe the lie.

I drank some beer, set the can down carefully on a rock, and got the chainsaw going again. About twenty minutes later I felt a light tap on my shoulder and turned, expecting to see Billy again. Instead it was Brent Norton. I turned off the chainsaw.

He didn't look the way Norton usually looks. He looked hot and tired and unhappy and a little bewildered.

"Hi, Brent," I said. Our last words had been hard ones, and I was a little unsure how to proceed. I had a funny feeling that he had been standing behind me for the last five minutes or so, clearing his throat decorously under the chainsaw's aggressive roar. I hadn't gotten a really good look at him this summer. He had lost weight, but it didn't look good. It should have, because he had been carrying around an extra twenty pounds, but it didn't. His wife had died the previous November. Cancer. Aggie Bibber told Steffy that. Aggie was our resident necrologist. Every neighborhood has one. From the casual way Norton had of ragging his wife and belittling her (doing it with the contemptuous ease of a veteran matador inserting *banderillas* in an old bull's lumbering body), I would have guessed he'd be glad to have her gone. If asked, I might even have speculated that he'd show up this summer with a girl twenty years younger than he was on his arm and a silly my-cock-has-died-and-gone-to-heaven grin on his face. But instead of the silly grin there was only a new batch of age lines, and the weight had come off in all the wrong places, leaving sags and folds and dewlaps that told their own story. For one passing moment I wanted only to lead Norton to a patch of sun and sit him beside one of the fallen trees with my can of beer in his hand, and do a charcoal sketch of him.

"Hi, Dave," he said, after a long moment of awkward silence—a silence that was made even louder by the absence of the chainsaw's racket and roar. He stopped, then blurted: "That tree. That damn tree. I'm sorry. You were right."

I shrugged.

He said, "Another tree fell on my car."

"I'm sorry to h—" I began, and then a horrid suspicion dawned. "It wasn't the T-Bird, was it?"

"Yeah. It was."

Norton had a 1960 Thunderbird in mint condition, only thirty thousand miles. It was a deep midnight blue inside and out. He drove it only summers, and then only rarely. He loved that Bird the way some men love electric trains or model ships or target-shooting pistols.

"That's a bitch," I said, and meant it.

He shook his head slowly. "I almost didn't bring it up. Almost brought the station wagon, you know. Then I said what the hell. I drove it up and a big old rotten pine fell on it. The roof of it's all bashed in. And I thought I'd cut it up . . . the tree, I mean . . . but I can't get my chainsaw to fire up . . . I paid two hundred dollars for that sucker . . . and . . . and . . ."

His throat began to emit little clicking sounds. His mouth worked as if he were toothless and chewing dates. For one helpless second I thought he was going to just stand there and bawl like a kid on a sandlot. Then he got himself under some halfway kind of control, shrugged, and turned away as if to look at the chunks of wood I had cut up.

"Well, we can look at your saw," I said. "Your T-Bird insured?"

"Yeah," he said, "like your boathouse."

I saw what he meant, and remembered again what Steff had said about insurance.

"Listen, Dave, I wondered if I could borrow your Saab and take a run up to town. I thought I'd get some bread and cold cuts and beer. A lot of beer."

"Billy and I are going up in the Scout," I said. "Come with us if you want. That is, if you'll give me a hand dragging the rest of this tree off to one side."

"Happy to."

He grabbed one end but couldn't quite lift it up. I had to do most of the work. Between the two of us we were able to tumble it into the underbrush. Norton was puffing and panting, his cheeks nearly purple. After all the yanking he had done on that chainsaw starter pull, I was a little worried about his ticker.

"Okay?" I asked, and he nodded, still breathing fast. "Come on back to the house, then. I can fix you up with a beer."

"Thank you," he said. "How is Stephanie?" He was regaining some of the old smooth pomposity that I disliked.

"Very well, thanks."

"And your son?"

"He's fine, too."

"Glad to hear it."

Steff came out, and a moment's surprise passed over her face when she saw who was with me. Norton smiled and his eyes crawled over her tight T-shirt. He hadn't changed that much after all.

"Hello, Brent," she said cautiously. Billy poked his head out from under her arm.

"Hello, Stephanie. Hi, Billy."

"Brent's T-Bird took a pretty good rap in the storm," I told her. "Stove in the roof, he says."

"Oh, no!"

Norton told it again while he drank one of our beers. I was sipping a third, but I had no kind of buzz on; apparently I had sweat the beer out as rapidly as I drank it.

"He's going to come to town with Billy and me."

"Well, I won't expect you for a while. You may have to go to the Shop-and-Save in Norway."

"Oh? Why?"

"Well, if the power's off in Bridgton—"

"Mom says all the cash registers and things run on electricity," Billy supplied.

It was a good point.

"Have you still got the list?"

I patted my hip pocket.

Her eyes shifted to Norton. "I'm very sorry about Carla, Brent. We all were."

"Thank you," he said. "Thank you very much."

There was another moment of awkward silence which Billy broke. "Can we go now, Daddy?" He had changed to jeans and sneakers.

"Yeah, I guess so. You ready, Brent?"

"Give me another beer for the road and I will be."

Steffy's brow creased. She had never approved of the one-for-the-road philosophy, or of men who drive with a can of Bud leaning against their crotches. I gave her a bare nod and she shrugged. I didn't want to reopen things with Norton now. She got him a beer.

"Thanks," he said to Steffy, not really thanking her but only mouthing a word. It was the way you thank a waitress in a restaurant. He turned back to me. "Lead on, Macduff."

"Be right with you," I said, and went into the living room.

Norton followed, and exclaimed over the birch, but I wasn't interested in that or in the cost of replacing the window just then. I was looking at the lake through the sliding glass panel that gave on our deck. The breeze had freshened a little and the day had warmed up five degrees or so while I was cutting wood. I thought the odd mist we'd noticed earlier would surely have broken up, but it hadn't. It was closer, too. Halfway across the lake now.

"I noticed that earlier," Norton said, pontificating. "Some kind of temperature inversion, that's my guess."

I didn't like it. I felt very strongly that I had never seen a mist exactly like this one. Part of it was the unnerving straight edge of its leading front. Nothing in nature is that even; man is the inventor of straight edges. Part of it was that pure, dazzling whiteness, with no variation but also without the sparkle of moisture. It was only half a mile or so off now, and the contrast between it and the blues of the lake and sky was more striking than ever.

"Come on, Dad!" Billy was tugging at my pants.

We all went back to the kitchen. Brent Norton spared one final glance at the tree that had crashed into our living room.

"Too bad it wasn't an apple tree, huh?" Billy remarked brightly. "That's what my mom said. Pretty funny, don't you think?"

"Your mother's a real card, Billy," Norton said. He ruffled Billy's hair in a perfunctory way and his eyes went to the front of Steff's T-shirt again. No, he was not a man I was ever going to be able to really like.

"Listen, why don't you come with us, Steff?" I asked. For no concrete reason I suddenly wanted her to come along.

"No, I think I'll stay here and pull some weeds in the garden," she said. Her eyes shifted toward Norton and then back to me. "This morning it seems like I'm the only thing around here that doesn't run on electricity."

Norton laughed too heartily.

I was getting her message, but tried one more time. "You sure?"

"Sure," she said firmly. "The old bend-and-stretch will do me good."

"Well, don't get too much sun."

"I'll put on my straw hat. We'll have sandwiches when you get back."

"Good."

She turned her face up to be kissed. "Be careful. There might be blowdowns on Kansas Road too, you know."

"I'll be careful."

"You be careful, too," she told Billy, and kissed his cheek.

"Right, Mom." He banged out of the door and the screen cracked shut behind him.

Norton and I walked out after him. "Why don't we go over to your place and cut the tree off your Bird?" I asked him. All of a sudden I could think of lots of reasons to delay leaving for town.

"I don't even want to look at it until after lunch and a few more of these," Norton said, holding up his beer can. "The damage has been done, Dave old buddy."

I didn't like him calling me buddy, either.

We all got into the front seat of the Scout (in the far corner of the garage my scarred Fisher plow blade sat glimmering yellow, like the ghost of Christmas yet-to-come) and I backed out, crunching over a litter of storm-blown twigs. Steff was standing on the cement path which leads to the vegetable patch at the extreme west end of our property. She had a pair of clippers in one gloved hand and the weeding claw in the other. She had put on her old floppy sunhat, and it cast a band of shadow over her face. I tapped the horn twice, lightly, and she raised the hand holding the clippers in answer. We pulled out. I haven't seen my wife since then.

We had to stop once on our way up to Kansas Road. Since the power truck had driven through, a pretty fair-sized pine had dropped across the road. Norton and I got out and moved it enough so I could inch the Scout by, getting our hands all pitchy in the process. Billy wanted to help but I waved him back. I was afraid he might get poked in the eye. Old trees have always reminded me of the Ents in Tolkien's wonderful Rings saga, only Ents that have gone bad. Old trees want to hurt you. It doesn't matter if you're snowshoeing, cross-country skiing, or just taking a walk in the woods. Old trees want to hurt you, and I think they'd kill you if they could.

Kansas Road itself was clear, but in several places we saw more lines down. About a quarter-mile past the Vicki-Linn Campground there was a power pole lying full-length in the ditch, heavy wires snarled around its top like wild hair.

"That was some storm," Norton said in his mellifluous, courtroom-trained voice; but he didn't seem to be pontificating now, only solemn.

"Yeah, it was."

"Look, Dad!"

He was pointing at the remains of the Ellitches' barn. For twelve years it had been sagging tiredly in Tommy Ellitch's back field, up to its hips in sunflowers, goldenrod, and Lolly-come-see-me. Every fall I would think it could not last through another winter. And every spring it would still be there. But it wasn't anymore. All that remained was a splintered wreckage and a roof that had been mostly stripped of shingles. Its number had come up. And for some reason that echoed solemnly, even ominously, inside me. The storm had come and smashed it flat.

Norton drained his beer, crushed the can in one hand, and dropped it indifferently to the floor of the Scout. Billy opened his mouth to say something and then closed it again—good boy. Norton came from New Jersey, where there was no bottle-and-can law; I guess he could be forgiven for squashing my nickel when I could barely remember not to do it myself.

Billy started fooling with the radio, and I asked him to see if WOXO was back on the air. He dialed up to FM 92 and got nothing but a blank hum. He looked at me and shrugged. I thought for a moment. What other stations were on the far side of that peculiar fog front?

"Try WBLM," I said.

He dialed down to the other end, passing WJBQ-FM and WIGY-FM on the way. They were there, doing business as usual . . . but WBLM, Maine's premier progressive-rock station, was off the air.

"Funny," I said.

"What's that?" Norton asked.

"Nothing. Just thinking out loud."

Billy had tuned back to the musical cereal on WJBQ. Pretty soon we got to town.

The Norge Washateria in the shopping center was closed, it being impossible to run a coin-op laundry without electricity, but both the Bridgton Pharmacy and the Federal Foods Supermarket were open. The parking lot was pretty full, and as always in the middle of the summer, a lot of the cars had out-of-state plates. Little knots of people stood here and there in the sun, noodling about the storm, women with women, men with men.

I saw Mrs. Carmody, she of the stuffed animals and the stump-water lore. She sailed into the supermarket decked out in an amazing canary-yellow pantsuit. A purse that looked the size of a small Samsonite suitcase was slung over one forearm. Then an idiot on a Yamaha roared past me, missing my front bumper by a few scant inches. He wore a denim jacket, mirror sunglasses, and no helmet.

"Look at that stupid shit," Norton growled.

I circled the parking lot once, looking for a good space. There were none. I was just resigning myself to a long walk from the far end of the lot when I got lucky. A lime-green Cadillac the size of a small cabin cruiser was easing out of a slot in the rank closest to the market's doors. The moment it was gone, I slid into the space.

I gave Billy Steff's shopping list. He was five, but he could read printing. "Get a cart and get started. I want to give your mother a jingle. Mr. Norton will help you. And I'll be right along."

We got out and Billy immediately grabbed Mr. Norton's hand. He'd been taught not to cross the parking lot without holding an adult's hand when he was younger and hadn't yet lost the habit. Norton looked surprised for a moment, and then smiled a little. I could almost forgive him for feeling Steff up with his eyes. The two of them went into the market.

I strolled over to the pay phone, which was on the wall between the drugstore and the Norge. A sweltering woman in a purple sunsuit was jogging the cutoff switch up and down.

I stood behind her with my hands in my pockets, wondering why I felt so uneasy about Steff, and why the unease should be all wrapped up with that line of white but unsparkling fog, the radio stations that were off the air . . . and the Arrowhead Project.

The woman in the purple sunsuit had a sunburn and freckles on her fat shoulders. She looked like a sweaty orange baby. She slammed the phone back down in its cradle, turned toward the drugstore and saw me there.

"Save your dime," she said. "Just dah-dah-dah." She walked grumpily away.

I almost slapped my forehead. The phone lines were down someplace, of course. Some of them were underground, but nowhere near all of them. I tried the phone anyway. The pay phones in the area are what Steff calls Paranoid Pay Phones. Instead of putting your dime right in, you get a dial tone and make your call. When someone answers, there's an automatic cutoff and you have to shove your dime in before your party hangs up. They're irritating, but that day it did save me my dime. There was no dial tone. As the lady had said, it was just dah-dah-dah.

I hung up and walked slowly toward the market, just in time to see an amusing little incident. An elderly couple walked toward the IN door, chatting together. And still chatting, they walked right into it. They stopped talking in a jangle and the woman squawked her surprise. They stared at each other comically. Then they laughed, and the old guy pushed the door open for his wife with some effort—those electric-eye doors are heavy—and they went in. When the electricity goes off, it catches you in a hundred different ways.

I pushed the door open myself and noticed the lack of air conditioning first thing. Usually in the summer they have it cranked up high enough to give you frostbite if you stay in the market more than an hour at a stretch.

Like most modern markets, the Federal was constructed like a Skinner box—modern marketing techniques turn all customers into white rats. The stuff you really needed, staples, like bread, milk, meat, beer, and frozen dinners, was all on the far side of the store. To get there you had to walk past all the impulse items known to modern man—everything from Cricket lighters to rubber dog bones.

Beyond the IN door is the fruit-and-vegetable aisle. I looked up it, but there was no sign of Norton or my son. The old lady who had run into the door was examining the grapefruits. Her husband had produced a net sack to store purchases in.

I walked up the aisle and went left. I found them in the third aisle, Billy mulling over the ranks of Jell-O packages and instant puddings. Norton was standing directly behind him, peering at Steff's list. I had to grin a little at his nonplussed expression.

I threaded my way down to them, past half-loaded carriages (Steff hadn't been the only one struck by the squirreling impulse, apparently) and browsing shoppers. Norton took two cans of pie filling down from the top shelf and put them in the cart.

"How are you doing?" I asked, and Norton looked around with unmistakable relief.

"All right, aren't we, Billy?"

"Sure," Billy said, and couldn't resist adding in a rather smug tone: "But there's lots of stuff Mr. Norton can't read either, Dad."

"Let me see." I took the list.

Norton had made a neat, lawyerly check beside each of the items he and Billy had picked up—half a dozen or so, including the milk and a six-pack of Coke. There were maybe ten other things that she wanted.

"We ought to go back to the fruits and vegetables," I said. "She wants some tomatoes and cucumbers."

Billy started to turn the cart around and Norton said, "You ought to go have a look at the checkout, Dave."

I went and had a look. It was the sort of thing you sometimes see photos of in the paper on a slow newsday, with a humorous caption beneath. Only two lanes were open, and the double line of people waiting to check their purchases out stretched past the mostly denuded bread racks, then made a jig to the right and went out of sight along the frozen-food coolers. All of the new computerized NCRs were hooded. At each of the two open positions, a harried-looking girl was totting up purchases on a battery-powered pocket calculator. Standing with each girl was one of the Federal's two managers, Bud Brown and Ollie Weeks. I liked Ollie but didn't care much for Bud Brown, who seemed to fancy himself the Charles de Gaulle of the supermarket world.

As each girl finished checking her order, Bud or Ollie would paperclip a chit to the customer's cash or check and toss it into the box he was using as a cash repository. They all looked hot and tired.

"Hope you brought a good book," Norton said, joining me. "We're going to be in line for a while."

I thought of Steff again, at home alone, and had another flash of unease. "You go on and get your stuff," I said. "Billy and I can handle the rest of this."

"Want me to grab a few more beers for you too?"

I thought about it, but in spite of the rapprochement, I didn't want to spend the afternoon with Brent Norton getting drunk. Not with the mess things were in around the house.

"Sorry," I said. "I've got to take a raincheck, Brent."

I thought his face stiffened a little. "Okay," he said shortly, and walked off. I watched him go, and then Billy was tugging at my shirt.

"Did you talk to Mommy?"

"Nope. The phone wasn't working. Those lines are down too, I guess."

"Are you worried about her?"

"No," I said, lying. I was worried, all right, but had no idea why I should be. "No, of course I'm not. Are you?"

"No-ooo . . ." But he was. His face had a pinched look. We should have gone back then. But even then it might have been too late.

III. The Coming of the Mist.

We worked our way back to the fruits and vegetables like salmon fighting their way upstream. I saw some familiar faces—Mike Hatlen, one of our selectmen, Mrs. Reppler from the grammar school (she who had terrified generations of third-graders was currently sneering at the cantaloupes), Mrs. Turman, who sometimes sat Billy when Steff and I went out—but mostly they were summer people stocking up on no-cook items and joshing each other about "roughing it." The cold cuts had been picked over as thoroughly as the dimebook tray at a rummage sale; there was nothing left but a few packages of bologna, some macaroni loaf, and one lonely, phallic kielbasa sausage.

I got tomatoes, cukes, and a jar of mayonnaise. She wanted bacon, but all the bacon was gone. I picked up some of the bologna as a substitute, although I've never been able to eat the stuff with any real enthusiasm since the FDA reported that each package contained a small amount of insect filth—a little something extra for your money.

"Look," Billy said as we rounded the corner into the fourth aisle. "There's some army guys."

There were two of them, their dun uniforms standing out against the much brighter background of summer clothes and sportswear. We had gotten used to seeing a scattering of army personnel with the Arrowhead Project only thirty miles or so away. These two looked hardly old enough to shave yet.

I glanced back down at Steff's list and saw that we had everything . . . no, almost but not quite. At the bottom, as an afterthought, she had scribbled: *Bottle of Lancers?* That sounded good to me. A couple of glasses of wine tonight after Billy had sacked out, then maybe a long slow bout of lovemaking before sleep.

I left the cart and worked my way down to the wine and got a bottle. As I walked back I passed the big double doors leading to the storage area and heard the steady roar of a good-sized generator.

I decided it was probably just big enough to keep the cold cases cold, but not large enough to power the doors and cash registers and all the other electrical equipment. It sounded like a motorcycle back there.

Norton appeared just as we got into line, balancing two six-packs of Schlitz Light, a loaf of bread, and the kielbasa I had spotted a few minutes earlier. He got in line with Billy and me. It seemed very warm in the market with the air conditioning off, and I wondered why none of the stockboys had at least chocked the doors open. I had seen Buddy Eagleton in his red apron two aisles back, doing nothing and piling it up. The generator roared monotonously. I had the beginnings of a headache.

"Put your stuff in here before you drop something," I said.

"Thanks."

The lines were up past the frozen food now; people had to cut through to get what they wanted and there was much excuse-me-ing and pardon-me-ing. "This is going to be a cunt," Norton said morosely, and I frowned a little. That sort of language is rougher than I'd like Billy to hear.

The generator's roar muted a little as the line shuffled forward. Norton and I made desultory conversation, skirting around the ugly property dispute that had landed us in district court and sticking with things like the Red Sox's chances and the weather. At last we exhausted our little store of small talk and fell silent. Billy fidgeted beside me. The line crawled along. Now we had frozen dinners on our right and the more expensive wines and champagnes on our left. As the line progressed down to the cheaper wines, I toyed briefly with the idea of picking up a bottle of Ripple, the wine of my flaming youth. I didn't do it. My youth never flamed that much anyway.

"Jeez, why can't they hurry up, Dad?" Billy asked. That pinched look was still on his face, and suddenly, briefly, the mist of disquiet that had settled over me rifted, and something terrible peered through from the other side—the bright and metallic face of terror. Then it passed.

"Keep cool, champ," I said.

We had made it up to the bread racks—to the point where the double line bent to the left. We could see the checkout lanes now, the two that were open and the other four, deserted, each with a little sign on the stationary conveyor belt, signs that read PLEASE CHOOSE ANOTHER LANE and WINSTON. Beyond the lanes was the big sectioned plate-glass window which gave a view of the parking lot and the intersection of

Routes 117 and 302 beyond. The view was partially obscured by the white-paper backs of signs advertising current specials and the latest giveaway, which happened to be a set of books called *The Mother Nature Encyclopedia.* We were in the line that would eventually lead us to the checkout where Bud Brown was standing. There were still maybe thirty people in front of us. The easiest one to pick out was Mrs. Carmody in her blazing-yellow pantsuit. She looked like an advertisement for yellow fever.

Suddenly a shrieking noise began in the distance. It quickly built up in volume and resolved itself into the crazy warble of a police siren. A horn blared at the intersection and there was a shriek of brakes and burning rubber. I couldn't see—the angle was all wrong—but the siren reached its loudest as it approached the market and then began to fade as the police car went past. A few people broke out of line to look, but not many. They had waited too long to chance losing their places.

Norton went; his stuff was tucked into my cart. After a few moments he came back and got into line again. "Local fuzz," he said.

Then the town fire whistle began to wail, slowly cranking up to a shriek of its own, falling off, then rising again. Billy grabbed my hand—clutched it. "What is it, Daddy?" he asked, and then, immediately: "Is Mommy all right?"

"Must be a fire on the Kansas Road," Norton said. "Those damned live lines from the storm. The fire trucks will go through in a minute."

That gave my disquiet something to crystallize on. There were live lines down in *our* yard.

Bud Brown said something to the checker he was supervising; she had been craning around to see what was happening. She flushed and began to run her calculator again.

I didn't want to be in this line. All of a sudden I very badly didn't want to be in it. But it was moving again, and it seemed foolish to leave now. We had gotten down by the cartons of cigarettes.

Someone pushed through the IN door, some teenager. I think it was the kid we almost hit coming in, the one on the Yamaha with no helmet. "The fog!" he yelled. "Y'oughta see the fog! It's rolling right up Kansas Road!" People looked around at him. He was panting, as if he had run a long distance. Nobody said anything. "Well, y'oughta see it," he repeated, sounding defensive this time. People eyed him and some of them shuffled, but no one wanted to lose his or her place in line. A few people who hadn't reached the lines yet left their carts and strolled through the empty checkout lanes to see if they could see what he was talking about. A big guy in a summer hat with a paisley band (the kind of hat you almost never see except in beer commercials with backyard barbecues as their settings) yanked open the OUT door and several people—ten, maybe a dozen—went out with him. The kid went along.

"Don't let out all the air conditioning," one of the army kids cracked, and there were a few chuckles. I wasn't chuckling. I had seen the mist coming across the lake.

"Billy, why don't you go have a look?" Norton said.

"No," I said at once, for no concrete reason.

The line moved forward again. People craned their necks, looking for the fog the kid had mentioned, but there was nothing on view except bright-blue sky. I heard someone say that the kid must have been joking. Someone else responded that he had seen a funny line of mist on Long Lake not an hour ago. The first whistle whooped and screamed. I didn't like it. It sounded like big-league doom blowing that way.

More people went out. A few even left their places in line,

which speeded up the proceedings a bit. Then grizzled old John Lee Frovin, who works as a mechanic at the Texaco station, came ducking in and yelled: "Hey! Anybody got a camera?" He looked around, then ducked back out again.

That caused something of a rush. If it was worth taking a picture of, it was worth seeing.

Suddenly Mrs. Carmody cried in her rusty but powerful old voice, "Don't go out there!"

People turned around to look at her. The orderly shape of the lines had grown fuzzy as people left to get a look at the mist, or as they drew away from Mrs. Carmody, or as they milled around, seeking out their friends. A pretty young woman in a cranberry-colored sweatshirt and dark-green slacks was looking at Mrs. Carmody in a thoughtful, evaluating way. A few opportunists were taking advantage of whatever the situation was to move up a couple of places. The checker beside Bud Brown looked over her shoulder again, and Brown tapped her shoulder with a long finger. "Keep your mind on what you're doing, Sally."

"Don't go out there!" Mrs. Carmody yelled. "It's death! I feel that it's death out there!"

Bud and Ollie Weeks, who both knew her, just looked impatient and irritated, but any summer people around her stepped smartly away, never minding their places in line. The bag-ladies in big cities seem to have the same effect on people, as if they were carriers of some contagious disease. Who knows? Maybe they are.

Things began to happen at an accelerating, confusing pace then. A man staggered into the market, shoving the IN door open. His nose was bleeding. "Something in the fog!" he screamed, and Billy shrank against me—whether because of the man's bloody nose or what he was saying, I don't know. "Something in the fog! Something in the fog took John Lee!

Something—" He staggered back against a display of lawn food stacked by the window and sat down there. *"Something in the fog took John Lee and I heard him screaming!"*

The situation changed. Made nervous by the storm, by the police siren and the fire whistle, by the subtle dislocation any power outage causes in the American psyche, and by the steadily mounting atmosphere of unease as things somehow . . . somehow *changed* (I don't know how to put it any better than that), people began to move in a body.

They didn't bolt. If I told you that, I would be giving you entirely the wrong impression. It wasn't exactly a panic. They didn't run—or at least, most of them didn't. But they went. Some of them just went to the big show window on the far side of the checkout lanes to look out. Others went out the IN door, some still carrying their intended purchases. Bud Brown, harried and officious, began yelling: "Hey! You haven't paid for that! Hey, you! Come back here with those hot-dog rolls!"

Someone laughed at him, a crazy, yodeling sound that made other people smile. Even as they smiled they looked bewildered, confused, and nervous. Then someone else laughed and Brown flushed. He grabbed a box of mushrooms away from a lady who was crowding past him to look out the window—the segments of glass were lined with people now, they were like the folks you see looking through loopholes into a building site—and the lady screamed, "Give me back my mushies!" This bizarre term of affection caused two men standing nearby to break into crazy laughter—and there was something of the old English Bedlam about all of it, now. Mrs. Carmody trumpeted again not to go out there. The fire whistle whooped breathlessly, a strong old woman who had scared up a prowler in the house. And Billy burst into tears.

"Daddy, what's that bloody man? Why is that bloody man?"

"It's okay, Big Bill, it's his nose, he's okay."

"What did he mean, something in the fog?" Norton asked. He was frowning ponderously, which was probably Norton's way of looking confused.

"Daddy, I'm scared," Billy said through his tears. "Can we please go home?"

Someone bumped past me roughly, jolting me off my feet, and I picked Billy up. I was getting scared, too. The confusion was mounting. Sally, the checker by Bud Brown, started away and he grabbed her back by the collar of her red smock. It ripped. She slap-clawed out at him, her face twisting. *"Get your fucking hands off me!"* she screamed.

"Oh, shut up, you little bitch," Brown said, but he sounded totally astounded.

He reached for her again and Ollie Weeks said sharply: "Bud! Cool it!"

Someone else screamed. It hadn't been a panic before—not quite—but it was getting to be one. People streamed out of both doors. There was a crash of breaking glass and Coke fizzed suddenly across the floor.

"What the Christ *is* this?" Norton exclaimed.

That was when it started getting dark . . . but no, that's not exactly right. My thought at the time was not that it was getting dark but that the lights in the market had gone out. I looked up at the fluorescents in a quick reflex action, and I wasn't alone. And at first, until I remembered the power failure, it seemed that was it, that was what had changed the quality of the light. Then I remembered they had been out all the time we had been in the market and things hadn't seemed dark before. Then I knew, even before the people at the window started to yell and point.

The mist was coming.

• • •

It came from the Kansas Road entrance to the parking lot, and even this close it looked no different than it had when we first noticed it on the far side of the lake. It was white and bright but nonreflecting. It was moving fast, and it had blotted out most of the sun. Where the sun had been there was now a silver coin in the sky, like a full moon in winter seen through a thin scud of cloud.

It came with lazy speed. Watching it reminded me somehow of last evening's waterspout. There are big forces in nature that you hardly ever see—earthquakes, hurricanes, tornadoes—I haven't seen them all but I've seen enough to guess that they all move with that lazy, hypnotizing speed. They hold you spellbound, the way Billy and Steffy had been in front of the picture window last night.

It rolled impartially across the two-lane blacktop and erased it from view. The McKeons' nice restored Dutch Colonial was swallowed whole. For a moment the second floor of the ramshackle apartment building next door jutted out of the whiteness, and then it went too. The KEEP RIGHT sign at the entrance and exit points to the Federal's parking lot disappeared, the black letters on the sign seeming to float for a moment in limbo after the sign's dirty-white background was gone. The cars in the parking lot began to disappear next.

"What the Christ *is* this?" Norton asked again, and there was a catch in his voice.

It came on, eating up the blue sky and the fresh black hottop with equal ease. Even twenty feet away the line of demarcation was perfectly clear. I had the nutty feeling that I was watching some extra-good piece of visual effects, something dreamed up by Willys O'Brian or Douglas Trumbull. It happened so quickly. The blue sky disappeared to a wide swipe, then to a stripe, then to a pencil line. Then it was gone. Blank white pressed against the glass of the wide show window. I could see as far as the litter barrel that stood maybe four feet away, but not much farther. I could see the front bumper of my Scout, but that was all.

A woman screamed, very loud and long. Billy pressed himself more tightly against me. His body was trembling like a loose bundle of wires with high voltage running through them.

A man yelled and bolted through one of the deserted lanes toward the door. I think that was what finally started the stampede. People rushed pell-mell into the fog.

"Hey!" Brown roared. I don't know if he was angry, scared, or both. His face was nearly purple. Veins stood out on his neck, looking almost as thick as battery cables. *"Hey you people, you can't take that stuff. Get back here with that stuff, you're shoplifting!"*

They kept going, but some of them tossed their stuff aside. Some were laughing and excited, but they were a minority. They poured out into the fog, and none of us who stayed ever saw them again. There was a faint, acrid smell drifting in through the open door. People began to jam up there. Some pushing and shoving started. I was getting an ache in my shoulders from holding Billy. He was good-sized; Steff sometimes called him her young heifer.

Norton started to wander off, his face preoccupied and rather bemused. He was heading for the door.

I switched Billy to the other arm so I could grab Norton's arm before he drifted out of reach. "No, man, I wouldn't," I said.

He turned back. "What?"

"Better wait and see."

"See what?"

"I don't know," I said.

"You don't think—" he began, and a shriek came out of the fog.

Norton shut up. The tight jam at the OUT door loosened and then reversed itself. The babble of excited conversation, shouts and calls, subsided. The faces of the people by the door suddenly looked flat and pale and two dimensional.

The shriek went on and on, competing with the fire whistle. It seemed impossible that any human pair of lungs could have enough air in them to sustain such a shriek. Norton muttered, "Oh my God," and ran his hands through his hair.

The shriek ended abruptly. It did not dwindle; it was cut off. One more man went outside, a beefy guy in chino workpants. I think he was set on rescuing the shrieker. For a moment he was out there, visible through the glass and the mist, like a figure seen through a milkscum on a tumbler. Then (and as far as I know, I was the only one to see this) something beyond him appeared to move, a gray shadow in all that white. And it seemed to me that instead of running into the fog, the man in the chino pants was *jerked* into it, his hands flailing upward as if in surprise.

For a moment there was total silence in the market.

A constellation of moons suddenly glowed into being outside. The parking-lot sodium lights, undoubtedly supplied by underground electrical cables, had just gone on.

"Don't go out there," Mrs. Carmody said in her best gorecrow voice. "It's death to go out there."

All at once, no one seemed disposed to argue or laugh.

Another scream came from outside, this one muffled and rather distant-sounding. Billy tensed against me again.

"David, what's going on?" Ollie Weeks asked. He had left his position. There were big beads of sweat on his round, smooth face. "What is this?"

"I'll be goddammed if I have any idea," I said. Ollie looked badly scared. He was a bachelor who lived in a nice little house up by Highland Lake and who liked to drink in the bar at Pleasant Mountain. On the pudgy little finger of his left hand was a star-sapphire ring. The February before, he won some money in the state lottery. He bought the ring out of his winnings. I always had the idea that Ollie was a little afraid of girls.

"I don't dig this," he said.

"No. Billy, I have to put you down. I'll hold your hand, but you're breaking my arms, okay?"

"Mommy," he whispered.

"She's okay," I told him. It was something to say.

The old geezer who runs the secondhand shop near Jon's Restaurant walked past us, bundled into the old collegiate letter-sweater he wears year-round. He said loudly: "It's one of those pollution clouds. The mills at Rumford and South Paris. Chemicals." With that, he made off up the Aisle 4, past the patent medicines and toilet paper.

"Let's get out of here, David," Norton said with no conviction at all. "What do you say we—"

There was a thud. An odd, twisting thud that I felt mostly in my feet, as if the entire building had suddenly dropped three feet. Several people cried out in fear and surprise. There was a musical jingle of bottles leaning off their shelves and destroying themselves upon the tile floor. A chunk of glass shaped like a pie wedge fell out of one of the segments of the wide front window, and I saw that the wooden frames banding the heavy sections of glass had buckled and splintered in some places.

The fire whistle stopped in mid-whoop.

The quiet that followed was the bated silence of people waiting for something else, something more. I was shocked and numb, and my mind made a strange cross-patch connection with the past. Back when Bridgton was little more than a crossroads, my dad would take me in with him and stand talking at the counter while I looked through the glass at the penny candy and two-cent chews. It was January thaw. No sound but the drip of meltwater falling from the galvanized tin gutters to the rain barrels on either side of the store. Me looking at the jawbreakers and buttons and pinwheels. The mystic yellow globes of light overhead showing up the monstrous, projected shadows of last summer's battalion of dead flies. A little boy named David Drayton with his father, the famous artist Andrew Drayton, whose painting *Christine Standing Alone* hung in the White House. A little boy named David Drayton looking at the candy and the Davy Crockett bubblegum cards and vaguely needing to go pee. And outside, the pressing, billowing yellow fog of January thaw.

The memory passed, but very slowly.

"You people!" Norton bellowed. "All you people, listen to me!"

They looked around. Norton was holding up both hands, the fingers splayed like a political candidate accepting accolades.

"It may be dangerous to go outside!" Norton yelled.

"Why?" a woman screamed back. "My kids're at home! I got to get back to my kids!"

"It's death to go out there!" Mrs. Carmody came back smartly. She was standing by the twenty-five-pound sacks of fertilizer stacked below the window, and her face seemed to bulge somehow, as if she were swelling.

A teenager gave her a sudden hard push and she sat down on the bags with a surprised grunt. "Stop saying that, you old bag! Stop rappin' that crazy bullshit!"

"Please!" Norton yelled. "If we just wait a few moments until it blows over and we can see—"

A babble of conflicting shouts greeted this.

"He's right," I said, shouting to be heard over the noise. "Let's just try to keep cool."

"I think that was an earthquake," a bespectacled man said. His voice was soft. In one hand he held a package of hamburger and a bag of buns. The other hand was holding the hand of a little girl, maybe a year younger than Billy. "I really think that was an earthquake."

"They had one over in Naples four years ago," a fat local man said.

"That was in Casco," his wife contradicted immediately. She spoke in the unmistakable tones of a veteran contradictor.

"Naples," the fat local man said, but with less assurance.

"Casco," his wife said firmly, and he gave up.

Somewhere a can that had been jostled to the very edge of its shelf by the thump, earthquake, whatever it had been, fell off with a delayed clatter. Billy burst into tears. "I want to go *home!* I want my MOTHER!"

"Can't you shut that kid up?" Bud Brown asked. His eyes were darting rapidly but aimlessly from place to place.

"Would you like a shot in the teeth, motormouth?" I asked him.

"Come on, Dave, that's not helping," Norton said distractedly.

"I'm sorry," the woman who had screamed earlier said. "I'm sorry, but I can't stay here. I've got to get home and see to my kids."

She looked around at us, a blond woman with a tired, pretty face.

"Wanda's looking after little Victor, you see. Wanda's only

eight and sometimes she forgets . . . forgets she's supposed to be . . . well, watching him, you know. And little Victor . . . he likes to turn on the stove burners to see the little red light come on . . . he likes that light . . . and sometimes he pulls out the plugs . . . little Victor does . . . and Wanda gets . . . bored watching him after a while . . . she's just eight . . ." She stopped talking and just looked at us. I imagine that we must have looked like nothing but a bank of merciless eyes to her right then, not human beings at all, just eyes. *"Isn't anyone going to help me?"* she screamed. Her lips began to tremble. "Won't . . . won't anybody here see a lady home?"

No one replied. People shuffled their feet. She looked from face to face with her own broken face. The fat local man took a hesitant half-step forward and his wife jerked him back with one quick tug, her hand clapped over his wrist like a manacle.

"You?" the blond woman asked Ollie. He shook his head. "You?" she said to Bud. He put his hand over the Texas Instruments calculator on the counter and made no reply. "You?" she said to Norton, and Norton began to say something in his big lawyer's voice, something about how no one should go off half-cocked, and . . . and she dismissed him and Norton just trailed off.

"You?" she said to me, and I picked Billy up again and held him in my arms like a shield to ward off her terrible broken face.

"I hope you all rot in hell," she said. She didn't scream it. Her voice was dead tired. She went to the OUT door and pulled it open, using both hands. I wanted to say something to her, call her back, but my mouth was too dry.

"Aw, lady, listen—" the teenage kid who had shouted at Mrs. Carmody began. He held her arm. She looked down at his hand and he let her go, shamefaced. She slipped out into the fog. We watched her go and no one said anything. We watched the fog overlay her and make her insubstantial, not a human being anymore but a pencil-ink sketch of a human being done on the world's whitest paper, and no one said anything. For a moment it was like the letters of the KEEP RIGHT sign that had seemed to float on nothingness; her arms and legs and pallid blond hair were all gone and only the misty remnants of her red summer dress remained, seeming to dance in white limbo. Then her dress was gone, too, and no one said anything.

IV. The Storage Area. Problems with the Generators. What Happened to the Bag-Boy.

Billy began to act hysterical and tantrummy, screaming for his mother in a hoarse, demanding way through his tears, instantly regressing to the age of two. Snot was lathered on his upper lip. I led him away, walking down one of the middle aisles with my arm around his shoulders, trying to soothe him. I took him back by the long white meat cabinet that ran the length of the store at the back. Mr. McVey, the butcher, was still there. We nodded at each other, the best we could do under the circumstances.

I sat down on the floor and took Billy on my lap and held his face against my chest and rocked him and talked to him. I told him all the lies parents keep in reserve for bad situations, the ones that sound so damn plausible to a child, and I told them in a tone of perfect conviction.

"That's not regular fog," Billy said. He looked up at me, his eyes dark-circled and tear-streaked. "It isn't, is it, Daddy?"

"No, I don't think so." I didn't want to lie about that.

Kids don't fight shock the way adults do; they go with it,

maybe because kids are in a semipermanent state of shock until they're thirteen or so. Billy started to doze off. I held him, thinking he might snap awake again, but his doze deepened into a real sleep. Maybe he had been awake part of the night before, when we had slept three-in-a-bed for the first time since Billy was an infant. And maybe—I felt a cold eddy slip through me at the thought—maybe he had sensed something coming.

When I was sure he was solidly out, I laid him on the floor and went looking for something to cover him up with. Most of the people were still up front, looking out into the thick blanket of mist. Norton had gathered a little crowd of listeners, and was busy spellbinding—or trying to. Bud Brown stood rigidly at his post, but Ollie Weeks had left his.

There were a few people in the aisles, wandering like ghosts, their faces greasy with shock. I went into the storage area through the big double doors between the meat cabinet and the beer cooler.

The generator roared steadily behind its plywood partition, but something had gone wrong. I could smell diesel fumes, and they were much too strong. I walked toward the partition, taking shallow breaths. At last I unbuttoned my shirt and put part of it over my mouth and nose.

The storage area was long and narrow, feebly lit by two sets of emergency lights. Cartons were stacked everywhere—bleach on one side, cases of soft drinks on the far side of the partition, stacked cases of Beefaroni and catsup. One of those had fallen over and the cardboard carton appeared to be bleeding.

I unlatched the door in the generator partition and stepped through. The machine was obscured in drifting, oily clouds of blue smoke. The exhaust pipe ran out through a hole in the wall. Something must have blocked off the outside end of the pipe. There was a simple on/off switch and I flipped it.

The generator hitched, belched, coughed, and died. Then it ran down in a diminishing series of popping sounds that reminded me of Norton's stubborn chainsaw.

The emergency lights faded out and I was left in darkness. I got scared very quickly, and I got disoriented. My breathing sounded like a low wind rattling in straw. I bumped my nose on the flimsy plywood door going out and my heart lurched. There were windows in the double doors, but for some reason they had been painted black, and the darkness was nearly total. I got off course and ran into a stack of the bleach cartons. They tumbled and fell. One came close enough to my head to make me step backward, and I tripped over another carton that had landed behind me. I fell down, thumping my head hard enough to see bright stars in the darkness. Good show.

I lay there cursing myself and rubbing my head, telling myself to just take it easy, just get up and get out of here, get back to Billy, telling myself nothing soft and slimy was going to close over my ankle or slip into one groping hand. I told myself not to lose control, or I would end up blundering around back here in a panic, knocking things over and creating a mad obstacle course for myself.

I stood up carefully, looking for a pencil line of light between the double doors. I found it, a faint but unmistakable scratch on the darkness. I started toward it, and then stopped.

There was a sound. A soft sliding sound. It stopped, then started again with a stealthy little bump. Everything inside me went loose. I regressed magically to four years of age. That sound wasn't coming from the market. It was coming from behind me. From outside. Where the mist was. Something that was slipping and sliding and scraping over the cinderblocks. And, maybe, looking for a way in.

Or maybe it was already in, and it was looking for me. Maybe in a moment I would feel whatever was making that sound on my shoe. Or on my neck.

It came again. I was positive it was outside. But that didn't make it any better. I told my legs to go and they refused the order. Then the quality of the noise changed. Something *rasped* across the darkness and my heart leaped in my chest and I lunged at that thin vertical line of light. I hit the doors straight-arm and burst through into the market.

Three or four people were right outside the double doors—Ollie Weeks was one of them—and they all jumped back in surprise. Ollie grabbed at his chest. "David!" he said in a pinched voice. "Jesus Christ, you want to take ten years off my—" He saw my face. "What's the matter with you?"

"Did you hear it?" I asked. My voice sounded strange in my own ears, high and squeaking. "Did any of you hear it?"

They hadn't heard anything, of course. They had come up to see why the generator had gone off. As Ollie told me that, one of the bag-boys bustled up with an armload of flashlights. He looked from Ollie to me curiously.

"I turned the generator off," I said, and explained why.

"What did you hear?" one of the other men asked. He worked for the town road department; his name was Jim something.

"I don't know. A scraping noise. Slithery. I don't want to hear it again."

"Nerves," the other fellow with Ollie said.

No. It was not nerves.

"Did you hear it before the lights went out?"

"No, only after. But . . ." But nothing. I could see the way they were looking at me. They didn't want any more bad news, anything else frightening or off-kilter. There was enough of that already. Only Ollie looked as if he believed me.

"Let's go in and start her up again," the bag-boy said, handing out the flashlights. Ollie took his doubtfully. The bag-boy offered me one, a slightly contemptuous shine in his eyes. He was maybe eighteen. After a moment's thought, I took the light. I still needed something to cover Billy with.

Ollie opened the doors and chocked them, letting in some light. The bleach cartons lay scattered around the half-open door in the plywood partition.

The fellow named Jim sniffed and said, "Smells pretty rank, all right. Guess you was right to shut her down."

The flashlight beams bobbed and danced across cartons of canned goods, toilet paper, dog food. The beams were smoky in the drifting fumes the blocked exhaust had turned back into the storage area. The bag-boy trained his light briefly on the wide loading door at the extreme right.

The two men and Ollie went inside the generator compartment. Their lights flashed uneasily back and forth, reminding me of something out of a boys' adventure story—and I illustrated a series of them while I was still in college. Pirates burying their bloody gold at midnight, or maybe the mad doctor and his assistant snatching a body. Shadows, made twisted and monstrous by the shifting, conflicting flashlight beams, bobbed on the walls. The generator ticked irregularly as it cooled.

The bag-boy was walking toward the loading door, flashing his light ahead of him. "I wouldn't go over there," I said.

"No, I know *you* wouldn't."

"Try it now, Ollie," one of the men said. The generator wheezed, then roared.

"Jesus! Shut her down! Holy crow, don't that *stink!*"

The generator died again.

The bag-boy walked back from the loading door just as they came out. "Something's plugged that exhaust, all right," one of the men said.

"I'll tell you what," the bag-boy said. His eyes were shining in the glow of the flashlights, and there was a devil-may-care expression on his face that I had sketched too many times as part of the frontispieces for my boys' adventure series. "Get it running long enough for me to raise the loading door back there. I'll go around and clear away whatever it is."

"Norm, I don't think that's a very good idea," Ollie said doubtfully.

"Is it an electric door?" the one called Jim asked.

"Sure," Ollie said. "But I just don't think it would be wise for—"

"That's okay," the other guy said. He tipped his baseball cap back on his head. "I'll do it."

"No, you don't understand," Ollie began again. "I really don't think anyone should—"

"Don't worry," he said indulgently to Ollie, dismissing him.

Norm, the bag-boy, was indignant. "Listen, it was my idea," he said.

All at once, by some magic, they had gotten around to arguing about who was going to do it instead of whether or not it should be done at all. But of course, none of them had heard that nasty slithering sound. "Stop it!" I said loudly.

They looked around at me.

"You don't seem to understand, or you're trying as hard as you can *not* to understand. This is no ordinary fog. Nobody has come into the market since it hit. If you open that loading door and something comes in—"

"Something like what?" Norm said with perfect eighteen-year-old macho contempt.

"Whatever made the noise I heard."

"Mr. Drayton," Jim said. "Pardon me, but I'm not convinced you heard anything. I know you're a big-shot artist with connections in New York and Hollywood and all, but that doesn't make you any different from anyone else, in my book. Way I figure, you got in here in the dark and maybe you just . . . got a little confused."

"Maybe I did," I said. "And maybe if you want to start screwing around outside, you ought to start by making sure that lady got home safe to her kids." His attitude—and that of his buddy and of Norm the bag-boy—was making me mad and scaring me more at the same time. They had the sort of light in their eyes that some men get when they go shooting rats at the town dump.

"Hey," Jim's buddy said. "When any of us here want your advice, we'll ask for it."

Hesitantly, Ollie said: "The generator really isn't that important, you know. The food in the cold cases will keep for twelve hours or more with absolutely no—"

"Okay, kid, you're it," Jim said brusquely. "I'll start the motor, you raise the door so that the place doesn't stink up too bad. Me and Myron will be standing by the exhaust outflow. Give us a yell when it's clear."

"Sure," Norm said, and bustled excitedly away.

"This is crazy," I said. "You let that lady go by herself—"

"I didn't notice you breaking your ass to escort her," Jim's buddy Myron said. A dull, brick-colored flush was creeping out of his collar.

"—but you're going to let this kid risk his life over a generator that doesn't even matter?"

"Why don't you just shut the fuck up!" Norm yelled.

"Listen, Mr. Drayton," Jim said, and smiled at me coldly. "I'll tell you what. If you've got anything else to say, I think you better count your teeth first, because I'm tired of listening to your bullshit."

Ollie looked at me, plainly frightened. I shrugged. They were crazy, that was all. Their sense of proportion was temporarily gone. Out there they had been confused and scared. In here was a straightforward mechanical problem: a balky generator. It was possible to solve this problem. Solving the problem would help make them feel less confused and helpless. Therefore they would solve it.

Jim and his friend Myron decided I knew when I was licked and went back into the generator compartment. "Ready, Norm?" Jim asked.

Norm nodded, then realized they couldn't hear a nod. "Yeah," he said.

"Norm," I said. "Don't be a fool."

"It's a mistake," Ollie added.

He looked at us, and suddenly his face was much younger than eighteen. It was the face of a boy. His Adam's apple bobbed convulsively, and I saw that he was scared green. He opened his mouth to say something—I think he was going to call it off—and then the generator roared into life again, and when it was running smoothly, Norm lunged at the button to the right of the door and it began to rattle upward on its dual steel tracks. The emergency lights had come back on when the generator started. Now they dimmed down as the motor which lifted the door sucked away the juice.

The shadows ran backward and melted. The storage area began to fill with the mellow white light of an overcast late-winter day. I noticed that odd, acrid smell again.

The loading door went up two feet, then four. Beyond I could see a square cement platform outlined around the edges with a yellow stripe. The yellow faded and washed out in just three feet. The fog was incredibly thick.

"Ho up!" Norm yelled.

Tendrils of mist, as white and fine as floating lace, eddied inside. The air was cold. It had been noticeably cool all morning long, especially after the sticky heat of the last three weeks, but it had been a summery coolness. This was *cold.* It was like March. I shivered. And I thought of Steff.

The generator died. Jim came out just as Norm ducked under the door. He saw it. So did I. So did Ollie.

A tentacle came over the far lip of the concrete loading platform and grabbed Norm around the calf. My mouth dropped wide open. Ollie made a very short glottal sound of surprise—*uk!* The tentacle tapered from a thickness of a foot—the size of a grass snake—at the point where it had wrapped itself around Norm's lower leg to a thickness of maybe four or five feet where it disappeared into the mist. It was slate gray on top, shading to a fleshy pink underneath. And there were rows of suckers on the underside. They were moving and writhing like hundreds of small, puckering mouths.

Norm looked down. He saw what had him. His eyes bulged. *"Get it off me! Hey, get it off me! Christ Jesus, get this frigging thing off me!"*

"Oh my God," Jim whimpered.

Norm grabbed the bottom edge of the loading door and yanked himself back in. The tentacle seemed to bulge, the way your arm will when you flex it. Norm was yanked back against the corrugated steel door—his head clanged against it. The tentacle bulged more, and Norm's legs and torso began to slip back out. The bottom edge of the loading door scraped the shirttail out of his pants. He yanked savagely and pulled himself back in like a man doing a chin-up.

"Help me," he was sobbing. "Help me, you guys, please, please."

"Jesus, Mary, and Joseph," Myron said. He had come out of the generator compartment to see what was going on.

I was the closest, and I grabbed Norm around the waist and yanked as hard as I could, rocking back on my heels. For a moment we moved backward, but only for a moment. It was like stretching a rubber band or pulling taffy. The tentacle yielded but gave up its basic grip not at all. Then three more tentacles floated out of the mist toward us. One curled around Norm's flapping red Federal apron and tore it away. It disappeared back into the mist with the red cloth curled in its grip and I thought of something my mother used to say when my brother and I would beg for something she didn't want us to have—candy, a comic book, some toy. "You need that like a hen needs a flag," she'd say. I thought of that, and I thought of that tentacle waving Norm's red apron around, and I got laughing. I got laughing, except my laughter and Norm's screams sounded about the same. Maybe no one even knew I was laughing except me.

The other two tentacles slithered aimlessly back and forth on the loading platform for a moment, making those low scraping sounds I had heard earlier. Then one of them slapped against Norm's left hip and slipped around it. I felt it touch my arm. It was warm and pulsing and smooth. I think now that if it had gripped me with those suckers, I would have gone out into the mist too. But it didn't. It grabbed Norm. And the third tentacle ringleted his other ankle.

Now he was being pulled away from me. "Help me!" I shouted. "Ollie! Someone! Give me a hand here!"

But they didn't come. I don't know what they were doing, but they didn't come.

I looked down and saw the tentacle around Norm's waist working into his skin. The suckers were *eating* him where his shirt had pulled out of his pants. Blood, as red as his missing apron, began to seep out of the trench the pulsing tentacle had made for itself.

I banged my head on the lower edge of the partly raised door.

Norm's legs were outside again. One of his loafers had fallen off. A new tentacle came out of the mist, wrapped its tip firmly around the shoe, and made off with it. Norm's fingers clutched at the door's lower edge. He had it in a death grip. His fingers were livid. He was not screaming anymore; he was beyond that. His head whipped back and forth in an endless gesture of negation, and his long black hair flew wildly.

I looked over his shoulder and saw more tentacles coming, dozens of them, a forest of them. Most were small but a few were gigantic, as thick as the moss-corseted tree that had been lying across our driveway that morning. The big ones had candy-pink suckers that seemed the size of manhole covers. One of these big ones struck the concrete loading platform with a loud and rolling *thrrrrap!* sound and moved sluggishly toward us like a great blind earthworm. I gave one gigantic tug, and the tentacle holding Norm's right calf slipped a little. That was all. But before it reestablished its grip, I saw that the thing was eating him away.

One of the tentacles brushed delicately past my cheek and then wavered in the air, as if debating. I thought of Billy then. Billy was lying asleep in the market by Mr. McVey's long white meat cooler. I had come in here to find something to cover him up with. If one of those things got hold of me, there would be no one to watch out for him—except maybe Norton.

So I let go of Norm and dropped to my hands and knees.

I was half in and half out, directly under the raised door. A tentacle passed by on my left, seeming to walk on its suckers. It attached itself to one of Norm's bulging upper arms, paused for a second, and then slid around it in coils.

Now Norm looked like something out of a madman's dream

of snake charming. Tentacles twisted over him uneasily almost everywhere . . . and they were all around me, as well. I made a clumsy leapfrog jump back inside, landed on my shoulder, and rolled. Jim, Ollie and Myron were still there. They stood like a tableau of waxworks in Madame Tussaud's, their faces pale, their eyes too bright. Jim and Myron flanked the door to the generator compartment.

"Start the generator!" I yelled at them.

Neither moved. They were staring with a drugged, thanatotic avidity at the loading bay.

I groped on the floor, picked up the first thing that came to hand—a box of Snowy bleach—and chucked it at Jim. It hit him in the gut, just above the belt buckle. He grunted and grabbed at himself. His eyes flickered back into some semblance of normality.

"Go start that fucking generator!" I screamed so loudly it hurt my throat.

He didn't move; instead he began to defend himself, apparently having decided that, with Norm being eaten alive by some insane horror from the mist, the time had come for rebuttals.

"I'm sorry," he whined. "I didn't know, how the hell was I supposed to know? You said you heard something but I didn't know what you meant, you should have said what you meant better. I thought, I dunno, maybe a bird, or something—"

So then Ollie moved, bunting him aside with one thick shoulder and blundering into the generator room. Jim stumbled over one of the bleach cartons and fell down, just as I had done in the dark. "I'm sorry," he said again. His red hair had tumbled over his brow. His cheeks were cheese-white. His eyes were those of a horrified little boy. Seconds later the generator coughed and rumbled into life.

I turned back to the loading door. Norm was almost gone,

yet he clung grimly with one hand. His body boiled with tentacles, and blood pattered serenely down on the concrete in dime-size droplets. His head whipped back and forth and his eyes bulged with terror as they stared off into the mist.

Other tentacles now crept and crawled over the floor inside. There were too many near the button that controlled the loading door to even think of approaching it. One of them closed around a half-liter bottle of Pepsi and carried it off. Another slipped around a cardboard carton and squeezed. The carton ruptured and rolls of toilet paper, two-packs of Delsey wrapped in cellophane, geysered upward, came down, and rolled everywhere. Tentacles seized them eagerly.

One of the big ones slipped in. Its tip rose from the floor and it seemed to sniff the air. It began to advance toward Myron and he stepped mincingly away from it, his eyes rolling madly in their sockets. A high-pitched little moan escaped his slack lips.

I looked around for something, anything at all long enough to reach over the questing tentacles and punch the SHUT button on the wall. I saw a janitor's push broom leaning against a stack-up of beer cases and grabbed it.

Norm's good hand was ripped loose. He thudded down onto the concrete loading platform and scrabbled madly for a grip with his one free hand. His eyes met mine for a moment. They were hellishly bright and aware. He knew what was happening to him. Then he was pulled, bumping and rolling, into the mist. There was another scream, choked off. Norm was gone.

I pushed the tip of the broom handle onto the button and the motor whined. The door began to slide back down. It touched the thickest of the tentacles first, the one that had been investigating in Myron's direction. It indented its hide—skin, whatever—and then pierced it. A black goo began to spurt from it. It writhed madly, whipping across the concrete storage-area floor like an obscene bullwhip, and then it seemed to flatten out. A moment later it was gone. The others began to withdraw.

One of them had a five-pound bag of Gaines dog food, and it wouldn't let go. The descending door cut it in two before thumping home in its grooved slot. The severed chunk of tentacle squeezed convulsively tighter, splitting the bag open and sending brown nuggets of dog food everywhere. Then it began to flop on the floor like a fish out of water, curling and uncurling, but ever more slowly, until it lay still. I prodded it with the tip of the broom. The piece of tentacle, maybe three feet long, closed on it savagely for a moment, then loosened and lay limp again in the confused litter of toilet paper, dog food, and bleach cartons.

There was no sound except the roar of the generator and Ollie, crying inside the plywood compartment. I could see him sitting on a stool in there with his face clutched in his hands.

Then I became aware of another sound. The soft, slithery sound I had heard in the dark. Only now the sound was multiplied tenfold. It was the sound of tentacles squirming over the outside of the loading door, trying to find a way in.

Myron took a couple of steps toward me. "Look," he said. "You got to understand—"

I looped a fist at his face. He was too surprised to even try to block it. It landed just below his nose and mashed his upper lip into his teeth. Blood flowed into his mouth.

"You got him killed!" I shouted. "Did you get a good look at it? Did you get a good look at what you did?"

I started to pummel him, throwing wild rights and lefts, not punching the way I had been taught in my college boxing classes but only hitting out. He stepped back, shaking some of them off, taking others with a numbness that seemed like a kind of resignation or penance. That made me angrier. I bloodied his nose. I raised a mouse under one of his eyes that was going to black just beautifully. I clipped him a hard one on the chin. After that one, his eyes went cloudy and semi-vacant.

"Look," he kept saying, "look, look," and then I punched him low in the stomach and the air went out of him and he didn't say "look, look" anymore. I don't know how long I would have gone on punching him, but someone grabbed my arms. I jerked free and turned around. I was hoping it was Jim. I wanted to punch Jim out, too.

But it wasn't Jim. It was Ollie, his round face dead pale, except for the dark circles around his eyes—eyes that were still shiny from his tears. "Don't, David," he said. "Don't hit him anymore. It doesn't solve anything."

Jim was standing off to one side, his face a bewildered blank. I kicked a carton of something at him. It struck one of his Dingo boots and bounced away.

"You and your buddy are a couple of stupid assholes," I said.

"Come on, David," Ollie said unhappily. "Quit it."

"You two assholes got that kid killed."

Jim looked down at his Dingo boots. Myron sat on the floor and held his beer belly. I was breathing hard. The blood was roaring in my ears and I was trembling all over. I sat down on a couple of cartons and put my head down between my knees and gripped my legs hard just above the ankles. I sat that way for a while with my hair in my face, waiting to see if I was going to black out or puke or what.

After a bit the feeling began to pass and I looked up at Ollie. His pinky ring flashed subdued fire in the glow of the emergency lights.

"Okay," I said dully. "I'm done."

"Good," Ollie said. "We've got to think what to do next."

The storage area was beginning to stink of exhaust again. "Shut the generator down. That's the first thing."

"Yeah, let's get out of here," Myron said. His eyes appealed to me. "I'm sorry about the kid. But you got to understand—"

"I don't got to understand anything. You and your buddy go back into the market, but you wait right there by the beer cooler. And don't say a word to anybody. Not yet."

They went willingly enough, huddling together as they passed through the swinging doors. Ollie killed the generator, and just as the lights started to fail, I saw a quilted rug—the sort of thing movers use to pad breakable things—flopped over a stack of returnable soda bottles. I reached up and grabbed it for Billy.

There was the shuffling, blundering sound of Ollie coming out of the generator compartment. Like a great many overweight men, his breathing had a slightly heavy wheezing sound.

"David?" His voice wavered a little. "You still here?"

"Right here, Ollie. You want to watch out for all those bleach cartons."

"Yeah."

I guided him with my voice and in thirty seconds or so he reached out of the dark and gripped my shoulder. He gave a long, trembling sigh.

"Christ, let's get out of here." I could smell the Rolaids he always chewed on his breath. "This dark is . . . is bad."

"It is," I said. "But hang tight a minute, Ollie. I wanted to talk to you and I didn't want those other two fuckheads listening."

"Dave . . . they didn't twist Norm's arm. You ought to remember that."

"Norm was a kid, and they weren't. But never mind, that's over. We've got to tell them, Ollie. The people in the market."

"If they panic—" Ollie's voice was doubtful.

"Maybe they will and maybe they won't. But it will make them think twice about going out, which is what most of them want to do. Why shouldn't they? Most of them will have people they left at home. I do myself. We have to make them understand what they're risking if they go out there."

His hand was gripping my arm hard. "All right," he said. "Yes, I just keep asking myself . . . all those tentacles . . . like a squid or something . . . David, what were they hooked to? *What were those tentacles hooked to?"*

"I don't know. But I don't want those two telling people on their own. That *would* start a panic. Let's go."

I looked around, and after a moment or two located the thin line of vertical light between the swing doors. We started to shuffle toward it, wary of scattered cartons, one of Ollie's pudgy hands clamped over my forearm. It occurred to me that all of us had lost our flashlights.

As we reached the doors, Ollie said flatly: "What we saw . . . it's impossible, David. You know that, don't you? Even if a van from the Boston Seaquarium drove out back and dumped out one of those gigantic squids like in *Twenty Thousand Leagues Under the Sea,* it would die. *It would just die."*

"Yes," I said. "That's right."

"So what happened? Huh? What happened? What is that damned mist?"

"Ollie, I don't know."

We went out.

V. An Argument with Norton.
A Discussion Near the Beer Cooler.
Verification.

Jim and his good buddy Myron were just outside the doors, each with a Budweiser in his fist. I looked at Billy, saw he was still asleep, and covered him with the ruglike mover's pad. He moved a little, muttered something, and then lay still again. I looked at my watch. It was 12:15 P.M. That seemed utterly impossible; it felt as if at least five hours had passed since I had first gone in there to look for something to cover him with. But the whole thing, from first to last, had taken only about thirty-five minutes.

I went back to where Ollie stood with Jim and Myron. Ollie had taken a beer and he offered me one. I took it and gulped down half the can at once, as I had that morning cutting wood. It bucked me up a little.

Jim was Jim Grondin. Myron's last name was LaFleur—that had its comic side, all right. Myron the flower had drying blood on his lips, chin, and cheek. The eye with the mouse under it was already swelling up. The girl in the cranberry-colored sweatshirt walked by aimlessly and gave Myron a cautious look. I could have told her that Myron was only dangerous to teenage boys intent on proving their manhood, but saved my breath. After all, Ollie was right—they *had* only been doing what they thought was best, although in a blind, fearful way rather than in any real common interest. And now I needed them to do what *I* thought was best. I didn't think that would be a problem. They had both had the stuffing knocked out of them. Neither—especially Myron the flower—was going to be good for anything for some time to come. Something that had been in their eyes when they were fixing to send Norm out to unplug the exhaust vent had gone now. Their peckers were no longer up.

"We're going to have to tell these people something," I said.

Jim opened his mouth to protest.

"Ollie and I will leave out any part you and Myron had in sending Norm out there if you'll back up what he and I say about . . . well, about what got him."

"Sure," Jim said, pitifully eager. "Sure, if we don't tell, people might go out there . . . like that woman . . . that woman who . . ." He wiped his hand across his mouth and then drank more beer quickly. "Christ, what a mess."

"David," Ollie said. "What—" He stopped, then made himself go on. "What if they get in? The tentacles?"

"How could they?" Jim asked. "You guys shut the door."

"Sure," Ollie said. "But the whole front wall of this place is plate glass."

An elevator shot my stomach down about twenty floors. I had known that, but had somehow been successfully ignoring it. I looked over at where Billy lay asleep. I thought of those tentacles swarming over Norm. I thought about that happening to Billy.

"Plate glass," Myron LaFleur whispered. "Jesus Christ in a chariot-driven sidecar."

I left the three of them standing by the cooler, each working a second can of beer, and went looking for Brent Norton. I found him in sober-sided conversation with Bud Brown at Register 2. The pair of them—Norton with his styled gray hair and his elderly-stud good looks, Brown with his dour New England phiz—looked like something out of a *New Yorker* cartoon.

As many as two dozen people milled restlessly in the space

between the end of the checkout lanes and the long show window. A lot of them were lined up at the glass, looking out into the mist. I was again reminded of the people that congregate at a building site.

Mrs. Carmody was seated on the stationary conveyor belt of one of the checkout lanes, smoking a Parliament in a One Step at a Time filter. Her eyes measured me, found me wanting, and passed on. She looked as if she might be dreaming awake.

"Brent," I said.

"David! Where did you get off to?"

"That's what I'd like to talk to you about."

"There are people back at the cooler drinking beer," Brown said grimly. He sounded like a man announcing that X-rated movies had been shown at the deacons' party. "I can see them in the security mirror. This has simply got to stop."

"Brent?"

"Excuse me for a minute, would you, Mr. Brown?"

"Certainly." He folded his arms across his chest and stared grimly up into the convex mirror. "It *is* going to stop, I can promise you that."

Norton and I headed toward the beer cooler in the far corner of the store, walking past the housewares and notions. I glanced back over my shoulder, noticing uneasily how the wooden beams framing the tall, rectangular sections of glass had buckled and twisted and splintered. And one of the windows wasn't even whole, I remembered. A pie-shaped chunk of glass had fallen out of the upper corner at the instant of that queer thump. Perhaps we could stuff it with cloth or something—maybe a bunch of those $3.59 ladies' tops I had noticed near the wine—

My thoughts broke off abruptly, and I had to put the back of my hand over my mouth, as if stifling a burp. What I was really stifling was the rancid flood of horrified giggles that wanted to escape me at the thought of stuffing a bunch of shirts into a hole to keep out those tentacles that had carried Norm away. I had seen one of those tentacles—a small one—squeeze a bag of dog food until it simply ruptured.

"David? Are you okay?"

"Huh?"

"Your face—you looked like you just had a good idea or a bloody awful one."

Something hit me then. "Brent, what happened to that man who came in raving about something in the mist getting John Lee Frovin?"

"The guy with the nosebleed?"

"Yes, him."

"He passed out and Mr. Brown brought him around with some smelling salts from the first-aid kit. Why?"

"Did he say anything else when he woke up?"

"He started in on that hallucination. Mr. Brown conducted him up to the office. He was frightening some of the women. He seemed happy enough to go. Something about the glass. When Mr. Brown said there was only one small window in the manager's office, and that that one was reinforced with wire, he seemed happy enough to go. I presume he's still there."

"What he was talking about is no hallucination."

"No, of course it isn't."

"And that thud we felt?"

"No, but, David—"

He's scared, I kept reminding myself. Don't blow up at him, you've treated yourself to one blowup this morning and that's enough. Don't blow up at him just because this is the way he was during that stupid property-line dispute . . . first patronizing, then sarcastic, and finally, when it became clear he was going to lose, ugly. Don't blow up at him because you're going to need him. He may not be able to start his own chainsaw, but he looks like the father figure of the Western world, and if he tells people not to panic, they won't. So don't blow up at him.

"You see those double doors up there beyond the beer cooler?"

He looked, frowning. "Isn't one of those men drinking beer the other assistant manager? Weeks? If Brown sees that, I can promise you that man will be looking for a job very soon."

"Brent, will you listen to me?"

He glanced back at me absently. "What were you saying, Dave? I'm sorry."

Not as sorry as he was going to be. "Do you see those doors?"

"Yes, of course I do. What about them?"

"They give on the storage area that runs all the way along the west face of the building. Billy fell asleep and I went back there to see if I could find something to cover him up with . . ."

I told him everything, only leaving out the argument about whether or not Norm should have gone out at all. I told him what had come in . . . and finally, what had gone out, screaming. Brent Norton refused to believe it. No—he refused to even entertain it. I took him over to Jim, Ollie, and Myron. All three of them verified the story, although Jim and Myron the flower were well on their way to getting drunk.

Again, Norton refused to believe or even to entertain it. He simply balked. "No," he said. "No, no, no. Forgive me, gentlemen, but it's completely ridiculous. Either you're having me on"—he patronized us with his gleaming smile to show that he could take a joke as well as the next fellow—"or you're suffering from some form of group hypnosis."

My temper rose again, and I controlled it—with difficulty. I don't think that I'm ordinarily a quick-tempered man, but these weren't ordinary circumstances. I had Billy to think about, and what was happening—or what had already happened—to Stephanie. Those things were constantly gnawing at the back of my mind.

"All right," I said. "Let's go back there. There's a chunk of tentacle on the floor. The door cut it off when it came down. And you can *hear* them. They're rustling all over that door. It sounds like the wind in ivy."

"No," he said calmly.

"What?" I really did believe I had misheard him. "What did you say?"

"I said no, I'm not going back there. The joke has gone far enough."

"Brent, I swear to you it's no joke."

"Of course it is," he snapped. His eyes ran over Jim, Myron, rested briefly on Ollie Weeks—who held his glance with calm impassivity—and at last came back to me. "It's what you locals probably call 'a real belly-buster.' Right, David?"

"Brent . . . look—"

"No, you look!" His voice began to rise toward a courtroom shout. It carried very, very well, and several of the people who were wandering around, edgy and aimless, looked over to see what was going on. Norton jabbed his finger at me as he spoke. "It's a joke. It's a banana skin and I'm the guy that's supposed to slip on it. None of you people are exactly crazy about out-of-towners, am I right? You all pretty much stick together. The way it happened when I hauled you into court to get what was rightfully mine. You won that one, all right. Why not? Your father was the famous artist, and it's your town. I only pay my taxes and spend my money here!"

He was no longer performing, hectoring us with the trained courtroom shout; he was nearly screaming and on the verge of losing all control. Ollie Weeks turned and walked away, clutching his beer. Myron and his friend Jim were staring at Norton with frank amazement.

"Am I supposed to go back there and look at some ninety-eight-cent rubber-joke novelty while these two hicks stand around and laugh their asses off?"

"Hey, you want to watch who you're calling a hick," Myron said.

"I'm *glad* that tree fell on your boathouse, if you want to know the truth. *Glad.*" Norton was grinning savagely at me. "Stove it in pretty well, didn't it? Fantastic. Now get out of my way."

He tried to push past me. I grabbed him by the arm and threw him against the beer cooler. A woman cawed in surprise. Two six-packs of Bud fell over.

"You dig out your ears and listen, Brent. There are lives at stake here. My kid's is not the least of them. So you listen, or I swear I'll knock the shit out of you."

"Go ahead," Norton said, still grinning with a kind of insane palsied bravado. His eyes, bloodshot and wide, bulged from their sockets. "Show everyone how big and brave you are, beating up a man with a heart condition who is old enough to be your father."

"Sock him anyway!" Jim exclaimed. "Fuck his heart condition. I don't even think a cheap New York shyster like him has got a heart."

"You keep out of it," I said to Jim, and then put my face down to Norton's. I was kissing distance, if that had been what I had in mind. The cooler was off, but it was still radiating a chill. "Stop throwing up sand. You know damn well I'm telling the truth."

"I know . . . no . . . such thing," he panted.

"If it was another time and place, I'd let you get away with it. I don't care how scared you are, and I'm not keeping score. I'm scared, too. But I need you, goddammit! Does that get through? I need you!"

"Let me *go!*"

I grabbed him by the shirt and shook him. "Don't you understand anything? People are going to start leaving and walk right into that thing out there! For Christ's sake, don't you understand?"

"Let me go!"

"Not until you come back there with me and see for yourself."

"I told you, *no!* It's all a trick, a joke, I'm not as stupid as you take me for—"

"Then I'll haul you back there myself."

I grabbed him by the shoulder and the scruff of his neck. The seam of his shirt under one arm tore with a soft purring sound. I dragged him toward the double doors. Norton let out a wretched scream. A knot of people, fifteen or eighteen, had gathered, but they kept their distance. None showed any signs of wanting to interfere.

"Help me!" Norton cried. His eyes bulged behind his glasses. His styled hair had gone awry again, sticking up in the same two little tufts behind his ears. People shuffled their feet and watched.

"What are you screaming for?" I said in his ear. "It's just a joke, right? That's why I took you to town when you asked to come and why I trusted you to cross Billy in the parking lot—because I had this handy fog all manufactured, I rented a fog machine from Hollywood, it cost me fifteen thousand dollars and another eight thousand dollars to ship it, all so I could play a joke on you. Stop bullshitting yourself and open your eyes!"

"Let . . . me . . . go!" Norton bawled. We were almost at the doors.

"Here, here! What is this? What are you doing?"

It was Brown. He bustled and elbowed his way through the crowd of watchers.

"Make him let me go," Norton said hoarsely. "He's crazy."

"No. He's not crazy. I wish he were, but he isn't." That was Ollie, and I could have blessed him. He came around the aisle behind us and stood there facing Brown.

Brown's eyes dropped to the beer Ollie was holding. "You're *drinking!"* he said, and his voice was surprised but not totally devoid of pleasure. "You'll lose your job for this."

"Come on, Bud," I said, letting Norton go. "This is no ordinary situation."

"Regulations don't change," Brown said smugly. "I'll see that the company hears of it. That's my responsibility."

Norton, meanwhile, had skittered away and stood at some distance, trying to straighten his shirt and smooth back his hair. His eyes darted between Brown and me nervously.

"Hey!" Ollie cried suddenly, raising his voice and producing a bass thunder I never would have suspected from this large but soft and unassuming man. *"Hey! Everybody in the store! You want to come up back and hear this! It concerns all of you!"* He looked at me levelly, ignoring Brown altogether. "Am I doing all right?"

"Fine."

People began to gather. The original knot of spectators to my argument with Norton doubled, then trebled.

"There's something you all had better know—" Ollie began.

"You put that beer down right now," Brown said.

"You shut up right now," I said, and took a step toward him.

Brown took a compensatory step back. "I don't know what

some of you think you are doing," he said, "but I can tell you it's going to be reported to the Federal Foods Company! All of it! And I want you to understand—*there may be charges!*" His lips drew nervously back from his yellowed teeth, and I could feel sympathy for him. Just trying to cope; that was all he was doing. As Norton was by imposing a mental gag order on himself. Myron and Jim had tried by turning the whole thing into a macho charade—if the generator could be fixed, the mist would blow over. This was Brown's way. He was . . . Protecting the Store.

"Then you go ahead and take down the names," I said. "But please don't talk."

"I'll take down plenty of names," he responded. "Yours will be head on the list, you . . . you *bohemian.*"

"Mr. David Drayton has got something to tell you," Ollie said, "and I think you had better all listen up, in case you were planning on going home."

So I told them what had happened, pretty much as I told Norton. There was some laughter at first, then a deepening uneasiness as I finished.

"It's a lie, you know," Norton said. His voice tried for hard emphasis and overshot into stridency. This was the man I'd told first, hoping to enlist his credibility. What a balls-up.

"Of course it's a lie," Brown agreed. "It's lunacy. Where do you suppose those tentacles came from, Mr. Drayton?"

"I don't know, and at this point, that's not even a very important question. They're here. There's—"

"I suspect they came out of a few of those beer cans. That's what I suspect." This got some appreciative laughter. It was silenced by the strong, rusty-hinge voice of Mrs. Carmody.

"Death!" she cried, and those who had been laughing quickly sobered.

She marched into the center of the rough circle that had formed, her canary pants seeming to give off a light of their own, her huge purse swinging against one elephantine thigh. Her black eyes glanced arrogantly around, as sharp and balefully sparkling as a magpie's. Two good-looking girls of about sixteen with CAMP WOODLANDS written on the back of their white rayon shirts shrank away from her.

"You listen but you don't hear! You hear but you don't believe! Which one of you wants to go outside and see for himself?" Her eyes swept them, and then fell on me. "And just what do you propose to do about it, Mr. David Drayton? What do you think you can do about it?"

She grinned, skull-like above her canary outfit.

"It's the end, I tell you. The end of everything. It's the Last Times. The moving finger has writ, not in fire, but in lines of mist. The earth has opened and spewed forth its abominations—"

"Can't you make her shut up?" one of the teenage girls burst out. She was beginning to cry. "She's scaring me!"

"Are you scared, dearie?" Mrs. Carmody asked, and turned on her. "You aren't scared now, no. But when the foul creatures the Imp has loosed upon the face of the earth come for you—"

"That's enough now, Mrs. Carmody," Ollie said, taking her arm. "That's just fine."

"You let go of me! It's the end, I tell you! It's death! Death!"

"It's a pile of shit," a man in a fishing hat and glasses said disgustedly.

"No, sir," Myron spoke up. "I know it sounds like something out of a dope-dream, but it's the flat-out truth. I saw it myself."

"I did, too," Jim said.

"And me," Ollie chipped in. He had succeeded in quieting Mrs. Carmody, at least for the time being. But she stood close by, clutching her big purse and grinning her crazy grin. No one wanted to stand too close to her—they muttered among themselves, not liking the corroboration. Several of them looked back at the big plate-glass windows in an uneasy, speculative way. I was glad to see it.

"Lies," Norton said. "You people all lie each other up. That's all."

"What you're suggesting is totally beyond belief," Brown said.

"We don't have to stand here chewing it over," I told him. "Come back into the storage area with me. Take a look. And a listen."

"Customers are not allowed in the—"

"Bud," Ollie said, "go with him. Let's settle this."

"All right," Brown said. "Mr. Drayton? Let's get this foolishness over with."

We pushed through the double doors into the darkness.

The sound was unpleasant—perhaps evil.

Brown felt it, too, for all his hardheaded Yankee manner; his hand clutched my arm immediately, his breath caught for a moment and then resumed more harshly.

It was a low whispering sound from the direction of the loading door—an almost caressing sound. I swept around gently with one foot and finally struck one of the flashlights. I bent down, got it, and turned it on. Brown's face was tightly drawn, and he hadn't even seen them—he was only hearing them. But I had seen, and I could imagine them twisting and climbing over the corrugated steel surface of the door like living vines.

"What do you think now? Totally beyond belief?"

Brown licked his lips and looked at the littered confusion of boxes and bags. "They did this?"

"Some of it. Most of it. Come over here."

He came—reluctantly. I spotted the flashlight on the shriveled and curled section of tentacle, still lying by the push broom. Brown bent toward it.

"Don't touch that," I said. "It may still be alive."

He straightened up quickly. I picked up the broom by the bristles and prodded the tentacle. The third or fourth poke caused it to unclench sluggishly and reveal two whole suckers and a ragged segment of a third. Then the fragment coiled again with muscular speed and lay still. Brown made a gagging, disgusted sound.

"Seen enough?"

"Yes," he said. "Let's get out of here."

We followed the bobbing light back to the double doors and pushed through them. All the faces turned toward us, and the hum of conversation died. Norton's face was like old cheese. Mrs. Carmody's black eyes glinted. Ollie was drinking beer; his face was still running with trickles of perspiration, although it had gotten rather chilly in the market. The two girls with CAMP WOODLANDS on their shirts were huddled together like young horses before a thunderstorm. Eyes. So many eyes. I could paint them, I thought with a chill. No faces, only eyes in the gloom. I could paint them but no one would believe they were real.

Bud Brown folded his long-fingered hands primly in front of him. "People," he said. "It appears we have a problem of some magnitude here."

VI. Further Discussion. Mrs. Carmody. Fortifications. What Happened to the Flat-Earth Society.

The next four hours passed in a kind of dream. There was a long and semihysterical discussion following Brown's confirmation, or maybe the discussion wasn't as long as it seemed; maybe it was just the grim necessity of people chewing over the same information, trying to see it from every possible point of view, working it the way a dog works a bone, trying to get at the marrow. It was a slow coming to belief. You can see the same thing at any New England town meeting in March.

There was the Flat-Earth Society, headed by Norton. They were a vocal minority of about ten who believed none of it. Norton pointed out over and over again that there were only four witnesses to the bag-boy being carried off by what he called the Tentacles from Planet X (it was good for a laugh the first time, but it wore thin quickly; Norton, in his increasing agitation, seemed not to notice). He added that he personally did not trust one of the four. He further pointed out that fifty percent of the witnesses were now hopelessly inebriated. That was unquestionably true. Jim and Myron LaFleur, with the entire beer cooler and wine rack at their disposal, were abysmally shitfaced. Considering what had happened to Norm, and their part in it, I didn't blame them. They would sober off all too soon.

Ollie continued to drink steadily, ignoring Brown's protests. After a while Brown gave up, contenting himself with an occasional baleful threat about the Company. He didn't seem to realize that Federal Foods, Inc., with its stores in Bridgton, North Windham, and Portland, might not even exist anymore. For all we knew, the Eastern Seaboard might no longer exist.

Ollie drank steadily, but didn't get drunk. He was sweating it out as rapidly as he could put it in.

At last, as the discussion with the Flat-Earthers was becoming acrimonious, Ollie spoke up. "If you don't believe it, Mr. Norton, that's fine. I'll tell you what to do. You go on out that front door and walk around to the back. There's a great big pile of returnable beer and soda bottles there. Norm and Buddy and I put them out this morning. You bring back a couple of those bottles so we know you really went back there. You do that and I'll personally take my shirt off and eat it."

Norton began to bluster.

Ollie cut him off in that same soft, even voice. "I tell you, you're not doing anything but damage talking the way you are. There's people here that want to go home and make sure their families are okay. My sister and her year-old daughter are at home in Naples right now. I'd like to check on them, sure. But if people start believing you and try to go home, what happened to Norm is going to happen to them."

He didn't convince Norton, but he convinced some of the leaners and fence sitters—it wasn't what he said so much as it was his eyes, his haunted eyes. I think Norton's sanity hinged on not being convinced, or that he thought it did. But he didn't take Ollie up on his offer to bring back a sampling of returnables from out back. None of them did. They weren't ready to go out, at least not yet. He and his little group of Flat-Earthers (reduced by one or two now) went as far away from the rest of us as they could get, over by the prepared-meats case. One of them kicked my sleeping son in the leg as he went past, waking him up.

I went over, and Billy clung to my neck. When I tried to put him down, he clung tighter and said, "Don't do that, Daddy. Please."

I found a shopping cart and put him in the baby seat. He looked very big in there. It would have been comical except for his pale face, the dark hair brushed across his forehead just above his eyebrows, his woeful eyes. He probably hadn't been up in the baby seat of the shopping cart for as long as two years. These little things slide by you, you don't realize at first, and when what has changed finally comes to you, it's always a nasty shock.

Meanwhile, with the Flat-Earthers having withdrawn, the argument had found another lightning rod—this time it was Mrs. Carmody, and understandably enough, she stood alone.

In the faded, dismal light she was witchlike in her blazing canary pants, her bright rayon blouse, her armloads of clacking junk jewelry—copper, tortoiseshell, adamantine—and her thyroidal purse. Her parchment face was grooved with strong vertical lines. Her frizzy gray hair was yanked flat with three horn combs and twisted in the back. Her mouth was a line of knotted rope.

"There is no defense against the will of God. This has been coming. I have seen the signs. There are those here that I have told, but there are none so blind as those who will not see."

"Well, what are you saying? What are you proposing?" Mike Hatlen broke in impatiently. He was a town selectman, although he didn't look the part now, in his yachtsman's cap and saggy-seated Bermudas. He was sipping at a beer; a great many men were doing it now. Bud Brown had given up protesting, but he was indeed taking names—keeping a rough tab on everyone he could.

"Proposing?" Mrs. Carmody echoed, wheeling toward Hatlen. "Proposing? Why, I am proposing that you prepare to meet your God, Michael Hatlen." She gazed around at all of us. "Prepare to meet your God!"

"Prepare to meet shit," Myron LaFleur said in a drunken snarl from the beer cooler. "Old woman, I believe your tongue must be hung in the middle so it can run on both ends."

There was a rumble of agreement. Billy looked around nervously, and I slipped an arm around his shoulders.

"I'll have my say!" she cried. Her upper lip curled back, revealing snaggle teeth that were yellow with nicotine. I thought of the dusty stuffed animals in her shop, drinking eternally at the mirror that served as their creek. "Doubters will doubt to the end! Yet a monstrosity did drag that poor boy away! Things in the mist! Every abomination out of a bad dream! Eyeless freaks! Pallid horrors! Do you doubt? Then go on out! Go on out and say howdy-do!"

"Mrs. Carmody, you'll have to stop," I said. "You're scaring my boy."

The man with the little girl echoed the sentiment. She, all plump legs and scabby knees, had hidden her face against her father's stomach and put her hands over her ears. Big Bill wasn't crying, but he was close.

"There's only one chance," Mrs. Carmody said.

"What's that, ma'am?" Mike Hatlen asked politely.

"A sacrifice," Mrs. Carmody said—she seemed to grin in the gloom. "A blood sacrifice."

Blood sacrifice—the words hung there, slowly turning. Even now, when I know better, I tell myself that then what she meant was someone's pet dog—there were a couple of them trotting around the market in spite of the regulations against them. Even now I tell myself that. She looked like some crazed remnant of New England Puritanism in the gloom . . . but I suspect that something deeper and darker than mere Puritanism motivated her. Puritanism had its own dark grandfather, old Adam with bloody hands.

She opened her mouth to say something more, and a small, neat man in red pants and a natty sport shirt struck her open-handed across the face. His hair was parted with ruler evenness on the left. He wore glasses. He also wore the unmistakable look of the summer tourist.

"You shut up that bad talk," he said softly and tonelessly.

Mrs. Carmody put her hand to her mouth and then held it out to us, a wordless accusation. There was blood on the palm. But her black eyes seemed to dance with mad glee.

"You had it coming!" a woman cried out. "I would have done it myself!"

"They'll get hold of you," Mrs. Carmody said, showing us her bloody palm. The trickle of blood was now running down one of the wrinkles from her mouth to her chin like a droplet of rain down a gutter. "Not today, maybe. Tonight. Tonight when the dark comes. They'll come with the night and take someone else. With the night they'll come. You'll hear them coming, creeping and crawling. And when they come, you'll beg for Mother Carmody to show you what to do."

The man in the red pants raised his hand slowly.

"You come on and hit me," she whispered, and grinned her bloody grin at him. His hand wavered. "Hit me if you dare." His hand dropped. Mrs. Carmody walked away by herself. Then Billy did begin to cry, hiding his face against me as the little girl had done with her father.

"I want to go home," he said. "I want to see my mommy."

I comforted him as best I could. Which probably wasn't very well.

The talk finally turned into less frightening and destructive channels. The plate-glass windows, the market's obvious weak point, were mentioned. Mike Hatlen asked what other entrances there were, and Ollie and Brown quickly ticked them off—two loading doors in addition to the one Norm had opened. The main IN/OUT doors. The window in the manager's office (thick, reinforced glass, securely locked).

Talking about these things had a paradoxical effect. It made the danger seem more real but at the same time made us feel better. Even Billy felt it. He asked if he could go get a candy bar. I told him it would be all right so long as he didn't go near the big windows.

When he was out of earshot, a man near Mike Hatlen said, "Okay, what are we going to do about those windows? The old lady may be as crazy as a bedbug, but she could be right about something moving in after dark."

"Maybe the fog will blow over by then," a woman said.

"Maybe," the man said. "And maybe not."

"Any ideas?" I asked Bud and Ollie.

"Hold on a sec," the man near Hatlen said. "I'm Dan Miller. From Lynn, Mass. You don't know me, no reason why you should, but I got a place on Highland Lake. Bought it just this year. Got held up for it, is more like it, but I had to have it." There were a few chuckles. "Anyway, I saw a whole pile of fertilizer and lawn-food bags down there. Twenty-five-pound sacks, most of them. We could put them up like sandbags. Leave loopholes to look out through . . ."

Now more people were nodding and talking excitedly. I almost said something, then held it back. Miller was right. Putting those bags up could do no harm, and might do some good. But my mind went back to that tentacle squeezing the dog-food bag. I thought that one of the bigger tentacles could probably do the same for a twenty-five-pound bag of Green Acres lawn food or Vigoro. But a sermon on that wouldn't get us out or improve anyone's mood.

People began to break up, talking about getting it done, and Miller yelled: "Hold it! Hold it! Let's thrash this out while we're all together!"

They came back, a loose congregation of fifty or sixty people in the corner formed by the beer cooler, the storage doors, and the left end of the meat case, where Mr. McVey always seems to put the things no one wants, like sweetbreads and Scotch eggs and sheep's brains and head cheese. Billy wove his way through them with a five-year-old's unconscious agility in a world of giants and held up a Hershey bar. "Want this, Daddy?"

"Thanks." I took it. It tasted sweet and good.

"This is probably a stupid question," Miller resumed, "but we ought to fill in the blanks. Anyone got any firearms?"

There was a pause. People looked around at each other and shrugged. An old man with grizzled white hair who introduced himself as Ambrose Cornell said he had a shotgun in the trunk of his car. "I'll try for it, if you want."

Ollie said, "Right now I don't think that would be a good idea, Mr. Cornell."

Cornell grunted. "Right now, neither do I, son. But I thought I ought to make the offer."

"Well, I didn't really think so," Dan Miller said. "But I thought—"

"Wait, hold it a minute," a woman said. It was the lady in the cranberry-colored sweatshirt and the dark-green slacks. She had sandy-blond hair and a good figure. A very pretty young woman. She opened her purse and from it she produced a medium-sized pistol. The crowd made an *ahhhh*-ing sound, as if they had just seen a magician do a particularly fine trick. The woman, who had been blushing, blushed that much the harder. She rooted in her purse again and brought out a box of Smith & Wesson ammunition.

"I'm Amanda Dumfries," she said to Miller. "This gun . . . my husband's idea. He thought I should have it for protection. I've carried it unloaded for two years."

"Is your husband here, ma'am?"

"No, he's in New York. On business. He's gone on business a lot. That's why he wanted me to carry the gun."

"Well," Miller said, "if you can use it, you ought to keep it. What is it, a thirty-eight?"

"Yes. And I've never fired it in my life except on a target range once."

Miller took the gun, fumbled around, and got the cylinder to open after a few moments. He checked to make sure it was not loaded. "Okay," he said. "We got a gun. Who shoots good? I sure don't."

People glanced at each other. No one said anything at first. Then, reluctantly, Ollie said: "I target-shoot quite a lot. I have a Colt .45 and a Llama .25."

"You?" Brown said. "Huh. You'll be too drunk to see by dark."

Ollie said very clearly, "Why don't you just shut up and write down your names?"

Brown goggled at him. Opened his mouth. Then decided, wisely, I think, to shut it again.

"It's yours," Miller said, blinking a little at the exchange. He handed it over and Ollie checked it again, more professionally. He put the gun into his right-front pants pocket and slipped the cartridge box into his breast pocket, where it made a bulge like a pack of cigarettes. Then he leaned back against the cooler, round face still trickling sweat, and cracked a fresh beer. The sensation that I was seeing a totally unsuspected Ollie Weeks persisted.

"Thank you, Mrs. Dumfries," Miller said.

"Don't mention it," she said, and I thought fleetingly that

if I were her husband and proprietor of those green eyes and that full figure, I might not travel so much. Giving your wife a gun could be seen as a ludicrously symbolic act.

"This may be silly, too," Miller said, turning back to Brown with his clipboard and Ollie with his beer, "but there aren't anything like flamethrowers in the place, are there?"

"Ohhh, *shit*," Buddy Eagleton said, and then went as red as Amanda Dumfries had done.

"What is it?" Mike Hatlen asked.

"Well . . . until last week we had a whole case of those little blowtorches. The kind you use around your house to solder leaky pipes or mend your exhaust systems or whatever. You remember those, Mr. Brown?"

Brown nodded, looking sour.

"Sold out?" Miller asked.

"No, they didn't go at all. We only sold three or four and sent the rest of the case back. What a pisser. I mean . . . what a shame." Blushing so deeply he was almost purple, Buddy Eagleton retired into the background again.

We had matches, of course, and salt (someone said vaguely that he had heard salt was the thing to put on bloodsuckers and things like that); and all kinds of O'Cedar mops and long-handled brooms. Most of the people continued to look heartened, and Jim and Myron were too plotzo to sound a dissenting note, but I met Ollie's eyes and saw a calm hopelessness in them that was worse than fear. He and I had seen the tentacles. The idea of throwing salt on them or trying to fend them off with the handles of O'Cedar mops was funny, in a ghastly way.

"Mike," Miller said, "why don't you crew this little adventure? I want to talk to Ollie and Dave here for a minute."

"Glad to." Hatlen clapped Dan Miller on the shoulder.

"Somebody had to take charge, and you did it good. Welcome to town."

"Does this mean I get a kickback on my taxes?" Miller asked. He was a banty little guy with red hair that was receding. He looked like the sort of guy you can't help liking on short notice and—just maybe—the kind of guy you can't help not liking after he's been around for a while. The kind of guy who knows how to do everything better than you do.

"No way," Hatlen said, laughing.

Hatlen walked off. Miller glanced down at my son.

"Don't worry about Billy," I said.

"Man, I've never been so worried in my whole life," Miller said.

"No," Ollie agreed, and dropped an empty into the beer cooler. He got a fresh one and opened it. There was a soft hiss of escaping gas.

"I got a look at the way you two glanced at each other," Miller said.

I finished my Hershey bar and got a beer to wash it down with.

"Tell you what I think," Miller said. "We ought to get half a dozen people to wrap some of those mop handles with cloth and then tie them down with twine. Then I think we ought to get a couple of those cans of charcoal lighter fluid all ready. If we cut the tops right off the cans, we could have some torches pretty quick."

I nodded. That was good. Almost surely not good enough—not if you had seen Norm dragged out—but it was better than salt.

"That would give them something to think about, at least," Ollie said.

Miller's lips pressed together. "That bad, huh?" he said.

"That bad," Ollie agreed, and worked his beer.

By four-thirty that afternoon the sacks of fertilizer and lawn food were in place and the big windows were blocked off except for narrow loopholes. A watchman had been placed at each of these, and beside each watchman was a tin of charcoal lighter fluid with the top cut off and a supply of mop-handle torches. There were five loopholes, and Dan Miller had arranged a rotation of sentries for each one. When four-thirty came around, I was sitting on a pile of bags at one of the loopholes, Billy at my side. We were looking out into the mist.

Just beyond the window was a red bench where people sometimes waited for their rides with their groceries beside them. Beyond that was the parking lot. The mist swirled slowly, thick and heavy. There *was* moisture in it, but how dull it seemed, and gloomy. Just looking at it made me feel gutless and lost.

"Daddy, do you know what's happening?" Billy asked.

"No, hon," I said.

He fell silent for a bit, looking at his hands, which lay limply in the lap of his Tuffskin jeans. "Why doesn't somebody come and rescue us?" he asked finally. "The State Police or the FBI or someone?"

"I don't know."

"Do you think Mom's okay?"

"Billy, I just don't know," I said, and put an arm around him.

"I want her awful bad," Billy said, struggling with tears. "I'm sorry about the times I was bad to her."

"Billy," I said, and had to stop. I could taste salt in my throat, and my voice wanted to tremble.

"Will it be over?" Billy asked. "Daddy? Will it?"

"I don't know," I said, and he put his face in the hollow of my shoulder and I held the back of his head, felt the delicate curve of his skull just under the thick growth of his hair. I found myself remembering the evening of my wedding day. Watching Steff take off the simple brown dress she had changed into after the ceremony. She had had a big purple bruise on one hip from running into the side of a door the day before. I remembered looking at the bruise and thinking, *When she got that, she was still Stephanie Stepanek*, and feeling something like wonder. Then we had made love, and outside it was spitting snow from a dull gray December sky.

Billy was crying.

"Shh, Billy, shh," I said, rocking his head against me, but he went on crying. It was the sort of crying that only mothers know how to fix right.

Premature night came inside the Federal Foods. Miller and Hatlen and Bud Brown handed out flashlights, the whole stock, about twenty. Norton clamored loudly for them on behalf of his group, and received two. The lights bobbed here and there in the aisles like uneasy phantoms.

I held Billy against me and looked out through the loophole. The milky, translucent quality of the light out there hadn't changed much; it was putting up the bags that had made the market so dark. Several times I thought I saw something, but it was only jumpiness. One of the others raised a hesitant false alarm.

Billy saw Mrs. Turman again, and went to her eagerly, even though she hadn't been over to sit for him all summer. She had one of the flashlights and handed it over to him amiably enough. Soon he was trying to write his name in light on the blank glass faces of the frozen-food cases. She seemed as happy to see him as he was to see her, and in a little while they came over. Hattie Turman was a tall, thin woman with lovely red hair just beginning to streak gray. A pair of glasses hung from an ornamental chain—the sort, I believe, it is illegal for anyone except middle-aged women to wear—on her breast.

"Is Stephanie here, David?" she asked.

"No. At home."

She nodded. "Alan, too. How long are you on watch here?"

"Until six."

"Have you seen anything?"

"No. Just the mist."

"I'll keep Billy until six, if you like."

"Would you like that, Billy?"

"Yes, please," he said, swinging the flashlight above his head in slow arcs and watching it play across the ceiling.

"God will keep your Steffy, and Alan, too," Mrs. Turman said, and led Billy away by the hand. She spoke with serene sureness, but there was no conviction in her eyes.

Around five-thirty the sounds of excited argument rose near the back of the store. Someone jeered at something someone else had said, and someone—it was Buddy Eagleton, I think—shouted, "You're crazy if you go out there!"

Several of the flashlight beams pooled together at the center of the controversy, and they moved toward the front of the store. Mrs. Carmody's shrieking, derisive laugh split the gloom, as abrasive as fingers drawn down a slate blackboard.

Above the babble of voices came the boom of Norton's courtroom tenor: "Let us pass, please! Let us pass!"

The man at the loophole next to mine left his place to see what the shouting was about. I decided to stay where I was. Whatever the concatenation was, it was coming my way.

"Please," Mike Hatlen was saying. "Please, let's talk this thing through."

"There is nothing to talk about," Norton proclaimed. Now his face swam out of the gloom. It was determined and haggard and wholly wretched. He was holding one of the two flashlights allocated to the Flat-Earthers. The corkscrewed tufts of hair still stuck up behind his ears like a cuckold's horns. He was at the head of an extremely small procession—five of the original nine or ten. "We are going out," he said.

"Don't stick to this craziness," Miller said. "Mike's right. We can talk it over, can't we? Mr. McVey is going to barbecue some chicken over the gas grill, we can all sit down and eat and just—"

He got in Norton's way and Norton gave him a push. Miller didn't like it. His face flushed and then set in a hard expression. "Do what you want, then," he said. "But you're as good as murdering these other people."

With all the evenness of great resolve or unbreakable obsession, Norton said: "We'll send help back for you."

One of his followers murmured agreement, but another quietly slipped away. Now there was Norton and four others. Maybe that wasn't so bad. Christ Himself could only find twelve.

"Listen," Mike Hatlen said. "Mr. Norton—Brent—at least stay for the chicken. Get some hot food inside you."

"And give you a chance to go on talking? I've been in too many courtrooms to fall for that. You've psyched out half a dozen of my people already."

"Your people?" Hatlen almost groaned it. "*Your* people? Good Christ, what kind of talk is that? They're *people,* that's all. This is no game, and it's surely not a courtroom. There are, for want of a better word, there are *things* out there, and what's the sense of getting yourself killed?"

"Things, you say," Norton said, sounding superficially amused. "Where? Your people have been on watch for a couple of hours now. Who's seen one?"

"Well, out back. In the—"

"No, no, no," Norton said, shaking his head. "That ground has been covered and covered. We're going out—"

"No," someone whispered, and it echoed and spread, sounding like the rustle of dead leaves at dusk of an October evening. *No, no, no . . .*

"Will you restrain us?" a shrill voice asked. This was one of Norton's "people," to use his word—an elderly lady wearing bifocals. "Will you restrain us?"

The soft babble of negatives died away.

"No," Mike said. "No, I don't think anyone will restrain you."

I whispered in Billy's ear. He looked at me, startled and questioning. "Go on, now," I said. "Be quick."

He went.

Norton ran his hands through his hair, a gesture as calculated as any ever made by a Broadway actor. I had liked him better pulling the cord of his chainsaw fruitlessly, cussing and thinking himself unobserved. I could not tell then and do not know any better now if he believed in what he was doing or not. I think, down deep, that he knew what was going to happen. I think that the logic he had paid lip service to all his life turned on him at the end like a tiger that has gone bad and mean.

He looked around restlessly, seeming to wish that there was more to say. Then he led his four followers through one of the checkout lanes. In addition to the elderly woman, there was a chubby boy of about twenty, a young girl, and a man in blue jeans wearing a golf cap tipped back on his head.

Norton's eyes caught mine, widened a little, and then started to swing away.

"Brent, wait a minute," I said.

"I don't want to discuss it any further. Certainly not with you."

"I know you don't. I just want to ask a favor." I looked around and saw Billy coming back toward the checkouts at a run.

"What's that?" Norton asked suspiciously as Billy came up and handed me a package done up in cellophane.

"Clothesline," I said. I was vaguely aware that everyone in the market was watching us now, loosely strung out on the other side of the cash registers and checkout lanes. "It's the big package. Three hundred feet."

"So?"

"I wondered if you'd tie one end around your waist before you go out. I'll let it out. When you feel it come up tight, just tie it around something. It doesn't matter what. A car door handle would do."

"What in God's name for?"

"It will tell me you got at least three hundred feet," I said.

Something in his eyes flickered . . . but only momentarily. "No," he said.

I shrugged. "Okay. Good luck, anyhow."

Abruptly the man in the golf cap said, "I'll do it, mister. No reason not to."

Norton swung on him, as if to say something sharp, and the man in the golf cap studied him calmly. There was nothing flickering in *his* eyes. He had made his decision and there was simply no doubt in him. Norton saw it too and said nothing.

"Thanks," I said.

I slit the wrapping with my pocketknife and the clothesline accordioned out in stiff loops. I found one loose end and tied it around Golf Cap's waist in a loose granny. He immediately untied it and cinched it tighter with a good quick sheet-bend knot. There was not a sound in the market. Norton shifted uneasily from foot to foot.

"You want to take my knife?" I asked the man in the golf cap.

"I got one." He looked at me with that same calm contempt. "You just see to paying out your line. If it binds up, I'll chuck her."

"Are we all ready?" Norton asked, too loud. The chubby boy jumped as if he had been goosed. Getting no response, Norton turned to go.

"Brent," I said, and held out my hand. "Good luck, man."

He studied my hand as if it were some dubious foreign object. "We'll send back help," he said finally, and pushed through the OUT door. That thin, acrid smell came in again. The others followed him out.

Mike Hatlen came down and stood beside me. Norton's party of five stood in the milky, slow-moving fog. Norton said something and I should have heard it, but the mist seemed to have an odd damping effect. I heard nothing but the sound of his voice and two or three isolated syllables, like the voice on the radio heard from some distance. They moved off.

Hatlen held the door a little way open. I paid out the clothesline, keeping as much slack in it as I could, mindful of the man's promise to chuck the rope if it bound him up. There was still not a sound. Billy stood beside me, motionless but seeming to thrum with his own inner current.

Again there was that weird feeling that the five of them did not so much disappear into the fog as become invisible. For a moment their clothes seemed to stand alone, and then they were gone. You were not really impressed with the unnatural density of the mist until you saw people swallowed up in a space of seconds.

I paid the line out. A quarter of it went, then a half. It stopped going out for a moment. It went from a live thing to a dead one in my hands. I held my breath. Then it started to go out again. I paid it through my fingers, and suddenly remembered my father taking me to see the Gregory Peck film of *Moby Dick* at the Brookside. I think I smiled a little.

Three-quarters of the line was gone now. I could see the end of it lying beside one of Billy's feet. Then the rope stopped moving through my hands again. It lay motionless for perhaps five seconds, and then another five feet jerked out. Then it suddenly whipsawed violently to the left, twanging off the edge of the OUT door.

Twenty feet of rope suddenly paid out, making a thin heat across my left palm. And from out of the mist there came a high, wavering scream. It was impossible to tell the sex of the screamer.

The rope whipsawed in my hands again. And again. It skated across the space in the doorway to the right, then back to the left. A few more feet paid out, and then there was a ululating howl from out there that brought an answering moan from my son. Hatlen stood aghast. His eyes were huge. One corner of his mouth turned down, trembling.

The howl was abruptly cut off. There was no sound at all for what seemed to be forever. Then the old lady cried out—this time there could be no doubt about who it was. *"Git it offa me!"* she screamed. *"Oh my Lord my Lord get it—"*

Then her voice was cut off, too.

Almost all of the rope abruptly ran out through my loosely closed fist, giving me a hotter burn this time. Then it went completely slack, and a sound came out of the mist—a thick, loud grunt—that made all the spit in my mouth dry up.

It was like no sound I've ever heard, but the closest approximation might be a movie set in the African veld or a South

American swamp. It was the sound of a big animal. It came again, low and tearing and savage. Once more . . . and then it subsided to a series of low mutterings. Then it was completely gone.

"Close the door," Amanda Dumfries said in a trembling voice. "Please."

"In a minute," I said, and began to yank the line back in.

It came out of the mist and piled up around my feet in untidy loops and snarls. About three feet from the end, the new white clothesline went barn-red.

"Death!" Mrs. Carmody screamed. "Death to go out there! Now do you see?"

The end of the clothesline was a chewed and frayed tangle of fiber and little puffs of cotton. The little puffs were dewed with minute drops of blood.

No one contradicted Mrs. Carmody.

Mike Hatlen let the door swing shut.

VII. The First Night.

Mr. McVey had worked in Bridgton cutting meat ever since I was twelve or thirteen, and I had no idea what his first name was or his age might be. He had set up a gas grill under one of the small exhaust fans—the fans were still now, but presumably they still gave some ventilation—and by 6:30 P.M. the smell of cooking chicken filled the market. Bud Brown didn't object. It might have been shock, but more likely he had recognized the fact that his fresh meat and poultry wasn't getting any fresher. The chicken smelled good, but not many people wanted to eat. Mr. McVey, small and spare and neat in his whites, cooked the chicken nevertheless and laid the pieces two by two on paper plates and lined them up cafeteria-style on top of the meat counter.

Mrs. Turman brought Billy and me each a plate, garnished with helpings of deli potato salad. I ate as best I could, but Billy would not even pick at his.

"You got to eat, big guy," I said.

"I'm not hungry," he said, putting the plate aside.

"You can't get big and strong if you don't—"

Mrs. Turman, sitting slightly behind Billy, shook her head at me.

"Okay," I said. "Go get a peach and eat it, at least. 'Kay?"

"What if Mr. Brown says something?"

"If he says something, you come back and tell me."

"Okay, Dad."

He walked away slowly. He seemed to have shrunk somehow. It hurt my heart to see him walk that way. Mr. McVey went on cooking chicken, apparently not minding that only a few people were eating it, happy in the act of cooking. As I think I have said, there are all ways of handling a thing like this. You wouldn't think it would be so, but it is. The mind is a monkey.

Mrs. Turman and I sat halfway up the patent-medicines aisle. People were sitting in little groups all over the store. No one except Mrs. Carmody was sitting alone; even Myron and his buddy Jim were together—they were both passed out by the beer cooler.

Six new men were watching the loopholes. One of them was Ollie, gnawing a leg of chicken and drinking a beer. The mop-handle torches leaned beside each of the watchposts, a can of charcoal lighter fluid next to each . . . but I don't think anyone really believed in the torches the way they had before. Not after that low and terribly vital grunting sound, not after the chewed and blood-soaked clothesline. If whatever was out there decided it wanted us, it was going to have us. It, or they.

"How bad will it be tonight?" Mrs. Turman asked. Her voice was calm, but her eyes were sick and scared.

"Hattie, I just don't know."

"You let me keep Billy as much as you can. I'm . . . Davey, I think I'm in mortal terror." She uttered a dry laugh. "Yes, I believe that's what it is. But if I have Billy, I'll be all right. I'll be all right for him."

Her eyes were glistening. I leaned over and patted her shoulder.

"I'm so worried about Alan," she said. "He's dead, Davey. In my heart, I'm sure he's dead."

"No, Hattie. You don't know any such thing."

"But I feel it's true. Don't you feel anything about Stephanie? Don't you at least have a . . . a feeling?"

"No," I said, lying through my teeth.

A strangled sound came from her throat and she clapped a hand to her mouth. Her glasses reflected back the dim, murky light.

"Billy's coming back," I murmured.

He was eating a peach. Hattie Turman patted the floor beside her and said that when he was done she would show him how to make a little man out of the peach pit and some thread. Billy smiled at her wanly, and Mrs. Turman smiled back.

At 8:00 P.M. six new men went on at the loopholes and Ollie came over to where I was sitting. "Where's Billy?"

"With Mrs. Turman, up back," I said. "They're doing crafts. They've run through peach-pit men and shopping-bag masks and apple dolls and now Mr. McVey is showing him how to make pipe-cleaner men."

Ollie took a long drink of beer and said, "Things are moving around out there."

I looked at him sharply. He looked back levelly.

"I'm not drunk," he said. "I've been trying but haven't been able to make it. I wish I could, David."

"What do you mean, things are moving around out there?"

"I can't say for sure. I asked Walter, and he said he had the same feeling, that parts of the mist would go darker for a minute—sometimes just a little smudge, sometimes a big dark place, like a bruise. Then it would fade back to gray. And the stuff is swirling around. Even Arnie Simms said he felt like something was going on out there, and Arnie's almost as blind as a bat."

"What about the others?"

"They're all out-of-staters, strangers to me," Ollie said. "I didn't ask any of them."

"How sure are you that you weren't just seeing things?"

"Sure," he said. He nodded toward Mrs. Carmody, who was sitting by herself at the end of the aisle. None of it had hurt her appetite any; there was a graveyard of chicken bones on her plate. She was drinking either blood or V-8 juice. "I think she was right about one thing," Ollie said. "We'll find out. When it gets dark, we'll find out."

But we didn't have to wait until dark. When it came, Billy saw very little of it, because Mrs. Turman kept him up back. Ollie was still sitting with me when one of the men up front gave out a shriek and staggered back from his post, pinwheeling his arms. It was approaching eight-thirty; outside the pearl-white mist had darkened to the dull slaty color of a November twilight.

Something had landed on the glass outside one of the loopholes.

"Oh my Jesus!" the man who had been watching there screamed. *"Let me out! Let me out of this!"*

He tore around in a rambling circle, his eyes starting from his face, a thin lick of saliva at one corner of his mouth glimmering in the deepening shadows. Then he took off straight up the far aisle past the frozen-food cases.

There were answering cries. Some people ran toward the front to see what had happened. Many others retreated toward the back, not caring and not wanting to see whatever was crawling on the glass out there.

I started down toward the loophole, Ollie by my side. His hand was in the pocket that held Mrs. Dumfries' gun. Now one of the other watchers let out a cry—not so much of fear as disgust.

Ollie and I slipped through one of the checkout lanes. Now I could see what had frightened the guy from his post. I couldn't tell what it was, but I could see it. It looked like one of the minor creatures in a Bosch painting—one of his hellacious murals. There was something almost horribly comic about it, too, because it also looked a little like one of those strange creations of vinyl and plastic you can buy for $1.89 to spring on your friends . . . in fact, exactly the sort of thing Norton had accused me of planting in the storage area.

It was maybe two feet long, segmented, the pinkish color of burned flesh that has healed over. Bulbous eyes peered in two different directions at once from the ends of short, limber stalks. It clung to the window on fat sucker-pads. From the opposite end there protruded something that was either a sexual organ or a stinger. And from its back there sprouted oversized, membranous wings, like the wings of a housefly. They were moving very slowly as Ollie and I approached the glass.

At the loophole to the left of us, where the man had made

the disgusted cawing sound, three of the things were crawling on the glass. They moved sluggishly across it, leaving sticky snail trails behind them. Their eyes—if that is what they were—joggled on the end of the finger-thick stalks. The biggest was maybe four feet long. At times they crawled right over each other.

"Look at those goddam things," Tom Smalley said in a sickened voice. He was standing at the loophole on our right. I didn't reply. The bugs were all over the loopholes now, which meant they were probably crawling all over the building . . . like maggots on a piece of meat. It wasn't a pleasant image, and I could feel what chicken I had managed to eat now wanting to come up.

Someone was sobbing. Mrs. Carmody was screaming about abominations from within the earth. Someone told her gruffly that she'd shut up if she knew what was good for her. Same old shit.

Ollie took Mrs. Dumfries' gun from his pocket and I grabbed his arm. "Don't be crazy."

He shook free. "I know what I'm doing," he said.

He tapped the barrel of the gun on the window, his face set in a nearly masklike expression of distaste. The speed of the creatures' wings increased until they were only a blur—if you hadn't known, you might have believed they weren't winged creatures at all. Then they simply flew away.

Some of the others saw what Ollie had done and got the idea. They used the mop handles to tap on the windows. The things flew away, but came right back. Apparently they had no more brains than your average housefly, either. The near-panic dissolved in a babble of conversation. I heard someone asking someone else what he thought those things would do if they landed on you. That was a question I had no interest in seeing answered.

The tapping on the windows began to die away. Ollie turned toward me and started to say something, but before he could do more than open his mouth, something came out of the fog and snatched one of the crawling things off the glass. I think I screamed. I'm not sure.

It was a flying thing. Beyond that I could not have said for sure. The fog appeared to darken in exactly the way Ollie had described, only the dark smutch didn't fade away; it solidified into something with flapping, leathery wings, an albino-white body, and reddish eyes. It thudded into the glass hard enough to make it shiver. Its beak opened. It scooped the pink thing in and was gone. The whole incident took no more than five seconds. I had a bare final impression of the pink thing wiggling and flapping as it went down the hatch, the way a small fish will wiggle and flap in the beak of a seagull.

Now there was another thud, and yet another. People began screaming again, and there was a stampede toward the back of the store. Then there was a more piercing scream, one of pain, and Ollie said, "Oh my God, that old lady fell down and they just ran over her."

He ran back through the checkout aisle. I turned to follow, and then I saw something that stopped me dead where I was standing.

High up and to my right, one of the lawn-food bags was sliding slowly backward. Tom Smalley was right under it, staring out into the mist through his loophole.

Another of the pink bugs landed on the thick plate glass of the loophole where Ollie and I had been standing. One of the flying things swooped down and grabbed it. The old woman who had been trampled went on screaming in a shrill, cracked voice.

That bag. That sliding bag.

"Smalley!" I shouted. "Look out! Heads up!"

In the general confusion, he never heard me. The bag teetered, then fell. It struck him squarely on the head. He went down hard, catching his jaw on the shelf that ran below the show window.

One of the albino flying things was squirming its way through the jagged hole in the glass. I could hear the soft scraping sound that it made, now that some of the screaming had stopped. Its red eyes glittered in its triangular head, which was slightly cocked to one side. A heavy, hooked beak opened and closed rapaciously. It looked a bit like the paintings of pterodactyls you may have seen in the dinosaur books, more like something out of a lunatic's nightmare.

I grabbed one of the torches and slam-dunked it into a can of charcoal lighter fluid, tipping it over and spilling a pool of the stuff across the floor.

The flying creature paused on top of the lawn-food bags, glaring around, shifting slowly and malignantly from one taloned foot to the other. It was a stupid creature, I am quite sure of that. Twice it tried to spread its wings, which struck the walls and then folded themselves over its hunched back like the wings of a griffin. The third time it tried, it lost its balance and fell clumsily from its perch, still trying to spread its wings. It landed on Tom Smalley's back. One flex of its claws and Tom's shirt ripped wide open. Blood began to flow.

I was there, less than three feet away. My torch was dripping lighter fluid. I was emotionally pumped up to kill it if I could . . . and then realized I had no matches to light it with. I had used the last one lighting a cigar for Mr. McVey an hour ago.

The place was in pandemonium now. People had seen the thing roosting on Smalley's back, something no one in the world had seen before. It darted its head forward at a questing angle, and tore a chunk of meat from the back of Smalley's neck.

I was getting ready to use the torch as a bludgeon when the cloth wrapped head of it suddenly blazed alight. Dan Miller was there, holding a Zippo lighter with a Marine emblem on it. His face was as harsh as a rock with horror and fury.

"Kill it," he said hoarsely. "Kill it if you can." Standing beside him was Ollie. He had Mrs. Dumfries' .38 in his hand, but he had no clear shot.

The thing spread its wings and flapped them once—apparently not to fly away but to secure a better hold on its prey—and then its leathery-white, membranous wings enfolded poor Smalley's entire upper body. Then the sounds came—mortal tearing sounds that I cannot bear to describe in any detail.

All of this happened in bare seconds. Then I thrust my torch at the thing. There was the sensation of striking something with no more real substance than a box kite. The next moment the entire creature was blazing. It made a screeching sound and its wings spread; its head jerked and its reddish eyes rolled with what I most sincerely hope was great agony. It took off with a sound like linen bedsheets flapping on a clothesline in a stiff spring breeze. It uttered that rusty shrieking sound again.

Heads turned up to follow its flaming, dying course. I think that nothing in the entire business stands in my memory so strongly as that bird-thing blazing a zigzagging course above the aisles of the Federal Supermarket, dropping charred and smoking bits of itself here and there. It finally crashed into the spaghetti sauces, splattering Ragú and Prince and Prima Salsa everywhere like gouts of blood. It was little more than ash and bone. The smell of its burning was high and sickening. And underlying it like a counterpoint was the thin and acrid stench of the mist, eddying in through the broken place in the glass.

For a moment there was utter silence. We were united in the black wonder of that brightly flaming deathflight. Then someone howled. Others screamed. And from somewhere in the back I could hear my son crying.

A hand grabbed me. It was Bud Brown. His eyes were bulging from their sockets. His lips were drawn back from his false teeth in a snarl. "One of those other things," he said, and pointed.

One of the bugs had come in through the hole and it now perched on a lawn-food bag, housefly wings buzzing—you could hear them; it sounded like a cheap department-store electric fan—eyes bulging from their stalks. Its pink and noxiously plump body was aspirating rapidly.

I moved toward it. My torch was guttering but not yet out. But Mrs. Reppler, the third-grade teacher, beat me to it. She was maybe fifty-five, maybe sixty, rope-thin. Her body had a tough, dried-out look that always makes me think of beef jerky.

She had a can of Raid in each hand like some crazy gunslinger in an existential comedy. She uttered a snarl of anger that would have done credit to a caveman splitting the skull of an enemy. Holding the pressure cans out at the full length of each arm, she pressed the buttons. A thick spray of insect-killer coated the thing. It went into throes of agony, twisting and turning crazily and at last falling from the bags, bouncing off the body of Tom Smalley—who was dead beyond any doubt or question—and finally landing on the floor. Its wings buzzed madly, but they weren't taking it anywhere; they were too heavily coated with Raid. A few moments later the wings slowed, then stopped. It was dead.

You could hear people crying now. And moaning. The old

lady who had been trampled was moaning. And you could hear laughter. The laughter of the damned. Mrs. Reppler stood over her kill, her thin chest rising and falling rapidly.

Hatlen and Miller had found one of those dollies that the stockboys use to trundle cases of things around the store, and together they heaved it atop the lawn-food bags, blocking off the wedge-shaped hole in the glass. As a temporary measure, it was a good one.

Amanda Dumfries came forward like a sleepwalker. In one hand she held a plastic floor bucket. In the other she held a whisk broom, still done up in its see-through wrapping. She bent, her eyes still wide and blank, and swept the dead pink thing—bug, slug, whatever it was—into the bucket. You could hear the crackle of the wrapping on the whisk broom as it brushed the floor. She walked over to the OUT door. There were none of the bugs on it. She opened it a little way and threw the bucket out. It landed on its side and rolled back and forth in ever-decreasing arcs. One of the pink things buzzed out of the night, landed on the floor pail, and began to crawl over it.

Amanda burst into tears. I walked over and put an arm around her shoulders.

At one-thirty the following morning I was sitting with my back against the white enamel side of the meat counter in a semidoze. Billy's head was in my lap. He was solidly asleep. Not far away Amanda Dumfries was sleeping with her head pillowed on someone's jacket.

Not long after the flaming death of the bird-thing, Ollie and I had gone back out to the storage area and had gathered up half a dozen of the pads such as the one I'd covered Billy with earlier. Several people were sleeping on these. We had also brought back several heavy crates of oranges and pears, and four of us working together had been able to swing them to the tops of the lawn-food bags in front of the hole in the glass. The bird-creatures would have a tough time shifting one of those crates; they weighed about ninety pounds each.

But the birds and the buglike things the birds ate weren't the only things out there. There was the tentacled thing that had taken Norm. There was the frayed clothesline to think about. There was the unseen thing that had uttered that low, guttural roar to think about. We had heard sounds like it since—sometimes quite distant—but how far was "distant" through the damping effect of the mist? And sometimes they were close enough to shake the building and make it seem as if the ventricles of your heart had suddenly been loaded up with ice water.

Billy started in my lap and moaned. I brushed his hair and he moaned more loudly. Then he seemed to find sleep's less dangerous waters again. My own doze was broken and I was staring wide awake again. Since dark, I had only managed to sleep about ninety minutes, and that had been dream-haunted. In one of the dream fragments it had been the night before again. Billy and Steffy were standing in front of the picture window, looking out at the black and slate-gray waters, out at the silver spinning waterspout that heralded the storm. I tried to get to them, knowing that a strong enough wind could break the window and throw deadly glass darts all the way across the living room. But no matter how I ran, I seemed to get no closer to them. And then a bird rose out of the waterspout, a gigantic scarlet *oiseau de mort* whose prehistoric wingspan darkened the entire lake from west to east. Its beak opened, revealing a maw the size of the Holland Tunnel. And as the bird came to gobble up my wife and son, a low, sinister voice began to whisper over and over again: *The Arrowhead Project . . . the Arrowhead Project . . . the Arrowhead Project . . .*

Not that Billy and I were the only ones sleeping poorly. Others screamed in their sleep, and some went on screaming after they woke up. The beer was disappearing from the cooler at a great rate. Buddy Eagleton had restocked it once from out back with no comment. Mike Hatlen told me the Sominex was gone. Not depleted but totally wiped out. He guessed that some people might have taken six or eight bottles.

"There's some Nytol left," he said. "You want a bottle, David?" I shook my head and thanked him.

And in the last aisle down by Register 5, we had our winos. There were about seven of them, all out-of-staters except for Lou Tattinger, who ran the Pine Tree Car Wash. Lou didn't need any excuse to sniff the cork, as the saying was. The wino brigade was pretty well anesthetized.

Oh yes—there were also six or seven people who had gone crazy.

Crazy isn't the best word; perhaps I just can't think of the proper one. But there were these people who had lapsed into a complete stupor without benefit of beer, wine, or pills. They stared at you with blank and shiny doorknob eyes. The hard cement of reality had come apart in some unimaginable earthquake, and these poor devils had fallen through. In time, some of them might come back. If there was time.

The rest of us had made our own mental compromises, and in some cases I suppose they were fairly odd. Mrs. Reppler, for instance, was convinced the whole thing was a dream—or so she said. And she spoke with some conviction.

I looked over at Amanda. I was developing an uncomfortably strong feeling for her—uncomfortable but not exactly unpleasant. Her eyes were an incredible, brilliant green . . . for a while I had kept an eye on her to see if she was going to take out a pair of contact lenses, but apparently the color was true. I wanted to make love to her. My wife was at home, maybe alive, more probably dead, alone either way, and I loved her; I wanted to get Billy and me back to her more than anything, but I also wanted to screw this lady named Amanda Dumfries. I tried to tell myself it was just the situation we were in, and maybe it was, but that didn't change the wanting.

I dozed in and out, then jerked awake more fully around three. Amanda had shifted into a sort of fetal position, her knees pulled up toward her chest, hands clasped between her thighs. She seemed to be sleeping deeply. Her sweatshirt had pulled up slightly on one side, showing clean white skin. I looked at it and began to get an extremely useless and uncomfortable erection.

I tried to divert my mind to a new track and got thinking about how I had wanted to paint Brent Norton yesterday. No, nothing as important as a painting, but . . . just sit him on a log with my beer in his hand and sketch his sweaty, tired face and the two wings of his carefully processed hair sticking up untidily in the back. It could have been a good picture. It took me twenty years of living with my father to accept the idea that being good could be good enough.

You know what talent is? The curse of expectation. As a kid you have to deal with that, beat it somehow. If you can write, you think God put you on earth to blow Shakespeare away. Of if you can paint, maybe you think—I did—that God put you on earth to blow your father away.

It turned out I wasn't as good as he was. I kept trying to be for longer than I should have, maybe. I had a show in New York and it did poorly—the art critics beat me over the head with my father. A year later I was supporting myself and Steff with the commercial stuff. She was pregnant and I sat down and talked to myself about it. The result of that conversation was a belief that serious art was always going to be a hobby for me, no more.

I did Golden Girl Shampoo ads—the one where the Girl is standing astride her bike, the one where she's playing Frisbee on the beach, the one where she's standing on the balcony of her apartment with a drink in her hand. I've done short-story illustrations for most of the big slicks, but I broke into that field doing fast illustrations for the stories in the sleazier men's magazines. I've done some movie posters. The money comes in. We keep our heads nicely above water.

I had one final show in Bridgton, just last summer. I showed nine canvases that I had painted in five years, and I sold six of them. The one I absolutely would not sell showed the Federal market, by some queer coincidence. The perspective was from the far end of the parking lot. In my picture, the parking lot was empty except for a line of Campbell's Beans and Franks cans, each one larger than the last as they marched toward the viewer's eye. The last one appeared to be about eight feet tall. The picture was titled *Beans and False Perspective.* A man from California who was a top exec in some company that makes tennis balls and rackets and who knows what other sports equipment seemed to want that picture very badly, and would not take no for an answer in spite of the NFS card tucked into the bottom left-hand corner of the spare wooden frame. He began at six hundred dollars and worked his way up to four thousand. He said he wanted it for his study. I would not let him have it, and he went away sorely puzzled. Even so, he didn't quite give up; he left his card in case I changed my mind.

I could have used the money—that was the year we put the addition on the house and bought the four-wheel-drive—but I just couldn't sell it. I couldn't sell it because I felt it was the best painting I had ever done and I wanted it to look at after someone would ask me, with totally unconscious cruelty, when I was going to do something serious.

Then I happened to show it to Ollie Weeks one day last fall. He asked me if he could photograph it and run it as an ad one week, and that was the end of my own false perspective. Ollie had recognized my painting for what it was, and by doing so, he forced me to recognize it, too. A perfectly good piece of slick commercial art. No more. And, thank God, no less.

I let him do it, and then I called the exec at his home in San Luis Obispo and told him he could have the painting for twenty-five hundred if he still wanted it. He did, and I shipped it UPS to the coast. And since then that voice of disappointed expectation—that cheated child's voice that can never be satisfied with such a mild superlative as good—has fallen pretty much silent. And except for a few rumbles—like the sounds of those unseen creatures somewhere out in the foggy night—it has been pretty much silent ever since. Maybe you can tell me—why should the silencing of that childish, demanding voice seem so much like dying?

Around four o'clock Billy woke up—partially, at least—and looked around with bleary, uncomprehending eyes. "Are we still here?"

"Yeah, honey," I said. "We are."

He started to cry with a weak helplessness that was horrible. Amanda woke up and looked at us.

"Hey, kid," she said, and pulled him gently to her. "Everything is going to look a little better come morning."

"No," Billy said. "No it won't. It won't. It won't."

"Shh," she said. Her eyes met mine over his head. "Shh, it's past your bedtime."

"I want my *mother!*"

"Yeah, you do," Amanda said. "Of course you do."

Billy squirmed around in her lap until he could look at me. Which he did for some time. And then slept again.

"Thanks," I said. "He needed you."

"He doesn't even know me."

"That doesn't change it."

"So what do you think?" she asked. Her green eyes held mine steadily. "What do you really think?"

"Ask me in the morning."

"I'm asking you now."

I opened my mouth to answer and then Ollie Weeks materialized out of the gloom like something from a horror tale. He had a flashlight with one of the ladies' blouses over the lens, and he was pointing it toward the ceiling. It made strange shadows on his haggard face. "David," he whispered.

Amanda looked at him, first startled, then scared again.

"Ollie, what is it?" I asked.

"David," he whispered again. Then: "Come on. Please."

"I don't want to leave Billy. He just went to sleep."

"I'll be with him," Amanda said. "You better go." Then, in a lower voice: "Jesus, this is never going to end."

VIII. What Happened to the Soldiers. With Amanda. A Conversation with Dan Miller.

I went with Ollie. He was headed for the storage area. As we passed the cooler, he grabbed a beer.

"Ollie, what is it?"

"I want you to see it."

He pushed through the double doors. They slipped shut behind us with a little backwash of air. It was cold. I didn't like this place, not after what had happened to Norm. A part of my mind insisted on reminding me that there was still a small scrap of dead tentacle lying around someplace.

Ollie let the blouse drop from the lens of his light. He trained it overhead. At first I had an idea that someone had hung a couple of mannequins from one of the heating pipes below the ceiling. That they had hung them on piano wire or something, a kid's Halloween trick.

Then I noticed the feet, dangling about seven inches off the cement floor. There were two piles of kicked-over cartons. I looked up at the faces and a scream began to rise in my throat because they were not the faces of department-store dummies. Both heads were cocked to the side, as if appreciating some horribly funny joke, a joke that had made them laugh until they turned purple.

Their shadows. Their shadows thrown long on the wall behind them. Their tongues. Their protruding tongues.

They were both wearing uniforms. They were the kids I had noticed earlier and had lost track of along the way. The army brats from—

The scream. I could hear it starting in my throat as a moan, rising like a police siren, and then Ollie gripped my arm just above the elbow. "Don't scream, David. No one knows about this but you and me. And that's how I want to keep it."

Somehow I bit it back.

"Those army kids," I managed.

"From the Arrowhead Project," Ollie said. "Sure." Something cold was thrust into my hand. The beer can. "Drink this. You need it."

I drained the can completely dry.

Ollie said, "I came back to see if we had any extra cartridges for that gas grill Mr. McVey has been using. I saw these guys. The way I figure, they must have gotten the nooses ready and stood on top of those two piles of cartons. They must have tied their hands for each other and then balanced each other while they stepped through the length of rope between their wrists. So . . . so that their hands would be behind them, you know. Then—this is the way I figure—they stuck their heads into the nooses and pulled them tight by jerking their heads to one side. Maybe one of them counted to three and they jumped together. I don't know."

"It couldn't be done," I said through a dry mouth. But their hands were tied behind them, all right. I couldn't seem to take my eyes away from that.

"It could. If they wanted to bad enough, David, they could."

"But why?"

"I think you know why. Not any of the tourists, the summer people—like that guy Miller—but there are people from around here who could make a pretty decent guess."

"The Arrowhead Project?"

Ollie said, "I stand by one of those registers all day long and I hear a lot. All this spring I've been hearing things about that damned Arrowhead thing, none of it good. The black ice on the lakes—"

I thought of Bill Giosti leaning in my window, blowing warm alcohol in my face. Not just atoms, but *different* atoms. Now these bodies hanging from that overhead pipe. The cocked heads. The dangling shoes. The tongues protruding like summer sausages.

I realized with fresh horror that new doors of perception were opening up inside. New? Not so. Old doors of perception. The perception of a child who has not yet learned to protect itself by developing the tunnel vision that keeps out ninety percent of the universe. Children see everything their eyes happen upon, hear everything in their ears' range. But if life is the rise of consciousness (as a crewel-work sampler my wife made in high school proclaims), then it is also the reduction of input.

Terror is the widening of perspective and perception. The horror was in knowing I was swimming down to a place most of us leave when we get out of diapers and into training pants. I could see it on Ollie's face, too. When rationality begins to break down, the circuits of the human brain can overload. Axons grow bright and feverish. Hallucinations turn real: the quicksilver puddle at the point where perspective makes parallel lines seem to intersect is really there; the dead walk and talk; a rose begins to sing.

"I've heard stuff from maybe two dozen people," Ollie said. "Justine Robards. Nick Tochai. Ben Michaelson. You can't keep secrets in small towns. Things get out. Sometimes it's like a spring—it just bubbles up out of the earth and no one has an idea where it came from. You overhear something at the library and pass it on, or at the marina in Harrison, Christ knows where else, or why. But all spring and summer I've been hearing Arrowhead Project, Arrowhead Project."

"But these two," I said. "Christ, Ollie, they're just kids."

"There were kids in Nam who used to take ears. I was there. I saw it."

"But . . . what would drive them to do this?"

"I don't know. Maybe they knew something. Maybe they only suspected. They must have known people in here would start asking them questions eventually. If there is an eventually."

"If you're right," I said, "it must be something really bad."

"That storm," Ollie said in his soft, level voice. "Maybe it knocked something loose up there. Maybe there was an accident. They could have been fooling around with anything. Some people claim they were messing with high-intensity lasers and masers. Sometimes I hear fusion power. And suppose . . . suppose they ripped a hole straight through into another dimension?"

"That's hogwash," I said.

"Are they?" Ollie asked, and pointed at the bodies.

"No. The question now is: What do we do?"

"I think we ought to cut them down and hide them," he said promptly. "Put them under a pile of stuff people won't want—dog food, dish detergent, stuff like that. If this gets out, it will only make things worse. That's why I came to you, David. I felt you are the only one I could really trust."

I muttered, "It's like the Nazi war criminals killing themselves in their cells after the war was lost."

"Yeah. I had that same thought."

We fell silent, and suddenly those soft shuffling noises began outside the steel loading door again—the sound of the tentacles feeling softly across it. We drew together. My flesh was crawling.

"Okay," I said.

"We'll make it as quick as we can," Ollie said. His sapphire ring glowed mutely as he moved his flashlight. "I want to get out of here fast."

I looked up at the ropes. They had used the same sort of clothesline the man in the golf cap had allowed me to tie around his waist. The nooses had sunk into the puffed flesh of their necks, and I wondered again what it could have been to make both of them go through with it. I knew what Ollie meant by saying that if the news of the double suicide got out, it would make things worse. For me it already had—and I wouldn't have believed that possible.

There was a snicking sound. Ollie had opened his knife, a good heavy job made for slitting open cartons. And, of course, cutting rope.

"You or me?" he asked.

I swallowed. "One each."

We did it.

When I got back, Amanda was gone and Mrs. Turman was with Billy. They were both sleeping. I walked down one of the aisles and a voice said: "Mr. Drayton. David." It was Amanda, standing by the stairs to the manager's office, her eyes like emeralds. "What was it?"

"Nothing," I said.

She came over to me. I could smell faint perfume. And oh how I wanted her. "You liar," she said.

"It was nothing. A false alarm."

"If that's how you want it." She took my hand. "I've just been up to the office. It's empty and there's a lock on the door." Her face was perfectly calm, but her eyes were lambent, almost feral, and a pulse beat steadily in her throat.

"I don't—"

"I saw the way you looked at me," she said. "If we need to talk about it, it's no good. The Turman woman is with your son."

"Yes." It came to me that this was a way—maybe not the best one, but a way, nevertheless—to take the curse off what Ollie and I had just done. Not the best way, just the only way.

We went up the narrow flight of stairs and into the office. It was empty, as she had said. And there was a lock on the door. I turned it. In the darkness she was nothing but a shape. I put my arms out, touched her, and pulled her to me. She was trembling. We went down on the floor, first kneeling, kissing, and I cupped one firm breast and could feel the quick thudding of her heart through her sweatshirt. I thought of Steffy telling Billy not to touch the live wires. I thought of the bruise that had been on her hip when she took off the brown dress on our wedding night. I thought of the first time I had seen her, biking across the mall of the University of Maine at Orono, me bound for one of Vincent Hartgen's classes with my portfolio under my arm. And my erection was enormous.

We lay down then, and she said, "Love me, David. Make me warm." When she came, she dug into my back with her nails and called me by a name that wasn't mine. I didn't mind. It made us about even.

When we came down, some sort of creeping dawn had begun. The blackness outside the loopholes went reluctantly to dull gray, then to chrome, then to the bright, featureless, and unsparkling white of a drive-in movie screen. Mike Hatlen was asleep in a folding chair he had scrounged somewhere. Dan Miller sat on the floor a little distance away, eating a Hostess donut. The kind that's powdered with white sugar.

"Sit down, Mr. Drayton," he invited.

I looked around for Amanda, but she was already halfway up the aisle. She didn't look back. Our act of love in the dark already seemed something out of a fantasy, impossible to believe even in this weird daylight. I sat down.

"Have a donut." He held the box out.

I shook my head. "All that white sugar is death. Worse than cigarettes."

That made him laugh a little bit. "In that case, have two."

I was surprised to find a little laughter left inside me—he had surprised it out, and I liked him for it. I did take two of his donuts. They tasted pretty good. I chased them with a cigarette, although it is not normally my habit to smoke in the mornings.

"I ought to get back to my kid," I said. "He'll be waking up."

Miller nodded. "Those pink bugs," he said. "They're all gone. So are the birds. Hank Vannerman said the last one hit the windows around four. Apparently the . . . the wildlife . . . is a lot more active when it's dark."

"You don't want to tell Brent Norton that," I said. "Or Norm."

He nodded again and didn't say anything for a long time. Then he lit a cigarette of his own and looked at me. "We can't stay here, Drayton," he said.

"There's food. Plenty to drink."

"The supplies don't have anything to do with it, and you know it. What do we do if one of the big beasties out there decides to break in instead of just going bump in the night? Do we try to drive it off with broom handles and charcoal lighter fluid?"

Of course he was right. Perhaps the mist was protecting us in a way. Hiding us. But maybe it wouldn't hide us for long, and there was more to it than that. We had been in the Federal for eighteen hours, more or less, and I could feel a kind of lethargy spreading over me, not much different from the lethargy I've felt on one or two occasions when I've tried to swim too far. There was an urge to play it safe, to just stay put, to take care of Billy (*and maybe to bang Amanda Dumfries in the middle of the night*, a voice murmured), to see if the mist wouldn't just lift, leaving everything as it had been.

I could see it on the other faces as well, and it suddenly occurred to me that there were people now in the Federal who probably wouldn't leave under any circumstance. The very thought of going out the door after all that had happened would freeze them.

Miller had been watching these thoughts cross my face, maybe. He said, "There were about eighty people in here when that damn fog came. From that number you subtract the bag-boy, Norton, and the four people that went out with him, and that man Smalley. That leaves seventy-three."

And subtracting the two soldiers, now resting under a stack of Purina Puppy Chow bags, it made seventy-one.

"Then you subtract the people who have just opted out," he went on. "There are ten or twelve of those. Say ten. That leaves about sixty-three. *But—*" He raised one sugar-powdered finger. "Of those sixty-three, we've got twenty or so that just won't leave. You'd have to drag them out kicking and screaming."

"Which all goes to prove what?"

"That we've got to get out, that's all. And I'm going. Around noon, I think. I'm planning to take as many people as will come. I'd like you and your boy to come along."

"After what happened to Norton?"

"Norton went like a lamb to the slaughter. That doesn't mean I have to, or the people who come with me."

"How can you prevent it? We have exactly one gun."

"And lucky to have that. But if we could make it across the intersection, maybe we could get down to the Sportsman's Exchange on Main Street. They've got more guns there than you could shake a stick at."

"That's one 'if' and one 'maybe' too many."

"Drayton," he said, "it's an iffy situation."

That rolled very smoothly off his tongue, but he didn't have a little boy to watch out for.

"Look, let it pass for now, okay? I didn't get much sleep last night, but I got a chance to think over a few things. Want to hear them?"

"Sure."

He stood up and stretched. "Take a walk over to the window with me."

We went through the checkout lane nearest the bread racks and stood at one of the loopholes. The man who was keeping watch there said, "The bugs are gone."

Miller slapped him on the back. "Go get yourself a coffee-and, fella. I'll keep an eye out."

"Okay. Thanks."

He walked away, and Miller and I stepped up to his loophole. "So tell me what you see out there," he said.

I looked. The litter barrel had been knocked over in the night, probably by one of the swooping bird-things, spilling a trash of papers, cans, and paper shake cups from the Dairy Queen down the road all over the hottop. Beyond that I could see the rank of cars closest to the market fading into whiteness. That was all I could see, and I told him so.

"That blue Chevy pickup is mine," he said. He pointed and I could see just a hint of blue in the mist. "But if you think back to when you pulled in yesterday, you'll remember that the parking lot was pretty jammed, right?"

I glanced back at my Scout and remembered I had only gotten the space close to the market because someone else had been pulling out. I nodded.

Miller said, "Now couple something else with that fact, Drayton. Norton and his four . . . what did you call them?"

"Flat-Earthers."

"Yeah, that's good. Just what they were. They go out, right? Almost the full length of that clothesline. Then we heard those roaring noises, like there was a goddam herd of elephants out there. Right?"

"It didn't sound like elephants," I said. "It sounded like—" *Like something from the primordial ooze* was the phrase that came to mind, but I didn't want to say that to Miller, not after he had clapped that guy on the back and told him to go get a coffee-and like the coach jerking a player from the big game. I might have said it to Ollie, but not to Miller. "I don't know what it sounded like," I finished lamely.

"But it sounded *big.*"

"Yeah." It had sounded pretty goddam big.

"So how come we didn't hear cars getting bashed around? Screeching metal? Breaking glass?"

"Well, because—" I stopped. He had me. "I don't know."

Miller said, "No way they were out of the parking lot when whatever-it-was hit them. I'll tell you what I think. I think we didn't hear any cars getting around because a lot of them might be gone. Just . . . gone. Fallen into the earth, vaporized, you name it. Strong enough to splinter these beams and twist them out of shape and knock stuff off the shelves. And the town whistle stopped at the same time."

I was trying to visualize half the parking lot gone. Trying to visualize walking out there and just coming to a brand-new drop in the land where the hottop with its neat yellow-lined parking slots left off. A drop, a slope . . . or maybe an out-and-out precipice falling away into the featureless white mist . . .

After a couple of seconds I said, "If you're right, how far do you think you're going to get in your pickup?"

"I wasn't thinking of my truck. I was thinking of your four-wheel-drive."

That was something to chew over, but not now. "What else is on your mind?"

Miller was eager to go on. "The pharmacy next door, that's on my mind. What about that?"

I opened my mouth to say I didn't have the slightest idea what he was talking about, and then shut it with a snap. The Bridgton Pharmacy had been doing business when we drove in yesterday. Not the laundromat, but the drugstore had been wide open, the doors chocked with rubber doorstops to let in a little cool air—the power outage had killed their air conditioning, of course. The door to the pharmacy could be no more than twenty feet from the door of the Federal market. So why—

"Why haven't any of those people turned up over here?" Miller asked for me. "It's been eighteen hours. Aren't they hungry? They're sure not over there eating Dristan and Stayfree Mini-pads."

"There's food," I said. "They're always selling food items on special. Sometimes it's animal crackers, sometimes it's those toaster pastries, all sorts of things. Plus the candy rack."

"I just don't believe they'd stick with stuff like that when there's all kinds of stuff over here."

"What are you getting at?"

"What I'm getting at is that I want to get out but I don't want to be dinner for some refugee from a grade-B horror picture. Four or five of us could go next door and check out the situation in the drugstore. As sort of a trial balloon."

"That's everything?"

"No, there's one other thing."

"What's that?"

"Her," Miller said simply, and jerked his thumb toward one of the middle aisles. "That crazy cunt. That witch."

It was Mrs. Carmody he had jerked his thumb at. She was no longer alone; two women had joined her. From their bright clothes I guessed they were probably tourists or summer people, ladies who had maybe left their families to "just run into town and get a few things" and were now eaten up with worry over their husbands and kids. Ladies eager to grasp at almost any straw. Maybe even the black comfort of a Mrs. Carmody.

Her pantsuit shone out with its same baleful resplendence. She was talking, gesturing, her face hard and grim. The two ladies in their bright clothes (but not as bright as Mrs. Carmody's pantsuit, no, and her gigantic satchel of a purse was still tucked firmly under one doughy arm) were listening raptly.

"She's another reason I want to get out, Drayton. By tonight she'll have six people sitting with her. If those pink bugs and the birds come back tonight, she'll have a whole congregation sitting with her by tomorrow morning. Then we can start worrying about who she'll tell them to sacrifice to make it all better. Maybe me, or you, or that guy Hatlen. Maybe your kid."

"That's idiocy," I said. But was it? The cold chill crawling up my back said not necessarily. Mrs. Carmody's mouth moved and moved. The eyes of the tourist ladies were fixed on her wrinkled lips. Was it idiocy? I thought of the dusty stuffed animals drinking at their looking-glass stream. Mrs. Carmody had power. Even Steff, normally hardheaded and straight-from-the-shoulder, invoked the old lady's name with unease.

That crazy cunt, Miller had called her. *That witch.*

"The people in this market are going through a section-eight experience for sure," Miller said. He gestured at the red-painted beams framing the show-window segments . . . twisted and splintered and buckled out of shape. "Their minds probably feel like those beams look. Mine sure as shit does. I spent half of last night thinking I must have flipped out of my gourd, that I was probably in a straitjacket in Danvers, raving my head off about bugs and dinosaur birds and tentacles and that it would all go away just as soon as the nice orderly came along and shot a wad of Thorazine into my arm." His small face was strained and white. He looked at Mrs. Carmody and then back at me. "I tell you it might happen. As people get flakier, she's going to look better and better to some of them. And I don't want to be around if that happens."

Mrs. Carmody's lips, moving and moving. Her tongue dancing around her old lady's snaggle teeth. She did look like a witch. Put her in a pointy black hat and she would be perfect. What was she saying to her two captured birds in their bright summer plumage?

Arrowhead Project? Black Spring? Abominations from the cellars of the earth? Human sacrifice?

Bullshit.

All the same—

"So what do you say?"

"I'll go this far," I answered him. "We'll try going over to the drug. You, me, Ollie if he wants to go, one or two others. Then we'll talk it over again." Even that gave me the feeling of walking out over an impossible drop on a narrow beam. I wasn't going to help Billy by killing myself. On the other hand, I wasn't going to help him by just sitting on my ass, either. Twenty feet to the drugstore. That wasn't so bad.

"When?" he asked.

"Give me an hour."

"Sure," he said.

IX. The Expedition to the Pharmacy.

I told Mrs. Turman, and I told Amanda, and then I told Billy. He seemed better this morning; he had eaten two donuts and a bowl of Special K for breakfast. Afterward I raced him up and down two of the aisles and even got him giggling a little. Kids are so adaptable that they can scare the living shit right out of you. He was too pale, the flesh under his eyes was still puffed from the tears he had cried in the night, and his face had a horribly *used* look. In a way it had become like an old man's face, as if too much emotional voltage had been running behind it for too long. But he was still alive and still able to laugh . . . at least until he remembered where he was and what was happening.

After the windsprints we sat down with Amanda and Hattie Turman and drank Gatorade from paper cups and I told him I was going over to the drugstore with a few other people.

"I don't want you to," he said immediately, his face clouding.

"It'll be all right, Big Bill. I'll bring you a *Spiderman* comic book."

"I want you to stay *here.*" Now his face was not just cloudy; it was thundery. I took his hand. He pulled it away. I took it again.

"Billy, we have to get out of here sooner or later. You see that, don't you?"

"When the fog goes away . . ." But he spoke with no conviction at all. He drank his Gatorade slowly and without relish.

"Billy, it's been almost one whole day now."

"I want Mommy."

"Well, maybe this is the first step on the way to getting back to her."

Mrs. Turman said, "Don't build the boy's hopes up, David."

"What the hell," I snapped at her, "the kid's got to hope for something."

She dropped her eyes. "Yes. I suppose he does."

Billy took no notice of this. "Daddy . . . Daddy, there are things out there. *Things.*"

"Yes, we know that. But a lot of them—not all, but a lot—don't seem to come out until it's nighttime."

"They'll wait," he said. His eyes were huge, centered on mine. "They'll wait in the fog . . . and when you can't get back inside, they'll come to eat you up. Like in the fairy stories." He hugged me with fierce, panicky tightness. "Daddy, please don't go."

I pried his arms loose as gently as I could and told him that I had to. "But I'll be back, Billy."

"All right," he said huskily, but he wouldn't look at me anymore. He didn't believe I would be back. It was on his face, which was no longer thundery but woeful and grieving. I wondered again if I could be doing the right thing, putting myself at risk. Then I happened to glance down the middle aisle and saw Mrs. Carmody there. She had gained a third listener, a man with a grizzled cheek and a mean and rolling bloodshot eye. His haggard brow and shaking hands almost screamed the word hangover. It was none other than your friend and his, Myron LaFleur. The fellow who had felt no compunction at all about sending a boy out to do a man's job.

That crazy cunt. That witch.

I kissed Billy and hugged him hard. Then I walked down to the front of the store—but not down the housewares aisle. I didn't want to fall under her eye.

Three-quarters of the way down, Amanda caught up with me. "Do you really have to do this?" she asked.

"Yes, I think so."

"Forgive me if I say it sounds like so much macho bullshit to me." There were spots of color high on her cheeks and her eyes were greener than ever. She was highly—no, royally—pissed.

I took her arm and recapped my discussion with Dan Miller.

The riddle of the cars and the fact that no one from the pharmacy had joined us didn't move her much. The business about Mrs. Carmody did.

"He could be right," she said.

"Do you really believe that?"

"I don't know. There's a poisonous feel to that woman. And if people are frightened badly enough for long enough, they'll turn to anyone that promises a solution."

"But human sacrifice, Amanda?"

"The Aztecs were into it," she said evenly. "Listen, David. You come back. If anything happens . . . *anything* . . . you come back. Cut and run if you have to. Not for me, what happened last night was nice, but that was last night. Come back for your boy."

"Yes. I will."

"I wonder," she said, and now she looked like Billy, haggard and old. It occurred to me that most of us looked that way. But not Mrs. Carmody. Mrs. Carmody looked younger somehow, and more vital. As if she had come into her own. As if . . . as if she were thriving on it.

We didn't get going until 9:30 A.M. Seven of us went: Ollie, Dan Miller, Mike Hatlen, Myron LaFleur's erstwhile buddy Jim (also hungover, but seemingly determined to find some way to atone), Buddy Eagleton, myself. The seventh was Hilda Reppler. Miller and Hatlen tried halfheartedly to talk her out of coming. She would have none of it. I didn't even try. I suspected she might be more competent than any of us, except maybe for Ollie. She was carrying a small canvas shopping basket, and it was loaded with an arsenal of Raid and Black Flag spray cans, all of them uncapped and ready for action. In her free hand she held a Spalding Jimmy Connors tennis racket from a display of sporting goods in Aisle 2.

"What you gonna do with that, Mrs. Reppler?" Jim asked.

"I don't know," she said. She had a low, raspy, competent voice. "But it feels right in my hand." She looked him over closely, and her eye was cold. "Jim Grondin, isn't it? Didn't I have you in school?"

Jim's lips stretched in an uneasy egg-suck grin. "Yes'm. Me and my sister Pauline."

"Too much to drink last night?"

Jim, who towered over her and probably outweighed her by one hundred pounds, blushed to the roots of his American Legion crewcut. "Aw, no—"

She turned away curtly, cutting him off. "I think we're ready," she said.

All of us had something, although you would have called it an odd assortment of weapons. Ollie had Amanda's gun, Buddy Eagleton had a steel pinchbar from out back somewhere. I had a broom handle.

"Okay," Dan Miller said, raising his voice a bit. "You folks want to listen up a minute?"

A dozen people had drifted down toward the OUT door to see what was going on. They were loosely knotted, and to their right stood Mrs. Carmody and her new friends.

"We're going over to the drugstore to see what the situation is there. Hopefully, we'll be able to bring something back to aid Mrs. Clapham." She was the lady who had been trampled yesterday, when the bugs came. One of her legs had been broken and she was in a great deal of pain.

Miller looked us over. "We're not going to take any chances," he said. "At the first sign of anything threatening, we're going to pop back into the market—"

"And bring all the fiends of hell down on our heads!" Mrs. Carmody cried.

"She's right!" one of the summer ladies seconded. "You'll make them notice us! You'll make them come! Why can't you just leave well enough alone?"

There was a murmur of agreement from some of the people who had gathered to watch us go.

I said, "Lady, is this what you call well enough?"

She dropped her eyes, confused.

Mrs. Carmody marched a step forward. Her eyes were blazing. "You'll die out there, David Drayton! Do you want to make your son an orphan?" She raised her eyes and raked all of us with them. Buddy Eagleton dropped his eyes and simultaneously raised the pinchbar, as if to ward her off.

"All of you will die out there! Haven't you realized that the end of the world has come? The Fiend has been let loose! Star Wormwood blazes and each one of you that steps out that door will be torn apart! And they'll come for those of us who are left, just as this good woman said! Are you people going to let that happen?" She was appealing to the onlookers now, and a little mutter ran through them. "After what happened to the unbelievers yesterday? It's death! *It's death! It's—*"

A can of peas flew across two of the checkout lanes suddenly and struck Mrs. Carmody on the right breast. She staggered backward with a startled squawk.

Amanda stood forward. "Shut up," she said. "Shut up, you miserable buzzard."

"She serves the Foul One!" Mrs. Carmody screamed. A jittery smile hung on her face. "Who did you sleep with last night, missus? Who did you lie down with last night? Mother Carmody sees, oh yes, Mother Carmody sees what others miss."

But the moment's spell she had created was broken, and Amanda's eyes never wavered.

"Are we going or are we going to stand here all day?" Mrs. Reppler asked.

And we went. God help us, we went.

Dan Miller was in the lead. Ollie came second, I was last, with Mrs. Reppler in front of me. I was as scared as I've ever been, I think, and the hand wrapped around my broom handle was sweaty-slick.

There was that thin, acrid, and unnatural smell of the mist. By the time I got out the door, Miller and Ollie had already faded into it, and Hatlen, who was third, was nearly out of sight.

Only twenty feet, I kept telling myself. *Only twenty feet.*

Mrs. Reppler walked slowly and firmly ahead of me, her tennis racket swinging lightly from her right hand. To our left was a red cinderblock wall. To our right the first rank of cars, looming out of the mist like ghost ships. Another trash barrel materialized out of the whiteness, and beyond that was a bench where people sometimes sat to wait their turn at the pay phone. *Only twenty feet, Miller's probably there by now, twenty feet is only ten or twelve paces, so—*

"Oh my God!" Miller screamed. "Oh dear sweet God, look at this!"

Miller had gotten there, all right.

Buddy Eagleton was ahead of Mrs. Reppler and he turned to run, his eyes wide and stary. She batted him lightly in the chest with her tennis racket. "Where do you think *you're* going?" she asked in her tough, slightly raspy voice, and that was all the panic there was.

The rest of us drew up to Miller. I took one glance back over my shoulder and saw that the Federal had been swallowed by the mist. The red cinderblock wall faded to a thin wash pink and then disappeared utterly, probably five feet on the Bridgton Pharmacy side of the OUT door. I felt more isolated, more simply alone, than ever in my life. It was as if I had lost the womb.

The pharmacy had been the scene of a slaughter.

Miller and I, of course, were very close to it—almost on top of it. All the things in the mist operated primarily by sense of smell. It stood to reason. Sight would have been almost completely useless to them. Hearing a little better, but as I've said, the mist had a way of screwing up the acoustics, making things that were close sound distant and—sometimes—things that were far away sound close. The things in the mist followed their truest sense. They followed their noses.

Those of us in the market had been saved by the power outage as much as by anything else. The electric-eye doors wouldn't operate. In a sense, the market had been sealed up when the mist came. But the pharmacy doors . . . they had been chocked open. The power failure had killed their air conditioning and they had opened the doors to let in the breeze. Only something else had come in as well.

A man in a maroon T-shirt lay facedown in the doorway. Or at first I thought his T-shirt was maroon; then I saw a few white patches at the bottom and understood that once it had been all white. The maroon was dried blood. And there was something else wrong with him. I puzzled it over in my mind. Even when Buddy Eagleton turned around and was noisily sick, it didn't come immediately. I guess when something that . . . that *final* happens to someone, your mind rejects it at first . . . unless maybe you're in a war.

His head was gone, that's what it was. His legs were splayed out inside the pharmacy doors, and his head should have been hanging over the low step. But his head just wasn't.

Jim Grondin had had enough. He turned away, his hands

over his mouth, his bloodshot eyes gazing madly into mine. Then he stumbled-staggered back toward the market.

The others took no notice. Miller had stepped inside. Mike Hatlen followed. Mrs. Reppler stationed herself at one side of the double doors with her tennis racket. Ollie stood on the other side with Amanda's gun drawn and pointing at the pavement.

He said quietly, "I seem to be running out of hope, David."

Buddy Eagleton was leaning weakly against the pay-phone stall like someone who has just gotten bad news from home. His broad shoulders shook with the force of his sobs.

"Don't count us out yet," I said to Ollie. I stepped up to the door. I didn't want to go inside, but I had promised my son a comic book.

The Bridgton Pharmacy was a crazy shambles. Paperbacks and magazines were everywhere. There was a *Spiderman* comic and an *Incredible Hulk* almost at my feet, and without thinking, I picked them up and jammed them into my back pocket for Billy. Bottles and boxes lay in the aisles. A hand hung over one of the racks.

Unreality washed over me. The wreckage . . . the *carnage*—that was bad enough. But the place also looked like it had been the scene of some crazy party. It was hung and festooned with what I at first took to be streamers. But they weren't broad and flat; they were more like very thick strings or very thin cables. It struck me that they were almost the same bright white as the mist itself, and a cold chill sketched its way up my back like frost. Not crepe. What? Magazines and books hung dangling in the air from some of them.

Mike Hatlen was prodding a strange black thing with one foot. It was long and bristly. "What the fuck is this?" he asked no one in particular.

And suddenly I knew. I knew what had killed all those

unlucky enough to be in the pharmacy when the mist came. The people who had been unlucky enough to get smelled out. *Out—*

"Out," I said. My throat was completely dry, and the word came out like a lint-covered bullet. "Get out of here."

Ollie looked at me. "David . . . ?"

"They're spiderwebs," I said. And then two screams came out of the mist. The first of fear, maybe. The second of pain. It was Jim. If there were dues to be paid, he was paying them.

"Get out!" I shouted at Mike and Dan Miller.

Then something looped out of the mist. It was impossible to see it against that white background, but I could hear it. It sounded like a bullwhip that had been halfheartedly flicked. And I could see it when it twisted around the thigh of Buddy Eagleton's jeans.

He screamed and grabbed for the first thing handy, which happened to be the telephone. The handset flew the length of its cord and then swung back and forth. *"Oh Jesus that HURTS!"* Buddy screamed.

Ollie grabbed for him, and I saw what was happening. At the same instant I understood why the head of the man in the doorway was missing. The thin white cable that had twisted around Buddy's leg like a silk rope *was sinking into his flesh.* That leg of his jeans had been neatly cut off and was sliding down his leg. A neat, circular incision in his flesh was brimming blood as the cable went deeper.

Ollie pulled him hard. There was a thin snapping sound and Buddy was free. His lips had gone blue with shock.

Mike and Dan were coming, but too slowly. Then Dan ran into several hanging threads and got stuck, exactly like a bug on flypaper. He freed himself with a tremendous jerk, leaving a flap of his shirt hanging from the webbing.

Suddenly the air was full of those languorous bullwhip cracks, and the thin white cables were drifting down all around us. They were coated with the same corrosive substance. I dodged two of them, more by luck than by skill. One landed at my feet and I could hear a faint hiss of bubbling hottop. Another floated out of the air and Mrs. Reppler calmly swung her tennis racket at it. The thread stuck fast, and I heard a high-pitched *twing! twing! twing!* as the corrosive ate through the racket's strings and snapped them. It sounded like someone rapidly plucking the strings of a violin. A moment later a thread wrapped around the upper handle of the racket and it was jerked into the mist.

"Get back!" Ollie screamed.

We got moving. Ollie had an arm around Buddy. Dan Miller and Mike Hatlen were on each side of Mrs. Reppler. The white strands of web continued to drift out of the fog, impossible to see unless your eye could pick them out against the red cinderblock background.

One of them wrapped around Mike Hatlen's left arm. Another whipped around his neck in a series of quick winding-up snaps. His jugular went in a jetting, jumping explosion and he was dragged away, head lolling. One of his Bass loafers fell off and lay there on its side.

Buddy suddenly slumped forward, almost dragging Ollie to his knees. "He's passed out, David. Help me."

I grabbed Buddy around the waist and we pulled him along in a clumsy, stumbling fashion. Even in unconsciousness, Buddy kept his grip on his steel pinchbar. The leg that the strand of web had wrapped around hung away from his body at a terrible angle.

Mrs. Reppler had turned around. "Ware!" she screamed in her rusty voice. "Ware behind you!"

As I started to turn, one of the web-strands floated down on top of Dan Miller's head. His hands beat at it, tore at it.

One of the spiders had come out of the mist from behind us. It was the size of a big dog. It was black with yellow piping. *Racing stripes,* I thought crazily. Its eyes were reddish-purple, like pomegranates. It strutted busily toward us on what might have been as many as twelve or fourteen many-jointed legs—it was no ordinary earthly spider blown up to horror-movie size; it was something totally different, perhaps not really a spider at all. Seeing it, Mike Hatlen would have understood what that bristly black thing he had been prodding at in the pharmacy really was.

It closed in on us, spinning its webbing from an oval-shaped orifice on its upper belly. The strands floated out toward us in what was nearly a fan shape. Looking at this nightmare, so like the death-black spiders brooding over their dead flies and bugs in the shadows of our boathouse, I felt my mind trying to tear completely loose from its moorings. I believe now that it was only the thought of Billy that allowed me to keep any semblance of sanity. I was making some sound. Laughing. Crying. Screaming. I don't know.

But Ollie Weeks was like a rock. He raised Amanda's pistol as calmly as a man on a target range and emptied it in spaced shots into the creature at point-blank range. Whatever hell it came from, it wasn't invulnerable. A black ichor splattered from its body and it made a terrible mewling sound, so low it was more felt than heard, like a bass note from a synthesizer. Then it scuttered back into the mist and was gone. It might have been a phantasm from a horrible drug-dream . . . except for the puddles of sticky black stuff it had left behind.

There was a clang as Buddy finally dropped his steel pinch-bar.

"He's dead," Ollie said. "Let him go, David. The fucking thing got his femoral artery, he's dead. Let's get the Christ out of here." His face was once more running with sweat and his eyes bulged from his big round face. One of the web-strands floated easily down on the back of his hand and Ollie swung his arm, snapping it. The strand left a bloody weal.

Mrs. Reppler screamed "Ware!" again, and we turned toward her. Another of them had come out of the mist and had wrapped its legs around Dan Miller in a mad lover's embrace. He was striking at it with his fists. As I bent and picked up Buddy's pinchbar, the spider began to wrap Dan in its deadly thread, and his struggles became a grisly, jittering death dance.

Mrs. Reppler walked toward the spider with a can of Black Flag insect repellent held outstretched in one hand. The spider's legs reached for her. She depressed the button and a cloud of the stuff jetted into one of its sparkling, jewel-like eyes. That low-pitched mewling sound came again. The spider seemed to shudder all over and then it began to lurch backward, hairy legs scratching at the pavement. It dragged Dan's body, bumping and rolling, behind it. Mrs. Reppler threw the can of bug spray at it. It bounced off the spider's body and clattered to the hottop. The spider struck the side of a small sports car hard enough to make it rock on its springs, and then it was gone.

I got to Mrs. Reppler, who was swaying on her feet and dead pale. I put an arm around her. "Thank you, young man," she said. "I feel a bit faint."

"That's okay," I said hoarsely.

"I would have saved him if I could."

"I know that."

Ollie joined us. We ran for the market doors, the threads falling all around us. One lit on Mrs. Reppler's marketing basket and sank into the canvas side. She tussled grimly for what was hers, dragging back on the strap with both hands, but she lost it. It went bumping off into the mist, end over end.

As we reached the IN door, a smaller spider, no bigger than a cocker spaniel puppy, raced out of the fog along the side of the building. It was producing no webbing; perhaps it wasn't mature enough to do so.

As Ollie leaned one beefy shoulder against the door so Mrs. Reppler could go through, I heaved the steel bar at the thing like a javelin and impaled it. It writhed madly, legs scratching at the air, and its red eyes seemed to find mine, and mark me . . .

"David!" Ollie was still holding the door.

I ran in. He followed me.

Pallid, frightened faces stared at us. Seven of us had gone out. Three of us had come back. Ollie leaned against the heavy glass door, barrel chest heaving. He began to reload Amanda's gun. His white assistant manager's shirt was plastered to his body, and large gray sweat-stains had crept out from under his arms.

"What?" someone asked in a low, hoarse voice.

"Spiders," Mrs. Reppler answered grimly. "The dirty bastards snatched my market basket."

Then Billy hurled his way into my arms, crying. I held on to him. Tight.

X. The Spell of Mrs. Carmody. The Second Night in the Market. The Final Confrontation.

It was my turn to sleep, and for four hours I remember nothing at all. Amanda told me I talked a lot, and screamed once or twice, but I remember no dreams. When I woke up it was afternoon. I was terribly thirsty. Some of the milk had gone over, but some of it was still okay. I drank a quart.

Amanda came over to where Billy, Mrs. Turman, and I were. The old man who had offered to make a try for the shotgun in the trunk of his car was with her—Cornell, I remembered. Ambrose Cornell.

"How are you, son?" he asked.

"All right." But I was still thirsty and my head ached. Most of all, I was scared. I slipped an arm around Billy and looked from Cornell to Amanda. "What's up?"

Amanda said, "Mr. Cornell is worried about that Mrs. Carmody. So am I."

"Billy why don't you take a walk over here with me?" Hattie asked.

"I don't want to," Billy said.

"Go on, Big Bill," I told him, and he went—reluctantly.

"Now what about Mrs. Carmody?" I asked.

"She's stirrin things up," Cornell said. He looked at me with an old man's grimness. "I think we got to put a stop to it. Just about any way we can."

Amanda said, "There are almost a dozen people with her now. It's like some crazy kind of a church service."

I remembered talking with a writer friend who lived in Otisfield and supported his wife and two kids by raising chickens and turning out one paperback original a year—spy stories. We had gotten talking about the bulge in popularity of books concerning themselves with the supernatural. Gault pointed out that in the forties *Weird Tales* had only been able to pay a pittance, and that in the fifties it went broke. When the machines fail, he had said (while his wife candled eggs and roosters crowed querulously outside), when the technologies fail, when the conventional religious systems fail, people have got to have something. Even a zombie lurching through the night can seem pretty cheerful compared to the existential comedy/horror of the ozone layer dissolving under the combined assault of a million fluorocarbon spray cans of deodorant.

We had been trapped here for twenty-six hours and we hadn't been able to do diddlyshit. Our one expedition outside had resulted in fifty-seven percent losses. It wasn't so surprising that Mrs. Carmody had turned into a growth stock, maybe.

"Has she really got a dozen people?" I asked.

"Well, only eight," Cornell said. "But she never shuts up! It's like those ten-hour speeches Castro used to make. It's a goddam filibuster."

Eight people. Not that many, not even enough to fill up a jury box. But I understood the worry on their faces. It was enough to make them the single largest political force in the market, especially now that Dan and Mike were gone. The thought that the biggest single group in our closed system was listening to her rant on about the pits of hell and the seven vials being opened made me feel pretty damn claustrophobic.

"She's started talking about human sacrifice again," Amanda said. "Bud Brown came over and told her to stop talking that drivel in his store. And two of the men that are with her—one of them was that man Myron LaFleur—told him he was the one who better shut up because it was still a free country. He wouldn't shut up and there was a . . . well, a shoving match, I guess you'd say."

"Brown got a bloody nose," Cornell said. "They mean business."

I said, "Surely not to the point of actually killing someone."

Cornell said softly, "I don't know how far they'll go if that mist doesn't let up. But I don't want to find out. I intend to get out of here."

"Easier said than done." But something had begun to tick over in my mind. *Scent.* That was the key. We had been left pretty much alone in the market. The bugs might have been attracted to the light, as more ordinary bugs were. The birds had simply followed their food supply. But the bigger things had left us alone unless we unbuttoned for some reason. The slaughter in the Bridgton Pharmacy had occurred because the doors had been left chocked open—I was sure of that. The thing or things that had gotten Norton and his party had sounded as big as a house, but it or they hadn't come near the market. And that meant that maybe . . .

Suddenly I wanted to talk to Ollie Weeks. I needed to talk to him.

"I intend to get out or die trying," Cornell said. "I got no plans to spend the rest of the summer in here."

"There have been four suicides," Amanda said suddenly.

"What?" The first thing to cross my mind, in a semiguilty flash, was that the bodies of the soldiers had been discovered.

"Pills," Cornell said shortly. "Me and two or three other guys carried the bodies out back."

I had to stifle a shrill laugh. We had a regular morgue going back there.

"It's thinning out," Cornell said. "I want to get gone."

"You won't make it to your car. Believe me."

"Not even to that first rank? That's closer than the drugstore."

I didn't answer him. Not then.

About an hour later I found Ollie holding up the beer cooler and drinking a Busch. His face was impassive but he also seemed to be watching Mrs. Carmody. She was tireless, apparently. And she was indeed discussing human sacrifice again, only now no one was telling her to shut up. Some of the people who had told her to shut up yesterday were either with her today or at least willing to listen—and the others were outnumbered.

"She could have them talked around to it by tomorrow morning," Ollie remarked. "Maybe not . . . but if she did, who do you think she'd single out for the honor?"

Bud Brown had crossed her. So had Amanda. There was the man who had struck her. And then, of course, there was me.

"Ollie," I said, "I think maybe half a dozen of us could get out of here. I don't know how far we'd get, but I think we could at least get out."

"How?"

I laid it out for him. It was simple enough. If we dashed across to my Scout and piled in, they would get no human scent. At least not with the windows rolled up.

"But suppose they're attracted to some other scent?" Ollie asked. "Exhaust, for instance?"

"Then we'd be cooked," I agreed.

"Motion," he said. "The motion of a car through fog might also draw them, David."

"I don't think so. Not without the scent of prey. I really believe that's the key to getting away."

"But you don't know."

"No, not for sure."

"Where would you want to go?"

"First? Home. To get my wife."

"David—"

"All right. To check. To be *sure.*"

"The things out there could be everyplace, David. They could get you the minute you stepped out of your Scout into your dooryard."

"If that happened, the Scout would be yours. All I'd ask would be that you take care of Billy as well as you could for as long as you could."

Ollie finished his Busch and dropped the can back into the cooler, where it clattered among the empties. The butt of the gun Amanda's husband had given her protruded from his pocket.

"South?" he asked, meeting my eyes.

"Yeah, I would," I said. "Go south and try to get out of the mist. Try like hell."

"How much gas you got?"

"Almost full."

"Have you thought that it might be impossible to get out?"

I had. Suppose what they had been fooling with at the Arrowhead Project had pulled this entire region into another dimension as easily as you or I would turn a sock inside out?

"It had crossed my mind," I said, "but the alternative seems to be waiting around to see who Mrs. Carmody taps for the place of honor."

"Were you thinking about today?"

"No, it's afternoon already and those things get active at night. I was thinking about tomorrow, very early."

"Who would you want to take?"

"Me and you and Billy. Hattie Turman. Amanda Dumfries. That old guy Cornell and Mrs. Reppler. Maybe Bud Brown, too. That's eight, but Billy can sit on someone's lap and we can all squash together."

He thought it over. "All right," he said finally. "We'll try. Have you mentioned this to anyone else?"

"No, not yet."

"My advice would be not to, not until about four tomorrow morning. I'll put a couple of bags of groceries under the checkout nearest the door. If we're lucky we can squeak out before anyone knows what's happening." His eyes drifted to Mrs. Carmody again. "If she knew, she might try to stop us."

"You think so?"

Ollie got another beer. "I think so," he said.

That afternoon—yesterday afternoon—passed in a kind of slow motion. Darkness crept in, turning the fog to that dull chrome color again. What world was left outside slowly dissolved to black by eight-thirty.

The pink bugs returned, then the bird-things, swooping into the windows and scooping them up. Something roared occasionally from the dark, and once, shortly before midnight, there was a long, drawn-out *Aaaaa-roooooooo!* that caused people to turn toward the blackness with frightened, searching faces. It was the sort of sound you'd imagine a bull alligator might make in a swamp.

It went pretty much as Miller had predicted. By the small hours, Mrs. Carmody had gained another half a dozen souls. Mr. McVey the butcher was among them, standing with his arms folded, watching her.

She was totally wound up. She seemed to need no sleep. Her sermon, a steady stream of horrors out of Doré, Bosch, and Jonathan Edwards, went on and on, building toward some climax. Her group began to murmur with her, to rock back and forth unconsciously, like true believers at a tent revival. Their eyes were shiny and blank. They were under her spell.

Around 3:00 A.M. (the sermon went on relentlessly, and the people who were not interested had retreated to the back to try to get some sleep) I saw Ollie put a bag of groceries on a shelf under the checkout nearest the OUT door. Half an hour later he put another bag beside it. No one appeared to notice him but me.

Billy, Amanda, and Mrs. Turman slept together by the denuded cold-cuts section. I joined them and fell into an uneasy doze.

At four-fifteen by my wristwatch, Ollie shook me awake. Cornell was with him, his eyes gleaming brightly from behind his spectacles.

"It's time, David," Ollie said.

A nervous cramp hit my belly and then passed. I shook Amanda awake. The question of what might happen with both Amanda and Stephanie in the car together passed into my mind, and then passed right out again. Today it would be best to take things just as they came.

Those remarkable green eyes opened and looked into mine. "David?"

"We're going to take a stab at getting out of here. Do you want to come?"

"What are you talking about?"

I started to explain, then woke up Mrs. Turman so I would only have to go through it the once.

"Your theory about scent," Amanda said. "It's really only an educated guess at this point, isn't it?"

"Yes."

"It doesn't matter to me," Hattie said. Her face was white and in spite of the sleep she'd gotten there were large discolored patches under her eyes. "I would do anything—take any chances—just to see the sun again."

Just to see the sun again. A little shiver coursed through me. She had put her finger on a spot that was very close to the center of my own fears, on the sense of almost foregone doom that had gripped me since I had seen Norm dragged out through the loading door. You could only see the sun through the mist as a little silver coin. It was like being on Venus.

It wasn't so much the monstrous creatures that lurked in

the mist; my shot with the pinchbar had shown me they were no Lovecraftian horrors with immortal life but only organic creatures with their own vulnerabilities. It was the mist itself that sapped the strength and robbed the will. *Just to see the sun again.* She was right. That alone would be worth going through a lot of hell.

I smiled at Hattie and she smiled tentatively back.

"Yes," Amanda said. "Me too."

I began to shake Billy awake as gently as I could.

"I'm with you," Mrs. Reppler said briefly.

We were all together by the meat counter, all but Bud Brown. He had thanked us for the invitation and then declined it. He would not leave his place in the market, he said, but added in a remarkably gentle tone of voice that he didn't blame Ollie for doing so.

An unpleasant, sweetish aroma was beginning to drift up from the white enamel case now, a smell that reminded me of the time our freezer went on the fritz while we were spending a week on the Cape. Perhaps, I thought, it was the smell of spoiling meat that had driven Mr. McVey over to Mrs. Carmody's team.

"—expiation! It's expiation we want to think about now! We have been scourged with whips and scorpions! We have been punished for delving into secrets forbidden by God of old! We have seen the lips of the earth open! We have seen the obscenities of nightmare! The rock will not hide them, the dead tree gives no shelter! And how will it end? What will stop it?"

"Expiation!" shouted good old Myron LaFleur.

"Expiation . . . expiation . . ." They whispered it uncertainly.

"Let me hear you say it like you mean it!" Mrs. Carmody shouted. The veins stood out on her neck in bulging cords.

Her voice was cracking and hoarse now, but still full of power. And it occurred to me that it was the mist that had given her that power—the power to cloud men's minds, to make a particularly apt pun—just as it had taken away the sun's power from the rest of us. Before, she had been nothing but a mildly eccentric old woman with an antiques store in a town that was lousy with antiques stores. Nothing but an old woman with a few stuffed animals in the back room and a reputation for

(that witch . . . that cunt)

folk medicine. It was said she could find water with an applewood stick, that she could charm warts, and sell you a cream that would fade freckles to shadows of their former selves. I had even heard—was it from old Bill Giosti?—that Mrs. Carmody could be seen (in total confidence) about your love life; that if you were having the bedroom miseries, she could give you a drink that would put the ram back in your rod.

"EXPIATION!" they all cried together.

"Expiation, that's right!" she shouted deliriously. *"It's expiation gonna clear away this fog! Expiation gonna clear off these monsters and abominations! Expiation gonna drop the scales of mist from our eyes and let us see!"* Her voice dropped a notch. *"And what does the Bible say expiation is? What is the only cleanser for sin in the Eye and Mind of God?"*

"Blood."

This time the chill shuddered up through my entire body, cresting at the nape of my neck and making the hairs there stiffen. Mr. McVey had spoken that word, Mr. McVey the butcher who had been cutting meat in Bridgton ever since I was a kid holding my father's talented hand. Mr. McVey taking orders and cutting meat in his stained whites. Mr. McVey, whose acquaintanceship with the knife was long—yes, and with the saw and cleaver as well. Mr. McVey who would understand better than anyone else that the cleanser of the soul flows from the wounds of the body.

"Blood . . ." they whispered.

"Daddy, I'm scared," Billy said. He was clutching my hand tightly, his small face strained and pale.

"Ollie," I said, "why don't we get out of this loony bin?"

"Right on," he said. "Let's go."

We started down the second aisle in a loose group—Ollie, Amanda, Cornell, Mrs. Turman, Mrs. Reppler, Billy, and I. It was a quarter to five in the morning and the mist was beginning to lighten again.

"You and Cornell take the grocery bags," Ollie said to me.

"Okay."

"I'll go first. Your Scout is a four-door, is it?"

"Yeah. It is."

"Okay, I'll open the driver's door and the back door on the same side. Mrs. Dumfries, can you carry Billy?"

She picked him up in her arms.

"Am I too heavy?" Billy asked.

"No, hon."

"Good."

"You and Billy get in front," Ollie went on. "Shove way over. Mrs. Turman in front, in the middle. David, you behind the wheel. The rest of us will—"

"Where did you think you were going?"

It was Mrs. Carmody.

She stood at the head of the checkout line where Ollie had hidden the bags of groceries. Her pantsuit was a yellow scream in the gloom. Her hair frizzed out wildly in all directions, reminding me momentarily of Elsa Lanchester in *The Bride of Frankenstein.* Her eyes blazed. Ten or fifteen people stood behind her, blocking the IN and OUT doors. They had the look of people who had been in car accidents, or who had seen a UFO land, or who had seen a tree pull its roots up and walk.

Billy cringed against Amanda and buried his face against her neck.

"Going out now, Mrs. Carmody," Ollie said. His voice was curiously gentle. "Stand away, please."

"You can't go out. That way is death. Don't you know that by now?"

"No one has interfered with you," I said. "All we want is the same privilege."

She bent and found the bags of groceries unerringly. She must have known what we were planning all along. She pulled them out from the shelf where Ollie had placed them. One ripped open, spilling cans across the floor. She threw the other and it smashed open with the sound of breaking glass. Soda ran fizzing every which way and sprayed off the chrome facing of the next checkout lane.

"These are the sort of people who brought it on!" she shouted. "People who will not bend to the will of the Almighty! Sinners in pride, haughty they are, and stiff-necked! It is from their number that the sacrifice must come! *From their number the blood of expiation!"*

A rising rumble of agreement spurred her on. She was in a frenzy now. Spittle flew from her lips as she screamed at the people crowding up behind her: *"It's the boy we want! Grab him! Take him! It's the boy we want!"*

They surged forward, Myron LaFleur in the lead, his eyes blankly joyous. Mr. McVey was directly behind him, his face blank and stolid.

Amanda faltered backward, holding Billy more tightly. His arms were wrapped around her neck. She looked at me, terrified. "David, what do I—"

"Get them both!" Mrs. Carmody screamed. *"Get his whore, too!"*

She was an apocalypse of yellow and dark joy. Her purse was still over her arm. She began to jump up and down. *"Get the boy, get the whore, get them both, get them all, get—"*

A single sharp report rang out.

Everything froze, as if we were a classroom full of unruly children and the teacher had just stepped back in and shut the door sharply. Myron LaFleur and Mr. McVey stopped where they were, about ten paces away. Myron looked back uncertainly at the butcher. He didn't look back or even seem to realize that LaFleur was there. Mr. McVey had a look I had seen on too many other faces in the last two days. He had gone over. His mind had snapped.

Myron backed up, staring at Ollie Weeks with widening, fearful eyes. His backing-up became a run. He turned the corner of the aisle, skidded on a can, fell down, scrambled up again, and was gone.

Ollie stood in the classic target shooter's position, Amanda's gun clasped in both hands. Mrs. Carmody still stood at the head of the checkout lane. Both of her liver-spotted hands were clasped over her stomach. Blood poured out between her fingers and splashed her yellow slacks.

Her mouth opened and closed. Once. Twice. She was trying to talk. At last she made it.

"You will all die out there," she said, and then she pitched slowly forward. Her purse slithered off her arm, struck the floor, and spilled its contents. A paper-wrapped tube rolled across the distance between us and struck one of my shoes. Without thinking, I bent over and picked it up. It was a half-used package of Rolaids. I threw it down again. I didn't want to touch anything that belonged to her.

The "congregation" was backing away, spreading out, their

focus broken. None of them took their eyes from the fallen figure and the dark blood spreading out from beneath her body. "You murdered her!" someone cried out in fear and anger. But no one pointed out that she had been planning something similar for my son.

Ollie was still frozen in his shooter's position, but now his mouth was trembling. I touched him gently. "Ollie, let's go. And thank you."

"I killed her," he said hoarsely. "Damn if I didn't kill her."

"Yes," I said. "That's why I thanked you. Now let's go."

We began to move again.

With no grocery bags to carry—thanks to Mrs. Carmody—I was able to take Billy. We paused for a moment at the door, and Ollie said in a low, strained voice, "I wouldn't have shot her, David. Not if there had been any other way."

"Yeah."

"You believe it?"

"Yeah, I do."

"Then let's go."

We went out.

XI. The End.

Ollie moved fast, the pistol in his right hand. Before Billy and I were more than out the door he was at my Scout, an insubstantial Ollie, like a ghost in a television movie. He opened the driver's door. Then the back door. Then something came out of the mist and cut him nearly in half.

I never got a good look at it, and for that I think I'm grateful. It appeared to be red, the angry color of a cooked lobster.

It had claws. It was making a low grunting sound, not much different from the sound we had heard after Norton and his little band of Flat-Earthers went out.

Ollie got off one shot, and then the thing's claws scissored forward and Ollie's body seemed to unhinge in a terrible glut of blood. Amanda's gun fell out of his hand, struck the pavement, and discharged. I caught a nightmare glimpse of huge black lusterless eyes, the size of giant handfuls of sea grapes, and then the thing lurched back into the mist with what remained of Ollie Weeks in its grip. A long, multi-segmented scorpion's body dragged harshly on the paving.

There was an instant of choices. Maybe there always is, no matter how short. Half of me wanted to run back into the market with Billy hugged to my chest. The other half was racing for the Scout, throwing Billy inside, lunging after him. Then Amanda screamed. It was a high, rising sound that seemed to spiral up and up until it was nearly ultrasonic. Billy cringed against me, digging his face against my chest.

One of the spiders had Hattie Turman. It was big. It had knocked her down. Her dress had pulled up over her scrawny knees as it crouched over her, its bristly, spiny legs caressing her shoulders. It began to spin its web.

Mrs. Carmody was right, I thought. *We're going to die out here, we are really going to die out here.*

"Amanda!" I yelled.

No response. She was totally gone. The spider straddled what remained of Billy's babysitter, who had enjoyed jigsaw puzzles and those damned Double-Crostics that no normal person can do without going nuts. Its threads crisscrossed her body, the white strands already turning red as the acid coating sank into her.

Cornell was backing slowly toward the market, his eyes as big as dinner plates behind his specs. Abruptly he turned and ran. He clawed the IN door open and ran inside.

The split in my mind closed as Mrs. Reppler stepped briskly forward and slapped Amanda, first forehand, then backhand. Amanda stopped screaming. I went to her, spun her around to face the Scout, and screamed "GO!" into her face.

She went. Mrs. Reppler brushed past me. She pushed Amanda into the Scout's back seat, got in after her, and slammed the door shut.

I yanked Billy loose and threw him in. As I climbed in myself, one of those spider threads drifted down and lit on my ankle. It burned the way a fishing line pulled rapidly through your closed fist will burn. And it was strong. I gave my foot a hard yank and it broke. I slipped in behind the wheel.

"Shut it, oh shut the door, dear God!" Amanda screamed.

I shut the door. A bare instant later, one of the spiders thumped softly against it. I was only inches from its red, viciously stupid eyes. Its legs, each as thick as my wrist, slipped back and forth across the square bonnet. Amanda screamed ceaselessly, like a firebell.

"Woman, shut your head," Mrs. Reppler told her.

The spider gave up. It could not smell us, ergo we were no longer there. It strutted back into the mist on its unsettling number of legs, became a phantasm, and then was gone.

I looked out the window to make sure it was gone and then opened the door.

"What are you doing?" Amanda screamed, but I knew what I was doing. I like to think Ollie would have done exactly the same thing. I half-stepped, half-leaned out, and got the gun. Something came rapidly toward me, but I never saw it. I pulled back in and slammed the door shut.

Amanda began to sob. Mrs. Reppler put an arm around her and comforted her briskly.

Billy said, "Are we going home, Daddy?"

"Big Bill, we're gonna try."

"Okay," he said quietly.

I checked the gun and then put it into the glove compartment. Ollie had reloaded it after the expedition to the drugstore. The rest of the shells had disappeared with him, but that was all right. He had fired at Mrs. Carmody, he had fired once at the clawed thing, and the gun had discharged once when it hit the ground. There were four of us in the Scout, but if push came right down to shove, I'd find some other way out for myself.

I had a terrible moment when I couldn't find my key ring. I checked all my pockets, came up empty, and then checked them all again, forcing myself to go slowly and calmly. They were in my jeans pocket; they had gotten down under the coins, as keys sometimes will. The Scout started easily. At the confident roar of the engine, Amanda burst into fresh tears.

I sat there, letting it idle, waiting to see what was going to be drawn by the sound of the engine or the smell of the exhaust. Five minutes, the longest five of my life, drifted by. Nothing happened.

"Are we going to sit here or are we going to go?" Mrs. Reppler asked at last.

"Go," I said. I backed out of the slot and put on the low beams.

Some urge—probably a base one—made me cruise past the Federal market as close as I could get. The Scout's right bumper bunted the trash barrel to one side. It was impossible to see in except through the loopholes—all those fertilizer and lawn-food bags made the place look as if it were in the throes of some mad garden sale—but at each loophole there were two or three pale faces, staring out at us.

Then I swung to the left, and the mist closed impenetrably behind us. And what has become of those people I do not know.

I drove back down Kansas Road at five miles an hour, feeling my way. Even with the Scout's headlights and running lights on, it was impossible to see more than seven or ten feet ahead.

The earth had been through some terrible contortion; Miller had been right about that. In places the road was merely cracked, but in others the ground itself seemed to have caved in, tilting up great slabs of paving. I was able to get over with the help of the four-wheel drive. Thank God for that. But I was terribly afraid that we would soon come to an obstacle that even the four-wheel drive couldn't get us over.

It took me forty minutes to make a drive that usually only took seven or eight. At last the sign that marked our private road loomed out of the mist. Billy, roused at a quarter of five, had fallen solidly asleep inside this car that he knew so well it must have seemed like home to him.

Amanda looked at the road nervously. "Are you really going down there?"

"I'm going to try," I said.

But it was impossible. The storm that had whipped through had loosened a lot of trees, and that weird, twisting drop had finished the job of tumbling them. I was able to crunch over the first two; they were fairly small. Then I came to a hoary old pine lying across the road like an outlaw's barricade. It was still almost a quarter of a mile to the house. Billy slept on beside me, and I put the Scout in Park, put my hands over my eyes, and tried to think what to do next.

• • •

Now, as I sit in the Howard Johnson's near Exit 3 of the Maine Turnpike, writing all of this down on HoJo stationery, I suspect that Mrs. Reppler, that tough and capable old broad, could have laid out the essential futility of the situation in a few quick strokes. But she had the kindness to let me think it through for myself.

I couldn't get out. I couldn't leave them. I couldn't even kid myself that all the horror-movie monsters were back at the Federal; when I cracked the window I could hear them in the woods, crashing and blundering around on the steep fall of land they call the Ledges around these parts. The moisture drip-drip-dripped from the overhanging leaves. Overhead the mist darkened momentarily as some nightmarish and half-seen living kite overflew us.

I tried to tell myself—then and now—that if she was very quick, if she buttoned up the house with herself inside, that she had enough food for ten days to two weeks. It only works a little bit. What keeps getting in the way is my last memory of her, wearing her floppy sunhat and gardening gloves, on her way to our little vegetable patch with the mist rolling inexorably across the lake behind her.

It is Billy I have to think about now. Billy, I tell myself. Big Bill, Big Bill . . . I should write it maybe a hundred times on this sheet of paper, like a child condemned to write *I will not throw spitballs in school* as the sunny three-o'clock stillness spills through the windows and the teacher corrects homework papers at her desk and the only sound is her pen, while somewhere, far away, kids pick up teams for scratch baseball.

Anyway, at last I did the only thing I could do. I reversed the Scout carefully back to Kansas Road. Then I cried.

Amanda touched my shoulder timidly. "David, I'm so sorry," she said.

"Yeah," I said, trying to stop the tears and not having much luck. "Yeah, so am I."

I drove to Route 302 and turned left, toward Portland. This road was also cracked and blasted in places, but was, on the whole, more passable than Kansas Road had been. I was worried about the bridges. The face of Maine is cut with running water, and there are bridges everywhere, big and small. But the Naples Causeway was intact, and from there it was plain—if slow—sailing all the way to Portland.

The mist held thick. Once I had to stop, thinking that trees were lying across the road. Then the trees began to move and undulate and I understood they were more tentacles. I stopped, and after a while they drew back. Once a great green thing with an iridescent green body and long transparent wings landed on the hood. It looked like a grossly misshapen dragonfly. It hovered there for a moment, then took wing again and was gone.

Billy woke up about two hours after we had left Kansas Road behind and asked if we had gotten Mommy yet. I told him I hadn't been able to get down our road because of fallen trees.

"Is she all right, Dad?"

"Billy, I don't know. But we'll come back and see."

He didn't cry. He dozed off again instead. I would have rather had his tears. He was sleeping too damn much and I didn't like it.

I began to get a tension headache. It was driving through the fog at a steady five or ten miles an hour that did it, the tension of knowing that anything might come out of it, anything at all—a washout, a landspill, or Ghidra the Three-headed Monster. I think I prayed. I prayed to God that Stephanie was alive and that He wouldn't take my adultery out on her. I prayed to God to let me get Billy to safety because he had been through so much.

Most people had pulled to the side of the road when the mist came, and by noon we were in North Windham. I tried the River Road, but about four miles down, a bridge spanning a small and noisy stream had fallen into the water. I had to reverse for nearly a mile before I found a spot wide enough to turn around. We went to Portland by Route 302 after all.

When we got there, I drove the cutoff to the turnpike. The neat line of tollbooths guarding the access had been turned into vacant-eyed skeletons of smashed Pola-Glas. All of them were empty. In the sliding glass doorway of one was a torn jacket with Maine Turnpike Authority patches on the sleeves. It was drenched with tacky, drying blood. We had not seen a single living person since leaving the Federal.

Mrs. Reppler said, "David, try your radio."

I slapped my forehead in frustration and anger at myself, wondering how I could have been stupid enough to forget the Scout's AM/FM for so long.

"Don't do that," Mrs. Reppler said curtly. "You can't think of everything. If you try, you will go mad and be of no use at all."

I got nothing but a shriek of static all the way across the AM band, and the FM yielded nothing but a smooth and ominous silence.

"Does that mean everything's off the air?" Amanda asked. I knew what she was thinking, maybe. We were far enough south now so that we should have been picking up a selection of strong Boston stations—WRKO, WBZ, WMEX. But if Boston had gone—

"It doesn't mean anything for sure," I said. "That static on the AM band is pure interference. The mist is having a damping effect on radio signals, too."

"Are you sure that's all it is?"

"Yes," I said, not sure at all.

We went south. The mileposts rolled past, counting down from about forty. When we reached Mile 1, we would be at the New Hampshire border. Going on the turnpike was slower; a lot of the drivers hadn't wanted to give up, and there had been rear-end collisions in several places. Several times I had to use the median strip.

At about twenty past one—I was beginning to feel hungry—Billy clutched my arm. "Daddy, what's that? *What's that!*"

A shadow loomed out of the mist, staining it dark. It was as tall as a cliff and coming right at us. I jammed on the brakes. Amanda, who had been catnapping, was thrown forward.

Something came; again, that is all I can say for sure. It may have been the fact that the mist only allowed us to glimpse things briefly, but I think it just as likely that there are certain things that your brain simply disallows. There are things of such darkness and horror—just, I suppose, as there are things of such great beauty—that they will not fit through the puny human doors of perception.

It was six-legged, I know that; its skin was slaty gray that mottled to dark brown in places. Those brown patches reminded me absurdly of the liver spots on Mrs. Carmody's hands. Its skin was deeply wrinkled and grooved, and clinging to it were scores, hundreds, of those pinkish "bugs" with the stalk-eyes. I don't know how big it actually was, but it passed directly over us. One of its gray, wrinkled legs smashed down right beside my window, and Mrs. Reppler said later she could not see the underside of its body, although she craned her neck up to look. She saw only two Cyclopean legs going up and up into the mist like living towers until they were lost to sight.

For the moment it was over the Scout I had an impression

of something so big that it might have made a blue whale look the size of a trout—in other words, something so big that it defied the imagination. Then it was gone, sending a seismological series of thuds back. It left tracks in the cement of the Interstate, tracks so deep I could not see the bottoms. Each single track was nearly big enough to drop the Scout into.

For a moment no one spoke. There was no sound but our breathing and the diminishing thud of that great Thing's passage.

Then Billy said, "Was it a dinosaur, Dad? Like the bird that got into the market?"

"I don't think so. I don't think there was ever an animal that big, Billy. At least not on earth."

I thought of the Arrowhead Project and wondered again what crazy damned thing they could have been doing up there.

"Can we go on?" Amanda asked timidly. "It might come back."

Yes, and there might be more up ahead. But there was no point in saying so. We had to go somewhere. I drove on, weaving in and out between those terrible tracks until they veered off the road.

That is what happened. Or nearly all—there is one final thing I'll get to in a moment. But you mustn't expect some neat conclusion. There is no *And they escaped from the mist into the good sunshine of a new day;* or *When we awoke the National Guard had finally arrived;* or even that great old standby: *It was all a dream.*

It is, I suppose, what my father always frowningly called "an Alfred Hitchcock ending," by which he meant a conclusion in ambiguity that allowed the reader or viewer to make up his own mind about how things ended. My father had nothing but contempt for such stories, saying they were "cheap shots."

We got to this Howard Johnson's near Exit 3 as dusk began to close in, making driving a suicidal risk. Before that, we took a chance on the bridge that spans the Saco River. It looked badly twisted out of shape, but in the mist it was impossible to tell if it was whole or not. That particular game we won.

But there's tomorrow to think of, isn't there?

As I write this, it is a quarter to one in the morning, July the twenty-third. The storm that seemed to signal the beginning of it all was only four days ago. Billy is sleeping in the lobby on a mattress that I dragged out for him. Amanda and Mrs. Reppler are close by. I am writing by the light of a big Delco flashlight, and outside the pink bugs are ticking and thumping off the glass. Every now and then there is a louder thud as one of the birds takes one off.

The Scout has enough gas to take us maybe another ninety miles. The alternative is to try to gas up here; there is an Exxon out on the service island, and although the power is off, I believe I could siphon some up from the tank. But—

But it means being outside.

If we can get gas—here or further along—we'll keep going. I have a destination in mind now, you see. It's that last thing I wanted to tell you about.

I couldn't be sure. That is the thing, the damned thing. It might have been my imagination, nothing but wish fulfillment. And even if not, it is such a long chance. How many miles? How many bridges? How many things that would love to tear up my son and eat him even as he screamed in terror and agony?

The chances are so good that it was nothing but a daydream that I haven't told the others . . . at least, not yet.

In the manager's apartment I found a large battery-operated multiband radio. From the back of it, a flat antenna wire led out through the window. I turned it on, switched over to BAT., fiddled with the tuning dial, with the SQUELCH knob, and still got nothing but static or dead silence.

And then, at the far end of the AM band, just as I was reaching for the knob to turn it off, I thought I heard, or dreamed I heard, one single word.

There was no more. I listened for an hour, but there was no more. If there was that one word, it came through some minute shift in the damping mist, an infinitesimal break that immediately closed again.

One word.

I've got to get some sleep . . . if I can sleep and not be haunted until daybreak by the faces of Ollie Weeks and Mrs. Carmody and Norm the bag-boy . . . and by Steff's face, half-shadowed by the wide brim of her sunhat.

There is a restaurant here, a typical HoJo restaurant with a dining room and a long, horseshoe-shaped lunch counter. I am going to leave these pages on the counter and perhaps someday someone will find them and read them.

One word.

If I only really heard it. If only.

I'm going to bed now. But first I'm going to kiss my son and whisper two words in his ear. Against the dreams that may come, you know.

Two words that sound a bit alike.

One of them is Hartford.

The other is hope.

ABOUT THE AUTHOR

Stephen King is the author of more than fifty books, all of them worldwide bestsellers. His recent work includes *The Outsider*; *Sleeping Beauties* (co-written with his son Owen King); the short story collection *The Bazaar of Bad Dreams;* the Bill Hodges Trilogy—*End of Watch*, *Finders Keepers*, and *Mr. Mercedes* (an Edgar Award winner for Best Novel and now an AT&T Audience Network original television series); *Doctor Sleep;* and *Under the Dome*. His novel *11/22/63*—a Hulu original television series event—was named a top ten book of 2011 by the *New York Times Book Review* and won the Los Angeles Times Book Prize for Mystery/Thriller. His epic works The Dark Tower and *It* are the basis for major motion pictures. He is the recipient of the 2018 PEN America Literary Service Award, the 2014 National Medal of Arts, and the 2003 National Book Foundation Medal for Distinguished Contribution to American Letters. He lives in Bangor, Maine, with his wife, novelist Tabitha King.

ALSO BY STEPHEN KING

FICTION

Carrie
'Salem's Lot
The Shining
Night Shift
The Stand
The Dead Zone
Firestarter
Cujo
Creepshow
Different Seasons
The Body
Cycle of the Werewolf
Christine
Pet Sematary
IT
Skeleton Crew
The Mist
The Eyes of the Dragon
Misery
The Tommyknockers
The Dark Half
Four Past Midnight
The Sun Dog
Needful Things
Gerald's Game
Dolores Claiborne
Nightmares & Dreamscapes
Insomnia
Rose Madder
The Green Mile
Desperation
The Girl Who Loved Tom Gordon
Hearts in Atlantis
Dreamcatcher
Everything's Eventual
From a Buick 8
The Colorado Kid
Cell
Lisey's Story
Duma Key
Just After Sunset
Stephen King Goes to the Movies
Under the Dome
Full Dark, No Stars
11/22/63
Doctor Sleep
Mr. Mercedes
Revival
Finders Keepers
The Bazaar of Bad Dreams
End of Watch
The Outsider
Elevation

NOVELS IN THE DARK TOWER SERIES

The Dark Tower I: The Gunslinger
The Dark Tower II: The Drawing of the Three
The Dark Tower III: The Waste Lands
The Dark Tower IV: Wizard and Glass
The Dark Tower V: Wolves of the Calla
The Dark Tower VI: Song of Susannah
The Dark Tower VII: The Dark Tower
The Wind Through the Keyhole: A Dark Tower Novel

BY STEPHEN KING AS RICHARD BACHMAN

Thinner
The Running Man
The Long Walk
Roadwork
The Regulators
Blaze

WITH OWEN KING

Sleeping Beauties

WITH PETER STRAUB

The Talisman
Black House

NONFICTION

Danse Macabre
On Writing (A Memoir of the Craft)

STEPHEN KING

APT PUPIL

SCRIBNER
New York London Toronto Sydney New Delhi

Scribner
An Imprint of Simon & Schuster, Inc.
1230 Avenue of the Americas
New York, NY 10020

This Scribner trade paperback edition December 2018

Manufactured in the United States of America

7 9 10 8 6

Library of Congress Cataloging-in-Publication Data is available.

ISBN 978-1-9821-1544-9
ISBN 978-1-9821-1545-6 (ebook)

For Elaine Koster and Herbert Schnall

1

He looked like the total all-American kid as he pedaled his twenty-six-inch Schwinn with the apehanger handlebars up the residential suburban street, and that's just what he was: Todd Bowden, thirteen years old, five-feet-eight and a healthy one hundred and forty pounds, hair the color of ripe corn, blue eyes, white even teeth, lightly tanned skin marred by not even the first shadow of adolescent acne.

He was smiling a summer vacation smile as he pedaled through the sun and shade not too far from his own house. He looked like the kind of kid who might have a paper route, and as a matter of fact, he did—he delivered the Santo Donato *Clarion.* He also looked like the kind of kid who might sell greeting cards for premiums, and he had done that, too. They were the kind that come with your name printed inside—JACK AND MARY BURKE, OR DON AND SALLY, OR THE MURCHISONS. He looked like the sort of boy who might whistle while he worked, and he often did so. He whistled quite prettily, in fact. His dad was an architectural engineer who made forty thousand dollars a year. His mom had majored in French in college and had met Todd's father when he desperately needed a tutor. She typed manuscripts in her spare time. She had kept all of Todd's old school report cards in a folder. Her favorite was his final fourth-grade card, on which Mrs. Upshaw had scratched: "Todd is an extremely apt pupil." He was, too. Straight A's and B's all the way up the line. If he'd done any better—straight A's, for example—his friends might have begun to think he was weird.

Now he brought his bike to a halt in front of 963 Claremont Street and stepped off it. The house was a small bungalow set discreetly back on its lot. It was white with green shutters and green trim. A hedge ran around the front. The hedge was well-watered and well-clipped.

Todd brushed his blonde hair out of his eyes and walked the Schwinn up the cement path to the steps. He was still smiling, and his smile was open and expectant and beautiful. He pushed down the bike's kickstand with the toe of one Nike running-shoe and then picked the folded newspaper off the bottom step. It wasn't the *Clarion;* it was the *LA. Times.* He put it under his arm and mounted the steps. At the top was a heavy wooden door with no window inside of a latched screen door. There was a doorbell on the right-hand doorframe, and below the bell were two small signs, each neatly screwed into the wood and covered with protective plastic so they wouldn't yellow or waterspot. German efficiency, Todd thought, and his smile widened a little. It was an adult thought, and he always mentally congratulated himself when he had one of those.

The top sign said ARTHUR DENKER.

The bottom one said NO SOLICITORS, NO PEDDLERS, NO SALESMEN.

Smiling still, Todd rang the bell.

He could barely hear its muted burring, somewhere far off inside the small house. He took his finger off the bell and cocked his head a little, listening for footsteps. There were none. He looked at his Timex watch (one of the premiums he had gotten for selling personalized greeting cards) and saw that it was twelve past ten. The guy should be up by now. Todd himself was always up by seven-thirty at the latest, even during summer vacation. The early bird catches the worm.

He listened for another thirty seconds and when the house remained silent he leaned on the bell, watching the sweep second hand on his Timex as he did so. He had been pressing the doorbell for exactly seventy-one seconds when he finally heard shuffling footsteps. Slippers, he deduced from the soft *wish-wish* sound. Todd was into deductions. His current ambition was to become a private detective when he grew up.

"All right! All right!" the man who was pretending to be Arthur Denker called querulously. "I'm coming! Let it go! I'm coming!"

Todd stopped pushing the doorbell button.

A chain and bolt rattled on the far side of the windowless inner door. Then it was pulled open.

An old man, hunched inside a bathrobe, stood looking out through the screen. A cigarette smouldered between his fingers. Todd thought the man looked like a cross between Albert Einstein and Boris Karloff. His hair was long and white but beginning to yellow in an unpleasant way that was more nicotine than ivory. His face was wrinkled and pouched and puffy with sleep, and Todd saw with some distaste that he hadn't bothered shaving for the last couple of days. Todd's father was fond of saying, "A shave puts a shine on the morning." Todd's father shaved every day, whether he had to work or not.

The eyes looking out at Todd were watchful but deeply sunken, laced with snaps of red. Todd felt an instant of deep disappointment. The guy *did* look a little bit like Albert Einstein, and he *did* look a little bit like Boris Karloff, but what he looked like more than anything else was one of the seedy old winos that hung around down by the railroad yard.

But of course, Todd reminded himself, the man had just gotten up. Todd had seen Denker many times before today (although he had been very careful to make sure that Denker hadn't seen *him, no way,* Jose), and on his public occasions, Denker looked very natty, every inch an officer in retirement, you might say, even though he was seventy-six if the articles Todd had read at the library had his birth-date right. On the days when Todd had shadowed him to the Shoprite where Denker did his shopping or to one of the three movie theaters on the bus line—Denker had no car—he was always dressed in one of three neatly kept suits, no matter how warm the weather. If the weather looked threatening he carried a furled umbrella under one arm like a swagger stick. He sometimes wore a trilby hat. And on the occasions when Denker went out, he was always neatly shaved and his white moustache (worn to conceal an imperfectly corrected harelip) was carefully trimmed.

"A boy," he said now. His voice was thick and sleepy. Todd saw with new disappointment that his robe was faded and tacky. One rounded collar point stood up at a drunken angle to poke at his wattled neck. There was a splotch of something that might have been chili or possibly A-1 Steak Sauce on the left lapel, and he smelled of cigarettes and stale booze.

"A boy," he repeated. "I don't need anything, boy. Read the sign. You can read, can't you? Of course you can. All American boys can read. Don't be a nuisance, boy. Good day."

The door began to close.

He might have dropped it right there, Todd thought much later on one of the nights when sleep was hard to find. His disappointment at seeing the man for the first time at close range, seeing him with his street-face put away—hanging in the closet, you might say, along with his umbrella and his trilby—might have done it. It could have ended in that moment, the tiny, unimportant snicking sound of the latch cutting off everything that happened later as neatly as a pair of shears. But, as the man himself had observed, he was an American boy, and he had been taught that persistence is a virtue.

"Don't forget your paper, Mr. Dussander," Todd said, holding the *Times* out politely.

The door stopped dead in its swing, still inches from the jamb. A tight and watchful expression flitted across Kurt Dussander's face and was gone at once. There might have been fear in that expression. It was good, the way he had made that expression disappear, but Todd was disappointed for the third time. He hadn't expected Dussander to be good; he had expected Dussander to be *great.*

Boy, Todd thought with real disgust. *Boy oh boy.*

He pulled the door open again. One hand, bunched with arthritis, unlatched the screen door. The hand pushed the screen door open just enough to wriggle through like a spider and close over the edge of the paper Todd was holding out. The boy saw with distaste that the old man's fingernails were long and yellow and horny. It was a hand that had spent most of its waking hours holding one cigarette after another. Todd thought smoking was a filthy dangerous habit, one he himself would never take up. It really was a wonder that Dussander had lived as long as he had.

The old man tugged. "Give me my paper."

"Sure thing, Mr. Dussander." Todd released his hold on the paper. The spider-hand yanked it inside. The screen closed.

"My name is Denker," the old man said. "Not this Doo-Zander. Apparently you cannot read. What a pity. Good day."

The door started to close again. Todd spoke rapidly into the narrowing gap. "Bergen-Belsen, January 1943 to June 1943. Auschwitz, June 1943 to June of 1944, *Unterkommandant.* Patin—"

The door stopped again. The old man's pouched and pallid face hung in the gap like a wrinkled, half-deflated balloon. Todd smiled.

"You left Patin just ahead of the Russians. You got to Buenos Aires. Some people say you got rich there, investing the gold you took out of Germany in the drug trade. Whatever, you were in Mexico City from 1950 to 1952. Then—"

"Boy, you are crazy like a cuckoo bird." One of the arthritic fingers twirled circles around a misshapen ear. But the toothless mouth was quivering in an infirm, panicky way.

"From 1952 until 1958, I don't know," Todd said, smiling more widely still. "No one does, I guess, or at least they're not telling. But an Israeli agent spotted you in Cuba, working as the concierge in a big hotel just before Castro took over. They lost you when the rebels came into Havana. You popped up in West Berlin in 1965. They almost got you." He pronounced the last two words as one: *gotcha.* At the same time he squeezed all of his fingers together into one large, wriggling fist. Dussander's eyes dropped to those well-made and well-nourished American hands, hands that were made for building soapbox racers and Aurora models. Todd had done both. In fact, the year before, he and his dad had built a model of the *Titanic.* It had taken almost four months, and Todd's father kept it in his office.

"I don't know what you are talking about," Dussander said. Without his false teeth, his words had a mushy sound Todd didn't like. It didn't sound . . . well, authentic. Colonel Klink on *Hogan's Heroes* sounded more like a Nazi than Dussander did. But in his time he must have been a real whiz. In an article on the death-camps in *Men's Action,* the writer had called him The Blood-Fiend of Patin. "Get out of here, boy. Before I call the police."

"Gee, I guess you better call them, Mr. Dussander. Or Herr Dussander, if you like that better." He continued to smile, showing perfect teeth that had been fluoridated since the beginning of his life and bathed thrice a day in Crest toothpaste for almost as long. "After 1965, no one saw you again . . . until I did, two months ago, on the downtown bus."

"You're insane."

"So if you want to call the police," Todd said, smiling, "you go right ahead. I'll wait on the stoop. But if you don't want to call them right away, why don't I come in? We'll talk."

There was a long moment while the old man looked at the smiling boy. Birds twitted in the trees. On the next block a power mower was running, and far off, on busier streets, horns honked out their own rhythm of life and commerce.

In spite of everything, Todd felt the onset of doubt. He couldn't be wrong, could he? Was there some mistake on his part? He didn't think so, but this was no schoolroom exercise. It was real life. So he felt a surge of relief (*mild* relief, he assured himself later) when Dussander said: "You may come in for a moment, if you like. But only because I do not wish to make trouble for you, you understand?"

"Sure, Mr. Dussander," Todd said. He opened the screen and came into the hall. Dussander closed the door behind them, shutting off the morning.

The house smelled stale and slightly malty. It smelled the way Todd's own house smelled sometimes the morning after his folks had thrown a party and before his mother had had a chance to air it out. But this smell was worse. It was lived-in and ground-in. It was liquor, fried food, sweat, old clothes, and some stinky medicinal smell like Vick's or Mentholatum. It was dark in the hallway, and Dussander was standing too close, his head hunched into the collar of his robe like the head of a vulture waiting for some hurt animal to give up the ghost. In that instant, despite the stubble and the loosely hanging flesh, Todd could see the man who had stood inside the black SS uniform more clearly than he had ever seen him on the street. And he felt a sudden lancet of fear slide into his belly. *Mild* fear, he amended later.

"I should tell you that if anything happens to me—" he began, and then Dussander shuffled past him and into the living room, his slippers *wish-wishing* on the floor. He flapped a contemptuous hand at Todd, and Todd felt a flush of hot blood mount into his throat and cheeks.

Todd followed him, his smile wavering for the first time. He had not pictured it happening quite like this. But it would work out. Things would come into focus. Of course they would. Things always did. He began to smile again as he stepped into the living room.

It was another disappointment—and how!—but one he supposed he should have been prepared for. There was of course no oil portrait of Hitler with his forelock dangling and eyes that followed you. No medals in cases, no ceremonial sword mounted on the wall, no Luger or PPK Walther on the mantel (there was, in fact, no mantel). Of course,

Todd told himself, the guy would have to be crazy to put any of those things out where people could see them. Still, it was hard to put everything you saw in the movies or on TV out of your head. It looked like the living room of any old man living alone on a slightly frayed pension. The fake fireplace was faced with fake bricks. A Westclox hung over it. There was a black and white Motorola TV on a stand; the tips of the rabbit ears had been wrapped in aluminum foil to improve reception. The floor was covered with a gray rug; its nap was balding. The magazine rack by the sofa held copies of *National Geographic, Reader's Digest,* and the *L.A. Times.* Instead of Hitler or a ceremonial sword hung on the wall, there was a framed certificate of citizenship and a picture of a woman in a funny hat. Dussander later told him that sort of hat was called a cloche, and they had been popular in the twenties and thirties.

"My wife," Dussander said sentimentally. "She died in 1955 of a lung disease. At that time I was working at the Menschler Motor Works in Essen. I was heartbroken."

Todd continued to smile. He crossed the room as if to get a better look at the woman in the picture. Instead of looking at the picture, he fingered the shade on a small table-lamp.

"Stop that!" Dussander barked harshly. Todd jumped back a little.

"That was good," he said sincerely. "Really commanding. It was Ilse Koch who had the lampshades made out of human skin, wasn't it? And she was the one who had the trick with the little glass tubes."

"I don't know what you're talking about," Dussander said. There was a package of Kools, the kind with no filter, on top of the TV. He offered them to Todd. "Cigarette?" he asked, and grinned. His grin was hideous.

"No. They give you lung cancer. My dad used to smoke, but he gave it up. He went to Smokenders."

"Did he." Dussander produced a wooden match from the

pocket of his robe and scratched it indifferently on the plastic case of the Motorola. Puffing, he said: "Can you give me one reason why I shouldn't call the police and tell them of the monstrous accusations you've just made? One reason? Speak quickly, boy. The telephone is just down the hall. Your father would spank you, I think. You would sit for dinner on a cushion for a week or so, eh?"

"My parents don't believe in spanking. Corporal punishment causes more problems than it cures." Todd's eyes suddenly gleamed. "Did you spank any of them? The women? Did you take off their clothes and—"

With a muffled exclamation, Dussander started for the phone.

Todd said coldly: "You better not do that."

Dussander turned. In measured tones that were spoiled only slightly by the fact that his false teeth were not in, he said: "I tell you this once, boy, and once only. My name is Arthur Denker. It has never been anything else; it has not even been Americanized. I was in fact named Arthur by my father, who greatly admired the stories of Arthur Conan Doyle. It has never been Doo-Zander, or Himmler, or Father Christmas. I was a reserve lieutenant in the war. I never joined the Nazi party. In the battle of Berlin I fought for three weeks. I will admit that in the late thirties, when I was first married, I supported Hitler. He ended the depression and returned some of the pride we had lost in the aftermath of the sickening and unfair Treaty of Versailles. I suppose I supported him mostly because I got a job and there was tobacco again, and I didn't need to hunt through the gutters when I needed to smoke. I thought, in the late thirties, that he was a great man. In his own way, perhaps he was. But at the end he was mad, directing phantom armies at the whim of an astrologer. He even gave Blondi, his dog, a death-capsule. The act of a madman; by the end they were all madmen, singing the 'Horst Wessel Song' as they fed poison to their children. On May 2nd, 1945, my regiment gave up to the Americans. I remember that a private soldier named Hackermeyer gave me a chocolate bar. I wept. There was no reason to fight on; the war was over, and really had been since February. I was interned at Essen and was treated very well. We listened to the Nuremberg trials on the radio, and when Goering committed suicide, I traded fourteen American cigarettes for half a bottle of *Schnaps* and got drunk. When I was released, I put wheels on cars at the Essen Motor Works until 1963, when I retired. Later I emigrated to the United States. To come here was a lifelong ambition. In 1967 I became a citizen. I am an American. I vote. No Buenos Aires. No drug dealing. No Berlin. No Cuba." He pronounced it *Koo-ba.* "And now, unless you leave, I make my telephone call."

He watched Todd do nothing. Then he went down the hall and picked up the telephone. Still Todd stood in the living room, beside the table with the small lamp on it.

Dussander began to dial. Todd watched him, his heart speeding up until it was drumming in his chest. After the fourth number, Dussander turned and looked at him. His shoulders sagged. He put the phone down.

"A boy," he breathed, "A *boy*."

Todd smiled widely but rather modestly.

"How did you find out?"

"One piece of luck and a lot of hard work," Todd said. "There's this friend of mine, Harold Pegler his name is, only all the kids call him Foxy. He plays second base for our team. His dad's got all these magazines out in his garage. Great big stacks of them. War magazines. They're old. I looked for some new ones, but the guy who runs the newsstand across from the school says most of them went out of business. In most of them there's pictures of krauts—German soldiers, I mean—and Japs torturing these women. And articles about the concentration camps. I really groove on all that concentration camp stuff."

"You . . . groove on it." Dussander was staring at him, one

hand rubbing up and down on his cheek, producing a very small sandpapery sound.

"Groove. You know. I get off on it. I'm interested."

He remembered that day in Foxy's garage as clearly as anything in his life—more clearly, he suspected. He remembered in the fifth grade, before Careers Day, how Mrs. Anderson (all the kids called her Bugs because of her big front teeth) had talked to them about what she called finding YOUR GREAT INTEREST.

"It comes all at once," Bugs Anderson had rhapsodized. "You see something for the first time, and right away you know you have found YOUR GREAT INTEREST. It's like a key turning in a lock. Or falling in love for the first time. That's why Careers Day is so important, children—it may be the day on which you find YOUR GREAT INTEREST." And she had gone on to tell them about her own GREAT INTEREST, which turned out not to be teaching the fifth grade but collecting nineteenth-century postcards.

Todd had thought Mrs. Anderson was full of bullspit at the time, but that day in Foxy's garage, he remembered what she had said and wondered if maybe she hadn't been right after all.

The Santa Anas had been blowing that day, and to the east there were brush-fires. He remembered the smell of burning, hot and greasy. He remembered Foxy's crewcut, and the flakes of Butch Wax clinging to the front of it. He remembered *everything.*

"I know there's comics here someplace," Foxy had said. His mother had a hangover and had kicked them out of the house for making too much noise. "Neat ones. They're Westerns, mostly, but there's some *Turok, Son of Stone* and—"

"What are those?" Todd asked, pointing at the bulging cardboard cartons under the stairs.

"Ah, they're no good," Foxy said. "True war stories, mostly. Boring."

"Can I look at some?"

"Sure. I'll find the comics."

But by the time fat Foxy Pegler found them, Todd no longer wanted to read comics. He was lost. Utterly lost.

It's like a key turning in a lock. Or falling in love for the first time.

It *had* been like that. He had known about the war, of course—not the stupid one going on now, where the Americans had gotten the shit kicked out of them by a bunch of gooks in black pajamas—but World War II. He knew that the Americans wore round helmets with net on them and the krauts wore sort of square ones. He knew that the Americans won most of the battles and that the Germans had invented rockets near the end and shot them from Germany onto London. He had even known something about the concentration camps.

The difference between all of that and what he found in the magazines under the stairs in Foxy's garage was like the difference between being *told* about germs and then actually *seeing* them in a microscope, squirming around and alive.

Here was Ilse Koch. Here were crematoriums with their doors standing open on their soot-clotted hinges. Here were officers in SS uniforms and prisoners in striped uniforms. The smell of the old pulp magazines was like the smell of the brush-fires burning out of control on the east of Santo Donato, and he could feel the old paper crumbling against the pads of his fingers, and he turned the pages, no longer in Foxy's garage but caught somewhere crosswise in time, trying to cope with the idea that *they had really done those things,* that *somebody had really done those things,* and that *somebody had let them do those things,* and his head began to ache with a mixture of revulsion and excitement, and his eyes were hot and strained, but he read on, and from a column of print beneath a picture of tangled bodies at a place called Dachau, this figure jumped out at him:

6,000,000.

And he thought: *Somebody goofed there, somebody added a zero or two, that's twice as many people as there are in L.A.!* But then, in another magazine (the cover of this one showed a woman chained to a wall while a guy in a Nazi uniform approached her with a poker in his hand and a grin on his face), he saw it again:

6,000,000.

His headache got worse. His mouth went dry. Dimly, from some distance, he heard Foxy saying he had to go in for supper. Todd asked Foxy if he could stay here in the garage and read while Foxy ate. Foxy gave him a look of mild puzzlement, shrugged, and said sure. And Todd read, hunched over the boxes of the old true war magazines, until his mother called and asked if he was *ever* going to go home.

Like a key turning in a lock.

All the magazines said it was bad, what had happened. But all the stories were continued at the back of the book, and when you turned to those pages, the words saying it was bad were surrounded by ads, and these ads sold German knives and belts and helmets as well as Magic Trusses and Guaranteed Hair Restorer. These ads sold German flags emblazoned with swastikas and Nazi Lugers and a game called Panzer Attack as well as correspondence lessons and offers to make you rich selling elevator shoes to short men. They said it was bad, but it seemed like a lot of people must not mind.

Like falling in love.

Oh yes, he remembered that day very well. He remembered everything about it—a yellowing pin-up calendar for a defunct year on the back wall, the oil-stain on the cement floor, the way the magazines had been tied together with orange twine. He remembered how his headache had gotten a little worse each time he thought of that incredible number,

6,000,000.

He remembered thinking: *I want to know about everything that happened in those places. Everything. And I want to know which is more true—the words, or the ads they put beside the words.*

He remembered Bugs Anderson as he at last pushed the boxes back under the stairs and thought: *She was right. I've found my GREAT INTEREST.*

Dussander looked at Todd for a long time. Then he crossed the living room and sat down heavily in a rocking chair. He looked at Todd again, unable to analyze the slightly dreamy, slightly nostalgic expression on the boy's face.

"Yeah. It was the magazines that got me interested, but I figured a lot of what they said was just, you know, bullspit. So I went to the library and found out a lot more stuff. Some of it was even neater. At first the crummy librarian didn't want me to look at any of it because it was in the adult section of the library, but I told her it was for school. If it's for school they have to let you have it. She called my dad, though." Todd's eyes turned up scornfully. "Like she thought Dad didn't know what I was doing, if you can dig that."

"He did know?"

"Sure. My dad thinks kids should find out about life as soon as they can—the bad as well as the good. Then they'll be ready for it. He says life is a tiger you have to grab by the tail, and if you don't know the nature of the beast it will eat you up."

"Mmmm," Dussander said.

"My mom thinks the same way."

"Mmmmm." Dussander looked dazed, not quite sure where he was.

"Anyhow," Todd said, "the library stuff was real good. They must have had a hundred books with stuff in them about the Nazi concentration camps, just here in the Santo Donato library. A *lot* of people must like to read about that stuff. There weren't as many pictures as in Foxy's dad's magazines, but the other stuff was real gooshy. Chairs with spikes sticking up through the seats. Pulling out gold teeth with pliers. Poison gas that came out of the showers." Todd shook his head. "You guys just went overboard, you know that? You really did."

"Gooshy," Dussander said heavily.

"I really *did* do a research paper, and you know what I got on it? An A-plus. Of course I had to be careful. You have to write that stuff in a certain way. You got to be careful."

"Do you?" Dussander asked. He took another cigarette with a hand that trembled.

"Oh yeah. All those library books, they read a certain way. Like the guys who wrote them got puking sick over what they were writing about." Todd was frowning, wrestling with the thought, trying to bring it out. The fact that *tone,* as that word is applied to writing, wasn't yet in his vocabulary, made it more difficult. "They all write like they lost a lot of sleep over it. How we've got to be careful so nothing like that ever happens again. I made my paper like that, and I guess the teacher gave me an A just cause I read the source material without losing my lunch." Once more, Todd smiled winningly.

Dussander dragged heavily on his unfiltered Kool. The tip trembled slightly. As he feathered smoke out of his nostrils, he coughed an old man's dank, hollow cough. "I can hardly believe this conversation is taking place," he said. He leaned forward and peered closely at Todd. "Boy, do you know the word 'existentialism'?"

Todd ignored the question. "Did you ever meet Ilse Koch?"

"Ilse Koch?" Almost inaudibly, Dussander said: "Yes, I met her."

"Was she beautiful?" Todd asked eagerly. "I mean . . ." His hands described an hourglass in the air.

"Surely you have seen her photograph?" Dussander asked. "An aficionado such as yourself?"

"What's an af . . . aff . . ."

"An aficionado," Dussander said, "is one who grooves. One who . . . gets off on something."

"Yeah? Cool." Todd's grin, puzzled and weak for a moment, shone out triumphantly again. "Sure, I've seen her picture. But you know how they are in those books." He spoke as if Dussander had them all. "Black and white, fuzzy . . . just snapshots. None of those guys knew they were taking pictures for, you know, *history.* Was she really stacked?"

"She was fat and dumpy and she had bad skin," Dussander said shortly. He crushed his cigarette out half-smoked in a Table Talk pie-dish filled with dead butts.

"Oh. Golly." Todd's face fell.

"Just luck," Dussander mused, looking at Todd. "You saw my picture in a war-adventures magazine and happened to ride next to me on the bus. *Tcha!*" He brought a fist down on the arm of his chair, but without much force.

"No sir, Mr. Dussander. There was more to it than that. A *lot,*" Todd added earnestly, leaning forward.

"Oh? Really?" The bushy eyebrows rose, signalling polite disbelief.

"Sure. I mean, the pictures of you in my scrapbook were all thirty years old, at least. I mean, it *is* 1974."

"You keep a . . . a scrapbook?"

"Oh, yes, sir! It's a good one. Hundreds of pictures. I'll show it to you sometime. You'll go ape."

Dussander's face pulled into a revolted grimace, but he said nothing.

"The first couple of times I saw you, I wasn't sure at all. And then you got on the bus one day when it was raining, and you had this shiny black slicker on—"

"That," Dussander breathed.

"Sure. There was a picture of you in a coat like that in one of the magazines out in Foxy's garage. Also, a photo of you in your SS greatcoat in one of the library books. And when I saw you that day, I just said to myself, 'It's for sure. That's Kurt Dussander.' So I started to shadow you—"

"You did *what?*"

"Shadow you. Follow you. My ambition is to be a private detective like Sam Spade in the books, or Mannix on TV. Anyway, I was super careful. I didn't want you to get wise. Want to look at some pictures?"

Todd took a folded-over manila envelope from his back pocket. Sweat had stuck the flap down. He peeled it back carefully. His eyes were sparkling like a boy thinking about his birthday, or Christmas, or the firecrackers he will shoot off on the Fourth of July.

"You took pictures of me?"

"Oh, you bet. I got this little camera. A Kodak. It's thin and flat and fits right into your hand. Once you get the hang of it, you can take pictures of the subject just by holding the camera in your hand and spreading your fingers enough to let the lens peek through. Then you hit the button with your thumb." Todd laughed modestly. "I got the hang of it, but I took a lot of pictures of my fingers while I did. I hung right in there, though. I think a person can do anything if they try hard enough, you know it? It's corny but true."

Kurt Dussander had begun to look white and ill, shrunken inside his robe. "Did you have these pictures finished by a commercial developer, boy?"

"Huh?" Todd looked shocked and startled, then contemptuous. "No! What do you think I am, stupid? My dad's got a darkroom. I've been developing my own pictures since I was nine."

Dussander said nothing, but he relaxed a little and some color came back into his face.

Todd handed him several glossy prints, the rough edges confirming that they had been home-developed. Dussander went through them, silently grim. Here he was sitting erect in a window seat of the downtown bus, with a copy of the latest James Michener, *Centennial,* in his hands. Here he was at the Devon Avenue bus stop, his umbrella under his arm and his head cocked back at an angle which suggested De Gaulle at his most imperial. Here he was standing on line just under the marquee of the Majestic Theater, erect and silent, conspicuous among the leaning teenagers and blank-faced housewives in curlers by his height and his bearing. Finally, here he was peering into his own mailbox.

"I was scared you might see me on that one," Todd said. "It was a calculated risk. I was right across the street. Boy oh boy, I wish I could afford a Minolta with a telephoto lens. Someday . . ." Todd looked wistful.

"No doubt you had a story ready, just in case."

"I was going to ask you if you'd seen my dog. Anyway, after I developed the pix, I compared them to these."

He handed Dussander three Xeroxed photographs. He had seen them all before, many times. The first showed him in his office at the Patin resettlement camp; it had been cropped so nothing showed but him and the Nazi flag on its stand by his desk. The second was a picture that had been taken on the day of his enlistment. The last showed him shaking hands with Heinrich Gluecks, who had been subordinate only to Himmler himself.

"I was pretty sure then, but I couldn't see if you had the harelip because of your goshdamn moustache. But I had to be sure, so I got this."

He handed over the last sheet from his envelope. It had been folded over many times. Dirt was grimed into the creases. The corners were lopped and milled—the way papers get when they spend a long time in the pockets of young boys who have no shortage of things to do and places to go. It was a copy of the Israeli want-sheet on Kurt Dussander. Holding it in his hands, Dussander reflected on corpses that were unquiet and refused to stay buried.

"I took your fingerprints," Todd said, smiling. "And then I did the compares to the one on the sheet."

Dussander gaped at him and then uttered the German word for shit. "You did not!"

"Sure I did. My mom and dad gave me a fingerprint set for Christmas last year. A real one, not just a toy. It had the powder and three brushes for three different surfaces and special paper for lifting them. My folks know I want to be a PI when I grow up. Of course, they think I'll grow out of it." He dismissed this idea with a disinterested lift and drop of his shoulders. "The book explained all about whorls and lands and points of similarity. They're called *compares.* You need eight compares for a fingerprint to get accepted in court.

"So anyway, one day when you were at the movies, I came here and dusted your mailbox and doorknob and lifted all the prints I could. Pretty smart, huh?"

Dussander said nothing. He was clutching the arms of his chair, and his toothless, deflated mouth was trembling. Todd didn't like that. It made him look like he was on the verge of tears. That, of course, was ridiculous. The Blood-Fiend of Patin in tears? You might as well expect Chevrolet to go bankrupt or McDonald's to give up burgers and start selling caviar and truffles.

"I got two sets of prints," Todd said. "One of them didn't look anything like the ones on the wanted poster. I figured those were the postman's. The rest were yours. I found more than eight compares. I found fourteen good ones." He grinned. "And that's how I did it."

"You are a little *bastard*," Dussander said, and for a moment his eyes shone dangerously. Todd felt a tingling little thrill, as he had in the hall. Then Dussander slumped back again.

"Whom have you told?"

"No one."

"Not even this friend? This Cony Pegler?"

"Foxy. Foxy Pegler. Nah, he's a blabbermouth. I haven't told anybody. There's nobody I trust that much."

"What do you want? Money? There is none, I'm afraid. In South America there was, although it was nothing as romantic or dangerous as the drug trade. There is—there *was*—a kind of 'old boy network' in Brazil and Paraguay and Santo Domingo. Fugitives from the war. I became part of their circle and did modestly well in minerals and ores—tin, copper, bauxite. Then the changes came. Nationalism, anti-Americanism. I might have ridden out the changes, but then Wiesenthal's men caught my scent. Bad luck follows bad luck, boy, like dogs after a bitch in heat. Twice they almost had me; once I heard the Jew-bastards in the next room.

"They hanged Eichmann," he whispered. One hand went to his neck, and his eyes had become as round as the eyes of a child listening to the darkest passage of a scary tale—"Hansel and Gretel," perhaps, or "Bluebeard." "He was an old man, of no danger to anyone. He was apolitical. Still, they hanged him."

Todd nodded.

"At last, I went to the only people who could help me. They had helped others, and I could run no more."

"You went to the Odessa?" Todd asked eagerly.

'To the Sicilians," Dussander said dryly, and Todd's face fell again. "It was arranged. False papers, false past. Would you care for a drink, boy?"

"Sure. You got a Coke?"

"No Coke." He pronounced it *Kök.*

"Milk?"

"Milk." Dussander went through the archway and into the kitchen. A fluorescent bar buzzed into life. "I live now on stock dividends," his voice came back. "Stocks I picked up after the war under yet another name. Through a bank in the State of Maine, if you please. The banker who bought them for me went to jail for murdering his wife a year after I bought them . . . life is sometimes strange, boy, *hein*?"

A refrigerator door opened and closed.

"The Sicilian jackals didn't know about those stocks," he said. "Today the Sicilians are everywhere, but in those days, Boston was as far north as they could be found. If they had known, they would have had those as well. They would have picked me clean and sent me to America to starve on welfare and food stamps."

Todd heard a cupboard door opened; he heard liquid poured into a glass.

"A little General Motors, a little American Telephone and Telegraph, a hundred and fifty shares of Revlon. All this banker's choices. Dufresne, his name was—I remember, because it sounds a little like mine. It seems he was not so smart at wife-killing as he was at picking growth stocks. The *crime passionel,* boy. It only proves that all men are donkeys who can read."

He came back into the room, slippers whispering. He held two green plastic glasses that looked like the premiums they sometimes gave out at gas station openings. When you filled your tank, you got a free glass. Dussander thrust a glass at Todd.

"I lived adequately on the stock portfolio this Dufresne had set up for me for the first five years I was here. But then I sold my Diamond Match stock in order to buy this house and a small cottage not far from Big Sur. Then, inflation. Recession. I sold the cottage and one by one I sold the stocks, many of them at fantastic profits. I wish to God I had bought more. But I thought I was well-protected in other directions; the stocks were, as you Americans say, a 'flier . . .'" He made a toothless hissing sound and snapped his fingers.

Todd was bored. He had not come here to listen to Dussander whine about his money or mutter about his stocks. The thought of blackmailing Dussander had never even crossed Todd's mind. Money? What would he do with it? He had his allowance; he had his paper route. If his monetary needs went higher than what these could provide during any given week, there was always someone who needed his lawn mowed.

Todd lifted his milk to his lips and then hesitated. His smile shone out again . . . an admiring smile. He extended the gas station premium glass to Dussander.

"*You* have some of it," he said slyly.

Dussander stared at him for a moment, uncomprehending, and then rolled his bloodshot eyes. *"Grüss Gott!"* He took the glass, swallowed twice, and handed it back. "No gasping for breath. No clawing at the t'roat. No smell of bitter almonds. It is milk, boy. *Milk.* From the Dairylea Farms. On the carton is a picture of a smiling cow."

Todd watched him warily for a moment, then took a small sip. Yes, it *tasted* like milk, sure did, but somehow he didn't feel very thirsty anymore. He put the glass down. Dussander shrugged, raised his own glass, and took a swallow. He smacked his lips over it.

"Schnaps?" Todd asked.

"Bourbon. Ancient Age. Very nice. And cheap."

Todd fiddled his fingers along the seams of his jeans.

"So," Dussander said, "if you have decided to have a 'flier' of your own, you should be aware that you have picked a worthless stock."

"Huh?"

"Blackmail," Dussander said. "Isn't that what they call it on *Mannix* and *Hawaii Five-0* and *Barnaby Jones*? Extortion. If that was what—"

But Todd was laughing—hearty, boyish laughter. He shook his head, tried to speak, could not, and went on laughing.

"No," Dussander said, and suddenly he looked gray and more frightened than he had since he and Todd had begun to speak. He took another large swallow of his drink, grimaced, and shuddered. "I see that is not it . . . at least, not the extortion of money. But, though you laugh, I smell extortion in it somewhere. What is it? Why do you come here and disturb an old man? Perhaps, as you say, I was once a Nazi. SS, even. Now I am only old, and to have a bowel movement I have to use a suppository. So what do you want?"

Todd had sobered again. He stared at Dussander with an open and appealing frankness. "Why . . . I want to hear about it. That's all. That's all I want. Really."

"*Hear* about it?" Dussander echoed. He looked utterly perplexed.

Todd leaned forward, tanned elbows on bluejeaned knees. "Sure. The firing squads. The gas chambers. The ovens. The guys who had to dig their own graves and then stand on the ends so they'd fall into them. The . . ." His tongue came out and wetted his lips. "The examinations. The experiments. Everything. All the gooshy stuff."

Dussander stared at him with a certain amazed detachment, the way a veterinarian might stare at a cat who was giving birth to a succession of two-headed kittens. "You are a monster," he said softly.

Todd sniffed. "According to the books I read for my report, *you're* the monster, Mr. Dussander. Not me. You sent them to the ovens, not me. Two thousand a day at Patin before you came, three thousand after, thirty-five hundred before the Russians came and made you stop. Himmler called you an efficiency expert and gave you a medal. So you call me a monster. Oh *boy*."

"All of that is a filthy American lie," Dussander said, stung. He set his glass down with a bang, slopping bourbon onto his hand and the table. "The problem was not of my making, nor was the solution. I was given orders and directives, which I followed."

Todd's smile widened; it was now almost a smirk.

"Oh, I know how the Americans have distorted that," Dussander muttered. "But your own politicians make our Dr. Goebbels look like a child playing with picture books in a kindergarten. They speak of morality while they douse screaming children and old women in burning napalm. Your draft-resisters are called cowards and 'peaceniks.' For refusing to follow orders they are either put in jails or scourged from the country. Those who demonstrate against this country's unfortunate Asian adventure are clubbed down in the streets. The GI soldiers who kill the innocent are decorated by

Presidents, welcomed home from the bayoneting of children and the burning of hospitals with parades and bunting. They are given dinners, Keys to the City, free tickets to pro football games." He toasted his glass in Todd's direction. "Only those who lose are tried as war criminals for following orders and directives." He drank and then had a coughing fit that brought thin color to his cheeks.

Through most of this Todd fidgeted the way he did when his parents discussed whatever had been on the news that night—good old Walter Klondike, his dad called him. He didn't care about Dussander's politics any more than he cared about Dussander's stocks. His idea was that people made up politics so they could do things. Like when he wanted to feel around under Sharon Ackerman's dress last year. Sharon said it was bad for him to want to do that, even though he could tell from her tone of voice that the idea sort of excited her. So he told her he wanted to be a doctor when he grew up and then she let him. That was politics. He wanted to hear about German doctors trying to mate women with dogs, putting identical twins into refrigerators to see whether they would die at the same time or if one of them would last longer, and electroshock therapy, and operations without anesthetic, and German soldiers raping all the women they wanted. The rest was just so much tired bullspit to cover up the gooshy stuff after someone came along and put a stop to it.

"If I hadn't followed orders, I would have been dead." Dussander was breathing hard, his upper body rocking back and forth in the chair, making the springs squeak. A little cloud of liquor-smell hung around him. "There was always the Russian front, *nicht wahr*? Our leaders were madmen, granted, but does one argue with madmen . . . especially when the maddest of them all has the luck of Satan. He escaped a brilliant assassination attempt by inches. Those who conspired were strangled with piano-wire, strangled slowly. Their death-agonies were filmed for the edification of the elite—"

"Yeah! Neat!" Todd cried impulsively. "Did you see that movie?"

"Yes. I saw. We all saw what happened to those unwilling or unable to run before the wind and wait for the storm to end. What we did then was the right thing. For that time and that place, it was the right thing. I would do it again. But . . ."

His eyes dropped to his glass. It was empty.

". . . but I don't wish to speak of it, or even think of it. What we did was motivated only by survival, and nothing about survival is pretty. I had dreams . . ." He slowly took a cigarette from the box on the TV. "Yes. For years I had them. Blackness, and sounds in the blackness. Tractor engines. Bulldozer engines. Gunbutts thudding against what might have been frozen earth, or human skulls. Whistles, sirens, pistol-shots, screams. The doors of cattle-cars rumbling open on cold winter afternoons.

"Then, in my dreams, all sounds would stop—and eyes would open in the dark, gleaming like the eyes of animals in a rainforest. For many years I lived on the edge of the jungle, and I suppose that is why it is always the jungle I smelled and felt in those dreams. When I woke from them I would be drenched with sweat, my heart thundering in my chest, my hand stuffed into my mouth to stifle the screams. And I would think: *The dream is the truth.* Brazil, Paraguay, Cuba . . . those places are the dream. In the reality I am still at Patin. The Russians are closer today than yesterday. Some of them are remembering that in 1943 they had to eat frozen German corpses to stay alive. Now they long to drink hot German blood. There were rumors, boy, that some of them did just that when they crossed into Germany: cut the t'roats of some prisoners and drank their blood out of a boot. I would wake up and think: *The work must go on, if only so there is no evidence of what we did here, or so little that the world, which doesn't want to believe it, won't have to.* I would think: *The work must go on if we are to survive.*"

Todd listened to this with close attention and great interest.

This was pretty good, but he was sure there would be better stuff in the days ahead. All Dussander needed was a little prodding. Heck, he was lucky. Lots of men his age were senile.

Dussander dragged deeply on his cigarette. "Later, after the dreams went away, there were days when I would think I had seen someone from Patin. Never guards or fellow officers, always inmates. I remember one afternoon in West Germany, ten years ago. There was an accident on the Autobahn. Traffic was frozen in every lane. I sat in my Morris, listening to the radio, waiting for the traffic to move. I looked to my right. There was a very old Simca in the next lane, and the man behind the wheel was looking at me. He was perhaps fifty, and he looked ill. There was a scar on his cheek. His hair was white, short, cut badly. I looked away. The minutes passed and still the traffic didn't move. I began snatching glances at the man in the Simca. Every time I did, he was looking at me, his face as still as death, his eyes sunken in their sockets. I became convinced he had been at Patin. He had been there and he had recognized me."

Dussander wiped a hand across his eyes.

"It was winter. The man was wearing an overcoat. But I was convinced that if I got out of my car and went to him, made him take off his coat and push up his shirtsleeves, I would see the number on his arm.

"At last the traffic began to move again. I pulled away from the Simca. If the jam had lasted another ten minutes, I believe I would have gotten out of my car and pulled the old man out of his. I would have beaten him, number or no number. I would have beaten him for looking at me that way.

"Shortly after that, I left Germany forever."

"Lucky for you," Todd said.

Dussander shrugged. "It was the same everywhere. Havana, Mexico City, Rome. I was in Rome for three years, you know. I would see a man looking at me over his *cappucino* in a café . . . a woman in a hotel lobby who seemed more interested in me than in her magazine . . . a waiter in a restaurant who would keep glancing at me no matter whom he was serving. I would become convinced that these people were studying me, and that night the dream would come—the sounds, the jungle, the eyes.

"But when I came to America I put it out of my mind. I go to movies. I eat out once a week, always at one of those fast-food places that are so clean and so well-lighted by fluorescent bars. Here at my house I do jigsaw puzzles and I read novels—most of them bad ones—and watch TV. At night I drink until I'm sleepy. The dreams don't come anymore. When I see someone looking at me in the supermarket or the library or the tobacconist's, I think it must be because I look like their grandfather . . . or an old teacher . . . or a neighbor in a town they left some years ago." He shook his head at Todd. "Whatever happened at Patin, it happened to another man. Not to me."

"Great!" Todd said. "I want to hear all about it."

Dussander's eyes squeezed closed, and then opened slowly. "You don't understand. I do not wish to speak of it."

"You will, though. If you don't, I'll tell everyone who you are."

Dussander stared at him, gray-faced. "I knew," he said, "that I would find the extortion sooner or later."

"Today I want to hear about the gas ovens," Todd said. "How you baked them after they were dead." His smile beamed out, rich and radiant. "But put your teeth in before you start. You look better with your teeth in."

Dussander did as he was told. He talked to Todd about the gas ovens until Todd had to go home for lunch. Every time he tried to slip over into generalities, Todd would frown severely and ask him specific questions to get him back on the track. Dussander drank a great deal as he talked. He didn't smile. Todd smiled. Todd smiled enough for both of them.

2

August, 1974.

They sat on Dussander's back porch under a cloudless, smiling sky. Todd was wearing jeans, Keds, and his Little League shirt. Dussander was wearing a baggy gray shirt and shapeless khaki pants held up with suspenders—wino-pants, Todd thought with private contempt; they looked like they had come straight from a box in the back of the Salvation Army store downtown. He was really going to have to do something about the way Dussander dressed when he was at home. It spoiled some of the fun.

The two of them were eating Big Macs that Todd had brought in his bike-basket, pedaling fast so they wouldn't get cold. Todd was sipping a Coke through a plastic straw. Dussander had a glass of bourbon.

His old man's voice rose and fell, papery, hesitant, sometimes nearly inaudible. His faded blue eyes, threaded with the usual snaps of red, were never still. An observer might have thought them grandfather and grandson, the latter perhaps attending some rite of passage, a handing down.

"And that's all I remember," Dussander finished presently, and took a large bite of his sandwich. McDonald's Secret Sauce dribbled down his chin.

"You can do better than that," Todd said softly.

Dussander took a large swallow from his glass. "The uniforms were made of paper," he said finally, almost snarling. "When one inmate died, the uniform was passed on if it could still be worn. Sometimes one paper uniform could dress as many as forty inmates. I received high marks for my frugality."

"From Gluecks?"

"From Himmler."

"But there was a clothing factory in Patin. You told me that just last week. Why didn't you have the uniforms made there? The inmates themselves could have made them."

"The job of the factory in Patin was to make uniforms for German soldiers. And as for us . . ." Dussander's voice faltered for a moment, and then he forced himself to go on. "We were not in the business of rehabilitation," he finished.

Todd smiled his broad smile.

"Enough for today? Please? My throat is sore."

"You shouldn't smoke so much, then," Todd said, continuing to smile. "Tell me some more about the uniforms."

"Which? Inmate or SS?" Dussander's voice was resigned.

Smiling, Todd said: "Both."

3

September, 1974.

Todd was in the kitchen of his house, making himself a peanut butter and jelly sandwich. You got to the kitchen by going up half a dozen redwood steps to a raised area that gleamed with chrome and stainless steel. His mother's electric typewriter had been going steadily ever since Todd had gotten home from school. She was typing a master's thesis for a grad student. The grad student had short hair, wore thick glasses, and looked like a creature from outer space, in Todd's humble opinion. The thesis was on the effect of fruit-flies in the Salinas Valley after World War II, or some good shit like that. Now her typewriter stopped and she came out of her office.

"Todd-baby," she greeted him.

"Monica-baby," he hailed back, amiably enough.

His mother wasn't a bad-looking chick for thirty-six, Todd thought; blonde hair that was streaked ash in a couple of places, tall, shapely, now dressed in dark red shorts and a sheer blouse of a warm whiskey color—the blouse was casually knotted below her breasts, putting her flat, unlined midriff on show. A typewriter eraser was tucked into her hair, which had been pinned carelessly back with a turquoise clip.

"So how's school?" she asked him, coming up the steps into the kitchen. She brushed his lips casually with hers and then slid onto one of the stools in front of the breakfast counter.

"School's cool."

"Going to be on the honor roll again?"

"Sure." Actually, he thought his grades might slip a notch this first quarter. He had been spending a lot of time with Dussander, and when he wasn't actually with the old kraut, he was thinking about the things Dussander had told him. Once or twice he had dreamed about the things Dussander had told him. But it was nothing he couldn't handle.

"Apt pupil," she said, ruffling his shaggy blonde hair. "How's that sandwich?"

"Good," he said.

"Would you make me one and bring it into my office?"

"Can't," he said, getting up. "I promised Mr. Denker I'd come over and read to him for an hour or so."

"Are you still on *Robinson Crusoe*?"

"Nope." He showed her the spine of a thick book he had bought in a junkshop for twenty cents. *"Tom Jones."*

"Ye gods and little fishes! It'll take you the whole school-year to get through that, Toddy-baby. Couldn't you at least find an abridged edition, like with *Crusoe*!"

"Probably, but he wanted to hear all of this one. He said so."

"Oh." She looked at him for a moment, then hugged him. It was rare for her to be so demonstrative, and it made Todd a little uneasy. "You're a peach to be taking so much of your spare time to read to him. Your father and I think it's just . . . just exceptional."

Todd cast his eyes down modestly.

"And to not want to tell anybody," she said. "Hiding your light under a bushel."

"Oh, the kids I hang around with—they'd probably think I was some kind of weirdo," Todd said, smiling modestly down at the floor. "All that good shit."

"Don't say that," she admonished absently. Then: "Do you think Mr. Denker would like to come over and have dinner with us some night?"

"Maybe," Todd said vaguely. "Listen, I gotta put an egg in my shoe and beat it."

"Okay. Supper at six-thirty. Don't forget."

"I won't."

"Your father's got to work late so it'll just be me and thee again, okay?"

"Crazy, baby."

She watched him go with a fond smile, hoping there was nothing in *Tom Jones* he shouldn't be reading; he was only thirteen. She didn't suppose there was. He was growing up in a society where magazines like *Penthouse* were available to anyone with a dollar and a quarter, or to any kid who could reach up to the top shelf of the magazine rack and grab a quick peek before the clerk could shout for him to put that up and get lost. In a society that seemed to believe most of all in the creed of hump thy neighbor, she didn't think there could be much in a book two hundred years old to screw up Todd's head—although she supposed the old man might get off on it a little. And as Richard liked to say, for a kid the whole world's a laboratory. You have to let them poke around in it. And if the kid in question has a healthy home life and loving parents, he'll be all the stronger for having knocked around a few strange corners.

And there went the healthiest kid she knew, pedaling up the street on his Schwinn. *We did okay by the lad,* she thought, turning to make her sandwich. *Damned if we didn't do okay.*

4

October, 1974.

Dussander had lost weight. They sat in the kitchen, the shopworn copy of *Tom Jones* between them on the oilcloth-covered table (Todd, who tried never to miss a trick, had purchased the Cliff's Notes on the book with part of his allowance and had carefully read the entire summary against the possibility that his mother or father might ask him questions about the plot). Todd was eating a Ring Ding he had bought at the market. He had bought one for Dussander, but Dussander hadn't touched it. He only looked at it morosely from time to time as he drank his bourbon. Todd hated to see anything as tasty as Ring Dings go to waste. If he didn't eat it pretty quick, Todd was going to ask him if he could have it.

"So how did the stuff get to Patin?" he asked Dussander.

"In railroad cars," Dussander said. "In railroad cars labelled medical supplies. It came in long crates that looked like coffins. Fitting, I suppose. The inmates off-loaded the crates and stacked them in the infirmary. Later, our own men stacked them in the storage sheds. They did it at night. The storage sheds were behind the showers."

"Was it always Zyklon-B?"

"No, from time to time we would be sent something else. Experimental gases. The High Command was always interested in improving efficiency. Once they sent us a gas code-named PEGASUS. A nerve-gas. Thank God they never sent it again. It—" Dussander saw Todd lean forward, saw those eyes sharpen, and he suddenly stopped and gestured casually with his gas station premium glass. "It didn't work very well," he said. "It was . . . quite boring."

But Todd was not fooled, not in the least. "What did it do?"

"It killed them—what did you think it did, made them walk on water? It killed them, that's all."

'Tell me."

"No," Dussander said, now unable to hide the horror he felt. He hadn't thought of PEGASUS in . . . how long? Ten years? Twenty? "I won't tell you! I refuse!"

"Tell me," Todd repeated, licking chocolate icing from his fingers. "Tell me or you know what."

Yes, Dussander thought. *I know what. Indeed I do, you putrid little monster.*

"It made them dance," he said reluctantly.

"Dance?"

"Like the Zyklon-B, it came in through the shower-heads. And they . . . they began to leap about. Some were screaming. Most of them were laughing. They began to vomit, and to . . . to defecate helplessly."

"Wow," Todd said. "Shit themselves, huh?" He pointed at the Ring Ding on Dussander's plate. He had finished his own. "You going to eat that?"

Dussander didn't reply. His eyes were hazed with memory. His face was far away and cold, like the dark side of a planet which does not rotate. Inside his mind he felt the *queerest* combination of revulsion and—could it be?—*nostalgia?*

"They began to twitch all over and to make high, strange sounds in their throats. My men . . . they called PEGASUS the Yodeling Gas. At last they all collapsed and just lay there on the floor in their own filth, they lay there, yes, they lay there on the concrete, screaming and yodeling, with bloody noses. But I lied, boy. The gas didn't kill them, either because it wasn't strong enough or because we couldn't bring ourselves to wait long enough. I suppose it was that. Men and women like that could not have lived long. Finally I sent in five men with rifles to end their agonies. It would have looked bad on my record if it had shown up, I've no doubt of that—it would have looked like a waste of cartridges at a time when the Fuehrer had declared every cartridge a national resource. But those five men I trusted. There were times, boy, when I thought I would never forget the sound they made. The yodeling sound. The laughing."

"Yeah, I bet," Todd said. He finished Dussander's Ring Ding in two bites. Waste not, want not, Todd's mother said on the rare occasions when Todd complained about left-overs. "That was a good story, Mr. Dussander. You always tell them good. Once I get you going."

Todd smiled at him. And incredibly—certainly not because he wanted to—Dussander found himself smiling back.

5

November, 1974.

Dick Bowden, Todd's father, looked remarkably like a movie and TV actor named Lloyd Bochner. He—Bowden, not Bochner—was thirty-eight. He was a thin, narrow man who liked to dress in Ivy League–style shirts and solid-color suits, usually dark. When he was on a construction site, he wore khakis and a hard-hat that was a souvenir of his Peace Corps days, when he had helped to design and build two dams in Africa. When he was working in his study at home, he wore half-glasses that had a way of slipping down to the end of his nose and making him look like a college dean. He was wearing these glasses now as he tapped his son's first-quarter report card against his desk's gleaming glass top.

"One B. Four C's. One D. A *D,* for Christ's sake! Todd, your mother's not showing it, but she's really upset."

Todd dropped his eyes. He didn't smile. When his dad swore, that wasn't exactly the best of news.

"My God, you've *never* gotten a report like this. A *D* in Beginning Algebra? What *is* this?"

"I don't know, Dad." He looked humbly at his knees.

"Your mother and I think that maybe you've been spending a little too much time with Mr. Denker. Not hitting the books enough. We think you ought to cut it down to weekends, slugger. At least until we see where you're going academically . . ."

Todd looked up, and for a single second Bowden thought he saw a wild, pallid anger in his son's eyes. His own eyes widened, his fingers clenched on Todd's buff-colored report card . . . and then it was just Todd, looking at him openly if rather unhappily. Had that anger really been there? Surely not. But the moment had unsettled him, made it hard for him to know exactly how to proceed. Todd hadn't been mad, and Dick Bowden didn't want to *make* him mad. He and his son were friends, always had been friends, and Dick wanted things to stay that way. They had no secrets from each other, none at all (except for the fact that Dick Bowden was sometimes unfaithful with his secretary, but that wasn't exactly the sort of thing you told your thirteen-year-old son, was it? . . . and besides, that had absolutely no bearing on his home life, his *family* life). That was the way it was supposed to be, the way it *had* to be in a cockamamie world where murderers went unpunished, high school kids skin-popped heroin, and junior high schoolers—kids Todd's age—turned up with VD.

"No, Dad, please don't do that. I mean, don't punish Mr. Denker for something that's my fault. I mean, he'd be lost without me. I'll do better. Really. That algebra . . . it just threw me to start with. But I went over to Ben Tremaine's, and after we studied together for a few days, I started to get it. I just . . . I dunno, I sorta choked at first."

"I think you're spending too much time with him," Bowden said, but he was weakening. It was hard to refuse Todd, hard to disappoint him, and what he said about punishing the old man for Todd's falling-off . . . goddammit, it made sense. The old man looked forward to his visits so much.

"That Mr. Storrman, the algebra teacher, is really hard," Todd said. "Lots of kids got D's. Three or four got F's."

Bowden nodded thoughtfully.

"I won't go Wednesdays anymore. Not until I bring my

grades up." He had read his father's eyes. "And instead of going out for anything at school, I'll stay after every day and study. I promise."

"You really like the old guy that much?"

"He's really neat," Todd said sincerely.

"Well . . . okay. We'll try it your way, slugger. But I want to see a big improvement in your marks come January, you understand me? I'm thinking of your future. You may think junior high's too soon to start thinking about that, but it's not. Not by a long chalk." As his mother liked to say *Waste not, want not,* so Dick Bowden liked to say *Not by a long chalk.*

"I understand, Dad," Todd said gravely. Man-to-man stuff.

"Get out of here and give those books a workout then." He pushed his half-glasses up on his nose and clapped Todd on the shoulder.

Todd's smile, broad and bright, broke across his face. "Right on, Dad!"

Bowden watched Todd go with a prideful smile of his own. One in a million. And that hadn't been anger on Todd's face. For sure. Pique, maybe . . . but not that high-voltage emotion he had at first thought he'd seen there. If Todd was that mad, he would have known; he could read his son like a book. It had always been that way.

Whistling, his fatherly duty discharged, Dick Bowden unrolled a blueprint and bent over it.

6

December, 1974.

The face that came in answer to Todd's insistent finger on the bell was haggard and yellowed. The hair, which had been lush in July, had now begun to recede from the bony brow; it looked lusterless and brittle. Dussander's body, thin to begin with, was now gaunt . . . although, Todd thought, he was nowhere near as gaunt as the inmates who had once been delivered into his hands.

Todd's left hand had been behind his back when Dussander came to the door. Now he brought it out and handed a wrapped package to Dussander. "Merry Christmas!" he yelled.

Dussander had cringed from the box; now he took it with no expression of pleasure or surprise. He handled it gingerly, as if it might contain explosive. Beyond the porch, it was raining. It had been raining off and on for almost a week, and Todd had carried the box inside his coat. It was wrapped in gay foil and ribbon.

"What is it?" Dussander asked without enthusiasm as they went to the kitchen.

"Open it and see."

Todd took a can of Coke from his jacket pocket and put it on the red and white checked oilcloth that covered the kitchen table. "Better pull down the shades," he said confidentially.

Distrust immediately leaked onto Dussander's face. "Oh? Why?"

"Well . . . you can never tell who's lookin," Todd said, smiling. "Isn't that how you got along all those years? By seeing the people who might be lookin before they saw you?"

Dussander pulled down the kitchen shades. Then he poured himself a glass of bourbon. Then he pulled the bow off the package. Todd had wrapped it the way boys so often wrap Christmas packages—boys who have more important things on their minds, things like football and street hockey and the Friday Nite Creature Feature you'll watch with a friend who's sleeping over, the two of you wrapped in a blanket and crammed together on one end of the couch, laughing. There were a lot of ragged corners, a lot of uneven seams, a lot of Scotch tape. It spoke of impatience with such a womanly thing.

Dussander was a little touched in spite of himself. And later, when the horror had receded a little, he thought: *I should have known.*

It was a uniform. An SS uniform. Complete with jackboots.

He looked numbly from the contents of the box to its cardboard cover: PETER'S QUALITY COSTUME CLOTHIERS—AT THE SAME LOCATION SINCE 1951!

"No," he said softly. "I won't put it on. This is where it ends, boy. I'll die before I put it on."

"Remember what they did to Eichmann," Todd said solemnly. "He was an old man and he had no politics. Isn't that what you said? Besides, I saved the whole fall for it. It cost over eighty bucks, with the boots thrown in. You didn't mind wearing it in 1944, either. Not at all."

"You little *bastard*!" Dussander raised one fist over his head. Todd didn't flinch at all. He stood his ground, eyes shining.

"Yeah," he said softly. "Go ahead and touch me. You just touch me *once.*"

Dussander lowered the hand. His lips were quivering. "You are a fiend from hell," he muttered.

"Put it on," Todd invited.

Dussander's hands went to the tie of his robe and paused there. His eyes, sheeplike and begging, looked into Todd's. "Please," he said. "I am an old man. No more."

Todd shook his head slowly but firmly. His eyes were still shining. He liked it when Dussander begged. The way they must have begged him once. The inmates at Patin.

Dussander let the robe fall to the floor and stood naked except for his slippers and his boxer shorts. His chest was sunken, his belly slightly bloated. His arms were scrawny old man's arms. But the uniform, Todd thought. The uniform will make a difference.

Slowly, Dussander took the tunic out of the box and began to put it on.

Ten minutes later he stood fully dressed in the SS uniform. The cap was slightly askew, the shoulders slumped, but still the death's-head insignia stood out clearly. Dussander had a dark dignity—at least in Todd's eyes—that he had not possessed earlier. In spite of his slump, in spite of the cockeyed angle of his feet, Todd was pleased. For the first time Dussander looked to Todd as Todd believed he should look. Older, yes. Defeated, certainly. But in uniform again. Not an old man spinning away his sunset years watching Lawrence Welk on a cruddy black and white TV with tinfoil on the rabbit ears, but Kurt Dussander, The Blood-Fiend of Patin.

As for Dussander, he felt disgust, discomfort . . . and a mild, sneaking sense of relief. He partly despised this latter emotion, recognizing it as the truest indicator yet of the psychological domination the boy had established over him. He was the boy's prisoner, and every time he found he could live through yet another indignity, every time he felt that mild relief, the boy's power grew. And yet he *was* relieved. It was only cloth and buttons and snaps . . . and it was a sham at that. The fly was a zipper; it should have been buttons. The marks of rank were wrong, the tailoring sloppy, the boots a cheap grade of imitation leather. It was only a trumpery uniform after all, and it wasn't exactly *killing* him, was it? No. It—

"Straighten your cap!" Todd said loudly.

Dussander blinked at him, startled.

"Straighten your cap, soldier!"

Dussander did so, unconsciously giving it that final small insolent twist that had been the trademark of his *Oberleutnants*—and, sadly wrong as it was, this was an *Oberleutnant's* uniform.

"Get those feet together!"

He did so, bringing the heels together with a smart rap, doing the correct thing with hardly a thought, doing it as if the intervening years had slipped off along with his bathrobe.

"Achtung!"

He snapped to attention, and for a moment Todd was scared—really scared. He felt like the sorcerer's apprentice, who had brought the brooms to life but who had not possessed enough wit to stop them once they got started. The old man living in genteel poverty was gone. Dussander was here.

Then his fear was replaced by a tingling sense of power.

"About face!"

Dussander pivoted neatly, the bourbon forgotten, the torment of the last four months forgotten. He heard his heels click together again as he faced the grease-splattered stove. Beyond it, he could see the dusty parade ground of the military academy where he had learned his soldier's trade.

"About face!"

He whirled again, this time not executing the order as well, losing his balance a little. Once it would have been ten demerits and the butt of a swagger stick in his belly, sending his breath out in a hot and agonized gust. Inwardly he smiled a little. The boy didn't know all the tricks. No indeed.

"Now *march*!" Todd cried. His eyes were hot, glowing.

The iron went out of Dussander's shoulders; he slumped forward again. "No," he said. "Please—"

"March! March! March, I said!"

With a strangled sound, Dussander began to goose-step across the faded linoleum of his kitchen floor. He right-faced to avoid the table, right-faced again as he approached the wall. His face was uptilted slightly, expressionless. His legs rammed out before him, then crashed down, making the cheap china rattle in the cabinet over the sink. His arms moved in short arcs.

The image of the walking brooms recurred to Todd, and his fright recurred with it. It suddenly struck him that he didn't want Dussander to be enjoying any part of this, and that perhaps—just perhaps—he had wanted to make Dussander appear ludicrous even more than he had wanted to make him appear authentic. But somehow, despite the man's age and the cheap dime-store furnishings of the kitchen, he didn't look ludicrous in the least. He looked frightening. For the first time the corpses in the ditches and the crematoriums seemed to take on their own reality for Todd. The photographs of the tangled arms and legs and torsos, fishbelly white in the cold spring rains of Germany, were not something staged like a scene in a horror film—a pile of bodies created from department-store dummies, say, to be picked up by the grips and propmen when the scene was done—but simply a real fact, stupendous and inexplicable and evil. For a moment it seemed to him that he could smell the bland and slightly smoky odor of decomposition.

Terror gathered him in.

"Stop!" he shouted.

Dussander continued to goose-step, his eyes blank and far away. His head had come up even more, pulling the scrawny chicken-tendons of his throat tight, tilting his chin at an arrogant angle. His nose, blade-thin, jutted obscenely.

Todd felt sweat in his armpits. *"Halt!"* he cried out.

Dussander halted, right foot forward, left coming up and then down beside the right with a single pistonlike stamp. For a moment the cold lack of expression held on his face—robotic, mindless—and then it was replaced by confusion. Confusion was followed by defeat. He slumped.

Todd let out a silent breath of relief and for a moment he was furious with himself. *Who's in charge here, anyway?* Then his self-confidence flooded back in. *I am, that's who. And he better not forget it.*

He began to smile again. "Pretty good. But with a little practice, I think you'll be a lot better."

Dussander stood mute, panting, his head hanging.

"You can take it off now," Todd added generously . . . and couldn't help wondering if he really wanted Dussander to put it on again. For a few seconds there—

7

January, 1975.

Todd left school by himself after the last bell, got his bike, and pedaled down to the park. He found a deserted bench, set his Schwinn up on its kickstand, and took his report card out of his hip pocket. He took a look around to see if there was anyone in the area he knew, but the only other people in sight were two high school kids making out by the pond and a pair of gross-looking winos passing a paper bag back and forth. Dirty fucking winos, he thought, but it wasn't the winos that had upset him. He opened his card.

English: C. American History: C. Earth Science: D. Your Community and You: B. Primary French: F. Beginning Algebra: F.

He stared at the grades, unbelieving. He had known it was going to be bad, but this was disaster.

Maybe that's best, an inner voice spoke up suddenly. *Maybe you even did it on purpose, because a part of you wants it to end.* Needs *for it to end. Before something bad happens.*

He shoved the thought roughly aside. Nothing bad was going to happen. Dussander was under his thumb. Totally under his thumb. The old man thought one of Todd's friends had a letter, but he didn't know which friend. If anything happened to Todd—*anything*—that letter would go to the police. Once he supposed Dussander might have tried it anyway. Now he was too old to run, even with a head start.

"He's under control, dammit," Todd whispered, and then pounded his thigh hard enough to make the muscle knot. Talking to yourself was bad shit—crazy people talked to themselves. He had picked up the habit over the last six weeks or so, and didn't seem able to break it. He'd caught several people looking at him strangely because of it. A couple of them had been teachers. And that asshole Bernie Everson had come right out and asked him if he was going fruitcrackers. Todd had come very, very close to punching the little pansy in the mouth, and that sort of stuff—brawls, scuffles, punch-outs—was no good. That sort of stuff got you noticed in all the wrong ways. Talking to yourself was bad, right, okay, but—

"The dreams are bad, too," he whispered. He didn't catch himself that time.

Just lately the dreams had been very bad. In the dreams he was always in uniform, although the type varied. Sometimes it was a paper uniform and he was standing in line with hundreds of gaunt men; the smell of burning was in the air and he could hear the choppy roar of bulldozer engines. Then Dussander would come up the line, pointing out this one or that one. They were left. The others were marched away toward the crematoriums. Some of them kicked and struggled, but most were too undernourished, too exhausted. Then Dussander was standing in front of Todd. Their eyes met for a long, paralyzing moment, and then Dussander levelled a faded umbrella at Todd.

"Take this one to the laboratories," Dussander said in the dream. His lip curled back to reveal his false teeth. "Take this American *boy*."

In another dream he wore an SS uniform. His jackboots were shined to a mirrorlike reflecting surface. The death's-head insignia and the lightning-bolts glittered. But he was standing in the middle of Santo Donato Boulevard and everyone was looking at him. They began to point. Some of them began to laugh. Others looked shocked, angry, or revolted. In this dream an old car came to a squalling, creaky halt and Dussander peered out at him, a Dussander who looked two hundred years old and nearly mummified, his skin a yellowed scroll.

"I know you!" the dream-Dussander proclaimed shrilly. He looked around at the spectators and then back to Todd. "You were in charge at Patin! Look, everybody! This is The Blood-Fiend of Patin! Himmler's 'Efficiency Expert'! I denounce you, murderer! I denounce you, butcher! I denounce you, killer of infants! I denounce you!"

In yet another dream he wore a striped convict's uniform and was being led down a stone-walled corridor by two guards who looked like his parents. Both wore conspicuous yellow armbands with the Star of David on them. Walking behind them was a minister, reading from the Book of Deuteronomy. Todd looked back over his shoulder and saw that the minister was Dussander, and he was wearing the black tunic of an SS officer.

At the end of the stone corridor, double doors opened on an octagonal room with glass walls. There was a scaffold in the center of it. Behind the glass walls stood ranks of emaciated men and women, all naked, all watching with the same dark, flat expression. On each arm was a blue number.

"It's all right," Todd whispered to himself. "It's okay, really, everything's under control."

The couple that had been making out glanced over at him. Todd stared at them fiercely, daring them to say anything. At last they looked back the other way. Had the boy been grinning?

Todd got up, jammed his report card into his hip pocket, and mounted his bike. He pedaled down to a drugstore two blocks away. There he bought a bottle of ink eradicator and a fine-point pen that dispensed blue ink. He went back to the park (the make-out couple was gone, but the winos were still there, stinking the place up) and changed his English grade to a B, American History to A, Earth Science to B, Primary French to C, and Beginning Algebra to B. Your Community and You he eradicated and then simply wrote in again, so the card would have a uniform look.

Uniforms, right.

"Never mind," he whispered to himself. "That'll hold them. That'll hold them, all right."

One night late in the month, sometime after two o'clock, Kurt Dussander awoke struggling with the bedclothes, gasping and moaning, into a darkness that seemed close and terrifying. He felt half-suffocated, paralyzed with fear. It was as if a heavy stone lay on his chest, and he wondered if he could be having a heart attack. He clawed in the darkness for the bedside lamp and almost knocked it off the nightstand turning it on.

I'm in my own room, he thought, my own bedroom, here in Santo Donato, here in California, here in America. See, the same brown drapes pulled across the same window, the same bookshelves filled with dime paperbacks from the bookshop on Soren Street, same gray rug, same blue wallpaper. No heart attack. No jungle. No eyes.

But the terror still clung to him like a stinking pelt, and his heart went on racing. The dream had come back. He had known that it would, sooner or later, if the boy kept on. The cursed boy. He thought the boy's letter of protection was only a bluff, and not a very good one at that; something he had picked up from the TV detective programs. What friend would the boy trust not to open such a momentous letter? No friend, that was who. Or so he thought. If he could be *sure*—

His hands closed with an arthritic, painful snap and then opened slowly.

He took the packet of cigarettes from the table and lit one, scratching the wooden match on the bedpost. The clock's hands stood at 2:41. There would be no more sleep for him this night. He inhaled smoke and then coughed it out in a series of racking spasms. No more sleep unless he wanted to go downstairs and have a drink or two. Or three. And there had been altogether too much drinking over the last six weeks or so. He was no longer a young man who could toss them off one after the other, the way he had when he had been an officer on leave in Berlin in '39, when the scent of victory had been in the air and everywhere you heard the Fuehrer's voice, saw his blazing, commanding eyes—

The boy . . . the cursed boy!

"Be honest," he said aloud, and the sound of his own voice in the quiet room made him jump a little. He was not in the habit of talking to himself, but neither was it the first time he had ever done so. He remembered doing it off and on during the last few weeks at Patin, when everything had come down around their ears and in the east the sound of Russian thunder grew louder first every day and then every hour. It had been natural enough to talk to himself then. He had been under stress, and people under stress often do strange things—cup their testicles through the pockets of their pants, click their teeth together . . . Wolff had been a great teeth-clicker. He grinned as he did it. Huffmann had been a finger-snapper and a thigh-patter, creating fast, intricate rhythms that he seemed utterly unaware of. He, Kurt Dussander, had sometimes talked to himself. But now—

"You are under stress again," he said aloud. He was aware that he had spoken in German this time. He hadn't spoken German in many years, but the language now seemed warm and comfortable. It lulled him, eased him. It was sweet and dark.

"Yes. You are under stress. Because of the boy. But be honest with yourself. It is too early in the morning to tell lies. You have not entirely regretted talking. At first you were terrified that the boy could not or would not keep his secret. He would have to tell a friend, who would tell another friend, and that friend would tell two. But if he has kept it this long, he will keep it longer. If I am taken away, he loses his . . . his talking book. Is that what I am to him? I think so."

He fell silent, but his thoughts went on. He had been lonely—no one would ever know just how lonely. There had been times when he thought almost seriously of suicide. He made a bad hermit. The voices he heard came from the radio. The only people who visited were on the other side of a dirty glass square. He was an old man, and although he was afraid of death, he was more afraid of being an old man who is alone.

His bladder sometimes tricked him. He would be halfway to the bathroom when a dark stain spread on his pants. In wet weather his joints would first throb and then begin to cry out, and there had been days when he had chewed an entire tin of Arthritis Pain Formula between sunrise and sunset . . . and still the aspirin only subdued the aches. Even such acts as taking a book from the shelf or switching the TV channel became an essay in pain. His eyes were bad; sometimes he knocked things over, barked his shins, bumped his head. He lived in fear of breaking a bone and not being able to get to the telephone, and he lived in fear of getting there and having some doctor uncover his real past as he became suspicious of Mr. Denker's nonexistent medical history.

The boy had alleviated some of those things. When the boy was here, he could call back the old days. His memory of those days was perversely clear; he spilled out a seemingly endless catalogue of names and events, even the weather of such and such a day. He remembered Private Henreid, who manned a machine-gun in the northeast tower and the wen Private Henreid had had between his eyes. Some of the men called him Three-Eyes, or Old Cyclops. He remembered Kessel, who had a picture of his girlfriend naked, lying on a sofa with her hands behind her head. Kessel charged the men to look at it. He remembered the names of the doctors and their experiments—thresholds of pain, the brainwaves of dying men and women, physiological retardation, effects of different sorts of radiation, dozens more. *Hundreds* more.

He supposed he talked to the boy as all old men talk, but he guessed he was luckier than most old men, who had impatience, disinterest, or outright rudeness for an audience. *His* audience was endlessly fascinated.

Were a few bad dreams too high a price to pay?

He crushed out his cigarette, lay looking at the ceiling for a moment, and then swung his feet out onto the floor. He and the boy were loathsome, he supposed, feeding off each other . . . eating each other. If his own belly was sometimes sour with the dark but rich food they partook of in his afternoon kitchen, what was the boy's like? Did he sleep well? Perhaps not. Lately Dussander thought the boy looked rather pale, and thinner than when he had first come into Dussander's life.

He walked across the bedroom and opened the closet door.

He brushed hangers to the right, reached into the shadows, and brought out the sham uniform. It hung from his hand like a vulture-skin. He touched it with his other hand. Touched it . . . and then stroked it.

After a very long time he took it down and put it on, dressing slowly, not looking into the mirror until the uniform was completely buttoned and belted (and the sham fly zipped).

He looked at himself in the mirror, then, and nodded.

He went back to bed, lay down, and smoked another cigarette. When it was finished, he felt sleepy again. He turned off the bedlamp, not believing it, that it could be this easy. But he was asleep, five minutes later, and this time his sleep was dreamless.

8

February, 1975.

After dinner, Dick Bowden produced a cognac that Dussander privately thought dreadful. But of course he smiled broadly and complimented it extravagantly. Bowden's wife served the boy a chocolate malted. The boy had been unusually quiet all through the meal. Uneasy? Yes. For some reason the boy seemed very uneasy.

Dussander had charmed Dick and Monica Bowden from the moment he and the boy had arrived. The boy had told his parents that Mr. Denker's vision was much worse than it actually was (which made poor old Mr. Denker in need of a Seeing Eye Dog, Dussander thought dryly), because that explained all the reading the boy had supposedly been doing. Dussander had been very careful about that, and he thought there had been no slips.

He was dressed in his best suit, and although the evening was damp, his arthritis had been remarkably mellow—nothing but an occasional twinge. For some absurd reason the boy had wanted him to leave his umbrella home, but Dussander had insisted. All in all, he had had a pleasant and rather exciting evening. Dreadful cognac or no, he had not been out to dinner in nine years.

During the meal he had discussed the Essen Motor Works, the rebuilding of postwar Germany—Bowden had asked several intelligent questions about that, and had seemed impressed by Dussander's answers—and German writers. Monica Bowden had asked him how he had happened to come to America so late in life and Dussander, adopting the proper expression of myopic sorrow, had explained about the death of his fictitious wife. Monica Bowden was meltingly sympathetic.

And now, over the absurd cognac, Dick Bowden said: "If this is too personal, Mr. Denker, please don't answer . . . but I couldn't help wondering what you did in the war."

The boy stiffened ever so slightly.

Dussander smiled and felt for his cigarettes. He could see them perfectly well, but it was important to make not the tiniest slip. Monica put them in his hand.

"Thank you, dear lady. The meal was superb. You are a fine cook. My own wife never did better."

Monica thanked him and looked flustered. Todd gave her an irritated look.

"Not personal at all," Dussander said, lighting his cigarette and turning to Bowden. "I was in the reserves from 1943 on, as were all able-bodied men too old to be in the active services. By then the handwriting was on the wall for the Third Reich, and for the madmen who created it. One madman in particular, of course."

He blew out his match and looked solemn.

"There was great relief when the tide turned against Hitler. Great relief. Of course," and here he looked at Bowden disarmingly, as man to man, "one was careful not to express such a sentiment. Not aloud."

"I suppose not," Dick Bowden said respectfully.

"No," Dussander said gravely. "Not aloud. I remember one evening when four or five of us, all friends, stopped at a local *Ratskeller* after work for a drink—by then there was not always *Schnaps,* or even beer, but it so happened that night there were both. We had all known each other for upwards of twenty years. One of our number, Hans Hassler, mentioned in passing that perhaps the Fuehrer had been ill-advised to open a second front against the Russians. I said, 'Hans, God in Heaven, watch what you say!' Poor Hans went pale and changed the subject entirely. Yet three days later he was gone. I never saw him again, nor, as far as I know, did anyone else who was sitting at our table that night."

"How awful!" Monica said breathlessly. "More cognac, Mr. Denker?"

"No thank you." He smiled at her. "My wife had a saying from her mother: 'One must never overdo the sublime.'"

Todd's small, troubled frown deepened slightly.

"Do you think he was sent to one of the camps?" Dick asked. "Your friend Hessler?"

"Hassler," Dussander corrected gently. He grew grave. "Many were. The camps . . . they will be the shame of the German people for a thousand years to come. They are Hitler's real legacy."

"Oh, I think that's too harsh," Bowden said, lighting his pipe and puffing out a choking cloud of Cherry Blend. "According to what I've read, the majority of the German people had no idea of what was going on. The locals around Auschwitz thought it was a sausage plant."

"Ugh, how *terrible,*" Monica said, and pulled a grimacing that's-enough-of-that expression at her husband. Then she turned to Dussander and smiled. "I just love the smell of a pipe, Mr. Denker, don't you?"

"Indeed I do, madam," Dussander said. He had just gotten an almost insurmountable urge to sneeze under control.

Bowden suddenly reached across the table and clapped

his son on the shoulder. Todd jumped. "You're awfully quiet tonight, son. Feeling all right?"

Todd offered a peculiar smile that seemed divided between his father and Dussander. "I feel okay. I've heard most of these stories before, remember."

"Todd!" Monica said. "That's hardly—"

"The boy is only being honest," Dussander said. "A privilege of boys which men often have to give up. Yes, Mr. Bowden?"

Dick laughed and nodded.

"Perhaps I could get Todd to walk back to my house with me now," Dussander said. "I'm sure he has his studies."

"Todd is a very apt pupil," Monica said, but she spoke almost automatically, looking at Todd in a puzzled sort of way. "All A's and B's, usually. He got a C this last quarter, but he's promised to bring his French up to snuff on his March report. Right, Todd-baby?"

Todd offered the peculiar smile again and nodded.

"No need for you to walk," Dick said. "I'll be glad to run you back to your place."

"I walk for the air and the exercise," Dussander said. "Really, I must insist . . . unless Todd prefers not to."

"Oh, no, I'd like a walk," Todd said, and his mother and father beamed at him.

They were almost to Dussander's corner when Dussander broke the silence. It was drizzling, and he hoisted his umbrella over both of them. And yet still his arthritis lay quiet, dozing. It was amazing.

"You are like my arthritis," he said.

Todd's head came up. "Huh?"

"Neither of you have had much to say tonight. What's got your tongue, boy? Cat or cormorant?"

"Nothing," Todd muttered. They turned down Dussander's street.

"Perhaps I could guess," Dussander said, not without a

touch of malice. "When you came to get me, you were afraid I might make a slip . . . 'let the cat out of the bag,' you say here. Yet you were determined to go through with the dinner because you had run out of excuses to put your parents off. Now you are disconcerted that all went well. Is that not the truth?"

"Who cares?" Todd said, and shrugged sullenly.

"Why shouldn't it go well?" Dussander demanded. "I was dissembling before you were born. You keep a secret well enough, I give you that. I give it to you most graciously. But did you see me tonight? I charmed them. *Charmed* them!"

Todd suddenly burst out: "You didn't have to do that!"

Dussander came to a complete stop, staring at Todd.

"Not do it? *Not?* I thought that was what you wanted, boy! Certainly they will offer no objections if you continue to come over and 'read' to me."

"You're sure taking a lot for granted!" Todd said hotly. "Maybe I've got all I want from you. Do you think there's anybody *forcing* me to come over to your scuzzy house and watch you slop up booze like those old wino pusbags that hang around the old trainyards? Is that what you think?" His voice had risen and taken on a thin, wavering, hysterical note. "Because there's nobody *forcing* me. If I want to come, I'll come, and if I don't, I won't."

"Lower your voice. People will hear."

"Who cares?" Todd said, but he began to walk again. This time he deliberately walked outside the umbrella's span.

"No, nobody forces you to come," Dussander said. And then he took a calculated shot in the dark: "In fact, you are welcome to stay away. Believe me, boy, I have no scruples about drinking alone. None at all."

Todd looked at him scornfully. "You'd like that, wouldn't you?"

Dussander only smiled noncommittally.

"Well, don't count on it." They had reached the concrete

walk leading up to Dussander's stoop. Dussander fumbled in his pocket for his latchkey. The arthritis flared a dim red in the joints of his fingers and then subsided, waiting. Now Dussander thought he understood what it was waiting for: for him to be alone again. Then it could come out.

"I'll tell you something," Todd said. He sounded oddly breathless. "If they knew what you were, if I ever told them, they'd spit on you and then kick you out on your skinny old ass."

Dussander looked at Todd closely in the drizzling dark. The boy's face was turned defiantly up to his, but the skin was pallid, the sockets under the eyes dark and slightly hollowed—the skin-tones of someone who has brooded long while others are asleep.

"I am sure they would have nothing but revulsion for me," Dussander said, although he privately thought that the elder Bowden might stay his revulsion long enough to ask many of the questions his son had asked already. "Nothing but revulsion. But what would they feel for you, boy, when I told them you had known about me for eight months . . . and said nothing?"

Todd stared at him wordlessly in the dark.

"Come and see me if you please," Dussander said indifferently, "and stay home if you don't. Goodnight, boy."

He went up the walk to his front door, leaving Todd standing in the drizzle and looking after him with his mouth slightly ajar.

The next morning at breakfast, Monica said: "Your dad liked Mr. Denker a lot, Todd. He said he reminded him of your grandfather."

Todd muttered something unintelligible around his toast. Monica looked at her son and wondered if he had been sleeping well. He looked pale. And his grades had taken that inexplicable dip. Todd *never* got C's.

"You feeling okay these days, Todd?"

He looked at her blankly for a moment, and then that radiant smile spread over his face, charming her . . . comforting her. There was a dab of strawberry preserves on his chin. "Sure," he said. "Four-oh."

"Todd-baby," she said.

"Monica-baby," he responded, and they both started to laugh.

9

March, 1975.

"Kitty-kitty," Dussander said. "*Heeere,* kitty-kitty. Puss-puss? Puss-puss?"

He was sitting on his back stoop, a pink plastic bowl by his right foot. The bowl was full of milk. It was one-thirty in the afternoon; the day was hazy and hot. Brush-fires far to the west tinged the air with an autumnal smell that jagged oddly against the calendar. If the boy was coming, he would be here in another hour. But the boy didn't always come now. Instead of seven days a week he came sometimes only four times, or five. An intuition had grown in him, little by little, and his intuition told him that the boy was having troubles of his own.

"Kitty-kitty," Dussander coaxed. The stray cat was at the far end of the yard, sitting in the ragged verge of weeds by Dussander's fence. It was a tom, and every bit as ragged as the weeds it sat in. Every time he spoke, the cat's ears cocked forward. Its eyes never left the pink bowl filled with milk.

Perhaps, Dussander thought, the boy was having troubles with his studies. Or bad dreams. Or both.

That last made him smile.

"Kitty-kitty," he called softly. The cat's ears cocked forward again. It didn't move, not yet, but it continued to study the milk.

Dussander had certainly been afflicted with problems of his

own. For three weeks or so he had worn the SS uniform to bed like grotesque pajamas, and the uniform had warded off the insomnia and the bad dreams. His sleep had been—at first—as sound as a lumberjack's. Then the dreams had returned, not little by little, but all at once, and worse than ever before. Dreams of running as well as the dreams of the eyes. Running through a wet, unseen jungle where heavy leaves and damp fronds struck his face, leaving trickles that felt like sap . . . or blood. Running and running, the luminous eyes always around him, peering soullessly at him, until he broke into a clearing. In the darkness he sensed rather than saw the steep rise that began on the clearing's far side. At the top of that rise was Patin, its low cement buildings and yards surrounded by barbed wire and electrified wire, its sentry towers standing like Martian dreadnoughts straight out of *War of the Worlds.* And in the middle, huge stacks billowed smoke against the sky, and below these brick columns were the furnaces, stoked and ready to go, glowing in the night like the eyes of fierce demons. They had told the inhabitants of the area that the Patin inmates made clothes and candles, and of course the locals had believed that no more than the locals around Auschwitz had believed that the camp was a sausage factory. It didn't matter.

Looking back over his shoulder in the dream, he would at last see *them* coming out of hiding, the restless dead, the *Juden,* shambling toward him with blue numbers glaring from the livid flesh of their outstretched arms, their hands hooked into talons, their faces no longer expressionless but animated with hate, lively with vengeance, vivacious with murder. Toddlers ran beside their mothers and grandfathers were borne up by their middle-aged children. And the dominant expression on all their faces was desperation.

Desperation? Yes. Because in the dreams he knew (and so did they) that if he could climb the hill, he would be safe. Down here in these wet and swampy lowlands, in this jungle where the night-flowering plants extruded blood instead of sap, he was a hunted animal . . . prey. But up there, he was in command. If this was a jungle, then the camp at the top of the hill was a zoo, all the wild animals safely in cages, he the head keeper whose job it was to decide which would be fed, which would live, which would be handed over to the vivisectionists, which would be taken to the knacker's in the remover's van.

He would begin to run up the hill, running in all the slowness of nightmare. He would feel the first skeletal hands close about his neck, feel their cold and stinking breath, smell their decay, hear their birdlike cries of triumph as they pulled him down with salvation not only in sight but almost at hand—

"Kitty-kitty," Dussander called. "Milk. Nice milk."

The cat came at last. It crossed half of the back yard and then sat again, but lightly, its tail twitching with worry. It didn't trust him; no. But Dussander knew the cat could smell the milk and so he was sanguine. Sooner or later it would come.

At Patin there had never been a contraband problem. Some of the prisoners came in with their valuables poked far up their asses in small chamois bags (and how often their valuables turned out not to be valuable at all—photographs, locks of hair, fake jewelry), often pushed up with sticks until they were past the point where even the long fingers of the trusty they had called Stinky-Thumbs could reach. One woman, he remembered, had had a small diamond, flawed, it turned out, really not valuable at all—but it had been in her family for six generations, passed from mother to eldest daughter (or so she said, but of course she was a Jew and all of them lied). She swallowed it before entering Patin. When it came out in her waste, she swallowed it again. She kept doing this, although eventually the diamond began to cut her insides and she bled.

There had been other ruses, although most only involved petty items such as a hoard of tobacco or a hair-ribbon or two. It didn't matter. In the room Dussander used for prisoner interrogations there was a hot plate and a homely kitchen table covered with a red checked cloth much like the one in his own kitchen. There was always a pot of lamb stew bubbling mellowly away on that hotplate. When contraband was suspected (and when was it not?) a member of the suspected clique would be brought to that room. Dussander would stand them by the hotplate, where the rich fumes from the stew wafted. Gently, he would ask them *Who.* Who is hiding gold? Who is hiding jewelry? Who has tobacco? Who gave the Givenet woman the pill for her baby? Who? The stew was never specifically promised; but always the aroma eventually loosened their tongues. Of course, a truncheon would have done the same, or a gun-barrel jammed into their filthy crotches, but the stew was . . . was *elegant.* Yes.

"Kitty-kitty," Dussander called. The cat's ears cocked forward. It half-rose, then half-remembered some long-ago kick, or perhaps a match that had burned its whiskers, and it settled back on its haunches. But soon it would move.

He had found a way of propitiating his nightmare. It was, in a way, no more than wearing the SS uniform . . . but raised to a greater power. Dussander was pleased with himself, only sorry that he had never thought of it before. He supposed he had the boy to thank for this new method of quieting himself, for showing him that the key to the past's terrors was not in rejection but in contemplation and even something like a friend's embrace. It was true that before the boy's unexpected arrival last summer he hadn't had any bad dreams for a long time, but he believed now that he had come to a coward's terms with his past. He had been forced to give up a part of himself. Now he had reclaimed it.

"Kitty-kitty," called Dussander, and a smile broke on his face, a kindly smile, a reassuring smile, the smile of all old men who have somehow come through the cruel courses of life to a safe place, still relatively intact, and with at least some wisdom.

The tom rose from its haunches, hesitated only a moment

longer, and then trotted across the remainder of the back yard with lithe grace. It mounted the steps, gave Dussander a final mistrustful look, laying back its chewed and scabby ears; then it began to drink the milk.

"*Nice* milk," Dussander said, pulling on the Playtex rubber gloves that had lain in his lap all the while. "*Nice* milk for a *nice* kitty." He had bought these gloves in the supermarket. He had stood in the express lane, and older women had looked at him approvingly, even speculatively. The gloves were advertised on TV. They had cuffs. They were so flexible you could pick up a dime while you were wearing them.

He stroked the cat's back with one green finger and talked to it soothingly. Its back began to arch with the rhythm of his strokes.

Just before the bowl was empty, he seized the cat.

It came electrically alive in his clenching hands, twisting and jerking, clawing at the rubber. Its body lashed limberly back and forth, and Dussander had no doubt that if its teeth or claws got into him, it would come off the winner. It was an old campaigner. It takes one to know one, Dussander thought, grinning.

Holding the cat prudently away from his body, the painful grin stamped on his face, Dussander pushed the back door open with his foot and went into the kitchen. The cat yowled and twisted and ripped at the rubber gloves. Its feral, triangular head flashed down and fastened on one green thumb.

"Nasty kitty," Dussander said reproachfully.

The oven door stood open. Dussander threw the cat inside. Its claws made a ripping, prickly sound as they disengaged from the gloves. Dussander slammed the oven door shut with one knee, provoking a painful twinge from his arthritis. Yet he continued to grin. Breathing hard, nearly panting, he propped himself against the stove for a moment, his head hanging down. It was a gas stove. He rarely used it for anything fancier than TV dinners and killing stray cats.

Faintly, rising up through the gas burners, he could hear the cat scratching and yowling to be let out.

Dussander twisted the oven dial over to 500°. There was an audible *pop!* as the oven pilot-light lit two double rows of hissing gas. The cat stopped yowling and began to scream. It sounded . . . yes . . . almost like a young boy. A young boy in terrible pain. The thought made Dussander smile even more broadly. His heart thundered in his chest. The cat scratched and whirled madly in the oven, still screaming. Soon, a hot, furry, burning smell began to seep out of the oven and into the room.

He scraped the remains of the cat out of the oven half an hour later, using a barbecue fork he had acquired for two dollars and ninety-eight cents at the Grant's in the shopping center a mile away.

The cat's roasted carcass went into an empty flour sack. He took the sack down cellar. The cellar floor had never been cemented. Shortly, Dussander came back up. He sprayed the kitchen with Glade until it reeked of artificial pine scent. He opened all the windows. He washed the barbecue fork and hung it up on the pegboard. Then he sat down to wait and see if the boy would come. He smiled and smiled.

Todd did come, about five minutes after Dussander had given up on him for the afternoon. He was wearing a warm-up jacket with his school colors on it; he was also wearing a San Diego Padres baseball cap. He carried his schoolbooks under his arm.

"Yucka-ducka," he said, coming into the kitchen and wrinkling his nose. "What's that smell? It's awful."

"I tried the oven," Dussander said, lighting a cigarette. "I'm afraid I burned my supper. I had to throw it out."

One day later that month the boy came much earlier than usual, long before school usually let out. Dussander was sitting in the kitchen, drinking Ancient Age bourbon from a chipped and discolored cup that had the words HERE'S YER CAWFEE MAW, HAW! HAW! HAW! written around the rim. He had his rocker out in the kitchen now and he was just drinking and rocking, rocking and drinking, bumping his slippers on the faded linoleum. He was pleasantly high. There had been no more bad dreams at all until just last night. Not since the tomcat with the chewed ears. Last night's had been particularly horrible, though. That could not be denied. *They* had dragged him down after he had gotten halfway up the hill, and *they* had begun to do unspeakable things to him before he was able to wake himself up. Yet, after his initial thrashing return to the world of real things, he had been confident. He could end the dreams whenever he wished. Perhaps a cat would not be enough this time. But there was always the dog pound. Yes. Always the pound.

Todd came abruptly into the kitchen, his face pale and shiny and strained. He had lost weight, all right, Dussander thought. And there was a queer white look in his eyes that Dussander did not like at all.

"You're going to help me," Todd said suddenly and defiantly.

"Really?" Dussander said mildly, but sudden apprehension leaped inside of him. He didn't let his face change as Todd slammed his books down on the table with a sudden, vicious overhand stroke. One of them spun-skated across the oilcloth and landed in a tent on the floor by Dussander's foot.

"Yes, you're fucking-A right!" Todd said shrilly. "You better believe it! Because this is your fault! All your fault!" Hectic spots of red mounted into his cheeks. "But you're going to have to help me get out of it, because I've got the goods on you! *I've got you right where I want you!*"

"I'll help you in any way I can," Dussander said quietly. He saw that he had folded his hands neatly in front of himself without even thinking about it—just as he had once done.

He leaned forward in the rocker until his chin was directly over his folded hands—as he had once done. His face was calm and friendly and enquiring; none of his growing apprehension showed. Sitting just so, he could almost imagine a pot of lamb stew simmering on the stove behind him. 'Tell me what the trouble is."

"This is the fucking *trouble,*" Todd said viciously, and threw a folder at Dussander. It bounced off his chest and landed in his lap, and he was momentarily surprised by the heat of the anger which leaped up in him; the urge to rise and backhand the boy smartly. Instead, he kept the mild expression on his face. It was the boy's school-card, he saw, although the school seemed to be at ridiculous pains to hide the fact. Instead of a school-card, or a Grade Report, it was called a "Quarterly Progress Report." He grunted at that, and opened the card.

A typed half-sheet of paper fell out. Dussander put it aside for later examination and turned his attention to the boy's grades first.

"You seem to have fallen on the rocks, my boy," Dussander said, not without some pleasure. The boy had passed only English and American History. Every other grade was an F.

"It's not my fault," Todd hissed venomously. "It's *your* fault. All those *stories.* I have nightmares about them, do you know that? I sit down and open my books and I start thinking about whatever you told me that day and the next thing I know, my mother's telling me it's time to go to bed. Well, that's not my fault! *It isn't! You hear me? It isn't!*"

"I hear you very well," Dussander said, and read the typed note that had been tucked into Todd's card.

Dear Mr. and Mrs. Bowden,

This note is to suggest that we have a group conference concerning Todd's second- and third-quarter grades. In light of Todd's previous good work in this school, his current grades suggest a specific problem which may be affecting his academic performance in a deleterious way. Such a problem can often be solved by a frank and open discussion.

I should point out that although Todd has passed the half-year, his final grades may be failing in some cases unless his work improves radically in the fourth quarter. Failing grades would entail summer school to avoid being kept back and causing a major scheduling problem.

I must also note that Todd is in the college division, and that his work so far this year is far below college acceptance levels. It is also below the level of academic ability assumed by the SAT tests.

Please be assured that I am ready to work out a mutually convenient time for us to meet. In a case such as this, earlier is usually better.

Sincerely yours,
Edward French

"Who is this Edward French?" Dussander asked, slipping the note back inside the card (part of him still marvelled at the American love of jargon; such a rolling missive to inform the parents that their son was flunking out!) and then refolding his hands. His premonition of disaster was stronger than ever, but he refused to give in to it. A year before, he would have done; a year ago he had been ready for disaster. Now he was not, but it seemed that the cursed boy had brought it to him anyway. "Is he your headmaster?"

"Rubber Ed? Hell, no. He's the guidance counsellor."

"*Guidance* counsellor? What is that?"

"You can figure it out," Todd said. He was nearly hysterical. "You read the goddam note!" He walked rapidly around the room, shooting sharp, quick glances at Dussander. "Well, I'm not going to let any of this shit go down. I'm just not. I'm not going to any summer school. My dad and mom are going to

Hawaii this summer and I'm going with them." He pointed at the card on the table. "Do you know what my dad will do if he sees that?"

Dussander shook his head.

"He'll get everything out of me. *Everything.* He'll know it was you. It couldn't be anything else, because nothing else has changed. He'll poke and pry and he'll get it all out of me. And then . . . then I'll . . . I'll be in dutch."

He stared at Dussander resentfully.

"They'll watch me. Hell, they might make me see a doctor, I don't know. How should *I* know? But I'm not getting in dutch. And I'm not going to any fucking summer school."

"Or to the reformatory," Dussander said. He said it very quietly.

Todd stopped circling the room. His face became very still. His cheeks and forehead, already pale, became even whiter. He stared at Dussander, and had to try twice before he could speak. "*What? What* did you just say?"

"My dear boy," Dussander said, assuming an air of great patience, "for the last five minutes I have listened to you pule and whine, and what all your puling and whining comes down to is this. *You* are in trouble. *You* might be found out. *You* might find yourself in adverse circumstances." Seeing that he had the boy's complete attention—at last—Dussander sipped reflectively from his cup.

"My boy," he went on, "that is a very dangerous attitude for you to have. And dangerous for me. The potential harm is much greater for me. You worry about your school-card. Pah! *This* for your school-card."

He flicked it off the table and onto the floor with one yellow finger.

"I am worried about my *life.*"

Todd did not reply; he simply went on looking at Dussander with that white-eyed, slightly crazed stare.

"The Israelis will not scruple at the fact that I am seventy-six. The death-penalty is still very much in favor over there, you know, especially when the man in the dock is a Nazi war criminal associated with the camps."

"You're a U.S. citizen," Todd said. "America wouldn't let them take you. I read up on that. I—"

"You read, but you don't *listen*! I am *not* a U.S. citizen! My papers came from *la cosa nostra.* I would be deported, and Mossad agents would be waiting for me wherever I deplaned."

"I wish they *would* hang you," Todd muttered, curling his hands into fists and staring down at them. "I was crazy to get mixed up with you in the first place."

"No doubt," Dussander said, and smiled thinly. "But you *are* mixed up with me. We must live in the present, boy, not in the past of 'I-should-have-nevers.' You must realize that your fate and my own are now inextricably entwined. If you 'blow the horn on me,' as your saying goes, do you think I will hesitate to blow the horn on you? Seven hundred thousand died at Patin. To the world at large I am a criminal, a monster, even the butcher your scandal-rags would have me. You are an accessory to all of that, my boy. You have criminal knowledge of an illegal alien, but you have not reported it. And if I am caught, I will tell the world all about you. When the reporters put their microphones in my face, it will be your name I'll repeat over and over again. 'Todd Bowden, yes, that is his name . . . how long? Almost a year. He wanted to know everything . . . all the gooshy parts. That's how he put it, yes: "All the gooshy parts." ' "

Todd's breath had stopped. His skin appeared transparent. Dussander smiled at him. He sipped bourbon.

"I think they will put you in jail. They may call it a reformatory, or a correctional facility—there may be a fancy name for it, like this 'Quarterly Progress Report' "—his lip curled—"but no matter what they call it, there will be bars on the windows."

Todd wet his lips. "I'd call you a liar. I'd tell them I just found out. They'd believe me, not you. You just better remember that."

Dussander's thin smile remained. "I thought you told me your father would get it all out of you."

Todd spoke slowly, as a person speaks when realization and verbalization occur simultaneously. "Maybe not. Maybe not this time. This isn't just breaking a window with a rock."

Dussander winced inwardly. He suspected that the boy's judgment was right—with so much at stake, he might indeed be able to convince his father. After all, when faced with such an unpleasant truth, what parent would not want to be convinced?

"Perhaps. Perhaps not. But how are you going to explain all those books you had to read to me because poor Mr. Denker is half-blind? My eyes are not what they were, but I can still read fine print with my spectacles. I can prove it."

"I'd say you fooled me!"

"Will you? And what reason will you be able to give for my fooling?"

"For . . . for friendship. Because you were lonely."

That, Dussander reflected, was just close enough to the truth to be believable. And once, in the beginning, the boy might have been able to bring it off. But now he was ragged; now he was coming apart in strings like a coat that has reached the end of its useful service. If a child shot off his cap pistol across the street, this boy would jump into the air and scream like a girl.

"Your school-card will also support my side of it," Dussander said. "It was not *Robinson Crusoe* that caused your grades to fall down so badly, my boy, was it?"

"Shut up, why don't you? Just shut up about it!"

"No," Dussander said. "I won't shut up about it." He lit a cigarette, scratching the wooden match alight on the gas oven door. "Not until I make you see the simple truth. We are in this together, sink or swim." He looked at Todd through the raftering smoke, not smiling, his old, lined face reptilian. "I will drag you down, boy. I promise you that. If anything comes out, *everything* will come out. That is my promise to you."

Todd stared at him sullenly and didn't reply.

"Now," Dussander said briskly, with the air of a man who has put a necessary unpleasantness behind him, "the question is, what are we going to do about this situation? Have you any ideas?"

"This will fix the report card," Todd said, and took a new bottle of ink eradicator from his jacket pocket. "About that fucking letter, I don't know."

Dussander looked at the ink eradicator approvingly. He had falsified a few reports of his own in his time. When the quotas had gone up to the point of fantasy . . . and far, far beyond. And . . . more like the situation they were now in—there had been the matter of the invoices . . . those which enumerated the spoils of war. Each week he would check the boxes of valuables, all of them to be sent back to Berlin in special train-cars that were like big safes on wheels. On the side of each box was a manila envelope, and inside the envelope there had been a verified invoice of that box's contents. So many rings, necklaces, chokers, so many grams of gold. Dussander, however, had had his own box of valuables—not very valuable valuables, but not insignificant, either. Jades. Tourmalines. Opals. A few flawed pearls. Industrial diamonds. And when he saw an item invoiced for Berlin that caught his eye or seemed a good investment, he would remove it, replace it with an item from his own box, and use ink eradicator on the invoice, changing their item for his. He had developed into a fairly expert forger . . . a talent that had come in handy more than once after the war was over.

"Good," he told Todd. "As for this other matter . . ."

Dussander began to rock again, sipping from his cup. Todd pulled a chair up to the table and began to go to work on his report card, which he had picked up from the floor without a word. Dussander's outward calm had had its effect on him and now he worked silently, his head bent studiously over the card, like any American boy who has set out to do the best by God job he can, whether that job be planting corn, pitching a no-hitter in the Little League World Series, or forging grades on his report card.

Dussander looked at the nape of his neck, lightly tanned and cleanly exposed between the fall of his hair and the round neck of his tee-shirt. His eyes drifted from there to the top counter drawer where he kept the butcher knives. One quick thrust—he knew where to put it—and the boy's spinal cord would be severed. His lips would be sealed forever. Dussander smiled regretfully. There would be questions asked if the boy disappeared. Too many of them. Some directed at him. Even if there was no letter with a friend, close scrutiny was something he could not afford. Too bad.

"This man French," he said, tapping the letter. "Does he know your parents in a social way?"

"Him?" Todd edged the word with contempt. "My mom and dad don't go anywhere that he could even get in."

"Has he ever met them in his professional capacity? Has he ever had conferences with them before?"

"No. I've always been near the top of my classes. Until now."

"So what does he know about them?" Dussander said, looking dreamily into his cup, which was now nearly empty. "Oh, he knows about *you.* He no doubt has all the records on you that he can use. Back to the fights you had in the kindergarten play yard. But what does he know about *them*?"

Todd put his pen and the small bottle of ink eradicator away. "Well, he knows their names. Of course. And their ages. He knows we're all Methodists. You don't have to fill that line out, but my folks always do. We don't go much, but he'd know that's what we are. He must know what my dad does for a living; that's on the forms, too. All that stuff they have to fill out every year. And I'm pretty sure that's all."

"Would he know if your parents were having troubles at home?"

"What's that supposed to mean?"

Dussander tossed off the last of the bourbon in his cup. "Squabbles. Fights. Your father sleeping on the couch. Your mother drinking too much." His eyes gleamed. "A divorce brewing."

Indignantly, Todd said: "There's nothing like that going on! No way!"

"I never said there was. But just think, boy. Suppose that things at your house were 'going to hell in a streetcar,' as the saying is."

Todd only looked at him, frowning.

"You would be worried about them," Dussander said. "Very worried. You would lose your appetite. You would sleep poorly. Saddest of all, your schoolwork would suffer. True? Very sad for the children, when there are troubles in the home."

Understanding dawned in the boy's eyes—understanding and something like dumb gratitude. Dussander was gratified.

"Yes, it is an unhappy situation when a family totters on the edge of destruction," Dussander said grandly, pouring more bourbon. He was getting quite drunk. "The daytime television dramas, they make this absolutely clear. There is acrimony. Backbiting and lies. Most of all, there is pain. Pain, my boy. You have no idea of the hell your parents are going through. They are so swallowed up by their own troubles that they have little time for the problems of their own son. His problems seem minor compared to theirs, *hein*? Someday, when the scars have begun to heal, they will no doubt take a fuller interest in him once again. But now the only concession they can make is to send the boy's kindly grandfather to Mr. French."

Todd's eyes had been gradually brightening to a glow that was nearly fervid. "Might work," he was muttering. "Might, yeah, might work, might—" He broke off suddenly. His eyes darkened again. "No, it won't. You don't look like me, not even a little bit. Rubber Ed will never believe it."

"Himmel! Gott im Himmel!" Dussander cried, getting to his feet, crossing the kitchen (a bit unsteadily), opening the cellar door, and pulling out a fresh bottle of Ancient Age. He spun off the cap and poured liberally. "For a smart boy, you are such a *Dummkopf.* When do grandfathers ever look like their grandsons? Huh? I got white hair. Do you have white hair?"

Approaching the table again, he reached out with surprising quickness, snatched an abundant handful of Todd's blonde hair, and pulled briskly.

"Cut it out!" Todd snapped, but he smiled a little.

"Besides," Dussander said, settling back into his rocker, "you have yellow hair and blue eyes. My eyes are blue, and before my hair turned white, it was yellow. You can tell me your whole family history. Your aunts and uncles. The people your father works with. Your mother's little hobbies. I will remember. I will study and remember. Two days later it will all be forgotten again—these days my memory is like a cloth bag filled with water—but I will remember for long enough." He smiled grimly. "In my time I have stayed ahead of Wiesenthal and pulled the wool over the eyes of Himmler himself. If I cannot fool one American public school teacher, I will pull my winding-shroud around me and crawl down into my grave."

"Maybe," Todd said slowly, and Dussander could see he had already accepted it. His eyes were luminous with relief.

"No—*surely*!" Dussander cried.

He began to cackle with laughter, the rocking chair squeaking back and forth. Todd looked at him, puzzled and a little frightened, but after a bit he began to laugh, too. In Dussander's kitchen they laughed and laughed, Dussander by the open window where the warm California breeze wafted in, and Todd rocked back on the rear legs of his kitchen chair, so that its back rested against the oven door, the white enamel of which was crisscrossed by the dark, charred-looking streaks made by Dussander's wooden matches as he struck them alight.

• • •

Rubber Ed French (his nickname, Todd had explained to Dussander, referred to the rubbers he always wore over his sneakers during wet weather) was a slight man who made an affectation of always wearing Keds to school. It was a touch of informality which he thought would endear him to the one hundred and six children between the ages of twelve and fourteen who made up his counselling load. He had five pairs of Keds, ranging in color from Fast Track Blue to Screaming Yellow Zonkers, totally unaware that behind his back he was known not only as Rubber Ed but as Sneaker Pete and The Ked Man, as in The Ked Man Cometh. He had been known as Pucker in college, and he would have been most humiliated of all to learn that even that shameful fact had somehow gotten out.

He rarely wore ties, preferring turtleneck sweaters. He had been wearing these ever since the mid-sixties, when David McCallum had popularized them in *The Man from U.N.C.L.E.* In his college days his classmates had been known to spy him crossing the quad and remark, "Here comes Pucker in his U.N.C.L.E. sweater." He had majored in Educational Psychology, and he privately considered himself to be the only good guidance counsellor he had ever met. He had real *rapport* with his kids. He could *get right down to it* with them; he could *rap* with them and be silently sympathetic if they had to do some shouting and *kick out the jams.* He could *get into their hangups* because he understood what a *bummer* it was to be thirteen when someone was *doing a number on your head* and you couldn't *get your shit together.*

The thing was, he had a damned hard time remembering what it had been like to be thirteen himself. He supposed that was the ultimate price you had to pay for growing up in the fifties. That, and travelling into the brave new world of the sixties nicknamed Pucker.

Now, as Todd Bowden's grandfather came into his office, closing the pebbled-glass door firmly behind him, Rubber Ed stood up respectfully but was careful not to come around his desk to greet the old man. He was aware of his sneakers. Sometimes the old-timers didn't understand that the sneakers were a psychological aid with kids who had teacher hangups—which was to say that some of the older folks couldn't *get behind* a guidance counsellor in Keds.

This is one fine-looking dude, Rubber Ed thought. His white hair was carefully brushed back. His three-piece suit was spotlessly clean. His dove-gray tie was impeccably knotted. In his left hand he held a furled black umbrella (outside, a light drizzle had been falling since the weekend) in a manner that was almost military. A few years ago Rubber Ed and his wife had gone on a Dorothy Sayers jag, reading everything by that estimable lady that they could lay their hands upon. It occurred to him now that this was her brainchild, Lord Peter Wimsey, to the life. It was Wimsey at seventy-five, years after both Bunter and Harriet Vane had passed on to their rewards. He made a mental note to tell Sondra about this when he got home.

"Mr. Bowden," he said respectfully, and offered his hand.

"A pleasure," Bowden said, and shook it. Rubber Ed was careful not to put on the firm and uncompromising pressure he applied to the hands of the fathers he saw; it was obvious from the gingerly way the old boy offered it that he had arthritis.

"A pleasure, Mr. French," Bowden repeated, and took a seat, carefully pulling up the knees of his trousers. He propped the umbrella between his feet and leaned on it, looking like an elderly, extremely urbane vulture that had come in to roost in Rubber Ed French's office. He had the slightest touch of an accent, Rubber Ed thought, but it wasn't the clipped intonation of the British upper class, as Wimsey's would have been; it was broader, more European. Anyway, the resemblance to Todd was quite striking. Especially through the nose and eyes.

"I'm glad you could come," Rubber Ed told him, resuming his own seat, "although in these cases the student's mother or father—"

This was the opening gambit, of course. Almost ten years

of experience in the counselling business had convinced him that when an aunt or an uncle or a grandparent showed up for a conference, it usually meant trouble at home—the sort of trouble that invariably turned out to be the root of the problem. To Rubber Ed, this came as a relief. Domestic problems were bad, but for a boy of Todd's intelligence, *a heavy drug trip* would have been much, much worse.

"Yes, of course," Bowden said, managing to look both sorrowful and angry at the same time. "My son and his wife asked me if I could come and talk this sorry business over with you, Mr. French. Todd is a good boy, believe me. This trouble with his school marks is only temporary."

"Well, we all hope so, don't we, Mr. Bowden? Smoke if you like. It's supposed to be off-limits on school property, but I'll never tell."

"Thank you."

Mr. Bowden took a half-crushed package of Camel cigarettes from his inner pocket, put one of the last two zigzagging smokes in his mouth, found a Diamond Blue-Tip match, scratched it on the heel of one black shoe, and lit up. He coughed an old man's dank cough over the first drag, shook the match out, and put the blackened stump into the ashtray Rubber Ed had produced. Rubber Ed watched this ritual, which seemed almost as formal as the old man's shoes, with frank fascination.

"Where to begin," Bowden said, his distressed face looking at Rubber Ed through a swirling raft of cigarette smoke.

"Well," Rubber Ed said kindly, "the very fact that you're here instead of Todd's parents tells me something, you know."

"Yes, I suppose it does. Very well." He folded his hands. The Camel protruded from between the second and third fingers of his right. He straightened his back and lifted his chin. There was something almost Prussian in his mental coming to terms, Rubber Ed thought, something that made him think of all those war movies he'd seen as a kid.

"My son and my daughter-in-law are having troubles in their home," Bowden said, biting off each word precisely. "Rather bad troubles, I should think." His eyes, old but amazingly bright, watched as Rubber Ed opened the folder centered in front of him on the desk blotter. There were sheets of paper inside, but not many.

"And you feel that these troubles are affecting Todd's academic performance?"

Bowden leaned forward perhaps six inches. His blue eyes never left Rubber Ed's brown ones. There was a heavily charged pause, and then Bowden said: "The mother drinks."

He resumed his former ramrod-straight position.

"Oh," Rubber Ed said.

"Yes," Bowden replied, nodding grimly. "The boy has told me that he has come home on two occasions and has found her sprawled out on the kitchen table. He knows how my son feels about her drinking problem, and so the boy has put dinner in the oven himself on these occasions, and has gotten her to drink enough black coffee so she will at least be awake when Richard comes home."

"That's bad," Rubber Ed said, although he had heard worse—mothers with heroin habits, fathers who had abruptly taken it into their heads to start banging their daughters . . . or their sons. "Has Mrs. Bowden thought about getting professional help for her problem?"

"The boy has tried to persuade her that would be the best course. She is much ashamed, I think. If she was given a little time . . ." He made a gesture with his cigarette that left a dissolving smoke-ring in the air. "You understand?"

"Yes, of course." Rubber Ed nodded, privately admiring the gesture that had produced the smoke-ring. "Your son . . . Todd's father . . ."

"He is not without blame," Bowden said harshly. "The hours he works, the meals he has missed, the nights when he must leave suddenly . . . I tell you, Mr. French, he is more married to his job than he is to Monica. I was raised to believe that a man's family came before everything. Was it not the same for you?"

"It sure was," Rubber Ed responded heartily. His father had been a night watchman for a large Los Angeles department store and he had really only seen his pop on weekends and vacations.

"That is another side of the problem," Bowden said.

Rubber Ed nodded and thought for a moment. "What about your other son, Mr. Bowden? Uh . . ." He looked down at the folder. "Harold. Todd's uncle."

"Harry and Deborah are in Minnesota now," Bowden said, quite truthfully. "He has a position there at the University medical school. It would be quite difficult for him to leave, and very unfair to ask him." His face took on a righteous cast. "Harry and his wife are quite happily married."

"I see." Rubber Ed looked at the file again for a moment and then closed it. "Mr. Bowden, I appreciate your frankness. I'll be just as frank with you."

"Thank you," Bowden said stiffly.

"We can't do as much for our students in the counselling area as we would like. There are six counsellors here, and we're each carrying a load of over a hundred students. My newest colleague, Hepburn, has a hundred and fifteen. At this age, in our society, all children need help."

"Of course." Bowden mashed his cigarette brutally into the ashtray and folded his hands once more.

"Sometimes bad problems get by us. Home environment and drugs are the two most common. At least Todd isn't mixed up with speed or mescaline or PCP."

"God forbid."

"Sometimes," Rubber Ed went on, "there's simply nothing we can do. It's depressing, but it's a fact of life. Usually the ones that are first to get spit out of the machine we're running here are the class troublemakers, the sullen, uncommunicative kids, the ones who refuse to even try. They are simply warm bodies waiting for the system to buck them up through the grades or waiting to get old enough so they can quit without their parents' permission and join the Army or get a job at the Speedy-Boy Carwash or marry their boyfriends. You understand? I'm being blunt. Our system is, as they say, not all it's cracked up to be."

"I appreciate your frankness."

"But it hurts when you see the machine starting to mash up someone like Todd. He ran out a ninety-two average for last year's work, and that puts him in the ninety-fifth percentile. His English averages are even better. He shows a flair for writing, and that's something special in a generation of kids that think culture begins in front of the TV and ends in the neighborhood movie theater. I was talking to the woman who had Todd in Comp last year. She said Todd passed in the finest term-paper she'd seen in twenty years of teaching. It was on the German death-camps during World War Two. She gave him the only A-plus she's ever given a composition student."

"I have read it," Bowden said. "It is very fine."

"He has also demonstrated above-average ability in the life sciences and social sciences, and while he's not going to be one of the great math whizzes of the century, all the notes I have indicate that he's given it the good old college try . . . until this year. Until this year. That's the whole story, in a nutshell."

"Yes."

"I hate like *hell* to see Todd go down the tubes this way, Mr. Bowden. And summer school . . . well, I said I'd be frank. Summer school often does a boy like Todd more harm than good. Your usual junior high school summer session is a zoo. All the monkeys and the laughing hyenas are in attendance, plus a full complement of dodo birds. Bad company for a boy like Todd."

"Certainly."

"So let's get to the bottom line, shall we? I suggest a series of appointments for Mr. and Mrs. Bowden at the Counselling Center downtown. Everything in confidence, of course. The man in charge down there, Harry Ackerman, is a good friend of mine. And I don't think Todd should go to them with the idea; I think you should." Rubber Ed smiled widely. "Maybe we can get everybody back on track by June. It's not impossible."

But Bowden looked positively alarmed by this idea.

"I believe they might resent the boy if I took that proposal to them now," he said. "Things are very delicate. They could go either way. The boy has promised me he will work harder in his studies. He is very alarmed at this drop in his marks." He smiled thinly, a smile Ed French could not quite interpret. "More alarmed than you know."

"But—"

"And they would resent *me,*" Bowden pressed on quickly. "God knows they would. Monica already regards me as something of a meddler. I try not to be, but you see the situation. I feel that things are best left alone . . . for now."

"I've had a great deal of experience in these matters," Rubber Ed told Bowden. He folded his hands on Todd's file and looked at the old man earnestly. "I really think counselling is in order here. You'll understand that my interest in the marital problems your son and daughter-in-law are having begins and ends with the effect they're having on Todd . . . and right now, they're having quite an effect."

"Let me make a counter-proposal," Bowden said. "You have, I believe, a system of warning parents of poor grades?"

"Yes," Rubber Ed agreed cautiously. "Interpretation of Progress cards—IOP cards. The kids, of course, call them Flunk Cards. They only get them if their grade in a given course falls below seventy-eight. In other words, we give out IOP cards to kids who are pulling a D or an F in a given course."

"Very good," Bowden said. "Then what I suggest is this: if the boy gets one of those cards . . . even *one*"—he held up one gnarled finger—"I will approach my son and his wife about your counselling. I will go further." He pronounced it *furdah.* "If the boy receives one of your Flunk Cards in April—"

"We give them out in May, actually."

"Yes? If he receives one then, I guarantee that they will accept the counselling proposal. They are worried about their son, Mr. French. But now they are so wrapped up in their own problem that . . ." He shrugged.

"I understand."

"So let us give them that long to solve their own problems. Pulling one's self up by one's own shoelaces . . . that is the American way, is it not?"

"Yes, I guess it is," Rubber Ed told him after a moment's thought . . . and after a quick glance at the clock, which told him he had another appointment in five minutes. "I'll accept that."

He stood, and Bowden stood with him. They shook hands again, Rubber Ed being carefully mindful of the old party's arthritis.

"But in all fairness, I ought to tell you that very few students can pull out of an eighteen-week tailspin in just four weeks of classes. There's a huge amount of ground to be made up—a *huge* amount. I suspect you'll have to come through on your guarantee, Mr. Bowden."

Bowden offered his thin, disconcerting smile again. "Do you?" was all he said.

Something had troubled Rubber Ed through the entire interview, and he put his finger on it during lunch in the cafeteria, more than an hour after "Lord Peter" had left, umbrella once again neatly tucked under his arm.

He and Todd's grandfather had talked for fifteen minutes at least, probably closer to twenty, and Ed didn't think the old man had once referred to his grandson by name.

Todd pedaled breathlessly up Dussander's walk and parked his bike on its kickstand. School had let out only fifteen minutes before. He took the front steps at one jump, used his doorkey, and hurried down the hall to the sunlit kitchen. His face was a mixture of hopeful sunshine and gloomy clouds. He stood in the kitchen doorway for a moment, his stomach and his vocal cords knotted, watching Dussander as he rocked with his cupful of bourbon in his lap. He was still dressed in his best, although he had pulled his tie down two inches and loosened the top button of his shirt. He looked at Todd expressionlessly, his lizardlike eyes at half-mast.

"Well?" Todd finally managed.

Dussander left him hanging a moment longer, a moment that seemed at least ten years long to Todd. Then, deliberately, Dussander set his cup on the table next to his bottle of Ancient Age and said:

"The fool believed everything."

Todd let out his pent-up breath in a whooping gust of relief.

Before he could draw another breath in, Dussander added: "He wanted your poor, troubled parents to attend counselling sessions downtown with a friend of his. He was really quite insistent."

"Jesus! Did you . . . what did you . . . how did you handle it?"

"I thought quickly," Dussander replied. "Like the little girl in the Saki story, invention on short notice is one of my strong points. I promised him your parents would go in for such counselling if you received even one Flunk Card when they are given in May."

The blood fell out of Todd's face.

"You did *what*?" he nearly screamed. "I've already flunked two algebra quizzes and a history test since the marking period started!" He advanced into the room, his pale face now growing shiny with breaking sweat. "There was a French quiz this afternoon and I flunked that, too . . . I know I did. All I could think about was that goddamned Rubber Ed and whether or not you were taking care of him. You took care of him, all right," he finished bitterly. "Not get one Flunk Card? I'll probably get five or six."

"It was the best I could do without arousing suspicions," Dussander said. "This French, fool that he is, is only doing his job. Now you will do yours."

"What's that supposed to mean?" Todd's face was ugly and thunderous, his voice truculent.

"You will work. In the next four weeks you will work harder than you have ever worked in your life. Furthermore, on Monday you will go to each of your instructors and apologize to them for your poor showing thus far. You will—"

"It's impossible," Todd said. "You don't get it, man. It's *impossible.* I'm at least five weeks behind in science and history. In algebra it's more like ten."

"Nevertheless," Dussander said. He poured more bourbon.

"You think you're pretty smart, don't you?" Todd shouted at him. "Well, I don't take orders from you. The days when you gave orders are long over. *Do you get it?*" He lowered his voice abruptly. "The most lethal thing you've got around the house these days is a Shell No-Pest Strip. You're nothing but a broken-down old man who farts rotten eggs if he eats a taco. I bet you even pee in your bed."

"Listen to me, snotnose," Dussander said quietly.

Todd's head jerked angrily around at that.

"Before today," Dussander said carefully, "it was possible, *just barely* possible, that you could have denounced me and come out clean yourself. I don't believe you would have been up to the job with your nerves in their present state, but never mind that. It would have been technically possible. But now things have changed. Today I impersonated your grandfather, one Victor Bowden. No one can have the slightest doubt that I did it with . . . how is the word? . . . your connivance. If it comes out now, boy, you will look blacker than ever. And you will have no defense. I took care of that today."

"I wish—"

"You *wish*! You *wish*!" Dussander roared. "Never mind your wishes, your wishes make me *sick,* your wishes are no more than little piles of dogshit in the gutter! *All I want from you is to know if you understand the situation we are in!*"

"I understand it," Todd muttered. His fists had been tightly clenched while Dussander shouted at him—he was not used to being shouted at. Now he opened his hands and dully observed that he had dug bleeding half-moons into his palms. The cuts would have been worse, he supposed, but in the last four months or so he had taken up biting his nails.

"Good. Then you will make your sweet apologies, and you will study. In your free time at school you will study. During your lunch hours you will study. After school you will come here and study, and on your weekends you will come here and do more of the same."

"Not here," Todd said quickly. "At home."

"No. At home you will dawdle and daydream as you have all along. If you are here I can stand over you if I have to and watch you. I can protect my own interests in this matter. I can quiz you. I can listen to your lessons."

"If I don't want to come here, you can't make me."

Dussander drank. "That is true. Things will then go on as they have. You will fail. This guidance person, French, will expect me to make good on my promise. When I don't, he will call your parents. They will find out that kindly Mr. Denker impersonated your grandfather at your request. They will find out about the altered grades. They—"

"Oh, shut up. I'll come."

"You're already here. Begin with algebra."

"No *way*! It's Friday afternoon!"

"You study *every* afternoon now," Dussander said softly. "Begin with algebra."

Todd stared at him—only for a moment before dropping his eyes and fumbling his algebra text out of his bookbag—and Dussander saw murder in the boy's eyes. Not figurative murder; literal murder. It had been years since he had seen that dark, burning, speculative glance, but one never forgot it. He supposed he would have seen it in his own eyes if there had been a mirror at hand on the day he had looked at the white and defenseless nape of the boy's neck.

I must protect myself, he thought with some amazement. *One underestimates at one's own risk.*

He drank his bourbon and rocked and watched the boy study.

It was nearly five o'clock when Todd biked home. He felt washed out, hot-eyed, drained, impotently angry. Every time his eyes had wandered from the printed page—from the maddening, incomprehensible, fucking *stupid* world of sets, subsets, ordered pairs, and Cartesian co-ordinates—Dussander's sharp old man's voice had spoken. Otherwise he had remained completely silent . . . except for the maddening bump of his slippers on the floor and the squeak of the rocker. He sat there like a vulture waiting for its prey to expire. Why had he ever gotten into this? *How* had he gotten into it? This was a mess, a terrible mess. He had picked up some ground this afternoon—some of the set theory that had stumped him so badly just before the Christmas break had fallen into place with an almost audible click—but it was impossible to think he could pick up enough to scrape through next week's algebra test with even a D.

It was four weeks until the end of the world.

On the corner he saw a bluejay lying on the sidewalk, its beak slowly opening and closing. It was trying vainly to get onto its birdy-feet and hop away. One of its wings had been crushed, and Todd supposed a passing car had hit it and flipped it up onto the sidewalk like a tiddlywink. One of its beady eyes stared up at him.

Todd looked at it for a long time, holding the grips of his bike's apehanger handlebars lightly. Some of the warmth had gone out of the day and the air felt almost chilly. He supposed his friends had spent the afternoon goofing off down at the

Babe Ruth diamond on Walnut Street, maybe playing a little scrub, more likely playing pepper or three-flies-six-grounders or rolly-bat. It was the time of year when you started working your way up to baseball. There was some talk about getting up their own sandlot team this year to compete in the informal city league; there were dads enough willing to shlepp them around to games. Todd, of course, would pitch. He had been a Little League pitching star until he had grown out of the Senior Little League division last year. *Would have pitched.*

So what? He'd just have to tell them no. He'd just have to tell them: *Guys, I got mixed up with this war criminal. I got him right by the balls, and then—ha-ha, this'll killya, guys—then I found out he was holding my balls as tight as I was holding his. I started having funny dreams and the cold sweats. My grades went to hell and I changed them on my report card so my folks wouldn't find out and now I've got to hit the books really hard for the first time in my life. I'm not afraid of getting grounded, though. I'm afraid of going to the reformatory. And that's why I can't play any sandlot with you guys this year. You see how it is, guys.*

A thin smile, much like Dussander's and not at all like his former broad grin, touched his lips. There was no sunshine in it; it was a shady smile. There was no fun in it; no confidence. It merely said: *You see how it is, guys.*

He rolled his bike forward over the jay with exquisite slowness, hearing the newspaper crackle of its feathers and the crunch of its small hollow bones as they fractured inside it. He reversed, rolling over it again. It was still twitching. He rolled over it again, a single bloody feather stuck to his front tire, revolving up and down, up and down. By then the bird had stopped moving, the bird had kicked the bucket, the bird had punched out, the bird had gone to that great aviary in the sky, but Todd kept going forwards and backwards across its mashed body just the same. He did it for almost five minutes, and that thin smile never left his face. You see how it is, guys.

10

April, 1975.

The old man stood halfway down the compound's aisle, smiling broadly, as Dave Klingerman walked up to meet him. The frenzied barking that filled the air didn't seem to bother him in the slightest, or the smells of fur and urine, or the hundred different strays yapping and howling in their cages, dashing back and forth, leaping against the mesh. Klingerman pegged the old guy as a dog-lover right off the bat. His smile was sweet and pleasant. He offered Dave a swollen, arthritis-bunched hand carefully, and Klingerman shook it in the same spirit.

"Hello, sir!" he said, speaking up. "Noisy as hell, isn't it?"

"I don't mind," the old man said. "Not at all. My name is Arthur Denker."

"Klingerman. Dave Klingerman."

"I am pleased to meet you, sir. I read in the paper—I could not believe it—that you *give* dogs away here. Perhaps I misunderstood. In fact, I think I must have misunderstood."

"No, we give em away, all right," Dave said. "If we can't, we have to destroy em. Sixty days, that's what the State gives us. Shame. Come on in the office here. Quieter. Smells better, too."

In the office, Dave heard a story that was familiar (but nonetheless affecting): Arthur Denker was in his seventies. He had come to California when his wife died. He was not rich, but he tended what he did have with great care. He was lonely. His only friend was the boy who sometimes came to his house and read to him. In Germany he had owned a beautiful Saint Bernard. Now, in Santo Donato, he had a house with a good-sized back yard. The yard was fenced. And he had read in the paper . . . would it be possible that he could . . .

"Well, we don't have any Bernards," Dave said. "They go fast because they're so good with kids—"

"Oh, I understand. I didn't mean that—"

"—but I do have a half-grown shepherd pup. How would that be?"

Mr. Denker's eyes grew bright, as if he might be on the verge of tears. "Perfect," he said. "That would be perfect."

"The dog itself is free, but there are a few other charges. Distemper and rabies shots. A city dog license. All of it goes about twenty-five bucks for most people, but the State pays half if you're over sixty-five—part of the California Golden Ager program."

"Golden Ager . . . is that what I am?" Mr. Denker said, and laughed. For just a moment—it was silly—Dave felt a kind of chill.

"Uh . . . I guess so, sir."

"It is very reasonable."

"Sure, we think so. The same dog would cost you a hundred and twenty-five dollars in a pet shop. But people go to those places instead of here. They are paying for a set of papers, of course, not the dog." Dave shook his head. "If they only understood how many fine animals are abandoned every year."

"And if you can't find a suitable home for them within sixty days, they are destroyed?"

"We put them to sleep, yes."

"Put them to . . . ? I'm sorry, my English—"

"It's a city ordinance," Dave said. "Can't have dog-packs running the streets."

"You shoot them."

"No, we give them gas. It's very humane. They don't feel a thing."

"No," Mr. Denker said. "I am sure they don't."

Todd's seat in Beginning Algebra was four desks down in the second row. He sat there, trying to keep his face expressionless, as Mr. Storrman passed back the exams. But his ragged fingernails were digging into his palms again, and his entire body seemed to be running with a slow and caustic sweat.

Don't get your hopes up. Don't be such a goddam chump. There's no way you could have passed. You know *you didn't pass.*

Nevertheless, he could not completely squash the foolish hope. It had been the first algebra exam in weeks that looked as if it had been written in something other than Greek. He was sure that in his nervousness (nervousness? no, call it what it had really been: outright terror) he had not done that well, but maybe . . . well, if it had been anyone else but Storrman, who had a Yale padlock for a heart . . .

STOP IT! he commanded himself, and for a moment, a coldly horrible moment, he was positive he had screamed those two words aloud in the classroom. *You flunked, you know you did, not a thing in the world is going to change it.*

Storrman handed him his paper expressionlessly and moved on. Todd laid it face down on his initial-scarred desk. For a moment he didn't think he possessed sufficient will to even turn it over and know. At last he flipped it with such convulsive suddenness that the exam sheet tore. His tongue stuck to the roof of his mouth as he stared at it. His heart seemed to stop for a moment.

The number 83 was written in a circle at the top of the sheet. Below it was a letter-grade: C+. Below the letter-grade was a brief notation: *Good improvement! I think I'm twice as relieved as you should be. Check errors carefully. At least three of them are arithmetical rather than conceptual.*

His heartbeat began again, at triple-time. Relief washed over him, but it was not cool—it was hot and complicated and strange. He closed his eyes, not hearing the class as it buzzed over the exam and began the pre-ordained fight for an extra point here or there. Todd saw redness behind his eyes. It pulsed like flowing blood with the rhythm of his heartbeat. In that instant he hated Dussander more than he ever had before. His hands snapped shut into fists and he only wished, wished, wished, that Dussander's scrawny chicken neck could have been between them.

• • •

Dick and Monica Bowden had twin beds, separated by a nightstand with a pretty imitation Tiffany lamp standing on it. Their room was done in genuine redwood, and the walls were comfortably lined with books. Across the room, nestled between two ivory bookends (bull elephants on their hind legs), was a round Sony TV. Dick was watching Johnny Carson with the earplug in while Monica read the new Michael Crichton that had come from the book club that day.

"Dick?" She put a bookmark (THIS IS WHERE I FELL ASLEEP, it said) into the Crichton and closed it.

On the TV, Buddy Hackett had just broken everyone up. Dick smiled.

"Dick?" she said more loudly.

He pulled the earplug out. "What?"

"Do you think Todd's all right?"

He looked at her for a moment, frowning, then shook his head a little. *"Je ne comprends pas, chérie."* His limping French was a joke between them. His father had sent him an extra two hundred dollars to hire a tutor when he was flunking French. He had gotten Monica Darrow, picking her name at random from the cards tacked up on the Union bulletin board. By Christmas she had been wearing his pin . . . and he had managed a C in French.

"Well . . . he's lost weight."

"He looks a little scrawny, sure," Dick said. He put the TV earplug in his lap, where it emitted tiny squawking sounds. "He's growing up, Monica."

"So soon?" she asked uneasily.

He laughed. "So soon. I shot up seven inches as a teenager—from a five-foot-six shrimp at twelve to the beautiful six-foot-one mass of muscle you see before you today. My mother said that when I was fourteen you could hear me growing in the night."

"Good thing not all of you grew that much."

"It's all in how you use it."

"Want to use it tonight?"

"The wench grows bold," Dick Bowden said, and threw the earplug across the room.

After, as he was drifting off to sleep:

"Dick, he's having bad dreams, too."

"Nightmares?" he muttered.

"Nightmares. I've heard him moaning in his sleep two or three times when I've gone down to use the bathroom in the night. I didn't want to wake him up. It's silly, but my grandmother used to say you could drive a person insane if you woke them up in the middle of a bad dream."

"She was the Polack, wasn't she?"

"The Polack, yeah, the Polack. Nice talk!"

"You know what I mean. Why don't you just use the upstairs john?" He had put it in himself two years ago.

"You know the flush always wakes you up," she said.

"So don't flush it."

"Dick, that's nasty."

He sighed.

"Sometimes when I go in, he's sweating. And the sheets are damp."

He grinned in the dark. "I bet."

"What's *that* . . . oh." She slapped him lightly. "That's nasty, too. Besides, he's only thirteen."

"Fourteen next month. He's not too young. A little precocious, maybe, but not too young."

"How old were you?"

"Fourteen or fifteen. I don't remember exactly. But I remember I woke up thinking I'd died and gone to heaven."

"But you were older than Todd is now."

"All that stuff's happening younger. It must be the milk . . . or the fluoride. Do you know they have sanitary napkin dispensers in all the girls' rooms of the school we built in Jackson

Park last year? And that's a *grammar school.* Now your average sixth-grader is only eleven. How old were you when you started?"

"I don't remember," she said. "All I know is Todd's dreams don't sound like . . . like he died and went to heaven."

"Have you asked him about them?"

"Once. About six weeks ago. You were off playing golf with that horrible Ernie Jacobs."

"That horrible Ernie Jacobs is going to make me a full partner by 1977, if he doesn't screw himself to death with that high-yellow secretary of his before then. Besides, he always pays the greens fees. What did Todd say?"

"That he didn't remember. But a sort of . . . shadow crossed his face. I think he *did* remember."

"Monica, I don't remember everything from my dear dead youth, but one thing I do remember is that wet dreams are not always pleasant. In fact, they can be downright unpleasant."

"How can that be?"

"Guilt. All kinds of guilt. Some of it maybe all the way from babyhood, when it was made very clear to him that wetting the bed was wrong. Then there's the sex thing. Who knows what brings a wet dream on? Copping a feel on the bus? Looking up a girl's skirt in study hall? I don't know. The only one I can really remember was going off the high board at the YMCA pool on co-ed day and losing my trunks when I hit the water."

"You got off on that?" she asked, giggling a little.

"Yeah. So if the kid doesn't want to talk to you about his John Thomas problems, don't force him."

"We did our damn best to raise him without all those needless guilts."

"You can't escape them. He brings them home from school like the colds he used to pick up in the first grade. From his friends, or the way his teachers mince around certain subjects. He probably got it from my dad, too. 'Don't touch it in the night, Todd, or your hands'll grow hair and you'll go blind and you'll start to lose your memory, and after awhile your thing will turn black and rot off. So be careful, Todd.' "

"Dick Bowden! Your dad would never—"

"He wouldn't. Hell, he *did.* Just like your Polack grandmother told you that waking somebody up in the middle of a nightmare might drive them nuts. He also told me to always wipe off the ring of a public toilet before I sat on it so I wouldn't get 'other people's germs.' I guess that was his way of saying syphilis. I bet your grandmother laid that one on you, too."

"No, my mother," she said absently. "And she told me to always flush. Which is why I go downstairs."

"It still wakes me up," Dick mumbled.

"What?"

"Nothing."

This time he had actually drifted halfway over the threshold of sleep when she spoke his name again.

"What?" he asked, a little impatiently.

"You don't suppose . . . oh, never mind. Go back to sleep."

"No, go on, finish. I'm awake again. I don't suppose what?"

"That old man. Mr. Denker. You don't think Todd's seeing too much of him, do you? Maybe he's . . . oh, I don't know . . . filling Todd up with a lot of stories."

"The real heavy horrors," Dick said. "The day the Essen Motor Works dropped below quota." He snickered.

"It was just an idea," she said, a little stiffly. The covers rustled as she turned over on her side. "Sorry I bothered you."

He put a hand on her bare shoulder. "I'll tell you something, babe," he said, and stopped for a moment, thinking carefully, choosing his words. "I've been worried about Todd, too, sometimes. Not the same things you've been worried about, but worried is worried, right?"

She turned back to him. "About what?"

"Well, I grew up a lot different than he's growing up. My dad had the store. Vic the Grocer, everyone called him. He had a book where he kept the names of the people who owed him, and how much they owed. You know what he called it?"

"No." Dick rarely talked about his boyhood; she had always thought it was because he hadn't enjoyed it. She listened carefully now.

"He called it the Left Hand Book. He said the right hand was business, but the right hand should never know what the left hand was doing. He said if the right hand *did* know, it would probably grab a meat-cleaver and chop the left hand right off."

"You never told me that."

"Well, I didn't like the old man very much when we first got married, and the truth is I still spend a lot of time not liking him. I couldn't understand why I had to wear pants from the Goodwill box while Mrs. Mazursky could get a ham on credit with that same old story about how her husband was going back to work next week. The only work that fucking wino Bill Mazursky ever had was holding onto a twelve-cent bottle of musky so it wouldn't fly away.

"All I ever wanted in those days was to get out of the neighborhood and away from my old man's life. So I made grades and played sports I didn't really like and got a scholarship at UCLA. And I made damn sure I stayed in the top ten per cent of my classes because the only Left Hand Book the colleges kept in those days was for the GIs that fought the war. My dad sent me money for my textbooks, but the only other money I ever took from him was the time I wrote home in a panic because I was flunking funnybook French. I met you. And I found out later from Mr. Halleck down the block that my dad put a lien on his car to scare up that two hundred bucks.

"And now I've got you, and we've got Todd. I've always thought he was a damned fine boy, and I've tried to make sure he's always had everything he ever needed . . . anything that would help him grow into a fine man. I used to laugh at that old wheeze about a man wanting his son to be better than he was, but as I get older it seems less funny and more true. I never want Todd to have to wear pants from a Goodwill box because some wino's wife got a ham on credit. You understand?"

"Yes, of course I do," she said quietly.

"Then, about ten years ago, just before my old man finally got tired of fighting off the urban renewal guys and retired, he had a minor stroke. He was in the hospital for ten days. And the people from the neighborhood, the guineas and the krauts, even some of the jigs that started to move in around 1955 or so . . . they paid his bill. Every fucking cent. I couldn't believe it. They kept the store open, too. Fiona Castellano got four or five of her friends who were out of work to come in on shifts. When my old man got back, the books balanced out to the cent."

"Wow," she said, very softly.

"You know what he said to me? My old man? That he'd always been afraid of getting old—of being scared and hurting and all by himself. Of having to go into the hospital and not being able to make ends meet anymore. Of dying. He said that after the stroke he wasn't scared anymore. He said he thought he could die well. 'You mean die happy, Pap?' I asked him. 'No,' he said. 'I don't think anyone dies happy, Dickie.' He always called me Dickie, still does, and that's another thing I guess I'll never be able to like. He said he didn't think anyone died happy, but you could die well. That impressed me."

He was silent for a long, thoughtful time.

"The last five or six years I've been able to get some perspective on my old man. Maybe because he's down there in San Remo and out of my hair. I started thinking that maybe the Left Hand Book wasn't such a bad idea. That was when I started to worry about Todd. I kept wanting to tell him about how there was maybe something more to life than me being able to take all of you to Hawaii for a month or being able to buy Todd pants that don't smell like the mothballs they used to put in the Goodwill box. I could never figure out how to tell him those things. But I think maybe he knows. And it takes a load off my mind."

"Reading to Mr. Denker, you mean?"

"Yes. He's not getting anything for that. Denker can't pay him. Here's this old guy, thousands of miles from any friends or relatives that might still be living, here's this guy that's everything my father was afraid of. And there's Todd."

"I never thought of it just like that."

"Have you noticed the way Todd gets when you talk to him about that old man?"

"He gets very quiet."

"Sure. He gets tongue-tied and embarrassed, like he was doing something nasty. Just like my pop used to when someone tried to thank him for laying some credit on them. We're Todd's right hand, that's all. You and me and all the rest—the house, the ski-trips to Tahoe, the Thunderbird in the garage, his color TV. All his right hand. And he doesn't want us to see what his left hand is up to."

"You don't think he's seeing too much of Denker, then?"

"Honey, look at his grades! If *they* were falling off, I'd be the first one to say Hey, enough is enough, already, don't go overboard. His grades are the first place trouble would show up. And how have they been?"

"As good as ever, after that first slip."

"So what are we talking about? Listen, I've got a conference at nine, babe. If I don't get some sleep, I'm going to be sloppy."

"Sure, go to sleep," she said indulgently, and as he turned over, she kissed him lightly on one shoulderblade. "I love you."

"Love you too," he said comfortably, and closed his eyes. "Everything's fine, Monica. You worry too much."

"I know I do. Goodnight."

They slept.

"Stop looking out the window," Dussander said. "There is nothing out there to interest you."

Todd looked at him sullenly. His history text was open on

the table, showing a color plate of Teddy Roosevelt cresting San Juan Hill. Helpless Cubans were falling away from the hooves of Teddy's horse. Teddy was grinning a wide American grin, the grin of a man who knew that God was in His heaven and everything was bully. Todd Bowden was not grinning.

"You like being a slave-driver, don't you?" he asked.

"I like being a free man," Dussander said. "Study."

"Suck my cock."

"As a boy," Dussander said, "I would have had my mouth washed out with lye soap for saying such a thing."

"Times change."

"Do they?" Dussander sipped his bourbon. "Study."

Todd stared at Dussander. "You're nothing but a goddamned rummy. You know that?"

"Study."

"Shut up!" Todd slammed his book shut. It made a riflecrack sound in Dussander's kitchen. "I can never catch up, anyway. Not in time for the test. There's fifty pages of this shit left, all the way up to World War One. I'll make a crib in Study Hall Two tomorrow."

Harshly, Dussander said: "You will do no such thing!"

"Why not? Who's going to stop me? You?"

"Boy, you are still having a hard time comprehending the stakes we play for. Do you think I enjoy keeping your snivelling brat nose in your books?" His voice rose, whipsawing, demanding, commanding. "Do you think I enjoy listening to your tantrums, your kindergarten swears? 'Suck my cock,'" Dussander mimicked savagely in a high, falsetto voice that made Todd flush darkly. "'Suck my cock, so what, who cares, I'll do it tomorrow, suck my cock'!"

"Well, you *like* it!" Todd shouted back. "Yeah, you *like* it! The only time you don't feel like a zombie is when you're on my back! So give me a fucking break!"

"If you are caught with one of these cribbing papers, what do you think will happen? Who will be told first?"

Todd looked at his hands with their ragged, bitten fingernails and said nothing.

"Who?"

"Jesus, you know. Rubber Ed. Then my folks, I guess."

Dussander nodded. "Me, I guess that too. Study. Put your cribbing paper in your head, where it belongs."

"I hate you," Todd said dully. "I really do." But he opened his book again and Teddy Roosevelt grinned up at him, Teddy galloping into the twentieth century with his saber in his hand, Cubans falling back in disarray before him—possibly before the force of his fierce American grin.

Dussander began to rock again. He held his teacup of bourbon in his hands. "That's a good boy," he said, almost tenderly.

Todd had his first wet dream on the last night of April, and he awoke to the sound of rain whispering secretly through the leaves and branches of the tree outside his window.

In the dream, he had been in one of the Patin laboratories. He was standing at the end of a long, low table. A lush young girl of amazing beauty had been secured to this table with clamps. Dussander was assisting him. Dussander wore a white butcher's apron and nothing else. When he pivoted to turn on the monitoring equipment, Todd could see Dussander's scrawny buttocks grinding at each other like misshapen white stones.

He handed something to Todd, something he recognized immediately, although he had never actually seen one. It was a dildo. The tip of it was polished metal, winking in the light of the overhead fluorescents like heartless chrome. The dildo was hollow. Snaking out of it was a black electrical cord that ended in a red rubber bulb.

"Go ahead," Dussander said. "The Fuehrer says it's all right. He says it's your reward for studying."

Todd looked down at himself and saw that he was naked. His small penis was fully erect, jutting plumply up at an angle from the thin peachdown of his pubic hair. He slipped the dildo on. The fit was tight but there was some sort of lubricant in there. The friction was pleasant. No; it was more than pleasant. It was delightful.

He looked down at the girl and felt a strange shift in his thoughts . . . as if they had slipped into a perfect groove. Suddenly all things seemed right. Doors had been opened. He would go through them. He took the red rubber bulb in his left hand, put his knees on the table, and paused for just a moment, gauging the angle while his Norseman's prick made its own angle up and out from his slight boy's body.

Dimly, far off, he could hear Dussander reciting: "Test run eighty-four. Electricity, sexual stimulus, metabolism. Based on the Thyssen theories of negative reinforcement. Subject is a young Jewish girl, approximately sixteen years of age, no scars, no identifying marks, no known disabilities—"

She cried out when the tip of the dildo touched her. Todd found the cry pleasant, as he did her fruitless struggles to free herself, or, lacking that, to at least bring her legs together.

This is what they can't show in those magazines about the war, he thought, *but it's there, just the same.*

He thrust forward suddenly, parting her with no grace. She shrieked like a fireball.

After her initial thrashings and efforts to expel him, she lay perfectly still, enduring. The lubricated interior of the dildo pulled and slid against Todd's engorgement. Delightful. Heavenly. His ringers toyed with the rubber bulb in his left hand.

Far away, Dussander recited pulse, blood pressure, respiration, alpha waves, beta waves, stroke count.

As the climax began to build inside him, Todd became perfectly still and squeezed the bulb. Her eyes, which had been closed, flew open, bulging. Her tongue fluttered in the pink cavity of her mouth. Her arms and legs thrummed. But the real action was in her torso, rising and falling, vibrating, every muscle

(oh every muscle every muscle moves tightens closes every)
every muscle and the sensation at climax was
(ecstasy)
oh it was, it was

(the end of the world thundering outside)

He woke to that sound and the sound of rain. He was huddled on his side in a dark ball, his heart beating at a sprinter's pace. His lower belly was covered with a warm, sticky liquid. There was an instant of panicky horror when he feared he might be bleeding to death . . . and then he realized what it *really* was, and he felt a fainting, nauseated revulsion. Semen. Come. Jizz. Jungle-juice. Words from fences and locker rooms and the walls of gas station bathrooms. There was nothing here he wanted.

His hands balled helplessly into fists. His dream-climax recurred to him, pallid now, senseless, frightening. But nerve-endings still tingled, retreating slowly from their spike-point. That final scene, fading now, was disgusting and yet somehow compulsive, like an unsuspecting bite into a piece of tropical fruit which, you realized (a second too late), had only tasted so amazingly sweet because it was rotten.

It came to him then. What he would have to do.

There was only one way he could get himself back again. He would have to kill Dussander. It was the only way. Games were done; storytime was over. This was survival.

"Kill him and it's all over," he whispered in the darkness, with the rain in the tree outside and semen drying on his belly. Whispering it made it seem real.

Dussander always kept three or four fifths of Ancient Age on a shelf over the steep cellar stairs. He would go to the door, open it (half-crocked already, more often than not), and go down two steps. Then he would lean out, put one hand on the shelf, and grip the fresh bottle by the neck with his other hand. The cellar floor was not paved, but the dirt was hard-packed and Dussander, with a machinelike efficiency that Todd now thought of as Prussian rather than German, oiled it once every two months to keep bugs from breeding in the dirt. Cement or no cement, old bones break easily. And old men have accidents. The post-mortem would show that "Mr. Denker" had had a skinful of booze when he "fell."

What happened, Todd?

He didn't answer the door so I used the key he gave me. Sometimes he falls asleep. I went into the kitchen and saw the cellar door was open. I went down the stairs and he . . . he . . .

Then, of course, tears.

It would work.

He would have himself back again.

For a long time Todd lay awake in the dark, listening to the thunder retreat westward, out over the Pacific, listening to the secret sound of the rain. He thought he would stay awake the rest of the night, going over it and over it. But he fell asleep only moments later and slept dreamlessly with one fist curled under his chin. He woke on the first of May fully rested for the first time in months.

11

May, 1975.

For Todd, that Friday was the longest of his life. He sat in class after class, hearing nothing, waiting only for the last five minutes, when the instructor would take out his or her small pile of Flunk Cards and distribute them. Each time an instructor approached Todd's desk with that pile of cards, he grew cold. Each time he or she passed him without stopping, he felt waves of dizziness and semi-hysteria.

Algebra was the worst. Storrman approached . . . hesitated . . . and just as Todd became convinced he was going to pass on, he laid a Flunk Card face down on Todd's desk. Todd looked at it coldly, with no feelings at all. Now that it had happened, he was only cold. *Well, that's it,* he thought. *Point, game, set, and match. Unless Dussander can think of something else. And I have my doubts.*

Without much interest, he turned the Flunk Card over to see by how much he had missed his C. It must have been close, but trust old Stony Storrman not to give anyone a break. He saw that the grade-spaces were utterly blank—both the letter-grade space and the numerical-grade space. Written in the comments section was this message: *I'm sure glad I don't have to give you one of these for* real! *Chas. Storrman.*

The dizziness came again, more savagely this time, roaring through his head, making it feel like a balloon filled with helium. He gripped the sides of his desk as hard as he could, holding one thought with total obsessive tightness: *You will not faint, not faint, not faint.* Little by little the waves of dizziness passed, and then he had to control an urge to run up the aisle after Storrman, turn him around, and poke his eyes out with the freshly sharpened pencil he held in his hand. And through it all his face remained carefully blank. The only sign that anything at all was going on inside was a mild tic in one eyelid.

School let out for the week fifteen minutes later. Todd walked slowly around the building to the bike-racks, his head down, his hands shoved into his pockets, his books tucked into the crook of his right arm, oblivious of the running, shouting students. He tossed the books into his bike-basket, unlocked the Schwinn, and pedaled away. Toward Dussander's house.

Today, he thought. *Today is your day, old man.*

"And so," Dussander said, pouring bourbon into his cup as Todd entered the kitchen, "the accused returns from the dock. How said they, prisoner?" He was wearing his bathrobe and a pair of hairy wool socks that climbed halfway up his shins. Socks like that, Todd thought, would be easy to slip in. He glanced at the bottle of Ancient Age Dussander was currently working. It was down to the last three fingers.

"No D's, no F's, no Flunk Cards," Todd said. "I'll still have to change some of my grades in June, but maybe just the averages. I'll be getting all A's and B's this quarter if I keep up my work."

"Oh, you'll keep it up, all right," Dussander said. "We will see to it." He drank and then tipped more bourbon into his cup. "This calls for a celebration." His speech was slightly blurred—hardly enough to be noticeable, but Todd knew the old fuck was as drunk as he ever got. Yes, today. It would have to be today.

But he was cool.

"Celebrate pigshit," he told Dussander.

"I'm afraid the delivery boy hasn't arrived with the beluga and the truffles yet," Dussander said, ignoring him. "Help is so unreliable these days. What about a few Ritz crackers and some Velveeta while we wait?"

"Okay," Todd said. "What the hell."

Dussander stood up (one knee banged the table, making him wince) and crossed to the refrigerator. He got out the cheese, took a knife from the drawer and a plate from the cupboard, and a box of Ritz crackers from the breadbox.

"All carefully injected with prussic acid," he told Todd as he set the cheese and crackers down on the table. He grinned, and Todd saw that he had left out his false teeth again today. Nevertheless, Todd smiled back.

"So quiet today!" Dussander exclaimed. "I would have expected you to turn handsprings all the way up the hall." He emptied the last of the bourbon into his cup, sipped, smacked his lips.

"I guess I'm still numb," Todd said. He bit into a cracker. He had stopped refusing Dussander's food a long time ago. Dussander thought there was a letter with one of Todd's friends—there was not, of course; he had friends, but none he trusted *that* much. He supposed Dussander had guessed that long ago, but he knew Dussander didn't quite dare put his guess to such an extreme test as murder.

"What shall we talk about today?" Dussander enquired, tossing off the last shot. "I give you the day off from studying, how's that? Uh? Uh?" When he drank, his accent became thicker. It was an accent Todd had come to hate. Now he felt okay about the accent; he felt okay about everything. He felt very cool all over. He looked at his hands, the hands which would give the push, and they looked just as they always did. They were not trembling; they were cool.

"I don't care," he said. "Anything you want."

"Shall I tell you about the special soap we made? Our experiments with enforced homosexuality? Or perhaps you would like to hear how I escaped Berlin after I had been foolish enough to go back. That was a close one, I can tell you." He pantomimed shaving one stubby cheek and laughed.

"Anything," Todd said. "Really." He watched Dussander examine the empty bottle and then get up with it in one hand. Dussander took it to the wastebasket and dropped it in.

"No, none of those, I think," Dussander said. "You don't seem to be in the mood." He stood reflectively by the wastebasket for a moment and then crossed the kitchen to the cellar door. His wool socks whispered on the hilly linoleum. "I think today I will instead tell you the story of an old man who was afraid."

Dussander opened the cellar door. His back was now to the table. Todd stood up quietly.

"He was afraid," Dussander went on, "of a certain young boy who was, in a queer way, his friend. A smart boy. His mother called this boy 'apt pupil,' and the old man had already discovered he *was* an apt pupil . . . although perhaps not in the way his mother thought."

Dussander fumbled with the old-fashioned electrical switch on the wall, trying to turn it with his bunched and clumsy fingers. Todd walked—almost glided—across the linoleum, not stepping on any of the places where it squeaked or creaked. He knew this kitchen as well as his own, now. Maybe better.

"At first, the boy was not the old man's friend," Dussander said. He managed to turn the switch at last. He descended the first step with a veteran drunk's care. "At first the old man disliked the boy a great deal. Then he grew to . . . to enjoy his company, although there was still a strong element of dislike there." He was looking at the shelf now but still holding the railing. Todd, cool—no, now he was *cold*—stepped behind him and calculated the chances of one strong push dislodging Dussander's hold on the railing. He decided to wait until Dussander leaned forward.

"Part of the old man's enjoyment came from a feeling of equality," Dussander went on thoughtfully. "You see, the boy and the old man had each other in mutual deathgrips. Each knew something the other wanted kept secret. And then . . . ah, then it became apparent to the old man that things were changing. Yes. He was losing his hold—some of it or all of it, depending on how desperate the boy might be, and how clever. It occurred to this old man on one long and sleepless night that it might be well for him to acquire a new hold on the boy. For his own safety."

Now Dussander let go of the railing and leaned out over the steep cellar stairs, but Todd remained perfectly still. The bone-deep cold was melting out of him, being replaced by a rosy flush of anger and confusion. As Dussander grasped his fresh bottle, Todd thought viciously that the old man had the stinkiest cellar in town, oil or no oil. It smelled as if something had died down there.

"So the old man got out of his bed right then. What is sleep to an old man? Very little. And he sat at his small desk, thinking about how cleverly he had enmeshed the boy in the very crimes the boy was holding over his own head. He sat thinking about how hard the boy had worked, how very hard, to bring his school marks back up. And how, when they *were* back up, he would have no further need for the old man alive. And if the old man were dead, the boy could be free."

He turned around now, holding the fresh bottle of Ancient Age by the neck.

"I heard you, you know," he said, almost gently. "From the moment you pushed your chair back and stood up. You are not as quiet as you imagine, boy. At least not yet."

Todd said nothing.

"So!" Dussander exclaimed, stepping back into the kitchen and closing the cellar door firmly behind him. "The old man wrote everything down, *nicht wahr*? From first word to last he wrote it down. When he was finally finished it was almost dawn and his hand was singing from the arthritis—the *verdammt* arthritis—but he felt good for the first times in weeks. He felt *safe.* He got back into his bed and slept until mid-afternoon. In fact, if he had slept any longer, he would have missed his favorite—*General Hospital.*"

He had regained his rocker now. He sat down, produced a worn jackknife with a yellow ivory handle, and began to cut painstakingly around the seal covering the top of the bourbon bottle.

"On the following day the old man dressed in his best suit and went down to the bank where he kept his little checking and savings accounts. He spoke to one of the bank officers, who was able to answer all the old man's questions most satisfactorily. He rented a safety deposit box. The bank officer explained to the old man that he would have a key and the bank would have a key. To open the box, both keys would be needed. No one but the old man could use the old man's key without a signed, notarized letter of permission from the old man himself. With one exception."

Dussander smiled toothlessly into Todd Bowden's white, set face.

"That exception is made in the event of the box-holder's death," he said. Still looking at Todd, still smiling, Dussander put his jackknife back into the pocket of his robe, unscrewed the cap of the bourbon bottle, and poured a fresh jolt into his cup.

"What happens then?" Todd asked hoarsely.

"Then the box is opened in the presence of a bank official and a representative of the Internal Revenue Service. The contents of the box are inventoried. In this case they will find only a twelve-page document. Non-taxable . . . but highly interesting."

The fingers of Todd's hands crept toward each other and locked tightly. "You can't do that," he said in a stunned and unbelieving voice. It was the voice of a person who observes another person walking on the ceiling. "You can't. . . can't do that."

"My boy," Dussander said kindly, "I have."

"But . . . I . . . you . . ." His voice suddenly rose to an agonized howl. "You're *old*! Don't you know that you're *old*? You could die! *You could die anytime!*"

Dussander got up. He went to one of the kitchen cabinets and took down a small glass. This glass had once held jelly. Cartoon characters danced around the rim. Todd recognized them all—Fred and Wilma Flintstone, Barney and Betty Rubble, Pebbles and Bamm-Bamm. He had grown up with them. He watched as Dussander wiped this jelly-glass almost ceremonially with a dishtowel. He watched as Dussander set it in front of him. He watched as Dussander poured a finger of bourbon into it.

"What's that for?" Todd muttered. "I don't drink. Drinking's for cheap stewbums like you."

"Lift your glass, boy. It is a special occasion. Today you drink."

Todd looked at him for a long moment, then picked up the glass. Dussander clicked his cheap ceramic cup smartly against it.

"I make a toast, boy—long life! Long life to both of us! *Prosit!*" He tossed his bourbon off at a gulp and then began to laugh. He rocked back and forth, stockinged feet hitting the linoleum, laughing, and Todd thought he had never looked so much like a vulture, a vulture in a bathrobe, a noisome beast of carrion.

"I hate you," he whispered, and then Dussander began to choke on his own laughter. His face turned a dull brick color; it sounded as if he were coughing, laughing, and strangling, all at the same time. Todd, scared, got up quickly and clapped him on the back until the coughing fit had passed.

"Danke schön," he said. "Drink your drink. It will do you good."

Todd drank it. It tasted like very bad cold-medicine and lit a fire in his gut.

"I can't believe you drink this shit all day," he said, putting the glass back on the table and shuddering. "You ought to quit it. Quit drinking *and* smoking."

"Your concern for my health is touching," Dussander said. He produced a crumpled pack of cigarettes from the same bathrobe pocket into which the jackknife had disappeared. "And I am equally solicitous of your own welfare, boy. Almost every day I read in the paper where a cyclist has been killed at a busy intersection. You should give it up. You should walk. Or ride the bus, like me."

"Why don't you go fuck yourself?" Todd burst out.

"My boy," Dussander said, pouring more bourbon and beginning to laugh again, "we are fucking each other—didn't you know that?"

One day about a week later, Todd was sitting on a disused mail platform down in the old trainyard. He chucked cinders out across the rusty, weed-infested tracks one at a time.

Why shouldn't I kill him anyway?

Because he was a logical boy, the logical answer came first. No reason at all. Sooner or later Dussander was going to die, and given Dussander's habits, it would probably be sooner. Whether he killed the old man or whether Dussander died of a heart attack in his bathtub, it was all going to come out. At least he could have the pleasure of wringing the old vulture's neck.

Sooner or later—that phrase defied logic.

Maybe it'll be later, Todd thought. *Cigarettes or not, booze or not, he's a tough old bastard. He's lasted this long, so . . . so maybe it'll be later.*

From beneath him came a fuzzy snort.

Todd jumped to his feet, dropping a handful of cinders he had been holding. That snorting sound came again.

He paused, on the verge of running, but the snort didn't recur. Nine hundred yards away, an eight-lane freeway swept across the horizon above this weed- and junk-strewn cul-de-sac with its deserted buildings, rusty Cyclone fences, and splintery, warped platforms. The cars up on the freeway glistened in the sun like exotic hard-shelled beetles. Eight lanes of traffic up there, nothing down here but Todd, a few birds . . . and whatever had snorted.

Cautiously, he bent down with his hands on his knees and peered under the mail platform. There was a wino lying up in there among the yellow weeds and empty cans and dusty old bottles. It was impossible to tell his age; Todd put him at somewhere between thirty and four hundred. He was wearing a strappy tee-shirt that was caked with dried vomit, green pants that were far too big for him, and gray leather workshoes cracked in a hundred places. The cracks gaped like agonized mouths. Todd thought he smelled like Dussander's cellar.

The wino's red-laced eyes opened slowly and stared at Todd with a bleary lack of wonder. As they did, Todd thought of the Swiss Army knife in his pocket, the Angler model. He had purchased it at a sporting goods store in Redondo Beach almost a year ago. He could hear the clerk that had waited on him in his mind: *You couldn't pick a better knife than that one, son—a knife like that could save your life someday. We sell fifteen hundred Swiss knives every damn year.*

Fifteen hundred a year.

He put his hand in his pocket and gripped the knife. In his mind's eye he saw Dussander's jackknife working slowly around the neck of the bourbon bottle, slitting the seal. A moment later he became aware that he had an erection.

Cold terror stole into him.

The wino swiped a hand over his cracked lips and then licked them with a tongue which nicotine had turned a permanent dismal yellow. "Got a dime, kid?"

Todd looked at him expressionlessly.

"Gotta get to L.A. Need another dime for the bus. I got a pointment, me. Got a job offertunity. Nice kid like you must have a dime. Maybe you got a quarter."

Yessir, you could clean out a damn bluegill with a knife like that . . . hell, you could clean out a damn marlin *with it if you had to. We sell fifteen hundred of those a year. Every sporting goods store and Army-Navy Surplus in America sells them, and if you decided to use this one to clean out some dirty, shitty old wino,* nobody *could trace it back to you, absolutely NOBODY.*

The wino's voice dropped; it became a confidential, tenebrous whisper. "For a buck I'd do you a blowjob, you never had a better. You'd come your brains out, kid, you'd—"

Todd pulled his hand out of his pocket. He wasn't sure what was in it until he opened it. Two quarters. Two nickles. A dime. Some pennies. He threw them at the wino and fled.

12

June, 1975.

Todd Bowden, now fourteen, came biking up Dussander's walk and parked his bike on the kickstand. The L.A. *Times* was on the bottom step; he picked it up. He looked at the bell, below which the neat legends ARTHUR DENKER and NO SOLICITORS, NO PEDDLERS, NO SALESMEN still kept their places. He didn't bother with the bell now, of course; he had his key.

Somewhere close by was the popping, burping sound of a Lawn-Boy. He looked at Dussander's grass and saw it could use a cutting; he would have to tell the old man to find a boy with a mower. Dussander forgot little things like that more often now. Maybe it was senility; maybe it was just the pickling influence of Ancient Age on his brains. That was an adult thought for a boy of fourteen to have, but such thoughts no longer struck Todd as singular. He had many adult thoughts these days. Most of them were not so great.

He let himself in.

He had his usual instant of cold terror as he entered the kitchen and saw Dussander slumped slightly sideways in his rocker, the cup on the table, a half-empty bottle of bourbon beside it. A cigarette had burned its entire length down to lacy gray ash in a mayonnaise cover where several other butts had been mashed out. Dussander's mouth hung open. His face was yellow. His big hands dangled limply over the rocker's arms. He didn't seem to be breathing.

"Dussander," he said, a little too harshly. "Rise and shine, Dussander."

He felt a wave of relief as the old man twitched, blinked, and finally sat up.

"Is it you? And so early?"

"They let us out early on the last day of school," Todd said. He pointed to the remains of the cigarette in the mayonnaise cover. "Someday you'll burn down the house doing that."

"Maybe," Dussander said indifferently. He fumbled out his cigarettes, shot one from the pack (it almost rolled off the edge of the table before Dussander was able to catch it), and at last got it going. A protracted fit of coughing followed, and Todd winced in disgust. When the old man really got going, Todd half-expected him to start spitting out grayish-black chunks of lung-tissue onto the table . . . and he'd probably grin as he did it.

At last the coughing eased enough for Dussander to say, "What have you got there?"

"Report card."

Dussander took it, opened it, and held it away from him at arm's length so he could read it. "English . . . A. American History . . . A. Earth Science . . . B-plus. Your Community and You . . . A. Primary French . . . B-minus. Beginning Algebra . . . B." He put it down. "Very good. What is the slang? We have saved your bacon, boy. Will you have to change any of these averages in the last column?"

"French and algebra, but no more than eight or nine points in all. I don't think any of this is ever going to come out. And I guess I owe that to you. I'm not proud of it, but it's the truth. So, thanks."

"What a touching speech," Dussander said, and began to cough again.

"I guess I won't be seeing you around too much from now on," Todd said, and Dussander abruptly stopped coughing.

"No?" he said, politely enough.

"No," Todd said. "We're going to Hawaii for a month starting on June twenty-fifth. In September I'll be going to school across town. It's this bussing thing."

"Oh yes, the *Schwarzen,*" Dussander said, idly watching a fly as it trundled across the red and white check of the oilcloth. "For twenty years this country has worried and whined about the *Schwarzen.* But we know the solution . . . don't we, boy?" He smiled toothlessly at Todd and Todd looked down, feeling the old sickening lift and drop in his stomach. Terror, hate, and a desire to do something so awful it could only be fully contemplated in his dreams.

"Look, I plan to go to college, in case you didn't know," Todd said. "I know that's a long time off, but I think about it. I even know what I want to major in. History."

"Admirable. He who will not learn from the past is—"

"Oh, shut up," Todd said.

Dussander did so, amiably enough. He knew the boy wasn't done . . . not yet. He sat with his hands folded, watching him.

"I could get my letter back from my friend," Todd suddenly blurted. "You know that? I could let you read it, and then you could watch me burn it. If—"

"—if I would remove a certain document from my safety deposit box."

"Well . . . yeah."

Dussander uttered a long, windy, rueful sigh. "My boy," he said. "Still you do not understand the situation. You never have, right from the beginning. Partly because you are only a boy, but not entirely . . . even in the beginning, you were a very *old* boy. No, the real villain was and is your absurd American self-confidence that never allowed you to consider the possible consequences of what you were doing . . . which does not allow it even now."

Todd began to speak and Dussander raised his hand adamantly, suddenly the world's oldest traffic cop.

"No, don't contradict me. It's true. Go on if you like. Leave the house, get out of here, never come back. Can I stop you? No. Of course I can't. Enjoy yourself in Hawaii while I sit in this hot, grease-smelling kitchen and wait to see if the *Schwarzen* in Watts will decide to start killing policemen and burning their shitty tenements again this year. I can't stop you any more than I can stop getting older a day at a time."

He looked at Todd fixedly, so fixedly that Todd looked away.

"Down deep inside, I don't like you. Nothing could make me like you. You forced yourself on me. You are an unbidden guest in my house. You have made me open crypts perhaps better left shut, because I have discovered that some of the corpses were buried alive, and that a few of those *still* have some wind left in them.

"You yourself have become enmeshed, but do I pity you because of that? *Gott im Himmel!* You have made your bed; should I pity you if you sleep badly in it? No . . . I don't pity you, and I don't like you, but I have come to respect you a little bit. So don't try my patience by asking me to explain this twice. We could obtain our documents and destroy them here in my kitchen. And still it would not be over. We would, in fact, be no better off than we are at this minute."

"I don't understand you."

"No, because you have never studied the consequences of what you have set in motion. But attend me, boy. If we burned our letters here, in this jar cover, how would I know you hadn't made a copy? Or two? Or three? Down at the library they have a Xerox machine, for a nickle anyone can make a photocopy. For a dollar, you could post a copy of my death-warrant on every streetcorner for twenty blocks. Two *miles* of death-warrants, boy! Think of it! Can you tell me how I would know you hadn't done such a thing?"

"I . . . well, I . . . I . . ." Todd realized he was floundering and forced himself to shut his mouth. All of a sudden his skin felt too warm, and for no reason at all he found himself remembering something that had happened when he was seven or eight. He and a friend of his had been crawling through a culvert which ran beneath the old Freight Bypass Road just out of town. The friend, skinnier than Todd, had had no problem . . . but Todd had gotten stuck. He had become suddenly aware of the feet of rock and earth over his head, all that dark *weight,* and when an L.A.-bound semi passed above, shaking the earth and making the corrugated pipe vibrate with a low, tuneless, and somehow sinister note, he had begun to cry and to struggle witlessly, throwing himself forward, pistoning with his legs, yelling for help. At last he had gotten moving again, and when he finally struggled out of the pipe, he had fainted.

Dussander had just outlined a piece of duplicity so fundamental that it had never even crossed his mind. He could feel his skin getting hotter, and he thought: *I won't cry.*

"And how would you know I hadn't made *two* copies for my safety deposit box . . . that I had burned one and left the other there?"

Trapped. I'm trapped just like in the pipe that time and who are you going to yell for now?

His heart speeded up in his chest. He felt sweat break on the backs of his hands and the nape of his neck. He remembered how it had been in that pipe, the smell of old water, the feel of the cool, ribbed metal, the way everything shook when the truck passed overhead. He remembered how hot and desperate the tears had been.

"Even if there were some impartial third party we could go to, always there would be doubts. The problem is insoluble, boy. Believe it."

Trapped. Trapped in the pipe. No way out of this one.

He felt the world go gray. *Won't cry. Won't faint.* He forced himself to come back.

Dussander took a deep drink from his cup and looked at Todd over the rim.

"Now I tell you two more things. First, that if your part in this matter came out, your punishment would be quite small. It is even possible—no, more than that, *likely*—that it would never come out in the papers at all. I frightened you with reform school once, when I was badly afraid you might crack and tell everything. But do I believe that? No—I used it the way a father will use the 'boogerman' to frighten a child into coming home before dark. I don't believe that they would send you there, not in this country where they spank killers on the wrist and send them out onto the streets to kill again after two years of watching color TV in a penitentiary.

"But it might well ruin your life all the same. There are records . . . and people talk. Always, they talk. Such a juicy scandal is not allowed to wither; it is bottled, like wine. And, of course, as the years pass, your culpability will grow with you. Your silence will grow more damning. If the truth came out today, people would say, 'But he is just a child!' . . . not knowing, as I do, what an *old* child you are. But what would they say, boy, if the truth about me, coupled with the fact that you knew about me as early as 1974 *but kept silent,* came out while you are in high school? That would be bad. For it to come out while you are in college would be disaster. As a young man just starting out in business . . . Armageddon. You understand this first thing?"

Todd was silent, but Dussander seemed satisfied. He nodded.

Still nodding, he said: "Second, I don't believe you *have* a letter."

Todd strove to keep a poker face, but he was terribly afraid his eyes had widened in shock. Dussander was studying him avidly, and Todd was suddenly, nakedly aware that this old man had interrogated hundreds, perhaps *thousands* of people. He was an expert. Todd felt that his skull had turned to window-glass and all things were flashing inside in large letters.

"I asked myself whom you would trust so much. Who are your friends . . . whom do you run with? Whom does this boy, this self-sufficient, coldly controlled little *boy,* go to with his loyalty? The answer is, nobody."

Dussander's eyes gleamed yellowly.

"Many times I have studied you and calculated the odds. I know you, and I know much of your character—no, not all, because one human being can never know everything that is in another human being's heart—but I know so little about what you do and whom you see outside of this house. So I think, 'Dussander, there is a chance that you are wrong. After all these years, do you want to be captured and maybe killed because you misjudged a boy?' Maybe when I was younger I would have taken the chance—the odds are good odds, and the chance is a small chance. It is very strange to me, you know—the older one becomes, the less one has to lose in matters of life and death . . . and yet, one becomes more and more conservative."

He looked hard into Todd's face.

"I have one more thing to say, and then you can go when you want. What I have to say is that, while I doubt the existence of your letter, never doubt the existence of mine. *The document I have described to you exists.* If I die today . . . tomorrow . . . everything will come out. *Everything.*"

"Then there's nothing for me," Todd said. He uttered a dazed little laugh. "Don't you see that?"

"But there is. Years will go by. As they pass, your hold on me will become worth less and less, because no matter how important my life and liberty remain to me, the Americans and—yes, even the Israelis—will have less and less interest in taking them away."

"Yeah? Then why don't they let that guy Hess go?"

"If the Americans had sole custody of him—the Americans who let killers out with a spank on the wrist—they *would* have let him go," Dussander said. "Are the Americans going to allow the Israelis to extradite an eighty-year-old man so they can hang him as they hanged Eichmann? I think not. Not in a country where they put photographs of firemen rescuing kittens from trees on the front pages of city newspapers.

"No, your hold over me will weaken even as mine over you grows stronger. No situation is static. And there will come a time—if I live long enough—when I will decide what you know no longer matters. Then I will destroy the document."

"But so many things could happen to you in between! Accidents, sickness, disease—"

Dussander shrugged. " 'There will be water if God wills it, and we will find it if God wills it, and we will drink it if God wills it.' What happens is not up to us."

Todd looked at the old man for a long time—for a very long time. There were flaws in Dussander's arguments—there had to be. A way out, an escape hatch either for both of them or for Todd alone. A way to cry it off—times, guys, I hurt my foot, allee-allee-in-free. A black knowledge of the years ahead trembled somewhere behind his eyes; he could feel it there, waiting to be born as conscious thought. Everywhere he went, everything he did—

He thought of a cartoon character with an anvil suspended over its head. By the time he graduated from high school, Dussander would be eighty-one, and that would not be the end; by the time he collected his B.A., Dussander would be eighty-five and he would still feel that he wasn't old enough, he would finish his master's thesis and graduate school the year Dussander turned eighty-seven . . . and Dussander still might not feel safe.

"No," Todd said thickly. "What you're saying . . . I can't face that."

"My boy," Dussander said gently, and Todd heard for the first time and with dawning horror the slight accent the old man had put on the first word. "My boy . . . you must."

Todd stared at him, his tongue swelling and thickening in his mouth until it seemed it must fill his throat and choke him. Then he wheeled and blundered out of the house.

Dussander watched all of this with no expression at all, and when the door had slammed shut and the boy's running footsteps stopped, meaning that he had mounted his bike, he lit a cigarette. There was, of course, no safe deposit box, no document. But the boy believed those things existed; he had believed utterly. He was safe. It was ended.

But it was not ended.

That night they both dreamed of murder, and both of them awoke in mingled terror and exhilaration.

Todd awoke with the now familiar stickiness of his lower belly. Dussander, too old for such things, put on the SS uniform and then lay down again, waiting for his racing heart to slow. The uniform was cheaply made and already beginning to fray.

In Dussander's dream he had finally reached the camp at the top of the hill. The wide gate slid open for him and then rumbled shut on its steel track once he was inside. Both the gate and the fence surrounding the camp were electrified. His scrawny, naked pursuers threw themselves against the fence in wave after wave; Dussander had laughed at them and he had strutted back and forth, his chest thrown out, his cap cocked at exactly the right angle. The high, winey smell of burning flesh filled the black air, and he had awakened in southern California thinking of jack-o'-lanterns and the night when vampires seek the blue flame.

Two days before the Bowdens were scheduled to fly to Hawaii, Todd went back to the abandoned trainyard where folks had once boarded trains for San Francisco, Seattle, and Las Vegas; where other, older folks had once boarded the trolley for Los Angeles.

It was nearly dusk when he got there. On the curve of freeway nine hundred yards away, most of the cars were now showing their parking lights. Although it was warm, Todd was wearing a light jacket. Tucked into his belt under it was a butcher knife wrapped in an old hand-towel. He had purchased the knife in a discount department store, one of the big ones surrounded by acres of parking lot.

He looked under the platform where the wino had been the month before. His mind turned and turned, but it turned on nothing; everything inside him at that moment was shades of black on black.

What he found was the same wino or possibly another; they all looked pretty much the same.

"Hey!" Todd said. "Hey! You want some money?"

The wino turned over, blinking. He saw Todd's wide, sunny grin and began to grin back. A moment later the butcher knife descended, all whicker-snicker and chrome-white, slicker-slicing through the stubbly right cheek. Blood sprayed. Todd could see the blade in the wino's opening mouth . . . and then its tip caught for a moment in the left corner of the wino's lips, pulling his mouth into an insanely cockeyed grin. Then it was the knife that was making the grin; he was carving the wino like a Halloween pumpkin.

He stabbed the wino thirty-seven times. He kept count. Thirty-seven, counting the first strike, which went through the wino's cheek and then turned his tentative smile into a great grisly grin. The wino stopped trying to scream after the fourth stroke. He stopped trying to scramble away from Todd after the sixth. Todd then crawled all the way under the platform and finished the job.

On his way home he threw the knife into the river. His pants were bloodstained. He tossed them into the washing machine and set it to wash cold. There were still faint stains on the pants when they came out, but they didn't concern Todd. They would fade in time. He found the next day that he could barely lift his right arm to the level of his shoulder. He told his father he must have strained it throwing pepper with some of the guys in the park.

"It'll get better in Hawaii," Dick Bowden said, ruffling Todd's hair, and it did; by the time they came home, it was as good as new.

13

It was July again.

Dussander, carefully dressed in one of his three suits (not his best), was standing at the bus stop and waiting for the last local of the day to take him home. It was 10:45 p.m. He had been to a film, a light and frothy comedy that he had enjoyed a great deal. He had been in a fine mood ever since the morning mail. There had been a postcard from the boy, a glossy color photo of Waikiki Beach with bone-white highrise hotels standing in the background. There was a brief message on the reverse.

Dear Mr. Denker,

Boy this sure is some place. I've been swimming every day. My dad caught a big fish and my mom is catching up on her reading (joke). Tomorrow we're going to a volcano. I'll try not to fall in! Hope you're okay.

Stay healthy,
Todd

He was still smiling faintly at the significance of that last when a hand touched his elbow.

"Mister?"

"Yes?"

He turned, on his guard—even in Santo Donato, muggers were not unknown—and then winced at the aroma. It seemed to be a combination of beer, halitosis, dried sweat, and possibly Musterole. It was a bum in baggy pants. He—*it*—wore a flannel shirt and very old loafers that were currently being held together with dirty bands of adhesive tape. The face looming above this motley costume looked like the death of God.

"You got an extra dime, mister? I gotta get to L.A., me. Got a job offertunity. I need just a dime more for the express bus. I wudn't ask if it wadn't a big chance for me."

Dussander had begun to frown, but now his smile reasserted itself.

"Is it really a bus ride you wish?"

The wino smiled sickly, not understanding.

"Suppose you ride the bus home with me," Dussander proposed. "I can offer you a drink, a meal, a bath, and a bed. All I ask in return is a little conversation. I am an old man. I live alone. Company is sometimes very welcome."

The drunk's smile abruptly grew more healthy as the situation clarified itself. Here was a well-to-do old faggot with a taste for slumming.

"All by yourself! Bitch, innit?"

Dussander answered the broad, insinuating grin with a polite smile. "I only ask that you sit away from me on the bus. You smell rather strongly."

"Maybe you don't want me stinking up your place, then," the drunk said with sudden, tipsy dignity.

"Come, the bus will be here in a minute. Get off one stop after I do and then walk back two blocks. I'll wait for you on the corner. In the morning I will see what I can spare. Perhaps two dollars."

"Maybe even five," the drunk said brightly. His dignity, tipsy or otherwise, had been forgotten.

"Perhaps, perhaps," Dussander said impatiently. He could now hear the low diesel drone of the approaching bus. He pressed a quarter, the correct bus fare, into the bum's grimy hand and strolled a few paces away without looking back.

The bum stood undecided as the headlights of the local swept over the rise. He was still standing and frowning down at the quarter when the old faggot got on the bus without looking back. The bum began to walk away and then—at the last second—he reversed direction and boarded the bus just before the doors folded closed. He put the quarter into the fare-box with the expression of a man putting a hundred dollars down on a long shot. He passed Dussander without doing more than glancing at him and sat at the back of the bus. He dozed off a little, and when he woke up, the rich old faggot was gone. He got off at the next stop, not knowing if it was the right one or not, and not really caring.

He walked back two blocks and saw a dim shape under the streetlight. It was the old faggot, all right. The faggot was watching him approach, and he was standing as if at attention.

For just a moment the bum felt a chill of apprehension, an urge to just turn away and forget the whole thing.

Then the old man was gripping him by the arm . . . and his grip was surprisingly firm.

"Good," the old man said. "I'm very glad you came. My house is down here. It's not far."

"Maybe even ten," the bum said, allowing himself to be led.

"Maybe even ten," the old faggot agreed, and then laughed. "Who knows?"

14

The Bi-Centennial year arrived.

Todd came by to see Dussander half a dozen times between his return from Hawaii in the summer of 1975 and the trip he and his parents took to Rome just as all the drum-thumping, flag-waving, and Tall Ships-watching was approaching its climax.

These visits to Dussander were low-key and in no way unpleasant; the two of them found they could pass the time civilly enough. They spoke more in silences than they did in words, and their actual conversations would have put an FBI agent to sleep. Todd told the old man that he had been seeing a girl named Angela Farrow off and on. He wasn't nuts about her, but she was the daughter of one of his mother's friends. The old man told Todd he had taken up braiding rugs because he had read such an activity was good for arthritis. He showed Todd several samples of his work, and Todd dutifully admired them.

The boy had grown quite a bit, had he not? (Well, two inches.) Had Dussander given up smoking? (No, but he had been forced to cut down; they made him cough too much now.) How had his schoolwork been? (Challenging but exciting; he had made all A's and B's, had gone to the state finals with his Science Fair project on solar power, and was now thinking of majoring in anthropology instead of history when he got to college.) Who was mowing Dussander's lawn this year?

(Randy Chambers from just down the street—a good boy, but rather fat and slow.)

During that year Dussander had put an end to three winos in his kitchen. He had been approached at the downtown bus stop some twenty times, had made the drink-dinner-bath-and-bed offer seven times. He had been turned down twice, and on two other occasions the winos had simply walked off with the quarters Dussander gave them for the fare-box. After some thought, he had worked out a way around this; he simply bought a book of coupons. They were two dollars and fifty cents, good for fifteen rides, and non-negotiable at the local liquor stores.

On very warm days just lately, Dussander had noticed an unpleasant smell drifting up from his cellar. He kept his doors and windows firmly shut on these days.

Todd Bowden had found a wino sleeping it off in an abandoned drainage culvert behind a vacant lot on Cienaga Way—this had been in December, during the Christmas vacation. He had stood there for some time, hands stuffed into his pockets, looking at the wino and trembling. He had returned to the lot six times over a period of five weeks, always wearing his light jacket, zipped halfway up to conceal the Craftsman hammer tucked into his belt. At last he had come upon the wino again—that one or some other, and who really gave a fuck—on the first day of March. He had begun with the hammer end of the tool, and then at some point (he didn't really remember when; everything had been swimming in a red haze) he had switched to the claw end, obliterating the wino's face.

For Kurt Dussander, the winos were a half-cynical propitiation of gods he had finally recognized . . . or re-recognized. And the winos were fun. They made him feel alive. He was beginning to feel that the years he had spent in Santo Donato—the years before the boy had turned up on his doorstep with his big blue eyes and his wide American grin—had been years spent being old before his time. He had been just past his mid-sixties when he came here. And he felt much younger than that now.

The idea of propitiating gods would have startled Todd at first—but it might have gained eventual acceptance. After stabbing the wino under the train platform, he had expected his nightmares to intensify—to perhaps even drive him crazy. He had expected waves of paralyzing guilt that might well end with a blurted confession or the taking of his own life.

Instead of any of those things, he had gone to Hawaii with his parents and enjoyed the best vacation of his life.

He had begun high school last September feeling oddly new and refreshed, as if a different person had jumped into his Todd Bowden skin. Things that had made no particular impression on him since earliest childhood—the sunlight just after dawn, the look of the ocean off the Fish Pier, the sight of people hurrying on a downtown street at just that moment of dusk when the streetlights come on—these things now imprinted themselves on his mind again in a series of bright cameos, in images so clear they seemed electroplated. He tasted life on his tongue like a draught of wine straight from the bottle.

After he had seen the stewbum in the culvert, but before he killed him, the nightmares had begun again.

The most common one involved the wino he had stabbed to death in the abandoned trainyard. Home from school, he burst into the house, a cheery *Hi, Monica-baby!* on his lips. It died there as he saw the dead wino in the raised breakfast nook. He was sitting slumped over their butcher-block table in his puke-smelling shirt and pants. Blood had streaked across the bright tiled floor; it was drying on the stainless steel counters. There were bloody handprints on the natural pine cupboards.

Clipped to the note-board by the fridge was a message from his mother: *Todd—Gone to the store. Back by 3:30.* The hands of the stylish sunburst clock over the Jenn-Air range stood at 3:20 and the drunk was sprawled dead up there in the nook like some horrid oozing relic from the subcellar of a junkshop and there was blood everywhere, and Todd began trying to clean it up, wiping every exposed surface, all the time screaming at the dead wino that he had to *go,* had to leave him *alone,* and the wino just lolled there and stayed dead, grinning up at the ceiling, and freshets of blood kept pouring from the stab-wounds in his dirty skin. Todd grabbed the O Cedar mop from the closet and began to slide it madly back and forth across the floor, aware that he was not really getting the blood up, only diluting it, spreading it around, but unable to stop. And just as he heard his mother's Town and Country wagon turn into the driveway, he realized the wino was Dussander. He woke from these dreams sweating and gasping, clutching double handfuls of the bedclothes.

But after he finally found the wino in the culvert again—that wino or some other—and used the hammer on him, these dreams went away. He supposed he might have to kill again, and maybe more than once. It was too bad, but of course their time of usefulness as human creatures was over. Except their usefulness to Todd, of course. And Todd, like everyone else he knew, was only tailoring his lifestyle to fit his own particular needs as he grew older. Really, he was no different than anybody. You had to make your own way in the world; if you were going to get along, you had to do it by yourself.

15

In the fall of his junior year, Todd played varsity tailback for the Santo Donato Cougars and was named All-Conference. And in the second quarter of that year, the quarter which ended in late January of 1977, he won the American Legion Patriotic Essay Contest. This contest was open to all city high school students who were taking American history courses. Todd's piece was called "An American's Responsibility." During the baseball season that year he was the school's star pitcher, winning four and losing none. His batting average was .361. At the awards assembly in June he was named Athlete of the Year and given a plaque by Coach Haines (Coach Haines, who had once taken him aside and told him to keep practicing his curve "because none of these niggers can hit a curve-ball, Bowden, not one of them"). Monica Bowden burst into tears when Todd called her from school and told her he was going to get the award. Dick Bowden strutted around his office for two weeks following the ceremony, trying not to boast. That summer they rented a cabin in Big Sur and stayed there for two weeks and Todd snorkled his brains out. During that same year Todd killed four derelicts. He stabbed two of them and bludgeoned two of them. He had taken to wearing two pairs of pants on what he now acknowledged to be hunting expeditions. Sometimes he rode the city busses, looking for likely spots. The best two, he found, were the Santo Donato Mission for the Indigent on Douglas Street, and around the corner from the Salvation Army on Euclid. He would walk slowly through both of these neighborhoods, waiting to be panhandled. When a wino approached him, Todd would tell him that he, Todd, wanted a bottle of whiskey, and if the wino would buy it, Todd would share the bottle. He knew a place, he said, where they could go. It was a different place every time, of course. He resisted a strong urge to go back either to the trainyard or to the culvert behind the vacant lot on Cienaga Way. Revisiting the scene of a previous crime would have been unwise.

During the same year Dussander smoked sparingly, drank Ancient Age bourbon, and watched TV. Todd came by once in awhile, but their conversations became increasingly arid. They were growing apart. Dussander celebrated his seventy-ninth birthday that year, which was also the year Todd turned sixteen. Dussander remarked that sixteen was the best year of a young man's life, forty-one the best year of a middle-aged man's, and seventy-nine the best of an old man's. Todd nodded politely. Dussander had been quite drunk, and cackled in a way that made Todd distinctly uneasy.

Dussander had dispatched two winos during Todd's academic year of 1976–77. The second had been livelier than he looked; even after Dussander had gotten the man soddenly drunk he had tottered around the kitchen with the haft of a steak-knife jutting from the base of his neck, gushing blood down the front of his shirt and onto the floor. The wino had re-discovered the front hall after two staggering circuits of the kitchen and had almost escaped the house.

Dussander had stood in the kitchen, eyes wide with shocked unbelief, watching the wino grunt and puff his way toward the door, rebounding from one side of the hall to the other and knocking cheap Currier & Ives reproductions to the floor. His paralysis had not broken until the wino was actually groping for the doorknob. Then Dussander had bolted across the room, jerked open the utility drawer, and pulled out his meat-fork. He ran down the hall with the meat-fork held out in front of him and drove it into the wino's back.

Dussander had stood over him, panting, his old heart racing in a frightening way . . . racing like that of a heart-attack victim on that Saturday night TV program he enjoyed, *Emergency!* But at last it had slowed back into a normal rhythm and he knew he was going to be all right.

There had been a great deal of blood to clean up.

That had been four months ago, and since then he had not made his offer at the downtown bus stop. He was frightened of the way he had almost bungled the last one . . . but when he remembered the way he had handled things at the last moment, pride rose in his heart. In the end the wino had never made it out the door, and that was the important thing.

16

In the fall of 1977, during the first quarter of his senior year, Todd joined the Rifle Club. By June of 1978 he had qualified as a marksman. He made All-Conference in football again, won five and lost one during the baseball season (the loss coming as the result of two errors and one unearned run), and made the third highest Merit Scholarship score in the school's history. He applied to Berkeley and was promptly accepted. By April he knew he would either be valedictorian or salutatorian on graduation night. He very badly wanted to be valedictorian.

During the latter half of his senior year, an odd impulse came on him—one which was as frightening to Todd as it was irrational. He seemed to be clearly and firmly in control of it, and *that* at least was comforting, but that such a thought should have occurred at all was scary. He had made an arrangement with life. He had worked things out. His life was much like his mother's bright and sunshiny kitchen, where all the surfaces were dressed in chrome, Formica, or stainless steel—a place where everything worked when you pressed the buttons. There were deep and dark cupboards in this kitchen, of course, but many things could be stored in them and their doors still be closed.

This new impulse reminded him of the dream in which he had come home to discover the dead and bleeding wino in his mother's clean, well-lighted place. It was as if, in the bright and careful arrangement he had made, in that a-place-for-everything-and-everything-in-its-place kitchen of his mind, a dark and bloody intruder now lurched and shambled, looking for a place to die conspicuously . . .

A quarter of a mile from the Bowden house was the freeway, running eight lanes wide. A steep and brushy bank led down to it. There was plenty of good cover on the bank. His father had given him a Winchester .30-.30 for Christmas, and it had a removable telescopic sight. During rush hour, when all eight lanes were jammed, he could pick a spot on that bank and . . . why, he could easily . . .

Do what?

Commit suicide?

Destroy everything he had worked for these last four years?

Say *what?*

No *sir,* no *ma'am,* no *way.*

It is, as they say, to laugh.

Sure it was . . . but the impulse remained.

One Saturday a few weeks before his high school graduation, Todd cased the .30-.30 after carefully emptying the magazine. He put the rifle in the back seat of his father's new toy—a used Porsche. He drove to the spot where the brushy slope dropped steeply down to the freeway. His mother and father had taken the station wagon and had driven to L.A. for the weekend. Dick, now a full partner, would be holding discussions with the Hyatt people about a new Reno hotel.

Todd's heart bumped in his chest and his mouth was full of sour, electric spit as he worked his way down the grade with the cased rifle in his arms. He came to a fallen tree and sat cross-legged behind it. He uncased the rifle and laid it on the dead tree's smooth trunk. A branch jutting off at an angle made a nice rest for the barrel. He snugged the buttplate into the hollow of his right shoulder and peered into the telescopic sight.

Stupid! his mind screamed at him. *Boy, this is really stupid! If someone sees you, it's not going to matter if the gun's loaded or not! You'll get in plenty of trouble, maybe even end up with some Chippie shooting at you!*

It was mid-morning and the Saturday traffic was light. He settled the crosshairs on a woman behind the wheel of a blue Toyota. The woman's window was half-open and the round collar of her sleeveless blouse was fluttering. Todd centered the crosshairs on her temple and dry-fired. It was bad for the firing-pin, but what the fuck.

"Pow," he whispered as the Toyota disappeared beneath the underpass half a mile up from the slope where Todd sat. He swallowed around a lump that tasted like a stuck-together mass of pennies.

Here came a man behind the wheel of a Subaru Brat pickup truck. This man had a scuzzy-looking gray beard and was wearing a San Diego Padres baseball hat.

"You're . . . you're a dirty rat . . . the dirty rat that shot my bruddah," Todd whispered, giggling a little, and dry-fired the .30-.30 again.

He shot at five others, the impotent snap of the hammer spoiling the illusion at the end of each "kill." Then he cased the rifle again. He carried it back up the slope, bending low to keep from being seen. He put it into the back of the Porsche. There was a dry hot pounding in his temples. He drove home. Went up to his room. Masturbated.

17

The stewbum was wearing a ragged, unravelling reindeer sweater that looked so startling it almost seemed surreal here in southern California. He also wore seaman's issue bluejeans which were out at the knees, showing white, hairy flesh and a number of peeling scabs. He raised the jelly-glass—Fred and Wilma, Barney and Betty dancing around the rim in what might have been some grotesque fertility rite—and tossed off the knock of Ancient Age at a gulp. He smacked his lips for the last time in this world.

"Mister, that hits the old spot. I don't mind saying so."

"I always enjoy a drink in the evening," Dussander agreed from behind him, and then rammed the butcher knife into the stewbum's neck. There was the sound of ripping gristle, a sound like a drumstick being torn enthusiastically from a freshly roasted chicken. The jelly-glass fell from the stewbum's hand and onto the table. It rolled toward the edge, its movement enhancing the illusion that the cartoon characters on it were dancing.

The stewbum threw his head back and tried to scream.

Nothing came out but a hideous whistling sound. His eyes widened, widened . . . and then his head thumped soggily onto the red and white oilcloth check that covered Dussander's kitchen table. The stewbum's upper plate slithered halfway out of his mouth like a semi-detachable grin.

Dussander yanked the knife free—he had to use both hands to do it—and crossed to the kitchen sink. It was filled with hot water, Lemon Fresh Joy, and dirty supper dishes. The knife disappeared into a billow of citrus-smelling suds like a very small fighter plane diving into a cloud.

He crossed to the table again and paused there, resting one hand on the dead stewbum's shoulder while a spasm of coughing rattled through him. He took his handkerchief from his back pocket and spat yellowish-brown phlegm into it. He had been smoking too much lately. He always did when he was making up his mind to do another one. But this one had gone smoothly; really very smoothly. He had been afraid after the mess he had made with the last one that he might be tempting fate sorely to try it again.

Now, if he hurried, he would still be able to watch the second half of *Lawrence Welk.*

He bustled across the kitchen, opened the cellar door, and turned on the light switch. He went back to the sink and got the package of green plastic garbage bags from the cupboard beneath. He shook one out as he walked back to the slumped wino. Blood had run across the oilcloth in all directions. It had puddled in the wino's lap and on the hilly, faded linoleum. It would be on the chair, too, but all of those things would clean up.

Dussander grabbed the stewbum by the hair and yanked his head up. It came with boneless ease, and a moment later the wino was lolling backwards, like a man about to get a pre-haircut shampoo. Dussander pulled the garbage bag down over the wino's head, over his shoulders, and down his arms to the elbows. That was as far as it would go. He unbuckled his late guest's belt and pulled it free of the fraying belt-loops. He wrapped the belt around the garbage bag two or three inches above the elbows and buckled it tight. Plastic rustled. Dussander began to hum under his breath.

The wino's feet were clad in scuffed and dirty Hush Puppies. They made a limp V on the floor as Dussander seized the belt and dragged the corpse toward the cellar door. Something white tumbled out of the plastic bag and clicked on the floor. It was the stewbum's upper plate, Dussander saw. He picked it up and stuffed it into one of the wino's front pockets.

He laid the wino down in the cellar doorway with his head now lolling backward onto the second stair-level. Dussander climbed around the body and gave it three healthy kicks. The body moved slightly on the first two, and the third sent it slithering bonelessly down the stairs. Halfway down, the feet flew up over the head and the body executed an acrobatic roll. It belly-whopped onto the packed dirt of the cellar floor with a solid thud. One Hush Puppy flew off, and Dussander made a mental note to pick it up.

He went down the stairs, skirted the body, and approached his toolbench. To the left of the bench a spade, a rake, and a hoe leaned against the wall in a neat rank. Dussander selected the spade. A little exercise was good for an old man. A little exercise could make you feel young.

The smell down here was not good, but it didn't bother him much. He limed the place once a month (once every three days after he had "done" one of his winos) and he had gotten a fan which he ran upstairs to keep the smell from permeating the house on very warm still days. Josef Kramer, he remembered, had been fond of saying that the dead speak, but we hear them with our noses.

Dussander picked a spot in the cellar's north corner and went to work. The dimensions of the grave were two and a half feet by six feet. He had gotten to a depth of two feet, half deep enough, when the first paralyzing pain struck him in the chest like a shotgun blast. He straightened up, eyes flaring wide. Then the pain rolled down his arm . . . unbelievable pain, as if an invisible hand had seized all the blood-vessels in there and was now pulling them. He watched the spade tumble sideways and felt his knees buckle. For one horrible moment he felt sure that he was going to fall into the grave himself.

Somehow he staggered backwards three paces and sat down on his workbench with a plop. There was an expression of stupid surprise on his face—he could feel it—and he thought he must look like one of those silent movie comedians after he'd been hit by the swinging door or stepped in the cow patty. He put his head down between his knees and gasped.

Fifteen minutes crawled by. The pain had begun to abate somewhat, but he did not believe he would be able to stand. For the first time he understood all the truths of old age which he had been spared until now. He was terrified almost to the point of whimpering. Death had brushed by him in this dank, smelly cellar; it had touched Dussander with the hem of its robe. It might be back for him yet. But he would not die down here; not if he could help it.

He got up, hands crossed on his chest, as if to hold the fragile machinery together. He staggered across the open space between the workbench and the stairs. His left foot tripped over the dead wino's outstretched leg and he went to his knees with a small cry. There was a sullen flare of pain in his chest. He looked up the stairs—the steep, steep stairs. Twelve of them. The square of light at the top was mockingly distant.

"Ein," Kurt Dussander said, and pulled himself grimly up onto the first stair-level. *"Zwei, Drei, Vier."*

It took him twenty minutes to reach the linoleum floor of the kitchen. Twice, on the stairs, the pain had threatened to come back, and both times Dussander had waited with his eyes closed to see what would happen, perfectly aware that if it came back as strongly as it had come upon him down there, he would probably die. Both times the pain had faded away again.

He crawled across the kitchen floor to the table, avoiding the pools and streaks of blood, which were now congealing. He got the bottle of Ancient Age, took a swallow, and closed his eyes. Something that had been cinched tight in his chest seemed to loosen a little. The pain faded a bit more. After another five minutes he began to work his way slowly down the hall. His telephone sat on a small table halfway down.

It was quarter past nine when the phone rang in the Bowden house. Todd was sitting cross-legged on the couch, going over his notes for the trig final. Trig was a bitch for him, as all maths were and probably always would be. His father was seated across the room, going through the checkbook stubs with a portable calculator on his lap and a mildly disbelieving expression on his face. Monica, closest to the phone, was watching the James Bond movie Todd had taped off HBO two evenings before.

"Hello?" She listened. A faint frown touched her face and she held the handset out to Todd. "It's Mr. Denker. He sounds excited about something. Or upset."

Todd's heart leaped into his throat, but his expression hardly changed. "Really?" He went to the phone and took it from her. "Hi, Mr. Denker."

Dussander's voice was hoarse and short. "Come over right away, boy. I've had a heart attack. Quite a bad one, I think."

"Gee," Todd said, trying to collect his flying thoughts, to see around the fear that now bulked huge in his own mind. "That's interesting, all right, but it's pretty late and I was studying—"

"I understand that you cannot talk," Dussander said in that harsh, almost barking voice. "But you can listen. I cannot call an ambulance or dial two-two-two, boy . . . at least not yet. There is a mess here. I need help . . . and that means *you* need help."

"Well . . . if you put it that way . . ." Todd's heartbeat had reached a hundred and twenty beats a minute, but his face was calm, almost serene. Hadn't he known all along that a night like this would come? Yes, of course he had.

"Tell your parents I've had a letter," Dussander said. "An important letter. You understand?"

"Yeah, okay," Todd said.

"Now we see, boy. We see what you are made of."

"Sure," Todd said. He suddenly became aware that his mother was watching him instead of the movie, and he forced a stiff grin onto his face. "Bye."

Dussander was saying something else now, but Todd hung up on it.

"I'm going over to Mr. Denker's for awhile," he said, speaking to both of them but looking at his mother—that faint expression of concern was still on her face. "Can I pick up anything for either of you at the store?"

"Pipe cleaners for me and a small package of fiscal responsibility for your mother," Dick said.

"Very funny," Monica said. "Todd, is Mr. Denker—"

"What in the name of *God* did you get at Fielding's?" Dick interrupted.

"That knick-knack shelf in the closet. I told you that. There's nothing wrong with Mr. Denker, is there, Todd? He sounded a little strange."

"There really *are* such things as knick-knack shelves? I thought those crazy women who write British mysteries made them up so there would always be a place where the killer could find a blunt instrument."

"Dick, can I get a word in edgeways?"

"Sure. Be my guest. But for the *closet*?"

"He's okay, I guess," Todd said. He put on his letter jacket and zipped it up. "But he *was* excited. He got a letter from a nephew of his in Hamburg or Düsseldorf or someplace. He hasn't heard from any of his people in years, and now he's got this letter and his eyes aren't good enough for him to read it."

"Well isn't that a *bitch,*" Dick said. "Go on, Todd. Get over there and ease the man's mind."

"I thought he had someone to read to him," Monica said. "A new boy."

"He does," Todd said, suddenly hating his mother, hating the half-informed intuition he saw swimming in her eyes. "Maybe he wasn't home, or maybe he couldn't come over this late."

"Oh. Well . . . go on, then. But be careful."

"I will. You don't need anything at the store?"

"No. How's your studying for that calculus final going?"

"It's trig," Todd said. "Okay, I guess. I was just getting ready to call it a night." This was a rather large lie.

"You want to take the Porsche?" Dick asked.

"No, I'll ride my bike." He wanted the extra five minutes to collect his thoughts and get his emotions under control—to try, at least. And in his present state, he would probably drive the Porsche into a telephone pole.

"Strap your reflector-patch on your knee," Monica said, "and tell Mr. Denker hello for us."

"Okay."

That doubt was still in his mother's eyes but it was less evident now. He blew her a kiss and then went out to the garage where his bike—a racing-style Italian bike rather than a Schwinn now—was parked. His heart was still racing in his chest, and he felt a mad urge to take the .30-.30 back into the house and shoot both of his parents and then go down to the slope overlooking the freeway. No more worrying about Dussander. No more bad dreams, no more winos. He would shoot and shoot and shoot, only saving one bullet back for the end.

Then reason came back to him and he rode away toward Dussander's, his reflector-patch revolving up and down just above his knee, his long blonde hair streaming back from his brow.

• • •

"Holy *Christ*!" Todd nearly screamed.

He was standing in the kitchen door. Dussander was slumped on his elbows, his china cup between them. Large drops of sweat stood out on his forehead. But it was not Dussander Todd was looking at. It was the blood. There seemed to be blood everywhere—it was puddled on the table, on the empty kitchen chair, on the floor.

"Where are you bleeding?" Todd shouted, at last getting his frozen feet to move again—it seemed to him that he had been standing in the doorway for at least a thousand years. *This is the end,* he was thinking, *this is the absolute end of everything. The balloon is going up high, baby, all the way to the sky, baby, and it's toot-toot-tootsie, goodbye.* All the same, he was careful not to step in any of the blood. "I thought you said you had a fucking heart attack!"

"It's not my blood," Dussander muttered.

"What?" Todd stopped. "What did you say?"

"Go downstairs. You will see what has to be done."

"What the hell *is* this?" Todd asked. A sudden terrible idea had come into his head.

"Don't waste our time, boy. I think you will not be too surprised at what you find downstairs. I think you have had experience in such matters as the one in my cellar. First-hand experience."

Todd looked at him, unbelieving, for another moment, and then he plunged down the cellar stairs two by two. His first look in the feeble yellow glow of the basement's only light made him think that Dussander had pushed a bag of garbage down here. Then he saw the protruding legs, and the dirty hands held down at the sides by the cinched belt.

"Holy Christ," he repeated, but this time the words had no force at all—they emerged in a slight, skeletal whisper.

He pressed the back of his right hand against lips that were as dry as sandpaper. He closed his eyes for a moment . . . and when he opened them again, he felt in control of himself at last.

Todd started moving.

He saw the spade-handle protruding from a shallow hole in the far corner and understood at once what Dussander had been doing when his ticker had seized up. A moment later he became fully aware of the cellar's fetid aroma—a smell like rotting tomatoes. He had smelled it before, but upstairs it was much fainter—and, of course, he hadn't been here very often over the past couple of years. Now he understood *exactly* what that smell meant and for several moments he had to struggle with his gorge. A series of choked gagging sounds, muffled by the hand he had clapped over his mouth and nose, came from him.

Little by little he got control of himself again.

He seized the wino's legs and dragged him across to the edge of the hole. He dropped them, skidded sweat from his forehead with the heel of his left hand, and stood absolutely still for a moment, thinking harder than he ever had in his life.

Then he seized the spade and began to deepen the hole. When it was five feet deep, he got out and shoved the derelict's body in with his foot. Todd stood at the edge of the grave, looking down. Tattered bluejeans. Filthy, scab-encrusted hands. It was a stewbum, all right. The irony was almost funny. So funny a person could scream with laughter.

He ran back upstairs.

"How are you?" he asked Dussander.

"I'll be all right. Have you taken care of it?"

"I'm doing it, okay?"

"Be quick. There's still up here."

"I'd like to find some pigs and feed you to them," Todd said, and went back down cellar before Dussander could reply.

He had almost completely covered the wino when he began to think there was something wrong. He stared into the grave, grasping the spade's handle with one hand. The wino's legs stuck partway out of the mound of dirt, as did the tips of his feet—one old shoe, possibly a Hush Puppy, and one filthy athletic sock that might actually have been white around the time that Taft was President.

One Hush Puppy? *One?*

Todd half-ran back around the furnace to the foot of the stairs. He glanced around wildly. A headache was beginning to thud against his temples, dull drillbits trying to work their way out. He spotted the old shoe five feet away, overturned in the shadow of some abandoned shelving. Todd grabbed it, ran back to the grave with it, and threw it in. Then he started to shovel again. He covered the shoe, the legs, everything.

When all the dirt was back in the hole, he slammed the spade down repeatedly to tamp it. Then he grabbed the rake and ran it back and forth, trying to disguise the fact the earth here had been recently turned. Not much use; without good camouflage, a hole that has been recently dug and then filled in always looks like a hole that has been recently dug and then filled in. Still, no one would have any occasion to come down here, would they? He and Dussander would damn well have to hope not.

Todd ran back upstairs. He was starting to pant.

Dussander's elbows had spread wide and his head had sagged down to the table. His eyes were closed, the lids a shiny purple—the color of asters.

"Dussander!" Todd shouted. There was a hot, juicy taste in his mouth—the taste of fear mixed with adrenaline and pulsing hot blood. "Don't you *dare* die on me, you old fuck!"

"Keep your voice down," Dussander said without opening his eyes. "You'll have everyone on the block over here."

"Where's your cleaner? Lestoil . . . Top Job . . . something like that. And rags. I need rags."

"All that is under the sink."

A lot of the blood had now dried on. Dussander raised his head and watched as Todd crawled across the floor, scrubbing first at the puddle on the linoleum and then at the drips that had straggled down the legs of the chair the wino had been sitting in. The boy was biting compulsively at his lips, champing at them, almost, like a horse at a bit. At last the job was finished. The astringent smell of cleaner filled the room.

"There is a box of old rags under the stairs," Dussander said. "Put those bloody ones on the bottom. Don't forget to wash your hands."

"I don't need your advice. You got me into this."

"Did I? I must say you took hold well." For a moment the old mockery was in Dussander's voice, and then a bitter grimace pulled his face into a new shape. "Hurry."

Todd took care of the rags, then hurried up the cellar stairs for the last time. He looked nervously down the stairs for a moment, then snapped off the light and closed the door. He went to the sink, rolled up his sleeves, and washed in the hottest water he could stand. He plunged his hands into the suds . . . and came up holding the butcher knife Dussander had used.

"I'd like to cut your throat with this," Todd said grimly.

"Yes, and then feed me to the pigs. I have no doubt of it."

Todd rinsed the knife, dried it, and put it away. He did the rest of the dishes quickly, let the water out, and rinsed the sink. He looked at the clock as he dried his hands and saw it was twenty minutes after ten.

He went to the phone in the hallway, picked up the receiver, and looked at it thoughtfully. The idea that he had forgotten something—something as potentially damning as the wino's shoe—nagged unpleasantly at his mind. What? He didn't know. If not for the headache, he might be able to get it. The triple-damned headache. It wasn't like him to forget things, and it was scary.

He dialed 222 and after a single ring, a voice answered: "This is Santo Donato MED-Q. Do you have a medical problem?"

"My name is Todd Bowden. I'm at 963 Claremont Street. I need an ambulance."

"What's the problem, son?"

"It's my friend, Mr. D—" He bit down on his lip so hard that it squirted blood, and for a moment he was lost, drowning in the pulses of pain from his head. *Dussander.* He had almost given this anonymous MED-Q voice Dussander's real name.

"Calm down, son," the voice said. 'Take it slow and you'll be fine."

"My friend Mr. Denker," Todd said. "I think he's had a heart attack."

"His symptoms?"

Todd began to give them, but the voice had heard enough as soon as Todd described the chest pain that had migrated to the left arm. He told Todd the ambulance would arrive in ten to twenty minutes, depending on the traffic. Todd hung up and pressed the heels of his hands against his eyes.

"Did you get it?" Dussander called weakly.

"Yes!" Todd screamed. *"Yes, I got it! Yes goddammit yes! Yes yes yes! Just shut up!"*

He pressed his hands even harder against his eyes, creating first senseless starflashes of light and then a bright field of red. *Get hold of yourself, Todd-baby. Get down, get funky, get cool. Dig it.*

He opened his eyes and picked up the telephone again. Now the hard part. Now it was time to call home.

"Hello?" Monica's soft, cultured voice in his ear. For a moment—just a moment—he saw himself slamming the muzzle of the .30-.30 into her nose and pulling the trigger into the first flow of blood.

"It's Todd, Mommy. Let me talk to Dad, quick."

He didn't call her mommy anymore. He knew she would get that signal quicker than anything else, and she did. "What's the matter? Is something wrong, Todd?"

"Just let me talk to him!"

"But what—"

The phone rattled and clunked. He heard his mother saying something to his father. Todd got ready.

"It's Mr. Denker, Daddy. He . . . it's a heart attack, I think. I'm pretty sure it is."

"Jesus!" His father's voice lagged away for a moment and Todd heard him repeating the information to his wife. Then he was back. "He's still alive? As far as you can tell?"

"He's alive. Conscious."

"All right, thank God for that. Call an ambulance."

"I just did."

"Two-two-two?"

"Yes."

"Good boy. How bad is he, can you tell?"

"I don't know, Dad. They said the ambulance would be here soon, but . . . I'm sorta scared. Can you come over and wait with me?"

"You bet. Give me four minutes."

Todd could hear his mother saying something else as his father hung up, breaking the connection. Todd replaced the receiver on his end.

Four minutes.

Four minutes to do anything that had been left undone. Four minutes to remember whatever it was that had been forgotten. Or *had* he forgotten anything? Maybe it was just nerves. God, he wished he hadn't had to call his father. But it was the natural thing to do, wasn't it? Sure. Was there some natural thing that he *hadn't* done? Something—?

"Oh, you shit-for-brains!" he suddenly moaned, and bolted back into the kitchen. Dussander's head lay on the table, his eyes half-open, sluggish.

"Dussander!" Todd cried. He shook Dussander roughly, and the old man groaned. "Wake up! Wake up, you stinking old bastard!"

"What? Is it the ambulance?"

"The letter! My father is coming over, he'll be here in no time. *Where's the fucking letter?*"

"What . . . what letter?"

"You told me to tell them you got an important letter. I said . . ." His heart sank. "I said it came from overseas . . . from Germany. Christ!" Todd ran his hands through his hair.

"A letter." Dussander raised his head with slow difficulty. His seamed cheeks were an unhealthy yellowish-white, his lips blue. "From Willi, I think. Willi Frankel. Dear . . . dear Willi."

Todd looked at his watch and saw that already two minutes had passed since he had hung up the phone. His father would not, *could* not make it from their house to Dussander's in four minutes, but he could do it damn fast in the Porsche. Fast, that was it. Everything was moving too fast. And there was still something wrong here; he *felt* it. But there was no time to stop and hunt around for the loophole.

"Yes, okay, I was reading it to you, and you got excited and had this heart attack. Good. Where is it?"

Dussander looked at him blankly.

"The letter! Where is it?"

"What letter?" Dussander asked vacantly, and Todd's hands itched to throttle the drunken old monster.

"The one I was reading to you! The one from Willi What's-his-face! Where is it?"

They both looked at the table, as if expecting to see the letter materialize there.

"Upstairs," Dussander said finally. "Look in my dresser. The third drawer. There is a small wooden box in the bottom of that drawer. You will have to break it open. I lost the key a long time ago. There are some very old letters from a friend of mine. None signed. None dated. All in German. A page or two will serve for window-fittings, as you would say. If you hurry—"

"Are you *crazy*?" Todd raged. "I don't understand German! How could I read you a letter written in German, you numb fuck?"

"Why would Willi write me in English?" Dussander countered wearily. "If you read me the letter in German, *I* would understand it even if *you* did not. Of course your pronunciation would be butchery, but still, I could—"

Dussander was right—right again, and Todd didn't wait to hear more. Even after a heart attack the old man was a step ahead. Todd raced down the hall to the stairs, pausing just long enough by the front door to make sure his father's Porsche wasn't pulling up even now. It wasn't, but Todd's watch told him just how tight things were getting; it had been five minutes now.

He took the stairs two at a time and burst into Dussander's bedroom. He had never been up here before, hadn't even been curious, and for a moment he only looked wildly around at the unfamiliar territory. Then he saw the dresser, a cheap item done in the style his father called Discount Store Modern. He fell on his knees in front of it and yanked at the third drawer. It came halfway out, then jigged sideways in its slot and stuck firmly.

"Goddam you," he whispered at it. His face was dead pale except for the spots of dark, bloody color flaring at each cheek and his blue eyes, which looked as dark as Atlantic stormclouds. "Goddam you fucking thing come *out*!"

He yanked so hard that the entire dresser tottered forward and almost fell on him before deciding to settle back. The drawer shot all the way out and landed in Todd's lap. Dussander's socks and underwear and handkerchiefs spilled out all around him. He pawed through the stuff that was still in the drawer and came out with a wooden box about nine inches long and three inches deep. He tried to pull up the lid. Nothing happened. It was locked, just as Dussander had said. Nothing was free tonight.

He stuffed the spilled clothes back into the drawer and then rammed the drawer back into its oblong slot. It stuck again. Todd worked to free it, wiggling it back and forth, sweat running freely down his face. At last he was able to slam it shut. He got up with the box. How much time had passed now?

Dussander's bed was the type with posts at the foot and Todd brought the lock side of the box down on one of these posts as hard as he could, grinning at the shock of pain that vibrated in his hands and travelled all the way up to his elbows. He looked at the lock. The lock looked a bit dented, but it was intact. He brought it down on the post again, even harder this time, heedless of the pain. This time a chunk of wood flew off the bedpost, but the lock still didn't give. Todd uttered a little shriek of laughter and took the box to the other end of the bed. He raised it high over his head this time and brought it down with all his strength. This time the lock splintered.

As he flipped the lid up, headlights splashed across Dussander's window.

He pawed wildly through the box. Postcards. A locket. A much-folded picture of a woman wearing frilly black garters and nothing else. An old billfold. Several sets of ID. An empty leather passport folder. At the bottom, letters.

The lights grew brighter, and now he heard the distinctive beat of the Porsche's engine. It grew louder . . . and then cut off.

Todd grabbed three sheets of airmail-type stationery, closely written in German on both sides of each sheet, and ran out of the room again. He had almost gotten to the stairs when he realized he had left the forced box lying on Dussander's bed. He ran back, grabbed it, and opened the third dresser drawer.

It stuck again, this time with a firm shriek of wood against wood.

Out front, he heard the ratchet of the Porsche's emergency brake, the opening of the driver's-side door, the slam shut.

Faintly, Todd could hear himself moaning. He put the box in the askew drawer, stood up, and lashed out at it with his foot. The drawer closed neatly. He stood blinking at it for a moment and then fled back down the hall. He raced down the stairs. Halfway down them, he heard the rapid rattle of his father's shoes on Dussander's walk. Todd vaulted over the bannister, landed lightly, and ran into the kitchen, the airmail pages fluttering from his hand.

A hammering on the door. "Todd? Todd, it's me!"

And he could hear an ambulance siren in the distance as well. Dussander had drifted away into semi-consciousness again.

"Coming, Dad!" Todd shouted.

He put the airmail pages on the table, fanning them a little as if they had been dropped in a hurry, and then he went back down the hall and let his father in.

"Where is he?" Dick Bowden asked, shouldering past Todd.

"In the kitchen."

"You did everything just right, Todd," his father said, and hugged him in a rough, embarrassed way.

"I just hope I remembered everything," Todd said modestly, and then followed his father down the hall and into the kitchen.

In the rush to get Dussander out of the house, the letter was almost completely ignored. Todd's father picked it up briefly, then put it down when the medics came in with the stretcher. Todd and his father followed the ambulance, and his explanation of what had happened was accepted without question by the doctor attending Dussander's case. "Mr. Denker" was, after all, eighty years old, and his habits were not the best. The doctor also offered Todd a brusque commendation for his quick thinking and action. Todd thanked him wanly and then asked his father if they could go home.

As they rode back, Dick told him again how proud of him he was. Todd barely heard him. He was thinking about his .30-.30 again.

18

That was the same day Morris Heisel broke his back.

Morris had never *intended* to break his back; all he had

intended to do was nail up the corner of the rain-gutter on the west side of his house. Breaking his back was the furthest thing from his mind, he had had enough grief in his life without that, thank you very much. His first wife had died at the age of twenty-five, and both of their daughters were also dead. His brother was dead, killed in a tragic car accident not far from Disneyland in 1971. Morris himself was nearing sixty, and had a case of arthritis that was worsening early and fast. He also had warts on both hands, warts that seemed to grow back as fast as the doctor could burn them off. He was *also* prone to migraine headaches, and in the last couple of years, that *potzer* Rogan next door had taken to calling him "Morris the Cat." Morris had wondered aloud to Lydia, his second wife, how Rogan would like it if Morris took up calling him "Rogan the hemorrhoid."

"Quit it, Morris," Lydia said on these occasions. "You can't take a joke, you never *could* take a joke, sometimes I wonder how I could marry a man with absolutely *no* sense of humor. We go to Las Vegas," Lydia had said, addressing the empty kitchen as if an invisible horde of spectators which only she could see were standing there, "we see Buddy Hackett, and Morris doesn't laugh *once*."

Besides arthritis, warts, and migraines, Morris also had Lydia, who, God love her, had developed into something of a nag over the last five years or so . . . ever since her hysterectomy. So he had plenty of sorrows and plenty of problems without adding a broken back.

"Morris!" Lydia cried, coming to the back door and wiping suds from her hands with a dishtowel. "Morris, you come down off that ladder right now!"

"What?" He twisted his head so he could see her. He was almost at the top of his aluminum stepladder. There was a bright yellow sticker on this step which said: DANGER! BALANCE MAY SHIFT WITHOUT WARNING ABOVE THIS STEP! Morris was wearing his carpenter's apron with the wide pockets, one of the pockets filled with nails and the other filled with heavy-duty staples. The ground under the stepladder's feet was slightly uneven and the ladder rocked a little when he moved. His neck ached with the unlovely prelude to one of his migraines. He was out of temper. *"What?"*

"Come down from there, I said, before you break your back."

"I'm almost finished."

"You're rocking on that ladder like you were on a boat, Morris. Come down."

"I'll come down when I'm done!" he said angrily. "Leave me alone!"

"You'll break your back," she reiterated dolefully, and went into the house again.

Ten minutes later, as he was hammering the last nail into the rain-gutter, tipped back nearly to the point of overbalancing, he heard a feline yowl followed by fierce barking.

"What in God's name—?"

He looked around and the stepladder rocked alarmingly. At that same moment, their cat—it was named Lover Boy, *not* Morris—tore around the corner of the garage, its fur bushed out into hackles and its green eyes flaring. The Rogans' collie pup was in hot pursuit, its tongue hanging out and its leash dragging behind it.

Lover Boy, apparently not superstitious, ran under the stepladder. The collie pup followed.

"Look out, look out, you dumb mutt!" Morris shouted.

The ladder rocked. The pup bunted it with the side of its body. The ladder tipped over and Morris tipped with it, uttering a howl of dismay. Nails and staples flew out of his carpenter's apron. He landed half on and half off the concrete driveway, and a gigantic agony flared in his back. He did not so much hear his spine snap as feel it happen. Then the world grayed out for awhile.

When things swam back into focus, he was still lying half on and half off the driveway in a litter of nails and staples.

Lydia was kneeling over him, weeping. Rogan from next door was there, too, his face as white as a shroud.

"I told you!" Lydia babbled. "I told you to come down off that ladder! Now look! Now look at this!"

Morris found he had absolutely no desire to look. A suffocating, throbbing band of pain had cinched itself around his middle like a belt, and that was bad, but there was something much worse: he could feel nothing below that belt of pain—nothing at all.

"Wail later," he said huskily. "Call the doctor now."

"I'll do it," Rogan said, and ran back to his own house.

"Lydia," Morris said. He wet his lips.

"What? What, Morris?" She bent over him and a tear splashed on his cheek. It was touching, he supposed, but it had made him flinch, and the flinch had made the pain worse.

"Lydia, I also have one of my migraines."

"Oh, poor darling! Poor Morris! But I *told* you—"

"I've got the headache because that *potzer* Rogan's dog barked all night and kept me awake. Today the dog chases my cat and knocks over my ladder and I think my back is broken."

Lydia shrieked. The sound made Morris's head vibrate.

"Lydia," he said, and wet his lips again.

"What, darling?"

"I have suspected something for many years. Now I am sure."

"My poor Morris! What?"

"There is no God," Morris said, and fainted.

They took him to Santo Donato and his doctor told him, at about the same time that he would have ordinarily been sitting down to one of Lydia's wretched suppers, that he would never walk again. By then they had put him in a body-cast. Blood and urine samples had been taken. Dr. Kemmelman had peered into his eyes and tapped his knees with a little rubber hammer—but no reflexive twitch of the leg answered the taps. And at every turn there was Lydia, the tears streaming from her eyes, as she used up one handkerchief after another. Lydia, a woman who would have been at home married to Job, went everywhere well-supplied with little lace snotrags, just in case reason for an extended crying spell should occur. She had called her mother, and her mother would be here soon ("That's nice, Lydia"—although if there was anyone on earth Morris honestly loathed, it was Lydia's mother). She had called the rabbi, he would be here soon, too ("That's nice, Lydia"—although he hadn't set foot inside the synagogue in five years and wasn't sure what the rabbi's name was). She had called his boss, and while he wouldn't be here soon, he sent his greatest sympathies and condolences ('That's nice, Lydia"—although if there was anyone in a class with Lydia's mother, it was that cigar-chewing *putz* Frank Haskell). At last they gave Morris a Valium and took Lydia away. Shortly afterward, Morris just drifted away—no worries, no migraines, no nothing. If they kept giving him little blue pills like that, went his last thought, he would go on up that stepladder and break his back again.

When he woke up—or regained consciousness, that was more like it—dawn was just breaking and the hospital was as quiet as Morris supposed it ever got. He felt very calm . . . almost serene. He had no pain; his body felt swaddled and weightless. His bed had been surrounded by some sort of contraption like a squirrel cage—a thing of stainless steel bars, guy wires, and pulleys. His legs were being held up by cables attached to this gadget. His back seemed to be bowed by something beneath, but it was hard to tell—he had only the angle of his vision to judge by.

Others have it worse, he thought. *All over the world, others have it worse. In Israel, the Palestinians kill busloads of farmers who were committing the political crime of going into town to see a movie. The Israelis cope with this injustice by dropping bombs on the Palestinians and killing children along with whatever terrorists may be there.*

Others have it worse than me . . . which is not to say this is good, *don't get that idea, but others have it worse.*

He lifted one hand with some effort—there was pain somewhere in his body, but it was very faint—and made a weak fist in front of his eyes. There. Nothing wrong with his hands. Nothing wrong with his arms, either. So he couldn't feel anything below the waist, so what? There were people all over the world paralyzed from the *neck* down. There were people with leprosy. There were people dying of syphilis. Somewhere in the world right now, there might be people walking down the jetway and onto a plane that was going to crash. No, this wasn't good, but there were worse things in the world.

And there had been, once upon a time, *much* worse things in the world.

He raised his left arm. It seemed to float, disembodied, before his eyes—a scrawny old man's arm with the muscles deteriorating. He was in a hospital johnny but it had short sleeves and he could still read the numbers on the forearm, tattooed there in faded blue ink. P499965214. Worse things, yes, worse things than falling off a suburban stepladder and breaking your back and being taken to a clean and sterile metropolitan hospital and being given a Valium that was guaranteed to bubble your troubles away.

There were the showers, they were worse. His first wife, Ruth, had died in one of their filthy showers. There were the trenches that became graves—he could close his eyes and still see the men lined up along the open maw of the trenches, could still hear the volley of rifle-fire, could still remember the way they flopped backwards into the earth like badly made puppets. There were the crematoriums, they were worse, too, the crematoriums that filled the air with the steady sweet smell of Jews burning like torches no one could see. The horror-struck faces of old friends and relatives . . . faces that melted away like guttering candles, faces that seemed to melt away *before your very eyes*—thin, thinner, thinnest. Then one day they were gone. Where? Where does a torch-flame go when the cold wind has blown it out? Heaven. Hell? Lights in the darkness, candles in the wind. When Job finally broke down and questioned, God asked him: *Where were you when I made the world?* If Morris Heisel had been Job, he would have responded: *Where were You when my Ruth was dying, You* potzer, *You? Watching the Yankees and the Senators? If You can't pay attention to Your business better than this, get out of my face.*

Yes, there were worse things than breaking your back, he had no doubt of it. But what sort of God would have allowed him to break his back and become paralyzed for life after watching his wife die, and his daughters, and his friends?

No God at all, that was Who.

A tear trickled from the corner of his eye and ran slowly down the side of his head to his ear. Outside the hospital room, a bell rang softly. A nurse squeaked by on white crepe-soled shoes. His door was ajar, and on the far wall of the corridor outside he could read the letters NSIVE CA and guessed that the whole sign must read INTENSIVE CARE.

There was movement in the room—a rustle of bedclothes.

Moving very carefully, Morris turned his head to the right, away from the door. He saw a night-table next to him with a pitcher of water on it. There were two call-buttons on the table. Beyond it was another bed, and in the bed was a man who looked even older and sicker than Morris felt. He was not hooked into a giant exercise-wheel for gerbils like Morris was, but an IV feed stood beside his bed and some sort of monitoring console stood at its foot. The man's skin was sunken and yellow. Lines around his mouth and eyes had driven deep. His hair was yellowish-white, dry and lifeless. His thin eyelids had a bruised and shiny look, and in his big nose Morris saw the burst capillaries of the life-long drinker.

Morris looked away . . . and then looked back. As the dawn-light grew stronger and the hospital began to wake up, he began to have the strangest feeling that he knew his roommate. Could that be? The man looked to be somewhere between seventy-five and eighty, and Morris didn't believe he knew anyone quite that old—except for Lydia's mother, a horror Morris sometimes believed to be older than the Sphinx, whom the woman closely resembled.

Maybe the guy was someone he had known in the past, maybe even before he, Morris, came to America. Maybe. Maybe not. And why all of a sudden did it seem to matter? For that matter, why had all his memories of the camp, of Patin, come flooding back tonight, when he always tried to—and most times succeeded in—keeping those things buried?

He broke out in a sudden rash of gooseflesh, as if he had stepped into some mental haunted house where old bodies were unquiet and old ghosts walked. Could that be, even here and now in this clean hospital, thirty years after those dark times had ended?

He looked away from the old man in the other bed, and soon he had begun to feel sleepy again.

It's a trick of your mind that this other man seems familiar. Only your mind, amusing you in the best way it can, amusing you the way it used to try to amuse you in—

But he would not think of that. He would not *allow* himself to think of that.

Drifting into sleep, he thought of a boast he had made to Ruth (but never to Lydia; it didn't pay to boast to Lydia; she was not like Ruth, who would always smile sweetly at his harmless puffing and crowing): *I never forget a face.* Here was his chance to find out if that was still so. If he had really known the man in the other bed at some time or other, perhaps he could remember when . . . and where.

Very close to sleep, drifting back and forth across its threshold, Morris thought: *Perhaps I knew him in the camp.*

That would be ironic indeed—what they called a "jest of God."

What God? Morris Heisel asked himself again, and slept.

19

Todd graduated salutatorian of his class, just possibly because of his poor grade on the trig final he had been studying for the night Dussander had his heart attack. It dragged his final grade in the course down to 89, one point below an A-minus average.

A week after graduation, the Bowdens went to visit Mr. Denker at Santo Donato General. Todd fidgeted through fifteen minutes of banalities and thank-yous and how-do-you-feels and was grateful for the break when the man in the other bed asked him if he could come over for a minute.

"You'll pardon me," the other man said apologetically. He was in a huge body-cast and was for some reason attached to an overhead system of pulleys and wires. "My name is Morris Heisel. I broke my back."

"That's too bad," Todd said gravely.

"*Oy,* too bad, he says! This boy has the gift of understatement!"

Todd started to apologize, but Heisel raised his hand, smiling a little. His face was pale and tired, the face of any old man in the hospital facing a life full of sweeping changes just ahead—and surely few of them for the better. In that way, Todd thought, he and Dussander were alike.

"No need," Morris said. "No need to answer a rude comment. You are a stranger. Does a stranger need to be inflicted with my problems?"

" 'No man is an island, entire of itself—' " Todd began, and Morris laughed.

"Donne, he quotes at me! A smart kid! Your friend there, is he very bad off?"

"Well, the doctors say he's doing fine, considering his age. He's eighty."

"That old!" Morris exclaimed. "He doesn't talk to me much,

you know. But from what he does say, I'd guess he's naturalized. Like me. I'm Polish, you know. Originally, I mean. From Radom."

"Oh?" Todd said politely.

"Yes. You know what they call an orange manhole cover in Radom?"

"No," Todd said, smiling.

"Howard Johnson's," Morris said, and laughed. Todd laughed, too. Dussander glanced over at them, startled by the sound and frowning a little. Then Monica said something and he looked back at her again.

"*Is* your friend naturalized?"

"Oh, yes," Todd said. "He's from Germany. Essen. Do you know that town?"

"No," Morris said, "but I was only in Germany once. I wonder if he was in the war."

"I really couldn't say." Todd's eyes had gone distant.

"No? Well, it doesn't matter. That was a long time ago, the war. In another three years there will be people in this country constitutionally eligible to become President—President!—who weren't even born until after the war was over. To them it must seem there is no difference between the Miracle of Dunkirk and Hannibal taking his elephants over the Alps."

"Were you in the war?" Todd asked.

"I suppose I was, in a manner of speaking. You're a good boy to visit such an old man . . . two old men, counting me."

Todd smiled modestly.

"I'm tired now," Morris said. "Perhaps I'll sleep."

"I hope you'll feel better very soon," Todd said.

Morris nodded, smiled, and closed his eyes. Todd went back to Dussander's bed, where his parents were just getting ready to leave—his dad kept glancing at his watch and exclaiming with bluff heartiness at how late it was getting.

• • •

Two days later, Todd came back to the hospital alone. This time, Morris Heisel, immured in his body-cast, was deeply asleep in the other bed.

"You did well," Dussander said quietly. "Did you go back to the house later?"

"Yes. I burned the damned letter. I don't think anyone was too interested in that letter, and I was afraid . . . I don't know." He shrugged, unable to tell Dussander he'd been almost superstitiously afraid about the letter—afraid that maybe someone would wander into the house who could read German, someone who would notice references in the letter that were ten, perhaps twenty years out of date.

"Next time you come, smuggle me in something to drink," Dussander said. "I find I don't miss the cigarettes, but—"

"I won't be back again," Todd said flatly. "Not ever. It's the end. We're quits."

"Quits." Dussander folded his hands on his chest and smiled. It was not a gentle smile . . . but it was perhaps as close as Dussander could come to such a thing. "I thought that was in the cards. They are going to let me out of this graveyard next week . . . or so they promise. The doctor says I may have a few years left in my skin yet. I ask him how many, and he just laughs. I suspect that means no more than three, and probably no more than two. Still, I may give him a surprise."

Todd said nothing.

"But between you and me, boy, I have almost given up my hopes of seeing the century turn."

"I want to ask you about something," Todd said, looking at Dussander steadily. 'That's why I came in today. I want to ask you about something you said once."

Todd glanced over his shoulder at the man in the other bed and then drew his chair closer to Dussander's bed. He could smell Dussander's smell, as dry as the Egyptian room in the museum.

"So ask."

"That wino. You said something about me having experience. First-hand experience. What was that supposed to mean?"

Dussander's smile widened a bit. "I read the newspapers, boy. Old men always read the newspapers, but not in the same way younger people do. Buzzards are known to gather at the ends of certain airport runways in South America when the crosswinds are treacherous, did you know that? That is how an old man reads the newspaper. A month ago there was a story in the Sunday paper. Not a front-page story, no one cares enough about bums and alcoholics to put them on the front page, but it was the lead story in the feature section, IS SOMEONE STALKING SANTO DONATO'S DOWN-AND-OUT?—that's what it was called. Crude. Yellow journalism. You Americans are famous for it."

Todd's hands were clenched into fists, hiding the butchered nails. He never read the Sunday papers, he had better things to do with his time. He had of course checked the papers every day for at least a week following each of his little adventures, and none of his stewbums had ever gotten beyond page three. The idea that someone had been making connections behind his back infuriated him.

"The story mentioned several murders, extremely brutal murders. Stabbings, bludgeonings. 'Subhuman brutality' was how the writer put it, but you know reporters. The writer of this lamentable piece admitted that there is a high death-rate among these unfortunates, and that Santo Donato has had more than its share of the indigent over the years. In any given year, not all of these men die naturally, or of their own bad habits. There are frequent murders. But in most cases the murderer is usually one of the deceased degenerate's compatriots, the motive no more than an argument over a penny-ante card-game or a bottle of muscatel. The killer is usually happy to confess. He is filled with remorse.

"But these recent killings have not been solved. Even more

ominous, to this yellow journalist's mind—or whatever passes for his mind—is the high disappearance rate over the last few years. Of course, he admits again, these men are not much more than modern-day hoboes. They come and go. But some of these left without picking up welfare checks or day-labor checks from Spell O' Work, which only pays on Fridays. Could some of these have been victims of this yellow journalist's Wino Killer, he asks? Victims who haven't been found? *Pah!*"

Dussander waved his hand in the air as if to dismiss such arrant irresponsibility.

"Only titillation, of course. Give people a comfortable little scare on Sunday morning. He calls up old bogies, threadbare but still useful—the Cleveland Torso Murderer, Zodiac, the mysterious Mr. X who killed the Black Dahlia, Springheel Jack. Such drivel. But it makes me think. What does an old man have to do but think when old friends don't come to visit anymore?"

Todd shrugged.

"I thought: 'If I wished to help this odious yellow-dog journalist, which I certainly do not, I could explain some of the disappearances. Not the corpses found stabbed or bludgeoned, not *them,* God rest their besotted souls, but some of the disappearances. Because at least some of the bums who disappeared are in my cellar.' "

"How many down there?" Todd asked in a low voice.

"Six," Dussander said calmly. "Counting the one you helped me dispose of, six."

"You're really nutso," Todd said. The skin below his eyes had gone white and shiny. "At some point you just blew all your fucking wheels."

" 'Blew my wheels.' What a charming idiom! Perhaps you're right! But then I said to myself: 'This newspaper jackal would love to pin the murders and the disappearances on the same somebody—his hypothetical Wino Killer.' But I think maybe that's not what happened at all.

"Then I say to myself: 'Do I know anybody who might be doing such things? Somebody who has been under as much strain as I have during the last few years? Someone who has also been listening to old ghosts rattle their chains?' And the answer is yes. I know *you,* boy."

"I've never killed anyone."

The image that came was not of the winos; they weren't people, not really people at all. The image that came was of himself crouched behind the dead tree, peering through the telescopic sight of his .30-.30, the crosshairs fixed on the temple of the man with the scuzzy beard, the man driving the Brat pickup.

"Perhaps not," Dussander agreed, amicably enough. "Yet you took hold so well that night. Your surprise was mostly anger at having been put in such a dangerous position by an old man's infirmity, I think. Am I wrong?"

"No, you're not wrong," Todd said. "I was pissed off at you and I still am. I covered it up for you because you've got something in a safety deposit box that could destroy my life."

"No. I do not."

"What? What are you talking about?"

"It was as much a bluff as your 'letter left with a friend.' You never wrote such a letter, there never was such a friend, and I have never written a single word about our . . . association, shall I call it? Now I lay my cards on the table. You saved my life. Never mind that you acted only to protect yourself; that does not change how speedily and efficiently you acted. I cannot hurt you, boy. I tell you that freely. I have looked death in the face and it frightens me, but not as badly as I thought it would. There is no document. It is as you say: we are quits."

Todd smiled: a weird upward corkscrewing of the lips. A strange, sardonic light danced and fluttered in his eyes.

"Herr Dussander," he said, "if only I could believe that."

In the evening Todd walked down to the slope overlooking the freeway, climbed down to the dead tree, and sat on it. It was just past twilight. The evening was warm. Car headlights cut through the dusk in long yellow daisy chains.

There is no document.

He hadn't realized how completely irretrievable the entire situation was until the discussion that had followed. Dussander suggested Todd search the house for a safety deposit key, and when he didn't find one, that would prove there was no safety deposit box and hence no document. But a key could be hidden anywhere—it could be put in a Crisco can and then buried, it could be put in a Sucrets tin and slid behind a board that had been loosened and then replaced; he might even have ridden the bus to San Diego and put it behind one of the rocks in the decorative stone wall which surrounded the bears' environmental area. For that matter, Todd went on, Dussander could even have thrown the key away. Why not? He had only needed it once, to put his written documents in. If he died, someone else would take it out.

Dussander nodded reluctantly at this, but after a moment's thought he made another suggestion. When he got well enough to go home, he would have the boy call every single bank in Santo Donato. He would tell each bank official he was calling for his grandfather. Poor grandfather, he would say, had grown lamentably senile over the last two years, and now he had misplaced the key to his safety deposit box. Even worse, he could no longer remember which bank the box was in. Could they just check their files for an Arthur Denker, no middle initial? And when Todd drew a blank at every bank in town—

Todd was already shaking his head again. First, a story like that was almost guaranteed to raise suspicions. It was too pat. They would probably suspect a con-game and get in touch with the police. Even if every one of them bought the story, it would do no good. If none of the almost nine dozen banks in Santo Donato had a box in the Denker name, it didn't mean that Dussander hadn't rented one in San Diego, L.A., or any town in between.

At last Dussander gave up.

"You have all the answers, boy. All, at least, but one. What would I stand to gain by lying to you? I invented this story to protect myself from you—that is a motive. Now I am trying to uninvent it. What possible gain do you see in that?"

Dussander got laboriously up on one elbow.

"For that matter, why would I need a document at all, at this point? I could destroy your life from this hospital bed, if that was what I wanted. I could open my mouth to the first passing doctor, they are all Jews, they would all know who I am, or at least who I was. But why would I do this? You are a fine student. You have a fine career ahead of you . . . unless you get careless with those winos of yours."

Todd's face froze. "I told you—"

"I know. You never heard of them, you never touched so much as a hair on their scaly, tick-ridden heads, all right, good, fine. I say no more about it. Only tell me, boy: why should I lie about this? We are quits, you say. But I tell you we can only be quits if we can trust each other."

Now, sitting behind the dead tree on the slope which ran down to the freeway, looking at all the anonymous headlights disappearing endlessly like slow tracer bullets, he knew well enough what he was afraid of.

Dussander talking about trust. That made him afraid.

The idea that Dussander might be tending a small but perfect flame of hatred deep in his heart, that made him afraid, too.

A hatred of Todd Bowden, who was young, clean-featured, unwrinkled; Todd Bowden, who was an apt pupil with a whole bright life stretching ahead of him.

But what he feared most was Dussander's refusal to use his name.

Todd. What was so hard about that, even for an old kraut whose teeth were mostly false? *Todd.* One syllable. Easy to say.

Put your tongue against the roof of your mouth, drop your teeth a little, replace your tongue, and it was out. Yet Dussander had always called him "boy." Only that. Contemptuous. *Anonymous.* Yes, that was it, anonymous. As anonymous as a concentration camp serial number.

Perhaps Dussander *was* telling the truth. No, not just perhaps; *probably.* But there were those fears . . . the worst of them being Dussander's refusal to use his name.

And at the root of it all was his own inability to make a hard and final decision. At the root of it all was a rueful truth: even after four years of visiting Dussander, he still didn't know what went on in the old man's head. Perhaps he wasn't such an apt pupil after all.

Cars and cars and cars. His fingers itched to hold his rifle. How many could he get? Three? Six? An even baker's dozen? And how many miles to Babylon?

He stirred restlessly, uneasily.

Only Dussander's death would tell the final truth, he supposed. Sometime during the next five years, maybe even sooner. Three to five . . . it sounded like a prison sentence. *Todd Bowden, this court hereby sentences you to three to five for associating with a known war criminal. Three to five at bad dreams and cold sweats.*

Sooner or later Dussander would simply drop dead. Then the waiting would begin. The knot in the stomach every time the phone or the doorbell rang.

He wasn't sure he could stand that.

His fingers itched to hold the gun and Todd curled them into fists and drove both fists into his crotch. Sick pain swallowed his belly and he lay for some time afterwards in a writhing ball on the ground, his lips pulled back in a silent shriek. The pain was dreadful, but it blotted out the endless parade of thoughts.

At least for awhile.

20

For Morris Heisel, that Sunday was a day of miracles.

The Atlanta Braves, his favorite baseball team, swept a double-header from the high and mighty Cincinnati Reds by scores of 7-1 and 8-0. Lydia, who boasted smugly of always taking care of herself and whose favorite saying was "An ounce of prevention is worth a pound of cure," slipped on her friend Janet's wet kitchen floor and sprained her hip. She was at home in bed. It wasn't serious, not at all, and thank God (what God) for that, but it meant she wouldn't be able to visit him for at least two days, maybe as long as four.

Four days without Lydia! Four days that he wouldn't have to hear about how she had warned him that the stepladder was wobbly and how he was up too high on it in the bargain. Four days when he wouldn't have to listen to her tell him how she'd always said the Rogans' pup was going to cause them grief, always chasing Lover Boy that way. Four days without Lydia asking him if he wasn't glad now that she had kept after him about sending in that insurance application, for if she had not, they would surely be on their way to the poorhouse now. Four days without having Lydia tell him that many people lived perfectly normal lives—almost, anyway—paralyzed from the waist down; why, every museum and gallery in the city had wheelchair ramps as well as stairs, and there were even special busses. After the observation, Lydia would smile bravely and then inevitably burst into tears.

Morris drifted off into a contented late afternoon nap.

When he woke up it was half-past five in the afternoon. His roommate was asleep. He still hadn't placed Denker, but all the same he felt sure that he had known the man at some time or other. He had begun to ask Denker about himself once or twice, but then something kept him from making more than the most banal conversation with the man—the weather, the last earthquake, the next earthquake, and yeah, the *Guide* says Myron Floren is going to come back for a special guest appearance this weekend on the Welk show.

Morris told himself he was holding back because it gave him a mental game to play, and when you were in a bodycast from your shoulders to your hips, mental games can come in handy. If you had a little mental contest going on, you didn't have to spend quite so much time wondering how it was going to be, pissing through a catheter for the rest of your life.

If he came right out and asked Denker, the mental game would probably come to a swift and unsatisfying conclusion. They would narrow their pasts down to some common experience—a train trip, a boat ride, possibly even the camp. Denker might have been in Patin; there had been plenty of German Jews there.

On the other hand, one of the nurses had told him Denker would probably be going home in a week or two. If Morris couldn't figure it out by then, he would mentally declare the game lost and ask the man straight out: *Say, I've had the feeling I know you—*

But there was more to it than just that, he admitted to himself. There was something in his feelings, a nasty sort of undertow, that made him think of that story "The Monkey's Paw," where every wish had been granted as the result of some evil turn of fate. The old couple who came into possession of the paw wished for a hundred dollars and received it as a gift of condolence when their only son was killed in a nasty mill accident. Then the mother had wished for the son to return to them. They had heard footsteps dragging up their walk shortly afterward; then pounding on the door. The mother, mad with joy, had gone rushing down the stairs to let in her only child. The father, mad with fear, scrabbled through the darkness for the dried paw, found it at last, and wished his son dead again. The mother threw the door open a moment later and found nothing on the stoop but an eddy of night wind.

In some way Morris felt that perhaps he *did* know where he and Denker had been acquainted, but that his knowledge was like the son of the old couple in the story—returned from the grave, but not as he was in his mother's memory; returned, instead, horribly crushed and mangled from his fall into the gnashing, whirling machinery. He felt that his knowledge of Denker might be a subconscious thing, pounding on the door between that area of his mind and that of rational understanding and recognition, demanding admittance . . . and that another part of him was searching frantically for the monkey's paw, or its psychological equivalent; for the talisman that would wish away the knowledge forever.

Now he looked at Denker, frowning.

Denker, Denker, Where have I known you, Denker? Was it Patin? Is that why I don't want to know? But surely, two survivors of a common horror do not have to be afraid of each other. Unless, of course . . .

He frowned. He felt very close to it, suddenly, but his feet were tingling, breaking his concentration, annoying him. They were tingling in just the way a limb tingles when you've slept on it and it's returning to normal circulation. If it wasn't for the damned body-cast, he could sit up and rub his feet until that tingle went away. He could—

Morris's eyes widened.

For a long time he lay perfectly still, Lydia forgotten, Denker forgotten, Patin forgotten, *everything* forgotten except that tingly feeling in his feet. Yes, *both* feet, but it was stronger in the right one. When you felt that tingle, you said *My foot went to sleep.*

But what you really meant, of course, was *My foot is waking up.*

Morris fumbled for a call-button. He pressed it again and again until the nurse came.

The nurse tried to dismiss it—she had had hopeful patients before. His doctor wasn't in the building, and the nurse didn't want to call him at home. Dr. Kemmelman had a vast reputation for evil temper . . . especially when he was called at home.

Morris wouldn't let her dismiss it. He was a mild man, but now he was prepared to make more than a fuss; he was prepared to make an uproar if that's what it took. The Braves had taken two. Lydia had sprained her hip. But good things came in threes, everyone knew that.

At last the nurse came back with an intern, a young man named Dr. Timpnell whose hair looked as if it had been cut by a Lawn Boy with very dull blades. Dr. Timpnell pulled a Swiss Army knife from the pocket of his white pants, folded out the Phillips screwdriver attachment, and ran it from the toes of Morris's right foot down to the heel. The foot did not curl, but his toes twitched—it was an obvious twitch, too definite to miss. Morris burst into tears.

Timpnell, looking rather dazed, sat beside him on the bed and patted his hand.

"This sort of thing happens from time to time," he said (possibly from his wealth of practical experience, which stretched back perhaps as far as six months). "No doctor predicts it, but it *does* happen. And apparently it's happened to you."

Morris nodded through his tears.

"Obviously, you're not totally paralyzed." Timpnell was still patting his hand. "But I wouldn't try to predict if your recovery will be slight, partial, or total. I doubt if Dr. Kemmelman will, either. I suspect you'll have to undergo a lot of physical therapy, and not all of it will be pleasant. But it will be more pleasant than . . . you know."

"Yes," Morris said through his tears. "I know. Thank God!" He remembered telling Lydia there was no God and felt his face fill up with hot blood.

"I'll see that Dr. Kemmelman is informed," Timpnell said, giving Morris's hand a final pat and rising.

"Could you call my wife?" Morris asked. Because, doomcrying and hand-wringing aside, he felt *something* for her. Maybe it was even love, an emotion which seemed to have little to do with sometimes feeling like you could wring a person's neck.

"Yes, I'll see that it's done. Nurse, would you—?"

"Of course, doctor," the nurse said, and Timpnell could barely stifle his grin.

"Thank you," Morris said, wiping his eyes with a Kleenex from the box on the nightstand. "Thank you very much."

Timpnell went out. At some point during the discussion, Mr. Denker had awakened. Morris considered apologizing for all the noise, or perhaps for his tears, and then decided no apology was necessary.

"You are to be congratulated, I take it," Mr. Denker said.

"We'll see," Morris said, but like Timpnell, he was barely able to stifle his grin. "We'll see."

"Things have a way of working out," Denker replied vaguely, and then turned on the TV with the remote control device. It was now quarter to six, and they watched the last of *Hee Haw.* It was followed by the evening news. Unemployment was worse. Inflation was not so bad. Billy Carter was thinking about going into the beer business. A new Gallup poll showed that, if the election were to be held right then, there were four Republican candidates who could beat Billy's brother Jimmy. And there had been racial incidents following the murder of a black child in Miami. "A night of violence," the newscaster called it. Closer to home, an unidentified man had been found in an orchard near Highway 46, stabbed and bludgeoned.

Lydia called just before six-thirty. Dr. Kemmelman had called her and, based on the young intern's report, he had been cautiously optimistic. Lydia was cautiously joyous. She vowed to come in the following day even if it killed her. Morris told her he loved her. Tonight he loved everyone—Lydia, Dr. Timpnell with his Lawn Boy haircut, Mr. Denker, even the young girl who brought in the supper trays as Morris hung up.

Supper was hamburgers, mashed potatoes, a carrots-and-peas combination, and small dishes of ice cream for dessert. The candy striper who served it was Felice, a shy blonde girl of perhaps twenty. She had her own good news—her boyfriend had landed a job as a computer programmer with IBM and had formally asked her to marry him.

Mr. Denker, who exuded a certain courtly charm that all the young ladies responded to, expressed great pleasure. "Really, how wonderful. You must sit down and tell us all about it. Tell us everything. Omit nothing."

Felice blushed and smiled and said she couldn't do that. "We've still got the rest of the B Wing to do and C Wing after that. And look, here it is six-thirty!"

"Then tomorrow night, for sure. We insist . . . don't we, Mr. Heisel?"

"Yes, indeed," Morris murmured, but his mind was a million miles away.

(you must sit down and tell us all about it)

Words spoken in that exact-same bantering tone. He had heard them before; of that there could be no doubt. But had Denker been the one to speak them? *Had* he?

(tell us everything)

The voice of an urbane man. A cultured man. But there was a threat in the voice. A steel hand in a velvet glove. Yes.

Where?

(tell us everything, omit nothing.)

(? PATIN ?)

Morris Heisel looked at his supper. Mr. Denker had already fallen to with a will. The encounter with Felice had left him in the best of spirits—the way he had been after the young boy with the blonde hair came to visit him.

"A nice girl," Denker said, his words muffled by a mouthful of carrots and peas.

"Oh yes—

(you must sit down)

—Felice, you mean. She's

(and tell us all about it.)

very sweet."

(tell us everything, omit nothing.)

He looked down at his own supper, suddenly remembering how it got to be in the camps after awhile. At first you would have killed for a scrap of meat, no matter how maggoty or green with decay. But after awhile, that crazy hunger went away and your belly lay inside your middle like a small gray rock. You felt you would never be hungry again.

Until someone showed you food.

("tell us everything, my friend, omit nothing, you must sit down and tell us AAALLLLL about it.")

The main course on Morris's plastic hospital tray was hamburger. Why should it suddenly make him think of lamb? Not mutton, not chops—mutton was often stringy, chops often tough, and a person whose teeth had rotted out like old stumps would perhaps not be overly tempted by mutton or a chop. No, what he thought of now was a savory lamb stew, gravy-rich and full of vegetables. Soft tasty vegetables. Why think of lamp stew? Why, unless—

The door banged open. It was Lydia, her face rosy with smiles. An aluminum crutch was propped in her armpit and she was walking like Marshal Dillon's friend Chester. *"Morris!"* she trilled. Trailing her and looking just as tremulously happy was Emma Rogan from next door.

Mr. Denker, startled, dropped his fork. He cursed softly under his breath and picked it up off the floor with a wince.

"It's so *WONDERFUL*!" Lydia was almost baying with excitement. "I called Emma and asked her if we could come tonight instead of tomorrow, I had the crutch already, and I said, 'Em,' I said, 'if I can't bear this agony for Morris, what kind of wife am I to him?' Those were my very words, weren't they, Emma?"

Emma Rogan, perhaps remembering that her collie pup had caused at least some of the problem, nodded eagerly.

"So I called the hospital," Lydia said, shrugging her coat off and settling in for a good long visit, "and *they* said it was past visiting hours but in my case they would make an exception, except we couldn't stay too long because we might bother Mr. Denker. We aren't bothering you, are we, Mr. Denker?"

"No, dear lady," Mr. Denker said resignedly.

"Sit down, Emma, take Mr. Denker's chair, he's not using it. Here, Morris, stop with the ice cream, you're slobbering it all over yourself, just like a baby. Never mind, we'll have you up and around in no time. I'll feed it to you. Goo-goo, ga-ga. Open wide . . . over the teeth, over the gums . . . look out, stomach, here it comes! . . . No, don't say a word, Mommy knows best. Would you look at him, Emma, he hardly has any hair left and I don't wonder, thinking he might never walk again. It's God's mercy. I told him that stepladder was wobbly. I said, 'Morris,' I said, 'come down off there before—' "

She fed him ice cream and chattered for the next hour and by the time she left, hobbling ostentatiously on the crutch while Emma held her other arm, thoughts of lamb stew and voices echoing up through the years were the last things in Morris Heisel's mind. He was exhausted. To say it had been a busy day was putting it mildly. Morris fell deeply asleep.

He awoke sometime between 3:00 and 4:00 a.m. with a scream locked behind his lips.

Now he knew. He knew exactly where and exactly when he had been acquainted with the man in the other bed. Except his name had not been Denker *then.* Oh no, not at all.

He had awakened from the most terrible nightmare of his whole life. Someone had given him and Lydia a monkey's paw, and they had wished for money. Then, somehow, a Western Union boy in a Hitler Youth uniform had been in the room with them. He handed Morris a telegram which read: REGRET TO INFORM YOU BOTH DAUGHTERS DEAD STOP PATIN CONCENTRATION CAMP STOP GREATEST REGRETS AT THIS FINAL SOLUTION STOP COMMANDANT'S LETTER FOLLOWS STOP WILL TELL YOU EVERYTHING AND OMIT NOTHING STOP PLEASE ACCEPT OUR CHECK FOR 100 REICHMARKS

ON DEPOSIT YOUR BANK TOMORROW STOP SIGNED ADOLF HITLER CHANCELLOR.

A great wail from Lydia, and although she had never even seen Morris's daughters, she held the monkey's paw high and wished for them to be returned to life. The room went dark. And suddenly, from outside, came the sound of dragging, lurching footfalls.

Morris was down on his hands and knees in a darkness that suddenly stank of smoke and gas and death. He was searching for the paw. One wish left. If he could find the paw he could wish this dreadful dream away. He would spare himself the sight of his daughters, thin as scarecrows, their eyes deep wounded holes, their numbers burning on the scant flesh of their arms.

Hammering on the door.

In the nightmare, his search for the paw became ever more frenzied, but it bore no fruit. It seemed to go on for years. And then, behind him, the door crashed open. *No,* he thought. *I won't look. I'll close my eyes. Rip them from my head if I have to, but I won't look.*

But he did look. He had to look. In the dream it was as if huge hands had grasped his head and wrenched it around.

It was not his daughters standing in the doorway; it was Denker. A much younger Denker, a Denker who wore a Nazi SS uniform, the cap with its death's-head insignia cocked rakishly to one side. His buttons gleamed heartlessly, his boots were polished to a killing gloss.

Clasped in his arms was a huge and slowly bubbling pot of lamb stew.

And the dream-Denker, smiling his dark, suave smile, said: *You must sit down and tell us all about it—as one friend to another,* hein? *We have heard that gold has been hidden. That tobacco has been hoarded. That it was not food-poisoning with Schneibel at all but powdered glass in his supper two nights ago. You must not insult our intelligence by pretending you know nothing. You knew EVERYTHING. So tell it all. Omit nothing.*

And in the dark, smelling the maddening aroma of the stew, he told them everything. His stomach, which had been a small gray rock, was now a ravening tiger. Words spilled helplessly from his lips. They spewed from him in the senseless sermon of a lunatic, truth and falsehood all mixed together.

Brodin has his mother's wedding ring taped below his scrotum!

("you must sit down")

Laslo and Herman Dorksy have talked about rushing guard tower number three!

("and tell us everything!")

Rachel Tannenbaum's husband has tobacco, he gave the guard who comes on after Zeickert, the one they call Booger-Eater because he is always picking his nose and then putting his fingers in his mouth. Tannenbaum, some of it to Booger-Eater so he wouldn't take his wife's pearl earrings!

("oh that makes no sense no sense at all you've mixed up two different stories I think but that's all right quite all right we'd rather have you mix up two stories than omit one completely you must omit NOTHING!")

There is a man who has been calling out his dead son's name in order to get double rations!

("tell us his name")

I don't know it but I can point him out to you please yes I can show him to you I will I will I will I

("tell us everything you know")

will I will I will I will I will I will I will I

Until he swam up into consciousness with a scream in his throat like fire.

Trembling uncontrollably, he looked at the sleeping form in the other bed. He found himself staring particularly at the wrinkled, caved-in mouth. Old tiger with no teeth. Ancient and vicious rogue elephant with one tusk gone and the other rotted loose in its socket. Senile monster.

"Oh my *God,*" Morris Heisel whispered. His voice was high and faint, inaudible to anyone but himself. Tears trickled down his cheeks toward his ears. "Oh dear *God,* the man who murdered my wife and my daughters is sleeping in the same room with me, my *God,* oh dear dear *God,* he is here with me now in this room."

The tears began to flow faster now—tears of rage and horror, hot, scalding.

He trembled and waited for morning, and morning did not come for an age.

21

The next day, Monday, Todd was up at six o'clock in the morning and poking listlessly at a scrambled egg he had fixed for himself when his father came down still dressed in his monogrammed bathrobe and slippers.

"Mumph," he said to Todd, going past him to the refrigerator for orange juice.

Todd grunted back without looking up from his book, one of the 87th Squad mysteries. He had been lucky enough to land a summer job with a landscaping outfit that operated out of Pasadena. That would have been much too far to commute ordinarily, even if one of his parents had been willing to loan him a car for the summer (neither was), but his father was working on-site not far from there, and he was able to drop Todd off at a bus stop on his way and pick him up at the same place on his way back. Todd was less than wild about the arrangement; he didn't like riding home from work with his father and absolutely detested riding to work with him in the morning. It was in the mornings that he felt the most naked, when the wall between what he was and what he might be seemed the thinnest. It was worse after a night of bad dreams, but even if no dreams had come in the night, it was bad. One morning he realized with a fright so suddenly it was almost terror that he had been seriously considering reaching across his father's briefcase, grabbing the wheel of the Porsche, and sending them corkscrewing into the two express lanes, cutting a swath of destruction through the morning commuters.

"You want another egg, Todd-O?"

"No thanks, Dad." Dick Bowden ate them fried. How could anyone stand to eat a fried egg? On the grill of the Jenn-Air for two minutes, then over easy. What you got on your plate at the end looked like a giant dead eye with a cataract over it, an eye that would bleed orange when you poked it with your fork.

He pushed his scrambled egg away. He had barely touched it.

Outside, the morning paper slapped the step.

His father finished cooking, turned off the grill, and came to the table. "Not hungry this morning, Todd-O?"

You call me that one more time and I'm going to stick my knife right up your fucking nose . . . Dad-O.

"Not much appetite, I guess."

Dick grinned affectionately at his son; there was still a tiny dab of shaving cream on the boy's right ear. "Betty Trask stole your appetite. That's my guess."

"Yeah, maybe that's it." He offered a wan smile that vanished as soon as his father went down the stairs from the breakfast nook to get the paper. *Would it wake you up if I told you what a cunt she is, Dad-O? How about if I said, "Oh, by the way, did you know your good friend Ray Trask's daughter is one of the biggest sluts in Santo Donato? She'd kiss her own twat if she was double-jointed, Dad-O. That's how much she thinks of it. Just a stinking little slut. Two lines of coke and she's yours for the night. And if you don't happen to have any coke, she's still yours for the night. She'd fuck a dog if she couldn't get a man." Think that'd wake you up, Dad-O? Get you a flying start on the day?*

He pushed the thoughts back away viciously, knowing they wouldn't stay gone.

His father came back with the paper. Todd glimpsed the headline: SPACE SHUTTLE WON'T FLY, EXPERT SAYS.

Dick sat down. "Betty's a fine-looking girl," he said. "She reminds me of your mother when I first met her."

"Is that so?"

"Pretty . . . young . . . fresh . . ." Dick Bowden's eyes had gone vague. Now they came back, focusing almost anxiously on his son. "Not that your mother isn't still a fine-looking woman. But at that age a girl has a certain . . . glow, I guess you'd say. It's there for awhile, and then it's gone." He shrugged and opened the paper. "*C'est la vie,* I guess."

She's a bitch in heat. Maybe that's what makes her glow.

"You're treating her right, aren't you, Todd-O?" His father was making his usual rapid trip through the paper toward the sports pages. "Not getting too fresh?"

"Everything's cool, Dad."

(if he doesn't stop pretty soon I'll I'll do something, scream, throw his coffee in his face, something.)

"Ray thinks you're a fine boy," Dick said absently. He had at last reached the sports. He became absorbed. There was blessed silence at the breakfast table.

Betty Trask had been all over him the very first time they went out. He had taken her to the local lovers' lane after the movie because he knew it would be expected of them; they could swap spits for half an hour or so and have all the right things to tell their respective friends the next day. She could roll her eyes and tell how she had fought off his advances—boys were so tiresome, really, and she never fucked on the first date, she wasn't that kind of girl. Her friends would agree and then all of them would troop into the girls' room and do whatever it was they did in there—put on fresh makeup, smoke Tampax, whatever.

And for a guy . . . well, you had to make out. You had to get at least to second base and try for third. Because there were reputations and reputations. Todd couldn't have cared less about having a stud reputation; he only wanted a reputation for being normal. And if you didn't at least *try,* word got around. People started to wonder if you were all right.

So he took them up on Jane's Hill, kissed them, felt their

tits, went a little further than that if they would allow it. And that was it. The girl would stop him, he would put up a little good-natured argument, and then take her home. No worries about what might be said in the girls' room the next day. No worries that anyone was going to think Todd Bowden was anything but normal. Except—

Except Betty Trask *was* the kind of girl who fucked on the first date. On every date. And in between dates.

The first time had been a month or so before the goddam Nazi's heart attack, and Todd thought he had done pretty well for a virgin . . . perhaps for the same reason a young pitcher will do well if he's tapped to throw the biggest game of the year with no forewarning. There had been no time to worry, to get all strung up about it.

Always before, Todd had been able to sense when a girl had made up her mind that on the next date she would just allow herself to be carried away. He was aware that he was personable and that both his looks and his prospects were good. The kind of boy their cunty mothers regarded as "a good catch." And when he sensed that physical capitulation about to happen, he would start dating some other girl. And whatever it said about his personality, Todd was able to admit to himself that if he ever started dating a truly frigid girl, he would probably be happy to date her for years to come. Maybe even marry her.

But the first time with Betty had gone fairly well—*she* was no virgin, even if he was. She had to help him get his cock into her, but she seemed to take that as a matter of course. And halfway through the act itself she had gurgled up from the blanket they were lying on: "I just *love* to fuck!" It was the tone of voice another girl might have used to express her love for strawberry whirl ice cream.

Later encounters—there had been five of them (five and a half, he supposed, if you wanted to count last night)—hadn't been so good. They had, in fact, gotten worse at what seemed an exponential rate . . . although he didn't believe even now that Betty had been aware of that (at least not until last night). In fact, quite the opposite. Betty apparently believed she had found the battering-ram of her dreams.

Todd hadn't felt any of the things he was supposed to feel at a time like that. Kissing her lips was like kissing warm but uncooked liver. Having her tongue in his mouth only made him wonder what kind of germs she was carrying, and sometimes he thought he could smell her fillings—an unpleasant metallic odor, like chrome. Her breasts were bags of meat. No more.

Todd had done it twice more with her before Dussander's heart attack. Each time he had more trouble getting erect. In both cases he had finally succeeded by using a fantasy. She was stripped naked in front of all their friends. Crying. Todd was forcing her to walk up and down before them while he cried out: *Show your tits! Let them see your snatch, you cheap slut! Spread your cheeks! That's right, bend over and SPREAD them!*

Betty's appreciation was not at all surprising. He was a good lover, not in spite of his problems but because of them. Getting hard was only the first step. Once you achieved erection, you had to have an orgasm. The fourth time they had done it—this was three days after Dussander's heart attack—he had pounded away at her for over ten minutes. Betty Trask thought she had died and gone to heaven; she had three orgasms and was trying for a fourth when Todd recalled an old fantasy . . . what was, in fact, the First Fantasy. The girl on the table, clamped and helpless. The huge dildo. The rubber squeeze-bulb. Only now, desperate and sweaty and almost insane with his desire to come and get this horror over with, the face of the girl on the table became Betty's face. That brought on a joyless, rubbery spasm that he supposed was, technically, at least, an orgasm. A moment later Betty was whispering in his ear, her breath warm and redolent of Juicy Fruit gum: "Lover, you do me any old time. Just call me."

Todd had nearly groaned aloud.

The nub of his dilemma was this: Wouldn't his reputation suffer if he broke off with a girl who obviously wanted to put out for him? Wouldn't people wonder why? Part of him said they would not. He remembered walking down the hall behind two senior boys during his freshman year and hearing one of them tell the other he had broken off with his girlfriend. The other wanted to know why. "Fucked 'er out," the first said, and both of them bellowed goatish laughter.

If someone asks me why I dropped her, I'll just say I fucked her out. But what if she says we only did it five times? Is that enough? What? . . . How much? . . . How many? . . . Who'll talk? . . . What'll they say?

So his mind ran on, as restless as a hungry rat in an insoluble maze. He was vaguely aware that he was turning a minor problem into a big problem, and that this very inability to solve the problem had something to say about how shaky he had gotten. But knowing it brought him no fresh ability to change his behavior, and he sank into a black depression.

College. College was the answer. College offered an excuse to break with Betty that no one could question. But September seemed so far away.

The fifth time it had taken him almost twenty minutes to get hard, but Betty had proclaimed the experience well worth the wait. And then, last night, he hadn't been able to perform at all.

"What are you, anyway?" Betty had asked petulantly. After twenty minutes of manipulating his lax penis, she was dishevelled and out of patience. "Are you one of those AC/DC guys?"

He very nearly strangled her on the spot. And if he'd had his .30-.30—

"Well, I'll be a son of a *gun*! Congratulations, son!"

"Huh?" He looked up and out of his black study.

"You made the Southern Cal High School All-Stars!" His father was grinning with pride and pleasure.

"Is that so?" For a moment he hardly knew what his father

was talking about; he had to grope for the meaning of the words. "Say, yeah, Coach Haines mentioned something to me about that at the end of the year. Said he was putting me and Billy DeLyons up. I never expected anything to happen."

"Well Jesus, you don't seem very excited about it!"

"I'm still trying

(who gives a ripe fuck?)

to get used to the idea." With a huge effort, he managed a grin. "Can I see the article?"

His father handed the paper across the table to Todd and got to his feet. "I'm going to wake Monica up. She's got to see this before we leave."

No, God—I can't face both of them this morning.

"Aw, don't do that. You know she won't be able to get back to sleep if you wake her up. We'll leave it for her on the table."

"Yes, I suppose we could do that. You're a damned thoughtful boy, Todd." He clapped Todd on the back, and Todd squeezed his eyes closed. At the same time he shrugged his shoulders in an aw-shucks gesture that made his father laugh. Todd opened his eyes again and looked at the paper.

4 BOYS NAMED TO SOUTHERN CAL ALL-STARS, the headline read. Beneath were pictures of them in their uniforms—the catcher and left-fielder from Fairview High, the harp southpaw from Mountford, and Todd to the far right, grinning openly out at the world from beneath the bill of his baseball cap. He read the story and saw that Billy DeLyons had made the second squad. That, at least, was something to feel happy about. DeLyons could claim he was a Methodist until his tongue fell out, if it made him feel good, but he wasn't fooling Todd. He knew perfectly well what Billy DeLyons was. Maybe he ought to introduce him to Betty Trask, she was another sheeny. He had wondered about that for a long time, and last night he had decided for sure. The Trasks were passing for white. One look at her nose and that olive complexion—her old man's was even worse—and you knew. That was probably why he hadn't been

able to get it up. It was simple: his cock had known the difference before his brain. Who did they think they were kidding, calling themselves Trask?

"Congratulations again, son."

He looked up and first saw his father's hand stuck out, then his father's foolishly grinning face.

Your buddy Trask is a yid! he heard himself yelling into his father's face. *That's why I was impotent with his slut of a daughter last night! That's the reason!* Then, on the heels of that, the cold voice that sometimes came at moments like this rose up from deep inside him, shutting off the rising flood of irrationality, as if

(GET HOLD OF YOURSELF RIGHT NOW)

behind steel gates.

He took his father's hand and shook it. Smiled guilelessly into his father's proud face. Said: "Jeez, thanks, Dad."

They left that page of the newspaper folded back and a note for Monica, which Dick insisted Todd write and sign *Your All-Star Son, Todd.*

22

Ed French, aka "Pucker" French, aka Sneaker Pete and The Ked Man, *also* aka Rubber Ed French, was in the small and lovely seaside town of San Remo for a guidance counsellors' convention. It was a waste of time if ever there had been one—all guidance counsellors could ever agree on was not to agree on anything—and he grew bored with the papers, seminars, and discussion periods after a single day. Halfway through the second day, he discovered he was also bored with San Remo, and that of the adjectives small, lovely, and seaside, the *key* adjective was probably *small.* Gorgeous views and redwood trees aside, San Remo didn't have a movie theater or a bowling alley, and Ed hadn't wanted to go in the place's only bar—it had a dirt parking lot filled with pickup trucks, and most of the pickups had Reagan stickers on their rusty bumpers and tailgates. He wasn't afraid of being picked on, but he hadn't wanted to spend an evening looking at men in cowboy hats and listening to Loretta Lynn on the jukebox.

So here he was on the third day of a convention which stretched out over an incredible four days; here he was in room 217 of the Holiday Inn, his wife and daughter at home, the TV broken, an unpleasant smell hanging around in the bathroom. There was a swimming pool, but his eczema was so bad this summer that he wouldn't have been caught dead in a bathing suit. From the shins down he looked like a leper. He had an hour before the next workshop (Helping the Vocally Challenged Child—what they meant was doing something for kids who stuttered or who had cleft palates, but we wouldn't want to come right out and *say* that, Christ no, someone might lower our salaries), he had eaten lunch at San Remo's only restaurant, he didn't feel like a nap, and the TV's one station was showing a re-run of *Bewitched.*

So he sat down with the telephone book and began to flip through it aimlessly, hardly aware of what he was doing, wondering distantly if he knew anyone crazy enough about either small, lovely, or seaside to live in San Remo. He supposed this was what all the bored people in all the Holiday Inns all over the world ended up doing—looking for a forgotten friend or relative to call up on the phone. It was that, *Bewitched,* or the Gideon Bible. And if you did happen to get hold of somebody, what the hell did you say? "Frank! How the hell are you? And by the way, which was it—small, lovely, or seaside?" Sure. Right. Give that man a cigar and set him on fire.

Yet, as he lay on the bed flipping through the thin San Remo white pages and half-scanning the columns, it seemed to him that he *did* know somebody in San Remo. A book salesman? One of Sondra's nieces or nephews, of which there were marching battalions? A poker buddy from college? The relative of a student? That seemed to ring a bell, but he couldn't fine it down any more tightly.

He kept thumbing, and found he was sleepy after all. He had almost dozed off when it came to him and he sat up, wide-awake again.

Lord Peter!

They were re-running those Wimsey stories on PBS just lately—*Clouds of Witness, Murder Must Advertise, The Nine Tailors.* He and Sondra were hooked. A man named Ian Carmichael played Wimsey, and Sondra was nuts for him. So nuts, in fact, that Ed, who didn't think Carmichael looked like Lord Peter at all, actually became quite irritated.

"Sandy, the shape of his face is all wrong. And he's wearing false teeth, for heaven's sake!"

"Poo," Sondra had replied airily from the couch where she was curled up. "You're just jealous. He's so *handsome.*"

"Daddy's jealous, Daddy's jealous," little Norma sang, prancing around the living room in her duck pajamas.

"You should have been in bed an hour ago," Ed told her, gazing at his daughter with a jaundiced eye. "And if I keep noticing you're *here,* I'll probably remember that you aren't *there.*"

Little Norma was momentarily abashed. Ed turned back to Sondra.

"I remember back three or four years ago. I had a kid named Todd Bowden, and his grandfather came in for a conference. Now *that* guy looked like Wimsey. A very *old* Wimsey, but the shape of his face was right, and—"

"Wim-zee, Wim-zee, *Dim*-zee, *Jim*-zee," little Norma sang. "*Wim*-zee, *Bim*-zee, doodle-oodle-ooo-doo—"

"Shh, both of you," Sondra said. "I think he's the most *beautiful* man." Irritating woman!

But hadn't Todd Bowden's grandfather retired to San Remo? Sure. It had been on the forms. Todd had been one of the brightest boys in that year's class. Then, all at once, his grades had gone to hell. The old man had come in, told a familiar tale of marital difficulties, and had persuaded Ed to let the situation alone for awhile and see if things didn't straighten themselves out. Ed's view was that the old *laissez-faire* bit didn't work—if you told a teenage kid to root, hog, or die, he or she usually died. But the old man had been almost eerily persuasive (it was the resemblance to Wimsey, perhaps), and Ed had agreed to give Todd to the end of the next Flunk Card period. And damned if Todd hadn't pulled through. The old man must have gone right through the whole family and really kicked some ass, Ed thought. He looked like the type who not only could do it, but who might derive a certain dour pleasure from it. Then, just two days ago, he had seen Todd's picture in the paper—he had made the Southern Cal All-Stars in baseball. No mean feat when you consider that about five hundred boys were nominated each spring. He supposed he might never have come up with the grandfather's name if he hadn't seen the picture.

He flicked through the white pages more purposefully now, ran his finger down a column of fine type, and there it was. BOWDEN, VICTOR S. 403 Ridge Lane. Ed dialed the number and it rang several times at the other end. He was just about to hang up when an old man answered. "Hello?"

"Hello, Mr. Bowden. Ed French. From Santo Donato Junior High."

"Yes?" Politeness, but no more. Certainly no recognition. Well, the old guy was three years further along (weren't they all!) and things undoubtedly slipped his mind from time to time.

"Do you remember me, sir?"

"Should I?" Bowden's voice was cautious, and Ed smiled. The old man forgot things, but he didn't want anybody to know if he could help it. His own old man had been that way when his hearing started to go.

"I was your grandson Todd's guidance counsellor at S.D.J.H.S. I called to congratulate you. He sure tore up the pea-patch when he got to high school, didn't he? And now he's All-Conference to top it off. Wow!"

"Todd!" the old man said, his voice brightening immediately. "Yes, he certainly did a fine job, didn't he? Second in his class! And the girl who was ahead of him took the business courses." A sniff of disdain in the old man's voice. "My son called and offered to take me to Todd's commencement, but I'm in a wheelchair now. I broke my hip last January. I didn't want to go in a wheelchair. But I have his graduation picture right in the hall, you bet! Todd's made his parents very proud. And me, of course."

"Yes, I guess we got him over the hump," Ed said. He was smiling as he said it, but his smile was a trifle puzzled—somehow Todd's grandfather didn't sound the same. But it had been a long time ago, of course.

"Hump? What hump?"

"The little talk we had. When Todd was having problems with his course-work. Back in ninth."

"I'm not following you," the old man said slowly. "I would never presume to speak for Richard's son. It would cause trouble . . . ho-ho, you don't *know* how much trouble it would cause. You've made a mistake, young fellow."

"But—"

"Some sort of mistake. Got me confused with another student and another grandfather, I imagine."

Ed was moderately thunderstruck. For one of the few times in his life, he could not think of a single thing to say. If there was confusion, it sure wasn't on *his* part.

"Well," Bowden said doubtfully, "it was nice of you to call, Mr.—"

Ed found his tongue. "I'm right here in town, Mr. Bowden. It's a convention. Guidance counsellors. I'll be done around ten tomorrow morning, after the final paper is read. Could I come around to . . ." He consulted the phone book again. ". . . to Ridge Lane and see you for a few minutes?"

"What in the world for?"

"Just curiosity, I guess. It's all water over the dam now. But about three years ago, Todd got himself into a real crack with his grades. They were so bad I had to send a letter home with his report card requesting a conference with a parent, or, ideally, with both of his parents. What I got was his grandfather, a very pleasant man named Victor Bowden."

"But I've already told you—"

"Yes. I know. Just the same, I talked to *somebody* claiming to be Todd's grandfather. It doesn't matter much now, I suppose, but seeing is believing. I'd only take a few minutes of your time. It's all I *can* take, because I'm expected home by suppertime."

"Time is all I have," Bowden said, a bit ruefully. "I'll be here all day. You're welcome to stop in."

Ed thanked him, said goodbye, and hung up. He sat on the end of the bed, staring thoughtfully at the telephone. After awhile he got up and took a pack of Phillies Cheroots from the sport coat hanging on the back of the desk chair. He ought to go; there was a workshop, and if he wasn't there, he would be missed. He lit his Cheroot with a Holiday Inn match and dropped the burnt stub into a Holiday Inn ashtray. He went to the Holiday Inn window and looked blankly out into the Holiday Inn courtyard.

It doesn't matter much now, he had told Bowden, but it mattered to him. He wasn't used to being sold a bill of goods by one of his kids, and this unexpected news upset him. Technically he supposed it could still turn out to be a case of an old man's senility, but Victor Bowden hadn't sounded as if he was drooling in his beard yet. And, damn it, he didn't sound the *same.*

Had Todd Bowden jobbed him?

He decided it could have been done. Theoretically, at least. Especially by a bright boy like Todd. He could have jobbed *everyone,* not just Ed French. He could have forged his mother or father's name to the Flunk Cards he had been issued during his bad patch. Lots of kids discovered a latent forging ability when they got Flunk Cards. He could have used ink eradicator on his second- and third-quarter reports, changing the grades up for his parents and then back down again so that his home-room teacher wouldn't notice anything weird if he or she glanced at his card. The double application of eradicator would be visible to someone who was really looking, but home-room teachers carried an average of sixty students each. They were lucky if they could get the entire roll called before the first bell, let alone spot-checking returned cards for tampering.

As for Todd's final class standing, it would have dipped perhaps no more than three points overall—two bad marking periods out of a total of twelve. His other grades had been lopsidedly good enough to make up most of the difference. And how many parents drop by the school to look at the student records kept by the California Department of Education? Especially the parents of a bright student like Todd Bowden?

Frown lines appeared on Ed French's normally smooth forehead.

It doesn't matter much now. That was nothing but the truth. Todd's high school work had been exemplary; there was no way in the world you could fake a 94 percent. The boy was going on to Berkeley, the newspaper article had said, and Ed supposed his folks were damned proud—as they had every right to be. More and more it seemed to Ed that there was a vicious downside of American life, a greased skid of opportunism, cut corners, easy drugs, easy sex, a morality that grew cloudier each year. When your kid got through in standout style, parents had a right to be proud.

It doesn't matter much now—but who was his frigging grandfather?

That kept sticking into him. Who, indeed? Had Todd Bowden gone to the local branch of the Screen Actors' Guild and hung a notice on the bulletin board? YOUNG MAN IN

GRADES TROUBLE NEEDS OLDER MAN, PREF. 70-80 YRS., TO GIVE BOFFO PERFORMANCE AS GRANDFATHER, will pay union scale? Uh-uh. No way, José. And just what sort of adult would have fallen in with such a crazy conspiracy, and for what reason?

Ed French, aka Pucker, aka Rubber Ed, just didn't know. And because it didn't really matter, he stubbed out his Cheroot and went to his workshop. But his attention kept wandering.

The next day he drove out to Ridge Lane and had a long talk with Victor Bowden. They discussed grapes; they discussed the retail grocery business and how the big chain stores were pushing the little guys out; they discussed the political climate in southern California. Mr. Bowden offered Ed a glass of wine. Ed accepted with pleasure. He felt that he needed a glass of wine, even if it was only ten-forty in the morning. Victor Bowden looked as much like Peter Wimsey as a machine-gun looks like a shillelagh. Victor Bowden had no trace of the faint accent Ed remembered, and he was quite fat. The man who had purported to be Todd's grandfather had been whip-thin.

Before leaving, Ed told him: "I'd appreciate it if you wouldn't mention any of this to Mr. or Mrs. Bowden. There may be a perfectly reasonable explanation for all of it . . . and even if there isn't, it's all in the past."

"Sometimes," Bowden said, holding his glass of wine up to the sun and admiring its rich dark color, "the past don't rest so easy. Why else do people study history?"

Ed smiled uneasily and said nothing.

"But don't you worry. I never meddle in Richard's affairs. And Todd is a good boy. Salutatorian of his class . . . he must be a good boy. Am I right?"

"As rain," Ed French said heartily, and then asked for another glass of wine.

23

Dussander's sleep was uneasy; he lay in a trench of bad dreams.

They were breaking down the fence. Thousands, perhaps millions of them. They ran out of the jungle and threw themselves against the electrified barbed wire and now it was beginning to lean ominously inward. Some of the strands had given way and now coiled uneasily on the packed earth of the parade ground, squirting blue sparks. And still there was no end to them, no end. The Fuehrer was as mad as Rommel had claimed if he thought now—if he had ever *thought—there could be a final solution to this problem. There were billions of them; they filled the universe; and they were all after* him.

"Old man. Wake up, old man. Dussander. Wake up, old man, wake up."

At first he thought this was the voice of the dream.

Spoken in German; it had to be part of the dream. That was why the voice was so terrifying, of course. If he awoke he would escape it, so he swam upward . . .

The man was sitting by his bed on a chair that had been turned around backwards—a real man. "Wake up, old man," this visitor was saying. He was young—no more than thirty. His eyes were dark and studious behind plain steel-framed glasses. His brown hair was longish, collar-length, and for a confused moment Dussander thought it was the boy in a disguise. But this was not the boy, wearing a rather old-fashioned blue suit much too hot for the California climate. There was a small silver pin on the lapel of the suit. Silver, the metal you used to kill vampires and werewolves. It was a Jewish star.

"Are you speaking to me?" Dussander asked in German.

"Who else? Your roommate is gone."

"Heisel? Yes. He went home yesterday."

"Are you awake now?"

"Of course. But you've apparently mistaken me for someone

else. My name is Arthur Denker. Perhaps you have the wrong room."

"My name is Weiskopf. And yours is Kurt Dussander."

Dussander wanted to lick his lips but didn't. Just possibly this was still all part of the dream—a new phase, no more. *Bring me a wino and a steak-knife, Mr. Jewish Star in the Lapel, and I'll blow you away like smoke.*

"I know no Dussander," he told the young man. "I don't understand you. Shall I ring for the nurse?"

"You understand," Weiskopf said. He shifted position slightly and brushed a lock of hair from his forehead. The prosiness of this gesture dispelled Dussander's last hope.

"Heisel," Weiskopf said, and pointed at the empty bed.

"Heisel, Dussander, Weiskopf—none of these names mean anything to me."

"Heisel fell off a ladder while he was nailing a new gutter onto the side of his house," Weiskopf said. "He broke his back. He may never walk again. Unfortunate. But that was not the only tragedy of his life. He was an inmate of Patin, where he lost his wife and daughters. Patin, which you commanded."

"I think you are insane," Dussander said. "My name is Arthur Denker. I came to this country when my wife died. Before that I was—"

"Spare me your tale," Weiskopf said, raising a hand. "He had not forgotten your face. This face."

Weiskopf flicked a photograph into Dussander's face like a magician doing a trick. It was one of those the boy had shown him years ago. A young Dussander in a jauntily cocked SS cap, seated behind his desk.

Dussander spoke slowly, in English now, enunciating carefully.

"During the war I was a factory machinist. My job was to oversee the manufacture of drive-columns and power-trains for armored cars and trucks. Later I helped to build Tiger tanks. My reserve unit was called up during the battle of Berlin and

I fought honorably, if briefly. After the war I worked in Essen, at the Menschler Motor Works until—"

"—until it became necessary for you to run away to South America. With your gold that had been melted down from Jewish teeth and your silver melted down from Jewish jewelry and your numbered Swiss bank account. Mr. Heisel went home a happy man, you know. Oh, he had a bad moment when he woke up in the dark and realized with whom he was sharing a room. But he feels better now. He feels that God allowed him the sublime privilege of breaking his back so that he could be instrumental in the capture of one of the greatest butchers of human beings ever to live."

Dussander spoke slowly, enunciating carefully.

"During the war I was a factory machinist—"

"Oh, why not drop it? Your papers will not stand up to a serious examination. I know it and you know it. You are found out."

"My job was to oversee the manufacture of—"

"Of corpses! One way or another, you will be in Tel Aviv before the new year. The authorities are cooperating with us this time, Dussander. The Americans want to make us happy, and you are one of the things that will make us happy."

"—the manufacture of drive-columns and power-trains for armored cars and trucks. Later I helped to build Tiger tanks."

"Why be tiresome? Why drag it out?"

"My reserve unit was called up—"

"Very well then. You'll see me again. Soon."

Weiskopf rose. He left the room. For a moment his shadow bobbed on the wall and then that was gone, too. Dussander closed his eyes. He wondered if Weiskopf could be telling the truth about American cooperation. Three years ago, when oil was tight in America, he wouldn't have believed it. But the current upheaval in Iran might well harden American support for Israel. It was possible. And what did it matter? One way or the other, legal or illegal, Weiskopf and his colleagues would have him. On the subject of Nazis they were intransigent, and on the subject of the camps they were lunatics.

He was trembling all over. But he knew what he must do now.

24

The school records for the pupils who had passed through Santo Donato Junior High were kept in an old, rambling warehouse on the north side. It was not far from the abandoned trainyard. It was dark and echoing and it smelled of wax and polish and 999 Industrial Cleaner—it was also the school department's custodial warehouse.

Ed French got there around four in the afternoon with Norma in tow. A janitor let them in, told Ed what he wanted was on the fourth floor, and showed them to a creeping, clanking elevator that frightened Norma into an uncharacteristic silence.

She regained herself on the fourth floor, prancing and capering up and down the dim aisles of stacked boxes and files while Ed searched for and eventually found the files containing report cards from 1975. He pulled the second box and began to leaf through the B's. BORK. BOSTWICK. BOSWELL. BOWDEN, TODD. He pulled the card, shook his head impatiently over it in the dim light, and took it across to one of the high, dusty windows.

"Don't run around in here, honey," he called over his shoulder.

"Why, Daddy?"

"Because the trolls will get you," he said, and held Todd's card up to the light.

He saw it at once. This report card, in those files for three years now, had been carefully, almost professionally, doctored.

"Jesus Christ," Ed French muttered.

"Trolls, trolls, trolls!" Norma sang gleefully, as she continued to dance up and down the aisles.

25

Dussander walked carefully down the hospital corridor. He was still a bit unsteady on his legs. He was wearing his blue bathrobe over his white hospital johnny. It was night now, just after eight o'clock, and the nurses were changing shifts. The next half hour would be confused—he had observed that all the shift changes were confused. It was a time for exchanging notes, gossip, and drinking coffee at the nurses' station, which was just around the corner from the drinking fountain.

What he wanted was just across from the drinking fountain.

He was not noticed in the wide hallway, which at this hour reminded him of a long and echoing train station minutes before a passenger train departs. The walking wounded paraded slowly up and down, some dressed in robes as he was, others holding the backs of their johnnies together. Disconnected music came from half a dozen different transistor radios in half a dozen different rooms. Visitors came and went. A man laughed in one room and another man seemed to be weeping across the hall. A doctor walked by with his nose in a paperback novel.

Dussander went to the fountain, got a drink, wiped his mouth with his cupped hand, and looked at the closed door across the hall. This door was always locked—at least, that was the theory. In practice he had observed that it was sometimes both unlocked and unattended. Most often during the chaotic half hour when the shifts were changing and the nurses were gathered around the corner. Dussander had observed all of this with the trained and wary eye of a man who has been on the jump for a long, long time. He only wished he could observe the unmarked door for another week or so, looking for dangerous breaks in the pattern—he would only have the one chance. But he didn't have another week. His status as Werewolf in Residence might not become known for another two or three days, but it might happen tomorrow. He did not dare wait. When it came out, he would be watched constantly.

He took another small drink, wiped his mouth again, and looked both ways. Then, casually, with no effort at concealment, he stepped across the hall, turned the knob, and walked into the drug closet. If the woman in charge had happened to already be behind her desk, he was only nearsighted Mr. Denker. So sorry, dear lady, I thought it was the W.C. Stupid of me.

But the drug closet was empty.

He ran his eye over the top shelf at his left. Nothing but eyedrops and eardrops. Second shelf: laxatives, suppositories. On the third shelf he saw both Seconal and Veronal. He slipped a bottle of Seconals into the pocket of his robe. Then he went back to the door and stepped out without looking around, a puzzled smile on his face—that certainly wasn't the W.C., was it? *There* it was, right next to the drinking fountain. Stupid me!

He crossed to the door labelled men, went inside, and washed his hands. Then he went back down the hall to the semi-private room that was now completely private since the departure of the illustrious Mr. Heisel. On the table between the beds was a glass and a plastic pitcher filled with water. Pity there was no bourbon; really, it was a shame. But the pills would float him off just as nicely no matter how they were washed down.

"Morris Heisel, *salud,*" he said with a faint smile, and poured himself a glass of water. After all those years of jumping at shadows, of seeing faces that looked familiar on park benches or in restaurants or bus terminals, he had finally been recognized and turned in by a man he wouldn't have known from Adam. It was almost funny. He had barely spared Heisel two glances, Heisel and his broken back from God. On second thought, it wasn't *almost* funny; it was *very* funny.

He put three pills in his mouth, swallowed them with water, took three more, then three more. In the room across the hall he could see two old men hunched over a night-table, playing a grumpy game of cribbage. One of them had a hernia, Dussander knew. What was the other? Gallstones? Kidney stones? Tumor? Prostate? The horrors of old age. They were legion.

He refilled his water glass but didn't take any more pills right away. Too many could defeat his purpose. He might throw them up and they would pump the residue out of his stomach, saving him for whatever indignities the Americans and the Israelis could devise. He had no intention of trying to take his life stupidly, like a *Hausfrau* on a crying jag. When he began to get drowsy, he would take a few more. That would be fine.

The quavering voice of one of the cribbage players came to him, thin and triumphant: "A double run of three for eight . . . fifteens for twelve . . . and the right jack for thirteen. How do you like *those* apples?"

"Don't worry," the old man with the hernia said confidently. "I got first count. I'll peg out."

Peg out, Dussander thought, sleepy now. An apt enough phrase—but the Americans had a turn of idiom. *I don't give a tin shit, get hip or get out, stick it where the sun don't shine, money talks, nobody walks.* Wonderful idiom.

They thought they had him, but he was going to peg out before their very eyes.

He found himself wishing, of all absurd things, that he could leave a note for the boy. Wishing he could tell him to be very careful. To listen to an old man who had finally overstepped himself. He wished he could tell the boy that in the end he, Dussander, had come to respect him, even if he could never like him, and that talking to him had been better than listening to the run of his own thoughts. But any note, no matter how innocent, might cast suspicion on the boy, and Dussander did not want that. Oh, he would have a bad month or two, waiting for some government agent to show up and question him about a certain document that had been found in a safety deposit box rented to Kurt Dussander, aka Arthur Denker . . . but after a time, the boy would come to believe he had been telling the truth. There was no need for the boy to be touched by any of this, as long as he kept his head.

Dussander reached out with a hand that seemed to stretch for miles, got the glass of water, and took another three pills. He put the glass back, closed his eyes, and settled deeper into his soft, soft pillow. He had never felt so much like sleeping, and his sleep would be long. It would be restful.

Unless there were dreams.

The thought shocked him. *Dreams? Please God, no. Not those dreams. Not for eternity, not with all possibility of awakening gone. Not—*

In sudden terror, he tried to struggle awake. It seemed that hands were reaching eagerly up out of the bed to grab him, hands with hungry fingers.

(!NO!)

His thoughts broke up in a steepening spiral of darkness, and he rode down that spiral as if down a greased slide, down and down, to whatever dreams there are.

His overdose was discovered at 1:35 a.m., and he was pronounced dead fifteen minutes later. The nurse on duty was young and had been susceptible to elderly Mr. Denker's slightly ironic courtliness. She burst into tears. She was a Catholic, and she could not understand why such a sweet old man, who had been getting better, would want to do such a thing and damn his immortal soul to hell.

26

On Saturday morning in the Bowden household, nobody got up until at least nine. This morning at nine-thirty Todd and his father were reading at the table and Monica, who was a slow waker, served them scrambled eggs, juice, and coffee without speaking, still half in her dreams.

Todd was reading a paperback science fiction novel and Dick was absorbed in *Architectural Digest* when the paper slapped against the door.

"Want me to get it, Dad?"

"I will."

Dick brought it in, started to sip his coffee, and then choked on it as he got a look at the front page.

"Dick, what's wrong?" Monica asked, hurrying toward him.

Dick coughed out coffee that had gone down the wrong pipe, and while Todd looked at him over the top of the paperback in mild wonder, Monica started to pound him on the back. On the third stroke, her eyes fell to the paper's headline and she stopped in mid-stroke, as if playing statues. Her eyes widened until it seemed they might actually fall out onto the table.

"Holy God up in heaven!" Dick Bowden managed in a choked voice.

"Isn't that . . . I can't believe . . ." Monica began, and then stopped. She looked at Todd. "Oh, honey—"

His father was looking at him, too.

Alarmed now, Todd came around the table. "What's the matter?"

"Mr. Denker," Dick said—it was all he could manage.

Todd read the headline and understood everything. In dark letters it read: FUGITIVE NAZI COMMITS SUICIDE IN SANTO DONATO HOSPITAL. Below were two photos, side by side. Todd had seen both of them before. One showed Arthur Denker, six years younger and spryer. Todd knew it had been taken by a hippie street photographer, and that the old man had bought it only to make sure it didn't fall into the wrong hands by chance. The other photo showed an SS officer named Kurt Dussander behind his desk at Patin, his cap cocked to one side.

If they had the photograph the hippie had taken, they had been in his house.

Todd skimmed the article, his mind whizzing frantically. No mention of the winos. But the bodies would be found, and when they were, it would be a worldwide story, PATIN COMMANDANT NEVER LOST HIS TOUCH. HORROR IN NAZI'S BASEMENT. HE NEVER STOPPED KILLING.

Todd Bowden swayed on his feet.

Far away, echoing, he heard his mother cry sharply: "Catch him, Dick! He's fainting!"

The word

(faintingfaintingfainting)

repeated itself over and over. He dimly felt his father's arms grab him, and then for a little while Todd felt nothing, heard nothing at all.

27

Ed French was eating a danish when he unfolded the paper. He coughed, made a strange gagging sound, and spat dismembered pastry all over the table.

"Eddie!" Sondra French said with some alarm. "Are you okay?"

"Daddy's chokun, Daddy's chokun," little Norma proclaimed with nervous good humor, and then happily joined her mother in slamming Ed on the back. Ed barely felt the blows. He was still goggling down at the newspaper.

"What's wrong, Eddie?" Sondra asked again.

"Him! Him!" Ed shouted, stabbing his finger down at the paper so hard that his fingernail tore all the way through the A section.

"That man! Lord Peter!"

"What in God's name are you t—"

"That's Todd Bowden's grandfather!"

"What? That war criminal? Eddie, that's *crazy*!"

"But it's *him,*" Ed almost moaned. "Jesus Christ *Almighty,* that's *him*!"

Sondra French looked at the picture long and fixedly.

"He doesn't look like Peter Wimsey at all," she said finally.

28

Todd, pale as window-glass, sat on a couch between his mother and father.

Opposite them was a graying, polite police detective named Richler. Todd's father had offered to call the police, but Todd had done it himself, his voice cracking through the registers as it had done when he was fourteen.

He finished his recital. It hadn't taken long. He spoke with a mechanical colorlessness that scared the hell out of Monica. He was seventeen, true enough, but he was still a boy in so many ways. This was going to scar him forever.

"I read him . . . oh, I don't know. *Tom Jones. The Mill on the Floss.* That was a boring one. I didn't think we'd ever get through it. Some stories by Hawthorne—I remember he especially liked 'The Great Stone Face' and 'Young Goodman Brown.' We started *The Pickwick Papers,* but he didn't like it. He said Dickens could only be funny when he was being serious, and *Pickwick* was only kittenish. That was his word, kittenish. We got along the best with *Tom Jones.* We both liked that one."

"And that was three years ago," Richler said.

"Yes. I kept stopping in to see him when I got the chance, but in high school we were bussed across town . . . and some of the kids got up a scratch ballteam . . . there was more homework . . . you know . . . things just came up."

"You had less time."

"Less time, that's right. The work in high school was a lot harder . . . making the grades to get into college."

"But Todd is a very apt pupil," Monica said almost automatically. "He graduated salutatorian. We were so proud."

"I'll bet you were," Richler said with a warm smile. "I've got two boys in Fairview, down in the Valley, and they're just about able to keep their sports eligibility." He turned back to Todd. "You didn't read him any more books after you started high school?"

"No. Once in awhile I'd read him the paper. I'd come over and he'd ask me what the headlines were. He was interested in Watergate when that was going on. And he always wanted to know about the stock market, and the print on that page used to drive him batshit—sorry, Mom."

She patted his hand.

"I don't know why he was interested in the stocks, but he was."

"He had a few stocks," Richler said. "That's how he was getting by. He also had five different sets of ID salted around that house. He was a cagey one, all right."

"I suppose he kept the stocks in a safe deposit box somewhere," Todd remarked.

"Pardon me?" Richler raised his eyebrows.

"His stocks," Todd said. His father, who had also looked puzzled, now nodded at Richler.

"His stock certificates, the few that were left, were in a footlocker under his bed," Richler said, "along with that photo of him as Denker. Did he have a safety deposit box, son? Did he ever say he did?"

Todd thought, and then shook his head. "I just thought that was where you kept your stocks. I don't know. This . . . this whole thing has just . . . you know . . . it blows my wheels." He shook his head in a dazed way that was perfectly real. He really *was* dazed. Yet, little by little, he felt his instinct of self-preservation surfacing. He felt a growing alertness, and the first stirrings of confidence. If Dussander had really taken a safety deposit box in which to store his insurance document, wouldn't he have transferred his remaining stock certificates there? And that photograph?

"We're working with the Israelis on this," Richler said. "In a very unofficial way. I'd be grateful if you didn't mention that if you decide to see any press people. They're real professionals. There's a man named Weiskopf who'd like to talk to you tomorrow, Todd. If that's okay by you and your folks."

"I guess so," Todd said, but he felt a touch of atavistic dread at the thought of being sniffed over by the same hounds that had chased Dussander for the last half of his life. Dussander had had a healthy respect for them, and Todd knew he would do well to keep that in mind.

"Mr. and Mrs. Bowden? Do you have any objections to Todd seeing Mr. Weiskopf?"

"Not if Todd doesn't," Dick Bowden said. "I'd like to be present, though. I've read about these Mossad characters—"

"Weiskopf isn't Mossad. He's what the Israelis call a special operative. In fact, he teaches Yiddish literature and English grammar. Also, he's written two novels." Richler smiled.

Dick raised a hand, dismissing it. "Whatever he is, I'm not going to let him badger Todd. From what I've read, these fellows can be a little *too* professional. Maybe he's okay. But I want you and this Weiskopf to remember that Todd tried to help that old man. He was flying under false colors, but Todd didn't know that."

"That's okay, Dad," Todd said with a wan smile.

"I just want you to help us all that you can," Richler said. "I appreciate your concern, Mr. Bowden. I think you're going to find that Weiskopf is a pleasant, low-pressure kind of guy. I've finished my own questions, but I'll break a little ground by telling you what the Israelis are most interested in. Todd was with Dussander when he had the heart attack that landed him in the hospital—"

"He asked me to come over and read him a letter," Todd said.

"We know." Richler leaned forward, elbows on his knees, tie swinging out to form a plumb-line to the floor. "The Israelis want to know about that letter. Dussander was a big fish, but he wasn't the last one in the lake—or so Sam Weiskopf says, and I believe him. They think Dussander might have known about a lot of other fish. Most of those still alive are probably in South America, but there may be others in a dozen countries . . . including the United States. Did you know they collared a man who had been an *Unterkommandant* at Buchenwald in the lobby of a Tel Aviv hotel?"

"Really!" Monica said, her eyes widening.

"Really." Richler nodded. "Two years ago. The point is just that the Israelis think the letter Dussander wanted Todd to read might have been from one of those other fish. Maybe they're right, maybe they're wrong. Either way, they want to know."

Todd, who had gone back to Dussander's house and burned the letter, said: "I'd help you—or this Weiskopf—if I could, Lieutenant Richler, but the letter was in German. It was really tough to read. I felt like a fool. Mr. Denker . . . Dussander . . . kept getting more excited and asking me to spell the words he couldn't understand because of my, you know, pronunciation. But I guess he was following all right. I remember once he laughed and said, 'Yes, yes, that is what you'd do, isn't it?' Then he said something in German. This was about two or three minutes before he had the heart attack. Something about *Dummkopf.* That means stupid in German, I think."

He was looking at Richler uncertainly, inwardly quite pleased with this lie.

Richler was nodding. "Yes, we understand that the letter was in German. The admitting doctor heard the story from you and corroborated it. But the letter *itself,* Todd . . . do you remember what happened to it?"

Here it is, Todd thought. *The crunch.*

"I guess it was still on the table when the ambulance came. When we all left. I couldn't testify to it in court, but—"

"I think there was a letter on the table," Dick said. "I picked something up and glanced at it. Airmail stationery, I think, but I didn't notice it was written in German."

"Then it should still be there," Richler said. "That's what we can't figure out."

"It's not?" Dick said. "I mean, it wasn't?"

"It wasn't, and it isn't."

"Maybe somebody broke in," Monica suggested.

"There would have been no need to *break* in," Richler said. "In the confusion of getting him out, the house was never locked. Dussander himself never thought to ask someone to lock up, apparently. His latchkey was still in the pocket of his pants when he died. His house was unlocked from the time the MED-Q attendants wheeled him out until we sealed it this morning at two-thirty a.m."

"Well, there you are," Dick said.

"No," Todd said. "I see what's bugging Lieutenant Richler." Oh yes, he saw it very well. You'd have to be blind to miss it. "Why would a burglar steal nothing but a letter? Especially one written in German? It doesn't listen. Mr. Denker didn't have much to steal, but a guy who broke in could find something better than that."

"You got it, all right," Richler said. "Not bad."

"Todd used to want to be a detective when he grew up," Monica said, and ruffled Todd's hair a bit. Since he had gotten big he seemed to object to that, but right now he didn't seem to mind. God, she hated to see him looking so pale. "I guess he's changed his mind to history these days."

"History is a good field," Richler said. "You can be an investigative historian. Have you ever read Josephine Tey?"

"No, sir."

"Doesn't matter. I just wish my boys had some ambition greater than seeing the Angels win the pennant this year."

Todd offered a wan smile and said nothing.

Richler turned serious again. "Anyway, I'll tell you the theory we're going on. We figure that someone, probably right here in Santo Donato, knew who and what Dussander was."

"Really?" Dick said.

"Oh yes. Someone who knew the truth. Maybe another fugitive Nazi. I know that sounds like Robert Ludlum stuff, but who would have thought there was even *one* fugitive Nazi in a quiet little suburb like this? And when Dussander was taken to the hospital, we think that Mr. X scooted over to the house and got that incriminating letter. And that by now it's so many decomposing ashes floating around in the sewer system."

"That doesn't make much sense either," Todd said.

"Why not, Todd?"

"Well, if Mr. Denk . . . if *Dussander* had an old buddy from the camps, or just an old Nazi buddy, why did he bother to have me come over and read him that letter? I mean, if you could have heard him correcting me, and stuff . . . at least this old Nazi buddy you're talking about would know how to speak German."

"A good point. Except maybe this other fellow is in a wheelchair, or blind. For all we know, it might be Bormann himself and he doesn't even dare go out and show his face."

"Guys that are blind or in wheelchairs aren't that good at scooting out to get letters," Todd said.

Richler looked admiring again. "True. But a blind man could steal a letter even if he couldn't read it, though. Or hire it done."

Todd thought this over, and nodded—but he shrugged at the same time to show how farfetched he thought the idea. Richler had progressed far beyond Robert Ludlum and into the land of Sax Rohmer. But how farfetched the idea was or wasn't didn't matter one fucking little bit, did it? No. What mattered was that Richler was still sniffing around . . . and that sheeny, Weiskopf, was also sniffing around. The letter, the goddam letter! Dussander's stupid goddam idea! And suddenly he was thinking of his .30-.30, cased and resting on its shelf in the cool, dark garage. He pulled his mind away from it quickly. The palms of his hands had gone damp.

"Did Dussander have any friends that you knew of?" Richler was asking.

"Friends? No. There used to be a cleaning lady, but she moved away and he didn't bother to get another one. In the summer he hired a kid to mow his lawn, but I don't think he'd gotten one this year. The grass is pretty long, isn't it?"

"Yes. We've knocked on a lot of doors, and it doesn't seem as if he'd hired anyone. Did he get phone calls?"

"Sure," Todd said off-handedly . . . here was a gleam of light, a possible escape-hatch that was relatively safe. Dussander's phone had actually rung only half a dozen times or so in all the time Todd had known him—salesmen, a polling organization asking about breakfast foods, the rest wrong numbers. He only had the phone in case he got sick . . . as he finally had, might his soul rot in hell. "He used to get a call or two every week."

"Did he speak German on those occasions?" Richler asked quickly. He seemed excited.

"No," Todd said, suddenly cautious. He didn't like Richler's excitement—there was something wrong about it, something dangerous. He felt sure of it, and suddenly Todd had to work furiously to keep himself from breaking out in a sweat. "He didn't talk much at all. I remember that a couple of times he said things like, 'The boy who reads to me is here right now. I'll call you back.'"

"I'll bet that's it!" Richler said, whacking his palms on his thighs. "I'd bet two weeks' pay that was the guy!" He closed his notebook with a snap (so far as Todd could see he had done nothing but doodle in it) and stood up. "I want to thank all three of you for your time. You in particular, Todd. I know all of this has been a hell of a shock to you, but it will be over soon. We're going to turn the house upside down this afternoon—cellar to attic and then back down to the cellar again.

We're bringing in all the special teams. We may find some trace of Dussander's phonemate yet."

"I hope so," Todd said.

Richler shook hands all around and left. Dick asked Todd if he felt like going out back and hitting the badminton birdie around until lunch. Todd said he didn't feel much like badminton *or* lunch, and went upstairs with his head down and his shoulders slumped. His parents exchanged sympathetic, troubled glances. Todd lay down on his bed, stared at the ceiling, and thought about his .30-.30. He could see it very clearly in his mind's eye. He thought about shoving the blued steel barrel right up Betty Trask's slimy Jewish cooze—just what she needed, a prick that never went soft. *How do you like it, Betty?* he heard himself asking her. *You just tell me if you get enough, okay?* He imagined her screams. And at last a terrible flat smile came to his face. *Sure, just tell me, you bitch . . . okay? Okay? Okay? . . .*

"So what do you think?" Weiskopf asked Richler when Richler picked him up at a luncheonette three blocks from the Bowden home.

"Oh, I think the kid was in on it somehow," Richler said. "Somehow, some way, to some degree. But is he cool? If you poured hot water into his mouth I think he'd spit out icecubes. I tripped him up a couple of times, but I've got nothing I could use in court. And if I'd gone much further, some smart lawyer might be able to get him off on entrapment a year or two down the road even if something *does* pull together. I mean, the courts are still going to look at him as a juvenile—the kid's only seventeen. In some ways, I'd guess he hasn't *really* been a juvenile since he was maybe eight. He's creepy, man." Richler stuck a cigarette in his mouth and laughed—the laugh had a shaky sound. "I mean, really fuckin creepy."

"What slips did he make?"

"The phone calls. That's the main thing. When I slipped

him the idea, I could see his eyes light up like a pinball machine." Richler turned left and wheeled the nondescript Chevy Nova down the freeway entrance ramp. Two hundred yards to their right was the slope and the dead tree where Todd had dry-fired his rifle at the freeway traffic one Saturday morning not long ago.

"He's saying to himself, 'This cop is off the wall if he thinks Dussander had a Nazi friend here in town, but if he *does* think that, it takes me off ground-zero.' So he says yeah, Dussander got one or two calls a week. Very mysterious. 'I can't talk now, Z-five, call later'—that type of thing. But Dussander's been getting a special 'quiet phone' rate for the last seven years. Almost no activity at all, and *no* long distance. He wasn't getting a call or two a week."

"What else?"

"He immediately jumped to the conclusion that the letter was gone and nothing else. He knew that was the only thing missing because he was the one who went back and took it."

Richler jammed his cigarette out in the ashtray.

"We *think* the letter was just a prop. We *think* that Dussander had the heart attack while he was trying to bury that body . . . the freshest body. There was dirt on his shoes and his cuffs, and so that's a pretty fair assumption. That means he called the kid *after* he had the heart attack, not before. He crawls upstairs and phones the kid. The kid flips out—as much as he ever flips out, anyway—and cooks up the letter story on the spur of the moment. It's not great, but not that bad, either . . . considering the circumstances. He goes over there and cleans up Dussander's mess for him. Now the kid is in fucking overdrive. MED-Q's coming, his father is coming, and he needs that letter for stage-dressing. He goes upstairs and breaks open that box—"

"You've got confirmation on that?" Weiskopf asked, lighting a cigarette of his own. It was an unfiltered Player, and to Richler it smelled like horseshit. No wonder the British

Empire fell, he thought, if they started smoking cigarettes like that.

"Yes, we've got confirmation right up the ying-yang," Richler said. "There are fingerprints on the box which match those in his school records. But his fingerprints are on almost *everything* in the goddam house!"

"Still, if you confront him with all of that, you can rattle him," Weiskopf said.

"Oh, listen, hey, you don't know this kid. When I said he was cool, I meant it. He'd say Dussander asked him to fetch the box once or twice so he could put something in it or take something out of it."

"His fingerprints are on the shovel."

"He'd say he used it to plant a rose-bush in the back yard." Richler took out his cigarettes but the pack was empty. Weiskopf offered him a Player. Richler took one puff and began coughing. "They taste as bad as they smell," he choked.

"Like those hamburgers we had for lunch yesterday," Weiskopf said, smiling. "Those Mac-Burgers."

"Big Macs," Richler said, and laughed. "Okay. So cross-cultural pollination doesn't always work." His smile faded. "He looks so clean-cut, you know?"

"Yes."

"This is no j.d. from Vasco with hair down to his asshole and chains on his motorcycle boots."

"No." Weiskopf stared at the traffic all around them and was very glad he wasn't driving. "He's just a boy. A white boy from a good home. And I find it difficult to believe that—"

"I thought you had them ready to handle rifles and grenades by the time they were eighteen. In Israel."

"Yes. But he was *fourteen* when all of this started. Why would a fourteen-year-old boy mix himself up with such a man as Dussander? I have tried and tried to understand that and still I can't."

"I'd settle for how," Richler said, and flicked the cigarette out the window. It was giving him a headache.

"Perhaps, if it did happen, it was just luck. A coincidence. Serendipity. I think there is black serendipity as well as white."

"I don't know what you're talking about," Richler said gloomily. "All I know is the kid is creepier than a bug under a rock."

"What I'm saying is simple. Any other boy would have been more than happy to tell his parents, or the police. To say, 'I have recognized a wanted man. He is living at this address. Yes, I am sure.' And then let the authorities take over. Or do you feel I am wrong?"

"No, I wouldn't say so. The kid would be in the limelight for a few days. Most kids would dig that. Picture in the paper, an interview on the evening news, probably a school assembly award for good citizenship." Richler laughed. "Hell, the kid would probably get a shot on *Real People.*"

"What's that?"

"Never mind," Richler said. He had to raise his voice slightly because ten-wheelers were passing the Nova on either side. Weiskopf looked nervously from one to the other. "You don't want to know. But you're right about most kids. *Most* kids."

"But not *this* kid," Weiskopf said. "This boy, probably by dumb luck alone, penetrates Dussander's cover. Yet instead of going to his parents or the authorities . . . he goes to Dussander. Why? You say you don't care, but I think you do. I think it haunts you just as it does me."

"Not blackmail," Richler said. "That's for sure. That kid's got everything a kid could want. There was a dune-buggy in the garage, not to mention an elephant gun on the wall. And even if he wanted to squeeze Dussander just for the thrill of it, Dussander was practically unsqueezable. Except for those few stocks, he didn't have a pot to piss in."

"How sure are you that the boy doesn't know you've found the bodies?"

"I'm sure. Maybe I'll go back this afternoon and hit him with that. Right now it looks like our best shot." Richler struck the steering wheel lightly. "If all of this had come out even one day sooner, I think I would have tried for a search warrant."

"The clothes the boy was wearing that night?"

"Yeah. If we could have found soil samples on his clothes that matched the dirt in Dussander's cellar, I almost think we could break him. But the clothes he was wearing that night have probably been washed six times since then."

"What about the other dead winos? The ones your police department has been finding around the city?"

"Those belong to Dan Bozeman. I don't think there's any connection anyhow. Dussander just wasn't that strong . . . and more to the point, he had such a neat little racket already worked out. Promise them a drink and a meal, take them home on the city bus—the fucking city bus!—and waste them right in his kitchen."

Weiskopf said quietly: "It wasn't *Dussander* I was thinking of."

"What do you mean by th—" Richler began, and then his mouth snapped suddenly closed. There was a long, unbelieving moment of silence, broken only by the drone of the traffic all around them. Then Richler said softly: "Hey. Hey, come on now. Give me a fucking br—"

"As an agent of my government, I am only interested in Bowden because of what, if anything, he may know about Dussander's remaining contacts with the Nazi underground. But as a human being, I am becoming more and more interested in the boy himself. I'd like to know what makes him tick. I want to know *why.* And as I try to answer that question to my own satisfaction, I find that more and more I am asking myself *What else.*"

"But—"

"Do you suppose, I ask myself, that the very atrocities in which Dussander took part formed the basis of some attraction between them? That's an unholy idea, I tell myself. The things that happened in those camps still have power enough to make the stomach flutter with nausea. I feel that way myself, although the only close relative I ever had in the camps was my grandfather, and he died when I was three. But maybe there is something about what the Germans did that exercises a deadly fascination over us—something that opens the catacombs of the imagination. Maybe part of our dread and horror comes from a secret knowledge that under the right—or wrong—set of circumstances, we ourselves would be willing to build such places and staff them. Black serendipity. Maybe we know that under the right set of circumstances the things that live in the catacombs would be glad to crawl out. And what do you think they would look like? Like mad Fuehrers with forelocks and shoe-polish moustaches, *heil*-ing all over the place? Like red devils, or demons, or the dragon that floats on its stinking reptile wings?"

"I don't know," Richler said.

"I think most of them would look like ordinary accountants," Weiskopf said. "Little mind-men with graphs and flow-charts and electronic calculators, all ready to start maximizing the kill ratios so that *next* time they could perhaps kill twenty or thirty million instead of only six. And some of them might look like Todd Bowden."

"You're damn near as creepy as he is," Richler said.

Weiskopf nodded. "It's a creepy subject. Finding those dead men and animals in Dussander's cellar . . . *that* was creepy, *nu*? Have you ever thought that maybe this boy began with a simple interest in the camps? An interest not much different from the interests of boys who collect coins or stamps or who like to read about Wild West desperados? And that he went to Dussander to get his information straight from the horse's head?"

"Mouth," Richler said automatically. "Man, at this point I could believe anything."

"Maybe," Weiskopf muttered. It was almost lost in the roar of another ten-wheeler passing them, BUDWEISER was printed on the side in letters six feet tall. *What an amazing country,* Weiskopf thought, and lit a fresh cigarette. *They don't understand how we can live surrounded by half-mad Arabs, but if I lived here for two years I would have a nervous breakdown.* "Maybe. And maybe it isn't possible to stand close to murder piled on murder and not be touched by it."

29

The short guy who entered the squadroom brought stench after him like a wake. He smelled like rotten bananas and Wildroot Cream Oil and cockroach shit and the inside of a city garbage truck at the end of a busy morning. He was dressed in a pair of ageing herringbone pants, a ripped gray institutional shirt, and a faded blue warmup jacket from which most of the zipper hung loose like a string of pygmy teeth. The uppers of his shoes were bound to the lowers with Krazy Glue. A pestiferous hat sat on his head.

"Oh Christ, get out of here!" the duty sergeant cried. "You're not under arrest, Hap! I swear to God! I swear it on my mother's name! Get out of here! I want to breathe again."

"I want to talk to Lieutenant Bozeman."

"He died, Hap. It happened yesterday. We're all really fucked up over it. So get out and let us mourn in peace."

"I want to talk to Lieutenant Bozeman!" Hap said more loudly. His breath drifted fragrantly from his mouth: a juicy, fermenting mixture of pizza, Hall's Mentho-lyptus lozenges, and sweet red wine.

"He had to go to Siam on a case, Hap. So why don't you just get out of here? Go someplace and eat a lightbulb."

"I want to talk to Lieutenant Bozeman and I ain't leaving until I do!"

The duty sergeant fled the room. He returned about five minutes later with Bozeman, a thin, slightly stooped man of fifty.

"Take him into your office, okay, Dan?" the duty sergeant begged. "Won't that be all right?"

"Come on, Hap," Bozeman said, and a minute later they were in the three-sided stall that was Bozeman's office. Bozeman prudently opened his only window and turned on his fan before sitting down. "Do something for you, Hap?"

"You still on those murders, Lieutenant Bozeman?"

"The derelicts? Yeah, I guess that's still mine."

"Well, I know who greased 'em."

"Is that so, Hap?" Bozeman asked. He was busy lighting his pipe. He rarely smoked the pipe, but neither the fan nor the open window was quite enough to overwhelm Hap's smell. Soon, Bozeman thought, the paint would begin to blister and peel. He sighed.

"You remember I told you Poley was talkin to a guy just a day before they found him all cut up in that pipe? You member me tellin you that, Lieutenant Bozeman?"

"I remember." Several of the winos who hung around the Salvation Army and the soup kitchen a few blocks away had told a similar story about two of the murdered derelicts, Charles "Sonny" Brackett and Peter "Poley" Smith. They had seen a guy hanging around, a young guy, talking to Sonny and Poley. Nobody knew for sure if Poley had gone off with the guy, but Hap and two others claimed to have seen Poley Smith walk off with him. They had the idea that the "guy" was underage and willing to spring for a bottle of musky in exchange for some juice. Several other winos claimed to have seen a "guy" like that around. The description of this "guy" was superb, bound to stand up in court, coming as it did from such unimpeachable sources. Young, blond, and white. What else did you need to make a bust?

"Well, last night I was in the park," Hap said, "and I just happened to have this old bunch of newspapers—"

"There's a law against vagrancy in this city, Hap."

"I was just collectin em up," Hap said righteously. "It's so awful the way people litter. I was doon a public surface, Lieutenant. A friggin public surface. Some of those papers was a week old."

"Yes, Hap," Bozeman said. He remembered—vaguely—being quite hungry and looking forward keenly to his lunch. That time seemed long ago now.

"Well, when I woke up, one of those papers had blew onto my face and I was lookin right *at* the guy. Gave me a hell of a jump, I can tell you. Look. This is the guy. This guy right here."

Hap pulled a crumpled, yellowed, water-spotted sheet of newspaper from his warmup jacket and unfolded it. Bozeman leaned forward, now moderately interested. Hap put the paper on his desk so he could read the headline: 4 BOYS NAMED TO SOUTHERN CAL ALL-STARS. Below the head were four photos.

"Which one, Hap?"

Hap put a grimy finger on the picture to the far right. "Him. It says his name is Todd Bowden."

Bozeman looked from the picture to Hap, wondering how many of Hap's brain-cells were still unfried and in some kind of working order after twenty years of being sautéed in a bubbling sauce of cheap wine seasoned with an occasional shot of sterno.

"How can you be sure, Hap? He's wearing a baseball cap in the picture. I can't tell if he's got blonde hair or not."

"The grin," Hap said. "It's the way he's grinnin. He was grinnin at Poley in just that same ain't-life-grand way when they walked off together. I couldn't mistake that grin in a million years. That's him, that's the guy."

Bozeman barely heard the last; he was thinking, and thinking hard. *Todd Bowden.* There was something very familiar about that name. Something that bothered him even worse than the thought that a local high school hero might be going around and offing winos. He thought he had heard that name just this morning in conversation. He frowned, trying to remember where.

Hap was gone and Dan Bozeman was still trying to figure it out when Richler and Weiskopf came in . . . and it was the sound of their voices as they got coffee in the squadroom that finally brought it home to him.

"Holy God," said Lieutenant Bozeman, and got up in a hurry.

Both of his parents had offered to cancel their afternoon plans—Monica at the market and Dick golfing with some business people—and stay home with him, but Todd told them he would rather be alone. He thought he would clean his rifle and just sort of think the whole thing over. Try to get it straight in his mind.

'Todd," Dick said, and suddenly found he had nothing much to say. He supposed if he had been his own father, he would have at this point advised prayer. But the generations had turned, and the Bowdens weren't much into that these days. "Sometimes these things happen," he finished lamely, because Todd was still looking at him. 'Try not to brood about it."

"It'll be all right," Todd said.

After they were gone, he took some rags and a bottle of Alpaca gun oil out onto the bench beside the roses. He went back into the garage and got the .30-.30. He took it to the bench and broke it down, the dusty-sweet smell of the flowers lingering pleasantly in his nose. He cleaned the gun thoroughly, humming a tune as he did it, sometimes whistling a snatch between his teeth. Then he put the gun together again. He could have done it just as easily in the dark. His mind wandered free. When it came back some five minutes later, he observed that he had loaded the gun. The idea of target-shooting didn't much appeal, not today, but he had still loaded it. He told himself he didn't know why.

Sure you do, Todd-baby. The time, so to speak, has come.

And that was when the shiny yellow Saab turned into the driveway. The man who got out was vaguely familiar to Todd, but it wasn't until he slammed the car door and started to walk toward him that Todd saw the sneakers—low-topped Keds, light blue. Talk about Blasts from the Past; here, walking up the Bowden driveway, was Rubber Ed French, The Ked Man.

"Hi, Todd. Long time no see."

Todd leaned the rifle against the side of the bench and offered his wide and winsome grin. "Hi, Mr. French. What are you doing out here on the wild side of town?"

"Are your folks home?"

"Gee, no. Did you want them for something?"

"No," Ed French said after a long, thoughtful pause. "No, I guess not. I guess maybe it would be better if just you and I talked. For starters, anyway. You may be able to offer a perfectly reasonable explanation for all this. Although God knows I doubt it."

He reached into his hip pocket and brought out a newsclipping. Todd knew what it was even before Rubber Ed passed it to him, and for the second time that day he was looking at the side-by-side pictures of Dussander. The one the street photographer had taken had been circled in black ink. The meaning was clear enough to Todd; French had recognized Todd's "grandfather." And now he wanted to tell everyone in the world all about it. He wanted to midwife the good news. Good old Rubber Ed, with his jive talk and his motherfucking sneakers.

The police would be very interested—but, of course, they already were. He knew that now. The sinking feeling had begun about thirty minutes after Richler left. It was as if he had been riding high in a balloon filled with happy-gas. Then a cold steel arrow had ripped through the balloon's fabric, and now it was sinking steadily.

The phone calls, that was the biggie. Richler had trotted that out just as slick as warm owlshit. *Sure,* he had said, practically breaking his neck to rush into the trap. *He gets one or two calls a week.* Let them go ranting all over southern California looking for geriatric ex-Nazis. Fine. Except maybe they had gotten a different story from Ma Bell. Todd didn't know if the phone company could tell how much your phone got used . . . but there had been a look in Richler's eyes . . .

Then there was the letter. He had inadvertently told Richler that the house hadn't been burgled, and Richler had no doubt gone away thinking that the only way Todd could have known that was if he had been back . . . as he had been, not just once but three times, first to get the letter and twice more looking for anything incriminating. There had been nothing; even the SS uniform was gone, disposed of by Dussander sometime during the last four years.

And then there were the bodies. Richler had never mentioned the bodies.

At first Todd had thought that was good. Let them hunt a little longer while he got his own head—not to mention his story—straight. No fear about the dirt that had gotten on his clothes burying the body; they had all been cleaned later that same night. He ran them through the washer-dryer himself, perfectly aware that Dussander might die and then everything might come out. You can't be too careful, boy, as Dussander himself would have said.

Then, little by little, he had realized it was *not* good. The weather had been warm, and the warm weather always made the cellar smell worse; on his last trip to Dussander's house it had been a rank presence. Surely the police would have been interested in that smell, and would have tracked it to its source. So why had Richler withheld the information? Was he saving it for later? Saving it for a nasty little surprise? And if Richler was into planning nasty little surprises, it could only mean that he suspected.

Todd looked up from the clipping and saw that Rubber Ed had half-turned away from him. He was looking into the street, although not much was happening out there. Richler could suspect, but suspicion was the best he could do.

Unless there was some sort of concrete evidence binding Todd to the old man.

Exactly the sort of evidence Rubber Ed French could give.

Ridiculous man in a pair of ridiculous sneakers. Such a ridiculous man hardly deserved to live. Todd touched the barrel of the .30-.30.

Yes, Rubber Ed was a link they didn't have. They could *never* prove that Todd had been an accessory to one of Dussander's murders. But with Rubber Ed's testimony they could prove conspiracy. And would even *that* end it? Oh, no. They would get his high school graduation picture next and start showing it to the stewbums down in the Mission district. A long shot, but one Richler could ill afford not to play. If we can't pin one bunch of winos on him, maybe we can get him for the other bunch.

What next? Court next.

His father would get him a wonderful bunch of lawyers, of course. And the lawyers would get him off, of course. Too much circumstantial evidence. He would make too favorable an impression on the jury. But by then his life would be ruined anyway, just as Dussander had said it would be. It would be all dragged through the newspapers, dug up and brought into the light like the half-decayed bodies in Dussander's cellar.

"The man in that picture is the man who came to my office when you were in the ninth grade," Ed told him abruptly, turning to Todd again. "He purported to be your grandfather. Now it turns out he was a wanted war criminal."

"Yes," Todd said. His face had gone oddly blank. It was the face of a department-store dummy. All the healthiness, life, and vivacity had drained from it. What was left was frightening in its vacuous emptiness.

"How did it happen?" Ed asked, and perhaps he intended his question as a thundering accusation, but it came out sounding plaintive and lost and somehow cheated. "How did this happen, Todd?"

"Oh, one thing just followed another," Todd said, and picked up the .30-.30. "That's really how it happened. One thing just . . . followed another." He pushed the safety catch to the off position with his thumb and pointed the rifle at Rubber Ed. "As stupid as it sounds, that's just what happened. That's all there was to it."

"Todd," Ed said, his eyes widening. He took a step backwards. "Todd, you don't want to . . . please, Todd. We can talk this over. We can disc—"

"You and the fucking kraut can discuss it down in hell," Todd said, and pulled the trigger.

The sound of the shot rolled away in the hot and windless quiet of the afternoon. Ed French was flung back against his Saab. His hand groped behind him and tore off a windshield wiper. He stared at it foolishly as blood spread on his blue turtleneck, and then he dropped it and looked at Todd.

"Norma," he whispered.

"Okay," Todd said. "Whatever you say, champ." He shot Rubber Ed again and roughly half of his head disappeared in a spray of blood and bone.

Ed turned drunkenly and began to grope toward the driver's-side door, speaking his daughter's name over and over again in a choked and failing voice. Todd shot him again, aiming for the base of the spine, and Ed fell down. His feet drummed briefly on the gravel and then were still.

Sure did die hard for a guidance counsellor, Todd thought, and brief laughter escaped him. At the same moment a burst of pain as sharp as an icepick drove into his brain and he closed his eyes.

When he opened them again, he felt better than he had in months—maybe better than he had felt in years. Everything was fine. Everything was together. The blankness left his face and a kind of wild beauty filled it.

He went back into the garage and got all the shells he had, better than four hundred rounds. He put them in his old knapsack and shouldered it. When he came back out into the sunshine he was smiling excitedly, his eyes dancing—it was the way boys smile on their birthdays, on Christmas, on the Fourth of July. It was a smile that betokened skyrockets, tree-houses, secret signs and secret meeting-places, the aftermath of the triumphal big game when the players are carried out of the stadium and into town on the shoulders of the exultant fans. The ecstatic smile of tow-headed boys going off to war in coal-scuttle helmets.

"I'm king of the world!" he shouted mightily at the high blue sky, and raised the rifle two-handed over his head for a moment. Then, switching it to his right hand, he started toward that place above the freeway where the land fell away and where the dead tree would give him shelter.

It was five hours later and almost dark before they took him down.

Also by Stephen King

FICTION

Carrie
'Salem's Lot
The Shining
Night Shift
The Stand
The Dead Zone
Firestarter
Cujo
Creepshow
Different Seasons
Cycle of the Werewolf
Christine
Pet Sematary
IT
Skeleton Crew
The Mist
The Eyes of the Dragon
Misery
The Tommyknockers
The Dark Half
Four Past Midnight
Needful Things
Gerald's Game
Dolores Claiborne
Nightmares & Dreamscapes
Insomnia
Rose Madder
The Green Mile
Desperation
Bag of Bones
The Girl Who Loved Tom Gordon
Hearts in Atlantis
Dreamcatcher
Everything's Eventual
From a Buick 8
The Colorado Kid
Cell
Lisey's Story
Duma Key
Just After Sunset
Stephen King Goes to the Movies
Under the Dome
Full Dark, No Stars
11/22/63
Doctor Sleep
Mr. Mercedes
Revival
Finders Keepers
The Bazaar of Bad Dreams
End of Watch
The Outsider

NOVELS IN THE DARK TOWER SERIES

The Dark Tower I: The Gunslinger
The Dark Tower II: The Drawing of the Three
The Dark Tower III: The Waste Lands
The Dark Tower IV: Wizard and Glass
The Dark Tower V: Wolves of the Calla
The Dark Tower VI: Song of Susannah
The Dark Tower VII: The Dark Tower
The Wind Through the Keyhole: A Dark Tower Novel

BY STEPHEN KING AS RICHARD BACHMAN

Thinner
The Running Man
The Long Walk
Roadwork
The Regulators
Blaze

WITH OWEN KING

Sleeping Beauties

WITH PETER STRAUB

The Talisman
Black House

NONFICTION

Danse Macabre
On Writing (A Memoir of the Craft)

STEPHEN KING

THE BODY

SCRIBNER
New York London Toronto Sydney New Delhi

Scribner
An Imprint of Simon & Schuster, Inc.
1230 Avenue of the Americas
New York, NY 10020

First Scribner trade paperback edition June 2018

Interior design by Erich Hobbing

Manufactured in the United States of America

15 17 19 20 18 16

Library of Congress Cataloging-in-Publication Data is available.

ISBN 978-1-9821-0353-8
ISBN 978-1-9821-0559-4 (ebook)

Permissions acknowledgments appear on page 181.

For George McLeod

THE BODY

1

The most important things are the hardest things to say. They are the things you get ashamed of, because words diminish them—words shrink things that seemed limitless when they were in your head to no more than living size when they're brought out. But it's more than that, isn't it? The most important things lie too close to wherever your secret heart is buried, like landmarks to a treasure your enemies would love to steal away. And you may make revelations that cost you dearly only to have people look at you in a funny way, not understanding what you've said at all, or why you thought it was so important that you almost cried while you were saying it. That's the worst, I think. When the secret stays locked within not for want of a teller but for want of an understanding ear.

I was twelve going on thirteen when I first saw a dead human being. It happened in 1960, a long time ago . . . although sometimes it doesn't seem that long to me. Especially on the nights I wake up from dreams where the hail falls into his open eyes.

2

We had a treehouse in a big elm which overhung a vacant lot in Castle Rock. There's a moving company on that lot today, and the elm is gone. Progress. It was a sort of social club, although it had no name. There were five, maybe six steady guys and some other wet ends who just hung around. We'd let them come up when there was a card game and we needed some fresh blood. The game was usually blackjack and we played for pennies, nickel limit. But you got double money on blackjack and five-card-under . . . *triple* money on six-card-under, although Teddy was the only guy crazy enough to go for that.

The sides of the treehouse were planks scavenged from the shitpile behind Mackey Lumber & Building Supply on Carbine Road—they were splintery and full of knotholes we plugged with either toilet paper or paper towels. The roof was a corrugated tin sheet we hawked from the dump, looking over our shoulders all the time we were hustling it out of there, because the dump custodian's dog was supposed to be a real kid-eating monster. We found a screen door out there on the same day. It was flyproof but really rusty—I mean, that rust was *extreme.* No matter what time of day you looked out that screen door, it looked like sunset.

Besides playing cards, the club was a good place to go and smoke cigarettes and look at girly books. There were half a dozen battered tin ashtrays that said camels on the bottom, a lot of centerfolds tacked to the splintery walls, twenty or thirty dog-eared packs of Bike cards (Teddy got them from his uncle, who ran the Castle Rock Stationery Shoppe—when Teddy's unc asked him one day what kind of cards we played, Teddy said we had cribbage tournaments and Teddy's unc thought that was just fine), a set of plastic poker chips, and a pile of ancient *Master Detective* murder magazines to leaf through if there was nothing else shaking. We also built a 12" x 10" secret compartment under the floor to hide most of this stuff in on the rare occasions when some kid's father decided it was time to do the we're-really-good-pals routine. When it rained, being in the club was like being inside a Jamaican steel drum . . . but that summer there had been no rain.

It had been the driest and hottest since 1907—or so the newspapers said, and on that Friday preceding the Labor Day weekend and the start of another school year, even the goldenrod in the fields and the ditches beside the backroads looked parched and poorly. Nobody's garden had done doodly-squat that year, and the big displays of canning stuff in the Castle Rock Red & White were still there, gathering dust. No one had anything to put up that summer, except maybe dandelion wine.

Teddy and Chris and I were up in the club on that Friday morning, glooming to each other about school being so near and playing cards and swapping the same old traveling salesman jokes and frenchman jokes. How do you know when a frenchman's been in your back yard? Well, your garbage cans are empty and your dog is pregnant. Teddy would try to look offended, but he was the first one to bring in a joke as soon as he heard it, only switching frenchman to polack.

The elm gave good shade, but we already had our shirts off so we wouldn't sweat them up too bad. We were playing three-penny-scat, the dullest card-game ever invented, but it was too hot to think about anything more complicated. We'd had a pretty fair scratch ballteam until the middle of August and then a lot of kids just drifted away. Too hot.

I was down to my ride and building spades. I'd started with thirteen, gotten an eight to make twenty-one, and nothing had happened since then. Chris knocked. I took my last draw and got nothing helpful.

"Twenty-nine," Chris said, laying down diamonds.

"Twenty-two," Teddy said, looking disgusted.

"Piss up a rope," I said, and tossed my cards onto the table face down.

"Gordie's out, ole Gordie just bit the bag and stepped out

the door," Teddy bugled, and then gave out with his patented Teddy Duchamp laugh—*Eeee-eee-eee,* like a rusty nail being slowly hauled out of a rotten board. Well, he was weird; we all knew it. He was close to being thirteen like the rest of us, but the thick glasses and the hearing aid he wore sometimes made him look like an old man. Kids were always trying to cadge smokes off him on the street, but the bugle in his shirt was just his hearing-aid battery.

In spite of the glasses and the flesh-colored button always screwed into his ear, Teddy couldn't see very well and often misunderstood the things people said to him. In baseball you had to have him play the fences, way beyond Chris in left field and Billy Greer in right. You just hoped no one would hit one that far because Teddy would go grimly after it, see it or not. Every now and then he got bonked a good one, and once he went out cold when he ran full-tilt-boogie into the fence by the treehouse. He lay there on his back with his eyes showing whites for almost five minutes, and I got scared. Then he woke up and walked around with a bloody nose and a huge purple lump rising on his forehead, trying to claim that the ball was foul.

His eyesight was just naturally bad, but there was nothing natural about what had happened to his ears. Back in those days, when it was cool to get your hair cut so that your ears stuck out like a couple of jug-handles, Teddy had Castle Rock's first Beatle haircut—four years before anyone in America had ever heard of the Beatles. He kept his ears covered because they looked like two lumps of warm wax.

One day when he was eight, Teddy's father got pissed at him for breaking a plate. His mother was working at the shoe factory in South Paris when it happened and by the time she found out about it, it was all over.

Teddy's dad took Teddy over to the big woodstove at the back of the kitchen and shoved the side of Teddy's head down against one of the cast-iron burner plates. He held it down there for about ten seconds. Then he yanked Teddy up by the hair of the head and did the other side. Then he called the Central Main General Emergency unit and told them to come get his boy. Then he hung up the phone, went into the closet, got his .410, and sat down to watch the daytime stories on TV with the shotgun laid across his knees. When Mrs. Burroughs from next door came over to ask if Teddy was all right—she'd heard the screaming—Teddy's dad pointed the shotgun at her. Mrs. Burroughs went out of the Duchamp house at roughly the speed of light, locked herself into her own house, and called the police. When the ambulance came, Mr. Duchamp let the orderlies in and then went out on the back porch to stand guard while they wheeled Teddy to the old portholed Buick ambulance on a stretcher.

Teddy's dad explained to the orderlies that while the fucking brass hats said the area was clear, there were still kraut snipers everywhere. One of the orderlies asked Teddy's dad if he thought he could hold on. Teddy's dad smiled tightly and told the orderly he'd hold until hell was a Frigidaire dealership, if that's what it took. The orderly saluted, and Teddy's dad snapped it right back at him. A few minutes after the ambulance left, the state police arrived and relieved Norman Duchamp of duty.

He'd been doing odd things like shooting cats and lighting fires in mailboxes for over a year, and after the atrocity he had visited upon his son, they had a quick hearing and sent him to Togus, which is a VA hospital. Togus is where you have to go if you're a section eight. Teddy's dad had stormed the beach at Normandy, and that's just the way Teddy always put it. Teddy was proud of his old man in spite of what his old man had done to him, and Teddy went with his mom to visit him every week.

He was the dumbest guy we hung around with, I guess, and

he was crazy. He'd take the craziest chances you can imagine, and get away with them. His big thing was what he called "truck-dodging." He'd run out in front of them on 196 and sometimes they'd miss him by bare inches. God knew how many heart attacks he'd caused, and he'd be laughing while the windblast from the passing truck rippled his clothes. It scared us because his vision was so lousy, Coke-bottle glasses or not. It seemed like only a matter of time before he misjudged one of those trucks. And you had to be careful what you dared him, because Teddy would do anything on a dare.

"Gordie's out, eeeeee-eee-eee!"

"Screw," I said, and picked up a *Master Detective* to read while they played it out. I turned to "He Stomped the Pretty Co-Ed to Death in a Stalled Elevator" and got right into it.

Teddy picked up his cards, gave them one brief look, and said: "I knock."

"You four-eyed pile of shit!" Chris cried.

"The pile of shit has a thousand eyes," Teddy said gravely, and both Chris and I cracked up. Teddy stared at us with a slight frown, as if wondering what had gotten us laughing. That was another thing about the cat—he was always coming out with weird stuff like "The pile of shit has a thousand eyes," and you could never be sure if he *meant* it to be funny or if it just happened that way. He'd look at the people who were laughing with that slight frown on his face, as if to say: *O Lord what is it this time?*

Teddy had a natural thirty—jack, queen, and king of clubs. Chris had only sixteen and went down to his ride.

Teddy was shuffling the cards in his clumsy way and I was just getting to the gooshy part of the murder story, where this deranged sailor from New Orleans was doing the Bristol Stomp all over this college girl from Bryn Mawr because he couldn't stand being in closed-in places, when we heard someone coming fast up the ladder nailed to the side of the elm. A fist rapped on the underside of the trapdoor.

"Who goes?" Chris yelled.

"Vern!" He sounded excited and out of breath.

I went to the trapdoor and pulled the bolt. The trapdoor banged up and Vern Tessio, one of the other regulars, pulled himself into the clubhouse. He was sweating buckets and his hair, which he usually kept combed in a perfect imitation of his rock and roll idol, Bobby Rydell, was plastered to his bullet head in chunks and strings.

"Wow, man," he panted. "Wait'll you hear this."

"Hear what?" I asked.

"Lemme get my breath. I ran all the way from my house."

"I ran all the way home," Teddy wavered in a dreadful Little Anthony falsetto, *"just to say I'm soh-ree—"*

"Fuck your hand, man," Vern said.

"Drop dead in a shed, Fred," Teddy returned smartly.

"You ran all the way from your place?" Chris asked unbelievingly. "Man, you're crazy." Vern's house was two miles down Grand Street. "It must be ninety out there."

"This is worth it," Vern said. "Holy Jeezum. You won't believe this. Sincerely." He slapped his sweaty forehead to show us how sincere he was.

"Okay, what?" Chris asked.

"Can you guys camp out tonight?" Vern was looking at us earnestly, excitedly. His eyes looked like raisins pushed into dark circles of sweat. "I mean, if you tell your folks we're gonna tent out in my back field?"

"Yeah, I guess so," Chris said, picking up his new hand and looking at it. "But my dad's on a mean streak. Drinkin, y'know."

"You got to, man," Vern said. "Sincerely. You won't *believe* this. Can you, Gordie?"

"Probably."

I was able to do most stuff like that—in fact, I'd been like the Invisible Boy that whole summer. In April my older brother, Dennis, had been killed in a Jeep accident. That was at Fort Benning, Georgia, where he was in Basic. He and another guy were on their way to the PX and an Army truck hit them broadside. Dennis was killed instantly and his passenger had been in a coma ever since. Dennis would have been twenty-two later that week. I'd already picked out a birthday card for him at Dahlie's over in Castle Green.

I cried when I heard, and I cried more at the funeral, and I couldn't believe that Dennis was gone, that anyone that used to knuckle my head or scare me with a rubber spider until I cried or give me a kiss when I fell down and scraped both knees bloody and whisper in my ear, "Now stop cryin, ya baby!"—that a person who had *touched* me could be dead. It hurt me and it scared me that he could be dead . . . but it seemed to have taken all the heart out of my parents. For me, Dennis was hardly more than an acquaintance. He was ten years older than me if you can dig it, and he had his own friends and classmates. We ate at the same table for a lot of years, and sometimes he was my friend and sometimes my tormentor, but mostly he was, you know, just a guy. When he died he'd been gone for a year except for a couple of furloughs. We didn't even look alike. It took me a long time after that summer to realize that most of the tears I cried were for my mom and dad. Fat lot of good it did them, or me.

"So what are you pissing and moaning about, Vern-O?" Teddy asked.

"I knock," Chris said.

"What?" Teddy screamed, immediately forgetting all about Vern. "You friggin liar! You ain't got no pat hand. I didn't deal you no pat hand."

Chris smirked. "Make your draw, shitheap."

Teddy reached for the top card on the pile of Bikes. Chris reached for the Winstons on the ledge behind him. I bent over to pick up my detective magazine.

Vern Tessio said: "You guys want to go see a dead body?"

Everybody stopped.

3

We'd all heard about it on the radio, of course. The radio, a Philco with a cracked case which had also been scavenged from the dump, played all the time. We kept it tuned to WALM in Lewiston, which churned out the super-hits and the boss oldies: "What in the World's Come Over You" by Jack Scott and "This Time" by Troy Shondell and "King Creole" by Elvis and "Only the Lonely" by Roy Orbison. When the news came on we usually switched some mental dial over to Mute. The news was a lot of happy horseshit about Kennedy and Nixon and Quemoy and Matsu and the missile gap and what a shit that Castro was turning out to be after all. But we had all listened to the Ray Brower story a little more closely, because he was a kid our age.

He was from Chamberlain, a town forty miles or so east of Castle Rock. Three days before Vern came busting into the clubhouse after a two-mile run up Grand Street, Ray Brower had gone out with one of his mother's pots to pick blueberries. When dark came and he still wasn't back, the Browers called the county sheriff and a search started—first just around the kid's house and then spreading to the surrounding towns of Motton and Durham and Pownal. Everybody got into the act—cops, deputies, game wardens, volunteers. But three days later the kid was still missing. You could tell, hearing about it on the radio, that they were never going to find that poor sucker alive; eventually the search would just peter away into nothing. He might have gotten smothered in a gravel pit slide or drowned in a brook, and ten years from now some hunter would find his bones. They were already dragging the ponds in Chamberlain, and the Motton Reservoir.

Nothing like that could happen in southwestern Maine today; most of the area has become suburbanized, and the bedroom communities surrounding Portland and Lewiston have spread out like the tentacles of a giant squid. The woods are still there, and they get heavier as you work your way west toward the White Mountains, but these days if you can keep your head long enough to walk five miles in one consistent direction, you're certain to cross two-lane blacktop. But in 1960 the whole area between Chamberlain and Castle Rock was undeveloped, and there were places that hadn't even been logged since before World War II. In those days it was still possible to walk into the woods and lose your direction there and die there.

4

Vern Tessio had been under his porch that morning, digging.

We all understood that right away, but maybe I should take just a minute to explain it to you. Teddy Duchamp was only about half-bright, but Vern Tessio would never be spending any of his spare time on *College Bowl* either. Still his brother Billy was even dumber, as you will see. But first I have to tell you why Vern was digging under the porch.

Four years ago, when he was eight, Vern buried a quart jar of pennies under the long Tessio front porch. Vern called the dark space under the porch his "cave." He was playing a pirate sort of game, and the pennies were buried treasure—only if you were playing pirate with Vern, you couldn't call it buried treasure, you had to call it "booty." So he buried the jar of pennies deep, filled in the hole, and covered the fresh dirt with some of the old leaves that had drifted under there over the years. He drew a treasure map which he put up in his room with the rest of his junk. He forgot all about it for a month or so. Then, being low on cash for a movie or something, he remembered the pennies and went to get his map. But his mom had been in to clean two or three times since then, and had collected all the old homework papers and candy wrappers and comic magazines and joke books. She burned them in the stove to start the cook-fire one morning, and Vern's treasure map went right up the kitchen chimney.

Or so he figured it.

He tried to find the spot from memory and dug there. No luck. To the right and the left of that spot. Still no luck. He gave up for the day but had tried off and on ever since. Four years, man. Four *years.* Isn't that a pisser? You didn't know whether to laugh or cry.

It had gotten to be sort of an obsession with him. The Tessio front porch ran the length of the house, probably forty feet long and seven feet wide. He had dug through damn near every inch of that area two, maybe three times and no pennies. The *number* of pennies began to grow in his mind. When it first happened he told Chris and me that there had been maybe three dollars' worth. A year later he was up to five and just lately it was running around ten, more or less, depending on how broke he was.

Every so often we tried to tell him what was so clear to us—that Billy had known about the jar and dug it up himself. Vern refused to believe it, although he hated Billy like the Arabs hate the Jews and probably would have cheerfully voted the death-penalty on his brother for shoplifting, if the opportunity had ever presented itself. He also refused to ask Billy point blank. Probably he was afraid Billy would laugh and say *Course I got them, you stupid pussy, and there was twenty bucks' worth of pennies in that jar and I spent every fuckin cent of it.* Instead, Vern went out and dug for the pennies whenever the spirit moved him (and whenever Billy wasn't around). He always crawled out from under the porch with his jeans dirty and his hair leafy and his hands empty. We ragged him about it something wicked, and his nickname was Penny—Penny Tessio. I think he came up to the club with his news as quick as he did not just to get it out but to show us that some good had finally come of his penny-hunt.

He had been up that morning before anybody, ate his cornflakes, and was out in the driveway shooting baskets through the old hoop nailed up on the garage, nothing much to do, no one to play Ghost with or anything, and he decided to have another dig for his pennies. He was under the porch when the screen door slammed up above. He froze, not making a sound. If it was his dad, he would crawl out; if it was Billy, he'd stay put until Billy and his j.d. friend Charlie Hogan had taken off.

Two pairs of footsteps crossed the porch, and then Charlie Hogan himself said in a trembling, crybaby voice: "Jesus Christ, Billy, what are we gonna do?"

Vern said that just hearing Charlie Hogan talk like that—Charlie, who was one of the toughest kids in town—made him prick up his ears. Charlie, after all, hung out with Ace Merrill and Eyeball Chambers, and if you hung out with cats like that, you had to be tough.

"Nuthin," Billy said. "That's all we're gonna do. Nuthin."

"We gotta do *somethin*," Charlie said, and they sat down on the porch close to where Vern was hunkered down. "Didn't you *see* him?"

Vern took a chance and crept a little closer to the steps,

practically slavering. At that point he thought that maybe Billy and Charlie had been really drunked up and had run somebody down. Vern was careful not to crackle any of the old leaves as he moved. If the two of them found out he was under the porch and had overheard them, you could have put what was left of him in a Ken-L Ration dogfood can.

"It's nuthin to us," Billy Tessio said. "The kid's dead so it's nuthin to him, neither. Who gives a fuck if they ever find him? I don't."

"It was that kid they been talkin about on the radio," Charlie said. "It was, sure as shit. Brocker, Brower, Flowers, whatever his name is. Fuckin train must have hit him."

"Yeah," Billy said. Sound of a scratched match. Vern saw it flicked into the gravel driveway and then smelled cigarette smoke. "It sure did. And you puked."

No words, but Vern sensed emotional waves of shame radiating off Charlie Hogan.

"Well, the girls didn't see it," Billy said after awhile. "Lucky break." From the sound, he clapped Charlie on the back to buck him up. "They'd blab it from here to Portland. We tore out of there fast, though. You think they knew there was something wrong?"

"No," Charlie said. "Marie don't like to go down that Back Harlow Road past the cemetery, anyway. She's afraid of ghosts." Then again in that scared crybaby voice: "Jesus, I wish we'd never boosted no car last night! Just gone to the show like we was gonna!"

Charlie and Billy went with a couple of scags named Marie Dougherty and Beverly Thomas; you never saw such gross-looking broads outside of a carnival show—pimples, moustaches, the whole works. Sometimes the four of them—or maybe six or eight if Fuzzy Bracowicz or Ace Merrill were along with their girls—would boost a car from a Lewiston parking lot and go joyriding out into the country with two or three bottles of Wild Irish Rose wine and a six-pack of ginger ale. They'd take the girls parking somewhere in Castle View or Harlow or Shiloh, drink Purple Jesuses, and make out. Then they'd dump the car somewhere near home. Cheap thrills in the monkey-house, as Chris sometimes said. They'd never been caught at it, but Vern kept hoping. He really dug the idea of visiting Billy on Sundays at the reformatory.

"If we told the cops, they'd want to know how we got way the hell out in Harlow," Billy said. "We ain't got no car, neither of us. It's better if we just keep our mouths shut. Then they can't touch us."

"We could make a nonnamus call," Charlie said.

"They trace those fuckin calls," Billy said ominously. "I seen it on *Highway Patrol.* And *Dragnet.*"

"Yeah, right," Charlie said miserably. "Jesus. I wish Ace'd been with us. We could have told the cops we was in his car."

"Well, he wasn't."

"Yeah," Charlie said. He sighed. "I guess you're right." A cigarette butt flicked into the driveway. "We hadda walk up and take a piss by the tracks, didn't we? Couldn't walk the other way, could we? And I got puke on my new P. F. Fliers." His voice sank a little. "Fuckin kid was laid right out, you know it? Didja see that sonofawhore, Billy?"

"I seen him," Billy said, and a second cigarette butt joined the first in the driveway. "Let's go see if Ace is up. I want some juice."

"We gonna tell him?"

"Charlie, we ain't gonna tell *nobody. Nobody never.* You dig me?"

"I dig you," Charlie said. "Christ Jesus, I wish we never boosted that fucking Dodge."

"Aw, shut the fuck up and come on."

Two pairs of legs clad in tight, wash-faded pegged jeans,

two pairs of feet in black engineer boots with side-buckles, came down the steps. Vern froze on his hands and knees ("My balls crawled up so high I thought they was trine to get back home," he told us), sure his brother would sense him beneath the porch and drag him out and kill him—he and Charlie Hogan would kick the few brains the good Lord had seen fit to give him right out his jug ears and then stomp him with their engineer boots. But they just kept going and when Vern was sure they were really gone, he had crawled out from under the porch and ran here.

5

"You're really lucky," I said. "They *would* have killed you."

Teddy said, "I know the Back Harlow Road. It comes to a dead end by the river. We used to fish for cossies out there."

Chris nodded. "There used to be a bridge, but there was a flood. A long time ago. Now there's just the train-tracks."

"Could a kid really have gotten all the way from Chamberlain to Harlow?" I asked Chris. "That's twenty or thirty miles."

"I think so. He probably happened on the train-tracks and followed them the whole way. Maybe he thought they'd take him out, or maybe he thought he could flag down a train if he had to. But that's just a freight run now—GS&WM up to Derry and Brownsville—and not many of those anymore. He'd have to've walked all the way to Castle Rock to get out. After dark a train must have finally come along . . . and el smacko."

Chris drove his right fist down against his left palm, making a flat noise. Teddy, a veteran of many close calls dodging the pulp-trucks on 196, looked vaguely pleased. I felt a little sick, imagining that kid so far away from home, scared to death but doggedly following the GS&WM tracks, probably walking on the ties because of the night-noises from the overhanging trees and bushes . . . maybe even from the culverts underneath the railroad bed. And here comes the train, and maybe the big headlight on the front hypnotized him until it was too late to jump. Or maybe he was just lying there on the tracks in a hunger-faint when the train came along. Either way, any way, Chris had the straight of it: el smacko had been the final result. The kid was dead.

"So anyway, you want to go see it?" Vern asked. He was squirming around like he had to go to the bathroom he was so excited.

We all looked at him for a long second, no one saying anything. Then Chris tossed his cards down and said: "Sure! And I bet you anything we get our pictures in the paper!"

"Huh?" Vern said.

"Yeah?" Teddy said, and grinning his crazy truck-dodging grin.

"Look," Chris said, leaning across the ratty card-table. "We can find the body and report it! We'll be on the news!"

"I dunno," Vern said, obviously taken aback. "Billy will know where I found out. He'll beat the living shit outta me."

"No he won't," I said, "because it'll be *us* guys that find that kid, not Billy and Charlie Hogan in a boosted car. Then they won't have to worry about it anymore. They'll probably pin a medal on you, Penny."

"Yeah?" Vern grinned, showing his bad teeth. It was a dazed sort of grin, as if the thought of Billy being pleased with anything he did had acted on him like a hard shot to the chin. "Yeah, you think so?"

Teddy was grinning, too. Then he frowned and said: "Oh-oh."

"What?" Vern asked. He was squirming again, afraid that some really basic objection to the idea had just cropped up in Teddy's mind . . . or what passed for Teddy's mind.

"Our folks," Teddy said. "If we find that kid's body over in South Harlow tomorrow, they're gonna know we didn't spend the night campin out in Vern's back field."

"Yeah," Chris said. "They'll know we went lookin for that kid."

"No they won't," I said. I felt funny—both excited and scared because I knew we could do it and get away with it. The mixture of emotions made me feel heatsick and headachy. I picked up the Bikes to have something to do with my hands and started box-shuffling them. That and how to play cribbage was about all I got for older brother stuff from Dennis. The other kids envied that shuffle, and I guess everyone I knew had asked me to show them how it went . . . everyone except Chris. I guess only Chris knew that showing someone would be like giving away a piece of Dennis, and I just didn't have so much of him that I could afford to pass pieces around.

I said: "We'll just tell em we got bored tenting in Vern's field because we've done it so many times before. So we decided to hike up the tracks and have a campout in the woods. I bet we don't even get hided for it because everybody'll be so excited about what we found."

"My dad'll hide me anyway," Chris said. "He's on a really mean streak this time." He shook his head sullenly. "To hell, it's worth a hiding."

"Okay," Teddy said, getting up. He was still grinning like crazy, ready to break into his high-pitched, cackling laugh at any second. "Let's all get together at Vern's house after lunch. What can we tell em about supper?"

Chris said, "You and me and Gordie can say we're eating at Vern's."

"And I'll tell my mom I'm eating over at Chris's," Vern said.

That would work unless there was some emergency we couldn't control or unless any of the parents got together. And neither Vern's folks or Chris's had a phone. Back then there were a lot of families which still considered a telephone a luxury, especially families of the shirttail variety. And none of us came from the upper crust.

My dad was retired. Vern's dad worked in the mill and was still driving a 1952 DeSoto. Teddy's mom had a house on Danberry Street and she took in a boarder whenever she could get one. She didn't have one that summer; the furnished room to let sign had been up in the parlor window since June. And Chris's dad was always on a "mean streak," more or less; he was a drunk who got welfare off and on—mostly on—and spent most of his time hanging out in Sukey's Tavern with Junior Merrill, Ace Merrill's old man, and a couple of other local rumpots.

Chris didn't talk much about his dad, but we all knew he hated him like poison. Chris was marked up every two weeks or so, bruises on his cheeks and neck or one eye swelled up and as colorful as a sunset, and once he came into school with a big clumsy bandage on the back of his head. Other times he never got to school at all. His mom would call him in sick because he was too lamed up to come in. Chris was smart, really smart, but he played truant a lot, and Mr. Halliburton, the town truant officer, was always showing up at Chris's house, driving his old black Chevrolet with the NO RIDERS sticker in the corner of the windshield. If Chris was being truant and Bertie (as we called him—always behind his back, of course) caught him, he would haul him back to school and see that Chris got detention for a week. But if Bertie found out that Chris was home because his father had beaten the shit out of him, Bertie just went away and didn't say boo to a cuckoo-bird. It never occurred to me to question this set of priorities until about twenty years later.

The year before, Chris had been suspended from school for

three days. A bunch of milk-money disappeared when it was Chris's turn to be room-monitor and collect it, and because he was a Chambers from those no-account Chamberses, he had to take a hike even though he always swore he never hawked that money. That was the time Mr. Chambers put Chris in the hospital for an overnight stay; when his dad heard Chris was suspended, he broke Chris's nose and his right wrist. Chris came from a bad family, all right, and everybody thought he would turn out bad . . . including Chris. His brothers had lived up to the town's expectations admirably. Frank, the eldest, ran away from home when he was seventeen, joined the Navy, and ended up doing a long stretch in Portsmouth for rape and criminal assault. The next-eldest, Richard (his right eye was all funny and jittery, which was why everybody called him Eyeball), had dropped out of high school in the tenth grade, and chummed around with Charlie and Billy Tessio and their j.d. buddies.

"I think all that'll work," I told Chris. "What about John and Marty?" John and Marty DeSpain were two other members of our regular gang.

'They're still away," Chris said. "They won't be back until Monday."

"Oh. That's too bad."

"So are we set?" Vern asked, still squirming. He didn't want the conversation sidetracked even for a minute.

"I guess we are," Chris said. "Who wants to play some more scat?"

No one did. We were too excited to play cards. We climbed down from the treehouse, climbed the fence into the vacant lot, and played three-flies-six-grounders for awhile with Vern's old friction-taped baseball, but that was no fun, either. All we could think about was that kid Brower, hit by a train, and how we were going to see him, or what was left of him. Around ten o'clock we all drifted away home to fix it with our parents.

6

I got to my house at quarter of eleven, after stopping at the drugstore to check out the paperbacks. I did that every couple of days to see if there were any new John D. MacDonalds. I had a quarter and I figured if there was, I'd take it along. But there were only the old ones, and I'd read most of those half a dozen times.

When I got home the car was gone and I remembered that my mom and some of her hen-party friends had gone to Boston to see a concert. A great old concert-goer, my mother. And why not? Her only kid was dead and she had to do something to take her mind off it. I guess that sounds pretty bitter. And I guess if you'd been there, you'd understand why I felt that way.

Dad was out back, passing a fine spray from the hose over his ruined garden. If you couldn't tell it was a lost cause from his glum face, you sure could by looking at the garden itself. The soil was a light, powdery gray. Everything in it was dead except for the corn, which had never grown so much as a single edible ear. Dad said he'd never known how to water a garden; it had to be mother nature or nobody. He'd water too long in one spot and drown the plants. In the next row, plants were dying of thirst. He could never hit a happy medium. But he didn't talk about it often. He'd lost a son in April and a garden in August. And if he didn't want to talk about either one, I guess that was his privilege. It just bugged me that he'd given up talking about everything else, too. That was taking democracy too fucking far.

"Hi, Daddy," I said, standing beside him. I offered him the Rollos I'd bought at the drugstore. "Want one?"

"Hello, Gordon. No thanks." He kept on flicking the fine spray over the hopeless gray earth.

"Be okay if I camp out in Vern Tessio's back field tonight with some of the guys?"

"What guys?"

"Vern. Teddy Duchamp. Maybe Chris."

I expected him to start right in on Chris—how Chris was bad company, a rotten apple from the bottom of the barrel, a thief, and an apprentice juvenile delinquent.

But he just sighed and said, "I suppose it's okay."

"Great! Thanks!"

I turned to go into the house and check out what was on the boob tube when he stopped me with: "Those are the only people you want to be with, aren't they, Gordon?"

I looked back at him, braced for an argument, but there was no argument in him that morning. It would have been better if there had been, I think. His shoulders were slumped. His face, pointed toward the dead garden and not toward me, sagged. There was a certain unnatural sparkle in his eyes that might have been tears.

"Aw, Dad, they're okay—"

"Of course they are. A thief and two feebs. Fine company for my son."

"Vern Tessio isn't feeble," I said. Teddy was a harder case to argue.

'Twelve years old and still in the fifth grade," my dad said. "And that time he slept over. When the Sunday paper came the next morning, he took an hour and a half to read the funny-pages."

That made me mad, because I didn't think he was being fair. He was judging Vern the way he judged all my friends, from having seen them off and on, mostly going in and out of the house. He was wrong about them. And when he called Chris a thief I always saw red, because he didn't know *anything* about Chris. I wanted to tell him that, but if I pissed him off he'd keep me home. And he wasn't really mad anyway, not like he got at the supper-table sometimes, ranting so loud that nobody wanted to eat. Now he just looked sad and tired and used. He was sixty-three years old, old enough to be my grandfather.

My mom was fifty-five—no spring chicken, either. When she and dad got married they tried to start a family right away and my mom got pregnant and had a miscarriage. She miscarried two more and the doctor told her she'd never be able to carry a baby to term. I got all of this stuff, chapter and verse, whenever one of them was lecturing me, you understand. They wanted me to think I was a special delivery from God and I wasn't appreciating my great good fortune in being conceived when my mother was forty-two and starting to gray. I wasn't appreciating my great good fortune and I wasn't appreciating her tremendous pain and sacrifices, either.

Five years after the doctor said Mom would never have a baby she got pregnant with Dennis. She carried him for eight months and then he just sort of fell out, all eight pounds of him—my father used to say that if she had carried Dennis to term, the kid would have weighed fifteen pounds. The doctor said: Well, sometimes nature fools us, but he'll be the only one you'll ever have. Thank God for him and be content. Ten years later she got pregnant with me. She not only carried me to term, the doctor had to use forceps to yank me out. Did you ever hear of such a fucked-up family? I came into the world the child of two Geritol-chuggers, not to go on and on about it, and my only brother was playing league baseball in the big kids' park before I even got out of diapers.

In the case of my mom and dad, one gift from God had been enough. I won't say they treated me badly, and they sure never beat me, but I was a hell of a big surprise and I guess when you get into your forties you're not as partial to surprises as you were in your twenties. After I was born, Mom got the operation her hen-party friends referred to as "The Band-Aid." I guess she wanted to make a hundred percent sure that there wouldn't be any more gifts from God. When I got to college I found out I'd beaten long odds just by not being born retarded . . . although I think my dad had his doubts when he saw my friend Vern taking ten minutes to puzzle out the dialogue in Beetle Baily.

This business about being ignored: I could never really pin it down until I did a book report in high school on this novel called *The Invisible Man.* When I agreed to do the book for Miss Hardy I thought it was going to be the science fiction story about the guy in bandages and Foster Grants—Claude Rains played him in the movies. When I found out this was a different story I tried to give the book back but Miss Hardy wouldn't let me off the hook. I ended up being real glad. This *Invisible Man* is about a Negro. Nobody ever notices him at all unless he fucks up. People look right through him. When he talks, nobody answers. He's like a black ghost. Once I got into it, I ate that book up like it was a John D. MacDonald, because that cat Ralph Ellison was writing about *me.* At the supper-table it was Denny how many did you strike out and Denny who asked you to the Sadie Hawkins dance and Denny I want to talk to you man to man about that car we were looking at. I'd say: "Pass the butter," and Dad would say: Denny, are you sure the Army is what you want? I'd say: "Pass the butter someone, okay?" and Mom would ask Denny if he wanted her to pick him up one of the Pendleton shirts on sale downtown, and I'd end up getting the butter myself. One night when I was nine, just to see what would happen: I said, "Please pass those goddam spuds." And my mom said: Denny, Auntie Grace called today and she asked after you and Gordon.

The night Dennis graduated with honors from Castle Rock

High School I played sick and stayed home. I got Stevie Darabont's oldest brother Royce to buy me a bottle of Wild Irish Rose and I drank half of it and puked in my bed in the middle of the night.

In a family situation like that, you're supposed to either hate the older brother or idolize him hopelessly—at least that's what they teach you in college psychology. Bullshit, right? But so far as I can tell, I didn't feel either way about Dennis. We rarely argued and never had a fist-fight. That would have been ridiculous. Can you see a fourteen-year-old boy finding something to beat up his four-year-old brother about? And our folks were always a little too impressed with him to burden him with the care of his kid brother, so he never resented me the way some older kids come to resent their sibs. When Denny took me with him somewhere, it was of his own free will, and those were some of the happiest times I can remember.

"Hey Lachance, who the fuck is that?"

"My kid brother and you better watch your mouth, Davis. He'll beat the crap out of you. Gordie's tough."

They gather around me for a moment, huge, impossibly tall, just a moment of interest like a patch of sun. They are so big, they are so old.

"Hey kid! This wet end really your big brother?"

I nod shyly.

"He's a real asshole, ain't he, kid?"

I nod again and everybody, Dennis included, roars with laughter. Then Dennis claps his hands together twice, briskly, and says: "Come on, we gonna have a practice or stand around here like a bunch of pussies?"

They run to their positions, already peppering the ball around the infield.

"Go sit over there on the bench, Gordie. Be quiet. Don't bother anybody."

I go sit over there on the bench. I am good. I feel impossibly small under the sweet summer clouds. I watch my brother pitch. I don't bother anybody.

But there weren't many times like that.

Sometimes he read me bedtime stories that were better than Mom's; Mom's stories were about The Gingerbread Man and The Three Little Pigs, okay stuff, but Dennis's were about stuff like Bluebeard and Jack the Ripper. He also had a version of Billy Goat's Gruff where the troll under the bridge ended up the winner. And, as I have already said, he taught me the game of cribbage and how to do a box-shuffle. Not that much, but hey! in this world you take what you can get, am I right?

As I grew older, my feelings of love for Dennis were replaced with an almost clinical awe, the kind of awe so-so Christians feel for God, I guess. And when he died, I was mildly shocked and mildly sad, the way I imagine those same so-so Christians must have felt when *Time* magazine said God was dead. Let me put it this way: I was as sad for Denny's dying as I was when I heard on the radio that Dan Blocker had died. I'd seen them both about as frequently, and Denny never even got any re-runs.

He was buried in a closed coffin with the American flag on top (they took the flag off the box before they finally stuck it in the ground and folded it—the flag, not the box—into a cocked hat and gave it to my mom). My parents just fell to pieces. Four months hadn't been long enough to put them back together again; I didn't know if they'd *ever* be whole again. Mr. and Mrs. Dumpty. Denny's room was in suspended animation just one door down from my room, suspended animation or maybe in a time-warp. The Ivy League college pennants were still on the walls, and the senior pictures of the girls he had dated were still tucked into the mirror where he had stood for what seemed like hours at a stretch, combing his hair back into a ducktail like Elvis's. The stack of *Trues* and *Sports Illustrated* remained on his desk, their dates looking more and more antique as time passed. It's the kind of thing you see in sticky-sentimental movies. But it wasn't sentimental to me; it was terrible. I didn't go into Dennis's room unless I had to because I kept expecting that he would be behind the door, or under the bed, or in the closet. Mostly it was the closet that preyed on my mind, and if my mother sent me in to get Denny's postcard album or his shoebox of photographs so she could look at them, I would imagine that door swinging slowly open while I stood rooted to the spot with horror. I would imagine him pallid and bloody in the darkness, the side of his head walloped in, a gray-veined cake of blood and brains drying on his shirt. I would imagine his arms coming up, his bloody hands hooking into claws, and he would be croaking: *It should have been you, Gordon. It should have been you.*

7

Stud City, by Gordon Lachance. Originally published in *Greenspun Quarterly,* Issue 45, Fall, 1970. Used by permission.

March.

Chico stands at the window, arms crossed, elbows on the ledge that divides upper and lower panes, naked, looking out, breath fogging the glass. A draft against his belly. Bottom right pane is gone. Blocked by a piece of cardboard.

"Chico."

He doesn't turn. She doesn't speak again. He can see a ghost of her in the glass, in his bed, sitting, blankets pulled up in apparent defiance of gravity. Her eye makeup has smeared into deep hollows under her eyes.

Chico shifts his gaze beyond her ghost, out beyond the house. Raining. Patches of snow sloughed away to reveal the bald ground underneath. He sees last year's dead grass, a plastic toy—Billy's—a rusty rake. His brother Johnny's Dodge is up on blocks, the detired wheels sticking out like stumps. He remembers times he and Johnny worked on it, listening to the super-hits and boss oldies from WLAM in Lewiston pour out of Johnny's old transistor radio—a couple of times Johnny would give him a beer. *She gonna run fast, Chico,* Johnny would say. *She gonna eat up everything on this road from Gates Falls to Castle Rock. Wait till we get that Hearst shifter in her!*

But that had been then, and this was now.

Beyond Johnny's Dodge was the highway. Route 14, goes to Portland and New Hampshire south, all the way to Canada north, if you turned left on U.S. 1 at Thomaston.

"Stud City," Chico says to the glass. He smokes his cigarette.

"What?"

"Nothing, babe."

"Chico?" Her voice is puzzled. He will have to change the sheets before Dad gets back. She bled.

"What?"

"I love you, Chico."

"That's right."

Dirty March. *You're some old whore,* Chico thinks. *Dirty, staggering old baggy-tits March with rain in her face.*

"This room used to be Johnny's," he says suddenly.

"Who?"

"My brother."

"Oh. Where is he?"

"In the Army," Chico says, but Johnny isn't in the Army. He had been working the summer before at Oxford Plains Speedway and a car went out of control and skidded across the infield toward the pit area, where Johnny had been changing the back tires on a Chevy Charger-class stocker. Some guys shouted at him to look out, but Johnny never heard them. One of the guys who shouted was Johnny's brother Chico.

"Aren't you cold?" she asks.

"No. Well, my feet. A little."

And he thinks suddenly: *Well, my God. Nothing happened to Johnny that isn't going to happen to you, too, sooner or later.* He sees it again, though: the skidding, skating Ford Mustang, the knobs of his brother's spine picked out in a series of dimpled shadows against the white of his Hanes tee-shirt; he had been hunkered down, pulling one of the Chevy's back tires. There had been time to see rubber flaying off the tires of the runaway Mustang, to see its hanging muffler scraping up sparks from the infield. It had struck Johnny even as Johnny tried to get to his feet. Then the yellow shout of flame.

Well, Chico thinks, *it could have been slow,* and he thinks of his grandfather. Hospital smells. Pretty young nurses bearing bedpans. A last papery breath. Were there any good ways?

He shivers and wonders about God. He touches the small silver St. Christopher's medal that hangs on a chain around his neck. He is not a Catholic and he's surely not a Mexican: his real name is Edward May and his friends all call him Chico because his hair is black and he greases it back with Brylcreem and he wears boots with pointed toes and Cuban heels. Not Catholic, but he wears this medallion. Maybe if Johnny had been wearing one, the runaway Mustang would have missed him. You never knew.

He smokes and stares out the window and behind him the girl gets out of bed and comes to him quickly, almost mincing, maybe afraid he will turn around and look at her. She puts a warm hand on his back. Her breasts push against his side. Her belly touches his buttock.

"Oh. It *is* cold."

"It's this place."

"Do you love me, Chico?"

"You bet!" he says off-handedly, and then, more seriously: "You were cherry."

"What does that—"

"You were a virgin."

The hand reaches higher. One finger traces the skin on the nape of his neck. "I said, didn't I?"

"Was it hard? Did it hurt?"

She laughs. "No. But I was scared."

They watch the rain. A new Oldsmobile goes by on 14, spraying up water.

"Stud City," Chico says.

"What?"

"That guy. He's going Stud City. In his new stud car."

She kisses the place her finger has been touching gently and he brushes at her as if she were a fly.

"What's the matter?"

He turns to her. Her eyes flick down to his penis and then up again hastily. Her arms twitch to cover herself, and then she remembers that they never do stuff like that in the movies and she drops them to her sides again. Her hair is black and her skin is winter white, the color of cream. Her breasts are firm, her belly perhaps a little too soft. One flaw to remind, Chico thinks, that this isn't the movies.

"Jane?"

"What?" He can feel himself getting ready. Not beginning, but getting ready.

"It's all right," he says. "We're friends." He eyes her deliberately, letting himself reach at her in all sorts of ways. When he looks at her face again, it is flushed. "Do you mind me looking at you?"

"I . . . no. No, Chico."

She steps back, closes her eyes, sits on the bed, and leans back, legs spread. He sees all of her. The muscles, the little muscles on the insides of her thighs . . . they're jumping, uncontrolled, and this suddenly excites him more than the taut cones of her breasts or the mild pink pearl of her cunt. Excitement trembles in him, some stupid Bozo on a spring. Love may be as divine as the poets say, he thinks, but sex is Bozo the Clown bouncing around on a spring. How could a woman look at an erect penis without going off into mad gales of laughter?

The rain beats against the roof, against the window, against the sodden cardboard patch blocking the glass-less lower pane. He presses his hand against his chest, looking for a moment like a stage Roman about to orate. His hand is cold. He drops it to his side.

"Open your eyes. We're friends, I said."

Obediently, she opens them. She looks at him. Her eyes appear violet now. The rainwater running down the window makes rippling patterns on her face, her neck, her breasts. Stretched across the bed, her belly has been pulled tight. She is perfect in her moment.

"Oh," she says. "Oh Chico, it feels so *funny."* A shiver goes through her. She has curled her toes involuntarily. He can see the insteps of her feet. Her insteps are pink. "Chico. Chico."

He steps toward her. His body is shivering and her eyes widen. She says something, one word, but he can't tell what it is. This isn't the time to ask. He half-kneels before her for just a second, looking at the floor with frowning concentration, touching her legs just above the knees. He measures the tide within himself. Its pull is thoughtless, fantastic. He pauses a little longer.

The only sound is the tinny tick of the alarm clock on the bedtable, standing brassy-legged atop a pile of Spiderman comic books. Her breathing flutters faster and faster. His muscles slide smoothly as he dives upward and forward. They begin. It's better this time. Outside, the rain goes on washing away the snow.

A half-hour later Chico shakes her out of a light doze. "We gotta move," he says. "Dad and Virginia will be home pretty quick."

She looks at her wristwatch and sits up. This time she makes no attempt to shield herself. Her whole tone—her body English—has changed. She has not matured (although she probably believes she has) or learned anything more complex than tying a shoe, but her tone has changed just the same. He nods and she smiles tentatively at him. He reaches for the cigarettes on the bedtable. As she draws on her panties, he thinks of a line from an old novelty song: *Keep playin till I shoot through, Blue . . . play your digeree, do.* "Tie Me Kangaroo Down," by Rolf Harris. He grins. That was a song Johnny used to sing. It ended: *So we tanned his hide when he died, Clyde, and that's it hanging on the shed.*

She hooks her bra and begins buttoning her blouse. "What are you smiling about, Chico?"

"Nothing," he says.

"Zip me up?"

He goes to her, still naked, and zips her up. He kisses her cheek. "Go on in the bathroom and do your face if you want," he says. "Just don't take too long, okay?"

She goes up the hall gracefully, and Chico watches her, smoking. She is a tall girl—taller than he—and she has to duck her head a little going through the bathroom door. Chico finds his underpants under the bed. He puts them in the dirty clothes bag hanging just inside the closet door, and gets another pair from the bureau. He puts them on, and then, while walking back to the bed, he slips and almost falls in a patch of wetness the square of cardboard has let in.

"Goddam," he whispers resentfully.

He looks around at the room, which had been Johnny's until Johnny died *(why did I tell her he was in the* Army, *for Christ's sake?* he wonders . . . a little uneasily). Fiberboard walls, so thin he can hear Dad and Virginia going at it at night, that don't quite make it all the way to the ceiling. The floor has a slightly crazy hipshot angle so that the room's door will only stay open if you block it open—if you forget, it swings stealthily closed as soon as your back is turned. On the far wall is a movie poster from *Easy Rider—Two Men Went Looking for America and Couldn't Find It Anywhere.* The room had more life when Johnny lived here. Chico doesn't know how or why; only that it's true. And he knows something else, as well. He knows that sometimes the room spooks him at night. Sometimes he thinks that the closet door will swing open and Johnny will be standing there, his body charred and twisted and blackened, his teeth yellow dentures poking out of wax that has partially melted and re-hardened; and Johnny will be whispering: *Get out of my room, Chico. And if you lay a hand on my Dodge, I'll fuckin kill you. Got it?*

Got it, bro, Chico thinks.

For a moment he stands still, looking at the rumpled sheet spotted with the girl's blood, and then he spreads the blankets up in one quick gesture. Here. Right here. How do you like that, Virginia? How does that grab your snatch? He puts on his pants, his engineer boots, finds a sweater.

He's dry-combing his hair in front of the mirror when she comes out of the john. She looks classy. Her too-soft stomach doesn't show in the jumper. She looks at the bed, does a couple of things to it, and it comes out looking made instead of just spread up.

"Good," Chico says.

She laughs a little self-consciously and pushes a lock of hair behind her ear. It is an evocative, poignant gesture.

"Let's go," he says.

They go out through the hall and the living room. Jane pauses in front of the tinted studio photograph on top of the TV. It shows his father and Virginia, a high-school-age Johnny, a grammar-school-age Chico, and an infant Billy—in the picture, Johnny is holding Billy. All of them have fixed, stone grins . . . all except Virginia, whose face is its sleepy, indecipherable self. That picture, Chico remembers, was taken less than a month after his dad married the bitch.

"That your mother and father?"

"It's my father," Chico says. "She's my stepmother, Virginia. Come on."

"Is she still that pretty?" Jane asks, picking up her coat and handing Chico his windbreaker.

"I guess my old man thinks so," Chico says.

They step out into the shed. It's a damp and drafty place—the wind hoots through the cracks in its slapstick walls. There is a pile of old bald tires, Johnny's old bike that Chico inherited when he was ten and which he promptly wrecked, a pile of detective magazines, returnable Pepsi bottles, a greasy monolithic engine block, an orange crate full of paperback books, an old paint-by-numbers of a horse standing on dusty green grass.

Chico helps her pick her way outside. The rain is falling with disheartening steadiness. Chico's old sedan stands in a driveway puddle, looking downhearted. Even up on blocks and with a piece of plastic covering the place where the windshield should go, Johnny's Dodge has more class. Chico's car is a Buick. The paint is dull and flowered with spots of rust. The front seat upholstery has been covered with a brown Army blanket. A large button pinned to the sun visor on the passenger side says: I WANT IT EVERY DAY. There is a rusty starter assembly on the back seat; if it ever stops raining he will clean it, he thinks, and maybe put it into the Dodge. Or maybe not.

The Buick smells musty and his own starter grinds a long time before the Buick starts up.

"Is it your battery?" she asks.

"Just the goddam rain, I guess." He backs out onto the road, flicking on the windshield wipers and pausing for a moment to look at the house. It is a completely unappetizing aqua color. The shed sticks off from it at a ragtag, double-jointed angle, tarpaper and peeled-looking shingles.

The radio comes on with a blare and Chico shuts it off at once. There is the beginning of a Sunday afternoon headache behind his forehead. They ride past the Grange hall and the Volunteer Fire Department and Brownie's Store. Sally Morrison's T-Bird is parked by Brownie's hi-test pump, and Chico raises a hand to her as he turns off onto the old Lewiston road.

"Who's that?"

"Sally Morrison."

"Pretty lady." Very neutral.

He feels for his cigarettes. "She's been married twice and divorced twice. Now she's the town pump, if you believe half the talk that goes on in this shitass little town."

"She looks young."

"She is."

"Have you ever—"

He slides his hand up her leg and smiles. "No," he says. "My brother, maybe, but not me. I like Sally, though. She's got her alimony and her big white Bird, she doesn't care what people say about her."

It starts to seem like a long drive. The Androscoggin, off to the right, is slaty and sullen. The ice is all out of it now. Jane has grown quiet and thoughtful. The only sound is the steady snap of the windshield wipers. When the car rolls through the dips in the road there is groundfog, waiting for evening when it will creep out of these pockets and take over the whole River Road.

They cross into Auburn and Chico drives the cutoff and swings onto Minot Avenue. The four lanes are nearly deserted, and all the suburban homes look packaged. They see one little boy in a yellow plastic raincoat walking up the sidewalk, carefully stepping in all the puddles.

"Go, man," Chico says softly.

"What?" Jane asks.

"Nothing, babe. Go back to sleep."

She laughs a little doubtfully.

Chico turns up Keston Street and into the driveway of one of the packaged houses. He doesn't turn off the ignition.

"Come in and I'll give you cookies," she says.

He shakes his head. "I have to get back."

"I know." She puts her arms around him and kisses him. "Thank you for the most wonderful time of my life."

He smiles suddenly. His face shines. It is nearly magical. "I'll see you Monday, Janey-Jane. Still friends, right?"

"You know we are," she says, and kisses him again . . . but when he cups a breast through her jumper, she pulls away. "Don't. My father might see."

He lets her go, only a little of the smile left. She gets out of the car quickly and runs through the rain to the back door. A second later she's gone. Chico pauses for a moment to light a cigarette and then he backs out of the driveway. The Buick stalls and the starter seems to grind forever before the engine manages to catch. It is a long ride home.

When he gets there, Dad's station wagon is parked in the driveway. He pulls in beside it and lets the engine die. For a moment he sits inside silently, listening to the rain. It is like being inside a steel drum.

Inside, Billy is watching Carl Stormer and His Country Buckaroos on the TV set. When Chico comes in, Billy jumps up, excited. "Eddie, hey Eddie, you know what Uncle Pete said? He said him and a whole mess of other guys sank a kraut sub in the war! Will you take me to the show next Saturday?"

"I don't know," Chico says, grinning. "Maybe if you kiss my shoes every night before supper all week." He pulls Billy's hair. Billy hollers and laughs and kicks him in the shins.

"Cut it out, now," Sam May says, coming into the room. "Cut it out, you two. You know how your mother feels about the rough-housing." He has pulled his tie down and unbuttoned the top button of his shirt. He's got a couple-three red hotdogs on a plate. The hotdogs are wrapped in white bread, and Sam May has put the old mustard right to them. "Where you been, Eddie?"

"At Jane's."

The toilet flushes in the bathroom. Virginia. Chico wonders briefly if Jane has left any hairs in the sink, or a lipstick, or a bobby pin.

"You should have come with us to see your Uncle Pete and Aunt Ann," his father says. He eats a frank in three quick bites. "You're getting to be like a stranger around here, Eddie. I don't like that. Not while we provide the bed and board."

"Some bed," Chico says. "Some board."

Sam looks up quickly, hurt at first, then angry. When he speaks, Chico sees that his teeth are yellow with French's mustard. He feels vaguely nauseated. "Your lip. Your goddam lip. You aren't too big yet, snotnose."

Chico shrugs, peels a slice of Wonder Bread off the loaf standing on the TV tray by his father's chair, and spreads it with ketchup. "In three months I'm going to be gone anyway."

"What the hell are you talking about?"

"I'm gonna fix up Johnny's car and go out to California. Look for work."

"Oh, yeah. Right." He is a big man, big in a shambling way, but Chico thinks now that he got smaller after he married Virginia, and smaller again after Johnny died. And in his mind he hears himself saying to Jane: *My brother, maybe, but not me.* And on the heels of that: *Play your dig-*

eree, do, Blue. "You ain't never going to get that car as far as Castle Rock, let alone California."

"You don't think so? Just watch my fucking dust."

For a moment his father only looks at him and then he throws the frank he has been holding. It hits Chico in the chest, spraying mustard on his sweater and on the chair.

"Say that word again and I'll break your nose for you, smartass."

Chico picks up the frank and looks at it. Cheap red frank, smeared with French's mustard. Spread a little sunshine. He throws it back at his father. Sam gets up, his face the color of an old brick, the vein in the middle of his forehead pulsing. His thigh connects with the TV tray and it overturns. Billy stands in the kitchen doorway watching them. He's gotten himself a plate of franks and beans and the plate has tipped and beanjuice runs onto the floor. Billy's eyes are wide, his mouth trembling. On the TV, Carl Stormer and His Country Buckaroos are tearing through "Long Black Veil" at a breakneck pace.

"You raise them up best you can and they spit on you," his father says thickly. "Ayuh. That's how it goes." He gropes blindly on the seat of his chair and comes up with the half-eaten hotdog. He holds it in his fist like a severed phallus. Incredibly, he begins to eat it . . . at the same time, Chico sees that he has begun to cry. "Ayuh, they spit on you, that's just how it goes."

"Well, why in the hell did you have to marry *her*?" he bursts out, and then has to bite down on the rest of it: *If you hadn't married her, Johnny would still be alive.*

"That's none of your goddam business!" Sam May roars through his tears. "That's my business!"

"Oh?" Chico shouts back. "Is that so? I only have to live with her! Me and Billy, we have to live with her! Watch her grind you down! And you don't even know—"

"What?" his father says, and his voice is suddenly low and ominous. The chunk of hotdog left in his closed fist is like a bloody chunk of bone. "What don't I know?"

"You don't know shit from Shinola," he says, appalled at what has almost come out of his mouth.

"You want to stop it now," his father says. "Or I'll beat the hell out of you, Chico." He only calls him this when he is very angry indeed.

Chico turns and sees that Virginia is standing at the other side of the room, adjusting her skirt minutely, looking at him with her large, calm, brown eyes. Her eyes are beautiful; the rest of her is not so beautiful, so self-renewing, but those eyes will carry her for years yet, Chico thinks, and he feels the sick hate come back—*So we tanned his hide when he died, Clyde, and that's it hanging on the shed.*

"She's got you pussywhipped and you don't have the guts to do anything about it!"

All of this shouting has finally become too much for Billy—he gives a great wail of terror, drops his plate of franks and beans, and covers his face with his hands. Beanjuice splatters his Sunday shoes and sprays across the rug.

Sam takes a single step forward and then stops when Chico makes a curt beckoning gesture, as if to say: *Yeah, come on, let's get down to it, what took you so fuckin long?* They stand like statues until Virginia speaks—her voice is low, as calm as her brown eyes.

"Have you had a girl in your room, Ed? You know how your father and I feel about that." Almost as an afterthought: "She left a handkerchief."

He stares at her, savagely unable to express the way he feels, the way she is dirty, the way she shoots unerringly at the back, the way she clips in behind you and cuts your hamstrings.

You could hurt me if you wanted to, the calm brown eyes say. *I know you know what was going on before he died. But that's the only way you can hurt me, isn't it, Chico? And only then if your father believed you. And if he believed you, it would kill him.*

His father lunges at the new gambit like a bear. "Have you been screwing in my house, you little bastard?"

"Watch your language, please, Sam," Virginia says calmly.

"Is that why you didn't want to come with us? So you could scr—so you could—"

"Say it!" Chico weeps. "Don't let her do it to you! Say it! Say what you mean!"

"Get out," he says dully. "Don't you come back until you can apologize to your mother and me."

"Don't you dare!" he cries. "Don't you dare call that bitch my mother! I'll kill you!"

"Stop it, Eddie!" Billy screams. The words are muffled, blurred through his hands, which still cover his face. "Stop yelling at Daddy! Stop it, *please*!"

Virginia doesn't move from the doorway. Her calm eyes remain on Chico.

Sam blunders back a step and the backs of his knees strike the edge of his easy chair. He sits down in it heavily and averts his face against a hairy forearm. "I can't even look at you when you got words like that in your mouth, Eddie. You are making me feel so bad."

"She makes you feel bad! Why don't you admit it?"

He does not reply. Still not looking at Chico, he fumbles another frank wrapped in bread from the plate on the TV tray. He fumbles for the mustard. Billy goes on crying. Carl Stormer and His Country Buckaroos are singing a truck-driving song. "My rig is old, but that don't mean she's slow," Carl tells all his western Maine viewers.

"The boy doesn't know what he's saying, Sam," Virginia says gently. "It's hard, at his age. It's hard to grow up."

She's whipped him. That's the end, all right.

He turns and heads for the door which leads first into the shed and then outdoors. As he opens it he looks back at Virginia, and she gazes at him tranquilly when he speaks her name.

"What is it, Ed?"

"The sheets are bloody." He pauses. "I broke her in."

He thinks something has stirred in her eyes, but that is probably only his wish. "Please go now, Ed. You're scaring Billy."

He leaves. The Buick doesn't want to start and he has almost resigned himself to walking in the rain when the engine finally catches. He lights a cigarette and backs out onto 14, slamming the clutch back in and racing the mill when it starts to jerk and splutter. The generator light blinks balefully at him twice, and then the car settles into a ragged idle. At last he is on his way, creeping up the road toward Gates Falls.

He spares Johnny's Dodge one last look.

Johnny could have had steady work at Gates Mills & Weaving, but only on the night shift. Nightwork didn't bother him, he had told Chico, and the pay was better than at the Plains, but their father worked days, and working nights at the mill would have meant Johnny would have been home with her, home alone or with Chico in the next room . . . and the walls were thin. *I can't stop and she won't let me try,* Johnny said. *Yeah, I know what it would do to him. But she's . . . she just won't stop and it's like I* can't *stop . . . she's always at me, you know what I mean, you've seen her, Billy's too young to understand, but you've seen her . . .*

Yes. He had seen her. And Johnny had gone to work at the Plains, telling their father it was because he could get parts for the Dodge on the cheap. And that's how it happened that he had been changing a tire when the Mustang came skidding and skating across the infield with its muffler draggin up sparks; that was how his stepmother had killed his brother, so just keep playing until I shoot through, Blue, cause we goin Stud City right here in this shitheap Buick, and he remembers how the rubber smelled, and how the knobs of Johnny's spine cast small crescent shadows on the bright white of his tee-shirt, he remembers seeing Johnny get halfway up from the squat he had been working in when the Mustang hit him, squashing him between it and the Chevy, and there had been a hollow bang as the Chevy came down off its jacks, and then the bright yellow flare of flame, the rich smell of gasoline—

Chico strikes the brakes with both feet, bringing the sedan to a crunching, juddering halt on the sodden shoulder. He leans wildly across the seat, throws open the passenger door, and sprays yellow puke onto the mud and snow. The sight of it makes him puke again, and the thought of it makes him dry-heave one more time. The car almost stalls, but he catches it in time. The generator light winks out reluctantly when he guns the engine. He sits, letting the shakes work their way out of him. A car goes by him fast, a new Ford, white, throwing up great dirty fans of water and slush.

"Stud City," Chico says. "In his new stud car. Funky."

He tastes puke on his lips and in his throat and coating his sinuses. He doesn't want a cigarette. Danny Carter will let him sleep over. Tomorrow will be time enough for further decisions. He pulls back onto Route 14 and gets rolling.

8

Pretty fucking melodramatic, right?

The world has seen one or two better stories, I know that—one or two hundred thousand better ones, more like it. It ought to have THIS IS A PRODUCT OF AN UNDERGRADUATE CREATIVE WRITING WORKSHOP stamped on every page . . . because that's just what it was, at least up to a certain point. It seems both painfully derivative and painfully sophomoric to me now; style by Hemingway (except we've got the whole thing in the present tense for some reason—how too fucking trendy), theme by Faulkner. Could anything be more *serious?* More *lit'ry*?

But even its pretensions can't hide the fact that it's an extremely sexual story written by an extremely inexperienced young man (at the time I wrote "Stud City," I had been to bed with two girls and had ejaculated prematurely all over one of them—not much like Chico in the foregoing tale, I guess). Its attitude toward women goes beyond hostility and to a point which verges on actual ugliness—two of the women in "Stud City" are sluts, and the third is a simple receptacle who says things like "I love you, Chico" and "Come in, I'll give you cookies." Chico, on the other hand, is a macho cigarette-smoking working-class hero who could have stepped whole and breathing from the grooves of a Bruce Springsteen record—although Springsteen was yet to be heard from when I published the story in the college literary magazine (where it ran between a poem called "Images of Me" and an essay on student parietals written entirely in lower case). It is the work of a young man every bit as insecure as he was inexperienced.

And yet it was the first story I ever wrote that felt like *my* story—the first one that really felt *whole,* after five years of trying. The first one that might still be able to stand up, even with its props taken away. Ugly but alive. Even now when I read it, stifling a smile at its pseudo-toughness and its pretensions, I can see the true face of Gordon Lachance lurking just behind the lines of print, a Gordon Lachance younger than the one living and writing now, one certainly more idealistic than the best-selling novelist who is more apt to have his paperback contracts reviewed than his books, but not so young as the one who went with his friends that day to see the body of a dead kid named Ray Brower. A Gordon Lachance halfway along in the process of losing the shine.

No, it's not a very good story—its author was too busy listening to other voices to listen as closely as he should have to the one coming from inside. But it was the first time I had ever really used the place I knew and the things I felt in a piece of fiction, and there was a kind of dreadful exhilaration in seeing things that had troubled me for years come out in a new form, *a form over which I had imposed control.* It had been years since that childhood idea of Denny being in the closet of his spookily preserved room had occurred to me; I would have honestly believed I had forgotten it. Yet there it is in "Stud City," only slightly changed . . . but *controlled.*

I've resisted the urge to change it a lot more, to rewrite it, to juice it up—and that urge was fairly strong, because I find the story quite embarrassing now. But there are still things in it I like, things that would be cheapened by changes made by this later Lachance, who has the first threads of gray in his hair. Things, like that image of the shadows on Johnny's white tee-shirt or that of the rain-ripples on Jane's naked body, that seem better than they have any right to be.

Also, it was the first story I never showed to my mother and father. There was too much Denny in it. Too much Castle Rock. And most of all, too much 1960. You always know the truth, because when you cut yourself or someone else with it, there's always a bloody show.

9

My room was on the second floor, and it must have been at least ninety degrees up there. It would be a hundred and ten by afternoon, even with all the windows open. I was really glad I wasn't sleeping there that night, and the thought of where we were going made me excited all over again. I made two blankets into a bedroll and tied it with my old belt. I collected all my money, which was sixty-eight cents. Then I was ready to go.

I went down the back stairs to avoid meeting my dad in front of the house, but I hadn't needed to worry; he was still out in the garden with the hose, making useless rainbows in the air and looking through them.

I walked down Summer Street and cut through a vacant lot to Carbine—where the offices of the Castle Rock *Call* stand today. I was headed up Carbine toward the clubhouse when a car pulled over to the curb and Chris got out. He had his old Boy Scout pack in one hand and two blankets rolled up and tied with clothesrope in the other.

"Thanks, mister," he said, and trotted over to join me as the car pulled away. His Boy Scout canteen was slung around his neck and under one arm so that it finally ended up banging on his hip. His eyes were sparkling.

"Gordie! You wanna see something?"

"Sure, I guess so. What?"

"Come on down here first." He pointed at the narrow space between the Blue Point Diner and the Castle Rock Drugstore.

"What is it, Chris?"

"Come on, I said!"

He ran down the alley and after a brief moment (that's all it took me to cast aside my better judgment) I ran after him. The two buildings were set slightly toward each other rather than running parallel, and so the alley narrowed as it went back. We waded through trashy drifts of old newspapers and stepped over cruel, sparkly nests of broken beer and soda bottles. Chris cut behind the Blue Point and put his bedroll down. There were eight or nine garbage cans lined up here and the stench was incredible.

"Phew! Chris! Come on, gimme a break!"

"Gimme your arm," Chris said, by rote.

"No, sincerely, I'm gonna throw u—"

The words broke off in my mouth and I forgot all about the smelly garbage cans. Chris had unslung his pack and opened it and reached inside. Now he was holding out a huge pistol with dark wood grips.

"You wanna be the Lone Ranger or the Cisco Kid?" Chris asked, grinning.

"Walking, talking Jesus! Where'd you get that?"

"Hawked it out of my dad's bureau. It's a forty-five."

"Yeah, I can see that," I said, although it could have been a .38 or a .357 for all I knew—in spite of all the John D. MacDonalds and Ed McBains I'd read, the only pistol I'd ever seen up close was the one Constable Bannerman carried . . . and although all the kids asked him to take it out of its holster, Bannerman never would. "Man, your dad's gonna hide you when he finds out. You said he was on a mean streak *anyway.*"

His eyes just went on dancing. "That's *it,* man. He ain't gonna find out *nothing.* Him and these other rummies are all laid up down in Harrison with six or eight bottles of wine. They won't be back for a week. Fucking rummies." His lip curled. He was the only guy in our gang who would never take a drink, even to show he had, you know, big balls. He said he wasn't going to grow up to be a fucking tosspot like his old man. And he told me once privately—this was after the DeSpain twins showed up with a six-pack they'd hawked from their old man and everybody teased Chris because he wouldn't take a beer or even a swallow—that he was *scared* to drink. He said his father never got his nose all the way out of the bottle anymore, that his older brother had been drunk out of his tits when he raped that girl, and that Eyeball was always guzzling Purple Jesuses with Ace Merrill and Charlie Hogan and Billy Tessio. What, he asked me, did I think his chances of letting go of the bottle would be once he picked it up? Maybe you think that's funny, a twelve-year-old worrying that he might be an incipient alcoholic, but it wasn't funny to Chris. Not at all. He'd thought about the possibility a lot. He'd had occasion to.

"You got shells for it?"

"Nine of them—all that was left in the box. He'll think he used em himself, shooting at cans while he was drunk."

"Is it loaded?"

"*No!* Chrissake, what do you think I *am?*"

I finally took the gun. I liked the heavy way it sat there in my hand. I could see myself as Steve Carella of the 87th Squad, going after that guy The Heckler or maybe covering Meyer Meyer or Kling while they broke into a desperate junkie's sleazy apartment. I sighted on one of the smelly trashcans and squeezed the trigger.

KA-BLAM!

The gun bucked in my hand. Fire licked from the end. It felt as if my wrist had just been broken. My heart vaulted nimbly into the back of my mouth and crouched there, trembling. A big hole appeared in the corrugated metal surface of the trashcan—it was the work of an evil conjuror.

"Jesus!" I screamed.

Chris was cackling wildly—in real amusement or hysterical terror I couldn't tell. "You did it, you did it! *Gordie did it!*" he bugled. *"Hey, Gordon Lachance is shooting up Castle Rock!"*

"Shut up! Let's get out of here!" I screamed, and grabbed him by the shirt.

As we ran, the back door of the Blue Point jerked open and Francine Tupper stepped out in her white rayon waitress's uniform. "Who did that? Who's letting off cherry-bombs back here?"

We ran like hell, cutting behind the drugstore and the hardware store and the Emporium Galorium, which sold antiques and junk and dime books. We climbed a fence, spiking our palms with splinters, and finally came out on Curran Street. I threw the .45 at Chris as we ran; he was killing himself laughing but caught it and somehow managed to stuff it back into his knapsack and close one of the snaps. Once around the corner of Curran and back on Carbine Street, we slowed to a walk so we wouldn't look suspicious, running in the heat. Chris was still giggling.

"Man, you shoulda seen your face. Oh man, that was priceless. That was really fine. My fucking-A." He shook his head and slapped his leg and howled.

"You knew it was loaded, didn't you? You wet! I'm gonna be in trouble. That Tupper babe saw me."

"Shit, she thought it was a firecracker. Besides, ole Thunderjugs Tupper can't see past the end of her own nose, you know that. Thinks wearing glasses would spoil her *pret*-ty *face.*" He put one palm against the small of his back and bumped his hips and got laughing again.

"Well, I don't care. That was a mean trick, Chris. Really."

"Come on, Gordie." He put a hand on my shoulder. "I didn't know it was loaded, honest to God, I swear on my mother's name I just took it out of my dad's bureau. He always unloads it. He must have been really drunk when he put it away the last time."

"You really didn't load it?"

"No sir."

"You swear it on your mother's name even if she goes to hell for you telling a lie?"

"I swear." He crossed himself and spit, his face as open and repentant as any choirboy's. But when we turned into the vacant lot where our treehouse was and saw Vern and Teddy sitting on their bedrolls waiting for us, he started to laugh again. He told them the whole story, and after everybody had had their yucks, Teddy asked him what Chris thought they needed a pistol for.

"Nothin," Chris said. "Except we might see a bear. Something like that. Besides, it's spooky sleeping out at night in the woods."

Everybody nodded at that. Chris was the biggest, toughest guy in our gang, and he could always get away with saying things like that. Teddy, on the other hand, would have gotten his ass ragged off if he even hinted he was afraid of the dark.

"Did you set your tent up in the field?" Teddy asked Vern.

"Yeah. And I put two turned-on flashlights in it so it'll look like we're there after dark."

"Hot shit!" I said, and clapped Vern on the back. For him, that was thinking. He grinned and blushed.

"So let's go," Teddy said. "Come on, it's almost twelve already!"

Chris got up and we gathered around him.

"We'll walk across Beeman's field and behind that furniture place by Sonny's Texaco," he said. "Then we'll get on the railroad tracks down by the dump and just walk across the trestle into Harlow."

"How far do you think it's gonna be?" Teddy asked.

Chris shrugged. "Harlow's big. We're gonna be walking at least twenty miles. That sound right to you, Gordie?"

"Yeah. It might even be thirty."

"Even if it's thirty we ought to be there by tomorrow afternoon, if no one goes pussy."

"No pussies here," Teddy said at once.

We all looked at each other for a second.

"Miaoww," Vern said, and we all laughed.

"Come on, you guys," Chris said, and shouldered his pack.

We walked out of the vacant lot together, Chris slightly in the lead.

10

By the time we got across Beeman's field and had struggled up the cindery embankment to the Great Southern and Western Maine tracks, we had all taken our shirts off and tied them around our waists. We were sweating like pigs. At the top of the embankment we looked down the tracks, toward where we'd have to go.

I'll never forget that moment, no matter how old I get. I was the only one with a watch—a cheap Timex I'd gotten as a premium for selling Cloverine Brand Salve the year before.

Its hands stood at straight up noon, and the sun beat down on the dry, shadeless vista before us with savage heat. You could feel it working to get in under your skull and fry your brains.

Behind us was Castle Rock, spread out on the long hill that was known as Castle View, surrounding its green and shady common. Further down Castle River you could see the stacks of the woollen mill spewing smoke into a sky the color of gun-metal and spewing waste into the water. The Jolly Furniture Barn was on our left. And straight ahead of us the railroad tracks, bright and heliographing in the sun. They paralleled the Castle River, which was on our left. To our right was a lot of overgrown scrubland (there's motorcycle track there today—they have scrambles every Sunday afternoon at 2:00 p.m.). An old abandoned water tower stood on the horizon, rusty and somehow scary.

We stood there for that one noontime moment and then Chris said impatiently, "Come on, let's get going."

We walked beside the tracks in the cinders, kicking up little puffs of blackish dust at every step. Our socks and sneakers were soon gritty with it. Vern started singing "Roll Me Over in the Clover" but soon quit it, which was a break for our ears. Only Teddy and Chris had brought canteens, and we were all hitting them pretty hard.

"We could fill the canteens again at the dump faucet," I said. "My dad told me that's a safe well. It's a hundred and ninety feet deep."

"Okay," Chris said, being the tough platoon leader. "That'll be a good place to take five, anyway."

"What about food?" Teddy asked suddenly. "I bet nobody thought to bring something to eat. I know I didn't."

Chris stopped. "Shit! I didn't, either. Gordie?"

I shook my head, wondering how I could have been so dumb.

"Vern?"

"Zip," Vern said. "Sorry."

"Well, let's see how much money we got," I said. I untied my shirt, spread it on the cinders, and dropped my own sixty-eight cents onto it. The coins glittered feverishly in the sun-light. Chris had a tattered dollar and two pennies. Teddy had two quarters and two nickels. Vern had exactly seven cents.

"Two-thirty-seven," I said. "Not bad. There's a store at the end of that little road that goes to the dump. Somebody'll have to walk down there and get some hamburger and some tonics while the others rest."

"Who?" Vern asked.

"We'll match for it when we get to the dump. Come on."

I slid all the money into my pants pocket and was just tying my shirt around my waist again when Chris hollered: *"Train!"*

I put my hand out on one of the rails to feel it, even though I could already hear it. The rail was thrumming crazily; for a moment it was like holding the train in my hand.

"Paratroops over the side!" Vern bawled, and leaped halfway down the embankment in one crazy, clownish stride. Vern was nuts for playing paratroops anyplace the ground was soft—a gravel pit, a haymow, an embankment like this one. Chris jumped after him. The train was really loud now, probably headed straight up our side of the river toward Lewiston. Instead of jumping, Teddy turned in the direction from which it was coming. His thick glasses glittered in the sun. His long hair flopped untidily over his brow in sweat-soaked stringers.

"Go on, Teddy," I said.

"No, huh-uh, I'm gonna dodge it." He looked at me, his magnified eyes frantic with excitement. "A train-dodge, dig it? What's trucks after a fuckin train-dodge?"

"You're crazy, man. You want to get killed?"

"Just like the beach at Normandy!" Teddy yelled, and strode out into the middle of the tracks. He stood on one of the cross-ties, lightly balanced.

I stood stunned for a moment, unable to believe stupidity of such width and breadth. Then I grabbed him, dragged him fighting and protesting to the embankment, and pushed him over. I jumped after him and Teddy caught me a good one in the guts while I was still in the air. The wind whooshed out of me, but I was still able to hit him in the sternum with my knee and knock him flat on his back before he could get all the way up. I landed, gasping and sprawling, and Teddy grabbed me around the neck. We went rolling all the way to the bottom of the embankment, hitting and clawing at each other while Chris and Vern stared at us, stupidly surprised.

"You little son of a bitch!" Teddy was screaming at me. "You fucker! Don't you throw your weight around on me! I'll kill you, you dipshit!"

I was getting my breath back now, and I made it to my feet. I backed away as Teddy advanced, holding my open hands up to slap away his punches, half-laughing and half-scared. Teddy was no one to fool around with when he went into one of his screaming fits. He'd take on a big kid in that state, and after the big kid broke both of his arms, he'd bite.

"Teddy, you can dodge anything you want after we see what we're going to see but

whack on the shoulder as one wildly swinging fist got past me

"until then no one's supposed to *see us,* you

whack on the side of the face, and then we might have had a real fight if Chris and Vern

"stupid wet end!"

hadn't grabbed us and kept us apart. Above us, the train roared by in a thunder of diesel exhaust and the great heavy clacking of boxcar wheels. A few cinders bounced down the embankment and the argument was over . . . at least until we could hear ourselves talk again.

It was only a short freight, and when the caboose had trailed by, Teddy said: "I'm gonna kill him. At least give him a fat lip." He struggled against Chris, but Chris only grabbed him tighter.

"Calm down, Teddy," Chris said quietly, and he kept saying it until Teddy stopped struggling and just stood there, his glasses hanging askew and his hearing-aid cord dangling limply against his chest on its way down to the battery, which he had shoved into the pocket of his jeans.

When he was completely still, Chris turned to me and said: "What the hell are you fighting with him about, Gordon?"

"He wanted to dodge the train. I figured the engineer would see him and report it. They might send a cop out."

"Ahhh, he'd be too busy makin chocolate in his drawers," Teddy said, but he didn't seem angry anymore. The storm had passed.

"Gordie was just trying to do the right thing," Vern said. "Come on, peace."

"Peace, you guys," Chris agreed.

"Yeah, okay," I said, and held out my hand, palm up. "Peace, Teddy?"

"I coulda dodged it," he said to me. "You know that, Gordie?"

"Yeah," I said, although the thought turned me cold inside. "I know it."

"Okay. Peace, then."

"Skin it, man," Chris ordered, and let go of Teddy.

Teddy slapped his hand down on mine hard enough to sting and then turned it over. I slapped his.

"Fuckin pussy Lachance," Teddy said.

"Meeiowww," I said.

"Come on, you guys," Vern said. "Let's go, okay?"

"Go anywhere you want, but don't go here," Chris said solemnly, and Vern drew back as if to hit him.

11

We got to the dump around one-thirty, and Vern led the way down the embankment with a *Paratroops over the side!* We went to the bottom in big jumps and leaped over the brackish trickle of water oozing listlessly out of the culvert which poked out of the cinders. Beyond this small boggy area was the sandy, trash-littered verge of the dump.

There was a six-foot security fence surrounding it. Every twenty feet weather-faded signs were posted. They said:

CASTLE ROCK DUMP
HOURS 4-8 P.M.
CLOSED MONDAYS
TRESPASSING STRICTLY FORBIDDEN

We climbed to the top of the fence, swung over, and jumped down. Teddy and Vern led the way toward the well, which you tapped with an old-fashioned pump—the kind from which you had to call the water with elbow-grease. There was a Crisco can filled with water next to the pump handle, and the great sin was to forget to leave it filled for the next guy to come along. The iron handle stuck off at an angle, looking a one-winged bird that was trying to fly. It had once been green, but almost all of the paint had been rubbed off by the thousands of hands that had worked that handle since 1940.

The dump is one of my strongest memories of Castle Rock. It always reminds me of the surrealist painters when I think of it—those fellows who were always painting pictures of clockfaces lying limply in the crotches of trees or Victorian living rooms standing in the middle of the Sahara or steam engines coming out of fireplaces. To my child's eye, *nothing* in the Castle Rock Dump looked as if it really belonged there.

We had entered from the back. If you came from the front, a wide dirt road came in through the gate, broadened out into a semicircular area that had been bulldozed as flat as a dirt landing-strip, and then ended abruptly at the edge of the dumping-pit. The pump (Teddy and Vern were currently standing there and squabbling about who was going to prime it) was at the back of this great pit. It was maybe eighty feet deep and filled with all the American things that get empty, wear out, or just don't work anymore. There was so much stuff that my eyes hurt just looking at it—or maybe it was your brain that actually hurt, because it could never quite decide what your eye should stop on. Then your eye *would* stop, or be stopped, by something that seemed as out of place as those limp clockfaces or the living room in the desert. A brass bedstead leaning drunkenly in the sun. A little girl's dolly looking amazedly between her thighs as she gave birth to stuffing. An overturned Studebaker automobile with its chrome bullet nose glittering in the sun like some Buck Rogers missile. One of those giant water bottles they have in office buildings, transformed by the summer sun into a hot, blazing sapphire.

There was plenty of wildlife there, too, although it wasn't the kind you see in the Walt Disney nature films or at those tame zoos where you can pet the animals. Plump rats, woodchucks grown sleek and lumbering on such rich chow as rotting hamburger and maggoty vegetables, seagulls by the thousands, and stalking among the gulls like thoughtful, introspective ministers, an occasional huge crow. It was also the place where the town's stray dogs came for a meal when they couldn't find any trashcans to knock over or any deer to run. They were a miserable, ugly-tempered, mongrel lot; slat-sided and grinning bitterly, they would attack each other over a flyblown piece of bologna or a pile of chicken guts fuming in the sun.

But these dogs never attacked Milo Pressman, the dump-keeper, because Milo was never without Chopper at his heel. Chopper was—at least until Joe Camber's dog Cujo went rabid twenty years later—the most feared and least seen dog in Castle Rock. He was the meanest dog for forty miles around (or so we heard), and ugly enough to stop a striking clock. The kids whispered legends about Chopper's meanness. Some said he was half German shepherd, some said he was mostly boxer, and a kid from Castle View with the unfortunate name of Harry Horr claimed that Chopper was a Doberman pinscher whose vocal cords had been surgically removed so you couldn't hear him when he was on the attack. There were other kids who claimed Chopper was a maniacal Irish wolfhound and Milo Pressman fed him a special mixture of Gaines Meal and chicken blood. These same kids claimed that Milo didn't dare take Chopper out of his shack unless the dog was hooded like a hunting falcon.

The most common story was that Pressman had trained Chopper not just to sic but to sic specific *parts* of the human anatomy. Thus an unfortunate kid who had illegally scaled the dump fence to pick up illicit treasures might hear Milo Pressman cry: "Chopper! Sic! Hand!" And Chopper would grab that hand and hold on, ripping skin and tendons, powdering bones between his slavering jaws, until Milo told him to quit. It was rumored that Chopper could take an ear, an eye, a foot, or a leg . . . and that a second offender who was surprised by Milo and the ever-loyal Chopper would hear the dread cry: "Chopper! Sic! Balls!" And that kid would be a soprano for the rest of his life. Milo himself was more commonly seen and thus more commonly regarded. He was just a half-bright working joe who supplemented his small town salary by fixing things people threw away and selling them around town.

There was no sign of either Milo or Chopper today.

Chris and I watched Vern prime the pump while Teddy worked the handle frantically. At last he was rewarded with a flood of clear water. A moment later both of them had their heads under the trough, Teddy still pumping away a mile a minute.

"Teddy's crazy," I said softly.

"Oh yeah," Chris said matter-of-factly. "He won't live to be twice the age he is now, I bet. His dad burnin his ears like that. That's what did it. He's crazy to dodge trucks the way he does. He can't see worth a shit, glasses or no glasses."

"You remember that time in the tree?"

"Yeah."

The year before, Teddy and Chris had been climbing the big pine tree behind my house. They were almost to the top and Chris said they couldn't go any further because all of the branches up there were rotten. Teddy got that crazy, stubborn look on his face and said fuck that, he had pine tar all over his hands and he was gonna go up until he could touch the top. Nothing Chris said could talk him out of it. So up he went, and he actually made it—he only weighed seventy-five pounds or so, remember. He stood there, clutching the top of the pine in one tar-gummy hand, shouting that he was king of the world or some stupid thing like that, and then there was a sickening, rotted crack as the branch he was standing on gave way and he plummeted. What happened next was one of those things that make you sure there must be a God. Chris reached out, purely on reflex, and what he caught was a fistful of Teddy Duchamp's hair. And although his wrist swelled up fat and he was unable to use his right hand very well for almost two weeks, Chris held him until Teddy, screaming and cursing, got his foot on a live branch thick enough to support his weight. Except for Chris's blind grab, he would have turned and crashed and smashed all the way to the foot of the tree, a hundred and twenty feet below. When they got down, Chris was gray-faced and almost puking with the fear reaction. And Teddy wanted to fight him for pulling his hair. They would have gone at it, too, if I hadn't been there to make peace.

"I dream about that every now and then," Chris said, and looked at me with strangely defenseless eyes. "Except in this dream I have, I always miss him. I just get a couple of hairs and Teddy screams and down he goes. Weird, huh?"

"Weird," I agreed, and for just one moment we looked in each other's eyes and saw some of the true things that made us friends. Then we looked away again and watched Teddy and Vern throwing water at each other, screaming and laughing and calling each other pussies.

"Yeah, but you didn't miss him," I said. "Chris Chambers never misses, am I right?"

"Not even when the ladies leave the seat down," he said. He winked at me, formed an O with his thumb and forefinger, and spat a neat white bullet through it.

"Eat me raw, Chambers," I said.

"Through a Flavor Straw," he said, and we grinned at each other.

Vern yelled: *"Come on and get your water before it runs back down the pipe!"*

"Race you," Chris said.

"In this heat? You're off your gourd."

"Come on," he said, still grinning. "On my go."

"Okay."

"Go!"

We raced, our sneakers digging up the hard, sunbaked dirt,

our torsos leaning out ahead of our flying bluejeaned legs, our fists doubled. It was a dead heat, with both Vern on Chris's side and Teddy on mine holding up their middle fingers at the same moment. We collapsed laughing in the still, smoky odor of the place, and Chris tossed Vern his canteen. When it was full, Chris and I went to the pump and first Chris pumped for me and then I pumped for him, the shocking cold water sluicing off the soot and the heat all in a flash, sending our suddenly freezing scalps four months ahead into January. Then I re-filled the lard can and we all walked over to sit down in the shade of the dump's only tree, a stunted ash forty feet from Milo Pressman's tarpaper shack. The tree was hunched slightly to the west, as if what it really wanted to do was pick up its roots the way an old lady would pick up her skirts and just get the hell out of the dump.

"The most!" Chris said, laughing, tossing his tangled hair back from his brow.

"A blast," I said, nodding, still laughing myself.

"This is really a good time," Vern said simply, and he didn't just mean being off-limits inside the dump, or fudging our folks, or going on a hike up the railroad tracks into Harlow; he meant those things but it seems to me now that there was more, and that we all knew it. Everything was there and around us. We knew exactly who we were and exactly where we were going. It was grand.

We sat under the tree for awhile, shooting the shit like we always did—who had the best ballteam (still the Yankees with Mantle and Maris, of course), what was the best car ('55 Thunderbird, with Teddy holding out stubbornly for the '58 Corvette), who was the toughest guy in Castle Rock who wasn't in our gang (we all agreed it was Jamie Gallant, who gave Mrs. Ewing the finger and then sauntered out of her class with his hands in his pockets while she shouted at him), the best

TV show (either *The Untouchables* or *Peter Gunn*—both Robert Stack as Eliot Ness and Craig Stevens as Gunn were cool), all that stuff.

It was Teddy who first noticed that the shade of the ash tree was getting longer and asked me what time it was. I looked at my watch and was surprised to see it was quarter after two.

"Hey man," Vern said. "Somebody's got to go for provisions. Dump opens at four. I don't want to still be here when Milo and Chopper make the scene."

Even Teddy agreed. He wasn't afraid of Milo, who had a pot belly and was at least forty, but every kid in Castle Rock squeezed his balls between his legs when Chopper's name was mentioned.

"Okay," I said. "Odd man goes?"

"That's you, Gordie," Chris said, smiling. "Odd as a cod."

"So's your mother," I said, and gave them each a coin. "Flip."

Four coins glittered up into the sun. Four hands snatched them from the air. Four flat smacks on four grimy wrists. We uncovered. Two heads and two tails. We flipped again and this time all four of us had tails.

"Oh Jesus, that's a goocher," Vern said, not telling us anything we didn't know. Four heads, or a moon, was supposed to be extraordinarily good luck. Four tails was a goocher, and that meant very bad luck.

"Fuck that shit," Chris said. "It doesn't mean anything. Go again."

"No, man," Vern said earnestly. "A goocher, that's really bad. You remember when Clint Bracken and those guys got wiped out on Sirois Hill in Durham? Billy tole me they was flippin for beers and they came up a goocher just before they got into the car. And bang! they all get fuckin totalled. I don't like that. Sincerely."

"Nobody believes that crap about moons and goochers,"

Teddy said impatiently. "It's baby stuff, Vern. You gonna flip or not?"

Vern flipped, but with obvious reluctance. This time he, Chris, and Teddy all had tails. I was showing Thomas Jefferson on a nickel. And I was suddenly scared. It was as if a shadow had crossed some inner sun. They still had a goocher, the three of them, as if dumb fate had pointed at them a second time. Abruptly I thought of Chris saying: *I just get a couple of hairs and Teddy screams and down he goes. Weird, huh?*

Three tails, one head.

Then Teddy was laughing his crazy, cackling laugh and pointing at me and the feeling was gone.

"I heard that only fairies laugh like that," I said, and gave him the finger.

"Eeee-eeee-eeee, Gordie," Teddy laughed. "Go get the provisions, you fuckin morphadite."

I wasn't really sorry to be going. I was rested up and didn't mind going down the road to the Florida Market.

"Don't call me any of your mother's pet names," I said to Teddy.

"Eeee-eee-eeee, what a fuckin wet you are, Lachance."

"Go on, Gordie," Chris said. "We'll wait over by the tracks."

"You guys better not go without me," I said.

Vern laughed. "Goin without you'd be like goin with Slitz instead of Budweiser's, Gordie."

"Ah, shut up."

They chanted together: "I don't shut up, I *grow* up. And when I look at you I *throw* up."

"Then your mother goes around the corner and licks it up," I said, and hauled ass out of there, giving them the finger over my shoulder as I went. I never had any friends later on like the ones I had when I was twelve. Jesus, did you?

12

Different strokes for different folks, they say now, and that's cool. So if I say *summer* to you, you get one set of private, personal images that are all the way different from mine. That's cool. But for me, *summer* is always going to mean running down the road to the Florida Market with change jingling in my pockets, the temperature in the gay nineties, my feet dressed in Keds. The word conjures an image of the GS&WM railroad tracks running into a perspective-point in the distance, burnished so white under the sun that when you closed your eyes you could still see them there in the dark, only blue instead of white.

But there was more to that summer than our trip across the river to look for Ray Brower, although that looms the largest. Sounds of The Fleetwoods singing, "Come Softly to Me" and Robin Luke singing "Susie Darlin" and Little Anthony popping the vocal on "I Ran All the Way Home." Were they all hits in that summer of 1960? Yes and no. Mostly yes. In the long purple evenings when rock and roll from WLAM blurred into night baseball from WCOU, time shifted. I think it was all 1960 and that the summer went on for a space of years, held magically intact in a web of sounds: the sweet hum of crickets, the machine-gun roar of playing-cards riffling against the spokes of some kid's bicycle as he pedaled home for a late supper of cold cuts and iced tea, the flat Texas voice of Buddy Knox singing "Come along and be my party doll, and I'll make love to you, to you," and the baseball announcer's voice mingling with the song and with the smell of freshly cut grass: "Count's three and two now. Whitey Ford leans over . . . shakes off the sign . . . now he's got it . . . Ford pauses . . . pitches . . . *and there it goes! Williams got all of that one! Kiss it goodbye! RED SOX LEAD, THREE TO ONE!*" Was Ted Williams still playing for the Red Sox in 1960? You bet your ass he was—.316 for my man Ted. I remember that very clearly. Baseball had become important to me in the last couple of years, ever since I'd had to face the knowledge that baseball players were as much flesh and blood as I was. That knowledge came when Roy Campanella's car overturned and the papers screamed mortal news from the front pages: his career was done, he was going to sit in a wheelchair for the rest of his life. How that came back to me, with that same sickening mortal thud, when I sat down to this typewriter one morning two years ago, turned on the radio, and heard that Thurman Munson had died while trying to land his airplane.

There were movies to go see at the Gem, which has long since been torn down; science fiction movies like *Gog* with Richard Egan and westerns with Audie Murphy (Teddy saw every movie Audie Murphy made at least three times; he believed Murphy was almost a god) and war movies with John Wayne. There were games and endless bolted meals, lawns to mow, places to run to, walls to pitch pennies against, people to clap you on the back. And now I sit here trying to look through an IBM keyboard and see that time, trying to recall the best and the worst of that green and brown summer, and I can almost feel the skinny, scabbed boy still buried in this advancing body and hear those sounds. But the apotheosis of the memory and the time is Gordon Lachance running down the road to the Florida Market with change in his pockets and sweat running down his back.

I asked for three pounds of hamburger and got some hamburger rolls, four bottles of Coke and a two-cent churchkey to open them with. The owner, a man named George Dusset, got the meat and then leaned by his cash register, one hammy hand planted on the counter by the big bottle of hardcooked eggs, a toothpick in his mouth, his huge beer belly rounding his white tee-shirt like a sail filled with a good wind. He stood right there as I shopped, making sure I didn't try to hawk anything. He didn't say a word until he was weighing up the hamburger.

"I know you. You're Denny Lachance's brother. Ain't you?" The toothpick journeyed from one corner of his mouth to the other, as if on ball bearings. He reached behind the cash register, picked up a bottle of S'OK cream soda, and chugged it.

"Yes, sir. But Denny, he—"

"Yeah, I know. That's a sad thing, kid. The Bible says: 'In the midst of life, we are in death.' Did you know that? Yuh. I lost a brother in Korea. You look just like Denny, people ever tell you that? Yuh. Spitting image."

"Yes, sir, sometimes," I said glumly.

"I remember the year he was All-Conference. Halfback, he played. Yuh. Could he run? Father God and Sonny Jesus! You're probably too young to remember." He was looking over my head, out through the screen door and into the blasting heat, as if he were having a beautiful vision of my brother.

"I remember. Uh, Mr. Dusset?"

"What, kid?" His eyes were still misty with memory; the toothpick trembled a little between his lips.

"Your thumb is on that scales."

"What?" He looked down, astounded, to where the ball of his thumb was pressed firmly on the white enamel. If I hadn't moved away from him a little bit when he started talking about Dennis, the ground meat would have hidden it. "Why, so it is. Yuh. I guess I just got thinkin about your brother, God love him." George Dusset signed a cross on himself. When he took his thumb off the scales, the needle sprang back six ounces. He patted a little more meat on top and then did the package up with white butcher's paper.

"Okay," he said past the toothpick. "Let's see what we got

here. Three pounds of hamburg, that's a dollar forty-four. Hamburg rolls, that's twenty-seven. Four sodas, forty cents. One churchkey, two pence. Comes to . . ." He added it up on the bag he was going to put the stuff in. "Two-twenty-nine."

"Thirteen," I said.

He looked up at me very slowly, frowning. "Huh?"

"Two-thirteen. You added it wrong."

"Kid, are you—"

"You added it wrong," I said. "First you put your thumb on the scales and then you overcharged on the groceries, Mr. Dusset. I was gonna throw some Hostess Twinkies on top of that order but now I guess I won't." I spanged two dollars and thirteen cents down on the Schlitz placemat in front of him.

He looked at the money, then at me. The frown was now tremendous, the lines on his face as deep as fissures. "What are you, kid?" he said in a low voice that was ominously confidential. "Are you some kind of smartass?"

"No, sir," I said. "But you ain't gonna jap me and get away with it. What would your mother say if she knew you was japping little kids?"

He thrust our stuff into the paper bag with quick stiff movements, making the Coke bottles clink together. He thrust the bag at me roughly, not caring if I dropped it and broke the sodas or not. His swarthy face was flushed and dull, the frown now frozen in place. "Okay, kid. Here you go. Now what you do is you get the Christ out of my store. I see you in here again and I going to throw you out, me. Yuh. Smartass little sonofawhore."

"I won't come in again," I said, walking over to the screen door and pushing it open. The hot afternoon buzzed somnolently along its appointed course outside, sounding green and brown and full of silent light. "Neither will none of my friends. I guess I got fifty or so."

"Your brother wasn't no smartass!" George Dusset yelled.

"Fuck you!" I yelled, and ran like hell down the road.

I heard the screen door bang open like a gunshot and his bull roar came after me: *"If you ever come in here again I'll fat your lip for you, you little punk!"*

I ran until I was over the first hill, scared and laughing to myself, my heart beating out a triphammer pulse in my chest. Then I slowed to a fast walk, looking back over my shoulder every now and then to make sure he wasn't going to take after me in his car, or anything.

He didn't, and pretty soon I got to the dump gate. I put the bag inside my shirt, climbed the gate, and monkeyed down the other side. I was halfway across the dump area when I saw something I didn't like—Milo Pressman's portholed '56 Buick was parked behind his tarpaper shack. If Milo saw me I was going to be in a world of hurt. As yet there was no sign of either him or the infamous Chopper, but all at once the chain-link fence at the back of the dump seemed very far away. I found myself wishing I'd gone around the outside, but I was now too far into the dump to want to turn around and go back. If Milo saw me climbing the dump fence, I'd probably be in dutch when I got home, but that didn't scare me as much as Milo yelling for Chopper to sic would.

Scary violin music started to play in my head. I kept putting one foot in front of the other, trying to look casual, trying to look as if I belonged here with a paper grocery sack poking out of my shirt, heading for the fence between the dump and the railroad tracks.

I was about fifty feet from the fence and just beginning to think that everything was going to be all right after all when I heard Milo shout: "Hey! Hey, you! Kid! Get away f'n that fence! Get outta here!"

The smart thing to have done would have been to just agree

with the guy and go around, but by then I was so keyed that instead of doing the smart thing I just broke for the fence with a wild yell, my sneakers kicking up dirt. Vern, Teddy, and Chris came out of the underbrush on the other side of the fence and stared anxiously through the chain-link.

"You come back here!" Milo bawled. *"Come back here or I'll sic my dawg on you, goddammit!"*

I did not exactly find that to be the voice of sanity and conciliation, and I ran even faster for the fence, my arms pumping, the brown grocery bag crackling against my skin. Teddy started to laugh his idiotic chortling laugh, *eee-eee-eeee* into the air like some reed instrument being played by a lunatic.

"Go, Gordie! Go!" Vern screamed.

And Milo yelled: "Sic 'im, Chopper! Go get 'im, boy!"

I threw the bag over the fence and Vern elbowed Teddy out of the way to catch it. Behind me I could hear Chopper coming, shaking the earth, blurting fire out of one distended nostril and ice out of the other, dripping sulphur from his champing jaws. I threw myself halfway up the fence with one leap, screaming. I made it to the top in no more than three seconds and simply leaped—I never thought about it, never even looked down to see what I might land on. What I *almost* landed on was Teddy, who was doubled over and laughing like crazy. His glasses had fallen off and tears were streaming out of his eyes. I missed him by inches and hit the clay-gravel embankment just to his left. At the same instant, Chopper hit the chain-link fence behind me and let out a howl of mingled pain and disappointment. I turned around, holding one skinned knee, and got my first look at the famous Chopper—and my first lesson in the vast difference between myth and reality.

Instead of some huge hellhound with red, savage eyes and teeth jutting out of his mouth like straight-pipes from a hotrod, I was looking at a medium-sized mongrel dog that was a perfectly common black and white. He was yapping and jumping fruitlessly, going up on his back legs to paw the fence.

Teddy was now strutting up and down in front of the fence, twiddling his glasses in one hand, and inciting Chopper to ever greater rage.

"Kiss my ass, Choppie!" Teddy invited, spittle flying from his lips. "Kiss my ass! Bite shit!"

He bumped his fanny against the chain-link fence and Chopper did his level best to take Teddy up on his invitation. He got nothing for his pains but a good healthy nose-bump. He began to bark crazily, foam flying from his snout. Teddy kept bumping his rump against the fence and Chopper kept lunging at it, always missing, doing nothing but racking out his nose, which was now bleeding. Teddy kept exhorting him, calling him by the somehow grisly diminutive "Choppie," and Chris and Vern were lying weakly on the embankment, laughing so hard that they could now do little more than wheeze.

And here came Milo Pressman, dressed in sweat-stained fatigues and a New York Giants baseball cap, his mouth drawn down in distracted anger.

"Here, here!" he was yelling. "You boys stop a-teasing that dawg! You hear me? *Stop it right now!*"

"Bite it, Choppie!" Teddy yelled, strutting up and down on our side of the fence like a mad Prussian reviewing his troops. "Come on and sic me! Sic me!"

Chopper went nuts. I mean it sincerely. He ran around in a big circle, yelping and barking and foaming, rear feet spewing up tough little dry clods. He went around about three times, getting his courage up, I guess, and then he launched himself straight at the security fence. He must have been going thirty miles an hour when he hit it, I kid you not—his doggy lips were stretched back from his teeth and his ears were flying in the slipstream. The whole fence made a low, musical sound as the chain-link was not just driven back against the posts but sort of *stretched* back. It was like a zither note—*yimmmmmmmm.* A strangled yawp came out of Chopper's mouth, both eyes came up blank and he did a totally amazing reverse snap-roll, landing on his back with a solid thump that sent dust puffing up around him. He just lay there for a moment and then he crawled off with his tongue hanging crookedly from the left side of his mouth.

At this, Milo himself went almost berserk with rage. His complexion darkened to a scary plum color—even his scalp was purple under the short hedgehog bristles of his flattop haircut. Sitting stunned in the dirt, both knees of my jeans torn out, my heart still thudding from the nearness of my escape, I thought that Milo looked like a human version of Chopper.

"I know you!" Milo raved. "You're Teddy Duchamp! I know *all* of you! Sonny, I'll beat your ass, teasing my dawg like that!"

"Like to see you try!" Teddy raved right back. "Let's see you climb over this fence and get me, fatass!"

"WHAT? WHAT DID YOU CALL ME?"

"FATASS!" Teddy screamed happily. *"LARD-BUCKET! TUBBAGUTS! COME ON! COME ON!"* He was jumping up and down, fists clenched, sweat flying from his hair. *"TEACH YOU TO SIC YOUR STUPID DOG ON PEOPLE! COME ON! LIKE TO SEE YOU TRY!"*

"You little tin-weasel peckerwood loony's son! I'll see your mother gets an invitation to go down and talk to the judge in court about what you done to my dawg!"

"What did you call me?" Teddy asked hoarsely. He had stopped jumping up and down. His eyes had gone huge and glassy, and his skin was the color of lead.

Milo had called Teddy a lot of things, but he was able to go back and get the one that had struck home with no trouble at all—since then I have noticed again and again what a genius people have for that . . . for finding the loony button down inside and not just pressing it but hammering on the fucker.

"Your dad was a loony," he said, grinning. "Loony up in Togus, that's what. Crazier'n a shithouse rat. Crazier'n a buck with tickwood fever. Nuttier'n a long-tailed cat in a room fulla rockin chairs. Loony. No wonder you're actin the way you are, with a loony for a f—"

"YOUR MOTHER BLOWS DEAD RATS!" Teddy screamed. *"AND IF YOU CALL MY DAD A LOONY AGAIN, I'LL FUCKING KILL YOU, YOU COCKSUCKER!"*

"Loony," Milo said smugly. He'd found the button, all right. "Loony's kid, loony's kid, your father's got toys in the attic, kid, tough break."

Vern and Chris had been getting over their laughing fit, perhaps getting ready to appreciate the seriousness of the situation and call Teddy off, but when Teddy told Milo that his mother blew dead rats, they went back into hysterics again, lying there on the bank, rolling from side to side, their feet kicking, holding their bellies. "No more," Chris said weakly. "No more, please, no more, I swear to God I'm gonna *bust*!"

Chopper was walking around in a large, dazed figure-eight behind Milo. He looked like the losing fighter about ten seconds after the ref has ended the match and awarded the winner a TKO. Meanwhile, Teddy and Milo continued their discussion of Teddy's father, standing nose to nose, with the wire fence Milo was too old and too fat to climb between them.

"Don't you say nothing else about my dad! My dad stormed the beach at Normandy, you fucking wet end!"

"Yeah, well, where is he now, you ugly little four-eyed turd? He's up to Togus, ain't he? He's up to Togus because *HE WENT FUCKING SECTION EIGHT!"*

"Okay, that's it," Teddy said. "That's it, that's the end, I'm gonna kill you." He threw himself at the fence and started up.

"You come on and try it, you slimy little bastard." Milo stood back, grinning and waiting.

"No!" I shouted. I got to my feet, grabbed Teddy by the loose seat of his jeans, and pulled him off the fence. We both staggered back and fell over, him on top. He squashed my balls pretty good and I groaned. Nothing hurts like having your balls squashed, you know it? But I kept my arms locked around Teddy's middle.

"Lemme up!" Teddy sobbed, writhing in my arms. "Lemme up, Gordie! Nobody ranks out my old man. *LEMME UP GODDAMMIT LEMME UP!*"

"That's just what he wants!" I shouted in his ear. "He wants to get you over there and beat the piss out of you and then take you to the cops!"

"Huh?" Teddy craned around to look at me, his face dazed.

"Never mind your smartmouth, kid," Milo said, advancing to the fence again with his hands curled into ham-sized fists. "Let'im fight his own battles."

"Sure," I said. "You only outweigh him by five hundred pounds."

"I know you, too," Milo said ominously. "Your name's Lachance." He pointed to where Vern and Chris were finally picking themselves up, still breathing fast from laughing so hard. "And those guys are Chris Chambers and one of those stupid Tessio kids. All your fathers are going to get calls from me, except for the loony up to Togus. You'll go to the 'formatory, every one of you. Juvenile delinquents!"

He stood flat on his feet, big freckled hands held out like a guy who wanted to play One Potato Two Potato, breathing hard, eyes narrow, waiting for us to cry or say we were sorry or maybe give him Teddy so he could feed Teddy to Chopper.

Chris made an O out of his thumb and index finger and spat neatly through it.

Vern hummed and looked at the sky.

Teddy said: "Come on, Gordie. Let's get away from this asshole before I puke."

"Oh, you're gonna get it, you foulmouthed little whoremaster. Wait'll I get you to the Constable."

"We heard what you said about his father," I told him. "We're all witnesses. And you sicced that dog on me. That's against the law."

Milo looked a trifle uneasy. "You was trespassin."

"The hell I was. The dump's public property."

"You climbed the fence."

"Sure I did, after you sicced your dog on me," I said, hoping that Milo wouldn't recall that I'd also climbed the gate to get in. "What'd you think I was gonna do? Stand there and let 'im rip me to pieces? Come on, you guys. Let's go. It stinks around here."

" 'Formatory," Milo promised hoarsely, his voice shaking. " 'Formatory for you wiseguys."

"Can't wait to tell the cops how you called a war vet a fuckin loony," Chris called back over his shoulder as we moved away. "What did *you* do in the war, Mr. Pressman?"

"NONE OF YOUR DAMN BUSINESS!" Milo shrieked. *"YOU HURT MY DAWG!"*

"Put it on your t.s. slip and send it to the chaplain," Vern muttered, and then we were climbing the railroad embankment again.

"Come back here!" Milo shouted, but his voice was fainter now and he seemed to be losing interest.

Teddy shot him the finger as we walked away. I looked back over my shoulder when we got to the top of the embankment. Milo was standing there behind the security fence, a big man in a baseball cap with his dog sitting beside him. His fingers were hooked through the small chain-link diamonds as he shouted at us, and all at once I felt very sorry for him—he looked like the biggest third-grader in the world, locked inside the playground by mistake, yelling for someone to come and let him out. He kept on yelling for awhile and then he either gave up or we got out of range. No more was seen or heard of Milo Pressman and Chopper that day.

13

There was some discussion—in righteous tones that were actually kind of forced-sounding—about how we had shown that creepy Milo Pressman we weren't just another bunch of pussies. I told how the guy at the Florida Market had tried to jap us, and then we fell into a gloomy silence, thinking it over.

For my part, I was thinking that maybe there was something to that stupid goocher business after all. Things couldn't have turned out much worse—in fact, I thought, it might be better to just keep going and spare my folks the pain of having one son in the Castle View Cemetery and one in South Windham Boys' Correctional. I had no doubt that Milo would go to the cops as soon as the importance of the dump having been closed at the time of the incident filtered into his thick skull. When that happened, he would realize that I really *had* been trespassing, public property or not. Probably that gave him every right in the world to sic his stupid dog on me. And while Chopper wasn't the hellhound he was cracked up to be, he sure would have ripped the sitdown out of my jeans if I hadn't won the race to the fence. All of it put a big dark crimp in the day. And there was another gloomy idea rolling around inside my head—the idea that this was no lark after all, and maybe we deserved our bad luck. Maybe it was even God warning us to go home. What were we doing, anyway, going to look at some kid that had gotten himself all mashed up by a freight train?

But we were doing it, and none of us wanted to stop.

We had almost reached the trestle which carried the tracks across the river when Teddy burst into tears. It was as if a great inner tidal wave had broken through a carefully constructed set of mental dykes. No bullshit—it was that sudden and that fierce. The sobs doubled him over like punches and he sort of collapsed into a heap, his hands going from his stomach to the mutilated gobs of flesh that were the remains of his ears. He went on crying in hard, violent bursts.

None of us knew what the fuck to do. It wasn't crying like when you got hit by a line drive while you were playing shortstop or smashed on the head playing tackle football on the common or when you fell off your bike. There was nothing physically wrong with him. We walked away a little and watched him, our hands in our pockets.

"Hey, man . . ." Vern said in a very thin voice. Chris and I looked at Vern hopefully. "Hey, man" was always a good start. But Vern couldn't follow it up.

Teddy leaned forward onto the crossties and put a hand over his eyes. Now he looked like he was doing the Allah bit—"Salami, salami, baloney," as Popeye says. Except it wasn't funny.

At last, when the force of his crying had trailed off a little, it was Chris who went to him. He was the toughest guy in our gang (maybe even tougher than Jamie Gallant, I thought privately), but he was also the guy who made the best peace. He had a way about it. I'd seen him sit down on the curb next to a little kid with a scraped knee, a kid he didn't even fucking *know,* and get him talking about something—the Shrine Circus that was coming to town or Huckleberry Hound on TV—

until the kid forgot he was supposed to be hurt. Chris was good at it. He was tough enough to be good at it.

"Lissen, Teddy, what do you care what a fat old pile of shit like him said about your father? Huh? I mean, sincerely! That don't change nothing, does it? What a fat old pile of shit like him says? Huh? Huh? Does it?"

Teddy shook his head violently. It changed nothing. But to hear it spoken of in bright daylight, something he must have gone over and over in his mind while he was lying awake in bed and looking at the moon off-center in one windowpane, something he must have thought about in his slow and broken way until it seemed almost holy, trying to make sense out of it, and then to have it brought home to him that everybody else had merely dismissed his dad as a loony . . . that had rocked him. But it changed nothing. Nothing.

"He still stormed the beach at Normandy, right?" Chris said. He picked up one of Teddy's sweaty, grimy hands and patted it.

Teddy nodded fiercely, crying. Snot was running out of his nose.

"Do you think that pile of shit was at Normandy?"

Teddy shook his head violently. *"Nuh-Nuh-No!"*

"Do you think that guy knows you?"

"Nuh-No! No, b-b-but—"

"Or your father? He one of your father's buddies?"

"NO!" Angry, horrified. The thought. Teddy's chest heaved and more sobs came out of it. He had pushed his hair away from his ears and I could see the round brown plastic button of the hearing aid set in the middle of his right one. The shape of the hearing aid made more sense than the shape of his ear, if you get what I mean.

Chris said calmly: "Talk is cheap."

Teddy nodded, still not looking up.

"And whatever's between you and your old man, talk can't change that."

Teddy's head shook without definition, unsure if this was true. Someone had redefined his pain, and redefined it in shockingly common terms. That would

(loony)

have to be examined

(fucking section eight)

later. In depth. On long sleepless nights.

Chris rocked him. "He was ranking you, man," he said in soothing cadences that were almost a lullaby. "He was tryin to rank you over that friggin fence, you know it? No strain, man. No fuckin strain. He don't know nothin about your old man. He don't know nothin but stuff he heard from those rumdums down at The Mellow Tiger. He's just dogshit, man. Right, Teddy? Huh? Right?"

Teddy's crying was down to sniffles. He wiped his eyes, leaving two sooty rings around them, and sat up.

"I'm okay," he said, and the sound of his own voice seemed to convince him. "Yeah, I'm okay." He stood up and put his glasses back on—dressing his naked face, it seemed to me. He laughed thinly and swiped his bare arm across the snot of his upper lip. "Fuckin crybaby, right?"

"No, man," Vern said uncomfortably. "If anyone was rankin out my dad—"

"Then you got to kill em!" Teddy said briskly, almost arrogantly. "Kill their asses. Right, Chris?"

"Right," Chris said amiably, and clapped Teddy on the back. "Right, Gordie?"

"Absolutely," I said, wondering how Teddy could care so much for his dad when his dad had practically killed him, and how I couldn't seem to give much of a shit one way or the other about my own dad, when so far as I could remember, he had never laid a hand on me since I was three and got some bleach from under the sink and started to eat it.

We walked another two hundred yards down the tracks and Teddy said in a quieter voice: "Hey, if I spoiled your good time, I'm sorry. I guess that was pretty stupid shit back there at that fence."

"I ain't sure I want it to be no good time," Vern said suddenly.

Chris looked at him. "You sayin you want to go back, man?"

"No, huh-uh!" Vern's face knotted in thought. "But going to see a dead kid—it shouldn't be a party, maybe. I mean, if you can dig it. I mean . . ." He looked at us rather wildly. "I mean, I could be a little scared. If you get me."

Nobody said anything and Vern plunged on:

"I mean, sometimes I get nightmares. Like . . . aw, you guys remember the time Danny Naughton left that pile of old funnybooks, the ones with the vampires and people gettin cut up and all that shit? Jeezum-crow, I'd wake up in the middle of the night dreamin about some guy hangin in a house with his face all green or somethin, you know, like that, and it seems like there's somethin under the bed and if I dangled a hand over the side, that thing might, you know, grab me . . ."

We all began to nod. We knew about the night shift. I would have laughed then, though, if you had told me that one day not too many years from then I'd parlay all those childhood fears and night-sweats into about a million dollars.

"And I don't dare say anything because my friggin *brother* . . . well, you know Billy . . . he'd broadcast it . . ." He shrugged miserably. "So I'm ascared to look at that kid cause if he's, you know, if he's really *bad* . . ."

I swallowed and glanced at Chris. He was looking gravely at Vern and nodding for him to go on.

"If he's really *bad,*" Vern resumed, "I'll have nightmares about *him* and wake up thinkin it's *him* under my bed, all cut up in a pool of blood like he just came out of one of those Saladmaster gadgets they show on TV, just eyeballs and hair, but *movin* somehow, if you can dig that, *mooovin* somehow, you know, and gettin ready to *grab*—"

"Jesus Christ," Teddy said thickly. "What a fuckin bedtime story."

"Well I can't *help* it," Vern said, his voice defensive. "But I feel like we *hafta* see him, even if there are bad dreams. You know? Like we *hafta.* But . . . but maybe it shouldn't be no good time."

"Yeah," Chris said softly. "Maybe it shouldn't."

Vern said pleadingly: "You won't tell none of the other guys, will you? I don't mean about the nightmares, everybody has those—I mean about wakin up and thinkin there might be somethin under the bed. I'm too fuckin old for the boogeyman."

We all said we wouldn't tell, and a glum silence fell over us again. It was only quarter to three, but it felt much later. It was too hot and too much had happened. We weren't even over into Harlow yet. We were going to have to pick them up and lay them down if we were going to make some real miles before dark.

We passed the railroad junction and a signal on a tall, rusty pole and all of us paused to chuck cinders at the steel flag on top, but nobody hit it. And around three-thirty we came to the Castle River and the GS&WM trestle which crossed it.

14

The river was better than a hundred yards across at that point in 1960; I've been back to look at it since then, and found it had narrowed up quite a bit during the years between. They're always fooling with the river, trying to make it work better for the mills, and they've put in so many dams that it's pretty well tamed. But in those days there were only three dams on the whole length of the river as it ran across New Hampshire and half of Maine. The Castle was still almost free back then, and every third spring it would overflow its banks and cover Route 136 in either Harlow or Danvers Junction or both.

Now, at the end of the driest summer western Maine had seen since the depression, it was still broad. From where we stood on the Castle Rock side, the bulking forest on the Harlow side looked like a different country altogether. The pines and spruces over there were bluish in the heat-haze of the afternoon. The rails went across the water fifty feet up, supported by an underpinning of tarred wooden support posts and criss-crossing beams. The water was so shallow you could look down and see the tops of the cement plugs which had been planted ten feet deep in the riverbed to hold up the trestle.

The trestle itself was pretty chintzy—the rails ran over a long, narrow wooden platform of six-by-fours. There was a four-inch gap between each pair of these beams where you could look all the way down into the water. On the sides, there was no more than eighteen inches between the rail and the edge of the trestle. If a train came, it was maybe enough room to avoid getting plastered . . . but the wind generated by a highballing freight would surely sweep you off to fall to a certain death against the rocks just below the surface of the shallow running water.

Looking at the trestle, we all felt fear start to crawl around in our bellies . . . and mixing uneasily with the fear was the excitement of a boss dare, a really big one, something you could brag on for weeks after you got home . . . *if* you got home. That queer light was creeping back into Teddy's eyes and I thought he wasn't seeing the GS&WM train trestle at all but a long sandy beach, a thousand LSTs aground in the foaming waves, ten thousand GIs charging up the sand, combat boots digging. They were leaping rolls of barbed wire! Tossing grenades at pillboxes! Overrunning machine-gun nests!

We were standing beside the tracks where the cinders sloped away toward the river's cut—the place where the embankment stopped and the trestle began. Looking down, I could see where the slope started to get steep. The cinders gave way to scraggly, tough-looking bushes and slabs of gray rock. Further down there were a few stunted firs with exposed roots writhing their way out of fissures in the plates of rock; they seemed to be looking down at their own miserable reflections in the running water.

At this point, the Castle River actually looked fairly clean; at Castle Rock it was just entering Maine's textile-mill belt. But there were no fish jumping out there, although the river was clear enough to see bottom—you had to go another ten miles upstream and toward New Hampshire before you could see any fish in the Castle. There were no fish, and along the edges of the river you could see dirty collars of foam around some of the rocks—the foam was the color of old ivory. The river's smell was not particularly pleasant, either; it smelled like a laundry hamper full of mildewy towels. Dragonflies stitched at the surface of the water and laid their eggs with impunity. There were no trout to eat them. Hell, there weren't even any shiners.

"Man," Chris said softly.

"Come on," Teddy said in that brisk, arrogant way. "Let's go." He was already edging his way out, walking on the six-by-fours between the shining rails.

"Say," Vern said uneasily, "any of you guys know when the next train's due?"

We all shrugged.

I said: "There's the Route 136 bridge . . ."

"Hey, come on, gimme a break!" Teddy cried. "That means walkin five miles down the river on this side and then five miles back up on the other side . . . it'll take us until dark! If we use the trestle, we can get to the same place in *ten minutes*!"

"But if a train comes, there's nowheres to go," Vern said. He wasn't looking at Teddy. He was looking down at the fast, bland river.

"Fuck there isn't!" Teddy said indignantly. He swung over the edge and held one of the wooden supports between the rails. He hadn't gone out very far—his sneakers were almost touching the ground—but the thought of doing that same thing above the middle of the river with a fifty-foot drop beneath and a train bellowing by just over my head, a train that would probably be dropping some nice hot sparks into my hair and down the back of my neck . . . none of that actually made me feel like Queen for a Day.

"See how easy it is?" Teddy said. He dropped to the embankment, dusted his hands, and climbed back up beside us.

"You tellin me you're gonna hang on that way if it's a two-hundred-car freight?" Chris asked. "Just sorta hang there by your hands for five or ten minutes?"

"You chicken?" Teddy shouted.

"No, just askin what you'd do," Chris said, grinning. "Peace, man."

"Go around if you want to!" Teddy brayed. "Who gives a fuck? I'll wait for you! I'll take a *nap*!"

"One train already went by," I said reluctantly. "And there probably isn't any more than one, two trains a day that go through Harlow. Look at this." I kicked the weeds growing up through the railroad ties with one sneaker. There were no weeds growing between the tracks which ran between Castle Rock and Lewiston.

"There. See?" Teddy triumphant.

"But still, there's a *chance,*" I added.

"Yeah," Chris said. He was looking only at me, his eyes sparkling. "Dare you, Lachance."

"Dares go first"

"Okay," Chris said. He widened his gaze to take in Teddy and Vern. "Any pussies here?"

"NO!" Teddy shouted.

Vern cleared his throat, croaked, cleared it again, and said "No" in a very small voice. He smiled a weak, sick smile.

"Okay," Chris said . . . but we hesitated for a moment, even Teddy, looking warily up and down the tracks. I knelt down and took one of the steel rails firmly in my hand, never minding that it was almost hot enough to blister the skin. The rail was mute.

"Okay," I said, and as I said it some guy pole-vaulted in my stomach. He dug his pole all the way into my balls, it felt like, and ended up sitting astride my heart.

We went out onto the trestle single file: Chris first, then Teddy, then Vern, and me playing tail-end Charlie because I was the one who said dares go first. We walked on the platform crossties between the rails, and you had to look at your feet whether you were scared of heights or not. A misstep and you would go down to your crotch, probably with a broken ankle to pay.

The embankment dropped away beneath me, and every step further out seemed to seal our decision more firmly . . . and to make it feel more suicidally stupid. I stopped to look up when I saw the rocks giving way to water far beneath me. Chris and Teddy were a long way ahead, almost out over the middle, and Vern was tottering slowly along behind them, peering studiously down at his feet. He looked like an old lady trying out stilts with his head poked downward, his back hunched, his arms held out for balance. I looked back over my shoulder. Too far, man. I had to keep going now, and not only because a train might come. If I went back, I'd be a pussy for life.

So I got walking again. After looking down at that endless series of crossties for awhile, with a glimpse of running water between each pair, I started to feel dizzy and disoriented. Each time I brought my foot down, part of my brain assured me it was going to plunge through into space, even though I could see it was not.

I became acutely aware of all the noises inside me and outside me, like some crazy orchestra tuning up to play. The steady thump of my heart, the bloodbeat in my ears like a drum being played with brushes, the creak of sinews like the strings of a violin that has been tuned radically upward, the steady hiss of the river, the hot hum of a locust digging into tight bark, the monotonous cry of a chickadee, and somewhere, far away, a barking dog. Chopper, maybe. The mildewy smell of the Castle River was strong in my nose. The long muscles in my thighs were trembling. I kept thinking how much safer it would be (probably faster, as well) if I just got down on my hands and knees and scuttered along that way. But I wouldn't do that—none of us would. If the Saturday matinee movies down to the Gem had taught us anything, it was that Only Losers Crawl. It was one of the central tenets of the Gospel According to Hollywood. Good guys walk firmly upright, and if your sinews are creaking like overtimed violin strings because of the adrenaline rush going on in your body, and if the long muscles in your thighs are trembling for the same reason, why, so be it.

I had to stop in the middle of the trestle and look up at the sky for awhile. That dizzy feeling had been getting worse. I saw phantom crossties—they seemed to float right in front of my nose. Then they faded out and I began to feel okay again. I looked ahead and saw I had almost caught up with Vern, who was slowpoking along worse than ever. Chris and Teddy were almost all the way across.

And although I've since written seven books about people who can do such exotic things as read minds and precognit the future, that was when I had my first and last psychic flash. I'm sure that's what it was; how else to explain it? I squatted and made a fist around the rail on my left. It thrummed in my hand. It was thrumming so hard that it was like gripping a bundle of deadly metallic snakes.

You've heard it said "His bowels turned to water"? I know what that phrase means—*exactly* what it means. It may be the most accurate cliché ever coined. I've been scared since, badly scared, but I've never been as scared as I was in that moment, holding that hot live rail. It seemed that for a moment all my works below throat level just went limp and lay there in an internal faint. A thin stream of urine ran listlessly down the inside of one thigh. My mouth opened. I didn't open it, it opened by itself, the jaw dropping like a trapdoor from which the hingepins had suddenly been removed. My tongue was plastered suffocatingly against the roof of my mouth. All my muscles were locked. That was the worst. My works went limp but my muscles were in a kind of dreadful lockbolt and I couldn't move at all. It was only for a moment, but in the subjective timestream, it seemed forever.

All sensory input became intensified, as if some power-surge had occurred in the electrical flow of my brain, cranking everything up from a hundred and ten volts to two-twenty. I could hear a plane passing in the sky somewhere near and had time to wish I was on it, just sitting in a window seat with a Coke in my hand and gazing idly down at the shining line of a river whose name I did not know. I could see every little splinter and gouge in the tarred crosstie I was squatting on. And out of the corner of my eye I could see the rail itself with my hand still clutched around it, glittering insanely. The vibration from that rail sank so deeply into my hand that when I took it away it still vibrated, the nerve-endings kicking each other over again and again, tingling the way a hand or foot tingles when it has been asleep and is starting to wake up. I could taste my saliva, suddenly all electric and sour and thickened to curds along my gums. And worst, somehow most horrible of all, I couldn't *hear* the train yet, could not know if it was rushing at me from ahead or behind, or how close it was. It was invisible. It was unannounced, except for that shaking rail. There was only that to advertise its imminent arrival. An image of Ray Brower, dreadfully mangled and thrown into a ditch somewhere like a ripped-open laundry bag, reeled before my eyes. We would join him, or at least Vern and I would, or at least I would. We had invited ourselves to our own funerals.

The last thought broke the paralysis and I shot to my feet. I probably would have looked like a jack-in-the-box to anyone watching, but to myself I felt like a boy in underwater slow motion, shooting up not through five feet of air but rather up through five hundred feet of water, moving slowly, moving with a dreadful languidness as the water parted grudgingly.

But at last I did break the surface.

I screamed: *"TRAIN!"*

The last of the paralysis fell from me and I began to run.

Vern's head jerked back over his shoulder. The surprise that distorted his face was almost comically exaggerated, written as large as the letters in a Dick and Jane primer. He saw me break into my clumsy, shambling run, dancing from one horribly high crosstie to the next, and knew I wasn't joking. He began to run himself.

Far ahead, I could see Chris stepping off the ties and onto the solid safe embankment and I hated him with a sudden bright green hate as juicy and as bitter as the sap in an April leaf. He was safe. *That* fucker was *safe.* I watched him drop to his knees and grab a rail.

My left foot almost slipped into the yaw beneath me. I flailed with my arms, my eyes as hot as ball bearings in some runaway piece of machinery, got my balance, and ran on. Now I was right behind Vern. We were past the halfway point and for the first time I heard the train. It was coming from behind us, coming from the Castle Rock side of the river. It was a low rumbling noise that began to rise slightly and sort itself into the diesel thrum of the engine and the higher, more sinister sound of big grooved wheels turning heavily on the rails.

"Awwwwwwww, *shit!*" Vern screamed.

"Run, you pussy!" I yelled, and thumped him on the back.

"I can't! I'll fall!"

"Run faster!"

"AWWWWWWWWW-SHIT!"

But he ran faster, a shambling scarecrow with a bare, sunburnt back, the collar of his shirt swinging and dangling below his butt. I could see the sweat standing out on his peeling shoulder-blades, standing out in perfect little beads. I could see the fine down on the nape of his neck. His muscles clenched and loosened, clenched and loosened, clenched and loosened. His spine stood out in a series of knobs, each knob casting its own crescent-shaped shadow—I could see that these knobs grew closer together as they approached his neck. He was still holding his bedroll and I was still holding mine. Vern's feet thudded on the crossties. He almost missed one, lunged forward with his arms out, and I whacked him on the back again to keep him going.

"Gordeee I can't AWWWWWWWWW-SHEEEEEEYIT—"

"RUN FASTER, DICKFACE!" I bellowed and was I *enjoying* this?

Yeah—in some peculiar, self-destructive way that I have experienced since only when completely and utterly drunk,

I was. I was driving Vern Tessio like a drover getting a particularly fine cow to market. And maybe he was enjoying his own fear in that same way, bawling like that self-same cow, hollering and sweating, his ribcage rising and falling like the bellows of a blacksmith on a speed-trip, clumsily keeping his footing, lurching ahead.

The train was very loud now, its engine deepening to a steady rumble. Its whistle sounded as it crossed the junction point where we had paused to chuck cinders at the rail-flag. I had finally gotten my hellhound, like it or not. I kept waiting for the trestle to start shaking under my feet. When that happened, it would be right behind us.

"GO FASTER, VERN! FAAASTER!"

"Oh Gawd Gordie oh Gawd Gordie oh Gawd *AWWWWWWW-SHEEEEYIT!"*

The freight's electric horn suddenly spanked the air into a hundred pieces with one long loud blast, making everything you ever saw in a movie or a comic book or one of your own daydreams fly apart, letting you know what both the heroes and the cowards really heard when death flew at them:

WHHHHHHHONNNNNNNNK! WHHHHHHHHONNNNNNNNK!

And then Chris was below us and to the right, and Teddy was behind him, his glasses flashing back arcs of sunlight, and they were both mouthing a single word and the word was *jump!* but the train had sucked all the blood out of the word, leaving only its shape in their mouths. The trestle began to shake as the train charged across it. We jumped.

Vern landed full-length in the dust and the cinders and I landed right beside him, almost on top of him. I never did see that train, nor do I know if its engineer saw us—when I mentioned the possibility that he hadn't seen us to Chris a couple of years later, he said: "They don't blow the horn like that just for chucks, Gordie." But he *could* have; he could have been blowing it just for the hell of it. I suppose. Right then, such fine points didn't much matter. I clapped my hands over my ears and dug my face into the hot dirt as the freight went by, metal squalling against metal, the air buffeting us. I had no urge to look at it. It was a long freight but I never looked at all. Before it had passed completely, I felt a warm hand on my neck and knew it was Chris's.

When it was gone—when I was *sure* it was gone—I raised my head like a soldier coming out of his foxhole at the end of a day-long artillery barrage. Vern was still plastered into the dirt, shivering. Chris was sitting cross-legged between us, one hand on Vern's sweaty neck, the other still on mine.

When Vern finally sat up, shaking all over and licking his lips compulsively, Chris said: "What you guys think if we drink those Cokes? Could anybody use one besides me?"

We all thought we could use one.

15

About a quarter of a mile along on the Harlow side, the GS&WM tracks plunged directly into the woods. The heavily wooded land sloped down to a marshy area. It was full of mosquitoes almost as big as fighter-planes, but it was cool . . . blessedly cool.

We sat down in the shade to drink our Cokes. Vern and I threw our shirts over our shoulders to keep the bugs off, but Chris and Teddy just sat naked to the waist, looking as cool and collected as two Eskimos in an icehouse. We hadn't been there five minutes when Vern had to go off into the bushes and take a squat, which led to a good deal of joking and elbowing when he got back.

"Train scare you much, Vern?"

"No," Vern said. "I was gonna squat when we got acrosst, anyway, I *hadda* take a squat, you know?"

"Verrrrrrn?" Chris and Teddy chorused.

"Come on, you guys, I *did.* Sincerely."

"Then you won't mind if we examine the seat of your Jockeys for Hershey-squirts, willya?" Teddy asked, and Vern laughed, finally understanding that he was getting ribbed.

"Go screw."

Chris turned to me. "That train scare you, Gordie?"

"Nope," I said, and sipped my Coke.

"Not much, you sucker." He punched my arm.

"Sincerely! I wasn't scared at all."

"Yeah? You wasn't scared?" Teddy was looking me over carefully.

"No. I was fuckin *petrified.*"

This slew all of them, even Vern, and we laughed long and hard. Then we just lay back, not goofing anymore, just drinking our Cokes and being quiet. My body felt warm, exercised, at peace with itself. Nothing in it was working crossgrain to anything else. I was alive and glad to be. Everything seemed to stand out with a special dearness, and although I never could have said that out loud I didn't think it mattered—maybe that sense of dearness was something I wanted just for myself.

I think I began to understand a little bit that day what makes men become daredevils. I paid twenty dollars to watch Evel Kneivel attempt his jump over the Snake River Canyon a couple of years ago and my wife was horrified. She told me that if I'd been born a Roman I would have been right there in the Colosseum, munching grapes and watching as the lions disemboweled the Christians. She was wrong, although it was hard for me to explain why (and, really, I think *she* thought I was just jiving her). I didn't cough up that twenty to watch the man die on coast-to-coast closed-circuit TV, although I was quite sure that was exactly what was going to happen. I went because of the shadows that are always somewhere behind our eyes, because of what Bruce Springsteen calls the darkness on the edge of town in one of his songs, and at one time or another I think everyone wants to dare that darkness in spite of the jalopy bodies that some joker of a God gave us human beings. No . . . not in *spite* of our jalopy bodies but *because* of them.

"Hey, tell that story," Chris said suddenly, sitting up.

"What story?" I asked, although I guess I knew.

I always felt uncomfortable when the talk turned to my stories, although all of them seemed to like them—wanting to tell stories, even wanting to write them down . . . that was just peculiar enough to be sort of cool, like wanting to grow up to be a sewer inspector or a Grand Prix mechanic. Richie Jenner, a kid who hung around with us until his family moved to Nebraska in 1959, was the first one to find out that I wanted to be a writer when I grew up, that I wanted to do that for my full-time job. We were up in my room, just fooling around, and he found a bunch of handwritten pages under the comic books in a carton in my closet. What's *this*? Richie asks. Nothin, I say, and try to grab them back. Richie held the pages up out of reach . . . and I must admit that I didn't try very *hard* to get them back. I wanted him to read them and at the same time I didn't—an uneasy mix of pride and shyness that has never changed in me very much when someone asks to look. The act of writing itself is done in secret, like masturbation—oh, I have one friend who has done things like write stories in the display windows of bookshops and department stores, but this is a man who is nearly crazy with courage, the kind of man you'd like to have with you if you just happened to fall down with a heart attack in a city where no one knew you. For me, it always wants to be sex and always falls short—

it's always that adolescent handjob in the bathroom with the door locked.

Richie sat right there on the end of my bed for most of the afternoon reading his way through the stuff I had been doing, most of it influenced by the same sort of comic books as the ones that had given Vern nightmares. And when he was done, Richie looked at me in a strange new way that made me feel very peculiar, as if he had been forced to re-appraise my whole personality. He said: You're pretty good at this. Why don't you show these to Chris? I said no, I wanted it to be a secret, and Richie said: Why? It ain't pussy. You ain't no queer. I mean, it ain't *poetry.*

Still, I made him promise not to tell anybody about my stories and of course he did and it turned out most of them liked to read the stuff I wrote, which was mostly about getting burned alive or some crook coming back from the dead and slaughtering the jury that had condemned him in Twelve Interesting Ways or a maniac that went crazy and chopped a lot of people into veal cutlets before the hero, Curt Cannon, "cut the subhuman, screeching madman to pieces with round after round from his smoking .45 automatic."

In my stories, there were always rounds. *Never* bullets.

For a change of pace, there were the Le Dio stories. Le Dio was a town in France, and during 1942, a grim squad of tired American dogfaces were trying to retake it from the Nazis (this was two years before I discovered that the Allies didn't land in France until 1944). They went on trying to retake it, fighting their way from street to street, through about forty stories which I wrote between the ages of nine and fourteen. Teddy was absolutely mad for the Le Dio stories, and I think I wrote the last dozen or so just for him—by then I was heartily sick of Le Dio and writing things like *Mon Dieu* and *Cherchez le Boche!* and *Fermez le porte!* In Le Dio, French peasants were always hissing to GI dogfaces to *Fermez le porte!* But Teddy would hunch over the pages, his eyes big, his brow beaded with sweat, his face twisting. There were times when I could almost hear air-cooled Brownings and whistling 88s going off in his skull. The way he clamored for more Le Dio stories was both pleasing and frightening.

Nowadays writing is my work and the pleasure has diminished a little, and more and more often that guilty, masturbatory pleasure has become associated in my head with the coldly clinical images of artificial insemination: I come according to the rules and regs laid down in my publishing contract. And although no one is ever going to call me the Thomas Wolfe of my generation, I rarely feel like a cheat: I get it off as hard as I can every fucking time. Doing less would, in an odd way, be like going faggot—or what that meant to us back then. What scares me is how often it hurts these days. Back then I was sometimes disgusted by how damned *good* it felt to write. These days I sometimes look at this typewriter and wonder when it's going to run out of good words. I don't want that to happen. I guess I can stay cool as long as I don't run out of good words, you know?

"What's this story?" Vern asked uneasily. "It ain't a horror story, is it, Gordie? I don't think I want to hear no horror stories. I'm not up for that, man."

"No, it ain't a horror," Chris said. "It's really funny. Gross, but funny. Go on, Gordie. Hammer that fucker to us."

"Is it about Le Dio?" Teddy asked.

"No, it ain't about Le Dio, you psycho," Chris said, and rabbit-punched him. "It's about this pie-eatin contest."

"Hey, I didn't even write it down yet," I said.

"Yeah, but tell it."

"You guys want to hear it?"

"Sure," Teddy said. "Boss."

"Well, it's about this made-up town. Gretna, I call it. Gretna, Maine."

"Gretna?" Vern said, grinning. "What kind of name is that? There ain't no *Gretna* in Maine."

"Shut up, fool," Chris said. "He just toldja it was made-up, didn't he?"

"Yeah, but *Gretna,* that sounds pretty stupid—"

"Lots of *real* towns sound stupid," Chris said. "I mean, what about *Alfred,* Maine? Or *Saco,* Maine? Or Jerusalem's Lot? Or Castle-fuckin-Rock? There ain't no castle here. *Most* town names are stupid. You just don't think so because you're used to em. Right, Gordie?"

"Sure," I said, but privately I thought Vern was right—Gretna was a pretty stupid name for a town. I just hadn't been able to think of another one. "So anyway, they're having their annual Pioneer Days, just like in Castle Rock—"

"Yeah, Pioneer Days, that's a fuckin *blast,*" Vern said earnestly. "I put my whole family in that jail on wheels they have, even fuckin Billy. It was only for half an hour and it cost me my whole allowance but it was worth it just to know where that sonofawhore was—"

"Will you shut up and let him tell it?" Teddy hollered.

Vern blinked. "Sure. Yeah. Okay."

"Go on, Gordie," Chris said.

"It's not really much—"

"Naw, we don't expect much from a wet end like you," Teddy said, "but tell it anyway."

I cleared my throat. "So anyway. It's Pioneer Days, and on the last night they have these three big events. There's an egg-roll for the little kids and a sack-race for kids that are like eight or nine, and then there's the pie-eating contest. And the main guy of the story is this fat kid nobody likes named Davie Hogan."

"Like Charlie Hogan's brother if he had one," Vern said, and then shrank back as Chris rabbit-punched him again.

"This kid, he's our age, but he's fat. He weighs like one-eighty and he's always gettin beat up and ranked out. And all the kids, instead of callin him Davie, they call him Lard Ass Hogan and rank him out wherever they get the chance."

They nodded respectfully, showing the proper sympathy for Lard Ass, although if such a guy ever showed up in Castle Rock, we all would have been out teasing him and ranking him to the dogs and back.

"So he decides to take revenge because he's, like, fed up, you know? He's only in the pie-eating contest, but that's like the final event during Pioneer Days and everyone really digs it. The prize is five bucks—"

"So he wins it and gives the finger to everybody!" Teddy said. "Boss!"

"No, it's better than that," Chris said. "Just shut up and listen."

"Lard Ass figures to himself, five bucks, what's that? If any-body remembers anything at all in two weeks, it'll just be that fuckin pig Hogan out-ate everybody, well, it figures, let's go over his house and rank the shit out of him, only now we'll call him Pie Ass instead of Lard Ass."

They nodded some more, agreeing that Davie Hogan was a thinking cat. I began to warm to my own story.

"But everybody expects him to enter the contest, you know. Even his mom and dad. Hey, they practically got that five bucks spent for him already."

"Yeah, right," Chris said.

"So he's thinkin about it and hating the whole thing, because being fat isn't really his fault. See, he's got these weird fuckin glands, somethin, and—"

"My cousin's like that!" Vern said excitedly. "Sincerely! She weighs close to three hundred pounds! Supposed to be Hyboid Gland or somethin like that. I dunno about her Hyboid Gland, but what a fuckin blimp, no shit, she looks like a fuckin Thanksgiving turkey, and this one time—"

"Will you shut the fuck *up,* Vern?" Chris cried violently. "For the last time! Honest to God!" He had finished his Coke and now he turned the hourglass-shaped green bottle upside down and brandished it over Vern's head.

"Yeah, right, I'm sorry. Go on, Gordie. It's a swell story."

I smiled. I didn't really mind Vern's interruptions, but of course I couldn't tell Chris that; he was the self-appointed Guardian of Art.

"So he's turnin it over in his mind, you know, the whole week before the contest. At school, kids keep comin up to him and sayin: Hey Lard Ass, how many pies ya gonna eat? Ya gonna eat ten? Twenty? Fuckin *eighty*? And Lard Ass, *he* says: How should I know. I don't even know what *kind* they are. And see, there's quite a bit of interest in the contest because the champ is this grownup whose name is, uh, Bill Traynor, I guess. And this guy Traynor, he ain't even fat. In fact, he's a real stringbean. But he can eat pies like a whiz, and the year before he ate six pies in five minutes."

"*Whole* pies?" Teddy asked, awe-struck.

"Right you are. And Lard Ass, he's the youngest guy to ever be in the contest."

"Go, Lard Ass!" Teddy cried excitedly. "Scoff up those fuckin pies!"

"Tell em about the other guys in it," Chris said.

"Okay. Besides Lard Ass Hogan and Bill Traynor, there was Calvin Spier, the fattest guy in town—he ran the jewelry store—"

"Gretna Jewels," Vern said, and snickered. Chris gave him a black look.

"And then there's this guy who's a disc jockey at a radio station up in Lewiston, he ain't exactly fat but he's sorta chubby, you know. And the last guy was Hubert Gretna the Third, who was the principal of Lard Ass Hogan's school."

"He was eatin against his own *princibal*?" Teddy asked.

Chris clutched his knees and rocked back and forth joyfully. "Ain't that *great*? Go on, Gordie!"

I had them now. They were all leaning forward. I felt an intoxicating sense of power. I tossed my empty Coke bottle into the woods and scrunched around a little bit to get comfortable. I remember hearing the chickadee again, off in the woods, farther away now, lifting its monotonous, endless call into the sky: *dee-dee-dee-dee* . . .

"So he gets this idea," I said. "The greatest revenge idea a kid ever had. The big night comes—the end of Pioneer Days. The pie-eating contest comes just before the fireworks. The Main Street of Gretna has been closed off so people can walk around in it, and there's this big platform set up right in the street. There's bunting hanging down and a big crowd in front. There's also a photographer from the paper, to get a picture of the winner with blueberries all over his face, because it turned out to be blueberry pies that year. Also, I almost forgot to tell you this, they had to eat the pies with their hands tied behind their backs. So, dig it, they come up onto the platform . . ."

16

From *The Revenge of Lard Ass Hogan,* by Gordon Lachance. Originally published in *Cavalier* magazine, March, 1975. Used by permission.

They came up onto the platform one by one and stood behind a long trestle table covered with a linen cloth. The table was stacked high with pies and stood at the edge of the platform. Above it were looped necklaces of bare 100-watt bulbs, moths and night-fliers banging softly against them and haloing them. Above the platform, bathed in spotlights, was a long sign which read: THE GREAT GRETNA PIE-EAT OF 1960! To either side of this sign hung battered loudspeakers, supplied by Chuck Day of the Great Day Appliance Shop. Bill Travis, the reigning champion, was Chuck's cousin.

As each contestant came up, his hands bound behind him and his shirtfront open, like Sydney Carton on his way to the guillotine, Mayor Charbonneau would announce his name over Chuck's PA system and tie a large white bib around his neck. Calvin Spier received token applause only; in spite of his belly, which was the size of a twenty-gallon waterbarrel, he was considered an underdog second only to the Hogan kid (most considered Lard Ass a comer, but too young and inexperienced to do much this year).

After Spier, Bob Cormier was introduced. Cormier was a disc jockey who did a popular afternoon program at WLAM in Lewiston. He got a bigger hand, accompanied by a few screams from the teenaged girls in the audience. The girls thought he was "cute." John Wiggins, principal of Gretna Elementary School, followed Cormier. He received a hearty cheer from the older section of the audience—and a few scattered boos from the fractious members of his student body. Wiggins managed to beam paternally and frown sternly down on the audience at the same time.

Next, Mayor Charbonneau introduced Lard Ass.

"A new participant in the annual Great Gretna Pie-Eat, but one we expect great things from in the future . . . *young Master David Hogan!"* Lard Ass got a big round of applause as Mayor Charbonneau tied on his bib, and as it was dying away, a rehearsed Greek chorus just beyond the reach of the 100-watt bulbs cried out in wicked unison: *"Go-get-'em-Lard-Ass!"*

There were muffled shrieks of laughter, running footsteps, a few shadows that no one could (or would) identify, some nervous laughter, some judicial frowns (the largest from Hizzoner Charbonneau, the most visible figure of authority). Lard Ass himself appeared to not even notice. The small smile greasing his thick lips and creasing his thick chops did not change as the Mayor, still frowning largely, tied his bib around his neck and told him not to pay any attention to fools in the audience (as if the Mayor had even the faintest inkling of what monstrous fools Lard Ass Hogan had suffered and would continue to suffer as he rumbled through life like a Nazi Tiger tank). The Mayor's breath was warm and smelled of beer.

The last contestant to mount the bunting-decorated stage drew the loudest and most sustained applause; this was the legendary Bill Travis, six feet five inches tall, gangling, voracious. Travis was a mechanic at the local Amoco station down by the railyard, a likeable fellow if there ever was one.

It was common knowledge around town that there was more involved in the Great Gretna Pie-Eat than a mere five dollars—at least, for Bill Travis there was. There were two reasons for this. First, people always came by the station to congratulate Bill after he won the contest, and most everyone who came to congratulate stayed to get his gas-tank filled. And the two garage-bays were sometimes booked up for a solid month after the contest. Folks would come in to get a muffler replaced or their wheelbearings greased, and would sit in the theater chairs ranged along one wall (Jerry Maling, who owned the Amoco, had salvaged them from the old Gem Theater when it was torn down in 1957), drinking Cokes and Moxies from out of the machine and gassing with Bill about the contest as he changed sparkplugs or rolled around on a crawlie-wheelie under someone's International Harvester pickup, looking for holes in the exhaust system. Bill always seemed willing to talk, which was one of the reasons he was so well-liked in Gretna.

There was some dispute around town as to whether Jerry Maling gave Bill a flat bonus for the extra business his yearly feat (or yearly eat, if you prefer) brought in, or if he got an out-and-out raise. Whatever way it was, there could be no doubt that Travis did much better than most small-town wrench jockies. He had a nice-looking two-story ranch out on the Sabbatus Road, and certain snide people referred to it as "the house that pies built." That was probably an exaggeration, but Bill had it coming another way—which brings us to the second reason there was more in it for Travis than just five dollars.

The Pie-Eat was a hot wagering event in Gretna. Perhaps most people only came to laugh, but a goodly minority also came to lay their money down. Contestants were observed and discussed by these bettors as ardently as thoroughbreds are observed and discussed by racing touts. The wagerers accosted contestants' friends, relatives, even mere acquaintances. They pried out any and all details concerning the contestants' eating habits. There was always a lot of discussion about that year's official pie—apple was considered a "heavy" pie, apricot a "light" one (although a contestant had to resign himself to a day or two of the trots after downing three or four apricot pies). That year's official pie, blueberry, was considered a happy medium. Bettors, of course, were particularly interested in their man's stomach for blueberry dishes. How did he do on blueberry buckle? Did he favor blueberry jam over strawberry preserves? Had he been known to sprinkle blueberries on his breakfast cereal, or was he strictly a bananas-and-cream sort of fellow?

There were other questions of some moment. Was he a fast eater who slowed down or a slow eater who started to speed up as things got serious or just a good steady all-around trencherman? How many hotdogs could he put away while watching a Babe Ruth League game down at the St. Dom's baseball field? Was he much of a beer-drinker, and, if so, how many bottles did he usually put away in the course of an evening? Was he a belcher? It was believed that a good belcher was a bit tougher to beat over the long haul.

All of this and other information was sifted, the odds laid, the bets made. How much money actually changed hands during the week or so following pie-night I have no way of knowing, but if you held a gun to my head and forced me to guess, I'd put it at close to a thousand dollars—that probably sounds like a pretty paltry figure, but it was a lot of money to be passing around in such a small town fifteen years ago.

And because the contest was honest and a strict time-limit of ten minutes was observed, no one objected to a competitor betting on himself, and Bill Travis did so every year. Talk was, as he nodded, smiling, to his audience on that summer night in 1960, that he had bet a substantial amount on himself again, and that the best he had been able to do this year was one-for-five odds. If you're not the betting type, let me explain it this way: he'd have to put two hundred and fifty dollars at risk to win fifty. Not a good deal at all, but it was the price of success—and as he stood there, soaking up the applause and smiling easy, he didn't look too worried about it.

"And the defending champeen," Mayor Charbonneau trumpeted, "Gretna's own *Bill Travis!*"

"Hoo, Bill!"

"How many you goin through tonight, Bill?"

"You goin for ten, Billy-boy?"

"I got a two-spot on you, Bill! Don't let me down, boy!"

"Save me one of those pies, Trav!"

Nodding and smiling with all proper modesty, Bill Travis allowed the mayor to tie his bib around his neck. Then he sat down at the far right end of the table, near the place where Mayor Charbonneau would stand during the contest. From right to left, then, the eaters were Bill Travis, David "Lard Ass" Hogan, Bob Cormier, principal John Wiggins, and Calvin Spier holding down the stool on the far left.

Mayor Charbonneau introduced Sylvia Dodge, who was even more of a contest figure than Bill Travis himself. She had been President of the Gretna Ladies' Auxiliary for years beyond telling (since the First Manassas, according to some town wits), and it was she who oversaw the baking of each year's pies, strictly subjecting each to her own rigorous quality control, which included a weigh-in ceremony on Mr. Bancichek's butcher's scales down at the Freedom Market—this to make sure that each pie weighed within an ounce of the others.

Sylvia smiled regally down at the crowd, her blue hair twinkling under the hot glow of the lightbulbs. She made a short speech about how glad she was that so much of the town had turned out to celebrate their hardy pioneer forebears, the people who made this country great, for it *was* great, not only on the grassroots level where Mayor Charbonneau would be leading the local Republicans to the hallowed seats of town government again in November, but on the national level where the team of Nixon and Lodge would take the torch of freedom from Our Great and Beloved General and hold it high for—

Calvin Spier's belly rumbled noisily—*goinnngg!* There was laughter and even some applause. Sylvia Dodge, who knew perfectly well that Calvin was both a Democrat and a Catholic (either would have been forgivable alone, but the two combined, never), managed to blush, smile, and look furious all at the same time. She cleared her throat and wound up with a ringing exhortation to every boy and girl in the audience, telling them to always hold the red, white, and blue high, both in their hands and in their hearts, and to remember that smoking was a dirty, evil habit which made you cough. The boys and girls in the audience, most of whom would be wearing peace medallions and smoking not Camels but marijuana in another eight years, shuffled their feet and waited for the action to begin.

"Less talk, more eatin!" someone in the back row called, and there was another burst of applause—it was heartier this time.

Mayor Charbonneau handed Sylvia a stopwatch and a silver police whistle, which she would blow at the end of the ten minutes of all-out pie-eating. Mayor Charbonneau would then step forward and hold up the hand of the winner.

"Are you *ready*??" Hizzoner's voice rolled triumphantly through the Great Day PA and off down Main Street.

The five pie-eaters declared they were ready.

"Are you *SET*??" Hizzoner enquired further.

The eaters growled that they were indeed set. Down-street, a boy set off a rattling skein of firecrackers.

Mayor Charbonneau raised one pudgy hand and then dropped it. *"GO!!!"*

Five heads dropped into five pie-plates. The sound was like five large feet stamping firmly into mud. Wet chomping noises rose on the mild night air and then were blotted out as the bettors and partisans in the crowd began to cheer on their favorites. And no more than the first pie had been demolished before most people realized that a possible upset was in the making.

Lard Ass Hogan, a seven-to-one underdog because of his age and inexperience, was eating like a boy possessed. His jaws machine-gunned up crust (the contest rules required that only the top crust of the pie be eaten, not the bottom), and when that had disappeared, a huge sucking sound issued from between his lips. It was like the sound of an industrial vacuum cleaner going to work. Then his whole head disappeared into the pie-plate. He raised it fifteen seconds later to indicate he was done. His cheeks and forehead were smeared with blueberry juice, and he looked like an extra in a minstrel show. He was done—done before the legendary Bill Travis had finished *half* of *his* first pie.

Startled applause went up as the Mayor examined Lard Ass's pie-plate and pronounced it clean enough. He whipped a second pie into place before the pace-maker. Lard Ass had gobbled a regulation-size pie in just forty-two seconds. It was a contest record.

He went at the second pie even more furiously yet, his head bobbing and smooching in the soft blueberry filling, and Bill Travis threw him a worried glance as he called for his second blueberry pie. As he told friends later, he felt he was in a real contest for the first time since 1957, when George Gamache gobbled three pies in four minutes and then fainted dead away. He had to wonder, he said, if he was up against a boy or a demon. He thought of the money he had riding on this and redoubled his efforts.

But if Travis had redoubled, Lard Ass had trebled. Blueberries flew from his second pie-dish, staining the tablecloth around him like a Jackson Pollock painting. There were blueberries in his hair, blueberries on his bib, blueberries standing out on his forehead as if, in an agony of concentration, he had actually begun to *sweat* blueberries.

"Done!" he cried, lifting his head from his second pie-dish before Bill Travis had even consumed the crust on his new pie.

"Better slow down, boy," Hizzoner murmured. Charbonneau himself had ten dollars riding on Bill Travis. "You got to pace yourself if you want to hold out."

It was as if Lard Ass hadn't heard. He tore into his third pie with lunatic speed, jaws moving with lightning rapidity. And then—

But I must interrupt for a moment to tell you that there was an empty bottle in the medicine cabinet at Lard Ass Hogan's house. Earlier, that bottle had been three-quarters full of pearl-yellow castor oil, perhaps the most noxious fluid that the good Lord, in His Infinite wisdom, ever allowed upon or beneath the face of the earth. Lard Ass had emptied the bottle himself, drinking every last drop and then licking the rim, his mouth twisting, his belly gagging sourly, his brain filled with thoughts of sweet revenge.

And as he rapidly worked his way through his third pie (Calvin Spier, dead last as predicted, had not yet finished his first), Lard Ass began to deliberately torture himself with grisly fantasies. He was not eating pies at all; he was eating cowflops. He was eating great big gobs of greasy grimy gopher-guts. He was eating diced-up woodchuck intestines with blueberry sauce poured over them. *Rancid* blueberry sauce.

He finished his third pie and called for his fourth, now one full pie ahead of the legendary Bill Travis. The fickle crowd, sensing a new and unexpected champ in the making, began to cheer him on lustily.

But Lard Ass had no hope or intention of winning. He could not have continued at the pace he was currently setting if his own mother's life had been the prize. And besides, winning for him was losing; revenge was the only blue ribbon he sought. His belly groaning with castor oil, his throat opening and closing sickly, he finished his fourth pie and called for his fifth, the Ultimate Pie—Blueberries Become Electra, so to speak. He dropped his head into the dish, breaking the crust, and snuffled blueberries up his nose. Blueberries went down his shirt. The contents of his stomach seemed to suddenly gain weight. He chewed up pasty pastry crust and swallowed it. He inhaled blueberries.

And suddenly the moment of revenge was at hand. His stomach, loaded beyond endurance, revolted. It clenched like a strong hand encased in a slick rubber glove. His throat opened.

Lard Ass raised his head.

He grinned at Bill Travis with blue teeth.

Puke rumbled up his throat like a six-ton Peterbilt shooting through a tunnel.

It roared out of his mouth in huge blue-and-yellow glurt, warm and gaily steaming. It covered Bill Travis, who only had time to utter one nonsense syllable—*"Goog!"* was what it sounded like. Women in the audience screamed. Calvin Spier, who had watched this unannounced event with a numb and surprised expression on his face, leaned conversationally over the table as if to explain to the gaping audience just what was happening, and puked on the head of Marguerite Charbonneau, the Mayor's wife. She screamed and backed away, pawing futilely at her hair, which was now covered with a mixture of crushed berries, baked beans, and partially digested frankfurters (the latter two had been Cal Spier's dinner). She turned to her good friend Maria Lavin and threw up on the front of Maria's buckskin jacket.

In rapid succession, like a replay of the firecrackers:

Bill Travis blew a great—and seemingly supercharged—jet of vomit out over the first two rows of spectators, his stunned face proclaiming to one and all, *Man, I just can't believe I'm doing this;*

Chuck Day, who had received a generous portion of Bill Travis's surprise gift, threw up on his Hush Puppies and then blinked at them wonderingly, knowing full well that stuff would *never* come off suede;

John Wiggins, principal of Gretna Elementary, opened his bluelined mouth and said reprovingly: "Really, this has . . . *YURRK!"* As befitted a man of his breeding and position, he did it in his own pie-plate;

Hizzoner Charbonneau, who found himself suddenly presiding over what must have seemed more like a stomach-flu hospital ward than a pie-eating contest, opened his mouth to call the whole thing off and upchucked all over the microphone.

"Jesus save us!" moaned Sylvia Dodge, and then her outraged supper—fried clams, cole slaw, butter-and-sugar corn (two ears' worth), and a generous helping of Muriel Harrington's Bosco chocolate cake—bolted out the emergency exit and landed with a large wet splash on the back of the Mayor's Robert Hall suitcoat.

Lard Ass Hogan, now at the absolute apogee of his young life, beamed happily out over the audience. Puke was everywhere. People staggered around in drunken circles, holding their throats and making weak cawing noises. Somebody's pet Pekingese ran past the stage, yapping crazily, and a man wearing jeans and a Western-style silk shirt threw up on it, nearly drowning it. Mrs. Brockway, the Methodist minister's wife, made a long, basso belching noise which was followed by a gusher of degenerated roast beef and mashed potatoes and apple cobbler. The cobbler looked as if it might have been good when it first went down. Jerry Maling, who had come to see his pet mechanic walk away with all the marbles again, decided to get the righteous fuck out of this madhouse. He got about fifteen yards before tripping over a kid's little red wagon and realizing he had landed in a puddle of warm bile. Jerry tossed his cookies in his own lap and told folks later he only thanked Providence he had been wearing his coveralls. And Miss Norman, who taught Latin and English Fundamentals at the Gretna Consolidated High School, vomited into her own purse in an agony of propriety.

Lard Ass Hogan watched it all, his large face calm and beaming, his stomach suddenly sweet and steady with a warm balm it might never know again—that balm was a feeling of utter and complete satisfaction. He stood up, took the slightly tacky microphone from the trembling hand of Mayor Charbonneau, and said . . .

17

" 'I declare this contest a draw.' Then he puts the mike down, walks off the back of the platform, and goes straight home. His mother's there, on account of she couldn't get a babysitter for Lard Ass's little sister, who was only two. And as soon as he comes in, all covered with puke and pie-drool, still wearing his bib, she says, 'Davie, did you win?' But he doesn't say a fuckin word, you know. Just goes upstairs to his room, locks the door, and lays down on his bed."

I downed the last swallow in Chris's Coke and tossed it into the woods.

"Yeah, that's cool, then what happened?" Teddy asked eagerly.

"I don't know."

"What do you mean, you don't *know*?" Teddy asked.

"It means it's the end. When you don't know what happens next, that's the end."

"Whaaaat?" Vern cried. There was an upset, suspicious look on his face, like he thought maybe he'd just gotten rooked playing penny-up Bingo at the Topsham Fair. "What's all this happy crappy? How'd it come *out!*"

"You have to use your imagination," Chris said patiently.

"No, I ain't!" Vern said angrily. "*He's* supposed to use *his* imagination! He made up the fuckin story!"

"Yeah, what happened to the cat?" Teddy persisted. "Come on, Gordie, tell us."

"I think his dad was at the Pie-Eat and when he came home he beat the living crap out of Lard Ass."

"Yeah, right," Chris said. "I bet that's just what happened."

"And," I said, "the kids went right on calling him Lard Ass. Except that maybe some of them started calling him Puke-Yer-Guts, too."

"That ending sucks," Teddy said sadly.

"That's why I didn't want to tell it."

"You could have made it so he shot his father and ran away and joined the Texas Rangers," Teddy said. "How about that?"

Chris and I exchanged a glance. Chris raised one shoulder in a barely perceptible shrug.

"I guess so," I said.

"Hey, you got any new Le Dio stories, Gordie?"

"Not just now. Maybe I'll think of some." I didn't want to upset Teddy, but I wasn't very interested in checking out what was happening in Le Dio, either. "Sorry you didn't go for this one better."

"Nah, it was good," Teddy said. "Right up to the end, it was good. All that pukin was really cool."

"Yeah, that was cool, really gross," Vern agreed. "But Teddy's right about the ending. It was sort of a gyp."

"Yeah," I said, and sighed.

Chris stood up. "Let's do some walking," he said. It was still bright daylight, the sky a hot, steely blue, but our shadows had begun to trail out long. I remember that as a kid, September days always seemed to end much too soon, catching me by surprise—it was as if something inside my heart expected it to always be June, with daylight lingering in the sky until almost nine-thirty. "What time is it, Gordie?"

I looked at my watch and was astonished to see it was after five.

"Yeah, let's go," Teddy said. "But let's make camp before dark so we can see to get wood and stuff. I'm getting hungry, too."

"Six-thirty," Chris promised. "Okay with you guys?"

It was. We started to walk again, using the cinders beside the tracks now. Soon the river was so far behind us we couldn't even hear its sound. Mosquitoes hummed and I slapped one off my neck. Vern and Teddy were walking up ahead, working out some sort of complicated comic-book trade. Chris was beside me, hands in his pockets, shirt slapping against his knees and thighs like an apron.

"I got some Winstons," he said. "Hawked em off my old man's dresser. One apiece. For after supper."

"Yeah? That's boss."

"That's when a cigarette tastes best," Chris said. "After supper."

"Right."

We walked in silence for awhile.

"That's a really fine story," Chris said suddenly. "They're just a little too dumb to understand."

"No, it's not that hot. It's a mumbler."

"That's what you always say. Don't give me that bullshit you don't believe. Are you gonna write it down? The story?"

"Probably. But not for awhile. I can't write em down right after I tell em. It'll keep."

"What Vern said? About the ending being a gyp?"

"Yeah?"

Chris laughed. "*Life's* a gyp, you know it? I mean, look at us."

"Nah, we have a great time."

"Sure," Chris said. "All the fuckin time, you wet."

I laughed. Chris did, too.

"They come outta you just like bubbles out of soda-pop," he said after awhile.

"What does?" But I thought I knew what he meant.

"The stories. That really bugs me, man. It's like you could tell a million stories and still only get the ones on top. You'll be a great writer someday, Gordie."

"No, I don't think so."

"Yeah, you will. Maybe you'll even write about us guys if you ever get hard up for material."

"Have to be pretty fuckin hard up." I gave him the elbow.

There was another period of silence and then he asked suddenly: "You ready for school?"

I shrugged. Who ever was? You got a little excited thinking about going back, seeing your friends; you were curious about your new teachers and what they would be like—pretty young things just out of teachers' college that you could rag or some old topkick that had been there since the Alamo. In a funny way you could even get excited about the long droning classes, because as the summer vacation neared its end you sometimes got bored enough to believe you could learn something. But summer boredom was nothing like the school boredom that always set in by the end of the second week, and by the beginning of the third week you got down to the *real* business: Could you hit Stinky Fiske in the back of the head with your Art-Gum while the teacher was putting The Principal Exports of South America on the board? How many good loud squeaks could you get off on the varnished surface of your desk if your hands were real sweaty? Who could cut the loudest farts in the locker room while changing up for phys ed? How many girls could you get to play Who Goosed the Moose during lunch hour? Higher learning, baby.

"Junior High," Chris said. "And you know what, Gordie? By next June, we'll all be quits."

"What are you talking about? Why would *that* happen?"

"It's not gonna be like grammar school, that's why. You'll be in the college courses. Me and Teddy and Vern, we'll all be in the shop courses, playing pocket-pool with the rest of the retards, making ashtrays and birdhouses. Vern might even have to go into Remedial. You'll meet a lot of new guys. Smart guys. That's just the way it works, Gordie. That's how they got it set up."

"Meet a lot of pussies is what you mean," I said.

He gripped my arm. "No, man. Don't say that. Don't even *think* that. They'll get your stories. Not like Vern and Teddy."

"Fuck the stories. I'm not going in with a lot of pussies. No sir."

"If you don't, then you're an asshole."

"What's asshole about wanting to be with your friends?"

He looked at me thoughtfully, as if deciding whether or not to tell me something. We had slowed down: Vern and Teddy had pulled almost half a mile ahead. The sun, lower now, came at us through the overlacing trees in broken, dusty shafts, turning everything gold—but it was a tawdry gold, dime-store gold, if you can dig that. The tracks stretched ahead of us in the gloom that was just starting to gather—they seemed almost to twinkle. Star-pricks of light stood out on them here and there, as if some nutty rich guy masquerading as a common laborer had decided to embed a diamond in the steel every sixty yards or so. It was still hot. The sweat rolled off us, slicking our bodies.

"It's asshole if your friends can drag you down," Chris said finally. "I know about you and your folks. They don't give a shit about you. Your big brother was the one they cared about. Like my dad, when Frank got thrown into the stockade in Portsmouth. That was when he started always bein mad at us other kids and hitting us all the time. Your dad doesn't beat on you, but maybe that's even worse. He's got you asleep. You could tell him you were enrolling in the fuckin shop division and you know what he'd do? He'd turn to the next page in his paper and say: Well, that's nice, Gordon, go ask your mother what's for dinner. And don't try to tell me different. I've met him."

I didn't try to tell him different. It's scary to find out that someone else, even a friend, knows just how things are with you.

"You're just a kid, Gordie—"

"Gee, thanks, Dad."

"I wish to fuck I *was* your father!" he said angrily. "You wouldn't go around talking about takin those stupid shop courses if I was! It's like God gave you something, all those stories you can make up, and He said: This is what we got for you, kid. Try not to lose it. But kids lose *everything* unless somebody looks out for them and if your folks are too fucked up to do it then maybe I ought to."

His face looked like he was expecting me to take a swing at him; it was set and unhappy in the green-gold late afternoon light. He had broken the cardinal rule for kids in those days. You could say anything about another kid, you could rank him to the dogs and back, but you didn't say a bad word *ever* about his mom and dad. That was the Fabled Automatic, the same way not inviting your Catholic friends home to dinner on Friday unless you'd checked first to make sure you weren't having meat was the Fabled Automatic. If a kid ranked out your mom and dad, you had to feed him some knuckles.

"Those stories you tell, they're no good to anybody but you, Gordie. If you go along with us just because you don't want the gang to break up, you'll wind up just another grunt, makin C's to get on the teams. You'll get to High and take the same fuckin shop courses and throw erasers and pull your meat along with the rest of the grunts. Get detentions. Fuckin *suspensions.* And after awhile all you'll care about is gettin a car so you can take some skag to the hops or down to the fuckin Twin Bridges Tavern. Then you'll knock her up and spend the rest of your life in the mill or some fuckin shoeshop in Auburn or maybe even up to Hillcrest pluckin chickens. And that pie story will never get written down. *Nothin*'ll get written down. Cause you'll just be another wiseguy with shit for brains."

Chris Chambers was twelve when he said all that to me. But while he was saying it his face crumpled and folded into something older, oldest, ageless. He spoke tonelessly, colorlessly, but nevertheless, what he said struck terror into my bowels. It was as if he had lived that whole life already, that life where they tell you to step right up and spin the Wheel of Fortune, and it spins so pretty and the guy steps on a pedal and it comes up double zeros, house number, everybody loses. They give you a free pass and then they turn on the rain machine, pretty funny, huh, a joke even Vern Tessio could appreciate.

He grabbed my naked arm and his fingers closed tight. They dug grooves in my flesh. They ground at the bones. His eyes were hooded and dead—so dead, man, that he might have just fallen out of his own coffin.

"I know what people think of my family in this town. I know what they think of me and what they expect. Nobody even *asked* me if I took the milk-money that time. I just got a three-day vacation."

"*Did* you take it?" I asked. I had never asked him before, and if you had told me I ever would, I would have called you crazy. The words came out in a little dry bullet.

"Yeah," he said. "Yeah, I took it." He was silent for a moment, looking ahead at Teddy and Vern. "You knew I took it, Teddy knew. *Everybody* knew. Even Vern knew, I think."

I started to deny it, and then closed my mouth. He was right. No matter what I might have said to my mother and father about how a person was supposed to be innocent until proved guilty, I had known.

"Then maybe I was sorry and tried to give it back," Chris said.

I stared at him, my eyes widening. "You tried to give it *back*?"

"*Maybe,* I said. Just *maybe.* And maybe I took it to old lady Simons and told her, and maybe the money was all there but I got a three-day vacation *anyway,* because the money never showed up. And maybe the next week old lady Simons had this brand-new skirt on when she came to school."

I stared at Chris, speechless with horror. He smiled at me, but it was a crimped, terrible smile that never touched his eyes.

"Just *maybe,*" he said, but I remembered the new skirt—a light brown paisley, sort of full. I remembered thinking that it made old lady Simons look younger, almost pretty.

"Chris, how much was that milk-money?"

"Almost seven bucks."

"Christ," I whispered.

"So just say that *I* stole the milk-money but then old lady Simons stole it from *me.* Just suppose I told that story. Me, Chris Chambers. Kid brother of Frank Chambers and Eyeball Chambers. You think anybody would have believed it?"

"No way," I whispered. "Jesus Christ!"

He smiled his wintry, awful smile. "And do you think that bitch would have dared try something like that if it had been one of those dootchbags from up on The View that had taken the money?"

"No," I said.

"Yeah, if it had been one of them, Simons would have said: 'Kay, 'kay, we'll forget it this time, but we're gonna spank your wrist real hard and if you ever do it again we'll have to spank *both* wrists. But *me* . . . well, maybe she had her eye on that skirt for a long time. Anyway, she saw her chance and she took it. I was the stupid one for even trying to give that money back. But I never thought . . . I never thought that a *teacher* . . . oh, who gives a fuck, anyway? Why am I even talkin about it?"

He swiped an arm angrily across his eyes and I realized he was almost crying.

"Chris," I said, "why don't you go into the college courses? You're smart enough."

"They decide all of that in the office. And in their smart little conferences. The teachers, they sit around in this big circle-jerk and all they say is Yeah, Yeah, Right, Right. All they give a fuck about is whether you behaved yourself in grammar school and what the town thinks of your family. All they're deciding is whether or not you'll contaminate all those precious college-course dootchbags. But maybe I'll try to work myself up. I don't know if I could do it, but I might try. Because I want to get out of Castle Rock and go to college and never see my old man or any of my brothers again. I want to go someplace where nobody knows me and I don't have any black marks against me before I start. But I don't know if I can do it."

"Why not?"

"People. People drag you down."

"Who?" I asked, thinking he must mean the teachers, or adult monsters like Miss Simons, who had wanted a new skirt, or maybe his brother Eyeball who hung around with Ace and Billy and Charlie and the rest, or maybe his own mom and dad.

But he said: "Your friends drag you down, Gordie. Don't you know that?" He pointed at Vern and Teddy, who were standing and waiting for us to catch up. They were laughing about something; in fact, Vern was just about busting a gut. "Your friends do. They're like drowning guys that are holding onto your legs. You can't save them. You can only drown with them."

"Come on, you fuckin slowpokes!" Vern shouted, still laughing.

"Yeah, comin!" Chris called, and before I could say anything else, he began to run. I ran, too, but he caught up to them before I could catch up to him.

18

We went another mile and then decided to camp for the night. There was still some daylight left, but nobody really wanted to use it. We were pooped from the scene at the dump and from our scare on the train trestle, but it was more than that. We were in Harlow now, in the woods. Somewhere up ahead was a dead kid, probably mangled and covered with flies. Maggots, too, by this time. Nobody wanted to get too close to him with the night coming on. I had read somewhere—in an Algernon Blackwood story, I think—that a guy's ghost hangs out around his dead body until that body is given a decent Christian burial, and there was no way I wanted to wake up in the night and confront the glowing, disembodied ghost of Ray Brower, moaning and gibbering and floating among the dark and rustling pines. By stopping here we figured there had to be at least ten miles between us and him, and of course all four of us knew there were no such things as ghosts, but ten miles seemed just about far enough in case what everybody knew was wrong.

Vern, Chris, and Teddy gathered wood and got a modest little campfire going on a bed of cinders. Chris scraped a bare patch all around the fire—the woods were powder-dry, and he didn't want to take any chances. While they were doing that I sharpened some sticks and made what my brother Denny used to call "Pioneer Drumsticks"—lumps of hamburger pushed onto the ends of green branches. The three of them laughed and bickered over their woodcraft (which was almost nil; there was a Castle Rock Boy Scout troop, but most of the kids who hung around our vacant lot considered it to be an organization made up mostly of pussies), arguing about whether it was better to cook over flames or over coals (a moot point; we were too hungry to wait for coals), whether dried moss would work as kindling, what they would do if they used up all the matches before they got the fire to stay lit. Teddy claimed he could make a fire by rubbing two sticks together. Chris claimed he was so full of shit he squeaked. They didn't have to try; Vern got the small pile of twigs and dry moss to catch from the second match. The day was perfectly still and there was no wind to puff out the light. We all took turns feeding the thin flames until they began to grow stouter on wrist-chunks of wood fetched from an old deadfall some thirty yards into the forest.

When the flames began to die back a little bit, I stuck the sticks holding the Pioneer Drumsticks firmly into the ground at an angle over the fire. We sat around watching them as they shimmered and dripped and finally began to brown. Our stomachs made pre-dinner conversation.

Unable to wait until they were really cooked, we each took one of them, stuck it in a roll, and yanked the hot stick out of the center. They were charred outside, raw inside, and totally delicious. We wolfed them down and wiped the grease from our mouths with our bare arms. Chris opened his pack and took out a tin Band-Aids box (the pistol was way at the bottom of his pack, and because he hadn't told Vern and Teddy, I guessed it was to be our secret). He opened it and gave each of us a battered Winston. We lit them with flaming twigs from the fire and then leaned back, men of the world, watching the cigarette smoke drift away into the soft twilight. None of us inhaled because we might cough and that would mean a day or two of ragging from the others. And it was pleasant enough just to drag and blow, hawking into the fire to hear the sizzle (that was the summer I learned how you can pick out someone who is just learning to smoke: if you're new at it you spit a lot). We were feeling good. We smoked the Winstons down to the filters, then tossed them into the fire.

"Nothin like a smoke after a meal," Teddy said.

"Fucking-A," Vern agreed.

Crickets had started to hum in the green gloom. I looked up at the lane of sky visible through the railroad cut and saw that the blue was now bruising toward purple. Seeing that outrider of twilight made me feel sad and calm at the same time, brave but not really brave, comfortably lonely.

We tromped down a flat place in the underbrush beside the embankment and laid out our bedrolls. Then, for an hour or so, we fed the fire and talked, the kind of talk you can never quite remember once you get past fifteen and discover girls. We talked about who was the best dragger in Castle Rock, if Boston could maybe stay out of the cellar this year, and about the summer just past. Teddy told about the time he had been at White's Beach in Brunswick and some kid had hit his head while diving off the float and almost drowned. We discussed at some length the relative merits of the teachers we had had. We agreed that Mr. Brooks was the biggest pussy in Castle Rock Elementary—he would just about cry if you sassed him back. On the other hand, there was Mrs. Cote (pronounced Cody)—she was just about the meanest bitch God had ever set down on the earth. Vern said he'd heard she hit a kid so hard two years ago that the kid almost went blind. I looked at Chris, wondering if he would say anything about Miss Simons, but he didn't say anything at all, and he didn't see me looking at him—he was looking at Vern and nodding soberly at Vern's story.

We didn't talk about Ray Brower as the dark drew down, but I was thinking about him. There's something horrible and fascinating about the way dark comes to the woods, its coming unsoftened by headlights or streetlights or houselights or neon. It comes with no mothers' voices, calling for their kids to leave off and come on in now, to herald it. If you're used to the town, the coming of the dark in the woods seems more like a natural disaster than a natural phenomenon; it rises like the Castle River rises in the spring.

And as I thought about the body of Ray Brower in this light—or lack of it—what I felt was not queasiness or fear that he would suddenly appear before us, a green and gibbering banshee whose purpose was to drive us back the way we had come before we could disturb his—*its*—peace, but a sudden and unexpected wash of pity that he should be so alone and so defenseless in the dark that was now coming over our side of the earth. If something wanted to eat on him, it would. His mother wasn't here to stop that from happening, and neither was his father, nor Jesus Christ in the company of all the saints. He was dead and he was all alone, flung off the railroad tracks and into the ditch, and I realized that if I didn't stop thinking about it I was going to cry.

So I told a Le Dio story, made up on the spot and not very good, and when it ended as most of my Le Dio stories did, with one lone American dogface coughing out a dying declaration of patriotism and love for the girl back home into the sad and wise face of the platoon sergeant, it was not the white, scared face of some pfc from Castle Rock or White River Junction I saw in my mind's eye but the face of a much younger boy, already dead, his eyes closed, his features troubled, a rill of blood running from the left corner of his mouth to his jawline. And in back of him, instead of the shattered shops and churches of my Le Dio dreamscape, I saw only dark forest and the cindered railway bed bulking against the starry sky like a prehistoric burial mound.

19

I came awake in the middle of the night, disoriented, wondering why it was so chilly in my bedroom and who had left the windows open. Denny, maybe. I had been dreaming of Denny, something about body-surfing at Harrison State Park. But it had been four years ago that we had done that.

This wasn't my room; this was someplace else. Somebody was holding me in a mighty bearhug, somebody else was pressed against my back, and a shadowy third was crouched beside me, head cocked in a listening attitude.

"What the fuck?" I asked in honest puzzlement.

A long-drawn-out groan in answer. It sounded like Vern.

That brought things into focus, and I remembered where I was . . . but what was everybody doing awake in the middle of the night? Or had I only been asleep for seconds? No, that couldn't be, because a thin sliver of moon was floating dead center in an inky sky.

"Don't let it get me!" Vern gibbered. "I swear I'll be a good boy, I won't do nothin bad, I'll put the ring up before I take a piss, I'll . . . I'll . . ." With some astonishment I realized that I was listening to a prayer—or at least the Vern Tessio equivalent of a prayer.

I sat bolt upright, scared. "Chris?"

"Shut up, Vern," Chris said. He was the one crouching and listening. "It's nothing."

"Oh, yes it is," Teddy said ominously. "It's something."

"*What* is?" I asked. I was still sleepy and disoriented, unstrung from my place in space and time. It scared me that I had come in late on whatever had developed—too late to defend myself properly, maybe.

Then, as if to answer my question, a long and hollow scream rose languidly from the woods—it was the sort of scream you might expect from a woman dying in extreme agony and extreme fear.

"Oh-dear-to-Jesus!" Vern whimpered, his voice high and filled with tears. He re-applied the bearhug that had awakened me, making it hard for me to breathe and adding to my own terror. I threw him loose with an effort but he scrambled right back beside me like a puppy which can't think of anyplace else to go.

"It's that Brower kid," Teddy whispered hoarsely. "His ghost's out walkin in the woods."

"Oh God!" Vern screamed, apparently not crazy about that

idea at all. "I promise I won't hawk no more dirty books out of Dahlie's Market! I promise I won't give my carrots to the dog no more! I . . . I . . . I . . ." He floundered there, wanting to bribe God with everything but unable to think of anything really good in the extremity of his fear. *"I won't smoke no more unfiltered cigarettes! I won't say no bad swears! I won't put my Bazooka in the offerin plate! I won't—"*

"Shut up, Vern," Chris said, and beneath his usual authoritative toughness I could hear the hollow boom of awe. I wondered if his arms and back and belly were as stiff with gooseflesh as my own were, and if the hair on the nape of his neck was trying to stand up in hackles, as mine was.

Vern's voice dropped to a whisper as he continued to expand the reforms he planned to institute if God would only let him live through this night.

"It's a bird, isn't it?" I asked Chris.

"No. At least, I don't think so. I think it's a wildcat. My dad says they scream bloody murder when they're getting ready to mate. Sounds like a woman, doesn't it?"

"Yeah," I said. My voice hitched in the middle of the word and two ice-cubes broke off in the gap.

"But no woman could scream that loud," Chris said . . . and then added helplessly: "Could she, Gordie?"

"It's his ghost," Teddy whispered again. His eyeglasses reflected the moonlight in weak, somehow dreamy smears. "I'm gonna go look for it."

I don't think he was serious, but we took no chances. When he started to get up, Chris and I hauled him back down. Perhaps we were too rough with him, but our muscles had been turned to cables with fear.

"Let me up, fuckheads!" Teddy hissed, struggling. "If I say I wanna go look for it, then I'm gonna go look for it! I wanna see it! I wanna see the ghost! I wanna see if—"

The wild, sobbing cry rose into the night again, cutting the air like a knife with a crystal blade, freezing us with our hands on Teddy—if he'd been a flag, we would have looked like that picture of the Marines claiming Iwo Jima. The scream climbed with a crazy ease through octave after octave, finally reaching a glassy, freezing edge. It hung there for a moment and then whirled back down again, disappearing into an impossible bass register that buzzed like a monstrous honeybee. This was followed by a burst of what sounded like mad laughter . . . and then there was silence again.

"Jesus H Baldheaded Christ," Teddy whispered, and he talked no more of going into the woods to see what was making that screaming noise. All four of us huddled up together and I thought of running. I doubt if I was the only one. If we had been tenting in Vern's field—where our folks *thought* we were—we probably *would* have run. But Castle Rock was too far, and the thought of trying to run across that trestle in the dark made my blood freeze. Running deeper into Harlow and closer to the corpse of Ray Brower was equally unthinkable. We were stuck. If there was a ha'ant out there in the woods—what my dad called a Goosalum—and it wanted us, it would probably get us.

Chris proposed we keep a guard and everyone was agreeable to that. We flipped for watches and Vern got the first one. I got the last. Vern sat up cross-legged by the husk of the campfire while the rest of us lay down again. We huddled together like sheep.

I was positive that sleep would be impossible, but I did sleep—a light, uneasy sleep that skimmed through unconsciousness like a sub with its periscope up. My half-sleeping dreams were populated with wild cries that might have been real or might have only been products of my imagination. I saw—or thought I saw—something white and shapeless steal through the trees like a grotesquely ambulatory bedsheet.

At last I slipped into something I knew was a dream. Chris and I were swimming at White's Beach, a gravel-pit in Brunswick that had been turned into a miniature lake when the gravel-diggers struck water. It was where Teddy had seen the kid hit his head and almost drown.

In my dream we were out over our heads, stroking lazily along, with a hot July sun blazing down. From behind us, on the float, came cries and shouts and yells of laughter as kids climbed and dived or climbed and were pushed. I could hear the empty kerosene drums that held the float up clanging and booming together—a sound not unlike that of churchbells, which are so solemn and emptily profound. On the sand-and-gravel beach, oiled bodies lay face down on blankets, little kids with buckets squatted on the verge of the water or sat happily flipping muck into their hair with plastic shovels, and teenagers clustered in grinning groups, watching the young girls promenade endlessly back and forth in pairs and trios, never alone, the secret places of their bodies wrapped in Jantzen tank suits. People walked up the hot sand on the balls of their feet, wincing, to the snackbar. They came back with chips, Devil Dogs, Red Ball Popsicles.

Mrs. Cote drifted past us on an inflatable rubber raft. She was lying on her back, dressed in her typical September-to-June school uniform: a gray two-piece suit with a thick sweater instead of a blouse under the jacket, a flower pinned over one almost nonexistent breast, thick support hose the color of Canada Mints on her legs. Her black old lady's high-heeled shoes were trailing in the water, making small V's. Her hair was blue-rinsed, like my mother's, and done up in those tight, medicinal-smelling clockspring curls. Her glasses flashed brutally in the sun.

"Watch your steps, boys," she said. "Watch your steps or I'll hit you hard enough to strike you blind. I can do that; I have been given that power by the school board. Now, Mr. Chambers, 'Mending Wall,' if you please. By rote."

"I tried to give the money back," Chris said. "Old lady Simons said okay, but she *took* it! Do you hear me? She *took* it! Now what are you going to do about it? Are you going to whack *her* blind?"

" 'Mending Wall,' Mr. Chambers, if you please. By *rote.*"

Chris threw me a despairing glance, as if to say *Didn't I tell you it would be this way?,* and then began to tread water. He began: " 'Something there is that doesn't love a wall, that sends the frozen-ground-swell under it—' " And then his head went under, his reciting mouth filling with water.

He popped back up, crying: "Help me, Gordie! Help me!"

Then he was dragged under again. Looking into the clear water I could see two bloated, naked corpses holding his ankles. One was Vern and the other was Teddy, and their open eyes were as blank and pupilless as the eyes of Greek statues. Their small pre-pubescent penises floated limply up from their distended bellies like albino strands of kelp. Chris's head broke water again. He held one hand up limply to me and voiced a screaming, womanish cry that rose and rose, ululating in the hot sunny summer air. I looked wildly toward the beach but nobody had heard. The lifeguard, his bronzed, athletic body lolling attractively on the seat at the top of his whitewashed cruciform wooden tower, just went on smiling down at a girl in a red bathing suit. Chris's scream turned into a bubbling water-choked gurgle as the corpses pulled him under again. And as they dragged him down to black water I could see his rippling, distorted eyes turned up to me in a pleading agony; I could see his white starfish hands held helplessly up to the sun-burnished roof of the water. But instead of diving down and trying to save him, I stroked madly for the shore, or at least to a place where the water would not be over my head.

Before I could get there—before I could even get close—I felt a soft, rotted, implacable hand wrap itself around my calf and begin to pull. A scream built up in my chest . . . but before I could utter it, the dream washed away into a grainy facsimile of reality. It was Teddy with his hand on my leg. He was shaking me awake. It was my watch.

Still half in the dream, almost talking in my sleep, I asked him thickly: "You alive, Teddy?"

"No. I'm dead and you're a black nigger," he said crossly. It dispelled the last of the dream. I sat up by the campfire and Teddy lay down.

20

The others slept heavily through the rest of the night. I was in and out, dozing, waking, dozing again. The night was far from silent; I heard the triumphant screech-squawk of a pouncing owl, the tiny cry of some small animal perhaps about to be eaten, a larger something blundering wildly through the undergrowth. Under all of this, a steady tone, were the crickets. There were no more screams. I dozed and woke, woke and dozed, and I suppose if I had been discovered standing such a slipshod watch in Le Dio, I probably would have been courtmartialed and shot.

I snapped more solidly out of my last doze and became aware that something was different. It took me a moment or two to figure it out: although the moon was down, I could see my hands resting on my jeans. My watch said quarter to five. It was dawn.

I stood, hearing my spine crackle, walked two dozen feet away from the limped-together bodies of my friends, and pissed into a clump of sumac. I was starting to shake the night-willies; I could feel them sliding away. It was a fine feeling.

I scrambled up the cinders to the railroad tracks and sat on one of the rails, idly chucking cinders between my feet, in no hurry to wake the others. At that precise moment the new day felt too good to share.

Morning came on apace. The noise of the crickets began to drop, and the shadows under the trees and bushes evaporated like puddles after a shower. The air had that peculiar lack of taste that presages the latest hot day in a famous series of hot days. Birds that had maybe cowered all night just as we had done now began to twitter self-importantly. A wren landed on top of the deadfall from which we had taken our firewood, preened itself, and then flew off.

I don't know how long I sat there on the rail, watching the purple steal out of the sky as noiselessly as it had stolen in the evening before. Long enough for my butt to start complaining anyway. I was about to get up when I looked to my right and saw a deer standing in the railroad bed not ten yards from me.

My heart went up into my throat so high that I think I could have put my hand in my mouth and touched it. My stomach and genitals filled with a hot dry excitement. I didn't move. I couldn't have moved if I had wanted to. Her eyes weren't brown but a dark, dusty black—the kind of velvet you see backgrounding jewelry displays. Her small ears were scuffed suede. She looked serenely at me, head slightly lowered in what I took for curiosity, seeing a kid with his hair in a sleep-scarecrow of whirls and many-tined cowlicks, wearing jeans with cuffs and a brown khaki shirt with the elbows mended and the collar turned up in the hoody tradition of the day. What I was seeing was some sort of gift, something given with a carelessness that was appalling.

We looked at each other for a long time . . . I *think* it was a long time. Then she turned and walked off to the other side of the tracks, white bobtail flipping insouciantly. She found grass and began to crop. I couldn't believe it. She had begun to *crop.* She didn't look back at me and didn't need to; I was frozen solid.

Then the rail started to thrum under my ass and bare seconds later the doe's head came up, cocked back toward Castle Rock. She stood there, her branch-black nose working on the air, coaxing it a little. Then she was gone in three gangling leaps, vanishing into the woods with no sound but one rotted branch, which broke with a sound like a track ref's starter-gun.

I sat there, looking mesmerized at the spot where she had been, until the actual sound of the freight came up through the stillness. Then I skidded back down the bank to where the others were sleeping.

The freight's slow, loud passage woke them up, yawning and scratching. There was some funny, nervous talk about "the case of the screaming ghost," as Chris called it, but not as much as you might imagine. In daylight it seemed more foolish than interesting—almost embarrassing. Best forgotten.

It was on the tip of my tongue to tell them about the deer, but I ended up not doing it. That was one thing I kept to myself. I've never spoken or written of it until just now, today. And I have to tell you that it seems a lesser thing written down, damn near inconsequential. But for me it was the best part of that trip, the cleanest part, and it was a moment I found myself returning to, almost helplessly, when there was trouble in my life—my first day in the bush in Vietnam, and this fellow walked into the clearing where we were with his hand over his nose and when he took his hand away there was no nose there because it had been shot off; the time the doctor told us our youngest son might be hydrocephalic (he turned out just to have an oversized head, thank God); the long, crazy weeks before my mother died. I would find my thoughts turning back to that morning, the scuffed suede of her ears, the white flash of her tail. But eight hundred million Red Chinese don't give a shit, right? The most important things are the hardest to say, because words diminish them. It's hard to make strangers care about the good things in your life.

21

The tracks now bent southwest and ran through tangles of second-growth fir and heavy underbrush. We got a breakfast of late blackberries from some of these bushes, but berries never fill you up; your stomach just gives them a thirty-minute option and then begins growling again. We went back to the tracks—it was about eight o'clock by then—and took five. Our mouths were a dark purple and our naked torsos were scratched from the blackberry brambles. Vern wished glumly aloud for a couple of fried eggs with bacon on the side.

That was the last day of the heat, and I think it was the worst of all. The early scud of clouds melted away and by nine o'clock the sky was a pale steel color that made you feel hotter just looking at it. The sweat rolled and ran from our chests and backs, leaving clean streaks through the accumulated soot and grime. Mosquitoes and blackflies whirled and dipped around our heads in aggravating clouds. Knowing that we had long miles to go didn't make us feel any better. Yet the fascination of the thing drew us on and kept us walking faster than we had any business doing, in that heat. We were all crazy to see that kid's body—I can't put it any more simply or honestly than that. Whether it was harmless or whether it turned out to have the power to murder sleep with a hundred mangled dreams, we wanted to see it. I think that we had come to believe we *deserved* to see it.

It was about nine-thirty when Teddy and Chris spotted

water up ahead—they shouted to Vern and me. We ran over to where they were standing. Chris was laughing, delighted. "Look there! Beavers did that!" He pointed.

It was the work of beavers, all right. A large-bore culvert ran under the railroad embankment a little way ahead, and the beavers had sealed the right end with one of their neat and industrious little dams—sticks and branches cemented together with leaves, twigs, and dried mud. Beavers are busy little fuckers, all right. Behind the dam was a clear and shining pool of water, brilliantly mirroring the sunlight. Beaver houses humped up and out of the water in several places—they looked like wooden igloos. A small creek trickled into the far end of the pool, and the trees which bordered it were gnawed a clean bone-white to a height of almost three feet in places.

"Railroad'll clean this shit out pretty soon," Chris said.

"Why?" Vern asked.

"They can't have a pool here," Chris said. "It'd undercut their precious railroad line. That's why they put that culvert in there to start with. They'll shoot them some beavers and scare off the rest and then knock out their dam. Then this'll go back to being a bog, like it probably was before."

"I think that eats the meat," Teddy said.

Chris shrugged. "Who cares about beavers? Not the Great Southern and Western Maine, that's for sure."

"You think it's deep enough to swim in?" Vern asked, looking hungrily at the water.

"One way to find out," Teddy said.

"Who goes first?" I asked.

"Me!" Chris said. He went running down the bank, kicking off his sneakers and untying his shirt from around his waist with a jerk. He pushed his pants and undershorts down with a single shove of his thumbs. He balanced, first on one leg and then on the other, to get his socks. Then he made a shallow dive. He came up shaking his head to get his wet hair out of his eyes. "It's fuckin *great*!" he shouted.

"How deep?" Teddy called back. He had never learned to swim.

Chris stood up in the water and his shoulders broke the surface. I saw something on one of them—a blackish-grayish something. I decided it was a piece of mud and dismissed it. If I had looked more closely I could have saved myself a lot of nightmares later on. "Come on in, you chickens!"

He turned and thrashed off across the pool in a clumsy breast-stroke, turned over, and thrashed back. By then we were all getting undressed. Vern was in next, then me.

Hitting the water was fantastic—clean and cool. I swam across to Chris, loving the silky feel of having nothing on but water. I stood up and we grinned into each other's faces.

"Boss!" We said it at exactly the same instant.

"Fuckin jerkoff," he said, splashed water in my face, and swam off the other way.

We goofed off in the water for almost half an hour before we realized that the pond was full of bloodsuckers. We dived, swam under water, ducked each other. We never knew a thing. Then Vern swam into the shallower part, went under, and stood on his hands. When his legs broke water in a shaky but triumphant V, I saw that they were covered with blackish-gray lumps, just like the one I had seen on Chris's shoulder. They were slugs—big ones.

Chris's mouth dropped open, and I felt all the blood in my body go as cold as dry ice. Teddy screamed, his face going pale. Then all three of us were thrashing for the bank, going just as fast as we could. I know more about freshwater slugs now than I did then, but the fact that they are mostly harmless has done nothing to allay the almost insane horror of them I've had ever since that day in the beaver-pool. They carry a local anesthetic and an anti-coagulant in their alien saliva, which means that the host never feels a thing when they attach themselves. If you don't happen to see them they'll go on feeding until their swelled, loathsome bodies fall off you, sated, or until they actually burst.

We pulled ourselves up on the bank and Teddy went into a hysterical paroxysm as he looked down at himself. He was screaming as he picked the leeches off his naked body.

Vern broke the water and looked at us, puzzled. "What the hell's wrong with h—"

"Leeches!" Teddy screamed, pulling two of them off his trembling thighs and throwing them just as far as he could. "Dirty mother-fuckin *bloodsuckers*!" His voice broke shrilly on the last word.

"OhGodOhGodOhGod!" Vern cried. He paddled across the pool and stumbled out.

I was still cold; the heat of the day had been suspended. I kept telling myself to catch hold. Not to get screaming. Not to be a pussy. I picked half a dozen off my arms and several more off my chest.

Chris turned his back to me. "Gordie? Are there any more? Take em off if there are, please, Gordie!" There *were* more, five or six, running down his back like grotesque black buttons. I pulled their soft, boneless bodies off him.

I brushed even more off my legs, then got Chris to do my back.

I was starting to relax a little—and that was when I looked down at myself and saw the granddaddy of them all clinging to my testicles, its body swelled to four times its normal size. Its blackish-gray skin had gone a bruised purplish-red. That was when I began to lose control. Not outside, at least not in any big way, but inside, where it counts.

I brushed its slick, glutinous body with the back of my hand.

It held on. I tried to do it again and couldn't bring myself to actually touch it. I turned to Chris, tried to speak, couldn't. I pointed instead. His cheeks, already ashy, went whiter still.

"I can't get it off," I said through numb lips. "You . . . can you . . ."

But he backed away, shaking his head, his mouth twisted. "I can't, Gordie," he said, unable to take his eyes away. "I'm sorry but I can't. No. Oh. No." He turned away, bowed with one hand pressed to his midsection like the butler in a musical comedy, and was sick in a stand of juniper bushes.

You got to hold onto yourself, I thought, looking at the leech that hung off me like a crazy beard. Its body was still visibly swelling. *You got to hold onto yourself and get him. Be tough. It's the last one. The. Last. One.*

I reached down again and picked it off and it burst between my fingers. My own blood ran across my palm and inner wrist in a warm flood. I began to cry.

Still crying, I walked back to my clothes and put them on. I wanted to stop crying, but I just didn't seem able to turn off the waterworks. Then the shakes set in, making it worse. Vern ran up to me, still naked.

"They off, Gordie? They off me? They off me?"

He twirled in front of me like an insane dancer on a carnival stage.

"They off? Huh? Huh? They off me, Gordie?"

His eyes kept going past me, as wide and white as the eyes of a plaster horse on a merry-go-round.

I nodded that they were and just kept on crying. It seemed that crying was going to be my new career. I tucked my shirt in and then buttoned it all the way to the neck. I put on my socks and my sneakers. Little by little the tears began to slow down. Finally there was nothing left but a few hitches and moans, and then they stopped, too.

Chris walked over to me, wiping his mouth with a handful of elm leaves. His eyes were wide and mute and apologetic.

When we were all dressed we just stood there looking at each other for a moment, and then we began to climb the railroad embankment. I looked back once at the burst leech lying on top of the tromped-down bushes where we had danced and screamed and groaned them off. It looked deflated . . . but still ominous.

Fourteen years later I sold my first novel and made my first trip to New York. "It's going to be a three-day celebration," my new editor told me over the phone. "People slinging bullshit will be summarily shot." But of course it was three days of unmitigated bullshit.

While I was there I wanted to do all the standard out-of-towner things—see a stage show at the Radio City Music Hall, go to the top of the Empire State Building (fuck the World Trade Center; the building King Kong climbed in 1933 is always gonna be the tallest one in the world for me), visit Times Square by night. Keith, my editor, seemed more than pleased to show his city off. The last touristy thing we did was to take a ride on the Staten Island Ferry, and while leaning on the rail I happened to look down and see scores of used condoms floating on the mild swells. And I had a moment of almost total recall—or perhaps it was an actual incidence of time-travel. Either way, for one second I was literally *in* the past, pausing halfway up that embankment and looking back at the burst leech: dead, deflated . . . but still ominous.

Keith must have seen something in my face because he said: "Not very pretty, are they?"

I only shook my head, wanting to tell him not to apologize, wanting to tell him that you didn't have to come to the Apple and ride the ferry to see used rubbers, wanting to say: *The only reason anyone writes stories is so they can understand the past and get ready for some future mortality; that's why all the verbs in stories have -ed endings, Keith my good man, even the ones that sell millions of paperbacks. The only two useful artforms are religion and stories.*

I was pretty drunk that night, as you may have guessed.

What I did tell him was: "I was thinking of something else, that's all." The most important things are the hardest things to say.

22

We walked further down the tracks—I don't know just how far—and I was starting to think: *Well, okay, I'm going to be able to handle it, it's all over anyway, just a bunch of leeches, what the fuck;* I was still thinking it when waves of whiteness suddenly began to come over my sight and I fell down.

I must have fallen hard, but landing on the crossties was like plunging into a warm and puffy feather bed. Someone turned me over. The touch of hands was faint and unimportant. Their faces were disembodied balloons looking down at me from miles up. They looked the way the ref's face must look to a fighter who has been punched silly and is currently taking a ten-second rest on the canvas. Their words came in gentle oscillations, fading in and out.

". . . him?"

". . . be all . . ."

". . . if you think the sun . . ."

"Gordie, are you . . ."

Then I must have said something that didn't make much sense because they began to look *really* worried.

"We better take him back, man," Teddy said, and then the whiteness came over everything again.

When it cleared, I seemed to be all right. Chris was squatting next to me, saying: "Can you hear me, Gordie? You there, man?"

"Yes," I said, and sat up. A swarm of black dots exploded in front of my eyes, and then went away. I waited to see if they'd come back, and when they didn't, I stood up.

"You scared the cheesly old shit outta me, Gordie," he said. "You want a drink of water?"

"Yeah."

He gave me his canteen, half-full of water, and I let three warm gulps roll down my throat.

"Why'd you faint, Gordie?" Vern asked anxiously.

"Made a bad mistake and looked at your face," I said.

"Eeee-eee-eeee!" Teddy cackled. "Fuckin Gordie! You wet!"

"You really okay?" Vern persisted.

"Yeah. Sure. It was . . . bad there for a minute. Thinking about those suckers."

They nodded soberly. We took five in the shade and then went on walking, me and Vern on one side of the tracks again, Chris and Teddy on the other. We figured we must be getting close.

23

We weren't as close as we thought, and if we'd had the brains to spend two minutes looking at a roadmap, we would have seen why. We knew that Ray Brower's corpse had to be near the Back Harlow Road, which dead-ends on the bank of the Royal River. Another trestle carries the GS&WM tracks across the Royal. So this is the way we figured: Once we got close to the Royal, we'd be getting close to the Back Harlow Road, where Billy and Charlie had been parked when they saw the boy. And since the Royal was only ten miles from the Castle River, we figured we had it made in the shade.

But that was ten miles as the crow flies, and the tracks didn't move on a straight line between the Castle and the Royal. Instead, they made a very shallow loop to avoid a hilly, crumbling region called The Bluffs. Anyway, we could have seen that loop quite clearly if we had looked on a map, and figured out that, instead of ten miles, we had about sixteen to walk.

Chris began to suspect the truth when noon had come and gone and the Royal still wasn't in sight. We stopped while he climbed a high pine tree and took a look around. He came down and gave us a simple enough report: it was going to be at least four in the afternoon before we got to the Royal, and we would only make it by then if we humped right along.

"Ah, *shit*!" Teddy cried. "So what're we gonna do now?"

We looked into each others' tired, sweaty faces. We were hungry and out of temper. The big adventure had turned into a long slog—dirty and sometimes scary. We would have been missed back home by now, too, and if Milo Pressman hadn't already called the cops on us, the engineer of the train crossing the trestle might have done it. We had been planning to hitchhike back to Castle Rock, but four o'clock was just three hours from dark, and *nobody* gives four kids on a back country road a lift after dark.

I tried to summon up the cool image of my deer, cropping at green morning grass, but even that seemed dusty and no good, no better than a stuffed trophy over the mantel in some guy's hunting lodge, the eyes sprayed to give them that phony lifelike shine.

Finally Chris said: "It's still closer out going ahead. Let's go."

He turned and started to walk along the tracks in his dusty sneakers, head down, his shadow only a puddle at his feet.

After a minute or so the rest of us followed him, strung out in Indian file.

24

In the years between then and the writing of this memoir, I've thought remarkably little about those two days in September, at least consciously. The associations the memories bring to the surface are as unpleasant as week-old river-corpses brought to the surface by cannonfire. As a result, I never really questioned our decision to walk down the tracks. Put another way, I've wondered sometimes about *what* we had decided to do but never how we did it.

But now a much simpler scenario comes to mind. I'm confident that if the idea *had* come up it would have been shot down—walking down the tracks would have seemed neater, *bosser,* as we said then. But if the idea had come up and *hadn't* been shot down in flames, none of the things which occurred later would have happened. Maybe Chris and Teddy and Vern would even be alive today. No, they didn't die in the woods or on the railroad tracks; nobody dies in this story except some bloodsuckers and Ray Brower, and if you want to be completely fair about it, he was dead before it even started. But it *is* true that, of the four of us who flipped coins to see who would go down to the Florida Market to get supplies, only the one who actually went is still alive. The Ancient Mariner at thirty-four, with you, Gentle Reader, in the role of Wedding Guest (at this point shouldn't you flip to the jacket photo to see if my eye holdeth you in its spell?). If you sense a certain flipness on my part, you're right—but maybe I have cause. At an age when all four of us would be considered too young and immature to be President, three of us are dead. And if small events really do echo up larger and larger through time, yes, maybe if we had done the simple thing and simply hitched into Harlow, they would still be alive today.

We could have hooked a ride all the way up Route 7 to the Shiloh Church, which stood at the intersection of the highway and the Back Harlow Road (at least until 1967, when it was levelled by a fire attributed to a tramp's smouldering cigarette butt). With reasonable luck we could have gotten to where the body was by sundown of the previous day.

But the idea wouldn't have lived. It wouldn't have been shot down with tightly buttressed arguments and debating society rhetoric, but with grunts and scowls and farts and raised middle fingers. The verbal part of the discussion would have been carried forward with such trenchant and sparkling contributions as "Fuck no," "That sucks," and that old reliable standby, "Did your mother ever have any kids that lived?"

Unspoken—maybe it was too fundamental to be spoken—was the idea that this was a *big* thing. It wasn't screwing around with firecrackers or trying to look through the knothole in the back of the girls' privy at Harrison State Park. This was something on a par with getting laid for the first time, or going into the Army, or buying your first bottle of legal liquor—just bopping into that state store, if you can dig it, selecting a bottle of good Scotch, showing the clerk your draft-card and driver's license, then walking out with a grin on your face and that brown bag in your hand, member of a club with just a few more rights and privileges than our old treehouse with the tin roof.

There's a high ritual to all fundamental events, the rites of passage, the magic corridor where the change happens. Buying the condoms. Standing before the minister. Raising your hand and taking the oath. Or, if you please, walking down the railroad tracks to meet a fellow your own age halfway, the same as I'd walk halfway over to Pine Street to meet Chris if he was coming over to my house, or the way Teddy would walk halfway down Gates Street to meet me if I was going to his. It seemed right to do it this way, because the rite of passage *is* a magic corridor and so we always provide an aisle—it's what you walk down when you get married, what they carry you down when you get buried. Our corridor was those twin rails, and we walked between them, just hopping along toward whatever this was supposed to mean. You don't hitchhike your way to a thing like that, maybe. And maybe we thought it was also right that it should have turned out to be harder than we had expected. Events surrounding our hike had turned it into what we had suspected it was all along: serious business.

What we *didn't* know as we walked around The Bluffs was that Billy Tessio, Charlie Hogan, Jack Mudgett, Norman "Fuzzy" Bracowicz, Vince Desjardins, Chris's older brother Eyeball, and Ace Merrill himself were all on their way to take a look at the body themselves—in a weird kind of way, Ray Brower had become famous, and our secret had turned into a regular roadshow. They were piling into Ace's chopped and channelled '52 Ford and Vince's pink '54 Studebaker even as we started on the last leg of our trip.

Billy and Charlie had managed to keep their enormous secret for just about thirty-six hours. Then Charlie spilled it to Ace while they were shooting pool, and Billy had spilled it to Jack Mudgett while they were fishing for steelies from the Boom Road Bridge. Both Ace and Jack had sworn solemnly on their mothers' names to keep the secret, and that was how everybody in their gang knew about it by noon. Guess you could tell what those assholes thought about their mothers.

They all congregated down at the pool hall, and Fuzzy Bracowicz advanced a theory (which you have heard before, Gentle Reader) that they could all become heroes—not to mention instant radio and TV personalities—by "discovering" the body. All they had to do, Fuzzy maintained, was to take two cars with a lot of fishing gear in the trunks. After they found the body, their story would be a hundred per cent. We was just plannin to take a few pickerel out of the Royal River, officer. Heh-heh-heh. Look what we found.

They were burning up the road from Castle Rock to the Back Harlow area just as we started to finally get close.

25

Clouds began to build in the sky around two o'clock, but at first none of us took them seriously. It hadn't rained since the early days of July, so why should it rain now? But they kept building to the south of us, up and up and up, thunderheads in great pillars as purple as bruises, and they began to move slowly our way. I looked at them closely, checking for that membrane beneath that means it's already raining twenty miles away, or fifty. But there was no rain yet. The clouds were still just building.

Vern got a blister on his heel and we stopped and rested while he packed the back of his left sneaker with moss stripped from the bark of an old oak tree.

"Is it gonna rain, Gordie?" Teddy asked.

"I think so."

"Pisser!" he said, and sighed. "The pisser good end to a pisser good day."

I laughed and he tipped me a wink.

We started to walk again, a little more slowly now out of respect for Vern's hurt foot. And in the hour between two and three, the quality of the day's light began to change, and we knew for sure that rain was coming. It was just as hot as ever, and even more humid, but we knew. And the birds did. They seemed to appear from nowhere and swoop across the sky, chattering and crying shrilly to each other. And the light. From a steady, beating brightness it seemed to evolve into something filtered, almost pearly. Our shadows, which had begun to grow long again, also grew fuzzy and ill-defined. The sun had begun to sail in and out through the thickening decks of clouds, and the southern sky had gone a coppery shade. We watched the thunderheads lumber closer, fascinated by their size and their mute threat. Every now and then it seemed that a giant flashbulb had gone off inside one of them, turning their purplish, bruised color momentarily to a light gray. I saw a jagged fork of lightning lick down from the underside of the closest. It was bright enough to print a blue tattoo on my retinas. It was followed by a long, shaking blast of thunder.

We did a little bitching about how we were going to get caught out in the rain, but only because it was the expected thing—of course we were all looking forward to it. It would be cold and refreshing . . . and leech-free.

At a little past three-thirty, we saw running water through a break in the trees.

"That's it!" Chris yelled jubilantly. "That's the Royal!"

We began to walk faster, taking our second wind. The storm was getting close now. The air began to stir, and it seemed that the temperature dropped ten degrees in a space of seconds. I looked down and saw that my shadow had disappeared entirely.

We were walking in pairs again, each two watching a side of the railroad embankment. My mouth was dry, throbbing with a sickish tension. The sun sailed behind another cloudbank and this time it didn't come back out. For a moment the bank's edges were embroidered with gold, like a cloud in an Old Testament Bible illustration, and then the wine-colored, dragging belly of the thunderhead blotted out all traces of the sun. The day became gloomy—the clouds were rapidly eating up the last of the blue. We could smell the river so clearly that we might have been horses—or perhaps it was the smell of rain impending in the air as well. There was an ocean above us, held in by a thin sac that might rupture and let down a flood at any second.

I kept trying to look into the underbrush, but my eyes were continually drawn back to that turbulent, racing sky; in its deepening colors you could read whatever doom you liked: water, fire, wind, hail. The cool breeze became more insistent, hissing in the firs. A sudden impossible bolt of lightning flashed down, seemingly from directly overhead, making me cry out and clap my hands to my eyes. God had taken my picture, a little kid with his shirt tied around his waist, duck-bumps on his bare chest and cinders on his cheeks. I heard the rending fall of some big tree not sixty yards away. The crack of thunder which followed made me cringe. I wanted to be at home reading a good book in a safe place . . . like down in the potato cellar.

"Jeezis!" Vern screamed in a high, fainting voice. "Oh my Jeezis Chrise, lookit *that*!"

I looked in the direction Vern was pointing and saw a blue-white fireball bowling its way up the lefthand rail of the GS&WM tracks, crackling and hissing for all the world like a scalded cat. It hurried past us as we turned to watch it go, dumbfounded, aware for the first time that such things could exist. Twenty feet beyond us it made a sudden—*pop!!*—and just disappeared, leaving a greasy smell of ozone behind.

"What am I *doin* here, anyway?" Teddy muttered.

"What a pisser!" Chris exclaimed happily, his face upturned. "This is gonna be a pisser like you wouldn't *believe*!" But I was with Teddy. Looking up at that sky gave me a dismaying sense of vertigo. It was more like looking into some deeply mysterious marbled gorge. Another lightning-bolt crashed down, making us duck. This time the ozone smell was hotter, more urgent. The following clap of thunder came with no perceptible pause at all.

My ears were still ringing from it when Vern began to screech triumphantly: *"THERE! THERE HE IS! RIGHT THERE! I SEE HIM!"*

I can see Vern right this minute, if I want to—all I have to do is sit back for a minute and close my eyes. He's standing there on the lefthand rail like an explorer on the prow of his ship, one hand shielding his eyes from the silver stroke of lightning that has just come down, the other extended and pointing.

We ran up beside him and looked. I was thinking to myself: *Vern's imagination just ran away with him, that's all. The suckers, the heat, now this storm . . . his eyes are dealing wild cards, that's all.* But that wasn't what it was, although there was a split second when I wanted it to be. In that split second I knew I never wanted to see a corpse, not even a runover woodchuck.

In the place where we were standing, early spring rains had washed part of the embankment away, leaving a gravelly, uncertain four-foot drop-off. The railroad maintenance crews had either not yet gotten around to it in their yellow diesel-operated repair carts, or it had happened so recently it hadn't yet been reported. At the bottom of this washout was a marshy, mucky tangle of undergrowth that smelled bad. And sticking out of a wild clockspring of blackberry brambles was a single pale white hand.

Did any of us breathe? I didn't.

The breeze was now a wind—harsh and jerky, coming at us from no particular direction, jumping and whirling, slapping at our sweaty skins and open pores. I hardly noticed. I think part of my mind was waiting for Teddy to cry out *Paratroops over the side!*, and I thought if he did that I might just go crazy. It would have been better to see the whole body, all at once, but instead there was only that limp outstretched hand, horribly white, the fingers limply splayed, like the hand of a drowned boy. It told us the truth of the whole matter. It explained every graveyard in the world. The image of that hand came back to me every time I heard or read of an atrocity. Somewhere, attached to that hand, was the rest of Ray Brower.

Lightning flickered and stroked. Thunder ripped in behind each stroke as if a drag race had started over our heads.

"Sheeeee . . ." Chris said, the sound not quite a cuss word, not quite the country version of *shit* as it is pronounced around a slender stem of timothy grass when the baler breaks down—instead it was a long, tuneless syllable without meaning; a sigh that had just happened to pass through the vocal cords.

Vern was licking his lips in a compulsive sort of way, as if he had tasted some obscure new delicacy, a Howard Johnson's 29th flavor, Tibetan Sausage Rolls, Interstellar Escargot, something so weird that it excited and revolted him at the same time.

Teddy only stood and looked. The wind whipped his greasy, clotted hair first away from his ears and then back over them. His face was a total blank. I could tell you I saw something there, and perhaps I did, in hindsight . . . but not then.

There were black ants trundling back and forth across the hand.

A great whispering noise began to rise in the woods on either side of the tracks, as if the forest had just noticed we were there and was commenting on it. The rain had started.

Dime-sized drops fell on my head and arms. They struck the embankment, turning the fill dark for a moment—and then the color changed back again as the greedy dry ground sucked the moisture up.

Those big drops fell for maybe five seconds and then they stopped. I looked at Chris and he blinked back at me.

Then the storm came all at once, as if a shower chain had been pulled in the sky. The whispering sound changed to loud contention. It was as if we were being rebuked for our discovery, and it was frightening. Nobody tells you about the pathetic fallacy until you're in college . . . and even then I noticed that nobody but the total dorks completely believed it *was* a fallacy.

Chris jumped over the side of the washout, his hair already soaked and clinging to his head. I followed. Vern and Teddy came close behind, but Chris and I were first to reach the body of Ray Brower. He was face down. Chris looked into my eyes, his face set and stern—an adult's face. I nodded slightly, as if he had spoken aloud.

I think he was down here and relatively intact instead of up there between the rails and completely mangled because he was trying to get out of the way when the train hit him, knocking him head over heels. He had landed with his head pointed toward the tracks, arms over his head like a diver about to execute. He had landed in this boggy cup of land that was becoming a small swamp. His hair was a dark reddish color. The moisture in the air had made it curl slightly at the ends. There was blood in it, but not a great deal, not a gross-out amount. The ants were grosser. He was wearing a solid color dark green tee-shirt and bluejeans. His feet were bare, and a few feet behind him, caught in tall blackberry brambles, I saw a pair of filthy low-topped Keds. For a moment I was puzzled—why was he here and his tennies there? Then I realized, and the realization was like a dirty punch below the belt. My wife, my kids, my friends—they all think that having an imagination like mine must be quite nice; aside from making all this dough, I can have a little mind-movie whenever things get dull. Mostly they're right. But every now and then it turns around and bites the shit out of you with these long teeth, teeth that have been filed to points like the teeth of a cannibal. You see things you'd just as soon not see, things that keep you awake until first light. I saw one of those things now, saw it with absolute clarity and certainty. He had been knocked spang out of his Keds. The train had knocked him out of his Keds just as it had knocked the life out of his body.

That finally rammed it all the way home for me. The kid was dead. The kid wasn't sick, the kid wasn't sleeping. The kid wasn't going to get up in the morning anymore or get the runs from eating too many apples or catch poison ivy or wear out the eraser on the end of his Ticonderoga No. 2 during a hard math test. The kid was dead; stone dead. The kid was never going to go out bottling with his friends in the spring, gunnysack over his shoulder to pick up the returnables the retreating snow uncovered. The kid wasn't going to wake up at two o'clock a.m. on the morning of November 1st this year, run to the bathroom, and vomit up a big glurt of cheap Holloween candy. The kid wasn't going to pull a single girl's braid in home room. The kid wasn't going to give a bloody nose, or get one. The kid was *can't, don't, won't, never, shouldn't, wouldn't, couldn't.* He was the side of the battery where the terminal says neg. The fuse you have to put a penny in. The wastebasket by the teacher's desk, which always smells of wood-shavings from the sharpener and dead orange peels from lunch. The haunted house outside of town where the windows are crashed out, the NO TRESPASSING signs whipped away across the fields, the attic full of bats, the cellar full of rats. The kid was dead, mister, ma'am, young sir, little miss. I could go on all day and never get it right about the distance between his bare feet on the ground and his dirty Keds hanging in the bushes. It was thirty-plus inches, it was a googol of light-years. The kid was disconnected from his Keds beyond all hope of reconciliation. He was dead.

We turned him face up into the pouring rain, the lightning, the steady crack of thunder.

There were ants and bugs all over his face and neck. They ran briskly in and out of the round collar of his tee-shirt. His eyes were open, but terrifyingly out of sync—one was rolled back so far that we could see only a tiny arc of iris; the other stared straight up into the storm. There was a dried froth of blood above his mouth and on his chin—from a bloody nose, I thought—and the right side of his face was lacerated and darkly bruised. Still, I thought, he didn't really look bad. I had once walked into a door my brother Dennis was shoving open, came off with bruises even worse than this kid's, *plus* the bloody nose, and still had two helpings of everything for supper after it happened.

Teddy and Vern stood behind us, and if there had been any sight at all left in that one upward-staring eye, I suppose we would have looked to Ray Brower like pallbearers in a horror movie.

A beetle came out of his mouth, trekked across his fuzzless cheek, stepped onto a nettle, and was gone.

"D'joo see that?" Teddy asked in a high, strange, fainting voice. "I bet he's fuckin *fulla* bugs! I bet his *brains*'re—"

"Shut up, Teddy," Chris said, and Teddy did, looking relieved.

Lightning forked blue across the sky, making the boy's single eye light up. You could almost believe he was glad to be found, and found by boys his own age. His torso had swelled up and there was a faint gassy odor about him, like the smell of old farts.

I turned away, sure I was going to be sick, but my stomach was dry, hard, steady. I suddenly rammed two fingers down my throat, trying to *make* myself heave, needing to do it, as if I could sick it up and get rid of it. But my stomach only hitched a little and then was steady again.

The roaring downpour and the accompanying thunder had

completely covered the sound of cars approaching along the Back Harlow Road, which lay bare yards beyond this boggy tangle. It likewise covered the crackle-crunch of the underbrush as they blundered through it from the dead end where they had parked.

And the first we knew of them was Ace Merrill's voice raised above the tumult of the storm, saying: "Well what the fuck do you know about this?"

26

We all jumped like we had been goosed and Vern cried out—he admitted later that he thought, for just a second, that the voice had come from the dead boy.

On the far side of the boggy patch, where the woods took up again, masking the butt end of the road, Ace Merrill and Eyeball Chambers stood together, half-obscured by a pouring gray curtain of rain. They were both wearing red nylon high school jackets, the kind you can buy in the office if you're a regular student, the same kind they give away free to varsity sports players. Their d.a. haircuts had been plastered back against their skulls and a mixture of rainwater and Vitalis ran down their cheeks like ersatz tears.

"Sumbitch!" Eyeball said. "That's my little brother!"

Chris was staring at Eyeball with his mouth open. His shirt, wet, limp, and dark, was still tied around his skinny middle. His pack, stained a darker green by the rain, was hanging against his naked shoulderblades.

"You get away, Rich," he said in a trembling voice. "We found him. We got dibs."

"Fuck your dibs. We're gonna report 'im."

"No you're not," I said. I was suddenly furious with them,

turning up this way at the last minute. If we'd thought about it, we'd have known something like this was going to happen . . . but this was one time, somehow, that the older, bigger kids weren't going to steal it—to take something they wanted as if by divine right, as if their easy way was the right way, the only way. They had come in *cars*—I think that was what made me angriest. They had come in *cars.* "There's four of us, Eyeball. You just try."

"Oh, we'll *try,* don't worry," Eyeball said, and the trees shook behind him and Ace. Charlie Hogan and Vern's brother Billy stepped through them, cursing and wiping water out of their eyes. I felt a lead ball drop into my belly. It grew bigger as Jack Mudgett, Fuzzy Bracowicz, and Vince Desjardins stepped out behind Charlie and Billy.

"Here we all are," Ace said, grinning. "So you just—"

"VERN!!" Billy Tessio cried in a terrible, accusing, my-judgment-cometh-and-that-right-early voice. He made a pair of dripping fists. "You little sonofawhore! You was under the porch! Cock-*knocker!*"

Vern flinched.

Charlie Hogan waxed positively lyrical: "You little keyhole-peeping cunt-licking *bungwipe!* I ought to beat the living shit out of you!"

"Yeah? Well, try it!" Teddy brayed suddenly. His eyes were crazily alight behind his rainspotted glasses. "Come on, fightcha for 'im! Come on! Come on, big men!"

Billy and Charlie didn't need a second invitation. They started forward together and Vern flinched again—no doubt visualizing the ghosts of Beatings Past and Beatings Yet to Come. He flinched . . . but hung tough. He was with his friends, and we had been through a lot, and we hadn't got here in a couple of *cars.*

But Ace held Billy and Charlie back, simply by touching each of them on the shoulder.

"Now listen, you guys," Ace said. He spoke patiently, just as if we weren't all standing in a roaring rainstorm. "There's more of us than there are of you. We're bigger. We'll give you one chance to just blow away. I don't give a fuck where. Just make like a tree and leave."

Chris's brother giggled and Fuzzy clapped Ace on the back in appreciation of his great wit. The Sid Caesar of the j.d. set.

"Cause *we're* takin him." Ace smiled gently, and you could imagine him smiling that same gentle smile just before breaking his cue over the head of some uneducated punk who had made the terrible mistake of lipping off while Ace was lining up a shot. "If you go, we'll take him. If you stay, we'll beat the piss outta you and still take him. Besides," he added, trying to gild the thuggery with a little righteousness, "Charlie and Billy found him, so it's their dibs anyway."

"They was chicken!" Teddy shot back. "Vern told us about it! They was fuckin chicken right outta their fuckin minds!" He screwed his face up into a terrified, snivelling parody of Charlie Hogan. " 'I wish we never boosted that car! I wish we never went out on no Back Harlow Road to whack off a piece! Oh, Billee, what are we gonna do? Oh Billee, I think I just turned my Fruit of the Looms into a fudge factory! Oh Billee—' "

"That's it," Charlie said, starting forward again. His face was knotted with rage and sullen embarrassment. "Kid, whatever your name is, get ready to reach down your fuckin throat the next time you need to pick your nose."

I looked wildly down at Ray Brower. He stared calmly up into the rain with his one eye, below us but above it all. The thunder was still booming steadily, but the rain had begun to slack off.

"What do you say, Gordie?" Ace asked. He was holding Charlie lightly by the arm, the way an accomplished trainer would restrain a vicious dog. "You must have at least some of your brother's sense. Tell these guys to back off. I'll let Charlie beat up the foureyes el punko a little bit and then we all go about our business. What do you say?"

He was wrong to mention Denny. I had wanted to reason with him, to point out what Ace knew perfectly well, that we had every right to take Billy and Charlie's dibs since Vern had heard them giving said dibs away. I wanted to tell him how Vern and I had almost gotten run down by a freight train on the trestle which spans the Castle River. About Milo Pressman and his fearless—if stupid—sidekick, Chopper the Wonder-Dog. About the bloodsuckers, too. I guess all I really wanted to tell him was Come on, Ace, fair is fair. You know that. But he had to bring Denny into it, and what I heard coming out of my mouth instead of sweet reason was my own death-warrant: "Suck my fat one, you cheap dimestore hood."

Ace's mouth formed a perfect O of surprise—the expression was so unexpectedly prissy that under other circumstances it would have been a laff riot, so to speak. All of the others—on both sides of the bog—stared at me, dumbfounded.

Then Teddy screamed gleefully: "That's telling 'im, Gordie! Oh boy! Too cool!"

I stood numbly, unable to believe it. It was like some crazed understudy had shot onstage at the critical moment and declaimed lines that weren't even in the play. Telling a guy to suck was as bad as you could get without resorting to his mother. Out of the corner of my eye I saw that Chris had unshouldered his knapsack and was digging into it frantically, but I didn't get it—not then, anyway.

"Okay," Ace said softly. "Let's take em. Don't hurt nobody but the Lachance kid. I'm gonna break both his fuckin arms."

I went dead cold. I didn't piss myself the way I had on the

railroad trestle, but it must have been because I had nothing inside to let out. He meant it, you see; the years between then and now have changed my mind about a lot of things, but not about that. When Ace said he was going to break both of my arms, he absolutely meant it.

They started to walk toward us through the slackening rain. Jackie Mudgett took a switchknife out of his pocket and hit the chrome. Six inches of steel flicked out, dove-gray in the afternoon half-light. Vern and Teddy dropped suddenly into fighting crouches on either side of me. Teddy did so eagerly, Vern with a desperate, cornered grimace on his face.

The big kids advanced in a line, their feet splashing through the bog, which was now one big sludgy puddle because of the storm. The body of Ray Brower lay at our feet like a water-logged barrel. I got ready to fight . . . and that was when Chris fired the pistol he had hawked out of his old man's dresser.

KA-BLAM!

God, what a wonderful sound that was! Charlie Hogan jumped right up into the air. Ace Merrill, who had been staring straight at me, now jerked around and looked at Chris. His mouth made that O again. Eyeball looked absolutely astounded.

"Hey, Chris, that's Daddy's," he said. "You're gonna get the tar whaled out of you—"

"That's nothing to what you'll get," Chris said. His face was horribly pale, and all the life in him seemed to have been sucked upward, into his eyes. They blazed out of his face.

"Gordie was right, you're nothing but a bunch of cheap hoods. Charlie and Billy didn't want their fuckin dibs and you all know it. We wouldn't have walked way to fuck out here if they said they did. They just went someplace and puked the story up and let Ace Merrill do their thinkin for them." His voice rose to a scream. *"But you ain't gonna get him, do you hear me?"*

"Now listen," Ace said. "You better put that down before you take your foot off with it. You ain't got the sack to shoot a woodchuck." He began to walk forward again, smiling his gentle smile as he came. "You're just a sawed-off pint-sized pissy-assed little runt and I'm gonna make you *eat* that fuckin gun.

"Ace, if you don't stand still I'm going to shoot you. I swear to God."

"You'll go to *jayy-ail,*" Ace crooned, not even hesitating. He was still smiling. The others watched him with horrified fascination . . . much the same way as Teddy and Vern and I were looking at Chris. Ace Merrill was the hardest case for miles around and I didn't think Chris could bluff him down. And what did that leave? Ace didn't think a twelve-year-old punk would actually shoot him. I thought he was wrong; I thought Chris would shoot Ace before he let Ace take his father's pistol away from him. In those few seconds I was sure there was going to be bad trouble, the worst I'd ever known. Killing trouble, maybe. And all of it over who got dibs on a dead body.

Chris said softly, with great regret: "Where do you want it, Ace? Arm or leg? I can't pick. You pick for me."

And Ace stopped.

27

His face sagged, and I saw sudden terror on it. It was Chris's tone rather than his actual words, I think; the real regret that things were going to go from bad to worse. If it was a bluff, it's still the best I've ever seen. The other big kids were totally convinced; their faces were squinched up as if someone had just touched a match to a cherry-bomb with a short fuse.

Ace slowly got control of himself. The muscles in his face tightened again, his lips pressed together, and he looked at Chris the way you'd look at a man who has made a serious business proposition—to merge with your company, or handle your line of credit, or shoot your balls off. It was a waiting, almost curious expression, one that made you know that the terror was either gone or tightly lidded. Ace had recomputed the odds on not getting shot and had decided that they weren't as much in his favor as he had thought. But he was still dangerous—maybe more than before. Since then I've thought it was the rawest piece of brinkmanship I've ever seen. Neither of them was bluffing, they both meant business.

"All right," Ace said softly, speaking to Chris. "But I know how you're going to come out of this, motherfuck."

"No you don't," Chris said.

"You little prick!" Eyeball said loudly. "You're gonna wind up in traction for this!"

"Bite my bag," Chris told him.

With an inarticulate sound of rage Eyeball started forward and Chris put a bullet into the water about ten feet in front of him. It kicked up a splash. Eyeball jumped back, cursing.

"Okay, now what?" Ace asked.

"Now you guys get into your cars and bomb on back to Castle Rock. After that I don't care. But you ain't getting him." He touched Ray Brower lightly, almost reverently, with the toe of one sopping sneaker. "You dig me?"

"But we'll get *you,*" Ace said. He was starting to smile again. "Don't you know that?"

"You might. You might not."

"We'll get you hard," Ace said, smiling. "We'll hurt you.

I can't believe you don't *know* that. We'll put you all in the fuckin hospital with fuckin ruptures. Sincerely."

"Oh, why don't you go home and fuck your mother some more? I hear she loves the way you do it."

Ace's smile froze. "I'll kill you for that. Nobody ranks my mother."

"I heard your mother fucks for bucks," Chris informed him, and as Ace began to pale, as his complexion began to approach Chris's own ghastly whiteness, he added: "In fact, I heard she throws blowjobs for jukebox nickels. I heard—"

Then the storm came back, viciously, all at once. Only this time it was hail instead of rain. Instead of whispering or talking, the woods now seemed alive with hokey B-movie jungle drums—it was the sound of big icy hailstones honking off treetrunks. Stinging pebbles began to hit my shoulders—it felt as if some sentient, malevolent force were throwing them. Worse than that, they began to strike Ray Brower's upturned face with an awful splatting sound that reminded us of him again, of his terrible and unending patience.

Vern caved in first, with a wailing scream. He fled up the embankment in huge, gangling strides. Teddy held out a minute longer, then ran after Vern, his hands held up over his head. On their side, Vince Desjardins floundered back under some nearby trees and Fuzzy Bracowicz joined him. But the others stood pat, and Ace began to grin again.

"Stick with me, Gordie," Chris said in a low, shaky voice. "Stick with me, man."

"I'm right here."

"Go on, now," Chris said to Ace, and he was able, by some magic, to get the shakiness out of his voice. He sounded as if he were instructing a stupid infant.

"We'll get you," Ace said. "We're not going to forget it, if that's what you're thinking. This is big time, baby."

"That's fine. You just go on and do your getting another day."

"We'll fuckin ambush you, Chambers. We'll—"

"Get out!" Chris screamed, and levelled the gun. Ace stepped back.

He looked at Chris a moment longer, nodded, then turned around. "Come on," he said to the others. He looked back over his shoulder at Chris and me once more. "Be seeing you."

They went back into the screen of trees between the bog and the road. Chris and I stood perfectly still in spite of the hail that was welting us, reddening our skins, and piling up all around us like summer snow. We stood and listened and above the crazy calypso sound of the hail hitting the treetrunks we heard two cars start up.

"Stay right here," Chris told me, and he started across the bog.

"Chris!" I said, panicky.

"I got to. Stay here."

It seemed he was gone a very long time. I became convinced that either Ace or Eyeball had lurked behind and grabbed him. I stood my ground with nobody but Ray Brower for company and waited for somebody—anybody—to come back. After a while, Chris did.

"We did it," he said. "They're gone."

"You sure?"

"Yeah. Both cars." He held his hands up over his head, locked together with the gun between them, and shook the double fist in a wry championship gesture. Then he dropped them and smiled at me. I think it was the saddest scaredest smile I ever saw. " 'Suck my fat one'—whoever told you you had a fat one, Lachance?"

"Biggest one in four counties," I said. I was shaking all over.

We looked at each other warmly for a second, and then, maybe embarrassed by what we were seeing, looked down together. A nasty thrill of fear shot through me, and the sudden *splash/splash* as Chris shifted his feet let me know that he had seen, too. Ray Brower's eyes had gone wide and white, starey and pupilless, like the eyes that look out at you from Grecian statuary. It only took a second to understand what had happened, but understanding didn't lessen the horror. His eyes had filled up with round white hailstones. Now they were melting and the water ran down his cheeks as if he were weeping for his own grotesque position—a tatty prize to be fought over by two bunches of stupid hick kids. His clothes were also white with hail. He seemed to be lying in his own shroud.

"Oh, Gordie, hey," Chris said shakily. "Say-hey, man. What a creepshow for him."

"I don't think he knows—"

"Maybe that *was* his ghost we heard. Maybe he knew this was gonna happen. What a fuckin creepshow, I'm sincere."

Branches crackled behind us. I whirled, sure they had flanked us, but Chris went back to contemplating the body after one short, almost casual glance. It was Vern and Teddy, their jeans soaked black and plastered to their legs, both of them grinning like dogs that have been sucking eggs.

"What are we gonna do, man?" Chris asked, and I felt a weird chill steal through me. Maybe he was talking to me, maybe he was . . . but he was still looking down at the body.

"We're gonna take him back, ain't we?" Teddy asked, puzzled. "We're gonna be heroes. Ain't that right?" He looked from Chris to me and back to Chris again.

Chris looked up as if startled out of a dream. His lip curled. He took big steps toward Teddy, planted both hands on Teddy's chest, and pushed him roughly backwards. Teddy stumbled, pinwheeled his arms for balance, then sat down with a soggy splash. He blinked up at Chris like a surprised muskrat. Vern was looking warily at Chris, as if he feared madness. Perhaps that wasn't far from the mark.

"You keep your trap shut," Chris said to Teddy. "Paratroops over the side my ass. You lousy rubber chicken."

"It was the *hail*!" Teddy cried out, angry and ashamed. "It wasn't those guys, Chris! I'm ascared of *storms*! I can't help it! I would have taken all of em on at once, I swear on my mother's name! But I'm ascared of *storms*! Shit! I can't help it!" He began to cry again, sitting there in the water.

"What about you?" Chris asked, turning to Vern. "Are you scared of storms, too?"

Vern shook his head vacuously, still astounded by Chris's rage. "Hey, man, I thought we was all runnin."

"You must be a mind-reader then, because you ran first."

Vern swallowed twice and said nothing.

Chris stared at him, his eyes sullen and wild. Then he turned to me. "Going to build him a litter, Gordie."

"If you say so, Chris."

"Sure! Like in Scouts." His voice had begun to climb into strange, reedy levels. "Just like in the fuckin Scouts. A litter—poles and shirts. Like in the handbook. Right, Gordie?"

"Yeah. If you want. But what if those guys—"

"Fuck those guys!" he screamed. *"You're all a bunch of chickens! Fuck off, creeps!"*

"Chris, they could call the Constable. To get back at us."

"He's ours and we're gonna take him OUT!"

"Those guys would say anything to get us in dutch," I told him. My words sounded thin, stupid, sick with the flu. "Say anything and then lie each other up. You know how people can get other people in trouble telling lies, man. Like with the milk-mo—"

"I DON'T CARE!" he screamed, and lunged at me with his fists up. But one of his feet struck Ray Brower's ribcage with a soggy thump, making the body rock. He tripped and fell full-length and I waited for him to get up and maybe punch me in

the mouth but instead he lay where he had fallen, head pointing toward the embankment, arms stretched out over his head like a diver about to execute, in the exact posture Ray Brower had been in when we found him. I looked wildly at Chris's feet to make sure his sneakers were still on. Then he began to cry and scream, his body bucking in the muddy water, splashing it around, fists drumming up and down in it, head twisting from side to side. Teddy and Vern were staring at him, agog, because nobody had ever seen Chris Chambers cry. After a moment or two I walked back to the embankment, climbed it, and sat down on one of the rails. Teddy and Vern followed me. And we sat there in the rain, not talking, looking like those three Monkeys of Virtue they sell in dime-stores and those sleazy gift-shops that always look like they are tottering on the edge of bankruptcy.

28

It was twenty minutes before Chris climbed the embankment to sit down beside us. The clouds had begun to break. Spears of sun came down through the rips. The bushes seemed to have gone three shades darker green in the last forty-five minutes. He was mud all the way up one side and down the other. His hair was standing up in muddy spikes. The only clean parts of him were the whitewashed circles around his eyes.

"You're right, Gordie," he said. "Nobody gets last dibs. Goocher all around, huh?"

I nodded. Five minutes passed. No one said anything. And I happened to have a thought—just in case they *did* call Bannerman. I went back down the embankment and over to where Chris had been standing. I got down on my knees and began to comb carefully through the water and marshgrass with my fingers.

"What you doing?" Teddy asked, joining me.

"It's to your left, I think," Chris said, and pointed.

I looked there and after a minute or two I found both shell casings. They winked in the fresh sunlight. I gave them to Chris. He nodded and stuffed them into a pocket of his jeans.

"Now we go," Chris said.

"Hey, come *on*!" Teddy yelled, in real agony. "I wanna *take* 'im!"

"Listen, dummy," Chris said, "if we take him back we could all wind up in the reformatory. It's like Gordie says. Those guys could make up any story they wanted to. What if they said *we* killed him, huh? How would you like that?"

"I don't give a damn," Teddy said sulkily. Then he looked at us with absurd hope. "Besides, we might only get a couple of months or so. As excessories. I mean, we're only twelve fuckin years old, they ain't gonna put us in Shawshank."

Chris said softly: "You can't get in the Army if you got a record, Teddy."

I was pretty sure that was nothing but a bald-faced lie—but somehow this didn't seem the time to say so. Teddy just looked at Chris for a long time, his mouth trembling. Finally he managed to squeak out: "No shit?"

"Ask Gordie."

He looked at me hopefully.

"He's right," I said, feeling like a great big turd. "He's right, Teddy. First thing they do when you volunteer is to check your name through R&I."

"Holy *God*!"

"We're gonna shag ass back to the trestle," Chris said. "Then we'll get off the tracks and come into Castle Rock from the other direction. If people ask where we were, we'll say we went campin up on Brickyard Hill and got lost."

"Milo Pressman knows better," I said. "That creep at the Florida Market does, too."

"Well, we'll say Milo scared us and that's when we decided to go up on the Brickyard."

I nodded. That might work. If Vern and Teddy could remember to stick to it.

"What about if our folks get together?" Vern asked.

"You worry about it if you want," Chris said. "My dad'll still be juiced up."

"Come on, then," Vern said, eyeing the screen of trees between us and the Back Harlow Road. He looked like he expected Bannerman, along with a brace of bloodhounds, to come crashing through at any moment. "Let's get while the gettin's good."

We were all on our feet now, ready to go. The birds were singing like crazy, pleased with the rain and the shine and the worms and just about everything in the world, I guess. We all turned around, as if pulled on strings, and looked back at Ray Brower.

He was lying there, alone again. His arms had flopped out when we turned him over and now he was sort of spread-eagled, as if to welcome the sunshine. For a moment it seemed all right, a more natural deathscene than any ever constructed for a viewing-room audience by a mortician. Then you saw the bruise, the caked blood on the chin and under the nose, and the way the corpse was beginning to bloat. You saw that the bluebottles had come out with the sun and that they were circling the body, buzzing indolently. You remembered that gassy smell, sickish but dry, like farts in a closed room. He was a boy our age, he was dead, and I rejected the idea that anything about it could be natural; I pushed it away with horror.

"Okay," Chris said, and he meant to be brisk but his voice came out of his throat like a handful of dry bristles from an old whiskbroom. "Double-time."

We started to almost-trot back the way we had come. We

didn't talk. I don't know about the others, but I was too busy thinking to talk. There were things that bothered me about the body of Ray Brower—they bothered me then and they bother me now.

A bad bruise on the side of his face, a scalp laceration, a bloody nose. No more—at least, no more visible. People walk away from bar-fights in worse condition and go right on drinking. Yet the train *must* have hit him; why else would his sneakers be off his feet that way? And how come the engineer hadn't seen him? Could it be that the train had hit him hard enough to toss him but not to kill him? I thought that, under just the right combination of circumstances, that could have happened. Had the train hit him a hefty, teeth-rattling sideswipe as he tried to get out of the way? Hit him and knocked him in a flying, backwards somersault over that caved-in banking? Had he perhaps lain awake and trembling in the dark for hours, not just lost now but disoriented as well, cut off from the world? Maybe he had died of fear. A bird with crushed tailfeathers once died in my cupped hands in just that way. Its body trembled and vibrated lightly, its beak opened and closed, its dark, bright eyes stared up at me. Then the vibration quit, the beak froze half-open and the black eyes became lackluster and uncaring. It could have been that way with Ray Brower. He could have died because he was simply too frightened to go on living.

But there was another thing, and that bothered me most of all, I think. He had started off to go berrying. I seemed to remember the news reports saying he'd been carrying a pot to put his berries in. When we got back I went to the library and looked it up in the newspapers just to be sure, and I was right. He'd been berrying, and he'd had a pail, or a pot—something like that. But we hadn't found it. We found him, and we found his sneakers. He must have thrown it away somewhere between Chamberlain and the boggy patch of ground in Harlow where he died. He perhaps clutched it even tighter at first, as though it linked him to home and safety. But as his fear grew, and with it that sense of being utterly alone, with no chance of rescue except for whatever he could do by himself, as the real cold terror set in, he maybe threw it away into the woods on one side of the tracks or the other, hardly even noticing it was gone.

I've thought of going back and looking for it—how does that strike you for morbid? I've thought of driving to the end of the Back Harlow Road in my almost new Ford van and getting out of it some bright summer morning, all by myself, my wife and children far off in another world where, if you turn a switch, lights come on in the dark. I've thought about how it would be. Pulling my pack out of the back and resting it on the customized van's rear bumper while I carefully remove my shirt and tie it around my waist. Rubbing my chest and shoulders with Muskol insect repellent and then crashing through the woods to where that boggy place was, the place where we found him. Would the grass grow up yellow there, in the shape of his body? Of course not, there would be no sign, but still you wonder, and you realize what a thin film there is between your rational man costume—the writer with leather elbow-patches on his corduroy jacket—and the capering, Gorgon myths of childhood. Then climbing the embankment, now overgrown with weeds, and walking slowly beside the rusted tracks and rotted ties toward Chamberlain.

Stupid fantasy. An expedition looking for a twenty-year-old blueberry bucket, which was probably cast deep into the woods or plowed under by a bulldozer readying a half-acre plot for a tract house or so deeply overgrown by weeds and brambles it had become invisible. But I feel sure it is still there, somewhere along the old discontinued GS&WM line, and at times the urge to go and look is almost a frenzy. It usually comes early in the morning, when my wife is showering and the kids are watching *Batman* and *Scooby-Doo* on channel 38 out of Boston, and I am feeling the most like the pre-adolescent Gordon Lachance that once strode the earth, walking and talking and occasionally crawling on his belly like a reptile. That boy was *me,* I think. And the thought which follows, chilling me like a dash of cold water, is: *Which boy do you mean?*

Sipping a cup of tea, looking at sun slanting through the kitchen windows, hearing the TV from one end of the house and the shower from the other, feeling the pulse behind my eyes that means I got through one beer too many the night before, I feel sure I could find it. I would see clear metal winking through rust, the bright summer sun reflecting it back to my eyes. I would go down the side of the embankment, push aside the grasses that had grown up and twined toughly around its handle, and then I would . . . what? Why, simply pull it out of time. I would turn it over and over in my hands, wondering at the feel of it, marvelling at the knowledge that the last person to touch it had been long years in his grave. Suppose there was a note in it? *Help me, I'm lost.* Of course there wouldn't be—boys don't go out to pick blueberries with paper and pencil—but just suppose. I imagine the awe I'd feel would be as dark as an eclipse. Still, it's mostly just the idea of holding that pail in my two hands, I guess—as much a symbol of my living as his dying, proof that I really do know which boy it was—which boy of the five of us. Holding it. Reading every year in its cake of rust and the fading of its bright shine. Feeling it, trying to understand the suns that shone on it, the rains that fell on it, and the snows that covered it. And to wonder where I was when each thing happened to it in its lonely place, where I was, what I was doing, who I was loving, how I was getting along, where I was. I'd hold it, read it, feel it . . . and look at my own face in whatever reflection might be left. Can you dig it?

29

We got back to Castle Rock a little past five o'clock on Sunday morning, the day before Labor Day. We had walked all night. Nobody complained, although we all had blisters and were all ravenously hungry. My head was throbbing with a killer headache, and my legs felt twisted and burning with fatigue. Twice we had to scramble down the embankment to get out of the way of freights. One of them was going our way, but moving far too fast to hop. It was seeping daylight when we got to the trestle spanning the Castle again. Chris looked at it, looked at the river, looked back at us.

"Fuck it. I'm walking across. If I get hit by a train I won't have to watch out for fuckin Ace Merrill."

We all walked across it—plodded might be the better verb. No train came. When we got to the dump we climbed the fence (no Milo and no Chopper, not this early, and not on a Sunday morning) and went directly to the pump. Vern primed it and we all took turns sticking our heads under the icy flow, slapping the water over our bodies, drinking until we could hold no more. Then we had to put our shirts on again because the morning seemed chilly. We walked—limped—back into town and stood for a moment on the sidewalk in front of the vacant lot. We looked at our treehouse so we wouldn't have to look at each other.

"Well," Teddy said at last, "seeya in school on Wednesday. I think I'm gonna sleep until then."

"Me too," Vern said. "I'm too pooped to pop."

Chris whistled tunelessly through his teeth and said nothing.

"Hey, man," Teddy said awkwardly. "No hard feelins, okay?"

"No," Chris said, and suddenly his somber, tired face broke into a sweet and sunny grin. "We did it, didn't we? We did the bastard."

"Yeah," Vern said. "You're fuckin-A. Now Billy's gonna do *me.*"

"So what?" Chris said. "Richie's gonna tool up on me and Ace is probably gonna tool up on Gordie and somebody else'll tool up on Teddy. But we *did* it."

"That's right," Vern said. But he still sounded unhappy.

Chris looked at me. "We did it, didn't we?" he asked softly. "It was worth it, wasn't it?"

"Sure it was," I said.

"Fuck this," Teddy said in his dry I'm-losing-interest way. "You guys sound like fuckin *Meet the Press.* Gimme some skin, man. I'm gonna toot home and see if Mom's got me on the Ten Most Wanted List."

We all laughed, Teddy gave us his surprised Oh-Lord-what-now look, and we gave him skin. Then he and Vern started off in their direction and I should have gone in mine . . . but I hesitated for a second.

"Walk with you," Chris offered.

"Sure, okay."

We walked a block or so without talking. Castle Rock was awesomely quiet in the day's first light, and I felt an almost holy tiredness-is-slipping-away sort of feeling. We were awake and the whole world was asleep and I almost expected to turn the corner and see my deer standing at the far end of Carbine Street, where the GS&WM tracks pass through the mill's loading yard.

Finally Chris spoke. "They'll tell," he said.

"You bet they will. But not today or tomorrow, if that's what you're worried about. It'll be a long time before they tell, I think. Years, maybe."

He looked at me, surprised.

"They're scared, Chris. Teddy especially, that they won't take him in the Army. But Vern's scared, too. They'll lose some sleep over it, and there's gonna be times this fall when it's right on the tips of their tongues to tell somebody, but I don't think they will. And then . . . you know what? It sounds fucking crazy, but . . . I think they'll almost forget it ever happened."

He was nodding slowly. "I didn't think of it just like that. You see through people, Gordie."

"Man, I wish I did."

"You do, though."

We walked another block in silence.

"I'm never gonna get out of this town," Chris said, and sighed. "When you come back from college on summer vacation, you'll be able to look me and Vern and Teddy up down at Sukey's after the seven-to-three shift's over. If you want to. Except you'll probably never want to." He laughed a creepy laugh.

"Quit jerking yourself off," I said, trying to sound tougher than I felt—I was thinking about being out there in the woods, about Chris saying: *And maybe I took it to old lady Simons and told her, and maybe the money was all there but I got a three-day vacation* anyway, *because the money never showed up. And maybe the next week old lady Simons had this brand-new skirt on when she came to school . . .* The look. The look in his eyes.

"No jerkoff, daddy-O," Chris said.

I rubbed my first finger against my thumb. "This is the world's smallest violin playing 'My Heart Pumps Purple Piss for You.' "

"He was *ours,*" Chris said, his eyes dark in the morning light.

We had reached the corner of my street and we stopped there. It was quarter past six. Back toward town we could see the Sunday *Telegram* truck pulling up in front of Teddy's uncle's stationery shop. A man in bluejeans and a tee-shirt threw off a bundle of papers. They bounced upside down on the sidewalk, showing the color funnies (always Dick Tracy and Blondie on the first page). Then the truck drove on, its driver intent on delivering the outside world to the rest of the whistlestops up the line—Otisfield, Norway-South Paris, Waterford, Stoneham. I wanted to say something more to Chris and didn't know how to.

"Gimme some skin, man," he said, sounding tired.

"Chris—"

"Skin."

I gave him some skin. "I'll see you."

He grinned—that same sweet, sunny grin. "Not if I see you first, fuckface."

He walked off, still laughing, moving easily and gracefully, as though he didn't hurt like me and have blisters like me and like he wasn't lumped and bumped with mosquito and chigger and blackfly bites like me. As if he didn't have a care in the world, as if he was going to some real boss place instead of just home to a three-room house (shack would have been closer to the truth) with no indoor plumbing and broken windows covered with plastic and a brother who was probably laying for him in the front yard. Even if I'd known the right thing to say, I probably couldn't have said it. Speech destroys the functions of love, I think—that's a hell of a thing for a writer to say, I guess, but I believe it to be true. If you speak to tell a deer you mean it no harm, it glides away with a single flip of its tail. The word is the harm. Love isn't what these asshole poets like McKuen want you to think it is. Love has teeth; they bite; the wounds never close. No word, no combination of words, can close those lovebites. It's the other way around, that's the joke. If those wounds dry up, the words die with them. Take it from me. I've made my life from the words, and I know that is so.

30

The back door was locked so I fished the spare key out from under the mat and let myself in. The kitchen was empty, silent, suicidally clean. I could hear the hum the fluorescent bars over the sink made when I turned on the switch. It had been literally years since I had been up before my mother; I couldn't even remember the last time such a thing had happened.

I took off my shirt and put it in the plastic clothesbasket behind the washing machine. I got a clean rag from under the sink and sponged off with it—face, neck, pits, belly. Then I unzipped my pants and scrubbed my crotch—my testicles in particular—until my skin began to hurt. It seemed I couldn't get clean enough down there, although the red weal left by the bloodsucker was rapidly fading. I still have a tiny crescent-shaped scar there. My wife once asked about it and I told her a lie before I was even aware I meant to do so.

When I was done with the rag, I threw it away. It was filthy.

I got out a dozen eggs and scrambled six of them together. When they were semi-solid in the pan, I added a side dish of crushed pineapple and half a quart of milk. I was just sitting down to eat when my mother came in, her gray hair tied in a knot behind her head. She was wearing a faded pink bathrobe and smoking a Camel.

"Gordon, where have you been?"

"Camping," I said, and began to eat. "We started off in Vern's field and then went up the Brickyard Hill. Vern's mom said she would call you. Didn't she?"

"She probably talked to your father," she said, and glided past me to the sink. She looked like a pink ghost. The fluorescent bars were less than kind to her face; they made her complexion look almost yellow. She sighed . . . almost sobbed. "I miss Dennis most in the mornings," she said. "I always look in his room and it's always empty, Gordon. Always."

"Yeah, that's a bitch," I said.

"He always slept with his window open and the blankets . . . Gordon? Did you say something?"

"Nothing important, Mom."

". . . and the blankets pulled up to his chin," she finished. Then she just stared out the window, her back to me. I went on eating. I was trembling all over.

31

The story never did get out.

Oh, I don't mean that Ray Brower's body was never found; it was. But neither our gang nor their gang got the credit. In the end, Ace must have decided that an anonymous phone call was the safest course, because that's how the location of the corpse was reported. What I meant was that none of our parents ever found out what we'd been up to that Labor Day weekend.

Chris's dad was still drinking, just as Chris had said he would be. His mom had gone off to Lewiston to stay with her sister, the way she almost always did when Mr. Chambers was on a bender. She went and left Eyeball in charge of the younger kids. Eyeball had fulfilled his responsibility by going off with Ace and his j.d. buddies, leaving nine-year-old Sheldon, five-year-old Emery, and two-year-old Deborah to sink or swim on their own.

Teddy's mom got worried the second night and called Vern's mom. Vern's mom, who was also never going to do the game-show circuit, said we were still out in Vern's tent. She knew because she had seen a light on in there the night before. Teddy's mom said she sure hoped no one was smoking cigarettes in there and Vern's mom said it looked like a flashlight to her, and besides, she was sure that none of Vern's or Billy's friends smoked.

My dad asked me some vague questions, looking mildly troubled at my evasive answers, said we'd go fishing together sometime, and that was the end of it. If the parents had gotten together in the week or two afterward, everything would have fallen down . . . but they never did.

Milo Pressman never spoke up, either. My guess is that he thought twice about it being our word against his, and how we would all swear that he sicced Chopper on me.

So the story never came out—but that wasn't the end of it.

32

One day near the end of the month, while I was walking home from school, a black 1952 Ford cut into the curb in front of me. There was no mistaking that car. Gangster white-walls and spinner hubcaps, highrise chrome bumpers and Lucite death-knob with a rose embedded in it clamped to the steering wheel. Painted on the back deck was a deuce and a one-eyed jack. Beneath them, in Roman Gothic script, were the words WILD CARD.

The doors flew open; Ace Merrill and Fuzzy Bracowicz stepped out.

"Cheap hood, right?" Ace said, smiling his gentle smile. "My mother loves the way I do it to her, right?"

"We're gonna rack you, baby," Fuzzy said.

I dropped my schoolbooks on the sidewalk and ran. I was busting my buns but they caught me before I even made the end of the block. Ace hit me with a flying tackle and I went full-length on the paving. My chin hit the cement and I didn't just see stars; I saw whole constellations, whole nebulae. I was already crying when they picked me up, not so much from my elbows and knees, both pairs scraped and bleeding, or even from fear—it was vast, impotent rage that made me cry. Chris was right. He had been ours.

I twisted and turned and almost squiggled free. Then Fuzzy hoicked his knee into my crotch. The pain was amazing, incredible, nonpareil; it widened the horizons of pain from plain old wide screen to Vista Vision. I began to scream. Screaming seemed to be my best chance.

Ace punched me twice in the face, long and looping haymaker blows. The first one closed my left eye; it would be four days before I was really able to see out of that eye again. The second broke my nose with a crunch that sounded the way crispy cereal sounds inside your head when you chew. Then old Mrs. Chalmers came out on her porch with her cane clutched in one arthritis-twisted hand and a Herbert Tareyton jutting from one corner of her mouth. She began to bellow at them:

"Hi! Hi there, you boys! You stop that! Police! Poleeeece!"

"Don't let me see you around, dipshit," Ace said, smiling, and they let go of me and backed off. I sat up and then leaned over, cupping my wounded balls, sickly sure I was going to throw up and then die. I was still crying, too. But when Fuzzy started to walk around me, the sight of his pegged jeans-leg snuggered down over the top of his motorcycle boot brought all the fury back. I grabbed him and bit his calf through his jeans. I bit him just as hard as I could. Fuzzy began to do a little screaming of his own. He also began hopping around on one leg, and, incredibly, he was calling me a dirty-fighter. I was watching him hop around and that was when Ace stamped down on my left hand, breaking the first two fingers. I heard them break. They didn't sound like crispy cereal. They sounded like pretzels. Then Ace and Fuzzy were going back to Ace's '52, Ace sauntering with his hands in his back pockets, Fuzzy hopping on one leg and throwing curses back over his shoulder at me. I curled up on the sidewalk, crying. Aunt Evvie Chalmers came down her walk, thudding her cane angrily as she came. She asked me if I needed the doctor. I sat up and managed to stop most of the crying. I told her I didn't.

"Bullshit," she bellowed—Aunt Evvie was deaf and bellowed everything. "I saw where that bully got you. Boy, your sweetmeats are going to swell up to the size of Mason jars."

She took me into her house, gave me a wet rag for my nose—it had begun to resemble a summer squash by then—and gave me a big cup of medicinal-tasting coffee that was somehow calming. She kept bellowing at me that she should call the doctor and I kept telling her not to. Finally she gave up and I walked home. Very slowly, I walked home. My balls weren't the size of Mason jars yet, but they were on their way.

My mom and dad got a look at me and wigged right out—I was sort of surprised that they noticed anything at all, to tell the truth. Who were the boys? Could I pick them out of a line-up? That from my father, who never missed *Naked City* and *The Untouchables.* I said I didn't think I could pick the boys out of a line-up. I said I was tired. Actually I think I was in shock—in shock and more than a little drunk from Aunt Evvie's coffee, which must have been at least sixty per cent VSOP brandy. I said I thought they were from some other town, or from "up the city"—a phrase everyone understood to mean Lewiston-Auburn.

They took me to Dr. Clarkson in the station wagon—Dr.

Clarkson, who is still alive today, was even then old enough to have quite possibly been on armchair-to-armchair terms with God. He set my nose and my fingers and gave my mother a prescription for painkiller. Then he got them out of the examining room on some pretext or other and came over to me, shuffling, head forward, like Boris Karloff approaching Igor.

"Who did it, Gordon?"

"I don't know, Dr. Cla—"

"You're lying."

"No, sir. Huh-uh."

His sallow cheeks began to flow with color. "Why should you protect the cretins who did this? Do you think they will respect you? They will laugh and call you stupid-fool! 'Oh,' they'll say, 'there goes the stupid-fool we beat up for kicks the other day. Ha-ha! Hoo-hoo! Har-de-har-har-har!' "

"I didn't know them. Really."

I could see his hands itching to shake me, but of course he couldn't do that. So he sent me out to my parents, shaking his white head and muttering about juvenile delinquents. He would no doubt tell his old friend God all about it that night over their cigars and sherry.

I didn't care if Ace and Fuzzy and the rest of those assholes respected me or thought I was stupid or never thought about me at all. But there was Chris to think of. His brother Eyeball had broken his arm in two places and had left his face looking like a Canadian sunrise. They had to set the elbow-break with a steel pin. Mrs. McGinn from down the road saw Chris staggering along the soft shoulder, bleeding from both ears and reading a Richie Rich comic book. She took him to the CMG Emergency Room where Chris told the doctor he had fallen down the cellar stairs in the dark.

"Right," the doctor said, every bit as disgusted with Chris

as Dr. Clarkson had been with me, and then he went to call Constable Bannerman.

While he did that from his office, Chris went slowly down the hall, holding the temporary sling against his chest so the arm wouldn't swing and grate the broken bones together, and used a nickel in the pay phone to call Mrs. McGinn—he told me later it was the first collect call he had ever made and he was scared to death that she wouldn't accept the charges—but she did.

"Chris, are you all right?" she asked.

"Yes, thank you," Chris said.

"I'm sorry I couldn't stay with you, Chris, but I had pies in the—"

"That's all right, Missus McGinn," Chris said. "Can you see the Buick in our dooryard?" The Buick was the car Chris's mother drove. It was ten years old and when the engine got hot it smelled like frying Hush Puppies.

"It's there," she said cautiously. Best not to mix in too much with the Chamberses. Poor white trash; shanty Irish.

"Would you go over and tell Mamma to go downstairs and take the lightbulb out of the socket in the cellar?"

"Chris, I really, my pies—"

"Tell her," Chris said implacably, "to do it right away. Unless she maybe wants my brother to go to jail."

There was a long, long pause and then Mrs. McGinn agreed. She asked no questions and Chris told her no lies. Constable Bannerman did indeed come out to the Chambers house, but Richie Chambers didn't go to jail.

Vern and Teddy took their lumps, too, although not as bad as either Chris or I. Billy was laying for Vern when Vern got home. He took after him with a stovelength and hit him hard enough to knock him unconscious after only four or five good licks. Vern was no more than stunned, but Billy got scared he might have killed him and stopped. Three of them caught

Teddy walking home from the vacant lot one afternoon. They punched him out and broke his glasses. He fought them, but they wouldn't fight him when they realized he was groping after them like a blindman in the dark.

We hung out together at school looking like the remains of a Korean assault force. Nobody knew exactly what had happened, but everybody understood that we'd had a pretty serious run-in with the big kids and comported ourselves like men. A few stories went around. All of them were wildly wrong.

When the casts came off and the bruises healed, Vern and Teddy just drifted away. They had discovered a whole new group of contemporaries that they could lord it over. Most of them were real wets—scabby, scrubby little fifth-grade assholes—but Vern and Teddy kept bringing them to the treehouse, ordering them around, strutting like Nazi generals.

Chris and I began to drop by there less and less frequently, and after awhile the place was theirs by default. I remember going up one time in the spring of 1961 and noticing that the place smelled like a shootoff in a haymow. I never went there again that I can recall. Teddy and Vern slowly became just two more faces in the halls or in three-thirty detention. We nodded and said hi. That was all. It happens. Friends come in and out of your life like busboys in a restaurant, did you ever notice that? But when I think of that dream, the corpses under the water pulling implacably at my legs, it seems right that it should be that way. Some people drown, that's all. It's not fair, but it happens. Some people drown.

33

Vern Tessio was killed in a housefire that swept a Lewiston apartment building in 1966—in Brooklyn and the Bronx, they call that sort of apartment building a slum tenement, I believe. The Fire Department said it started around two in the morning, and the entire building was nothing but cinders in the cellarhole by dawn. There had been a large drunken party; Vern was there. Someone fell asleep in one of the bedrooms with a live cigarette going. Vern himself, maybe, drifting off, dreaming of his pennies. They identified him and the four others who died by their teeth.

Teddy went in a squalid car crash. That was 1971, I think, or maybe it was early 1972. There used to be a saying when I was growing up: "If you go out alone you're a hero. Take somebody else with you and you're dogpiss." Teddy, who had wanted nothing but the service since the time he was old enough to want anything, was turned down by the Air Force and classified 4-F by the draft. Anyone who had seen his glasses and his hearing aid knew it was going to happen—anyone but Teddy. In his junior year at high school he got a three-day vacation from school for calling the guidance counselor a lying sack of shit. The g.o. had observed Teddy coming in every so often—like every day—and checking over his career-board for new service literature. He told Teddy that maybe he should think about another career, and that was when Teddy blew his stack.

He was held back a year for repeated absences, tardies, and the attendant flunked courses . . . but he *did* graduate. He had an ancient Chevrolet Bel Air, and he used to hang around the places where Ace and Fuzzy and the rest had hung around before him: the pool hall, the dance hall, Sukey's Tavern, which is closed now, and The Mellow Tiger, which isn't. He eventually got a job with the Castle Rock Public Works Department, filling up holes with hotpatch.

The crash happened over in Harlow. Teddy's Bel Air was full of his friends (two of them had been part of that group he and Vern took to bossing around way back in 1960), and they were all passing around a couple of joints and a couple of bottles of Popov. They hit a utility pole and sheared it off and the Chevrolet rolled six times. One girl came out technically still alive. She lay for six months in what the nurses and orderlies at Central Maine General call the C&T Ward—Cabbages and Turnips. Then some merciful phantom pulled the plug on her respirator. Teddy Duchamp was posthumously awarded the Dogpiss of the Year Award.

Chris enrolled in the college courses in his second year of junior high—he and I both knew that if he waited any longer it would be too late; he would never catch up. Everyone jawed at him about it: his parents, who thought he was putting on airs, his friends, most of whom dismissed him as a pussy, the guidance counsellor, who didn't believe he could do the work, and most of all the teachers, who didn't approve of this duck-tailed, leather-jacketed, engineer-booted apparition who had materialized without warning in their classrooms. You could see that the sight of those boots and that many-zippered jacket offended them in connection with such high-minded subjects as algebra, Latin, and earth science; such attire was meant for the shop courses only. Chris sat among the well-dressed, vivacious boys and girls from the middle class families in Castle View and Brickyard Hill like some silent, brooding Grendel that might turn on them at any moment, produce a horrible roaring like the sound of dual glass-pack mufflers, and gobble them up, penny loafers, Peter Pan collars, button-down paisley shirts, and all.

He almost quit a dozen times that year. His father in particular hounded him, accusing Chris of thinking he was better than his old man, accusing Chris of wanting "to go up there to the college so you can turn me into a bankrupt." He once broke a Rhinegold bottle over the back of Chris's head and Chris wound up in the CMG Emergency Room again, where it took four stitches to close his scalp. His old friends, most of whom were now majoring in Smoking Area, catcalled him on the streets. The guidance counsellor huckstered him to take at least *some* shop courses so he wouldn't flunk the whole slate. Worst of all, of course, was just this: he'd been fucking off for the entire first seven years of his public education, and now the bill had come due with a vengeance.

We studied together almost every night, sometimes for as long as six hours at a stretch. I always came away from those sessions exhausted, and sometimes I came away frightened as well—frightened by his incredulous rage at just how murderously high that bill was. Before he could even begin to understand introductory algebra, he had to re-learn the fractions that he and Teddy and Vern had played pocket-pool through in the fifth grade. Before he could even begin to understand *Pater noster qui est in caelis,* he had to be told what nouns and prepositions and objects were. On the inside of his English grammar, neatly lettered, were the words FUCK GERUNDS. His compositional ideas were good and not badly organized, but his grammar was bad and he approached the whole business of punctuation as if with a shotgun. He wore out his copy of Warriner's and bought another in a Portland bookstore—it was the first hardcover book he actually owned, and it became a queer sort of Bible to him.

But by our junior year in high school, he had been accepted. Neither of us made top honors, but I came out seventh and Chris stood nineteenth. We were both accepted at the University of Maine, but I went to the Orono campus while Chris enrolled at the Portland campus. Pre-law, can you believe that? More Latin.

We both dated through high school, but no girl ever came between us. Does that sound like we went faggot? It would have to most of our old friends, Vern and Teddy included.

But it was only survival. We were clinging to each other in deep water. I've explained about Chris, I think; my reasons for clinging to him were less definable. His desire to get away from Castle Rock and out of the mill's shadow seemed to me to be my best part, and I could not just leave him to sink or swim on his own. If he had drowned, that part of me would have drowned with him, I think.

Near the end of 1971, Chris went into a Chicken Delight in Portland to get a three-piece Snack Bucket. Just ahead of him, two men started arguing about which one had been first in line. One of them pulled a knife. Chris, who had always been the best of us at making peace, stepped between them and was stabbed in the throat. The man with the knife had spent time in four different institutions; he had been released from Shawshank State Prison only the week before. Chris died almost instantly.

I read about it in the paper—Chris had been finishing his second year of graduate studies. Me, I had been married a year and a half and was teaching high school English. My wife was pregnant and I was trying to write a book. When I read the news item—STUDENT FATALLY STABBED IN PORTLAND RESTAURANT—I told my wife I was going out for a milk-shake. I drove out of town, parked, and cried for him. Cried for damn near half an hour, I guess. I couldn't have done that in front of my wife, much as I love her. It would have been pussy.

34

Me?

I'm a writer now, like I said. A lot of critics think what I write is shit. A lot of the time I think they are right . . . but it still freaks me out to put those words, "Freelance Writer," down in the *Occupation* blank of the forms you have to fill out at credit desks and in doctors' offices. My story sounds so much like a fairytale that it's fucking absurd.

I sold the book and it was made into a movie and the movie got good reviews and it was a smash hit besides. This all had happened by the time I was twenty-six. The second book was made into a movie as well, as was the third. I told you—it's fucking absurd. Meantime, my wife doesn't seem to mind having me around the house and we have three kids now. They all seem perfect to me, and most of the time I'm happy.

But like I said, the writing isn't so easy or as much fun as it used to be. The phone rings a lot. Sometimes I get headaches, bad ones, and then I have to go into a dim room and lie down until they go away. The doctors say they aren't true migraines; he called them "stressaches" and told me to slow down. I worry about myself sometimes. What a stupid habit that is . . . and yet I can't quite seem to stop it. And I wonder if there is really any point to what I'm doing, or what I'm supposed to make of a world where a man can get rich playing "let's pretend."

But it's funny how I saw Ace Merrill again. My friends are dead but Ace is alive. I saw him pulling out of the mill parking lot just after the three o'clock whistle the last time I took my kids down home to see my dad.

The '52 Ford had become a '77 Ford station wagon. A faded bumper-sticker said REAGAN/BUSH 1980. His hair was mowed into a crewcut and he'd gotten fat. The sharp, handsome features I remembered were buried in an avalanche of flesh. I had left the kids with Dad long enough to go downtown and get the paper. I was standing on the corner of Main and Carbine and he glanced at me as I waited to cross. There was no sign of recognition on the face of this thirty-two-year-old man who had broken my nose in another dimension of time.

I watched him wheel the Ford wagon into the dirt parking lot beside The Mellow Tiger, get out, hitch at his pants, and walk inside. I could imagine the brief wedge of country-western as he opened the door, the brief sour whiff of Knick and Gansett on draft, the welcoming shouts of the other regulars as he closed the door and placed his large ass on the same stool which had probably held him up for at least three hours every day of his life—except Sundays—since he was twenty-one.

I thought: *So that's what Ace is now.*

I looked to the left, and beyond the mill I could see the Castle River not so wide now but a little cleaner, still flowing under the bridge between Castle Rock and Harlow. The trestle upstream is gone, but the river is still around. So am I.

ACKNOWLEDGMENTS

Grateful acknowledgment is made to the following for permission to reprint copyrighted material.

Beechwood Music Corporation and Castle Music Pty. Limited: Portions of lyrics from "Tie Me Kangaroo Down, Sport," by Rolf Harris. Copyright © Castle Music Pty. Limited, 1960. Assigned to and copyrighted Beechwood Music Corp., 1961 for the United States and Canada. Copyright © Castle Music Pty. Limited for other territories. Used by permission. All rights reserved.

Big Seven Music Corporation: Portions of lyrics from "Party Doll," by Buddy Knox and Jimmy Bowen. Copyright © Big Seven Music Corp., 1956. Portions of lyrics from "Sorry (I Ran All the Way Home)" by Zwirn/Giosasi. Copyright © Big Seven Music Corp., 1959. All rights reserved.

Holt, Rinehart and Winston, Publishers; Jonathan Cape Ltd.; and the Estate of Robert Frost: Two lines from "Mending Wall" from *The Poetry of Robert Frost*, edited by Edward Connery Lathem. Copyright © Holt, Rinehart and Winston, 1930, 1939, 1969. Copyright © Robert Frost, 1958. Copyright © Lesley Frost Ballantine, 1967.

ABOUT THE AUTHOR

Stephen King is the author of more than fifty books, all of them worldwide bestsellers. His recent work includes *The Outsider*; *Sleeping Beauties* (co-written with his son Owen King); the short story collection *The Bazaar of Bad Dreams;* the Bill Hodges Trilogy—*End of Watch*, *Finders Keepers*, and *Mr. Mercedes* (an Edgar Award winner for Best Novel and now an AT&T Audience Network original television series); *Doctor Sleep;* and *Under the Dome*. His novel *11/22/63*—a Hulu original television series event—was named a top ten book of 2011 by the *New York Times Book Review* and won the Los Angeles Times Book Prize for Mystery/Thriller. His epic works The Dark Tower and *It* are the basis for major motion pictures. He is the recipient of the 2018 PEN America Literary Service Award, the 2014 National Medal of Arts, and the 2003 National Book Foundation Medal for Distinguished Contribution to American Letters. He lives in Bangor, Maine, with his wife, novelist Tabitha King.

Read on for an excerpt from Stephen King's

Billy Summers

Available August 2021 from Scribner

"Two million. Five hundred thousand up front, the rest after."

Billy's whistle isn't part of the act, which he doesn't think of as an act but as his *dumb self*, the one he shows to guys like Nick and Frank and Paulie. It's like a seatbelt. You don't use it because you expect to be in a crash, but you never know who you might meet coming over a hill on your side of the road. This is also true on the road of life, where people veer all over the place and drive the wrong way on the turnpike.

"Why so much?" The most he's ever gotten on a contract was seventy K. "It's not a politician, is it? Because I don't do that."

"Not even close."

"Is it a bad person?"

Nick laughs, shakes his head, and looks at Billy with real affection. "Always the same question with you."

Billy nods.

The dumb self might be a shuck, but this is true: he only does bad people. It's how he sleeps at night. It goes without saying that he has made a living *working* for bad people, yes, but Billy doesn't see this as a moral conundrum. He has no problem with bad people paying to have other bad people killed. He basically sees himself as a garbageman with a gun.

"This is a very bad person."